# AMERICAN FRATERNITY MAN

a novel by
# Nathan Holic

Published 2013 by Beating Windward Press LLC

For contact information, please visit:
www.BeatingWindward.com

First Edition
ISBN: 978-0-9838252-8-9

"The culture of Greek life is both skewered and embraced in this take-no-prisoners coming of age novel from debut author Nathan Holic. Here, you'll meet one character who has reached the conclusion that goodness is just and that evil is easy to spot. But for Charles Washington, the dynamic hero of this compelling story, right and wrong are slippery things. In the end, it's a pleasure to tumble into Charles' world, even as we watch that world pulled out from under him. *American Fraternity Man* is, at once, satire and seriousness itself. But, more than anything, it is a compulsively readable book, a thrilling ride, beginning to end."
  -David James Poissant, author of *The Heaven of Animals*
  (Simon & Schuster)


"Nathan Holic writes with the precision and confidence of a true badass. Hide your valuables and DIG IN."
  -Lindsay Hunter, author of *Daddy's* (featherproof) and *Don't Kiss Me*
  (FSG)


"In a transnational tour of the college scene, it's Man versus the Fraternity World, and even the parents are too drunk to drive. Nathan Holic offers a fast-paced and multifaceted look at campus Greek culture and what it might take to effect change from within."
  -Alex Kudera, author of *Fight For Your Long Day* (Atticus Books)

For Heather, whose eventual book on the life of sorority consulting will be much sexier than this one.

And for Jeanne Leiby, who knew nothing about fraternity life, but damn, did she know how to tell a story and how to bring out the best in a writer.

# Part I

# The Wine Bottle

CHAPTER ONE

Three months ago, about the time that Florida's summer was overtaking spring, about the time that Obama was emerging from his slugfest with Hillary to assert himself as the *change we could believe in*, I was hoping I might be able to do the same: convince everyone—my girlfriend Jenn, my fraternity brothers at EU, my parents—that I'd become a new man, the very definition of "role model" and "leader."

I was graduating. I'd taken a job half a country away. I'd be leaving everything and everyone behind. And I had only one night when they'd all be gathered together: it would either be the most hopeful night of my life, a celebration of who I was and the great things I wanted to do, or it would be a confirmation of everything I'd hoped was not true about myself. Because that was the question, wasn't it: was I ready to be a leader, or was I just pretending?

\*

On the afternoon of my final day as president of Nu Kappa Epsilon fraternity, my father appeared at the front door of the house, cradling a bottle of red wine tight to his chest and glancing about nervously, as if some *National Lampoon's* Frat Guy stereotype—able to detect alcohol the way a police dog could sniff out pot—might come zipping through and snatch the bottle from his hands. It was early afternoon on a Friday, several hours before the start of the Senior Send-Off event I'd planned for the graduating brothers in the fraternity house, and my father was here alone, my mother nowhere in sight.

"Wine for the party," he said. "From our trip to Napa Valley."

"Wine for the party," I repeated. He wasn't yet holding it out for me so I wasn't sure if I was supposed to take it. "You shouldn't have."

"I know how much you fraternity boys love to drink," he said.

"Come on." I smiled to show good humor. "This is a family event."

Ordinarily, of course, the Senior Send-Off was *anything but* a family event. It was the final event of our Spring semester, the night when our fraternity would gather in the chapter room to toast the new graduates, to share old stories and drink long into the night. Sometimes the seniors drafted "Senior Wills" and bequeathed to the young members their old memories, their old hook-ups, their old nicknames; sometimes the seniors brought gigantic

Tupperware bins full of old fraternity t-shirts and jerseys and tossed them out to the crowd, one at a time. We ordered a stack of pizzas and sent someone to Super Wal-Mart to clear the shelves of Natty Ice, and we sat in the chapter room drinking and chanting and cheering and immersing ourselves in crude in-jokes and embellished narratives of past adventures, all of us smelling like spilled beer and Crazy Bread by the time the sun came up the next morning.

But this year, Nu Kappa Epsilon had won "Chapter of the Year" at Edison University's Greek Awards banquet. We'd also won the "Champions Trophy" for overall dominance on the intramural fields, and *Florida Leader* magazine had recognized our chapter's intense campus involvement. "That's a hell of a year," our campus Greek Advisor told me. "Invite your parents. Invite your families. This is a chance to celebrate the positive aspects of fraternity life, to really change some minds about what it is we do."

I was the outgoing President. It was my event to plan. So I figured, why fester in a stinky chapter room with cheap beer and pizza; why not celebrate in a way that *mattered?* And I invited the mothers and fathers of every member, our first parent-themed event in three years. We'd make it classy, mature. This would be a night for all of us to drink vodka tonics and give speeches and receive academic awards, a night to talk about how much the house had meant to our academic progress, our development as leaders and citizens, our futures. This would be a night that parents and students alike would remember for years to come, and I was a *President* whose legacy would be remembered forever.

"A family event," my father said. He ran his hands down the surface of the wine bottle. "That's what I'm afraid of."

"Dad," I said.

"I remember last time."

Again, I tried to laugh.

He stepped carefully up the steps to our front door, still holding the wine bottle close and looking down at the concrete as if there was sloppy danger everywhere at the fraternity house, as if he might slip on some errant splash of spilled beer or urine.

"I'm sure the other parents will appreciate the wine," I said. "Looks like a good one."

And I reached for it, but he held it back.

"Don't chill it," he said. "Remember: don't refrigerate reds."

"Okay. I'll just put it on the bar."

"Well," he said, still holding tight, "I'll hang onto it for now. Why don't you show me around the house before the party starts? Things look different."

He hadn't been to the fraternity house in three years, and in that time we'd remodeled the first floor, adding a fireplace and a stone floor and a series of patio-style tables—it all had an outdoorsy look, as if the interior of our house was actually the backyard. The alumni had grown weary at having to replace the furniture every three years; they'd reasoned that stone was easier to clean than carpet, and outdoor furniture less likely to be damaged by spilled beer than cloth or leather couches. But I didn't mention any of that. My father was giving me the opportunity to impress him. Maybe he wanted to believe that his son had grown and matured, and telling him that we now had lawn furniture because we were too destructive for regular furniture: not a good idea.

"Follow me," I said, and I led him around the fraternity house, pointing out the things I *did* think were important: that the stone floors had been mopped, that the counters were Windex-shiny and that the wood shelves smelled of Pine Spray. Walls were patched, repainted, free not only of holes and gashes, but also scratches and scuffs. Artwork on the walls, potted plants (living!), new exercise equipment in the game room.

Eventually we arrived at the bar, a stunning piece of furniture built by a group of alumni just one year before, the wood coming from a torn-down building in Naples, the original office space for a lawyer named Damon Jarred who'd founded the fraternity chapter at Edison University decades ago; the glass on the cabinet doors had come from the windows of our first fraternity house from the 1960s.

My father stroked his chin. "So your alumni built this for you, then? One more entitlement."

"Here," I said, "we can put your wine with the others." I'd bought a shopping cart full of wine from the liquor store, some whites, some reds. I had no idea the difference in the colors or names; Merlot meant as much to me as White Zinfandel or Chenin Blanc. But my father wasn't quite so nonchalant.

"Up there?" he asked. "With all of that?"

"Sure." I'd gone for affordable brands, too, nothing over $10, because I wasn't even sure if—given a choice between Yellow Tail Chardonnay and a Grey Goose martini—anyone at the party would even drink the wine.

My father shook his head. "Do you even have a corkscrew?"

"A corkscrew?"

"This bottle isn't twist-off, son."

"I guess I didn't think about it."

"Well." He was still holding the bottle tight. "I have one in the car. I'll just need it back."

"No problem. I'll guard it with my life."

"Charles," he said. "I don't want to have to search around for it tomorrow, or find out someone threw it into the pond."

"Dad, it's not an issue. It'll be all right. It's not that kind of event." I smiled, tried to give him the same "you can trust me" look I'd so recently used in my job interview. But he didn't look convinced. In fact, my father was now wearing an expression of such deep skepticism that I wondered if he'd actually brought along the corkscrew with the *expectation* that I'd be unprepared. Was this a test of my ability to plan an event for adults? Had I just failed?

"Not that kind of event," he repeated. "So tell me, Charles. Spare me the suspense. What *is* in store for my visit this time around? What madness can I expect?"

*

Three years prior, on the morning after I'd completed my first great leadership role as a freshman in the fraternity, I woke up in a puddle of vomit and a scrap heap of broken chunks of drywall on the fraternity house floor, my father staring down at me with a look struggling at indifference. He tossed me a towel, a ketchup-stained rag that he'd found discarded in a corner of the room. "So this is responsibility, then?" he asked.

It was 7:30 AM, and as usual, he was awake and alert, even held the signature metal coffee cup that he'd brought from home and had probably filled at his hotel's continental breakfast. No doubt he'd even brought his own sugar packets, and—if the hotel didn't have a carafe of 2% milk in place of creamer—had driven to the local 7-Eleven to buy a half-gallon, his coffee prep as precise and measured as any task in his professional life.

I rolled over and tried to sit up, sharp pieces of drywall under my palms, my back against one of the new couches we'd just purchased for the living room. Later, I'd think of a thousand ways to respond—a self-deprecating joke, an eloquent rebuttal, even a heartfelt acknowledgment of my own failings... maybe something simple, so pathetic it was tragic: "Hey, Dad," with heavy eyelids and a pained moan. But in the moment, my head was spinning and I still wasn't even sure why I was in the living room, why my father was here in my fraternity house, and so I opened my mouth and tried to speak but only managed a couple coughs.

"My God, what happened to your wall?"

Yes, it wasn't just the floor; there was also a powdering of drywall dust stretching from couch to wall like a light snow that refused to melt. Scattered throughout were fist-sized drywall rocks, all of them unnaturally bright in the direct sunlight of the foyer window. Follow the trail of the drywall pieces and you'd eventually find a crater in the wall (at that moment, I vaguely remembered two of my fraternity brothers wrestling the night before, one of them slamming the other against the wall), and above it, in the low hallway ceiling, a hole that you could have stuck your head inside comfortably. I hadn't been involved in any of this, I know that, but still...I was the only one my father had found passed-out on the floor.

"We must have gotten carried away last night after you all left," I said. The evening before had been the "meet 'n greet" portion of our Family Weekend, an event I—as a freshman—had planned as an effort to showcase to more than forty parents the benefits of life in Nu Kappa Epsilon Fraternity, and to dispel nasty misconceptions of "frat house" lifestyle. And the parents had been impressed, mothers commenting on our manners as they sampled from the tray of cheese cubes and crackers we'd set out, fathers smiling at the "Intramural Champion" banners hanging in the game room, clapping their sons on the back. My own fraternity brothers shook my hand and told me that this was the most important thing we'd done as a fraternity in years: bringing all of our families together to celebrate the brotherhood we'd built.

4

But the parents had all left by 10 PM, and we'd kept drinking, and now it was morning.

"Where's your mop?" my father asked.

"Dad," I said, and I finally pushed myself to my feet but I wobbled and had to hold onto the couch's arm rest for support. "You don't have to help me. I can do this."

"All right. But where is it?"

"I don't know if we have a mop," I said.

"You don't know?"

"The house is, like, owned by the university," I said and winced, held my head. "We pay a cleaning staff."

He exhaled with such disappointment that it almost didn't seem possible that he'd even bother to speak again. "You can't do these things yourself? In your own house?" At the time 49 years old, my father had adopted full-time the role of "hardened businessman," his every feature edged, leveled, set to exude unwavering determination...That such an attitude and approach paid off in his business dealings, there's no doubt: this was 2005, the height of the housing boom in Florida, but when the economy tanked my Senior year, he was still brokering deals to buy acres of scrub palm and convert it to Publix-anchored shopping centers that would service the new neighborhoods built at the farthest inland boundaries of Cypress Falls, all those neighborhoods and townhomes that no resident wanted but still were somehow built and sold. No money anywhere, but somehow my father came out all right, still had a boat, a screened-in Solar-heated pool, granite countertops, columns on his stucco house, timeshares across the country.

And there, resting against the couch, head still spinning, maybe I actually expected him to tell me that he admired my fraternity's savvy in having negotiated this arrangement with the university, the cleaning staff provided as part of our rental agreement. Maybe he'd say, "This isn't such a bad deal, this fraternity." Or maybe, "Congrats. Sounds like you guys have your act together." But I should've known better. There in the NKE house on that Saturday morning, eyes locked on mine, he said, "A cleaning staff. That's the most ridiculous thing I've ever heard."

"But it's a university requirement for all houses," I said. "They're the same ones who do the dorms and the classroom buildings."

"And you were just going to go up to your bedroom, then? Wait until they came by and cleaned this up?" He gestured toward the long puddle of slop on the living room tile; thankfully, only a small splash had tainted the red area rug, and nothing appeared to have hit the couches. "Hope they might patch up the drywall, even? While you slept it off?"

"I just woke up. I hadn't thought about it yet."

"Of course you hadn't." He walked toward our kitchen door, which was shut and dead-locked. "There's got to be a mop or paper towels in here," he said. "Windex and a sponge, at the very least."

I tried to stand, and managed shakily. "Dad, you can't go in there."

"Excuse me?" he asked. The door handle shook but wouldn't turn.

"They lock the door," I said.

"Who locks the door?"

"The kitchen staff."

He shook harder. "There's a kitchen staff, as well?"

"We're not allowed in there."

"You pay rent here. More accurately, *I* pay rent here," he said. "And you can't even go into your own kitchen for a paper towel?"

"Most of the equipment in there isn't even ours," I said. "It's, like, a catering company. They cook for all the fraternity and sorority houses."

"Let me make sure I'm understanding correctly. You don't clean. Don't cook."

"We're technically a university dorm," I said, "so we have to use their vendors."

"Don't clean. Don't cook. And you keep extolling the virtues of this house. How it's made you a better man? A leader? Etcetera."

"That's just, you know, two little things."

My father shook his head. "The first week I lived in my co-op in college, I had to replace a toilet. We had water coming out under the baseboards in two of the bedrooms, and the screws were stripped around the bottom of the toilet. We didn't have vendor lists, Charles, and we didn't have cleaning ladies. We were 19, and we had to work together to make things happen."

"I know, Dad."

"You don't know, Charles. I try to tell you, but you don't listen."

But I'm not entirely sure that was true. My father never talked much about his own past, except random memories (a stint as a farmer in the late '70s, a 9-month business trip to London in the mid-80s, a nagging pain in his shoulder about which he'd say only, "Use your seatbelt," or—here, now—his broken toilet at his co-op in college) revealed during pivotal points in conversations when he wanted to prove a point.

"I can clean this. Please. It's nothing."

"So this is what we've been paying for, then?" he asked. "I trusted you to do the research, Charles. But the big-screen TVs? The pool table? This is what the semester dues pay for? This is the 'leadership development' you brag about?"

He made it sound as if this was a new realization he'd just come to, but really, the fraternity had never stood a chance with my father. As a high school senior one year before, I'd worked out a deal with him so that I could attend Edison University, an expensive private school on the Gulf Coast. I'd pay tuition (student loans), and he'd pay room and board at the campus dorms for all four years. "I still think you'd be better off at the University of Florida," he said. "Hell, you've got scholarships that would cover the full tuition there. But this is the same deal I had with my father. So: room and board it is."

Then I joined a fraternity during the first week of classes. Didn't tell him. And—because the university owned all housing facilities and approved most transfer requests—I quietly moved to the freshman floor of the fraternity house. The cost of rent, which now included a full meal plan, National Fraternity insurance, and social budget dues, tripled. I kept my father unaware until Thanksgiving break in November, when I drove the four hours back to Cypress Falls and my father held in his hands the first semester's fraternity house bills. "Room and board," he'd said softly. "Really pushing this deal, aren't you?"

But I'd bullet-pointed the benefits of fraternity life to him as if I was an infomercial host ("But that's not all! We also have a chapter library full of old textbooks, so I can actually save money on books every semester!" "But that's not all! We designate two brothers each week as Sober Drivers, so we can call any time, any place, and get a safe ride!"). I'd insisted that the fraternity was the logical continuation of my old days in high school, a new leadership activity to take over for Varsity Baseball and Key Club and the Honor Society. But for every benefit, he'd countered with a news story about hazing, or alcoholism, something to suck the positive energy from my speech. The evening before had been his first visit to the fraternity house. First chance to see it up close, to document the *wrong* that had before been unseen, intangible, always elsewhere. And there on the floor at the end of my freshman year, I knew that he'd have enough ammunition to keep firing for my full college career.

I couldn't look him in the eyes anymore; I just made an "Unnh?" noise, the sort that someone makes when every available response feels wrong...the exhale of defeat.

"The things you learn," he said, "when you find your son sleeping in puke."

"I don't..." I started. "This isn't *me*."

"Who am I looking at, Charles?"

"I don't know. But this isn't...it's me, but it isn't me."

"I'm going back to the hotel," he said. "Your mother and I will be back at 10:30 for your Awards Brunch, as your Family Weekend schedule indicates. I assume you can find a way to clean this up before then."

"Yeah," I said.

"Good. I'm not bringing your mother back to this." And my father walked down the hallway, through the foyer and out the front door, taking a sip of his coffee while on our front porch, and then he was off and it was just me and the mess. It wasn't until fifteen minutes later, when I finally found some Windex stored in the upstairs bathroom, that I took the time to look at myself in the mirror and see what my father had been looking at during our conversation: at some point in the night, I'd rolled over into my own vomit, and now it was caked in my hair, caked in my sideburns, smeared across the front of my red polo. Yes, here was the model young man who'd just planned a splendid end-of-the-semester Family Weekend, full of presentations and live music and meet 'n greets and—soon—a Saturday brunch. Here was the young man who was supposed to win both "Freshman of the Year" and "Leader of the Year" honors at the upcoming brunch, the young man who wanted so badly for all the world to know how ambitious he was, even as a freshman, how responsible and dedicated, how smart and full of potential. I picked a piece of floor fuzz from my eyebrow, brushed some drywall from my forehead, and headed to the bathroom's paper towel dispenser, dutifully restocked the afternoon prior by a woman named Sonya who sometimes smiled at us, and to whom we sometimes nodded.

For the next three years, I tried to pretend that this moment hadn't happened, that maybe my father had never even come to visit the house, had never seen me on the floor, and that I was indeed the young "Leader of the Year" I was supposed to be.

For those three years, I worked my ass off to maintain a near-perfect GPA, to turn those grades into solid internships by my junior and senior years, to win spots in the Edison Student Government and on the fraternity's Executive Board. Freshman of the Year became Sophomore of the Year became Junior of the Year. For three years, whenever I'd talk to my father, my voice would sound like a bad Christmas letter, a list of updates on my leadership activities, my academic progress, my career development. Sure, I kept a few things to myself: no mention of how many 25-cent Beer Nights I'd conquered, how many Bladder Busts, how many Power Hours, how many Beer Pong tournament wins. I was a Public Relations expert when it came to my own persona. And whenever possible, fraternity took the spotlight: when we appeared on the front page of the campus newspaper for organizing a Toys For Tots event, I sent my father the cut-out article; when the EU school web site posted on their front page a photo of our Executive Board receiving the *Florida Leader* magazine "Organization of the Year" award (I stood dead-center in the photo, holding a framed magazine cover while my brothers crowded around me and held up #1 fingers), I captured the screen shot and convinced my mother to make the jpg into his computer's background image so that he'd see it every single day.

But still, I'd have to wait three full years before my parents would visit the fraternity house again, before I could change their minds by showing them who I'd become. By now, I was the outgoing President, a more accomplished student-leader than I'd ever imagined I could be. And yes, I'd just accepted a job offer, too, so it felt as if everything in my life was on schedule, as if I was passing each mile marker at the right time: college degree, first job, then up ahead, family and house and pool and all that. My mother even kept asking "how serious" it was with Jenn, and we were at that strange-but-exhilarating moment in a relationship when Jenn was receiving birthday cards and Christmas cards in the mail from my parents. At the Senior Send-Off, I was prepared to *lavalier* her, the first step toward a planned proposal around Thanksgiving. Everything on pace.

But there was something I still hadn't told him.

My job: it wasn't just any job.

I'd just taken a position with the National Fraternity Headquarters.

*

There at the bar on the afternoon before the Send-Off, my father still gripping the wine bottle tight, I finally gave voice to the one thing that could take the emphasis off of my own ambitions and failings. "Where's Mom?"

"What?" he said.

"Mom," I said. "Don't tell me she's in the car?"

My father looked up at the gigantic Greek letters painted onto the tall wall behind the living room staircase, took a deep breath. "I dropped her off at the hotel."

"That's a little bit out of the way," I said.

"Yes," he said.

"And why are you here so early?" I asked. "The event doesn't start for three hours."

My father exhaled, still staring at the wall...and suddenly everything clicked into place: he'd committed her to the event without clearing her Friday night schedule, hadn't he? He'd forgotten to tell her about the Senior Send-Off, and now—somehow, some way—she was making him pay for his oversight. Maybe she was shopping right now. Or maybe she would show up later in the night in a brand-new sports car she'd bought while his back was turned.

My father has always been the type to meet problems head-on, plowing directly through the thick of the continent, but my mother is the opposite: she has, over the course of many years, honed the fine art of circumnavigation. When I was a child playing with G.I. Joes, she'd help me with the A-B-C steps of building the tanks and armored vehicles, but when my imagination took over and I made a tank fly, she knew to back slowly away from my play-time rather than argue the impossibilities. "Oh, tanks can fly now?" she'd ask. Or: "Oh, his hands shoot lasers, do they?" My father would argue, try to explain that I should make the tank *roll* and the jetfighter *fly*, but my mother just let me live in my fantasy world. Even throughout my time in youth soccer, Little League, JV baseball, I might leave the field complaining of poor refereeing, blatantly missed calls, and she'd say only, "I know. Bad refs. Sorry." My father would sit me down and for thirty minutes explain the nature of the calls, the difficulty of refereeing, the need to accept the penalties. *Confrontation*. If my standardized test scores were low, he'd outline why I needed to change my study habits, and he'd tell me over and over how I should do it. Meanwhile, my mother would just sign me up for SAT prep courses and drop me off before I even knew where we were going. *Circumnavigation*.

To the casual observer, it seemed almost as if my mother lived in a constant state of defeat. At home, while she watched the evening news, my father might snatch the remote and change the channel. "I just want to see where that hurricane is headed," he'd say, and the station would remain fixed on the Weather Channel for the next hour. Out to dinner at Outback, my father might veto her appetizer recommendations, her drink ("You didn't like that the last time you ordered it."), or even her meal itself. "I suppose you're right," my mother would say, sighing. But then, while my father left town on business, she'd have the house painted. Or, at a silent auction, she'd buy a ten-day trip to Paris, signing her name and a too-high bid, committing my father to the bill while he was at the bar ordering drinks. Better to just act and then apologize, my mother told me once, and probably that's why I'd joined the fraternity without telling him.

"Your mother is at the Ritz-Carlton's Spa and Salon," my father said, and for a moment he placed the wine bottle on the bar's countertop. "She knew about your graduation ceremony tomorrow morning, but apparently she didn't know that we'd be getting a hotel room in town the night before. So she scheduled some extensive…activities. I'll need to pick her up in a bit."

"She is coming tonight, though?" I asked. "To the Senior Send-Off?"

"Your mother's made her own plans for the afternoon. But yes, she'll be here for your event." And I could tell from my father's careful language that the long-standing marital tug-of-war was as taut as ever, though perhaps the flag in the center of the rope was crossing the line to my mother's side.

"As long as you'll both be here," I said, "that's all that matters."

My father adjusted his belt, tried to straighten his posture.

"It means everything to me that you came," I said. "That you gave the fraternity another chance, that you'll see what we've become."

My father was looking me in the eyes, and I reached slowly for the wine—

But at that exact moment, two of my fraternity brothers burst through the front door, both of them carrying Gator-Ade bottles and stinking of the gym, neither caring that his shoes were leaving wet footprints on the stone floor from having walked through the front yard sprinklers. "Fake tits, bro!" one of them said, shaking his head with the sort of seriousness that you might expect during a debate about the unemployment rate or the housing bubble.

"No fucking way!" said the other. "Fake tits don't *feel* right. They feel like a muscle or something, all thick and solid."

They trudged from front door to staircase, voices so loud that it seemed like the words might hang in the air and haunt the house forever. "You're fucking crazy!"

"*I'm* crazy?"

"Real tits are, like, sloppy. If I grab something, I want *firmness*, brother. I don't want my hand to disappear."

"Please. *Please.*"

"Dude, there was this bitch who—" And then they were upstairs, voices faded by distance, and it was just me and my father again.

"So," he said, cleared his throat. "How about, um. How about I hold onto this wine. Bring it back later."

"Come on," I said and reached for it, but it was in his hands once again. "It's fine up there, with the rest."

"It's really good wine, Charles." He held it back.

"You don't want anyone drinking it?"

"It's supposed to be enjoyed, not chugged. It was for us."

"No one will chug the wine, Dad," I said. "We're not animals."

He didn't respond, but the look on his face—eyes like slits, forehead and cheeks smooth, lips stuck together at the edges of a mouth cracked open only slightly—suggested that this was *exactly* what he was thinking, that he did indeed imagine a National Lampoon's scene later that night, a house full of cartoon characters dumping all the wine together into a giant barrel, pumping their fists and chanting for someone to chug, someone else speeding through the living room in a banana costume and tossing out condoms, while in the backyard a group of brothers sloshed into a kiddy pool of Jell-o…

"No one can open it without your corkscrew," I said, then motioned to the bottles of gin and vodka. "And there's so much liquor, no one needs to *steal* your wine."

I held out my hands one last time.

"Well," he said. "I'll hang onto it for now."

I needed to say something that would alter the air, something that would lift the smog that had settled over the two of us there in the bar. So I finally said it: I was waiting for the right moment, but I was already feeling like I'd lost some sort of battle. "Dad," I said, "did I mention that I got a job?"

"Really?" he asked. "That's exciting. Where?"

I took a deep breath, ran my palm across the bar's countertop, and I told him the one thing that he didn't want to hear.

# The Job
## CHAPTER TWO

Halfway through my Senior year at Edison University, I'd received an email: at the top was a masterfully Photoshopped header, the words "Nu Kappa Epsilon National Fraternity" backgrounded by watermark-faint images of historic NKE chapter houses, of brothers in intramural jerseys huddled up after football victory, of alumni standing together at weddings, beautiful women with white carnations pinned to their gowns. Below the graphic, the words "Save the World."

It was the sort of email that made you stop breathing for a few minutes, the same as if I'd just been notified that I'd won some million-dollar prize…the sort of email that asked you to imagine a future full of possibilities you'd never before considered. "Save the World," and it continued below in plain text:

**Save the World…**
**The world of *fraternities* and *sororities*.**

Become an Educational Consultant with the Nu Kappa Epsilon National Fraternity Headquarters. Travel the country! Meet hundreds of your fraternity brothers at dozens of campuses! Network with alumni! Work hands-on with chapters facing difficulties! *Save fraternity life for future generations!*

Job Responsibilities include:
• Conducting leadership development workshops
• Hosting roundtables with Alumni Advisory Boards.
• Meet with campus Greek Advisors and other administrators.
• Maintaining the standards of NKE excellence at each chapter.
• Investigating and uncovering infractions of our fraternity Sacred Laws
• Acting as a Beacon of Leadership

**Do you have what it takes?**

What are you waiting for? We select three Educational Consultants for single-year contracts. NKE *depends* on you!

In a few months, I would be graduating and looking for jobs with my freshly pressed Organizational Communication degree, but suddenly I was receiving "Save the World" emails *and* phone calls from my National Fraternity Headquarters: I'd been scouted as one of the top student leaders in Florida, they said. Recommendations from my campus Director of Student Involvement, from the Student Government Advisor. *Scouted.* Apparently there was a permanent file somewhere, full of questionnaires and email interviews about me, about Charles Washington, about a kid who—when he got the phone call—was in a Publix supermarket buying margarita mix for his underage girlfriend's birthday party.

Someone thought I was important.

Scratch that.

Someone *important* thought I was important. That meant something.

*

To the outsider, maybe the words "National Fraternity" don't carry much weight. Maybe they feel small: just some frivolous college organization. Maybe they even feel outdated, a quaint relic of American history that has now become irrelevant. Fraternities, after all, started as six or seven-member orders, teenagers living and studying together in remote college towns; their collective history is captured in turn-of-the-century photographs, the corners yellowing around young faces eager for fraternal bonds, eager to share professed values through rituals and handshakes and ceremonies. What could be more out-of-touch with a youth culture immersed in Facebook and *Jersey Shore*?

To the outsider—to my father, especially—modern fraternity life is not just irrelevant, but destructive; the entire experience can be distilled down into the toxic stories found on the internet, hazing at this school, alcoholism at that one. But those stories of fringe elements don't reveal the scope of Greek Life, the power and potential of the National Fraternity. The outsider doesn't know, for instance, that there are more than sixty national fraternities, some with as many as two hundred undergraduate chapters sprinkled from coast to coast, and as many as ten thousand young men claiming allegiance to the same Greek letters. Sigma Chi, Beta Theta Pi, Sigma Nu, Tau Kappa Epsilon, so many Greek letter combinations that you wonder how any of them didn't accidentally duplicate one another. Each with millions of dollars invested in sprawling campus houses, each with its own foundation to distribute scholarships to worthy brothers, each with its own leadership conference in summer, maybe another at the start of Spring semester, each with its own philanthropic partnership, fundraising and service events with the Big Brothers or Habitat For Humanity or St. Jude's, some national fraternities so progressive they've even *started* their own charities or service organizations, like Pi Kappa Phi and its Push America outreach program for people with disabilities.

The outsider doesn't know that our dues not only go to social events, but also to Alcohol Responsibility Workshops, and charter buses to off-campus events so that our members don't drive drunk. The outsider doesn't know that, every year at EU, we rent a gigantic church van and stuff as many as *sixteen* of our brothers into it, and we drive from Fort Myers to Charlotte or Knoxville or Atlanta for the annual Regional Leadership Conclave, sixteen grown men—some of them goliaths who play for the EU football team and who take up two full seats—occupying every square inch of that van, long drives from 9 PM until noon the next day, limbs in one another's faces, knees bunched together, Jeff Simmons pissing in a Gatorade bottle so that we don't need to stop at a rest area, Edwin farting and nearly killing us all…and it's one of the best times of our lives, but it's still *sixteen fraternity men* on the road to a *leadership conference*, to spend a full weekend in hotel meeting rooms with NKE staffers drawing on dry erase boards and helping us to re-think our study habits, our time management skills…*Fraternity men*!

And it's bigger than that, even: the National Fraternities belong to professional associations: FEA, FIPG, ICE, NEA…And members attend interfraternity conferences, too: SEIFC, MGCA, Recruitment Boot Camp…

The outsider sees it as frivolous, but Greek Life is an industry, a world unto itself. It isn't quaint or outdated. It is thriving, a Grand Tradition stretching back more than two centuries, hundreds of thousands of alumni in the sixty national fraternities, an impressive list that reads like a "Who's Who" of influential American men. Drew Brees and Brad Pitt of Sigma Chi. Sam Walton and Ken Kesey of Beta Theta Pi. Dr. Seuss and Orel Hershiser of Sigma Phi Epsilon. George W. Bush and George Steinbrenner of Delta Kappa Epsilon. Astronauts, governors, CEOs, baseball players. Musicians, actors, writers, skyscraper owners, presidents. In our history, Nu Kappa Epsilon has seen five governors of South Carolina and four governors of North Carolina, twelve Major League Baseball All-Stars, three NFL All-Pros, one Academy Award Winner (cinematography), two Gold Star winners, two Emmy Award winners, the former CEO of Insight Marketing…

A Grand Tradition that—now—was recruiting *me* into the super-selective brain-trust of the "National Fraternity Headquarters," the 15- or 20-man teams of esteemed alumni staff members responsible for keeping the machinery going. Beat that.

*

The night before I flew to Indianapolis for my first interview with the executive directors of the National Fraternity Headquarters, I sat at my final Alumni Ball in a Tommy Hilfiger tuxedo with my girlfriend Jenn, at the Golden Crown Country Club a half-mile from Fort Myers Beach, dead-drunk from dirty martinis.

Halfway through the night, my good friend and fraternity brother Edwin Cambria stood up, clinked his glass, and informed all 250 of us in the room—fraternity brothers, dates, alumni—that he wanted to give a special dedication to Mr. Charles Washington, our departing chapter president. All eyes on me in that country club ballroom as Edwin spoke into the microphone. All those gigantic round tables—hanging white lace tablecloths, tall NKE-red candles on silver platters, white carnations the centerpiece—and young men in stiff tuxedos, dates with brilliant curled hair creations, with dresses shimmering on hour-glass EU-gym-sculpted bodies, with makeup borne of hour-long preparation, with sparkling earrings and heavy necklaces…all of this…the most intelligent, talented, attractive men and women of Edison University, each table of students buzzing with its own electricity…they could turn the lights off and still the room would glow, and this room, all eyes on me as Edwin held his hand over his heart and said that it was his honor to stand before us tonight. His honor to present me with a plaque recognizing my dedication to the university and the fraternity. A heavy applause followed, the brothers with whom I'd entered the fraternity as a pledge cheering the wildest, alumni clapping for the man whose name graced the "Update Letters" that our chapter mailed out each semester.

Later that night, I sat in the country club's outdoor hot tub with Jenn and a few other couples. For all the mad preparation for Alumni Ball, the dresses and hair appointments, the formal clothes slid off easily once the music ended and everyone returned to their rooms for after-parties. We'd brought a 12-pack to the hot tub, three bottles of champagne, and while the guys had no trouble ducking under the water and running our hands through our sloppy wet hair, our dates sat upright, barely allowing the water to rise as high as the swell of their breasts, trying to spare their makeup and their still-perfect hair.

"Did you ever think you'd be here, your last Alumni Ball?" Edwin asked me. He had one arm around his date, a girl who looked like Tara Reid (but who Edwin confessed to me was his second choice as a formal date). He looked to be weighting her down into the water, and she struggled to keep from sinking. "Did you ever think that this would all be over?"

"Got a few months left in the semester," I said.

"Still. It's close to being over."

"It's never over." I took a sip of my beer. "Fraternity is lifelong."

"Maybe for you," Edwin said. "You're going to work for Nationals."

"Are you really doing that?" one of the girls asked. "Jenn, you're going to let him do that?"

"It's just an interview," I said. "Nothing definite."

"It's his decision," Jenn said. She had one hand on my thigh, underwater, and the other held a plastic cup of champagne. The next day she'd have a terrible headache, but that night she spoke with such clarity that it didn't seem possible she'd finished more than a bottle of the stuff on her own. "I wish he wouldn't leave me"—under the bubbles, hand moving up my thigh—"but you've got to do what makes you happy."

"So mature, Jenn," one of the girls said, laughing. "Wise beyond your years."

"Do what makes you happy," Edwin said. "Ha ha. Four years of college, and I still don't know what the hell that is."

"You'll be fine," Jenn said. "Don't be dramatic, Edwin."

"So much school, so many classes," Edwin said, "and this is what you want as a career, Charles? This is what makes you happy?"

Such a simple question, and there in the hot tub, soaked and drunk and half-naked holding a cold beer, a hand so close to my underwater hard-on, I began and ended a number of Hallmark responses in my mind, all of them corny but rich in emotion...*I don't know what I'd do without this*...Or: *I never had real brothers*. Or: *This is where I found myself. This is where I was able to finally be myself.* But I prevented myself from saying any of that. Because I knew that once I started, I wouldn't be able to stop. "Who *was* I before this fraternity?" I might've asked (as if any of them could answer), and then I would have been forced to tell them that I was nothing, that I'd never really done anything for myself back in high school, would just come home to find out that my mother had signed me up for Key Club, or had talked to the JV baseball coach to find an extra roster spot for me, or had scheduled a meeting with my English teacher to discuss my grades, or had filled out the first several pages of paperwork for a college application, a crowded resume that looked great to university admissions staffs but was a blur of text that meant nothing to me...the same was true for my friends in high school, all of us moving from club to organization to sport to club to practice to class like animatronic Disney versions of young people—"helicopter parents" was the term my college advisor used, as if my mother had buzzed overhead from birth to graduation—and I never felt like anyone even believed I could accomplish something important by myself. "But fraternity?" I could've said to my friends in the hot tub. "This was a time in my life when everyone told me I would be hazed and humiliated, this was the institution that everyone told me would be worthless. Dangerous. But fraternity? You were different. You *made* me."

When I told my father about the job in the hours before the Senior Send-Off, I'd imply that it was the lure of Grand Tradition—important people, networks, job opportunities—that had attracted me to a job with the National Headquarters. But that was just the stainless steel fridge, the hardwood floors, the upgrades on a house hunt. Something else drew me in: the way my father said "waste of time." The way my Public Relations professor at Edison University said "Hmmm, a position with a fraternity. How will future employers view that?" when I asked for his opinion. As if it was not simply skepticism at my employer, but an indictment of the past four years of my life.

My father didn't understand. *No one* understood.

In fact, there is a consensus among undergraduates that the world is unfairly hostile toward fraternities. After all, the scandal at Arizona—where a pledge was pushed into a freezer during a party, the door locked behind him, and he was forgotten about despite cold-hardened hands beating against the door, and only saved when two other pledges were told to retrieve ice to pour atop the kegs upstairs—was no more than ordinary college idiocy, the sort of brainless tomfoolery resulting from *any* gathering of young men whose bodies were controlled by testosterone and alcohol. This is college, just college, and *everyone* does stupid shit in college. But when a fraternity makes a mistake, boom! Front page news.

Oh, everyone in the media loves to swoop in whenever we misstep so that they can deliver scathing O'Reilly-esque commentaries. We're easy fodder. Take the incident at Auburn several years back: the guys who, at a Halloween party, came dressed as lynched runaway slaves, complete with black-face and fake nooses round their necks. No, we didn't *like* hearing about it, but it's tough to believe there are no other such parties on these Deep South campuses, and yet...no reporter can resist such a story when spiked with the word "fraternity." Too potent to pass up. A fist fight at a football game between two fraternities? Front page! A drunk driving accident? Front page! Even a heart attack, an untimely death for a 22-year-old: investigated ad nauseum in local editorials, written about for years to come with the closing tagline, "He was also a member of a fraternity on campus, and although no charges were ever filed, some suspected hazing." And there was Alexandra Robbins' *Pledged*, that tell-all expose of sorority girls in Texas, and the *Rolling Stone* article on the "secret lives" of sorority girls at Ohio State. Yes: a feeling that fraternities are targeted by media outlets, discriminated against by professors and other university faculty/ staff, that we are perceived as little more than drunks and womanizers, as spoiled white rich kids with inferior GPAs, all of us with jobs lined up after graduation. The "Frat Guy" stereotype. A label that so affected us as undergraduates that we'd only refer to fraternity as "fraternity," never "frat" ("Just feeds the Frat Guy stereotype to use the word 'frat,'" my Big Brother told me in my first week as a pledge. "I mean, would you call your country a cunt?"). We'd joined a social organization on campus, only slightly different than so many others at EU, but because it had Greek letters, we'd now been branded alcoholics, or rapists, or racists, or...

Fraternity *stereotype*: that is the rallying cry of undergraduates.

And even there in the hot tub on the night before my first interview, I knew I wanted to battle that stereotype. Prove that I'd been right all along, that fraternity *is* something special, that this was family and it was essential to the lives of boys growing into men.

Hot tub, head swirling, and I was thinking of a dozen different stories that debunked the stereotype. The time when I was knocked unconscious at a football game by a random beer bottle dropped from the bleachers, and it was Edwin who caught me before I hit the ground, who tore off his shirt sleeve and pressed it to the cut on my temple and shouted for help. Dramatic but true. Or the time when Alex and Brandon and Chad—seniors when I was a freshman—sat me down and forced me to study for my Economics final, locked the door of the chapter library, wouldn't let me leave until I had my flashcards memorized. The Habitat For Humanity projects. The "Rally Against Discrimination" we organized with Kappa Delta sorority on the campus greens. "This is my home," I could've said to Jenn and Edwin and all the others sipping champagne, "and you are my family, and fraternity means everything to me."

But it just seemed like the sort of moment that you didn't want to ruin with some sobbing speech, so I finally said, "This isn't the end. This isn't going to end."

And the conversation moved on, and soon we were talking about our upcoming Spring Break cruise and duty-free liquor and cigars and free samples of tanning lotion, and everyone was happy and that's the way I wanted it to be.

Later in the night, the lens grew hazy.

Seven or eight of us finishing the final few beers and the last drops of the champagne we'd brought along, much of it warm by then. 2 AM or 3 AM, who knew? Our muscles so loosened that, if we stood up and tried to walk around, we'd just jello back into the Jacuzzi.

By now, Jenn was sitting on my lap.

Then she was facing me, kissing me, the rest of the world fading out.

"This is exciting, isn't it?" she asked.

I slid my hand up her bare back, let it rest on the strap of her bikini top.

"Not just *this*," she said, meaning the hot tub, "but all of it. You'll graduate soon."

"That's exciting?" I asked.

"Moving on to something new," she said. "We have the whole world in front of us, you know? We can do anything."

Suddenly, on the other end of the hot tub, one of the girls slipped underwater. There was a splash, a scream, then a spread-out seaweedy mass of blonde hair beneath the bubbles, and when she emerged, there was no more fabulous make-up; it was another face entirely that we saw, the glittery blues and blacks and reds all mixed up, hair in her eyes, hair in her mouth, and she said "Shit!" and then she was out of the hot tub, and Edwin was following her and saying "Sorry, sorry! The dance is over, though. We're just going back to the room anyway!" And then the whole hot tub crowd was dispersing, the other girls—terrified that they might be next—hopping out of the water and grabbing towels, the guys shrugging and surrendering. The party was over, and I picked up the now-empty cooler and followed Jenn back to the room and we ripped off our swimsuits and it was supposed to be amazing sex because we'd all paid so much for the Alumni Ball and for the rooms at the country club's historic hotel, but truth be told, we were still rubber-muscled and saturated to the bone with chlorine, and I was so drunk that I barely remember much of it. I just remember her face when she said "We can do anything," this look in her eyes like she believed in me, and it made me believe in myself, and I knew at that moment that I had to win the job with the National Fraternity because it had given me *all of this*, it had caused so many people to believe in me for the first time, almost like I'd truly been born again during my freshman-year initiation ceremony, during that symbolic ritual of death and rebirth as a Nu Kappa Epsilon man.

The next afternoon, the National Fraternity Headquarters flew me to Indianapolis for a weekend interview, introduced me to their strategic plan, stressing what fraternity *should* be: a learning laboratory to mold socially responsible citizens. As an Educational Consultant, I could be a "road warrior" on the "front lines" at America's universities, battling the fraternity stereotype, building the ideal leadership organization.

The Executive Director of Nu Kappa Epsilon—Dr. Jim Simpson, Delta Chapter, '68, a University of North Carolina graduate with a tobacco road accent so slow and soothing that everything he said sounded like a thought-out compliment—told me that I was a "Diamond Candidate." President of my chapter, Vice President of Student Government, Cum Laude. He shook his head respectfully, whistled. *Diamond Candidate.* "This is the next step," he said. "A job that means something. Protecting one of our nation's most sacred institutions. None of that selfish Wall Street nonsense that got us into the mess we're in now."

And when I interviewed with Walter LaFaber, the Director of Chapter Operations at the Headquarters, a man I'd seen on the cover of nearly every leadership magazine in the country...a man who commands over $5,000 per speaking engagement...the man who would be my boss and mentor...he put his hand on my shoulder and said that I reminded him of, well, *himself.* "I look at you," LaFaber said, his low voice a combination of linebacker grit and motivational speaker energy, "and I see a man ready to make a difference in the world."

I'm not even sure I saw that in myself. But as soon as he said it, I *wanted* to.

I wanted to be the Diamond Candidate they'd claimed that I was. I wanted to be the "Marathon Man," the hand-drawn diagram in our pledge books that represents everything the National Fraternity wants to build its members to be:

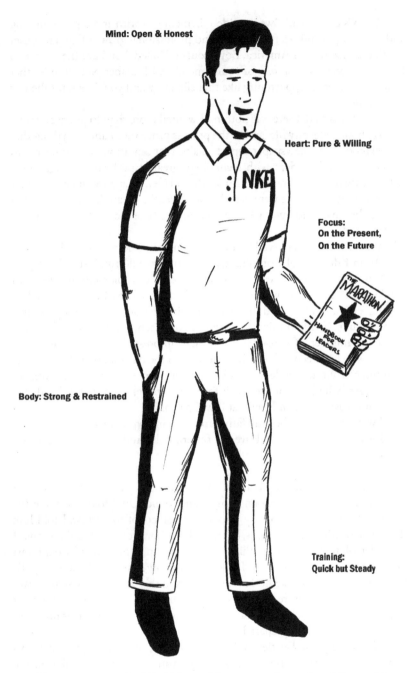

For our very survival, LaFaber told me, we—the national fraternities—cannot allow ourselves to be perceived as "drinking clubs" or as the fraternities of pop culture; we are not *Animal House* or *Revenge of the Nerds*. We have re-branded ourselves. We are *leadership* organizations.

"At NKE," he said, "we provide our members with more programming and more opportunities for personal and professional growth than any other youth organization in America, Boy Scouts included. You have the chance to be a role model to *thousands* of young men," and LaFaber paused to let that sink in. "You let an opportunity like that slip away and you'll regret it the rest of your life."

And I was sold: there was nothing I wanted more than to prove everyone wrong about fraternity life, and in the process prove that *I* am everything that the textbooks and newspaper reports claim that ambitious young people in America *should* be: adept with technology, great at problem-solving, armed with a sense of humor and a disdain for the old Gen-X apathy and unrelenting sarcasm. That's right: we were *not* a horde of Facebook-addicted zombies, but instead the smart and savvy youth who would change the world. That was me, that was *me*!

Walter LaFaber believed it already. Soon, so would everyone else.

As an Educational Consultant, my contract would run just a single year, but here was the bonus: career options were sure to blossom afterwards. I would sacrifice salary now, but after I finished consulting I could get a job at any university, LaFaber said. In college administrations, in student personnel or recruiting, in fundraising and alumni outreach. And he couldn't even count the number of consultants who had impressed our most influential alumni, who had been offered big-time jobs on the day that their Educational Consultant contracts ended. "This is a job for people who want to *work*, not for climbers who just want to use it for their own selfish purposes," LaFaber said. "But trust me when I say that it will pay off."

I wouldn't need to beg my father for a job in Cypress Falls.

I wouldn't even need to leave the fraternity behind. I took the challenge. I accepted.

*

So this—role model, diamond candidate, saving the world—is what I told my father on the afternoon of my Senior Send-Off. I told him about the mission, to develop the socially responsible leaders of tomorrow. I told him that I'd be starting in two weeks, but man, I was born for this. I told him that I wanted a job that meant something, but I wasn't an idiot, either; I would start investing my money, too, since I'd be receiving my first real-world salary; I'd be smart, shrewd, just like he'd always been, and this was my first step toward a financially secure future. I spoke so quickly and with such intensity that—at one point—I even had an out-of-body experience, looking down at myself as I recited the speech I'd prepared.

My father waited patiently for me to finish, his fingers pressed to his temple with increasing pressure, as though a migraine was hatching in the space between brain and skull, growing in strength, growing, and when I finally stopped speaking he said "Hold on, hold on. You're thinking about *investments*? Now?"

"I'll be making a salary. I want to start thinking about a house."

"How much is this job paying you?"

"Not much in base salary, but it's a traveling position," I said. "And the Headquarters owns a dorm in Indianapolis, so I don't have to worry about rent or utilities. I live free, and I make money."

"How much?"

"Well, like I said, the salary isn't impressive."

"Numbers, Charles. Specifics."

"Twelve thousand."

"Twelve thousand?"

"But that's not including per diem. And all gas is reimbursed. So."

"So you took a poverty-level job?"

"No, listen," I said. "I've got no expenses. That's the thing."

"How can they get away with paying you that? Even for a non-profit, that's criminal."

"But I'll have a job lined up afterward, see," I said. "It's a networking thing. It'll pay off. That's the, um, real value of the position."

"So you're using this job as a springboard?" he asked, hopeful.

"No, that's not it. I believe in this—"

"And in the meantime, you've still got car payments."

"Right. But that's...you know?"

"And your student loan payments will be coming."

"Starting soon, sure. Six months, I think?"

"Any other debt?"

"Minor credit card stuff," I said, but I didn't tell him about the thousands of dollars in debt I'd racked up during my Senior year, from the Alumni Ball to my Spring Break cruise to the ridiculous tab for this Senior Send-Off party. I'd wanted this to be a classy event; I was president, and I wouldn't have it any other way. No cheap beer, no kegs, no bottom-shelf bottles of turpentine-tasting liquor. No, we'd have Stoli's of all varieties, the whipped cream and the coffee and the blueberry flavors, Kahlua, Captain Morgan's, Tanqueray, Miller Lite by the—no, *Heineken* by the case...an ice-cold selection of mixers... cigars...catered barbecue, a custom cake...all of which I'd purchase with my own money. Everyone knew that I had a Real World job now, after all. The chapter had given me a sparing budget for food and decorations, but I'd max out my credit cards to make this a Senior Send-Off to be remembered. At the time, maybe I was hoping that the cost of the liquor would be reimbursed by some pass-the-hat contribution, but the semester was technically over. No more chapter meetings. No way to make an announcement that I could use a little help. And really, I wanted everyone to believe that this one was on me, no biggie. I was drunk with generosity. Afterwards, a few brothers dropped me ten or fifteen bucks as a courtesy, but I still had a debt so large that it didn't feel real.

"What's left to invest, then?" my father asked.

"I'll save. And, like, this job is about more than money, too."

"So you said. You're using it to get a different job."

"No," I said. "I'll be helping people."

"Oh yes," he said. "The Compassion Boom."

I told him that I didn't know what that meant.

"It's what all the kids are doing, isn't it?" he asked. "Taking jobs at not-for-profits. Sticking their middle fingers up at Wall Street? As if you're somehow bettering yourself by taking a smaller salary?"

"Well, isn't that a good thing?"

"There are so many non-profits," my father said, finally tired of the conversation. "If you're so intent on some save-the-world job, why don't you go to medical school? Join Doctors Without Borders? Anything. Why a *fraternity*?"

It was a non-profit, but my sacrifice wasn't big enough? At that moment, I could have said something about *his* job: where was the humanity in running a real estate speculation business, buying and leveling old Florida land? How many new developments were necessary, how many new fountains and entry gates and zero-plot-line yards, how many more Spanish-tiled roofs? His entire business, built on unaffordable homes whose owners now probably faced foreclosure, land deals that saw shopping centers intrude upon quiet communities, and *I* was the one who was doing something that *didn't matter*?

But I only said: "I believe in this, okay? Jobs aren't just about making money."

He sighed. "Okay. Just remember. You're on your own now, you understand?" And he gripped my shoulder, without hostility but also without encouragement, his few gray hairs seeming to shine in his thick black scalp like the white-hot embers beneath the spent logs of a bonfire. I couldn't tell if he wanted to sound condescending or helpful. "You're a college grad. You support yourself now, job or no job. That's the life of a professional."

I told him that I understood, that I was set for success. "They *wanted* me. They called me a Diamond Candidate."

"You might have fooled them into thinking you're someone else," he said, "but I know the *real* you."

"I can do this," I said. "You're wrong about me."

And that's when the conversation died and I led him back to the front door, and he drove back across town to unpack at the hotel and wait an hour or two while my mother finished at the spa and then showered and dressed for the Senior Send-Off dinner buffet.

The wine bottle wound up back in his car, in a cooler, leaving me to wonder if he'd brought the wine to my Senior Send-Off as a gift, if he'd even intended to open it, or if he just wanted to present it so that he could take it back and tell me that I wasn't responsible enough for it. Was it even possible to convince my father that I was anything but a toga-clad Bluto, shotgunning PBR cans, fireballing hard liquor like Ogre from *Revenge of the Nerds*? And if it wasn't possible to convince him, how could I convince anyone else?

The night hadn't even started, but already it felt desperate.

# The Jenn Outlook

## CHAPTER THREE

Sometime after my father left the house, and sometime before the first flood of parents poured through the front door, Jenn stopped by to help me put the finishing touches on the living room, the bar, and the back courtyard. Everything had been thought-out. The house was a showroom of fraternity accolades: photo albums on the wicker end tables opened to display brothers whose parents had RSVP'd, the handsome *Complete History of Nu Kappa Epsilon National Fraternity* on the long coffee table, several *Marathon* pledge manuals scattered about like magazines at a doctor's office, just in case some mother or father got curious about our policies, what their sons had been through as pledges. We had nothing to hide. We were fraternity re-defined, and the parents—in reading—would be left mouths agape by the nobility of it all.

I'd even worked with our Web Chairman to create "Parents' Guide to NKE" brochures, which Jenn and I had printed at the local copy shop and which she was now arranging in the foyer on an information table, and then skillfully leaving on random chairs inside and outside to make it seem as if the brochures had already been picked up and perused by other parents. The brochures were a wonder, a revelation conjured by Jenn: "The parents are a captive audience, Charles," she said, "so here's your chance to get your message out there." It was impossible to read one and not feel as if your son had made the best decision of his life: there were GPA statistics, a list of awards, blurbs about our alcohol workshops, run-downs of our Habitat For Humanity projects, a thank-you letter from Charles Washington on one inside flap.

As we walked through the house, Jenn helped me spot things I barely even saw anymore: a gash in one chair ("Move it over here, so the table hides the rip," she said), a long stain in the tile grout that almost looked like blood. "Give me the bleach," she said. "You're dressed already. I haven't showered yet, so I'll scrub it out."

She found bubblegum under tables, chiseled it off with a flat-head screwdriver. The nicer the house became, the more nervous I got. Certainly there would be *one* thing I'd miss, one thing made all the more glaring for the surrounding spotlessness. An extension cord I hadn't properly hid under a rug, maybe, and some mother would trip and break her neck and—

"You worry too much," Jenn said.

"You never get a second chance to make a last impression," I said. "This is it, Jenn. Last fraternity event. This is how they'll remember me."

"It'll be fine," she said. "Everyone's gonna have a great time." She looked toward the bar, the liquor store of bottles, and shook her head. "I mean, how could they *not*?"

The Jenn Outlook, we called this: an unfazeable optimism that seemed to always silence any doubts. Whether we were worried about making a movie's showtime, or burning burgers on the grill at DeLaney Park, or stressed about a Research Methods exam, Jenn would speak a single sentence and make our worries or complaints feel groundless.

"Are your parents in town yet?" she asked.

"My father already stopped by," I said.

"Where was I?"

"This was, like, twenty minutes before you came over. My mother was at the spa, so he was just stopping by to drop off some—" I paused. "He just wanted to hang out."

"Did he like it?"

"Did he like what?"

"The bar, the house, all this work you did. He's gotta be excited, right?"

"Sure," I said.

"Did you tell him about the job?"

"I did."

"I bet he was crazy-excited for you, wasn't he?" she said. "I told you not to worry."

I opened the Kahlua, sniffed inside and breathed deeply, dropped a few ice cubes into a rocks glass and set about making a White Russian. There were two options here: I could tell her the truth, and for once be honest about my imperfect life, or I could do the same thing I always did and convince her that Charles Washington's life was as happy and flawless as the feed on an average Facebook page. "*Crazy*-excited," I said. "He was proud that I was doing something I believed in."

"I told you," Jenn said. "I *told* you."

*

In late Fall at EU, when Dead Week hits and the semester's end comes into view, we drag the lawn furniture out of the fraternity house living room and onto (appropriately) our front lawn. We drag televisions outside, too, and we drink and watch college football; sometimes we grill hamburgers and set up lawn chairs on the grass and—if it's still sunny in December, which it usually is—kiddy pools, and we invite sorority girls over. We sit outside in the sunshine while the rest of the country is shivering in front of fireplaces, and we post pictures of ourselves (shirtless, arms around girls in bikinis) to Facebook so that all our friends up north can scream at the injustice of it all.

That was how I first met Jenn, actually. On a Thursday afternoon when nearly everyone had stopped studying for the day, a pack of Kappa Deltas strolled up our front walkway wearing thin t-shirts under which the bright straps of bikini tops were visible. If anyone still had a textbook open, this was the cue to shut it.

That Thursday, Jenn and I wound up sitting side-by-side on chaise lounges, and we spent hours drinking Pabst Blue Ribbon and discussing our favorite *Seinfeld* episodes, learning one another's childhoods through sitcom. Every time I saw the "Magic Loogie" episode, for instance, I remembered breaking my arm during a Little League game, spending my first night in a cast on the family room couch, eating pizza and watching *Seinfeld* reruns; I'd video-taped the Magic Loogie episode for some reason, and my father paused the tape again and again to explain the *JFK* references. Jenn would always remember the Soup Nazi episode because her parents had held a family conference after that specific show to tell Jenn and her sister that they'd all be moving from Dallas to Tampa, that her father was quitting his life as a truck driver so they could have stability. Even now, long after the sting of divorce has faded, Jenn told me that she still jokes with her older sister and says "No soup for you!" whenever discussing the buzzkill of trips back home for holidays.

We moved from *Seinfeld* to *Saturday Night Live*. Then *Friends* to *Futurama*. And holy shit, a sorority girl who watched *Futurama*? And *The Simpsons*? And could recite quotes from *The Monster Squad* and *The Goonies* as easily as most of her sisters could recite lines from *Dirty Dancing*? Who *was* this girl? We spent hours on those lawn chairs, following personal pop culture histories and getting lost in memory the same as if we were tumbling down into internet hyperlink loops, unsure where we started and how we'd wound up where we did, hours and hours of conversation so natural it shouldn't have been possible, and then—like any fantasy—she was gone, and the next day I wondered if she'd existed at all.

But just days later, Jenn's sorority organized an end-of-the-semester "Grab-A-Date," one of those affairs where each girl wakes up to learn that she has just 24 hours to find a date at some undisclosed venue: sometimes it's a beach bar, other times a bowling alley or even a movie theater. At the zero hour, desperate because she'd only heard about the Grab-A-Date with fifteen minutes to spare, Jenn rushed to the NKE house and asked everyone where she could find someone named Charles, the guy she'd met on the lawn days before. "Charles. Do you mean *the* Charles Washington?" one of my brothers asked. I was the Vice President of NKE at the time (pegged as president when elections rolled around next term), and the VP of ESG. My brothers jokingly called me "MOC," man on campus. "Didn't realize you were such a hot commodity," Jenn said when Edwin led her to my second-floor bedroom.

And that night at the Grab-A-Date, it didn't matter that I'd realized—at the start of the semester—that my Organizational Communication program was so vague I had no idea what I'd be doing after graduation. It didn't matter that I'd hated my internships. It didn't matter, because I entertained Jenn with story after story of my nearly three years of EU exploits, and she loved this exciting persona, the *Man on Campus*, a Charles Washington who seemed to have it all together. Hell, I loved him too.

\*

That was a persona, of course, and what I soon learned was this: there is only *one* Jenn, no façades, no deceptions, no performances. Just Jenn. Overwhelmingly optimistic, a little whacky, but only one Jenn, a girl who dances between two worlds and who—if you didn't know her—you might think is two different people.

There is Jenn who dances in the world of Kappa Delta, a girl who belongs to a sorority and attends Grab-A-Dates, who spends afternoons at Greek N Things putting together Big Sis – Lil Sis paddles, "Fam 34" paddles, painting the F, the A, the M, in the colors of KD. Jenn dancing in sundresses of fuschia during Rush Week, singing the sorority songs. Jenn dancing at semi-formals, at date functions to tiki bars, at hayride socials…She dances in the sorority house living room when the girls gather late-night in pajamas for chick flicks and re-enact full scenes from *Clueless* or *13 Going on 30*, *Centerstage* or *Showgirls*; she's fine with all of that. She dances at formals, too, in gowns that glide glistening over her body's curves, effortless though the dresses take forever to apply *just right*. She dances to every song at formals, the slow and serious—"On Bended Knee" and "Back to One" and "When Can I See You Again?"—and the freaky grindy hot-sex songs—Trick Daddy and Usher and maybe Snoop or 50 Cent. She dances with the other KDs when the *just the girls*! songs come on—"We are Family" and "I'm Every Woman"—and stays on the dance floor during the slapstick playlist—"YMCA" and "ABC," and sometimes even "Tubthumper" or "99 Red Balloons": every song, she's out of her seat, her hands in the air even when Outkast doesn't tell her to, dancing like a woman who's let her hair down even when it's still trapped in the stranglehold of pins and sticky-solid hairspray. She dances with her sorority girls, so in love with this brand of womanhood that you'd think there would be no energy left to dance elsewhere, but she does.

Jenn dances at the Indie Saloon and at Hip-Star, too, bars far from the top fraternity/sorority hang-outs, bars where every shirt is a slogan T, where the irony is so thick and suffocating that the crowds have forgotten that they're even being ironic. She dances to '90s Night, to Backstreet and Marcy Playground while drinking two-dollar vodka-cranberries. And Charles, you sit uncomfortable in this other-world, this outside-the-establishment refuge for Gulf Coast hipsters. Jenn doesn't care, doesn't know discomfort. She disappears to the front when the moody emo band plays Billy Idol, forces you to hop up and fist-pump and sing along to "867-5309 (Jenny)" and "Don't Stop Believing" and "Two Tickets to Paradise." She wears a Def Leppard t-shirt one day, but tomorrow it might be N'Sync or vintage Madonna or Poison or NKOTB, tight baby t's she found on the internet or at thrift stores and that might have looked ridiculous on anyone else…but *she is Jenn*. For her, it isn't sarcasm, really, just a style all her own, a sincere devotion to the things that make her happy no matter what anyone else tells her she should or shouldn't enjoy.

Dancing one night at Alumni Ball with her fraternity-president boyfriend, a week later at a Gin Blossoms Reunion Show, an outdoor block party in Port Charlotte you'd never have imagined existing if she hadn't found it, but at the end of the night you somehow feel as if your entire existence has been enriched by the time you've spent here with her, the two of you yell-singing "Hey Jealousy" and "Found Out About You." It's like eating couscous instead of French fries, a gator burger instead of ground beef. There is nothing quantitative about such experiences, but there is this: there is *you* being better than you would've been had you gone to the same old bar and said/done the same old things, and there is Jenn leading the way to that better version of you, dancing as she leads.

Once every couple months, she drags a whole crew—you, maybe Edwin or James Hawke, and a gaggle of sorority girls who would otherwise be hotly pursued at the Sigma Chi bar by well-muscled slicksters—she gets these whole crews together and re-directs them to '90s Grunge Night at Supernova, this ordinarily lame bar on the outskirts of Campus Town made bustling by Jenn and her entourage, and it's her favorite thing in the world, bands covering Pearl Jam and Nirvana and Soundgarden and Alice in Chains, maybe more morose than you'd picture for Jenn, "Black Hole Sun" and "Jeremy" and "Smells Like Teen Spirit." She was in elementary or middle school when these songs came out, but they all feel like the soundtrack for a high-schooler who spent his days draped in blacks and chains and world-doesn't-understand-me sadness. It doesn't seem very Jenn Outlook, but still, Jenn doesn't miss these nights. The best '90s Grunge Nights start with DJ request and move on to some featured cover band, the best of which has always been the Presidents of the United States of America Cover Band Cover Band, so bizarre because the Presidents of the United States of America weren't really grunge, and probably weren't ever deserving of one cover band, let alone another cover band to cover the cover band (?). For all you know, the old guys on the stage are the original band itself. They don't even restrict themselves to the Presidents of the United States of America, sometimes going off on wild tangents of hip-hop and early-'90s dance, but who can resist the wackiness of "Peaches" morphing into "Garden Grove" morphing into "Gin 'N Juice" morphing into "All That She Wants" morphing into "Lump." It makes no sense, but Jenn stands at the front of the room when the band takes the stage and she is a smile and an exclamation point in a bar that is mostly scowls and tortured ellipses.

She dances in these two worlds, happy-proper-girlie vs. dark-grunge-whacky, strange though the juxtaposition seems, but she is honesty personified. Jenn is Jenn is Jenn, and somehow she makes you feel like you should be proud to be Charles Washington even when you're not sure who that is.

\*

At some point over the past year, Jenn and I moved beyond the superficial quirks and platitudes of a college relationship's early days. We moved beyond sitcom discussions, and drove straight into full-speed-ahead discussions about family and future.

And no one else knew, but on the night of the Senior Send-Off, I was planning to give Jenn my fraternity letters.

It was called the "*lavalier* ceremony," and the act itself was simple. I bought the silver charm online, the letters NKE dangling straight down, and I'd get down on one knee and clasp the charm to her current necklace. Simple. But it was universally acknowledged at our campus: the lavalier was a promise of engagement (no one got engaged *in* college, of course), forever merging your girlfriend with your brotherhood, and even though NKE tradition mandated that the chapter was supposed to physically destroy any member who gave up his letters to a woman—they'd mob me, beat me, rip off my clothes, tie me to a street light on Greek Row, and dump sour milk and raw eggs and shaving cream and beer and toilet water all over me, good clean fun, just like Jerry O'Connell in *Scream 2* except without the unfortunate kill scene afterward—I wanted my parents to see that, too. To know how dedicated I was to taking such a step in my life. What I was willing to endure to do the right thing.

I'd be leaving for a full year on the road, but my parents loved her, and we already knew everything we needed to know about one another, Jenn and I. We knew the good and the bad, the nitty-gritty and the nitty-grittier, and we were still excited by everything we saw. There was no reason to delay the inevitable: when you know, you know.

She'd be at the Senior Send-Off, probably standing there with my parents, and then moments later she'd be wearing my letters.

*

"Charles, I've got something to say," Jenn told me as we arranged the final stack of napkins on one of the long fold-out tables in the dining room. We'd booked a caterer for the Senior Send-Off, just a local barbecue joint, but we'd gone to great lengths to make this as classy as BBQ could be: we wouldn't simply have plastic condiment packets, nor even cheap squeeze bottles, but decadent *serving bowls, ladles*, the barbecue sauce glistening in the glass like refrigerated pudding. There would be no torn and discarded packets across the floor, no errant squirts of mustard to ruin some mother's white shirt. We'd even arranged on the table—or rather, Jenn had arranged—stacks of napkins in alternating geometric designs, alternating colors. "And I just wanted to say it now," she said, "before everyone gets here and this whole house gets crazy."

"Talk to me," I said.

"I don't ever want to tell you what to do," she said. "The second that happens, a relationship—a friendship, even—is already over." Her hand on my chest, and she closed her fingers around the bottom of my collar, pulled me closer, kissed me, and how long had we been together at that point?, a year and a half?, and so it should've just been an average mid-afternoon kiss, an action no different than a handshake or high-five or chest-bump with a fraternity brother, but it somehow seemed like something more. Yes, I'd be leaving her soon. I'd be leaving all of this. Starting over sounds exciting until you realize that you're *ending* one life to begin the other. "But," she said, "I know how you get about this fraternity. The hours you spend with it. The energy."

"That's why it's the perfect job," I said.

"I know," she said. "But listen. You need to promise that you're going to call me."

"Of course I'll—"

"And you need to promise that you'll visit. That's the only way this will work. I've got experience with this sort of thing, someone I love hitting the road for weeks at a time."

"Plane tickets are expensive, gas is expensive," I said, "so I've got to be strategic."

"I understand that," she said. "But seriously, what else are you gonna spend your money on? A new TV? Can't lug that around in the Explorer, can you?" She laughed.

But I was thinking about engagement rings. My father had been right about how little money I'd pocket; already I'd done the math in my head and I knew I'd been too eager to believe Walter LaFaber when he told us that we'd save a ton of money on the road because our food and rent and electric and water was all covered by the National Headquarters. A thousand bucks a month in salary, and I was supposed to buy an engagement ring *and* plane tickets home? Already my head was caught in a loop of thought, but it was the night of my Senior Send-Off: I didn't *want* reality.

"Jenn," I said. "You know I'll do it."

"For your good as much as mine," she said. "Charles, I know how you get."

"How I get?"

She stopped, fingers now curled around the back of my neck. Closed her eyes and shook her head. "I know how frustrated you get when things don't work out the way you want them to. You try so hard."

And I said something, and then she said something else, and I know we kept talking, but damned if I remember what either of us said because my head was a frozen computer with hourglass spinning, and then Jenn was gone so she could shower and attend some early-evening sorority function for her own Senior sisters; she'd be back in a couple hours with her camera, ready to be our official photographer and capture our event and make permanent every shining moment, but for a minute—the short stretch of time before any of the parents arrived, and before any of the brothers emerged from their bedrooms upstairs—it was just me and the house living room, an image so lonely it belonged in some end-of-the-world zombie-apocalypse movie, the man who wakes up to discover that the world has died off while he slept.

# The Barbecue
CHAPTER FOUR

By the time my parents arrived back at the fraternity house for the Senior Send-Off, most of the other parents had already filtered inside, fifty or sixty total. They came two at a time, husbands wearing polo shirts tucked into khaki pants, a few still in shirt and tie, having driven here straight from work; wives in Florida weekend wear, skirts or jeans or white pants, all of them walking around our house hesitantly, led by sons unsure how to introduce them to their college world; mothers eventually stopping at the giant framed composite photos of the entire chapter, touching the glass, trying to locate the individual photos of their sons, saying, "Oh, why didn't he *tell* me he had his picture taken in a tuxedo? He looks so *nice*! I would have bought one!"; or touching the hanging portraits of our founders, or the charter, straightening the frames. Some of the fathers commented on the wicker couches, on the big-screen TV where the Magic game flashed with high-def crispness. They stepped over discolorations in the area rug, unaware that these were beer and vomit stains from their own sons. And over and over again, I heard parents repeating the same two questions: "Where's the bar?", and "Where's the food?"

The first question was easy to answer. "Right this way," I said to Mr. and Mrs. Cambria. "Right this way," I said to Mr. and Mrs. Simmons. Over and over, a handshake and a modest bottom-of-the-throat laugh when they said, "You're the president? Good work, son." And then I watched them shrink in awe of the grand display of alcohol at the bar. "Where's the bar?" they had asked, and my response had stunned them to silence.

For some reason, though, our caterer—a local barbecue restaurant—was late. "Still gonna be another hour," they told me when I called. "Sorry, bro. We're backed up."

"I've got over a hundred people waiting for food," I said. The house was full by this point, any minor error magnified, and I'd imagined a rigid schedule for the night: cocktail hour, barbecue, awards and cake, lavalier, ass-beating, immortality, all before midnight. "If you're late, there better be some sort of discount."

"You gave us a window," the clerk told me. "Your sheet says 7-9 PM. So we've got another two hours to fulfill the order. Like I said, busy busy busy over here."

"I never said anything about a *window*. That's the time of the event!"

"It was on the paperwork you signed. It said 'between these times.' That's how we plan ahead for use of our kitchen space, the times that our customers give us."

"I need the food," I said, summoning my presidential voice, something I wasn't very good at. "If we're satisfied, we'll use you guys for all our events. If not? We'll let everyone on campus know about our dissatisfaction. Trust me when I say that there will be no one ordering from Old Smoky ever again."

"We don't like threats," the man said. "You'll get your order in the time frame promised."

Click.

"Where's the food?" Edwin Cambria asked me. He'd helped me plan the night, might have even filled out the catering paperwork, and now that I was on the phone *he* was fielding those two questions over and over: *Where's the bar?* (easy) and *Where's the food?* (tougher). "It's coming, it's coming," he told them, trying to then introduce one set of parents to another, or trying to steer them all toward the bar instead of toward the long empty tables where the plates and napkins were stacked in anticipation of the barbecue.

"I just called," I told him, holding up my cell phone. "Running late."

"Don't worry, brother-man. As long as the bar's stocked, everything's kosher. I'll play bartender!" So here was Edwin, going from family to family to continue his assurances that food was coming, pointing out the bar and the beer tubs, then slipping behind the bar and conjuring a martini shaker and pointing to one mother and saying "I know *you* want a chocolate martini, am I right?"

And the minutes ticked past.

Eventually, Edwin's parents joined him at the bar, a semi-circle of genetic inheritance—the father's pointed nose on his son, the mother's comically round eyes. The entire room, in fact, had become a case study of shared traits, of parental features—hair colors or styles or texture, shoulder size, even clothing preference—passed onto children. Blonde hair came from *you*, thick forearms from you, freckles from you, bushy eyebrows from you. My mother with a drink in her hand, my father stolid and humorless. But everywhere, the same look of hunger.

Our Senior Send-Off featured only a short awards ceremony, planned for after dinner, but there were really no other activities on the agenda that I could cram into this empty over-long cocktail hour. I couldn't turn this into a college party, after all, and put on a Kanye CD, dim the lights, and let lust take over. I couldn't roll out the beer pong table, couldn't gather all of the brothers together to sing the dirty "Yogi Bear" song. And so—with no food yet delivered—the tiny father-mother-son clumps milled around, then drifted back to the bar with greater frequency, as if there was a riptide in the otherwise-stagnant waters of the living room that compelled them all to constantly circle back to the bar. And soon enough, the trashcans were full, sixty Baby Boomers holding beer bottles or cocktail cups, forty or so drinking-age children seizing the opportunity to grab alcohol and make sure their parents knew that—*yes*—they could drink casually too, they were capable of it, they did it well.

7:00 PM melted into 8:00, but the alcohol was easing minds, bringing us together without worry. Maybe this was reassuring. Maybe this was the modern fraternity. A happy family gathering, no one hanging from windows or chugging vodka. Maybe this is all the Send-Off needed to be.

But soon my own parents—after making the rounds and saying hello to the few brothers they knew, then introducing themselves to a few other parents—were standing before me, my father with a cup of ice water and my mother with a glass of red wine.

"Everyone drinking on an empty stomach," my father said. "This could get ugly."

"It's fine," I said. "The food will be here any minute."

"We could order take-out," my mother suggested.

"Please, no. Just enjoy the wine, and in no time—"

"Better be soon," my father said. He tapped his watch. "You're dealing with an older crowd, Charles. We don't drink like you college kids. We don't do 10:00 dinners."

"No time," I repeated.

But "no time" turned out to be the end of the "window."

\*

Jenn came back at some point, camera in hand.

And while I rushed around making phone calls and running my hands through my hair, she spent the evening sliding in and out of the different clumps, introducing herself to this set of parents, that set, to the Smiths, to the Gordons, one hand on Mr. Young's chest—"Would you like to pose for a picture?"—snapping photos for the NKE online photo album. She didn't need me to make the introductions. She was *Jenn*. She was the life of any party, dancing wherever she went, any crowd; if I was busy, she'd make her own way. Besides, she was a fiend with the camera, so focused on the task of artful documentation that nothing could detract her.

She wore a black cocktail dress that night, sexier than she needed to be, but I'm not even sure she was trying: it was the sort of dress that seemed both tight and loose, that clung to her body in all the right spots, that floated off in all the other right spots, so effortless that you figured she just woke up like this every morning. No one was complaining. All night long, as she navigated the room and appeared from nowhere, a lightning bolt of youthful energy and beauty suddenly striking directly next to you, camera in hand, face aglow and ready to make *you* the subject of her next picture, it must have seemed to these parents that they'd been singled out for some special honor. *Us? You picked us for your picture?*

Occasionally, in that long cocktail haze before dinner, she found me to relay some bit of round-the-house gossip from the evening ("Darrell's father just knocked into the trophy case" or "I found an empty vodka bottle in one of the planters on the back patio..."), but then she was gone just as quickly, always ending each exchange with a hug and a kiss and a "This turned out well, Charles. You should be proud."

The lavalier was upstairs. In hindsight, maybe I could have presented it to her then, while everyone waited for food and had nothing else to occupy their attention. Maybe it would have been productive, even, to unite 150 drunk-hungry people in a common task that pulled them momentarily from the bar and made them forget about their hunger. But there was still a full night ahead, a full awards ceremony, and who wants to be hog-tied before the food even arrived?

*

At some point there was a brief lapse in the noise and chaos of the cocktail hour, and I slunk outside to find my mother in the back courtyard. My father had disappeared somewhere else, likely to make phone calls or check his email on his Blackberry.

"If I didn't know better," I said and sipped my vodka-tonic, "I'd think you and Dad were avoiding one another."

My mother took too long to answer, and I realized in that moment that I shouldn't have made the joke. They'd arrived together, after all, but he hadn't had his arm around her, hadn't poured her a drink or said a word to her, and they never seemed to get close enough that their skin might touch even accidentally. They'd never been a giddy touchy-feely high-school couple, but it seemed strange to see my father speaking with another set of parents without even bothering to introduce his wife.

"That's crazy," my mother said eventually, then swirled her wine glass and finished off the last few ounces of red.

"Enjoy your massage?" I asked.

"I always enjoy my massages."

"I'm just glad you're enjoying yourself. That's all I want, really."

"Don't worry," my mother said and held up her empty cup. "Your father might be joyless, but I'll enjoy myself."

"That's the spirit!" I put my arm around her. She'd never had any problem with the fraternity, had never lectured me about it as my father had, never found newspaper articles about hazing accidents or alcohol deaths. Hell, she'd never even pulled her circumnavigation stunts with me: canceling payments to the fraternity so that I'd get kicked out. Three years before, she'd enjoyed herself at our Family Weekend, and tonight, she was sitting out in the courtyard with a glass of wine, striking up conversation with a crew of other women spread across the outdoor lawn chairs. "Let me get back to the bar, then," I told her, "and get you another drink. All that alcohol isn't going to drink itself."

My mother craned her neck, searched this way and that. "Get me something stronger," she said. "Vodka, maybe. Your father wouldn't want to hear this, but if I have more wine, I'll fall asleep."

*

Sometime after I took the first heavy-duty trash bag of liquor bottles and beer cans from behind the bar and out the back door, the van for Old Smoky BBQ finally arrived. I'd already sent Edwin to the local 7-Eleven to

36

pick up Doritos and pretzels so that the mothers—some of them three-deep on Edwin's chocolate martinis—would have something in their stomachs to absorb all the alcohol. "This is not acceptable," I said to the driver after the food had been unloaded. I said it loud enough for the entire house to hear me; I wanted to make sure the parents knew it wasn't my fault, that the fraternity and the Senior Send-Off were both still flawless.

"Huh?" the driver said.

"Tell your manager that we won't be using Old Smoky again," I said. "Tell him."

"Is something wrong? Is something missing?"

"It's...the time frame is *not acceptable*."

"Um," he said. "I got here as quick as I could. There were speed limits."

But no, of course he wasn't responsible. He'd probably delivered ten other orders that evening, all at the times noted on whatever paperwork his boss had given him. And now everyone was looking at the two of us, angry Charles Washington with a vodka-tonic in his hand, and perplexed 16-year-old delivery boy wearing a t-shirt with a cartoon pig on the front. All of the parents staring, even as the twelve disposable aluminum tubs, each covered in foil and arranged on the long tables of our dining room, waited to be opened and served. Fathers, mothers, and sons all inching closer to the food, but with marked restraint, no one wanting to jump the gun and dig in first. Twelve aluminum tubs, and several stacks of styrofoam to-go containers filled with Texas Toast and fried okra. Everyone staring, first at the two of us, then at the food. *What is he arguing about? Give us the motherfucking barbecue!*

"Here," I told the driver, and handed him his tip. "Just get out of here."

And I walked back inside. Edwin was just now bringing from his upstairs mini-fridge the small glass bowls of barbecue sauce and hot mustard and mayonnaise, balancing each precariously on his palms and forearms, arranging them around the carefully designed stacks of napkins. The food had been a long time coming, but our presentation was flawless.

"Barbecue?" my father asked. "Interesting choice."

I hadn't even noticed him approach me. "Thought it would be easiest for a large group."

"Couldn't just grill out yourselves?"

"You know about our kitchen," I said.

"Right. You guys can't use your own kitchen. House full of fraternity guys, and no one has a grill?"

So my father wasn't impressed with our catered meal...fine...I'd draw his attention back to the single element of the party that I knew was a hit. "You like the bar selection?" I asked, motioning toward the far end of the room, where—even with the food just delivered—a crowd still remained, a tall man in gray slacks holding the bottle of Grey Goose high, turning it around and examining it in the same way that a Revolutionary War musket or a piece of Confederate cash might be inspected on *Antique Roadshow*, before eventually nodding satisfactorily and pouring himself a drink.

"Your mother appreciates the wine," he said.

"Yeah. She told me."

He swirled the ice in his cup. "She'll drink too much and have a headache."

"She's fine."

"You're not the one who has to drive her," he said.

I pointed to his cup. "What are you drinking?"

"Water."

"There's a lot of stuff over there. You like martinis."

He crept toward the foil-covered metal tubs. Everyone else was still keeping their distance while I arranged the plates and plastic silverware, but there was an energy pulsing in that room: if I didn't get out of the way in the next minute, I would be stampeded. "Are you trying to get rid of me?" he asked.

"No. Of course not. I just..." I flung my arms out desperately, knocked over one of the napkin stacks. "I just want you to enjoy yourself," I said, and bent to gather the mess I'd created, smacked my hand on the side of the table.

"Well," he said and pinched the foil lightly; seeing that it wasn't too hot, he lifted the corner to peer inside. He'd found the tub of pulled pork, and we both stared at the tall piles of meat as if beholding an ancient wonder of the world. "I'd have a much better time if I had a plate full of barbecue," he said. "Want to get this party started, Charles?"

And finally it seemed as if the two of us were in agreement; it was just pulled pork, sure, but in that moment it became something more important: it was my choice of which university to attend, my choice to join the fraternity; it was the house, my brand-new career, my ability to save the world, all inside those steaming metal pans. And so I lifted the foil covers, curling them back on themselves to protect and keep warm as much of the meat as possible. Proud of the pulled pork. The baked beans. The roasted quarter-chickens. The mashed potatoes and macaroni and cheese! Cornbread! Green beans and almonds, sliced smoked ham, smoked sausages, dry-rub ribs! The entire menu of Old Smoky BBQ, ready to be consumed, ready to feed the appetites of all these parents, ready to assuage concerns, to give final confirmation that their sons had made the right choice when they'd joined this fraternity. Here it was!

Except—

"Serving spoons?" my father asked, and he had a sesame-seed bun opened on his plate. "Tongs?"

"Sure," I said. "Do you see a plastic bag around here anywhere?"

I fumbled, hit my hand again.

"I don't see anything," my father said, and behind him, other parents had formed a line, some grabbing plates and buns and napkins the same as he had, their moods and spirits high, men and women who were previously strangers now chatting and joking with one another, some holding full martini glasses, others with whiskey on the rocks. A woman in white pants was laughing so hard that it almost looked painful, and her husband was slapping her back. Another couple was clinking wine glasses, and Jenn stood at the bar with a group of her sorority sisters, girls who were dating Nikes; she topped off with a healthy pour of cranberry juice a set of glasses half-filled with vodka and ice. This was what a cocktail party was supposed to looked like. This was polished adulthood. Everything I'd wanted. But somehow I'd missed the smallest of details.

"I can't find any serving equipment," I said, madly searching beneath the table, under the trash bags we'd hung to collect dirty paper plates. "Edwin? See them anywhere?"

"I don't see anything," Edwin said from the bar. He was searching through cabinets as if—for whatever reason—the delivery man might have stashed a set of tongs up there.

"Something wrong, Charles?" Jenn called out, finishing her final pour.

"No, no!" I said. Crawling on the floor now, searching searching.

"Charles," my father said, and he looked back over his shoulder at the long line, where parents were taking notice of this situation. Standing in clumps of brand-new friends. Turning to one another, all of them asking the same questions. "What's wrong?" "Why won't he let us eat?" "What's the hold-up?" "Who's in charge, here?" The woman in the white pants had stopped laughing, face sucked of its humor.

And now my mother was wedging herself into the line, grabbing a plate. Cocktail cup in hand. "What's wrong?" she asked. "Charles, what are you doing?"

"Nothing!" I said from beneath the table. "I'm sure it's around!" Rising, banging my shoulder against the table again, nearly knocking over the cornbread.

"Oh, you can't find the spoons?" my mother asked.

"Sometimes you have to *ask* to rent serving equipment," my father said. "They don't always just *give* it to you. Did you ask?"

"Edwin," I said. "Did they say anything about serving equipment?"

And now Edwin was walking toward us empty-handed, disappointment etched into his face. "I don't know," he said. "I don't remember them saying anything."

"Didn't ask them many questions at all, did you, Charles?" my father asked.

"The two-hour window…that wasn't my fault."

"You've probably got something in your kitchen," he said.

"It's locked, Dad."

"Oh. Right."

But he knew. He knew.

"Why is the kitchen locked?" my mother asked.

"They pay a staff," my father said. "They're not allowed inside their own kitchen. Maybe next time I should bring my own utensils."

"That's silly," my mother said.

"Hungry!" someone shouted.

"I've *explained* this to you!" I said, trying to keep my voice down.

Jenn approaching now, cranberry-vodka in hand, her crew of sorority friends fanning out behind her with looks of mild puzzlement. As she passed the tall man in the gray slacks, I noticed that his drink was empty now, too; he was standing in a static line, eating ice cubes, eyebrows raised in frustration.

"Why don't we just use the plastic utensils?" my mother asked.

"That'll have to do," Edwin said. "No other option."

"Charles, just grab some spoons and forks," my father said. "It won't be pretty, but it's better than nothing."

"I'd prefer to use a serving spoon," I said. "It's got to be around here."

"Charles. We're hungry. A plastic fork will work."

"I can find it. The event *deserves* better."

"It's going to get cold, Charles."

The long, long line—over a hundred people by now, parents, children, all the khaki shorts and polo shirts and button-downs and ties and jean skirts and white pants, all of my fraternity brothers holding Heineken bottles, everyone pulled in from the living room and the courtyard and the game room—they were all looking at *him* now. My father. They knew what was happening, and what they saw was this: little Charles, the supposed president, rummaging around, panicked, an empty plastic bag in one hand. Parents looking at my father as if he was the sensible one, as if…as if…who the hell was *I?* Why couldn't I just clear out of the way and let the man do his job? As if my father had planned this event, as if I was his mere assistant. *For fuck's sake, let us eat!*

"Fine," I said. "Plastic utensils."

And a cheer arose from the crowd. "All *right!*" one man yelled.

"Teamwork," Edwin said, clapped my father's back. "Nice work, Mr. Washington."

My father opened the Ziploc bag of plastic utensils, dumped them out on the table beside our now-silly-looking glass bowls of barbecue sauce. And even though my father had been first in line, he stepped aside, motioning for the next couple to fill their plates, and as they stepped past him en route to pulled pork, they smiled and thanked my father, and he waited until the very end, a hundred people, two hundred, after the last couple—who shook his hand and called him a gentleman—before he finally stepped back into place in front of the pulled pork tub. But before doing so, he turned to me and said, "Come and grab something to eat, Charles," the same voice that any of the parents in the room would have used to reprimand a 10-year-old. And he didn't move to fill his own plate until I'd done so.

*

After dinner ended—only scraps of pork and burnt toast left at the tables, a line of trash bags stuffed with sloppy plastic plates and used silverware—it was time for the academic awards presentation, and then the cake. And, of course, the lavalier.

This was my farewell, my personal send-off, a memory that I hoped I could keep close for the full summer of training and then sixteen weeks of Fall travel and then sixteen weeks of Spring travel, like baby pictures in a grown man's wallet. This would be another Alumni Ball moment for me, my final bow. My night redeemed.

# After-Dinner Drinks
CHAPTER FIVE

"Your attention!" I shouted to the room, and there seemed to be a great deal of wobbling in the fraternity house by now. Mothers holding glasses of wine, hands on their husbands' shoulders. Fathers leaning against walls, bellies swollen from an ill-advised second or third trip to the buffet, a quarter-pound of extra brisket and four ribs too many, and still finishing another bottle of Heineken. Everyone engaged in sedated post-dinner conversations throughout the house, swirling as they talked, spilling beer and white wine.

"Your attention, please!" I said again, and now Jenn was standing five feet in front of me. Seeing her was a reminder: I was speaking to the room, but really I was speaking to Jenn. Or I would be *soon*, at least.

But the room continued to buzz in a hundred different conversations. I waved my arms for attention, a small table topped with a half-dozen engraved academic plaques waiting to be presented and distributed, and it was Jenn who smiled up at me and then placed her drink on the table to unleash a vigorous earthquake-clap that didn't seem possible from such tiny hands.

The room stopped, cups frozen at lips, mouths paused in mid-word, as if stuck in a *Saved By the Bell* time-out.

And it was Jenn who kissed me on the cheek, who projected her voice to reach the entire fraternity house, inside and out, upstairs and down, 150 people in all, Jenn who introduced me—"My boyfriend, the president of the fraternity, an amazing guy who planned this entire night, and he's just got a few words to say"—and it was Jenn who gripped my hand, the sort of soft squeeze that you can't misinterpret and you can't fake.

The room broke into polite applause, not nearly as loud as a single clap from Jenn.

"I want to thank you all for making the trip to attend our Senior Send-Off," I told the assembled crowd. I tried to keep my eye on my girlfriend. To let her slip away, back into the crowd, would be to dash my plans: she needed to be close so that I could bend casually to my knee and present her the charm. "This event took a lot of planning," I said, "and we wanted to make sure that we used this opportunity to spotlight some of the great aspects of our fraternity."

But as I spoke, the faces and bodies were already un-freezing, hands stuffing into pockets and backs slumping against walls in anticipation of some long and exhausting speech. *Please, do we have to listen to this?* "Diversity in our membership," I was saying, "a commitment to service, a National Headquarters that strongly believes"—mothers taking sips of wine, glassy eyes glossing further— "depiction of fraternities in the media and in Hollywood is *100 percent wrong*, and we wanted to show you that" —fathers whispering into the ears of their sons, my fraternity brothers patting their dads on the back and then slinking away to the bar to mix a couple more drinks. Cell phones out. Text messages.

But I continued speaking, said something about the mission and about the socially responsible citizens we were creating, and how proud I'd been to represent them all as their president, and my father stood in the back of the room, water in hand, never failing to make eye contact as I recited my prepared speech about the importance of scholarship to the fraternity mission; he sipped the water just the same as he sipped his morning coffee, stared directly into my eyes, perhaps already thinking of how he would call bullshit on my convictions.

"Enough from me," I said, and I dabbed my sweaty forehead with a napkin. "It's time to hand out the awards and the annual Nu Kappa Epsilon scholarships."

And then the room erupted into real applause, this time much heartier than the last, this time genuine. And before I could say another word, Todd Hampton—the newly elected president of our chapter, the man who would move into my presidential suite once I drove away to Indianapolis in two weeks—was beside me, arm around me, and he was saying "I'll take over from here, Charles. Why don't you step down?"

"Um," I said, but he nudged me back into the crowd. And from down here, surrounded by fraternity brothers and swaying mothers and 50-year-old men still chewing ribs, I could no longer see Jenn. She'd fallen to the thick of the crowd somehow, maybe all the way to the back of the room. And Todd passed out plaque after plaque, "Best G.P.A." and "Most Improved G.P.A." and "The Damon Jarred Memorial Scholarship," and it was supposed to be me up there, soaking in the applause and offering my commentary on the brothers who meant so much to me, the family, the power of fraternity, but it was Todd. "Thank you all so much for coming," Todd said. "We worked so hard on this night, and it means everything to have our families celebrate with us. And now, I'll—"

"Time to cut the cake!" I shouted over him. And I was motioning for everyone to follow me, and the room was a flood of parents and teenagers and twenty-somethings rushing to the next room, where—wobbling—I was soon cutting the giant cake with a tiny plastic knife, fingers slopping into the frosting, mothers taking slices of cake while trying (but not very hard, after all the wine they'd finished) to hide their grimaces when they noticed thumb prints in the icing, Jenn taking pictures, *Jenn taking pictures*! And I tried to elbow my way away from the table and toward her, but the mothers were too intent on their cake, and it was all arms and torsos and I was pushed back to the table and someone said, "Not so fast, buddy! Keep cutting that cake!" and Jenn was gone.

Minutes later, I escaped to the courtyard, but there was no sign of her. Not inside, not outside.

"Looking for Jenn?" Edwin asked. He was out here with a girl who looked like Lindsay Lohan, his hand on her ass while his parents were inside finishing another round of martinis.

"You seen her?" I asked.

"She went home," the Lindsay Lohan girl said and pouted her lips. "Back to the KD house."

"She went home? Without saying goodbye?" I asked. "She can't…"

"Christina was waaaa-sted," the girl said. "She, like, had to get her out of there."

"Christina?"

"His formal date," Lindsay said and slapped Edwin's chest. She said *formal* as if it had twelve syllables, the "foooorrrrrrr" lasting so long that Edwin was able to move his beer bottle to his lips, take a long gulp, then bring it down and toss the empty bottle into a trash can.

"What?" Edwin said nonchalantly. "I'm with *you* tonight."

"She's not coming back?"

The girl held up her palms, and the action was enough to make her stumble and almost fall into the fountain. Edwin caught her. "Take it easy, Charles," he said, "we don't want her thinking too hard tonight, buddy." And she laughed and fell into him and he caught her by the boobs and balanced her and grabbed her ass while doing so. "God, I love this house," he said.

*

"So proud of you," my mother said. "So proud, Charlie."

"Thank you," I said.

"Whoops." Splash of drink on the wall, on the floor.

"You all right?"

"Charlie Charlie," my mother said. "I was always hard on you, wasn't I?" And she had her hand on my shoulder, was leaning close as if this was a conversation we'd been putting off for far too long. "All the clubs, all the sports."

"No, Mom. You were fine."

"But it paid off, didn't it? Look at you now, Charlie!"

Splash of drink on my pants.

"Yes, Mom."

"Let me tell you something about your father," she said.

"Um. Please don't."

"He won't even let himself have a good time," she said. "It's so… it's *pathetic*."

"He's trying to be…I don't know…responsible," I said.

"We did all right as a family, didn't we, Charlie?"

"What are you talking about, Mom?"

"I'd like to think we did something right. You're going to do so well. Maybe you'll do better than we have."

"Do better? You did fine. What are you talking about?"

"Whoops," she said again.

\*

I still remember the first time I ever saw my parents drunk. When I was fifteen or so. They came home from a party, a housewarming party, my mother crashing through the front door, laughing and stumbling through the dim hallway to cook leftovers in the kitchen, my father trying to keep her quiet while I pretended to be asleep. She made ridiculous comments about doing yardwork at midnight, or about dusting fan blades, howled, but the next day appeared normal again, like a werewolf the morning after a full moon. My father, in the morning, was back to wearing pleated khaki shorts and a polo, sipping coffee on the front porch. Thinking about it now, I'm not sure if he'd even had a sip of alcohol the night before, but he *knew*, at least. Knew I'd heard. My mother, too. And I think they realized my mental picture was altered that night, irrevocably, and it wasn't a bad thing to them, just gave them license to resume "Saturday Nights on the Town," something they'd abandoned the moment I'd been born, gave my mother license to start a wine collection, a new red every few nights. As an only child, she was the one who'd kept me involved all throughout middle school and high school, in soccer and Key Club and Cypress Falls Service, always telling me about my potential and about how I could be *anything* but I needed to be *driven*, and so—starting, perhaps, that night when I was fifteen—she could see the credits rolling on her parental responsibilities. Perhaps she imagined a rewind to her youth. I would be off to college in two years, gone, a financial burden but no longer a physical one.

Out in Cypress Falls, many of my friends' parents one-upped my own; no longer needing large houses for their kids to spread out toys and textbooks, they moved into the city, into condos in Tampa and Orlando and Miami, or back up north to Chicago or New York. All those ideas we had about who our parents really were had been extinguished in an instant. They'd played a role for sixteen years, and now they'd called it curtains. Even the idea of "family" seemed to dissipate, divorce after divorce ravaging my friends' lives while they were in college, but at least my parents still held *that* together. That was the thing that kept the past meaningful, after all: to know that it was still alive, that it hadn't just been an act, that the world didn't need to re-start, that it had always been going.

\*

By 10:30 PM, the food was finished. Slop in pans. The cake a shredded mess, a slasher victim. Parents were sitting in the living room lawn furniture, cups still full, yawning and grasping for conversation. Glancing at their watches, at the front door.

My mother had refilled her glass, had grabbed some cake and retreated to the patio with a few other *Real Housewives* types with whom she'd somehow become instant best friends. But my father hadn't moved in fifteen minutes, just stood at a wicker coffee table flipping through *The Complete History of the Nu Kappa Epsilon Fraternity* that I'd placed out in hopes of wowing curious parents with our storied past; it was a leather-bound volume of black-and-

44

white photos assembled and published for the 90ᵗʰ anniversary celebration several years before, and it was a massive testament to the Grand Tradition. My father examined a photo, read a caption, registered no real reaction. Still taking sips of his water. Flipped a page, then sipped water.

"Interesting stuff?" I asked, approaching him.

"I remember this," he said, pointing to a photo of the NKE house at the University of Florida, the entire structure consumed in white flames. I'd remembered looking through the book on a few lazy afternoons, knew that this picture was taken in the early 1970s; at the bottom border of the photo, you could make out the silhouettes of a dozen onlookers, some of them crying, others with their hands digging deep into their wild Social Revolution hair, all of them wearing laughably tight jeans and t-shirts. "I was a student at the time," my father said.

"I didn't know that," I said. "They rebuilt the house, right?"

"Yes. This was almost a major tragedy."

"Looks like it." A house on fire, billowing smoke, campus in turmoil...

He stared back down into the photograph, eyes lost in the grayscale conflagration.

"So listen," I said, and I held out a vodka-tonic for my father. "I saw that you didn't have a cocktail. I made this for you." There was still an excess of alcohol, so many unopened or half-finished bottles looking like they would go to waste: I couldn't take it with me to Indianapolis where I'd literally be living in a dorm attached to the Nu Kappa Epsilon National Fraternity Headquarters, and I didn't want to just leave all this alcohol at the fraternity house where it would be consumed without any real memory of who had purchased it and why. This was for my Senior Send-Off, not for two dudes on August 15ᵗʰ who wanted to play *Halo* and get drunk for free. It was clear that the parents in the room had come to their middle-age senses, all of them adopting the same behavior as my father. Maybe a single drink in hand, but hey, it was 10:30 PM, and that was later than they'd even planned to stay, and they needed to get back to the hotel before they fell asleep, and listen, it was nice meeting everyone, thanks for a wonderful evening, good night, good night, good night.

The party was just moments from breaking up, and what had I accomplished? What would be the final impression with which these men and women would be left?

"I'm driving your mother," he said, waving his hand to decline my drink.

"You can have a single drink," I said. "I mean, you brought that wine, so I know you were planning on having a drink."

"I'm saving that wine," he said. "I don't need to drink."

"Just take this or it's going to go to waste." I pushed it closer to him, arm rigid, a drop or two splashing out and onto the black and white photos of the *Complete History*. This, I realized then and there, was as close as I'd ever come to telling my father what to do.

"Fine." He took the rocks glass. "One."

"One."

He sipped, nearly spit it back out. "Jesus! Could you make this any stronger?"

"It's not that bad, is it?"

"It's *all* vodka, Charles."

"Half and half," I said.

"There's no tonic in this. Are you trying to kill me?"

"Dad, take it easy. We can add more tonic. Just take a sip and make some room."

"Is this how you drink?" He shook his head, placed the drink on the coffee table.

"What do you mean?"

"No wonder."

"No wonder *what*?" And now I shook *my* head, something I wouldn't have done if I hadn't already finished several vodka-tonics myself, several Heinekens. But this was my Senior Send-Off; this was the night before my graduation; this was the night to celebrate my new job. This was not a night on which to receive lectures about alcohol responsibility. This was not a night for him to play Fun Nazi to me. The money I'd spent! The trouble with the caterer, the embarrassment with the serving spoons and the cake. *I* would have a good time, damn it! I would. He would. *Everyone would.* They would remember me, and they would remember how fucking *amazing*—in my head, I even heard Jenn saying that word, "a-*maaaz*-ing"—this fraternity was, that it wasn't the stereotype they'd heard; fraternity held us all together, fraternity was family, fraternity was protection and leadership development and career and citizenship and future, life itself, and they would see that, they would see what I had been seeing and preaching for four years, and fine, I wasn't going to be able to lavalier my girlfriend so the *least* you can all do is *fucking enjoy yourselves!*

"No wonder I found you on the floor, right over there," my father whispered, pointing to the living room floor, to the very spot. "You sure you want to be drinking so much? With all these parents here?"

"It's all right," I told him. "Trust me."

My father regarded me with narrowed eyes, sighed.

"I'm not the same kid I was three years ago. I *am* responsible now, Dad."

"Charles, I know that you're a smart young man."

"But?"

"But nothing. That's all I'll say."

"Somehow I doubt that."

He sighed again. "That's all, Charles. You graduate tomorrow. You're a big boy. Just make sure I don't have to wake you up."

"See?" I said. "See? You can't just let it go."

"I care about you," he said. "You want to have these sorts of conversations, you're going to hear things you don't like."

"What conversations, Dad? This is my"—and I whispered now—"*my* night, okay? My party, my celebration. For one night, can you just pretend to have a good time? Can you just pretend you're, like, proud of what I'm doing?"

And I'm not entirely sure what he heard at that moment, if he heard the indignation in my voice that I wanted him to hear, the anger. Or did I just sound like a whiny teenager, no longer even a fraternity stereotype but now an angsty *rebelling-against-my-awful-parents* stereotype? No matter what he was thinking, he just shrugged, sniffed at his drink but didn't take another swallow. "The job? What am I supposed to say, Charles? You're better than this."

"Better than this? Un-fucking-believable," I said. "I'm going to talk to mom for awhile." And on any other day, I might have turned and walked away without another word, just let it die, you've been bold enough for one evening, Charles, and in any case, you're not going to ever win, he's your father and that's what fathers do, they keep you in check, and you're making a big deal out of something that all good fathers do—but there on *my night*, after the wine and the barbecue and the awards plaques and Todd and the cake and Jenn leaving and now *this*, I had to say something: "I'm going to do something good with my life, okay? My career…I'm not going to be like you."

"Hmm." He didn't move. "Good to hear your opinion of my life. How this whole experience was paid for."

But I was already walking away.

Away from the coffee table, down the hallway, past Edwin and his parents and Lindsay Lohan still gripping him tight, out of the living room, out to the backyard and the patio, and there was my mother, sitting in a lawn chair and drinking her vodka tonic, chatting with another woman. Sipping, then flipping back her dark brown hair from her eyes as though she was once again a 20-year-old sorority girl. How did this happen, I wondered? How did my mother always find someone to befriend in social settings? Someone nearly identical in appearance? How was it that these newfound friends even seemed to exhibit the same mannerisms, that—no matter where we were—they would even have identical drinks?

The party had died inside, but my mother—and the small collection of women on the patio—they had the right idea. This was the Future Jenn out here, I realized; this was the older version of the Kappa Delta clan out here, all of them still drinking and still chatting and still enjoying themselves like they had in college. Husbands inside, collapsing from fifty-hour work-weeks and three or four alcoholic drinks.

If the party was dying, then maybe the men only needed a reminder of who they once were, permission to drop their facades and become fraternity guys again.

Strong gulp of my vodka tonic.

It didn't seem right that it could all end so against-plan, either: Charles pushed aside, Jenn jetting early. If the night ended now, all anyone would remember of me was that I'd screwed up the catering order and given a terrible speech. I needed to keep it going.

Head spinning, and from here the night turns to snapshots.

One second, I'm inside the house.

The next, I'm zooming down the hallway, faces a smudge of activity all around me.

Then: I find Edwin, leaning against the bar, Lindsay with her hand on his belt.

"Where's the beer pong table?"

"Why?" he asked. "The party—"

"It's dying, Edwin," I said.

Strong gulp of my vodka tonic.

Voices, doors opening and closing, smudge of faces.

"They're old," Edwin said. "This is what old people do. They go to sleep by 10."

"Not tonight," I said. "Tonight's different. Help me with the beer pong table."

"You sure?"

"I'm President for two more days," I said. "Of course I'm sure."

# Drinking Games
## CHAPTER SIX

The parents were already drunk and the night should have been fading gracefully to black, but now I was leading the house into a banned activity. Maybe something would happen along the way, I hoped: Jenn would return, or my father would join my team and grab a ping-pong ball.

Beer pong might not sound like a big deal, that label of "banned activity" maybe just an unseen administrator's way of issuing blanket zero-tolerance guidelines in case of emergency, but I'd later hear during my summer training at the headquarters that drinking games have become one of the greatest "risk management liabilities" for undergraduate fraternities, one of the greatest causes of student death/injury, one of the top sources of lawsuits brought against national fraternities: stick a bunch of 19-year-olds in a room together with cards or ping-pong balls or some other seemingly innocent toy, give them a cooler full of beer, issue a set of rules forcing them to drink (on average) five beers an hour (most of it chugged), let them think that it's an extreme sport, that Ability to Drink in Excess = Toughness, and then crank up the peer pressure in the room until everyone is chugging before they've even started playing the game and...Well. It was an activity banned by Edison University, by FIPG insurance guidelines, by Nu Kappa Epsilon National Sacred Laws, but probably you didn't need any formal regulations to know that bad things resulted from drinking games.

At the National Fraternity Headquarters, where each year insurance costs rise higher and higher, and where the staff spends the majority of its energy on preaching alcohol responsibility and enforcing strict guidelines, we use a simple graphic to educate members on how to avoid liability. It's called the Circles of Danger:

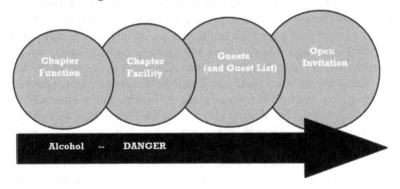

The basic idea is this: when alcohol is present, the danger for the fraternity chapter is greater in each new overlapping circle of danger.

Drinking games are so dangerous that they don't even warrant inclusion on the Circles of Danger. They're banned outright. Everyone knows: you get caught, and you're fucked.

And there I was at the Senior Send-Off, in my brand-new Banana Republic slacks and blue dress shirt, rolling the old warped ping-pong table from our storage closet to the center of the first-floor game room, Edwin rummaging through the bar cabinets for plastic cups and clean ping-pong balls. These were items, of course, that we'd *never* allow the cleaning staff to lock up in the kitchen: they needed to remain accessible. Always. Walk into the NKE house on any Saturday night and you might find this table in use, tournaments in progress, elaborate charts of team rosters and round-robin seating drawn on the dry erase board on the wall, brothers with sharpies writing their signatures and their team logos on the underside of the table after winning: crude sketches of machine guns ("The Automatics!") and fraternity/sorority letters ("TEAM NKE & AΔΠ), messages to future gamers: "Ten wins in a row. Good luck topping that."

"Beer pong?" someone asked. One of my fraternity brothers in the other room.

My head still spinning, but a smile returning to my face.

"Fathers and sons, doubles matches," Edwin said.

"Hell yeah!" someone else yelled.

Table wheeled into place.

"What's this?" one father asked.

"Beer pong!" someone else yelled.

Explanation of the rules under way.

"What are these signatures, here?" a father asked his son.

"We create team names, Dad."

"Interesting. And logos?"

"That's mine. We won the Super Bowl tournament."

"Atta boy!"

Hundreds of different drinking games: Asshole and "What the Fuck?" and Power Hour and Flip Cup and Quarters, but Beer Pong is the most notorious of them all, maybe the only one with national tournaments. All you need is a simple ping-pong table (really, though, any table can be manipulated for Beer Pong), some solo cups, beer, and a ping-pong ball. Usually you play in teams, two per side; half-fill a cluster of cups on each side of the table with beer (ten per side, usually in a triangle formation); then take turns bouncing a ping-pong ball from one side of the table to the other with the aim of plopping the ball directly into each of the cups of beer opposite you; accomplish the feat before the opposing team can do it first, and you win the game. And for each ball you plop in? Your opponent chugs the beer from that cup, then removes it from the table. Of course, that's just the basic concept, and the game is full of variations: *regional variations*, with South Floridians playing different than Central Floridians, Californians playing different than New Yorkers; *cultural variations*, with the campus Hillel and Filipino Student Organizations claiming different rules; or even *personal variations*, with some teams deciding upon a modified set of ground rules before ever squaring off. But the game itself, no matter the rules prohibiting it, is as universal on college campuses as the spiral-bound notebook.

And as crowds began moving from the bar and the courtyard and the living room to the game room, I checked for my father, looked to the coffee table and *The Complete History*. By now he was absorbed entirely in the photo narrative. Still standing, not even bothering to lounge with the book and get comfortable. Ice melting in his un-sipped vodka tonic.

"Push the table into the living room," someone said.

I backed up against the bar as the table was wheeled past me, a platoon of my fraternity brothers pushing it as quickly as a battering ram but as reverently as if it was a coffin and they were its pall-bearers.

And soon it was dead-center in the house, directly atop the area rug, in line with the front door. Now it was the centerpiece of the party, occupying the space where the cake had sat a short while before. Ordinarily, we never played Beer Pong anywhere except the game room, always made sure to tuck the forbidden drinking game away in the back corner of the house, even closed the door and made non-participants into look-outs so the Greek Row Resident Advisors—there were four of them, two fraternity members and two sorority members—would not feel obligated to report the infraction. Generally, the Greek Row Resident Advisors looked the other way. We had an understanding, so long as we were discrete.

But this particular Friday night?

"Round one," someone shouted, and I heard the squeak of the dry erase marker on the board. Names written, charts scribbled. "Edwin and David Cambria will take on James...and your name, sir?...Henry Betterman! Round one, everyone!"

Head spinning. Men rising from their chairs.

"Sign up, right up here!"

Marker squeaking. The pop and *psssh* of Miller Lite cans opening, sound of foam rising, beer into plastic cup, ping-pong ball knocking against painted particle board. Bottles of Heineken popped, perhaps the first time in our chapter history we'd used *Heineken* for Beer Pong.

And this was it. The fathers, sleepy a moment before, now had the wide-eyed looks of waking-life dreamers. *You want us to play drinking games? You're inviting us, the old men?* Here, now, in the fraternity house? *Oh yes, oh yes!* Designated drivers be damned. Wives, children...whatever. 10 PM bedtimes forsaken! It was now time for some serious father-son bonding over ten cups of Heineken! The party was undying, room full of stumbling zombies lurching toward more drink, ping-pong balls plopping into cups, sons showing fathers their tossing technique, how best to score.

51

I watched from a distance, alone, still drinking vodka-tonics. I'd let it go a few games, then I'd drag my father over and force him to play. No sitting on the sidelines. Everyone plays, even *you*, Dad.

*

It started with father-son teams, but soon it was couples: teams of husbands and wives. Ball splashing into Miller Lite, Mrs. Schell lamenting that the ping-pong ball was getting pretty dirty by now, but oh well, let's just dip it into the water cup, ha ha ha, *oh goodness*!

Then it was mothers and sons versus mothers and sons, cups raised for a long chug, and then it was one woman saying, "I'll just sit down over... over here," and then we were helping someone to stand, and Edwin and his Lindsay Lohan lookalike were beside me, and he was saying, "This might have been a bad idea."

"They're fine," I said. "We're all adults here."

And at that moment, someone's father—a man with garlic-colored hair, body-builder's arms and torso, but a gut that suggested that he'd long ago given up cardio—let out the sort of scream that I usually only hear at football and basketball games. "*Yeeeaaa*-aaahhhhh!" Low and angry, from far back in the darkest caverns of his body, a recess left unexplored for years. "How you like *that*, huh?" he screamed. Slapped his wife on the back, then pointed across the table at his opponent, a skinny sophomore named Marc who I hoped was his son. "*Drink it up!* You just lost to an old man!"

"Scary," Lindsay said.

"Marc bears no resemblance to his father," I said.

But then they were gone, and I was standing alone again and still talking and it took me how long to figure that out?

Head spinning again.

I took another strong gulp of my vodka tonic.

Screeching laughter from somewhere. And then Todd Hampton was at my side. The new president. A year younger than me. The boy who'd pushed me from the podium. He'd said some things during elections a few weeks back that I suddenly remembered, how *things* needed to change, "things" in quote fingers and I had no idea what he meant. "We're never doing this again," he said. "These parents cannot handle their alcohol."

"Relax," I said. "It's a good event." Swaying.

"Easy for you to say. You're graduating," he said.

"Nothing easy about life after graduation," I said.

"Someone's mom is passed out in the bathroom."

"Well," I said. "Just having fun, you know?"

"Whole house is a mess," he said, "and now that the pledges are initiated, we got no one to clean it up."

"Um. We can clean it up *ourselves*, maybe?" I said. "Since when do we make the pledges do everything around here?"

"Beer Pong at a family event. This is out of control." He shook his head. "Things will be different when I'm president."

52

There it was again, that word "things."

But drunk as I was, I couldn't argue. What was I to say?

So I nodded. "Whose bright idea was this, anyway?" I asked.

"You really don't understand what the brothers in this fraternity want," he said, and then he was gone, too.

*

And then there was my father. Five minutes later? Ten? Beside me.

"I need your help," he said.

"Help with what?" I asked, tried to stand, slipped and fell back into my seat. When had I sat down?

"Your mother," he said.

"What about her?"

"She can't walk."

"She's fine. I just saw her."

"She's on the bathroom floor, Charles."

"*What?*"

"Passed out on the bathroom floor. I need your help getting her to the car."

And when I followed him down the hallway, past the Beer Pong tournament and past a father and son sitting at one of the patio tables drinking whiskey and playing cards, all the way down the hall, hand up for support, past the now-crooked charter on the wall, into the women's bathroom, there was my mother, a knocked-over rocks glass with chunks of melting ice spilled across the tiles.

"Is there anyone else in here?" I asked.

"Does it *matter?*" my father said. "Help me get her to her feet."

Really, the only reason we even had a women's bathroom at our fraternity house was because this was a university-owned property; I'd lived here for four years, and I'd only ever stepped foot inside the women's room once or twice, both times searching for extra toilet paper, both times scrambling to get in and out post-haste just in case one of the other residents had brought a female guest. Women's bathrooms: they're like some mystical forbidden zone, made you paranoid and loopy, made you feel icky and naughty for your intrusion. I ducked and peered beneath the stall doors, gave the entire space a once-over—

"Help me out, Charles," my father said. "Come on." He'd rolled her forward so that she was now sitting.

"Whu—" my mother mumbled, eyelids opening then closing.

"Just needs some water," I said. "Give her a few minutes."

My father brushed her hair away from her eyes, pressed the back of his hand against her forehead, then leaned in to whisper something in her ear. He smoothed out the tangles in her shoulder-length hair, then adjusted her shirt from where it had stretched around her shoulder as she rolled on the floor.

I stood nearby, hands in my pockets, trying not to watch, eyeing the door.

Truthfully, I'd never seen anything like this before, had no idea how a son was supposed to act when his mother reverted to freshman sorority girl. Yes, I

53

knew my mother had built up her wine collection after I'd left for college, and I knew that she drank more now than she ever had while I lived back home, but still I thought that parents had…I don't know…some sort of emergency shut-off switch before they went too far, something that prevented them from the same stupid behavior as their children.

Her eyes were open now, and she was mumbling again.

"One arm around her shoulder," my father told me, and I did as he instructed. "One arm at her waist. And lift." And we did, my mother's legs jiggling beneath her as she rose, her head rolling from side to side before finally going rigid to stare me in the eyes. "Whoa!" my father said, because I nearly dropped her. I tightened my grip on her waist. My other arm brushed against my father's, both of us volleying for position at my mother's back; he tapped my forearm, a sort of "you okay?" gesture, and I nodded. We were standing now, an interlocked three-person unit. "All right," he said. "Going out the doors now, Kim. One foot in front of the other. I've already pulled the car up."

When had he done this? How long had he known about Mom, passed out, before finally enlisting my help? Where had I *been* for the last thirty minutes?

"One foot in front of the other, Kim," he said again.

We lumbered forward, but she was at least conscious now, legs regaining their stability but still bending like rubber swords poked into steel armor. If we loosened our grip, she'd take a hard spill.

"There you go, there you go," my father said.

"Charles," she said then, and I tried not to hear. "Charlie. Charlie boy." Words as haunting as a nightmare that you can't convince yourself wasn't real. "Oh, Charlie."

"Keep going," my father said, gripping the bathroom door now. He was sweating, fingers trembling as he pushed the door open.

Mother still staring into my face. "You've grown," she said and nodded sloppily, her body weight shifting. My father was letting her rest against my chest and shoulder so that he could keep the door open, his foot wedged into the doorway. Soon we were moving again, out into the hallway where the sounds of the ping-pong balls and the splashing and the midnight chatter of other parents and children replaced the wet empty echoes of the bathroom. "Oh," my mother said, "don't let them see." I held her tighter, already feeling the stares of Tim French and Bryan Hopper, both of them saying "oh shit!" in unison as they saw the three of us proceed through the hallway and toward the living room. Brand-new president, Todd Hampton, standing and watching with his arms crossed, rolling his eyes.

"Oh," my mother said, "I ruined your party, Charlie."

"No, you didn't," I said. "Just keep walking, Mom. You're doing fine."

I kept my gaze fixed to the ground before us, tried not to imagine what my fraternity brothers were seeing at that moment, how they were reacting, at what point the initial shock of a husband and son escorting a drunk mother outside would give way to laughtrack, as if we were just a couple of bumbling characters in a sitcom created for their enjoyment. One foot in front of the other, and finally we turned a corner and the front door was only yards away.

I saw the flash of a picture being taken, but tried to ignore it. Tried not to think of the comments I'd get on Facebook.

"Charlie," my mother said. "I'm so sorr-rrrry."

"Stop, Mom."

"Charlie. Charr-rrrrlie."

My father kept us moving. "Could you grab the door for us?" he asked someone who was standing in the foyer, and then we were outside, teetering down the steps and onto the sidewalk that slit through the front yard to the curb of Greek Park Drive. One foot in front of the other, and I knew that they were gathering in the doorway, men and women, boys and girls.

But there was my father's Lexus convertible at the curb, his shining *I've-made-it* toy. "Hold her," he said, and now I had her full weight again as he searched his keys and then opened the passenger-side door.

"Charlie Boy," my mother said, glassy eyes upon me once again, one hand now resting on my shoulder. I held her in a dancer's embrace: we were chest to chest, hands at one another's waists and necks. "I ruined your little party."

"No," I said. "Just...let's just get you into the car."

"I don't want to go," she said.

"Kim," my father said. "Please."

"No!" Voice like a petulant child ripped from the ball pit at Chuck E. Cheese at the end of her birthday party. "I don't want to *go*! I don't want to ruin the *party*!"

And now the front door of the fraternity house *did* close, any onlookers shrinking inside, likely sensing that this moment was becoming too personal, the sitcom humor now bleeding over into reality TV "should I laugh or should I cry?" horrorshow. A trainwreck scene on *The Real World* or *Rock of Love* that you turn the channel to avoid.

"I'm closing the door," my father said. We'd sat her down. "Pull your legs inside."

"Charles, *tell* him!"

"Pull your legs inside."

"Tell him I want to go back to the party!"

"Kim. We're going to the hotel. You're done drinking."

"Charles, help me." My father was now grabbing her legs, trying to manage them into the car, but my mother had been reinvigorated by all of this, had a burst of strength in which she was able to land one good kick to my father's chest. He stumbled back, hand to his shirt, face scrunched in pain...and then, just as suddenly, my mother's mood changed again and she was crying, feet inside the car. "Oh God, Charles, I just want to go. I just want to...I just want to..."

My father stood up straight, smoothed his shirt and closed the door as gently as he could. He took a deep breath, ran his hands through the grayest of his hair above his ears, and this was the closest I'd ever seen him to becoming unraveled.

"Is this..." I started, looking in at my sobbing mother. She was now attempting to buckle her seatbelt, but couldn't quite finish the job. "Does this happen often?"

"This?" he asked, and he touched the kick-mark on his shirt, the bits of grass and sand that had been deposited by the tip of her shoe. "I'd be lying if I said that I saw this as a possibility for the night."

"I guess this is how you know it's a good party, right?" I forced a smile, slapped my father's sore chest. "Aside from the violence, of course."

"Charles."

"Sorry. Bad joke."

He closed his eyes.

"Will she be okay?" I asked.

He went silent for a moment, looking back at the fraternity house behind us. Arms crossed over his chest even though he was still breathing heavy. "When do you move out?"

"Two weeks."

"And then you drive up to Indianapolis. To start your job?"

"That's right."

"Then you drive across the country, to fifty fraternity houses just like this one."

"That's the idea."

"So what would you do if you encountered this particular scene?"

"I don't know, Dad," I said through a long exhale, and now I leaned against the car with him, looked at the house also, trying to see something different than what he was seeing. I tried to invoke the same fraternity excitement as always; I could hear myself asking him where else in America you could go on a Friday night at midnight to find a well-kept *mansion*, first-floor popping with activity, a full bar and *no end to the night*...a party like *this*, a house like this, accessible to a common middle-class young man? Where else but fraternity rows? This was an *American institution*! Sounded nice in my head, of course, but all I could focus upon now were the empty bottles on the front steps, one of which I'd accidentally kicked over, and a long wet trail of... something...leading down the sidewalk. Silhouettes inside the house, young men fist-pumping to some sort of chugging chant. The sound of shattering glass from the backyard. "I assume there's some standard operating procedure for breaking up parties," I said. "It's parents, though? All grown-ups. Who am I to tell them not to drink? They're responsible."

"Are they?"

"I mean...for the most part?"

"Hmm," he said and went silent once again. "Your mother will feel like hell tomorrow. But yes, this is indeed her responsibility."

Still, my father looked as if he had more to say, as if he had full dissertations waiting to be delivered. His words were coming slow: was he pacing himself, saving something for later, afraid of saying something? He motioned toward the house. "You think you can stop a party like this from getting out-of-hand if it's all kids?"

"It'll be my job. I'll have to."

"It's your job right *now*, isn't it? President of the house. And you couldn't stop your own fraternity brothers, could you? There was a kid passed out in the men's bathroom, too, Charles."

"You're blaming me, aren't you?" I said.

"Blaming you?"

"For everything that happened in there. For Mom. You're blaming me."

"I'm not blaming you, Charles."

Head spinning again, now that I was leaning against the car, now that the unthinking labor of carrying my mother was finished. Harder to find the right words, harder to make any sense. "This was a *party*, all right?" I said. "Things happen at parties. But it's like...this is what we do *every* night. This is my life." Stop. Reconsider. "Not *every* night. It's not, you know, a lifestyle. It's just a party, is all I'm saying. A Friday night. Just a party. And I'm graduating tomorrow. And I have a job, which is, like, more than some of the other Seniors can say. So...like...why *wouldn't* I celebrate?"

He unfolded his arms, held them out. "So you celebrated."

"Right. I celebrated. That's all this is."

"So what happens next time?"

"What do you mean?"

"Every night isn't a celebration. What happens when you're on the road? What do you do, Charles? If you encounter this?"

"I told you. I'll act different when it's my actual job. That's what people do."

"I'm not an idiot, you know," he said. "I know you didn't plan *everything* in there. It's not as if you bought all that alcohol yourself."

And I realized at that moment that he didn't know: I'd made no speech, no declaration that these were all *my* purchases, this entire bar full of Stoli and Bacardi Limon. He assumed it was some sort of collaborative house effort. Hell, he probably didn't even know that I'd initiated the Beer Pong tournament. Who, after all, would take it upon himself—all by himself—to get five or six dozen parents wasted out of their minds? It was unthinkably dumb.

"I don't want you to fail, Charles, but you need to hear this." He was no longer looking up at the columns of the Nu Kappa Epsilon house, no longer looking through the car window at his wife. She'd passed out by now. No, my father was now pinning me to the door with the same Authority Figure look that he'd used in key moments throughout my life: when I'd gotten into my first fight at a soccer game in elementary school, when I'd been suspended from school in seventh-grade for swearing at a teacher, when he'd found a bottle of Aftershock hidden in my bedroom on the night before Senior Prom. His chin up, five o'clock shadow blooming across his cheeks, and even in the dark it seemed as if he could find a way to make every inch of his face illuminated. "When my own father sent me off to college, he told me—from the start—he told me I was on my own. Make your own mistakes, he said. This is where you learn to be the man you'll be for the rest of your life."

"And I think I *have*—"

"Don't talk. Listen," he said. "I worked landscaping in the afternoons, on the weekends. Lived in a co-op in Gainesville, cheaper than the dorms. Biked to campus for breakfast, lunch, and dinner. Had to find rides back to Jacksonville for Thanksgiving. Hitch-hiked a few times. Hated my father because he wouldn't come to visit, never gave an encouraging word. Made me pay my own tuition, even though he could afford to help. I hated the man, Charles. Hated him for many years, even when he tried to make nice." Chin still raised, breathing still heavy from the exertion of the struggle. "It wasn't until your freshman year that I understood his point. It wasn't until I saw you on the floor. I can live with myself if you hate me, Charles, because it was my father who *let* me become a man my own."

"I don't hate you," I said, pretending to be shocked that he would imply such a thing. But, of course, the faux-shock was betrayed by the fact that I had a response ready to fling: "But you have it out for fraternities. And fraternity is who I am. You don't recognize any of the good things we're doing."

"The good things?"

"We had this whole awards ceremony inside!" I shook my fist, traded the shocked look for one of pure anger. I gestured toward the sloping grass lawn, the house and the porch and the plantation shutters. But my father just sighed, again ran his fingers through the sweat-dampened gray hair on the sides of his head, smoothing it back. He didn't look at me, either, only stared straight ahead into the house windows for a few silent seconds before finally turning and peering through the passenger-side window of his Lexus.

After awhile, once he'd allowed the silence of the outdoors to smother the emotion of my words, he spoke again: "Did I ever stop you?"

"Stop me from *what*?" I snapped. I was holding onto the anger. I would not let it slip away.

"Stop you from joining." He rubbed his eyes, squinted.

"You never approved of it."

"I'm not shy about my opinions," he said. He rummaged in his pockets now, pulled out a small leather case and removed from it a pair of slender glasses. My father never wore glasses during the daytime, never even liked anyone to see him wearing reading glasses at work, hid the fact of his declining eyesight the way that other men his age tried to hide or conceal their bald spots, but once the world went dark and my father's vision went foggier, street signs turning to bright wordless bars, he'd finally submit. But always slowly, dramatically, unfolding the glasses, inspecting the lenses, polishing the glass even though they were spotless, positioning them over his ears, over his nose, blinking to adjust his vision, all of it an act to show the world that glasses were not *normal* for him. Finally, he looked up and stared me in the eyes. "I always share my thoughts," he said, "but I never told you *not* to join, did I?"

I still faced him, didn't break the eye contact that I'd fought so hard to gain, but I had no similar nonverbal gestures or practiced routines which I could force him to watch. No glasses in my pocket. I could only stand and shift my weight from foot to foot, could only slide my fingertips down my pants and rub the front of my legs. Again, again, over and over, until my fingertips were staticky hot.

"Did I?" he repeated.

"Not...you know, expressly."

"Do you know why I never joined a fraternity?"

I shook my head. As always, it had taken only a short exchange to wear me down, to wring the unthinking aggression from me, and even though I was still spinning I'd at least had some fight for a minute or two, had at least managed for a round. But—like my mother, after kicking him in the chest— now I felt defeated. He'd asked such a simple question—"Do you know why I never joined a fraternity?"—and the fact that I'd never even thought to ask it myself proved something about me, didn't it?

"For one thing, I had no money," he said and smiled, maybe drifting into some college-years memory to which I'd never have access; I didn't see my father smile often, committed as he was to showing the world that his actions were not dictated by emotion, that he had complete control over his feelings. But the smile would still creep out on occasion, just a subtle movement of his lips, but real joy overtaking his eyes and making them shine like freshly cleaned silver; it made you want to cry, seeing this, knowing that he had such happiness inside him but that he suppressed it so entirely.

But at the curb of the fraternity house, it faded quickly.

"My roommate—freshman year—he joined a fraternity. He joined Nu Kappa Epsilon." He stopped, stared me in the eyes again, and it was so sudden and his eyes so searing that I had to look away.

Behind us, on the long and winding campus roadway that snaked through Greek Row and the scattered upperclassmen residence halls, a patrol car rolled past, one portly security officer in the driver's seat with a Nextel phone in his hand. The "Night Patrol" was what this was called, and it wasn't an official police force, was really no different than mall cops with cars, but they did have long laminated sheets on their clipboards of every important campus phone number: the residence hall directors, the RAs for Greek Row, the off-campus police. And if you were having an event that maybe you didn't want the world to know was happening, the absolute worst thing was that they'd cruise past *without* a head-nod, without a wave, without any acknowledgment that they'd just called someone to investigate an incident they found suspicious. If the security officers stopped, then a fraternity president could at least shake hands, pat them on the back, assure them that calling the authorities would be a waste of time, and would you like to come inside and talk to a few girls, have a drink?

The Night Patrol car sped up after it passed, was gone around the corner.

What had he seen here at the curb? A father and son, a mother in the car? Had he seen us as who we were? Or had the relationships—even the ages of the participants—not registered? Had he seen only a fraternity house, a party, Greek Row a series of blind spots that his mind could fill in with the predictable generalizations of frat life: two drunk guys arguing over keys, a drunk sorority girl the prize whenever they got home.

"Campus police, Charles?" my father asked.

"Just the Night Patrol," I said. "They patrol for burglaries. Fights. You know."

"They're not looking for parties to bust?"

"This is a family event," I said. "They don't care."

My father shrugged and gave an *if you say so* look. "Your book had some dramatic photos of that Florida house fire, but the caption said nothing. Know how the fire started?"

"If it isn't in the caption," I said, "then no."

"The fraternity claimed it was electrical, but it wasn't," he said. And now his hands were in his pockets again, his most comfortable pose, even without a coffee mug in his right hand to finish the look. "I told you that it could have been a major tragedy. That's not because the fraternity brothers were sleeping upstairs, innocent and unsuspecting." He adjusted his glasses and squinted again, as if by moving them this way, that way, he could now see farther, deeper, through the walls of the fraternity house in front of us, into my mind, into my soul. "No, it could've been a major tragedy because your fraternity had the pledges blind-folded and locked in closets. It was a ceremony called 'Trust a Brother,' or something to that effect."

He paused, perhaps waiting for me to interject, but I just leaned against the car and tried to remain straight-faced, as emotionless and reaction-free as he always seemed. It was a performance, probably a bad one because I was still swaying, but he continued.

He told me that the pledges were supposed to wait in their closets all night long, no matter what happened, until a brother released them. And all night long, apparently, there were distractions and surprises meant to terrify the pledges. Banging pots and pans, fights between brothers, bugs dumped into the closets. And the whole house was dark to preserve a creepy haunted mansion feel for the blind-folded pledges, only a few rows of candles lining the hallways. And then someone knocked over a candle. And who knows how the fire grew? Maybe no one knew what had happened until it was too late. But can you guess what happened next?

"The house burnt down," I said. Shrugged. "Fine. An accident. But how is that—"

And then he was telling me that the house *started* to burn. But the pledges were still in the closets, the flames growing and growing in the rooms around them. Blind-folded. The house getting hotter.

"Come on."

They were still standing upright in those closets, three or four of them clumped together. Told not to make a sound, no matter what happened. *Trust your brothers.* And outside those doors, does that sound like *real* fire? And boy,

60

does that feel *hot*! How did the brothers manage this? Did they turn up the heat in the house? And the pledges stayed there, thinking it was still part of the game. Until one of the windows upstairs burst out, glass sprinkling far away on the sidewalk outside. And finally, one pledge decided—hell, this is getting *ridiculous*—and he took off his blindfold, come what may, and opened the door, and the house...was...*ablaze*. And it was this pledge brother, this single guy, who searched every closet—and he had no idea where everyone was, he'd been blindfolded the entire time—and he had to find every pledge in every closet, counting to make sure he'd reached them all, convince them this wasn't part of some elaborate scenario, it wasn't staged, and then they were all running out of the house, all these pledges in their underwear, and there were over a hundred people on the lawn by now, confused as hell as to why these twenty naked men were *just now* scurrying out of the burning house.

"I'm sure you've got it wrong," I said. "Our UF chapter is, like, legendary. They've never been suspended. They're—"

I was on the lawn, my father told me. Watching. Ten minutes before, he'd been in the library. Spent a lot of nights in the library, since he worked days. Someone comes screaming into the library, "Fire at the Nike house! Fire at the Nike house!" Nu Kappa Epsilon? Where his roommate was pledging? And he hurried over there. Saw the fire up close. Saw the pledges. The fire trucks. And you know what I remember most, Charles? I saw the brothers take the pledges aside. God knows what they said. A mixture of apologies and threats, no doubt, because there wasn't a single pledge who came forward to report the hazing. Why were they in their underwear, everyone wanted to know. The brothers had an easy answer: the pledges were on the top floor, already asleep, they said. We didn't even realize they'd gone to sleep so early. We feel *terrible*! My God, *we could have lost them all in the fire!*

And the campus bought it, and *oh*, the poor Nikes who suffered this outrageous house fire, and for the next two months, all you would hear on-campus is how lucky they were that no one had died, and could you spare some change for the House Restoration effort? Help put these guys back into their home?

"So how can you be sure it was hazing?" I asked. "You jump to *conclusions*."

"My roommate," my father said.

"Your roommate?"

"He came forward. Spoke to the campus newspaper, finally had the courage."

"So why does no one talk about this today?"

"Gerry—my roommate—he was blackballed as soon as he spoke. A liar, the fraternity brothers said. The National Fraternity? Your Headquarters? The place where you're going to start a career? They offered all sorts of support for the beleaguered fraternity chapter, as if they were the victims somehow. Gerry's name was dragged through the mud."

But I shook my head: this was just his perspective, one story from an outsider, and I imagined that there were dozens of other versions of that night's event that all conflicted with one another. Hell, how much of this story was sloppy foggy memory, a narrative he'd constructed out of the spare parts available to him? I'd listened to his story, but it was just campus gossip, the talk of outsiders jealous that they weren't part of what was going on behind that heavy front door. The GDIs, the Goddamn Independents who hated Greek Life, the privileges, the Grand Tradition, the roots of power that burrowed centuries-deep into the campus soil. They *needed* these stories, needed the Fraternity Stereotype and kept it alive as if—like deluded Southerners who speak of the "War of Northern Aggression"— the words and the myths confirm something about their own choices, that it was wise *not* to enter those doors during Rush, that it was wise *not* to pledge, that no one should have to *pay for friends*, etc., etc.

"And why are you telling me this *now*?" I asked finally. I waited for him to open his mouth, and then I shouted: "Things are different now, don't you understand? All of that stuff…it just feeds the stereotype, but you don't want to hear anything different." Oh, *this was it*. "We're all a bunch of drunks," I said. "Or we're all a bunch of hazers. Just a stereotype, and you eat it up! Do you know what we're doing at the Headquarters? Do you know that we have a mission? That we offer our members more leadership programming than any other men's group? Do you know how many community service hours we log? We're *different*. That—your little gossipy story—that's not who we are!" I stepped away from the car, from the curb, paced on the sidewalk with fists clenched at my sides and heart pounding. Yes: this was the moment I'd hoped would come, when impulse took over and the space between us was flooded with the rush of my true thoughts.

But as quickly as it had started, it was over, and my father didn't say a word for what felt like a very long time. I couldn't bring myself to make eye contact with him again, to see the reaction to such deep and intractable feelings. Just kept looking up at my house as if to gain some strength from the comforting columns, from the long green hedges, from those concrete steps. The black "Nu Kappa Epsilon" above the much-smaller address numbers on the white boards below the gutters. The laughter inside, the cracking glass. The bouncing ping-pong ball. The "Yeeeaa-aaaah!"

And at the far end of the road the Night Patrol car had returned, had parked in front of the quiet Kappa Delta sorority house, observing from a distance. Darkness behind the windshield. Only a black shape that made the tiniest of motions, head tilting slowly and curiously to the side…he wanted me to know that he was watching, and no, he didn't care who I was speaking with, what we were saying. The whole Row could hear the bouncing of ping-pong balls, and no matter what, there would be trouble.

"So why do you need to take this job?" my father asked finally.

I held out my hands, forced a look of confusion. "What do you mean?"

"A leadership organization. Role models. Responsible citizens. All the buzz words," he said. "And yet you are hired to *change* the culture?"

62

I held out my hands farther: why couldn't he understand? "The *fringe* elements!"

"You're hired to be a role model, you keep telling me," he said. "A role model."

"That's right. I'm going to be something important. Something positive."

"Is this how role models spend their Friday nights?"

"That isn't fair. This is a party."

"Yes, these are the good guys." Pointing at my house now. "These aren't the ones who would lock pledges in closets. But still, they love their alcohol. And now you're going to spend a year of your life trying to be a role model when, really, you don't want to change anything. You enjoy it too much."

"It's a party," I repeated, as if that somehow disarmed his argument. "A party."

My father raised his hand to his face, slid his thumb and forefinger beneath the glasses and pressed them to the corners of his eyes, squinted hard. "You asked me if I blamed you for your mother," my father said finally, and tapped on the window to remind me that she was mere feet away. Beyond the glass, she was still asleep, didn't stir; she remained a hunched-over middle-aged mess of brown hair and Ann Taylor clothing and sparkling Macy's jewelry. "I know how she gets, and this isn't even the worst I've seen." He paused again, stayed that way—eyes closed, fingers at his eyes—for another moment. "I didn't want you to see any of that, Charles. I didn't. I've always... I've always known who she is, and I've tried not to let her put herself into the sorts of situations that will bring out the wrong side of her. But she doesn't listen to me anymore." He paused again, peered back into the interior of the car. I now noticed that she hadn't ever finished buckling her seatbelt; it hung limply around her arm. "When we were carrying her, Charles, and she said your name, what did you think?"

"What did I think? I don't know."

"If she would have told you—looking like she did—to put down your beer, to stop drinking, that you'd had too much, what would you have thought?"

"Put down my beer?"

"This is my point, Charles. You can't be two different things at once. You can't be a parent and *also* be what you see in the car. You're one thing, or you're the other, and you make a choice and you stick with it. I look at your mother now, and I think..."

I pushed myself from the car and tried to stand of my own volition. "Are you okay?"

"You can't be the good guy *and* the party animal, Charles. And your fraternity? It can't be what you say it is, this remarkable leadership development organization, and also be what I *know* it is. It can't."

"It's a stereotype, Dad," I said, but softer now. "We're changing it."

"You'll never change a culture that doesn't want to change," he said.

"So I shouldn't try?"

"Not if everyone seems to like it broken," he said. "Not if *you* like it broken."

63

"How much of my life have I already invested in this?" I said. "It's not—"

"Four years, spit in the wind," he said. "I'm telling you. Sometimes it's best to remove yourself from situations that are damaging to you."

"It isn't *damaging* me," I said. "It's this fraternity that *made* me who I am."

"Who you are?" he asked and shrugged. "Who are you, really?"

"Please. You know me," I said. "I mean...I've been drinking tonight, but I'm—" And what was I going to say at that moment that didn't sound ridiculous? I'm the *Man on Campus*? Diamond Candidate, Marathon Man! I'm a cartoon diagram! The catered barbecue and the cake and the open bar were supposed to speak for me, but they'd only managed to turn my mother into a freshman sorority girl, the other fathers into frat stars. Who *was* I?

"Is this what you want to stand for?" he asked.

"You're wrong about me. About all of this."

"Maybe I am. Maybe I am," he said. He pushed himself from the car and started toward the driver side. "Either way, Charles, I've said what I can. I've got to get her home." He was now at the door, opening up. "You really want to accomplish something, I can see that. And you think there's something wrong with how I've done it. I understand that. But when I'm finished with a project, I see that something's been built. Blank space before, and something tangible after...a house, a parking lot...No two ways about it. You either agree that it was a good thing, or you disagree. I just want to make sure you can have that feeling, that your accomplishments aren't just empty words on paper." He shrugged again. "We'll see you tomorrow at graduation."

"Yeah," I said. "Tomorrow."

He slid into his car, just a flash of khaki pants and blue polo shirt and gold-and-silver watch, all of it disappearing behind the tinted windows of the Lexus. Behind the windshield, just a dark shape adjusting his glasses, turning the keys in the ignition, checking the rearview mirror and then the unconscious woman at his side, all of it as methodical as if it occurred each time he entered his vehicle. No final wave, no glance in my direction, and the car itself became a silver flash, pulling away from the curb and down the street and to the stop sign at the end of Greek Row, and then it stayed where it was for a moment, my father looking into his rearview—

Because another car had rolled up to take my father's spot at the curb.

The Night Patrol.

It had crept forward a tenth of a mile, lights off, from where it had been idling just moments ago. The dark shape behind the windshield now reaching to his left, opening his door, stepping from the car, a blue and white shirt stretched to its limits, coming untucked as the officer huffed his way toward me.

"Good evening," he said, and I returned the courtesy greeting, but really I was staring down the street at the fading lights of my father's Lexus. Part of me hoped he hadn't seen the security patrol car coming to life and rolling down the street to the curb of the Nu Kappa Epsilon house, that he was just checking his hair in the mirror, but I knew this was fantasy. My father had glanced in his rearview mirror and had seen his still-drunk son confronted by a patrol car—and no, this wasn't the police, but it damn sure *looked* like the police, black-and-blue painted vehicle, spotlights on the sides, emergency lights on the top—ready to bust up the party, ready to issue citations for public intoxication, disturbing the peace, whatever, all those things from which my father had removed himself.

Nothing happened, of course, just a standard questioning from Jarred the Night Patrol officer ("Got a party going inside?" "No, no, just parents." "Gonna be going on much longer?" "No, they're parents. Should be wrapping up soon." "Had a noise complaint, you know. I should probably call the RA." "Won't be necessary, Jarred. Why don't you come inside, check it out? We've got some cake left, could probably make you a vodka-tonic if you're game?"), and then it was over without any trouble. But it was the *image in the rearview* that had made my father linger at the stop sign for an extra three seconds, Charles Washington in the final hours of his college life, standing alone on the paved sidewalk to the fraternity house, law enforcement vehicle at the curb before him as he prepared in his mind some desperate appeal for the officer... the image, immortalized not in some Facebook photo album where I could un-tag or delete it, but immortalized instead in my father's memory next to the still-vivid image of a freshman boy laying in his own puke in the center of a living room. And hell, how did I know that Todd Hampton, the new chapter president, was not also watching out of the front windows of the fraternity house? Thousands of dollars spent for this epic send-off, and how would I be remembered?

And I did see my parents at graduation the next day. Pictures with the family, pictures with the cap and gown, my mother looking embarrassed in each photo, the two of them fidgeting the entire time, long spaces between us as we ate lunch at one of those "nice restaurants" my mother had wanted to visit while down in Fort Myers. At first, I just thought they were eager to leave Edison University and escape the constant reminders of what had happened the night before.

Jenn couldn't come out with us; she had a Mother's Brunch for the house Seniors. I'd thought about presenting her with the lavalier at dinner with my parents. Not the original plan, but still a moment with real potential.

But then, at lunch, it was time for another "talk." And very quickly it became clear that, even though the previous night had been the longest my father had ever spoken to me about college, about fraternities, about his own past, there was still more that he'd wanted to say. More that he'd swallowed and saved.

"We didn't want to ruin your night," my mother said, and even at my post-graduation lunch she had a glass of wine, "so we waited until today to talk."

*Oh no*, I said. This isn't about *me* again, is it? I mean, really. This is going to be a long afternoon, a long night, if you get started now. Can't we just enjoy ourselves?

"We aren't staying for dinner," my mother said.

Wait. Not staying for dinner? But we were supposed to go out with Jenn and—

"This is about *us*," my father said and motioned toward my mother. "This is about our marriage."

Your marriage?

"We've gotten a divorce, Charles," my father said.

Whoa, whoa. *What?*

"We want you to know that we both still love you," my mother said, "that nothing is going to change."

Hold on here. Is this…is this about last night?

"No, Charles," my father said. "This was a long time coming."

This doesn't make any sense. Where did this come from?

"Charles, this has nothing to do with last night."

That isn't true, either. Oh my God.

"Charles," my mother said. "We've been living separately for six months."

*Six months?*

Smoothing my pants, couldn't breathe. Knocked over my water glass.

How did this happen? You can't do this. You've been married for 25 years.

"There are a lot of things you don't know. It's better this way."

You're giving up, I said. You can't give up!

"Remember what I told you last night," my father said, "that sometimes it's best to remove yourself from unhealthy situations. We've recognized that, Charles."

This is a marriage, damn it! You've always told me: you wouldn't let yourselves become like everyone else. Don't you realize what this means to me?

"I know it's difficult, Charles," my mother said.

You tell me today? On my graduation day? What is this?

"Charles."

You were supposed to be *different!* This wasn't supposed to happen to you!

"College is over now, Charles," my father said. "You're a man, you have a job, you don't need a safety net."

This has been a long time coming? Six months separately? You've been *keeping this* from me! You've been lying to me? Shit, this means you weren't even living together when I visited for Christmas?

"Charles."

It's a lie. You are, I am. This entire family, just a lie. A long time coming?

And then I was thinking about what else they'd never told me. Six months? How many dinners, how many phone conversations? Had my father cheated? My mother? Was she drinking? Was that what had caused this, and had she been drinking all these years, a glass of wine in her car while she waited for me to finish baseball practice? *Who* were *these people?* How long had they been acting? Every Christmas a choreographed production, every Thanksgiving, stage actors in the presence of their son, living out different lives as soon as I left the building. Curtains: daily.

"Charles. There's no need to get dramatic."

Families don't *do* this! Families don't lie to one another!

"We had our reasons."

Families don't *say* that.

"You've had a good life, Charles. Everything you wanted."

Families don't say *that*, either. They don't congratulate themselves for fulfilling their responsibilities. They don't use the past tense. It's not like a birthday reminder on Facebook, an obligatory comment on someone's page. Family isn't like this!

And aside from scattered "How are things?" phone conversations, that was it: the last I've spoken with either of my parents before leaving town for Indianapolis.

# Goal-Setting
## CHAPTER SEVEN

After the Senior Send-Off, the Edison University campus emptied for the three-month summer break, dorms and apartment buildings and fraternity houses going silent and dark. The EU staff members and professors—what few remained—hung up their blazers and ties and came to campus wearing seersucker shorts and Tommy Bahama button-downs, zipping in and out of their offices only to sign year-end paperwork and lug boxes of student portfolios to the dumpster. EU is a private university, its enrollment always bobbing above or below 7,000, the classroom buildings ultra-modern three-story structures with reflective ground-to-roof glass facades which glaze over with air-conditioning condensation in the humid summers. Filled with students, the campus is lively and you hardly pay attention to the architecture; but without students wandering on every sidewalk and through every green, it feels instead like an office-park, like you're working on your Saturday off.

For my final two weeks in town, I slept in the fraternity house President's Room and each morning woke up to say goodbye to another carload of brothers who were heading back home till August. The left-over liquor from the Senior Send-Off lined the bar's countertop, sticky and heavy and unwanted, like a collection of extra pecan pies and fruitcakes after the end of the holiday season. For the first few days after the party, I found discarded cups and forks in the living room, in the bathrooms, in the courtyard, and I spent mornings Windexing the glass of the framed photos and paintings in our hallways, wiping away fruit-punch-colored fingerprints and spit-out Sprite; in the summer months, the cleaning staff came only once every two weeks, and the house would stink and fester if I didn't clean.

Jenn wasn't around for those two weeks. Over summers, she worked as a lifeguard in St. Pete, stayed at her sister's place and bought groceries in exchange for rent-free living in the guest room. She was coming back down to Fort Myers for my final two days in town, and we were going to spend a full forty-eight hours together before I left for Indianapolis: out at the beach with a cooler full of Miller Lite and Seadog Blueberry, out for dinner and drinks at one of the hotel steakhouses, lunch the next day at a tiki bar, then finally packing my car together on the last evening, keeping one another awake from dusk to dawn for our last night together in the President's Room. I still had the lavalier in a box in the glove compartment of my Explorer, but I couldn't give it to her. Not now. Not anymore. The letters required ceremony; they required that my brothers bruise me and bloody me, that they dump sour milk over my shoulders and crack rotten eggs on my scalp; to give her the letters while everyone was out of town…it would rob the moment of meaning, render the lavalier as procedural as a Tuesday afternoon courthouse marriage. I could hope for Thanksgiving, perhaps, or Labor Day, or Homecoming, sometime in the Fall semester when I might return to town and make my commitment with all of my brothers present and get my ass beaten to make it official, but for our last night in town, it would just be the two of us, no speeches or ceremonies or jewelry.

*

For those two weeks alone, I thought long and hard about the changes I needed to make in my life. I wanted to be this—

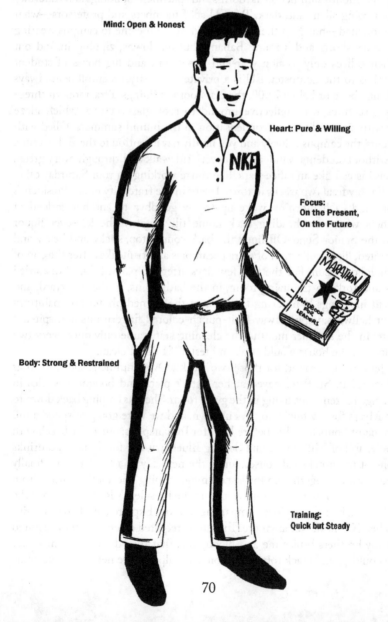

Mind: Open & Honest

Heart: Pure & Willing

NKD

Focus:
On the Present,
On the Future

Body: Strong & Restrained

THE MARATHON
HANDBOOK
FOR
LEADERS

Training:
Quick but Steady

70

—but I just seemed to keep fucking it up.

Two weeks alone in the fraternity house, and I spent my time creating goal sheets for my new professional life. I created key categories, "Exercise" and "Healthy Eating" and "Leadership Development," with individual goals like "Fast Food only four times/ weekly," "Jog three times/ weekly," and "No gas station candy purchases/ EVER." All of it printed out, easily accessible in my notebook, right beside the original form email I received from the National Fraternity Headquarters. *Save the World.*

Every aspect of my life organized, planned.

Maybe it was as simple as separating egg white from yolk, as simple as scraping congealed fat from the top of refrigerated gravy, the bad from the good of Charles Washington, the Frat Star from the Leader, a separation, a focusing—like the Jenn Outlook—on the best and not the worst.

I didn't want to think about the Senior Send-Off anymore, either. I wanted to believe that my memories were just the strobe light flashes of some different man that I could leave behind in college, the same way I could leave behind all the old college bars, all the booty music.

Leave the night behind. Leave the old family behind.

Create a new profile. New man. New status updates:

Charles is…going to do this right.

Charles is…going to do *everything* right.

Charles…doesn't care what his father said, doesn't give a damn, because who is that man anyway? What do I really know about him? About either of them? They're not who they're supposed to be. Nobody is who they're supposed to be. But I am. I can be. Charles Washington is Charles Washington.

Charles…doesn't need to lie.

Charles…just needs to start over.

I clipped a long metal rod to the hooks above each window in the backseat of my Explorer. The package claimed it would provide "order" and a "comforting sense of home" for my year of cross-country travel, my Explorer becoming my bedroom closet, my office, my whole life. I decided upon just the right clothes to bring and to buy, and just the right sequence in which to hang them: (from far right) my silver-black Ralph Lauren suit, two pairs dress pants (one pair black, one gray), four dress shirts (two white, one navy, one light blue), one black wool winter coat, one navy-and-white windbreaker, one pair jeans, two pairs khaki pants, two business-casual polo shirts (the letters NKE embroidered above their hearts).

I planned how to perfectly organize every square inch of the Explorer:

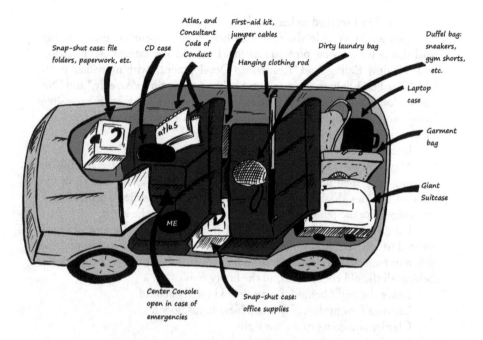

One full year as a role model; and starting in August, four straight months of fraternity house hopping. I would *not* drift back into the college lifestyle, into drinking games and late-night pizza and waking up at noon on someone's sofa. No slip-ups. Hell, I would eliminate the opportunity for slip-ups. I would be the man I was always supposed to be.

*

"It doesn't matter who you really are," Walter LaFaber wrote in the "Preparing For Life as a Fraternity Consultant" email that I received just days after the Senior Send-Off, "it only matters what people *think* you are." Just google yourselves, the email told us, so you can truly see what the world knows of you, how you might be perceived if anyone grows curious. "Think about Facebook profiles, twitter accounts, online photo albums. What was fun and cute a year ago is now professional suicide."

How true.

The first time I'd googled myself (back during freshman year of college, just for the hell of it), I wasn't expecting much. My name stretches back centuries, has been chiseled onto a thousand gravestones, and I've always relied on how easily I've been able to slink into anonymity should the need arise ("You must have the wrong Charles Washington," I can say. "There are quite a few of us."). At other times, I've relied on the more "famous" Charles Washington (the younger brother of America's first president) to steal attention and web traffic from me. Hell, I share a name with a hero, a patriot, a founder. We were Google buddies, and he wasn't going anywhere. But during freshman year, I found my own name on the third page of the Google results, an old high school web site I'd created for a world history project. I remember looking at the search result, the bold hypertext that would lead me to an online ghost town I'd built years before, and wondering if—like some abandoned general store, crumbling under stinging desert winds—it would ever disappear.

By my senior year at EU, I was on the *second* page of the search results, the fraternity letters "Nu Kappa Epsilon" following, image results accompanying, further demarcating this Charles Washington from all others.

So when asked to search my name online, anything seemed possible: was I on the first page by now? And what new results would await? Could the world know more about me than I knew about myself?

"You'll want to make sure that the image you've given the world is truly the image you want the world to see," the email said. "Everyone leaves a digital footprint, and it's hard to accomplish a mission—any mission—when you're sabotaging yourself."

Had anyone at the National Headquarters searched my name?

It scared the hell out of me.

After the email, this is what I found, in descending order of relevance, the first page of 49,400,000 results:

1. First, as expected, Wikipedia's entry for President George Washington's younger brother Charles, dead at age 60, shortly before his older brother passed, though records are sketchy. Also, some Google Image results displaying Charles Washington's only known portrait: his face feels vaguely recognizable, a blurry Xerox of a more famous patriot.

2. Next, a series of pages dedicated to 18th-Century Charles Washington's various historical markers across the Virginias, the Shenandoah Valley.

3, 4, 5. Scroll down the page. A few other Charles Washingtons, attorneys whose names are remembered in law reviews, actors whose names are preserved on imdb.com, authors catalogued on *Harper's Magazine's* database.

25. Then…keep scrolling down the page…ignore everything until you get to the very bottom of the first page. "Charles Washington," the search result tells you, offering a link to our national web site. "Educational Consultant, Nu Kappa Epsilon National Fraternity Headquarters."

Yes, that sounded respectable. A few weeks before, the Headquarters had posted a news release about my hiring, had created a full profile page on their web site to tout my college accolades. How exciting to find my name here on—

But, wait. Scroll back up.

Stop here. Right here.

6.

Because that listing at the bottom of the page was not my only search result. Here was another one. Much earlier. The *sixth* entry! My Facebook page and a choice selection of party photos blinking like a "red alert" sign in the center of the web page. Oh, you could still see the original historic photos right above mine, the Charles Washington oil painting, the place markers, the words "Charles Town" on an olde tyme hand-drawn 1770s map, and you could still see the professional Nu Kappa Epsilon site far down the page, but you wouldn't see any of it without also seeing a description of my full Facebook profile, my name and age and education and hometown, all paired with the digital images of the supposed "diamond candidate" standing on the arm rest of a sofa with beer bottles in each hand. Giving the thumbs-up sign at Bang-Shots while standing under a banner that said "Wet T-Shirt Contest," and behind me a girl shaking her slippery tits to the approval of the crowd. Pouring Everclear from a bottle and into the cut-out hole of a watermelon.

And a dozen other photos just like these.

Oh, and if you clicked onto the second page of search results, there was an old MySpace account, too. Hadn't been used in over a year, but full of vulgar *Anchorman* quotes ("I want to be on you!" "Mr. Burgundy, you have a massive erection!"), a profile page now stamped and spammed with comments from strippers and porn sites, bare-breasted women licking the web cam and asking me to visit the link below for some action. The sort of comments I would have deleted if I'd still cared about MySpace. But here was civilization left to the wind and snow and rain of the internet: junk comments piled high on my forgotten profile, one after the next, like weeds and topsoil over cold and irrelevant train tracks. And there was even a comment from Renee, my cousin in Georgia: "Wow, Charles. Haven't checked your MySpace in awhile?"

And so, like a criminal returning to the scene of his crime, I tried to wipe the internet clean of any trace that I'd been here, that I'd been there. A post on a Ft. Myers newspaper forum, lamenting the change in tailgate areas for EU football games? Deleted. An old string of back-and-forth comments about Eminem's rap feud with Ja Rule, posted on an entertainment gossip site? Deleted. How had I even ended up here, I wondered? How was it possible that these traces of myself were so widespread? Snapfish photo albums, Ancestry.com photos, Kodak.com photo albums, years and years of accumulated internet settlements, all of them open to the public.

I sent emails to the web technicians of the EU Intramural Sports Page, the Annual Shamrock Chicken-Wing-Eating Contest, the Memorial Day Drink Around the World Challenge: take my "Finishing Times" off your web sites, please, I'm no longer affiliated in any way with your organization.

Taking a towel to my fingerprints across the web, sweeping the floor, mopping my muddy footprints from the ground, finding any hint that I'd ever existed anywhere but right here, right now. MySpace account, deleted. Rivals.com profile, deleted. And soon, I'd eliminate my beloved Facebook account, too.

*

"You keep talking about how much you need to change," Jenn told me during our final day at EU, the two of us in the parking lot of the fraternity house packing my Explorer, arranging each suitcase and duffel bag and CD case into what I'd decided would be the perfect spots for easy access while I spent the next two days (and then sixteen straight weeks) on the road. Later, we'd stretch across the futon in the presidential suite of the house—my final night in my own bedroom—and Jenn would commandeer the television, force me to watch a *Sex and the City* marathon ("It's painful, isn't it?" she said, "But don't tell me you actually want to watch TV right now."), Carrie Bradshaw's voice-overs our porno soundtrack as we forever spoiled every square inch of the bedroom in anticipation of Todd Hampton's forthcoming presidency. But that—the TV, the ripping-off of clothes, the *Sex and the City* opening theme song playing again and again and again—would come later. After the packing.

"I'm graduating," I said. "That's what people do. They grow up. They change."

It had been two weeks since my father told me that he knew the *real me*, but I'd told Jenn nothing of our conversations. She didn't need to know. About them or about me.

One afternoon when we were first dating, Jenn had stopped by the fraternity house to ask if I knew how to change the oil in her car. (*Me?* Perform an at-home oil change? Obviously she didn't know me very well yet.) No, I said, but I'll go with you to the shop, and then we can grab a drink while the professionals do their thing.

"I should know how to do an oil change," Jenn said at the Ale House. "My father would be disappointed."

"Why's that?"

"He drove a semi," she said. "When I was a kid, I'd actually ride with him. Summers, Spring Breaks." They'd lived in Dallas back then, she said, and she'd tag along with her father from Dallas to Chicago, or to Kansas City, or to El Paso. Long trips that her mother didn't want to see her take, but what could she say? Daddy wanted to spend time with his two daughters the only way he could, and so Jenn and her sister would fight over who'd go next.

"We wore trucker hats before they were cool," Jenn said, "and we wore the *real* ones."

She'd share booths with her father at diners that smelled equally of hash browns and cigarette smoke, and they'd load their plates with chicken-fried steak and mashed potatoes at the Flying J dinner buffet. Jenn would sleep in the doghouse, sometimes curled up with her father if it was cold; sometimes he'd sleep in his driver seat and let her have the tiny bed all to herself. He'd stop at rest areas to show her their position on the map, how all of the roads of Middle America were connected, how one city fed into the next, how the highways (and before them, the railroads and the rivers) determined where and why the cities had grown in the first place. She saved a jar of sand from New Mexico, dipped her feet into the Mississippi, brought home Chicago sausage and Georgia peaches for her mother. Her father wouldn't let her touch the CB, but by the end of each trip she'd be speaking trucker language, pointing at highway patrolmen and calling them "smokey" and laughing at the local police, the "city kitties."

"And none of the garbage mouth in front of your mother or your teachers," he'd warn her, even though he'd allow the CB to expand her swear-word vocabulary: *Bunch 'a bullshit up ahead*, and *Some asshole on a crotch-rocket cut me off*, and *Goddamn these Utards, worst drivers in the country*.

But by the time high school came, road trips were no longer fun: life on the road was cramped, gross, and who wants to sleep with their father or eat those runny eggs or use those awful showers? For years, Jenn's mother had complained about the time away, how he was never home for the girls, and so the daughters now joined forces with their mother; the entire family was complaining about the absent father, and why couldn't he find a job where he could see his wife and children every night, because look at all the things he was missing, etc., and so they moved from Dallas to Tampa, where he could now work with his wife's brother and the family would be perfect.

"It was supposed to be better for us," Jenn said at the Ale House, swirling her glass of Cherry Wheat. "We were together. My father had a job in Tampa, a management position in some mattress store. My uncle pulled all sorts of strings to get him the job."

"So what happened?" I asked.

"He resented my mother for it," Jenn said. Became increasingly bitter and mean during his time at home, she said, and so he found some way to lose the job at the mattress store, then took control of a semi once again, and he was off, and they became a family of three. At first, he was just absent. Then, her mother grew exhausted and called it quits. Family split up, and then it was two Christmases, two Thanksgivings. "He's the kind of guy who needs to be moving. Always moving. The second he settles down, he's miserable. Maybe it rubbed off on me, too. Before high school, I loved my time in the big-rig. I loved moving to Tampa. I loved moving down here for EU. My old friends from high school…most of them just went to USF, right down the street. I don't know why you'd stay in any place for longer than four years."

"Exactly," I said.

"What about *your* parents? Still together?"

"Still together."

"Please tell me that *they* have a storybook romance," she said. "I need to be reassured that it's possible."

"They're about as close as you can come for old people," I said. I took a long drink of my beer, trying to decide what to say and what to leave out. She'd been honest about her own family dysfunction, but hers was real; mine, it seemed, was negligible. Helicopter parenting? Circumnavigation? My complaints seemed so minor, so I figured: if she wants storybook, I'll give her storybook. "My mother doesn't work anymore, and my father makes his own hours. So they're always taking trips. He golfs, and she shops." I was telling her the truth, really: they'd bought a couple timeshares after I graduated high school, their own "empty nester gift to themselves," and they seemed to be heading to a new state, a new golf club or lodge, every time I called home.

Asheville, North Carolina; Kalispell, Montana; Hilton Head, South Carolina. A dream life: who could argue?

"They've been together 25 years?" Jenn asked. "Shoot. That's what marriage is *supposed* to be. Two people who will stick together for a lifetime."

Later, when I brought Jenn back to Cypress Falls for Labor Day Weekend, everything she saw seemed to confirm my characterization. My father grilled turkey burgers in the backyard, mother cut tomatoes and peppers for salad, sliced gouda cheese and avocado for the burgers. There were four or five other couples in the porch, too, friends from around the neighborhood, and there were Amstel Lights and Newcastle Browns and cigars and those amazing jalapeno-cheddar potato chips and someone's Labrador retriever belly-flopping in the pool, the Clemson – Florida State football game on the big-screen, and my father sliding a burger onto Jenn's pre-sliced deli-fresh sesame-seed bun, and she told them that this was such a fun little party and she always wished her own parents could've had parties like this, but she hadn't gone home for Labor Day or Independence Day or Memorial Day since her freshman year at EU, because "back home" for her was just her mother's dumpy two-bedroom rental house in Hillsborough County that always smelled like Cheerio's, or it was her father's double-wide on a plot of gravel-weed-palmetto-scrub land and there were oil spots everywhere from his truck. Raccoons and fire ants. And Jenn told my parents that she didn't even like going home for Christmas or Thanksgiving, doing the whole drive-all-the-way-back-to-Tampa-and-then-spend-five-hours-at-my-Mom's-place-and-then-three-hours-at-my-Dad's-place-just-watching-CourtTV-or-USA-Network-and-then-driving-out-of-town-feeling-like-I've-been-robbed-of-a-good-family thing.

It was depressing, she said, and she didn't like going somewhere that she knew she'd be depressed. And my mother told Jenn that she was welcome here at their house for any holiday, for every holiday, and Charles, *we love Jenn*, bring her back for Thanksgiving! We have an extra bedroom! And my father slid a burger onto my plate, patted me on the back. And shit, of anything I'd ever accomplished, it seemed that acquiring Jenn was the only thing that had impressed him.

Jenn told my parents that their marriage was perfect, their family was perfect, and this was everything she wanted her own family to be someday. You two should, like, give lessons on marriage, she said. And all the neighbors laughed, even the Labrador retriever laughed as it snatched a hot dog from someone's plate.

So I *couldn't* let her know that my parents were now divorced. To have a fractured family, here on the eve of my new life as a role model, here on the eve of our new life as a "long-distance couple," was not an option.

"I can change, too," Jenn said in the parking lot as we packed my Explorer. "Do you want me to start dressing more like some 40-year-old office secretary?" She was wearing a black Britney Spears concert t-shirt and a pair of black yoga pants, the form-fitting kind with the bright teal waistband.

Same as she always wore whenever she spent the night, so she could head straight to the gym the next morning for muscle toning. Maybe the ensemble was comfortable for her, easy, but it showed her figure so completely that I appreciated the still moments—like this one, as she stood at my passenger-side door and searched for a place in the car where the tiny first-aid kit she'd made for me might fit—when I could listen to her, look at her, appreciate all that she was. "Or maybe I could dress like an elementary school teacher?" she asked. "Bad sweaters and *Golden Girls* pants? Mom Jeans?"

No, I couldn't imagine any change in my girlfriend, didn't even want to picture her in anything but these kitschy pop t-shirts. And right now, the sun was setting behind the pine trees at the edge of campus, and in this light her hair seemed perfectly straight and fairy-tale-golden.

For some reason, I stopped moving and just stared at her; Jenn brushed her hair from her shoulders with the grace of some actress in a Shampoo ad who models the silkiness of her strands as she runs along the beach and into the breeze. My God, this was a perfect woman.

Oh, sure, she was messy. Left bowls of half-eaten cereal in odd places in my bedroom until I had to investigate the source of the sour-milk smell. Wore lip gloss always, and was constantly drinking from my Tervis Tumbler cups and then leaving them half-full with water throughout the first floor of the fraternity house, each crescent-marked with lip gloss.

But she was perfect.

"I wouldn't change a thing about you," I said. "Well. Maybe your taste in TV shows. In movies."

She gasped dramatically. "I thought you *loved* my movies."

"I loved *Ferris Bueller* the first fifteen times I saw it. And *Sixteen Candles*, and *Uncle Buck*, and *Home Alone*. Back when I was in middle school."

"Be careful," she said. She owned only a dozen or so DVDs, and for some reason, all of them seemed to be John Hughes comedies. It was as if she'd refused to leave behind the PG-13 world of 1980s teenage suburbia and enter the R-rated world of '90s and 2000s pie-fucking gross-out comedies. Her sorority house roommate had bought her a book of social criticism called *The Twisted World of John Hughes' America* as a gag gift, but Jenn had never opened it.

"I rescind the comment. Wouldn't change a thing."

"That's all cosmetic stuff," she said. "Movies, clothes. But seriously, Charles. If you were a bad person, I wouldn't be with you. You know that."

"It's not about being a bad person," I said, pulling out my heavy suitcase to make room for the gym bag—tennis shoes, shorts, a few sweatshirts and pairs of sweatpants I'd bought so that I could jog outdoors in the winter. "I'm trying to, like, better myself."

"You said 're-invent yourself," she said. "That sounds so intense."

"It's just semantics."

"People can change in bad ways, too, you know."

"Sure. But I won't."

"Nobody ever *thinks* they're going to change for the worse," she said. "My parents. I heard them say the words 'change' and 're-invent' and 'renew' and all this other bullshit…I heard it over and over again, every day for two years, till it made me sick. And you know how *that* turned out. It was like listening to New Year's resolutions that you know aren't going to last. God, sometimes I wish my parents were more like yours."

"Right," I said.

"Speaking of which, should I come stay with you guys for Labor Day?"

"With…my parents?"

"Yeah. Or for Thanksgiving? We can spend the whole holiday in Cypress Falls."

"I don't…." I shrugged. "That's just so far away."

"More time to plan?" she said.

I nodded, but changed the subject. "Anyway, I'm taking a job where I have to act a certain way."

"Every job is like that."

"People are going to see me as a role model, Jenn. I have to *be* that person. All the time, I have to be that person." As I spoke, I stared at my suitcase, thought of the insides: on one half of the suitcase, one stack clean undershirts, one stack clean boxer shorts, six total pairs of socks, black toiletry bag, plastic bottle of vitamins, cell phone recharger, one pair pajama pants, three belts; on the other half of the suitcase, in the zipped-up pouch, my blue bath towel, three pairs of shoes, and a mesh laundry bag for my dirty clothes. This was the new Charles Washington. I'd packed and re-packed, measured pros against cons, multiplied to determine the number of possible outfit combinations of one shirt vs. another, before making my ultimate decisions and then boxing up everything I wouldn't take on the road and dumping it in a storage unit to wait for my return.

"I admire what you're doing. No question," Jenn said.

Her older sister had gone into an America Reads program after college, living in the Ukraine and teaching English to villagers or something (the village had even named a pig or a cow after her), before coming home to take an unrelated job with a health insurance company. So Jenn understood the fluidity of life, that career decisions need to make sense to *you* before they can make sense to everyone else. As soon as I'd told her about my mission—building young men into the socially responsible leaders of the next generation, beacon of leadership, all of it—she'd called it *noble*. Do you know how that feels? To have a beautiful woman call you noble?

"But you've got to promise me," she said, there in the fraternity house parking lot, "that the Charles Washington I see when you come back for Homecoming will be the same one that I know."

"I'll be the same guy, just new and improved. An extra scoop of raisins." I gave the suitcase one last shove, and boom: the Explorer was packed. "And you don't need to worry about *us*. I'm ready to do the right things to make this relationship work. I have goals."

"Do you know what my father told me when we moved to Tampa?" she asked.

"Jenn, I'm not your parents. I'm not your father."

"He told me, he told all of us: 'I'm ready to be the man.' And he had this look in his eye, this…determination? I don't know. Like he was listening to himself speak, and he was hearing his words as the voice-over in some movie trailer. 'I'm ready to be the man.' And he changed, all right. Sure, he quit driving semis so he could have a normal job and spend time with his family, but then he bitched about getting up for work, slept in, yelled at my mother that she'd ruined his life. Stopped coming home at night. Got fired for lord-knows-what. Ready to be the man? We believed him, and he probably believed himself, but it's like…the more determined you are to change, the worse it is when things go wrong."

"Jenn, listen to me," I said, and maybe *I* was hearing myself speak, too, maybe *I* was listening to a voice-over. "I would never let that happen. Not to my family."

"Oh yeah? Why not?"

"Because," I said. "I just won't let it happen. I see these other couples. If I'm going to do a relationship, I'm going to do it right. You look at our friends…look at Edwin. Thinks that he's Vinnie Chase or something. Has a girlfriend, but he goes out to Bang-Shots and he hooks up with a different girl every night. Look at Amanda. Tells everyone she doesn't want to get married until her 30s, wants to play the field. Thinks she's—and no offense to your show—she thinks she's in a *Sex and the City* episode."

"This coming from a guy who made out with three different girls on his 21$^{st}$ birthday?"

"That was *before*. No, I'll do this right."

"Yeah?"

"I don't want to be them. That's everyone around us. They either rush into a relationship because they're scared, or think they've got all their lives to figure it out and then avoid making commitments."

"Yeah?"

"And don't get me started on, like, Baby Boomers and their weak ideas about marriage and—" And I was thinking about my parents by that point, even though I hadn't told her anything I'd learned about their marriage. I was delivering speeches again, and maybe this one even sounded great, but because the speech pre-dated the challenges it spoke of meeting and overcoming, did the words matter at all? Whatever. I wasn't thinking of that at the time.

*Noble*, I was thinking. *I'm going to be noble.*

"I'll do this right," I said. "Trust me."

*

This was my last-gasp Facebook status update, typed just before I left the fraternity house in Fort Myers for good:

"**Charles Washington is**…headed to training at Headquarters today, and I'll be disabling my Facebook profile when I stop at a hotel tonight. Joining the 'real world' now, homeys, so no incriminating evidence. Sad but true. Leave one last comment on my wall, or drop me a text and wish me good luck."

By the time I checked my profile later that evening, unfurling below the status like the plastic-sheet baby pictures dropping from the inside of a father's wallet were nearly 50 comments.

**Lauren Vintner** – Are you really closing down your account? I don't get it.

**Andy Hitt** – Are you switching to MySpace or something? Wanna hang with the 14-year-olds? Are you pursuing a future in pedophilia?

**Josh Dorsey** – And I've written some awesome comments on your wall through the years, buddy. You sure you want to deprive the world of my amazing sense of humor?

**Jenn Barry** – I miss you already, Charles! You need to come back to Florida NOW!

**Edwin Cambria** – Ha ha, Jenn! He'll never be able to delete himself from those pictures at the Senior Send-Off. Drunk, cutting the cake.

**Jenn Barry** – So true. Don't worry, world! He's in, like, half of my Facebook photo albums, so you can get your Charlie Washington fix whenever you want!

**Harry Stewart** – Charles…I know what you mean. I got a friend request from my boss and my mom on the same day…almost made me cancel my account right there.

**Sean Farrow** – All these motherfucking political comments these days. I get it, man. It's fucking annoying. Fuck Obama, too! Why the hell does he get to have a Facebook account? That's like totally Big Brother. Fucking Nazi is what he is. Good call, Charles. You're a brave man. Delete delete delete!

**Jenn Barry** – I think it's silly that you're deleting your account. You should be allowed to have a social life, you know? Call me later.

On and on, the comments.
But then it was over. Click of a button, account de-activated at 5:44 PM, and it was done, everything vanished in an instant. "Charles is…clean," I thought.

\*

But on the day that I left Fort Myers and headed to Indianapolis for training, I texted Jenn to give her an update on my travels, and a strange thing happened. I started to type "I found the hotel that u booked for me," but the phone's auto-finish feature immediately completed the statement as "I fuck" and so I went back to erase the word "fuck" and start over, typed again, and then it auto-completed with "I found tits" and *tits? really?* so I went back, erased, typed "I found the hotel tits" and I erased and re-typed and before we were done with our text conversation, the phone had auto-finished the following additional words: "Booze," "Fucking," "Shitstorm," and "Fraternity." How many times must someone type "booze" in text messages, I wondered, before it becomes a phone's favorite choice for auto-finish?

*I know the real you.*

# **Orientation**

CHAPTER EIGHT

The sun had barely crept over the Indianapolis skyline and the consultant orientation was still sixty minutes from starting, but already I was convinced that my glorious new life as a role model was going to end in failure.

Earlier that morning at the hotel, I'd packed up and left before the staff had even finished setting out the continental breakfast. *Finally,* I'd thought. Finally my life was feeling like an Outlook calendar, not a Facebook page. Empty roads as I drove north, crisp skies free of jet trails, like the world was indeed offering me a chance to start a new profile, add new contacts, new tasks, new appointments, new goals.

But when I arrived at the gravel parking lot of the Henderson Memorial Auditorium a full hour early to the consultant orientation, expecting only empty spaces and cold rocks, expecting to beat my new colleagues to the first day of our new jobs, I found that several dozen of the other freshly hired educational consultants were already there, milling about the parking lot like early risers for Sunday service competing to show the still-sleeping pastor who was most devout.

My first day of summer training for the Nu Kappa Epsilon National Fraternity Headquarters. An hour early, but somehow I was still late.

They all stood outside in the mild heat of a Midwest summer morning, 22- and 23-year-old men and women straight from college or grad school, wandering and talking to one another as if this was an evening cocktail party and not an early morning in a parking lot. From the seat of my Explorer, I could see them shaking hands and introducing themselves; I could hear their strong leadership voices even from inside, names always paired with alma maters: *Jeff, from Michigan State, nice to meet you! Jeanna, from Bowling Green, nice to meet you! Tami, from Purdue, nice to meet you!* They—well, *we*— all wore brand-new suits, dresses, ensembles purchased with graduation gift money, all carried leather planners and portfolio notebooks, all of us trying our damndest to look like we'd been at this for awhile. Only it didn't look like they had to try. They had it together, every one of them.

One of the guys in the thick of the crowd saw that I was watching through my rearview mirror and that I was still buckled into my seat, and he waved me over, an emphatic flapping of his arm as if he was directing take-offs and landings on an aircraft carrier. So I smoothed my pants, adjusted my tie, told myself that this was the right choice, and I joined them in the gravel where they'd clumped together.

"Jeanna, from Bowling Green!" one girl said to me. Curly brown hair bouncing, eyes so wide and full of delight that she looked like Will Ferrell's *Elf* character, fed on a steady diet of gumdrops and pixie sticks. Clutching her portfolio notebook with such force that she was likely leaving permanent finger marks in the leather.

"Nice to meet you," I said. "Charles, from Edison University."

She cocked her head sideways, still smiling, but there was a disappointment darkening her eyes…disappointment, perhaps, that I wasn't displaying the same high-volume enthusiasm. Behind her, two young women had their hands on one another's shoulders, bobbing their heads so much as they talked that it didn't seem possible that they could keep eye contact without getting dizzy. So I tried again.

"Charles!" I said. "From Edison University!"

Her smile faded, deep dimples disappearing but still leaving faint parentheses in her cheeks…like maybe her face was unaccustomed to *not* smiling. "Um," she said. "Well, Charles. Nice to meet you." And she scampered off into the crowd to introduce herself to someone else, and I checked my tie again, my belt, smoothed my pants.

All around me, they smiled at one another in the same collegial fashion to which we'd all grown accustomed from weekends spent at SEIFC or the Gulf State Leadership Convocation or a score of other Greek-themed conferences, eyes lighting up as though they'd met a dozen times before *and it's fantastic to see you again*, and it seemed so easy and natural for all of them. The men stopped just short of raised-voice excitement, favoring firm handshakes and hands on shoulders and statements with only a single word or two extra-emphasized ("Looking *forward* to *working* with you."), but the women clapped and shouted. "You got the job!" Jeanna from Bowling Green said to another young woman, and she was now far away, but I could still hear her. "Oh my *God*! This is going to be the *best* year ever!"

In another conversation, one stout young man pounded his fist into his open palm, thundering the words, "And I said, you *buy in*…or you *get out*!"

Someone else said, "It's the drug culture. That's why I'm here. Stop! The! Drugs!"

And someone else: "—helped my fraternity to become the first on my campus to accept gay men without reservation—"

"—the house occupancy was dismal when I first got there, so I—"

"—so much opportunity to help the—"

"—and we need to really bring the *energy*, you know?"

The Henderson Memorial Auditorium is the centerpiece for the Indianapolis "National Greek Row," a single stretch of road in the unassuming heartland city of Indianapolis, where there is a carefully constructed corporate empire of national fraternities and sororities—headquarters buildings packed with full-time office staffs and file cabinets and three-ring binders and databases and spreadsheets—dedicated to maintaining the centuries of tradition within the world of "Greek Life," dedicated to reforming the fringe elements.

My headquarters building was a quarter-mile away, all the way at the far end of Founder's Row: a large gray triangle, the sharp point facing the road and the window-adorned wings spreading out in the grass behind it. Fierce like a Stealth fighter aimed straight for you. On the front lawn, distinctly visible from where we stood, was a gigantic set of concrete NKE letters, surrounded by white carnations (our national flower) and a small fountain which spurts water throughout the summer.

We stood in a giant clump in the gravel, all of us super-early on our first day of training with our respective national fraternities and sororities, fighting to show that our bodies were 90% excitement and only 10% flesh-and-bone. But even though we were all there for the same reason, a group orientation, I knew even then that some of us had more reasons than others…From fifteen feet away, I could hear the Lambda Chi Alpha fraternity consultant detailing how he'd cleaned up the alcohol culture in his house, how it had inspired him to want to make a difference in the lives of young people; I could hear the sorority consultant from Alpha Xi Delta telling someone that—when she was a freshman—they were the "nasty girls" on campus, the girls you picked up at the bar at 2 AM, but she took over as president and flushed out the "girls with the wrong priorities," changed the sorority from *nasty* to *classy*, changed the reputation, changed futures. "That's what I want to do as a consultant," she said. "Empower young women to make the *right* choices."

And yes, everyone around me had a story. Everyone around me sparkled with passion. They were born ready for this.

"Just what we need, right?" said the young man beside me, Southwestern cattle rancher's accent layering the words with down-home joviality.

I jumped, didn't realize he was there.

He looked familiar: the military-sharp blonde crewcut, the thick eyebrows and fist-sized Adam's apple. Maybe I'd met him already? Some other conference? Some other event? But he didn't seem to recognize me, seemed instead like he was the sort who was accustomed to striking up conversations with strangers, making them feel like they'd already been chatting for an hour. "Our first meeting is in an auditorium," he said, pointing at the doors. "We drive all weekend, and then we sit our asses right back down." He extended his hand so we could shake. "Brock London. From Central Texas University." And he had the sort of knuckle-cracking handshake that I should have expected from someone built like a tractor. I tried to match its energy.

"I'm Charles!" I said. "Edison University! Nice to meet you!"

"Whew. No need to shout, buddy," Brock said. "I'm right here."

"Sorry," I said. "It's just…loud. All around us."

"No biggie. Have a long drive?"

"Eighteen hours. All the way from Fort Myers, Florida."

"About the same for me. Guess we'd better get used to it. Part of the job."

"That's right," I said. "Part of our job." And it felt good to say this, the first moment that morning that hadn't felt forced, because yes, this is what

I *did* have in common with all the graduates gathered there: we came from everywhere. Florida and Texas, California and New York, Chicago and Seattle, each of us from different fraternities, different sororities—there are 29 national fraternities and sororities headquartered in Indianapolis, most of them represented in that gravel parking lot ("I'm with Zeta Tau Alpha sorority," one girl was saying in front of me, while behind me another said "Heather, from Alpha Xi Delta," and there were ten more introductions happening all around me, Theta Chi and Delta Delta Delta and Sigma Nu. When a name wasn't paired with an alma mater, it was paired with Greek letters.). Hundreds of gallons of gas for all of us to get there, hundreds of hours driving in our Altimas and Explorers and Corollas, some cars built for the travel and others in the lot clearly winded from the effort. Hundreds of gas station stops, bags of Cheetos and Chex Mix and 44-ounce Diet Cokes; dozens of hotel stays, bad coffee in styrofoam cups before hitting the road. We'd left behind vastly different campuses: Albright College, West Virginia Tech, LSU, Kansas. We'd left behind vastly different chapter houses, some of them four-bedroom homes in neighborhoods outside campus, some of them four-story mansions with eighty beds, boardrooms, libraries. We'd left behind friends, girlfriends/ boyfriends, fiancés. Or, like Jenn back at EU, someone we were *hoping* would become our fiancé if we could get through this year. We'd turned down offers for better jobs, better money. (Well. Not me. But most of *them*.). We'd argued and argued with our parents, with our professors, with everyone who told us that it was a foolish choice to spend the next full year employed by a national fraternity or sorority.

But we *knew* that we'd live from our cars, from airplanes, from suitcases, from the Starbucks and Panera cafes at which we'd soon type our reports, and we knew that our paychecks would be tight, that we were here together in a collective orientation because each national fraternity and sorority is a not-for-profit that operates from student dues, and a group orientation saves money, and as our web sites and brochures tout, "No matter the letter, we're all Greek together!" We knew it. We'd all signed up for this because...well, because we care about something greater than a "pay-off."

"I packed lots of CDs," I said. "But I should have subscribed to XM."

"Sure. Good for the long drives," Brock said. "So what's your letters, chief?"

"Nu Kappa Epsilon," I said. "I'm a Nike."

"Hey hey!" He slapped my back with one hard-as-a-board hand, like he was not a stranger but instead my older brother, and this rough-house exchange was an established part of our relationship. I fell forward a few steps. "Me too! Looks like we're gonna be working together!"

Brock London: and yes, I knew the name sounded familiar. There were dozens of consultants all around, but even on my first day of training I knew that I was one of just three new consultants hired by Nu Kappa Epsilon. And yes, I remembered the name Brock London. He'd already been hired before I was even interviewed.

"So," he said. Looked around, lowered his voice. "You know why we're here?"

"Why we're here? Like, the job responsibilities?"

"No, no," Brock said. "Heh. I'm a big dumb Texas boy, but I'm not that dense. I know why *I'm* here." And he smiled wide and slapped me on the back again, but this time I braced myself and didn't stumble. "I meant, why are we *here*? The auditorium?"

I stood straight, grimacing. "You didn't get a copy of the agenda?"

"Don't think so. I just knew that training starts today at 8 AM."

"And you got here early?"

"First day, buddy. Don't check my email too much, but I do know that you gotta make a solid first impression. You think you'd be the only one to show up early?"

"I guess not." But I pulled a sheet of paper from my leather portfolio, handed it to him. My first victory: fully prepared for the first day's training sessions. "Here you go. I try to print out all of my appointments. I think I have internet on my phone, but it costs an arm and leg, and it takes forever."

"Heh," Brock said. "We'll get along just fine, you and me. I don't even know how to send a text message. I just go with the flow." He read from the print-out: "'Consultant Orientation, 8 AM. The Mission of Greek Life, with W. LaFaber – H. M. Auditorium.' Well, damn. Walter's leading this session?" And now Brock looked all around, as if Walter LaFaber had perhaps materialized in the parking lot. "Hell of a start to the day! You've met him, right?"

"I have. During my interview."

And yes, if it is indeed a corporate empire of national fraternities and sororities there in Indianapolis, Walter LaFaber is not just my supervisor at NKE…he is at the forefront of the entire empire. The promise of what fraternity life could and should be.

With only a few minutes remaining before the start of the orientation, I said to Brock, "So what's your story? Why'd *you* take the job?"

"You might never heard of me," he said, running his hand over his buzzcut, "but you know why I'm here."

"I don't understand," I said.

"You heard the name Ashton Simon, I bet."

Ashton Simon. And it dawned on me that I shouldn't have asked for his story.

Because every fraternity man in the last decade knows the story of Ashton Simon. "The Ashton Simon Tragedy" had not just made headlines, but had become the sort of cautionary tale preached about at national conferences and in fraternity manuals. It had brought down an entire national fraternity. Everyone knew the name and the basic details, but now I was going to hear the full story.

This is what Brock told me:

During his freshman year at Central Texas University, a private school of about 2,500 outside of Fort Worth, Brock and his childhood best friend

Ashton Simon decided to pledge different fraternities. They'd been friends their whole lives, so they figured: why not branch out, meet new people? Brock chose Nu Kappa Epsilon. "Had some problems from the start," he told me. "Always been more of a leader than a follower," and the chapter hazed without abandon, subjected the pledges to all sorts of subservient activities. "Had to spend a night pretending to be a coffee table," he said. "Most humiliating night of my life." Ashton, though, chose a fraternity called Beta Beta Alpha and had a different experience entirely. Immersed himself in the chapter during this first semester, played intramural football, even became Pledge Class President. Never hazed, not once. Always bragged that this was fraternity the way it was supposed to be. But at the very pinnacle of the semester, just as all was going so well for him, Ashton was forced by an older brother to drink a full bottle of cheap vodka after a Big Brother-Little Brother ceremony, and afterward passed out. Asphyxiated on his own vomit.

And Brock stood tall as he told the story, eyes locked on mine, such gravity that I felt as if my body was liquefying and sinking into the Earth.

Without a pause or stutter, Brock told me that he'd fallen into a deep depression, had withdrawn from his classes, left campus. The two had known each other since preschool, had played Little League together. JV football. Varsity lettermen, Powder Puff cheerleaders. How could something like this have happened?

So when Brock returned to campus the following semester, he was a man on a mission: Beta Beta Alpha National Fraternity had crumbled from its legal battle, was now defunct, but Brock re-pledged Nu Kappa Epsilon and took a leadership role, rebelling against brothers when they attempted to haze him, tackling and pinning down the soft, spoiled Dallas and Houston brats when they tried to drive drunk after parties, counseling other pledges who were coping with peer pressure and alcoholism in their first year in college. By his junior year, he was president, had expelled the chapter troublemakers, and had convinced the administration *and* the students at Central Texas to ban alcohol in student housing; he even traveled Texas on a lecture tour with several anti-hazing and anti-binge-drinking presenters for CampuSpeak. Appeared on morning talk shows. Became a celebrity and advocate for values-based campus organizations. "That's how I met Walter LaFaber. He had me scouted for a long time, offered me the job after a speech I gave at Texas A&M."

Yes, that's Brock London. The sort of consultant who never had to change a thing about himself. Born for this.

"Start our summer training with a speech from Walter LaFaber," Brock said after finishing his story, face beaming with born-again intensity. "Gonna be good. Yessir."

"Yeah," I said. "I'm excited."

"Are you?" Brock asked, and his eyes suddenly darkened with the same skepticism that I'd seen in *Jeanna-from-Bowling-Green's* eyes. Buzz cut seeming somehow sharper, cheeks losing their jolly roundness and turning hard as elbows. And I thought that he might ask me if I had a similar story, something that compares, something dramatic and important. And if not, why the hell was I even there?

"Yes," I said to Brock. "Yes, of course."

"Show the excitement, then, buddy!" he said and slapped my back one more time, and this time I did fall forward again, knocked into someone in a suit who turned and scoffed as if I'd charged forward like a linebacker and had intentionally tried to tackle him. He brushed the back of his jacket even though it was clean and still wrinkle-free. I backed away, mouthed an apology, and meanwhile Brock was saying, "What a morning, what a morning. I'm ready to save the world, you better believe it. Let's get it on!"

Around us, the crowd was growing. Gravel crunching as cars parked. Doors opening, shutting. More shirts, more ties, more pantsuits and dresses, more portfolio notebooks, more introductions and handshakes and names paired with alma maters and Greek letters, more stories of leadership development and tough choices as the clock ticked closer to the start of the consultant orientation, more smiles that seemed more natural and genuine than mine, the purest of motives for every one of them because they were not hiding anything, no, they'd always been what I was seeing in front of me, their profiles always clean, lives always structured and disciplined and honest and good-hearted, and I straightened my tie again and hoped that no one was staring at me, seeing through me.

\*

Finally, as if in fulfillment of Brock's let's-get-it-on declaration, the doors of the Henderson Memorial Auditorium were unlocked from the inside, and all of us—all of the freshly hired consultants on our first day of training—were ushered into the auditorium, packed together like kids at a church camp ready to sing and praise the Lord.

We shuffled together toward the front row, knees bumping against seats as we side-walked down the tiny row. Beside me, Brock held his too-short tie against his shirt as he walked, like he was afraid that it might fall off if it kept swinging. But we barely had time to find a seat before the speakers at the front of the auditorium cackled from microphone feedback and Walter LaFaber burst onto stage, one clenched fist held out before him like a head football coach who has just watched his team execute a critical scoring drive. "Ladies and gentlemen," he yelled, "we are on a *mission!*"

We all stopped, asses still halfway out of our seats, the same awkward posture one might assume when a pastor finishes a prayer and the congregation opens its eyes and starts to re-settle...only to be forced back up when the pastor launches ahead with a new hymn.

"We have a mission," LaFaber said, "and that's what they don't understand out there." He motioned with one massive arm, pointing at the world outside the doors of this building. "We are creating positive change in the lives of young men and women all across the country. Do you believe it?"

We hovered, knees still bent, and I looked left, looked right to see if anyone else had sat down, if we were supposed to. But everyone else was still staring straight ahead.

"No, I don't think I need this," Walter LaFaber said, regarding the microphone in his hand as if it was an expended cigarette. "You all are going to be my voice this morning." And he placed the microphone back onto the podium, projected louder: "We are creating positive change. Do you *believe* it?"

And again, after LaFaber repeated his question, I took tentative glances at the graduates to my left and right. Beside me, Brock was nodding emphatically and clenching his fists in excitement, so when I turned my attention back to the stage, back to LaFaber, I nodded also and mouthed the word "yes." Brock said, "I believe!" and so I said those words, too.

"I want to really hear it," LaFaber said. "Do you believe in what you are doing?"

"I believe it!" Brock said, his blue eyes so clear that I could almost see the heroic consultant fantasies he was imagining. And there were other similar rumblings, too—one of the girls at the end of the row was cheerleader-clapping as she shouted, one clap for each syllable—but we still sounded disconnected.

"I don't know if I'm feeling you guys yet," LaFaber said, smiling. "But we'll work on it, we'll work on it. We've got all morning. Heck, we've got all summer."

He returned to the podium, flipped through a stack of notes.

LaFaber, who was once again pacing and summoning his energy, is not just the Director of Chapter Operations at Nu Kappa Epsilon National Fraternity Headquarters, but is a tremendous draw as a motivational speaker (even for a Monday morning group orientation in Indianapolis): though the front rows were occupied only by the newly hired consultants, the auditorium behind us appeared to be filling with the most important faces in all of fraternity and sorority life, twenty or thirty Greek Life staffers who'd crowded into the room to hear LaFaber and to meet this year's class of consultants, forty of them, fifty: there were National Fraternity CEOs back there, Foundation presidents, Alumni Board directors, rows upon rows filled with gray-haired men of sixty, their lapels graced with side-by-side Lambda Chi Alpha and American flag pins; there were rows of sorority administrators and volunteers, women with short dark hair and perfect ladylike posture; there were bespectacled motivational speakers, former consultants from years past who now—like LaFaber—were making commendable salaries for weekend speaking engagements, and they had their sleeves rolled up as if they'd just come from a stage; there were sorority and fraternity volunteers of every age, interns from DePauw or IUPUI younger than me, next to men and women so old that they likely remembered a time before this auditorium was built, before there even was a National Fraternity Row of headquarters buildings in Indianapolis.

"You know, the media loves to feast on Greek Life," LaFaber said, no longer smiling, but still walking back and forth across the stage slowly, his eyes meeting each of ours. He has a long and perfectly straight scar descending from his widow's peak, an old football injury that every magazine profile about his life seems to explore in-depth, as if the hard hit made him a prophet or gave him superhuman powers; when the light strikes this scar dead-on, as it did in this moment, his entire face glows, becomes electric. "Newspapers are always quick to point out the bad stuff," he said. "It's sexier, sells more copies when they find a way to make fraternity guys into a collection of binge drinkers and womanizers, or when they can find a story that makes our sorority women seem as if they all have eating disorders, or they're all—pardon the language—a bunch of sluts. Sorostitutes. These are the words we hear."

I nodded politely—*fraternity stereotype*—but beside me Brock's face had gone red, as though he was not just intense but angry. I held my breath and clenched my teeth, wondered what it would take to look the same way, vein popping out on my forehead.

"Hell, just google the word 'fraternity' and see what happens," LaFaber said, and he held the stack of papers high in front of him. "Here are three of the top results that came up this morning: 'Freshman student stuffed into freezer for three hours,' 'Two students forced to wear women's panties,' 'Orlando youth loses nose in freak hazing accident.'"

"Disgusting," Brock said. "Absolutely *disgusting*, some of these punks."

"And that's just the headlines!" LaFaber shouted to the room. "What about the YouTube videos of drunk men performing explicit dances on-stage to the song 'My Dingaling?' During university talent shows! Or the hundreds of thousands of photos from Facebook, from blog sites, photos of jell-o shots, photos of 'Sexy CEOs and Secretaries' parties, photos of men hanging from the windows and balconies of their houses?"

Brock was gritting his teeth, and though I've often heard people tell me that they are so upset that they "could burst," I'd never truly believed it until this moment.

"You all right?" I whispered.

"No, sir," he said. "Makes me sick to my stomach."

"But I don't think this perception is accurate," LaFaber said. "I think that you all are something very different, that our organizations are something very different."

He paused, one hand stroking his chin, and there was a deep silence in the room, a silence that shouldn't have been possible with more than 150 people gathered in one place. No rustling, no shifting in seats, no movement of pants or shirt fabric, no change jingling in pockets. A beneath-the-Earth silence, mystical, as if LaFaber had found a way to will away any competition for his attention, to make us all float above our seats. I'm not sure what I expected of my first day on the job. Paperwork? Office tours? Here's how to use the copy machine, here's the code to the fax machine, here's your cubicle, and we have a stapler around here somewhere, and oh, we're not sure how to unlock this old filing cabinet beside your desk, but if you figure it out, let us know. The sort of things that had taken up the entire first week of my internship at Gulf Coast Communications. But this was different. I found myself standing like a soldier at attention, the slightest fidget unacceptable.

"You are *not* the headlines!" LaFaber said. "You are the best and brightest. You were the presidents of your fraternities and sororities, the advisors in your residence halls, the senators in your schools' student governments. Best and the brightest on your campuses. And now? You're ready, aren't you?"

Brock was nodding again, trying to steady his breathing.

"You're going to save the world. I couldn't stop you if I tried!"

He shook his head comically, and everyone in the room laughed.

"You are *leaders*," LaFaber said, "and you cannot falter in your faith."

The Henderson Memorial Auditorium is an aging structure. Water spots on the ceiling, fading public service announcement posters on the walls. I was told on my initial tour that it was built as a joint project between the Indianapolis-based national fraternities and sororities in the mid-1980s, during a golden age of Greek Life when college enrollments were exploding in a way that hadn't been seen since the end of World War II, fraternity houses filled to capacity, expanding, adding new bedrooms and kitchens. A golden age when everyone wanted to join and anything seemed possible. Before the Liability Era came and ruined everything.

But even against the dated backdrop, LaFaber looked impressive as he walked the glossy floorboards on-stage before us. Towering above us, impossibly tall, and impossible the way he made eye contact with so many of us so quickly, each of us, one after the next, perhaps 50 consultants in all.

The power of Walter LaFaber. Larger than the stage on which he walks.

"Repeat after me," LaFaber said, and his voice was barely a whisper, but still the world held its breath to hear him speak. "We are leaders."

"We are leaders," the front-row echoed. And I still spoke so softly that I couldn't even hear my own voice over the din of dozens of other young men and women repeating the same words. But somehow, it didn't matter anymore.

"We are not stereotypes," LaFaber said softly.

"We are not stereotypes," we said.

Brock trembled, he was so excited.

"We are not stereotypes," LaFaber said and paused, searching our eyes, finger pointed directly at us. All of us, somehow. "You know you'll encounter groups that *just—don't—get it*." He shook his head sadly. "I want you to remember these words. The men and women in this room? The men and women in the organizations you will be consulting? We are *leaders*."

"We are leaders," we echoed.

"We are not stereotypes."

"We are not stereotypes."

"Forget the google search results," he said, fist held before him again, jaw clenched. "You know what we really are."

"We are leaders."

"And you know what we're *not*."

"We are not stereotypes."

Again. Again. Again.

There in the auditorium, with all of the other consultants, I stood as tall as I could.

"We are leaders," LaFaber said. "No matter what anyone wants to think!"

"We are leaders," we said, and it was becoming easier for me to join the chorus.

"And when we do encounter resistance," LaFaber said, "we will *change the culture*."

Penetrating silence.

"You're the top fraternity and sorority leaders in the nation," LaFaber said, face still ablaze, scar on his forehead still shining under the spotlight. Suddenly, though, he sighed. He looked disappointed, and this is a man whose every expression screams, *Do* not *disappoint me*. "I want you to tell me, with no uncertainty, what you will be doing out on the road."

The long row of consultants in the Henderson Memorial Auditorium looked from side to side again, then back up at LaFaber, then left, then right; beside me, Brock was mouthing "*I believe*" yet again, but he seemed unsure that this was what he should be repeating, so he didn't actually say a word. It was as if we were all performers in a dress rehearsal who'd suddenly realized that we'd been missing a page in our scripts.

And I don't know why, but the words came to me in that moment: "*Change the culture!*" I yelled, all by myself, and ran my hands through my hair like an athlete after a grueling game, absolute relief from mental exhaustion.

Up on stage, LaFaber nodded in confirmation. "Yes. We will *change* the culture."

"We will change the culture," we all said together. Taking my lead.

"I didn't catch that," LaFaber replied, scratching his chin, looking at the far wall. "This is your career now. This is your life. And that's all you got?"

"We will change the culture!" we tried. And now Brock was struggling to say it as loud as I was; now Jeanna from Bowling Green was trying to keep up with *me*.

"Louder! This is your *life!*"

"We will change the culture!" we shouted, digging deep within our lungs to convince him that we were serious, 40 of us, 50, and it was the sort of chant that could make a believer of every *Animal House* Bluto out there. If we'd been singing a hymn in church, we'd have had our hands outstretched, convinced we could feel the Holy Spirit on our fingertips.

LaFaber nodded, perhaps satisfied for the moment. "What is most important," he said from the stage, "is that *you believe* in *yourselves*. You can't do a damn thing if you don't believe that you are *leaders!*"

"We are leaders!"

*

93

During my first semester of senior year, I'd interned at Gulf Coast Communications, a Fort Myers-based marketing and public relations office whose main focus was on event planning. I'd been lured into this unpaid position at EU's annual "Internship Fest," where a man in a silver power-tie showed me a laptop presentation of the events with which I might assist: the Bank of America Southeast Regional Awards Banquet, the Sanderson Properties Parade of Homes, the Edison University Faculty and Staff Outreach Night. Ice cream socials, galas, chili cook-offs, barbecues, martini and mashed potato nights. Planning social events, mixers, dances, fundraisers? Hell, I'd been doing this for *three years* already. Now it could be my *career*?

But there was no way that the reality of daily office life at GCC could match what I'd imagined. It was long lines of cubicles, men in short-sleeved button-downs and ties who spent mornings emailing YouTube clips to one another, women who rarely moved from their computer chairs and their cubicle-shelf Beanie Baby collections, and who seemed always to be clicking through online photo albums. It was as if everyone at the office tried their damndest to avoid work, as if the 9-5 workday was no different than an average Spring day at a local high school, kids snoozing and passing notes and copying homework. *Why are you even here?* I wondered.

And, of course, my role at the office was to make copies, to update seemingly endless Excel spreadsheets one symbol at a time, to spend four hours searching online for novelty martini glasses for the Naples Health Care Association's "Roaring '20s"-themed fundraiser. Just before an event, the office descended into a frenzy, swept up in gossip about table settings and life-sized Ray Charles cardboard cut-outs and the 25 different toppings from which guests could choose to create their own designer mashed potatoes. But only four or five employees were ever allowed to attend the events, and these were the elusive and well-dressed executive types who hid behind the tinted glass windows of their enclosed offices, or who spent days, weeks, out of the office on supposed "business trips" to LA or New York or New Orleans. "Gotta put in your time," my fellow intern, a kid named Randy, told me. "This shit might be tedious right now, but someday, that could be *us* in those offices." I usually just smiled and nodded out of courtesy, but I also wondered: *Why?* Years of toil, so that hopefully I could plan a bank's holiday party, and then get the privilege of going to the party and eating the chicken fingers? Was this really it?

Often, I spent hours at GCC imagining others at their own jobs: had my father felt like he was accomplishing something important as he moved money from place to place, or were his tasks no different than when I moved stacks of papers from copy room to filing cabinet? The alumni who came back to visit the fraternity house during football season, who walked with such a profound sense of purpose as they inspected our furniture and our floors... what sort of jobs did they have?

And there in the Henderson Memorial Auditorium, body and voice seemingly possessed by purpose, I knew it: no matter what my father had said, no matter what the outsiders thought, this is a job that would actually mean something.

*

"Change starts with each one of you," LaFaber said from the stage. "I have faith in you. I know what you're capable of. I've read your bios, your resumes. But it's no longer about what you did in college. It's about what you're going to do now. And what are you going to do?"

"Change the culture!" we screamed.

"What are you going to do?"

"Change the culture!"

"You must be flawless. You must be angels. Wherever you go, students should be blinded by your haloes."

Laughter from all around the hall, from the back rows of fraternity and sorority legends, from the CEOs and Foundation Presidents, from the secretaries and interns. Laughter from the front rows, too, from all of us consultants. And I want to think that, because we were strangers from across the country, we'd *all* been hiding behind defensive armor this entire time. Not just me. And in this moment, because we all knew that we were part of something special, we began shedding that armor, revealing ourselves, and there was no one who was any better than me, any worse.

"If you don't have a halo," LaFaber said, and he seemed to be looking directly at me now, as if he feared that all the chants in the world would not change the man I was, the man I'd tried to erase, "you better hurry up and get one."

So I chanted even louder the next time. Louder. Louder.

Until nothing else mattered but this moment, when I was one of them.

And by the time we left this first session, it felt like we were all indestructible crusaders protected by God Himself, glowing and so full of energy that we no longer needed to breathe, we floated out of the auditorium. It seemed that so much of my life had been a search for some way to make myself matter to the world, some way to protect or preserve something I cared deeply for, a family, an organization, preserve it and make it perfect and pass it to others, and for this bright shining moment I knew I'd found it.

Two months of training before I was to hit the road, and here I was—here I *am*, now on my final night in Indianapolis—ready to be what I never could before. Ready to be the Marathon Man that they expect me to be. Ready to change the culture. Ready to save the world.

# Part II

## Alcohol Responsibility Workshop

CHAPTER NINE

At the National Fraternity Headquarters, we divide them neatly into two groups: the high-achieving leadership organizations who keep their houses clean and behave as gentlemen and raise money for charities and maintain stellar GPAs, and the *frat stars*, who seem to fuck everything up. And right now, at the end of my second week on the road as an Educational Consultant, I've fallen into a nest of frat stars.

I'm at the University of Pittsburgh now, in the Chapter Room of a crumbling two-story fraternity house so rife with a rotten-orange-juice smell that I've been fighting my gag reflex since I arrived two days ago. All around me, on deteriorating couches and rusty metal fold-out chairs, sit the twenty-five dues-paying, live-in brothers of the house. During the day, this is simply the Living Room, but when the fraternity gathers for meetings, the brothers drag couches and chairs from all the first-floor bedrooms and closets and construct a haphazard meeting facility. The "Chapter Room," they call it. Among my job responsibilities: document and report any damages to alumni-owned housing facilities. But where do I start? The burn marks on the front door, perhaps? The rotting railings of the front porch? The stagnant liquor-beer-trash-water in the dark corners of the basement?

And currently, I'm sitting on a sofa so saturated with beer, liquor, wine, soda, and cereal milk that the cushions are probably more liquid than solid. The assembled fraternity members are busy finishing an exercise I gave them ten minutes ago. I passed out Sharpie markers and tear-away sheets of paper from my portable presentation pad to every member. "I want you to create a timeline of your life," I told them all (and I could almost hear the squishy noise of everyone rolling their eyes in unison), "but I want the timeline to focus on your life with alcohol. Like, your *birth* would be your first drink, and major events might include a drunk driving experience, or a night where you made a poor choice because of alcohol." I checked my watch. "I'll give you fifteen minutes." Then I shifted from my front-and-center position as Presenter to my current position on the couch as Observer, watching the members attempt—with various degrees of awkwardness—to draw their

97

timelines, using the floor or the couch as desks, sharpies bleeding into the cushions, poking holes through the paper.

Pittsburgh is one of those groups that sets the fraternity stereotype, that puts *Animal House* to shame. "Very *fratty*," they say at Headquarters. "Frat-tastic." Eight members on academic ineligibility, four members serving university probation for underage drinking, two live-in brothers who aren't even enrolled in school. A group that lives in the '80s, a reckless lawless Wild West decade for fraternities.

And I'm staring straight up now, looking at nothing, looking at everything, while they draw. The ceiling fan rests motionless overhead, broken and beyond repair, its blades (and the ceiling itself) splashed with dried caramel-brown blotches. The chapter president told me that someone tossed an open beer into the fan as it spun, and instead of scrubbing the splattered mess with hot water and a sponge and 409, the chapter's elected House Manager pulled a can of spray-paint from the supply room and drenched the stain with a coat of white paint. The stain recently broke through the paint, the chapter president said, and was now growing larger. My face remained flat as he told this story. In the moment, I was too shocked to really say anything, though later I imagined a more productive reaction. A discussion about "respect for housing," about "personal responsibility," about "pride in the fraternity." I imagined unclasping my laptop and sitting down and working with the President and the House Manager to create a set of bullet-point action initiatives that could make this house into a clean and profitable unit.

"Yo, EC," someone calls from across the Chapter Room. *EC:* Educational Consultant. In the world of higher education, everything is shortened or abbreviated. Educational Consultant isn't tough to say, but no matter the title, someone will eventually acronym your position.

"My name is Charles," I say.

"Right," he says. "Sorry, man." He's wearing dirty gym shorts and an ash-gray shirt, cut-off sleeves, a faded slogan across the chest. Looks like it says *What's My Name* or *Ain't the Same.* Maybe *Play the Game.* When I met him yesterday he smelled like rusty barbells and weeks-old laundry, but we talked about the National Fraternity and the other Pennsylvania chapters for an hour. He *loves* this fraternity and all his brothers, he kept saying, but he *hates* "Nationals." We're always getting his chapter in trouble, he said. I told him that we weren't *getting* them into trouble, only enforcing standards because we *do* care about them as individuals. But I've already forgotten his name. Could be James or Joe or Jason. So many names, so quick, and no system to remember them all. "How much longer we got for this?" he asks.

"A few minutes," I say, and I struggle to lean forward on the sofa, to look professional, but I slip, sink back into the cushions. The couch is broken and the springs squeak. I smooth my dress pants again and again to make it seem as if I'm comfortable, but it feels like I'm getting eaten alive by a soggy stack of laundry. "Don't worry. I don't expect these timelines to be artistic masterpieces."

James (or Joe, or Jason) nods, goes back to darkening some gigantic black letters on his paper. And once again, even though the entire room looks like a kindergarten run by crack addicts, I have to tell myself that I'm making progress.

*

This is my schedule for the semester:

---

**TRAVEL SCHEDULE – CHARLES WASHINGTON**

~~Summer Training in Indianapolis~~

~~University of Kentucky~~
~~East Tennessee State University~~
~~University of Virginia—Great Valley~~ ///
University of Pittsburgh ///
Shippensburg University
St. Joseph's University
New Mexico State University
Texas Tech
California State University—Fresno
California State University—Highland
California State University—Long Beach
California State University—San Francisco
University of Delaware
Marshall University
Miami University (Ohio)
University of Toledo
Central Michigan University
University of Michigan
Bowling Green State University
Purdue University
Indiana University

Headquarters – Mid-Semester Debrief (Indianapolis)

University of Oklahoma
University of Kansas
University of Missouri—Columbia
University of Nebraska
Iowa State University

Thanksgiving Vacation

Bradley University
University of Iowa

Headquarters (Indianapolis)

Christmas Vacation

---

University after university, college after college for sixteen weeks. Three days at one school, pack up and drive, then three days at the next. Twenty-four hours a day at fraternity houses, reporting social infractions, documenting housing damages, living in them. The Headquarters doesn't have the money for plane tickets or hotels, so my car is my office, and my home is a scattered series of fraternity house guest rooms across the Midwest.

For the past three days, I've been sinking into the slippery-sided pit of Pittsburgh. When I've showered, I've done so in the dingy first-floor bathroom they usually use only during parties: I had to clear dead leaves and the pieces of a broken volleyball from the tub before stepping inside. When I've slept, I've done so in a guest bedroom with holes in the walls and piles of old Busch cans in the corners. I eat with the frat stars at their dented dinner table. In my spare time, I sit on the slimy couches and talk with them, even though the conversations are the same each night: *Family Guy* is hilarious, the BCS is evil, and it's absolute bullshit that Nationals won't allow them to have kegs at their parties. All the while, 24/7, acting the part of Marathon Man. A "beacon for leadership," instilling in the brothers of each chapter the mission of Nu Kappa Epsilon, to "develop our members into the socially responsible leaders of the next generation."

Three days at one school, pack up and drive, then three days at the next.

"Nobody said it'd be easy," Walter LaFaber told us during training. "But you are the face of the National Headquarters. The embodiment of our spirit. Without you, there is no national fraternity, no mission." There are three Educational Consultants at the Nu Kappa Epsilon Headquarters—Brock London, myself, and a kid from California named Nick—and we spent the summer in training with LaFaber, learning every word of every Sacred Law, every name and date in the fraternity's history, every number and decimal on the national budget, every story of fraternity life gone wild, the hazing, the alcohol and drug abuse and house fires and sexual abuse charges and gang warfare. Two years ago, we suffered three alcohol deaths in a single semester (Brandon Kane, Wisconsin, fell from a balcony during a Big Brother ceremony; Eddie Sandor, San Jose State, asphyxiated on his own vomit; and Kyle Benet, UTEP, died when, after a party, he drove his truck into the concrete divider in a Texas highway), three immediate lawsuits that threaten the financial foundation of the fraternity.

"It's the Sandor Lawsuit we're most concerned with," LaFaber confided to us. "His parents? They're going for the throat."

Millions of dollars each year pass through some individual fraternity chapters. My own chapter back at EU, sure, but especially the oldest chapters on historic campuses—Alabama, Illinois, Nebraska, Cornell—who live in ten-columned mansions, eighty live-in members, full breakfast-lunch-dinner meal plans, cleaning services, Spring Formals, alumni anniversary banquets, faculty luncheons. And each year, millions of dollars pass through our National Headquarters: student fees, alumni contributions, investments, grants,

100

conferences. We don't have an impressive travel budget for our employees, but if a lawyer sees these numbers…?

"What do they want?" I asked.

"I'll tell you what they don't want," LaFaber said. He leaned forward over the conference table and spoke with the same intense whisper he'd used during our first-day orientation, the one that could silence the entire world. "They don't want an easy cash settlement. And unlike the Kanes and the Benets, they don't want to admit that their own son might have been at fault."

"But Sandor was drunk, right? He had a choice about whether to drink—"

"That's what they want to prove," LaFaber said. "That he did *not* have a choice. That it was the fraternity's fault that he drank a bottle of rum. That the fraternity members *made* him do it, that the entire national fraternity is responsible for perpetuating a culture of alcoholism."

"That's ridiculous," I said.

But beside me, Brock London was shaking his head. "They got a hell of a case, don't they?" he asked. "Some older brother hands a freshman a drink, tells him to chug it…who wouldn't feel pressured?"

"This is the lawsuit that makes or breaks Nu Kappa Epsilon," LaFaber said. "They don't just want our financial resources. They want to end our existence."

"They can't do that," I said. "What did *we* ever do? Nationally, I mean."

"Just the same as my buddy Ashton," Brock said. "Parents wanted someone to blame, and they took down Beta Beta Alpha."

"This might seem bleak at times, but this is the fraternity world as it exists," LaFaber said, and he backed away from the conference table, the rugged intensity now replaced with a calm confidence. As if he had everything under control. "If you believe in the power and importance of our national brotherhood, though, you believe we can change the culture."

Change the culture.

And that is why tonight, a Friday night, at the end of my fourth chapter visit of the semester, I'm facilitating an alcohol education workshop, a cornerstone of the risk management component of the National Fraternity's newly hatched "DO IT!" initiative. This is how we show the world what we truly are, what we truly want to be.

*

I try to lean forward from the couch, try to reach my notebook on the condiment-stained coffee table, but I fall back into the damp cushions. I lean forward again, *stretch* with all the energy I can muster, grab the outline: "Life with Alcohol Timeline," it says, "15 min."

I've given them twenty.

"All right, guys," I say and push myself up, and this simple action—pushing myself from a broken couch—is an exercise much more difficult than it might sound, like shooting a basketball while sitting cross-legged. I stand and wobble, pat my behind—still dry, surprisingly—and walk to the center of the room. "Good job, guys. Very good," I say. I clap my hands, attempt to

101

make eye contact with as many of the fraternity brothers as possible, many of whom are still coloring or drawing unrelated pictures on their timelines. I keep my demeanor friendly, positive; I laugh, smile, bend the knees so I don't appear wooden like an old English teacher, keep one hand in pocket the same way that Walter LaFaber does. "So tell me," I say, "why I had you all participate in this exercise."

The brothers trudge back to their seats, timeline papers clenched in their hands, but no one immediately volunteers an answer. Most stare at the floor, look in different directions, check the time on their cell phones.

"Anyone?" I ask.

Several seconds pass. I can hear my own heartbeat in my ears.

The problem, as I've learned in the last two weeks, is that some chapters get it, and some don't. Some want to change the culture of fraternity life and live the mission, and some want to live the stereotype. This University of Pittsburgh chapter? For the past two days, they've treated me like an enemy spy attempting to learn their every secret, sneak a peek under their pillows, in their closets, and report the findings back to my superiors at the Death Star. In fact, one of them dropped a few homemade business cards on my suitcase, all of them printed with the job title "Fun Nazi." I forced myself to laugh when they asked me if I liked the gag, but I couldn't smile.

"We're a bunch of drunks, yo," someone says finally, and everyone laughs.

"Well, um," I say. "Thank you for confirming that. Anyone else?"

A couple seconds pass.

"So," I say, "how many of you were surprised by your timelines?"

No answer.

"Anyone?"

And such is the inherent flaw of interactive presentations for groups that have no desire to interact with you.

A few of them have cell phones in laps, are texting or checking Facebook or moving images around the interactive screens of their iPhones. Throughout the past three days, whenever I've made an educational suggestion for improving chapter operations, someone has said, "There's an app for that!" and everyone has snickered in a dirty-joke sort of way. And I've never before had to pretend that I understand technology-related gags, but I'm lost. Just months ago, before LaFaber told us to clean up our digital footprints, I'd spend hours every night updating my own Facebook profile, leaving comments across my network, over a thousand friends, dozens of groups, Farmville, Mafia Wars, zombie-ized profile pictures, Flixster movie reviews. But that Charles Washington doesn't exist anymore.

"Anyone?" I ask again. "Anyone who found your timeline surprising?"

And then, mercifully, one hand rises with measured reluctance, slinks upward like a periscope poking out of the water. Then, another hand rises. Three or four more. Not so bad. Very good response, in fact. Most of the hands then drop, flop back into laps as though I'd snake-charmed them all into the air and now my spell is broken. One of the brothers, though—I think

102

I met him, think his name is Tony—hasn't realized that he's the only one with his hand still raised. So I point at him and say, "Great. What surprised you about *your* timeline?"

"What?" Tony says, looks around. "Oh. I don't know. Guess I... guess I've had more good times than I thought?" A few random snickers throughout the room. I hold my breath: I think he's done. He's made a joke, and this is probably the best I'll get out of this workshop, just jokes and smart-ass comments.

"Putting it all on paper, I mean," he says. "I had some good times, but hell, I think I've spent more money on alcohol than I've ever had in my account at any one time, you know?"

Everyone laughs.

More jokes and smart-ass comments.

But there are several types of laughter, right? You can laugh when you make fun of someone, but you can also laugh when you realize something about yourself that's maybe a little disturbing and you've got no other way to cope with it in public. You joke and you laugh to relieve your own tension. So this could be productive laughter?

"Excellent!" I say. "*Putting it all on paper.* That's a great point. Anyone else?"

"These guys made me into an alcoholic," someone blurts out and everyone laughs again. And I'm about to scowl but then I'm thinking, *wait*, productive. "I'm just joking, you know," he says. "I ain't complaining. But I probably could've made a whole other timeline just from the time I've been living in this house. Maybe that says something."

"Interesting," I say. "Thank you. That's an honest observation. It seems to me that these timelines, more than anything else, allow us to see trends in our habits. When I created mine, you'd never believe the things I learned about myself."

And, amazingly, they're sitting forward in their seats, all thirty of them alert, elbows at angles and palms pressed against their knees, baseball caps lifted out of their eyes; for the first time in the presentation, their eyes are wide with interest. Like they actually want to talk about this, like they actually want to *get it*.

"Would anyone like to share their timelines?" I ask.

And now, without a moment's hesitation, someone stands from a fold-out chair, eager but nervous, like he's been recognized at a major awards show and must now deliver his speech. He's wearing a navy NYPD shirt and a Yankees hat turned backward, bill flipped up. He's either the "Vice President" or the "Director of Chairmen," one of the officers I met briefly.

"Thanks for volunteering," I say, and he nods and walks to the center of the Chapter Room, holds his paper high for everyone to see. It's the typical Life with Alcohol timeline, a bumpy black line from left to right across the page, sharp date-lines shooting upward like porcupine spikes, each carrying a barely-legible description.

I slip away, sink back into the couch.

"At first," NYPD says in a coughy coal miner's voice, "I was going to draw every time I've been drunk. But we only had fifteen minutes to do this. Time was limited, know what I'm saying? Had to pick and choose."

Everyone laughs.

"So I was like, well, I could just write the times when I've puked," he says. He waves his hand across his timeline. He says he can't even remember all the times he's puked, but he tried anyway. He says that it's pathetic, all this puking. No one laughs.

When I gave this presentation at the University of Kentucky, my very first visit, one of the brothers stood up and tore off his Wildcats hat and said in this ultra-bluegrass voice, "You calling us *alcoholics?*" Took me the rest of the presentation just to convince him that I wasn't trying to insult anyone, that I never said that alcohol was evil or that it made anyone a bad person or an alcoholic, that I was only trying to help them understand alcohol responsibility, that alcohol education is an important part of leadership development.

I wanted to talk to them about restraint and regrets, maybe share something from my own life, joke about how to avoid waking up on the living room floor. But you *do not* veer from the script, LaFaber said. Do you want to be a leader or a punchline?

Here, now, maybe I've got a stack of "Fun Nazi" business cards on my suitcase, but...I see opportunity.

Someone else stands and volunteers.

Says that his name is Gerry and he's an alcoholic, and everyone laughs.

Shows his timeline. Points to the major events in his college career. Big Brother night. Homecoming. End of Finals Week. End of freshman year. Sophomore year. Junior year. The night of his first sexual experience. The first night he got drunk with his parents. And he tells a story about the first night he lived in the dorms here at Pittsburgh, how his father left him with two 12-packs of Rolling Rock for his mini-fridge, how he and his roommate played Power Hour and they both got wasted and paranoid and didn't know how to get rid of the bottles and they spent the night sneaking the bottles and the caps and the cardboard cases out of the dorms and across campus to the Meal Hall dumpster, little by little, any way they could. Picture that movie *Shawshank Redemption*, he says, when Andy breaks out of prison over the course of many years by carrying chunks of his chiseled wall in his shoes and dumping them into the prison yard.

And it's a good story and everyone's into it, having fun. And I'm laughing, too, caught in the moment and laughing because I did almost the same thing my freshman year at Edison University. Carried a backpack of empty bottles out of the dorms. Got caught, too, and had to explain to my father why I was on university probation before classes had even started.

And he keeps going, listing each spike of his Life with Alcohol timeline, and I *do* understand this guy, Gerry. Part of progress is understanding, not just condemning.

He talks about his twenty-first birthday, and I'm thinking of my own.

Back at EU, back in Fort Myers, Florida. Back at Hem-Haw's on Central, sinking into the dark cushions of the back booth. Boom. Shot of Jack, from Ronnie. Boom. Sex on the Beach, from Tara. Boom. Three Wise Men, from Edwin. Boom boom boom. Knocking 'em down. Singing "Under the Bridge" along with the jukebox, making out with Natalie, telling somebody that I'm going to kick his ass cause he called me a pussy, and then it's boom boom boom and three more shots, and then I'm face down on the floor, under the booth's table, George grabbing me by my left arm, dragging me under the table, dragging me out the only way that he could get me. Dragging me out of Hem-Haw's *twenty* minutes before I turned twenty-one.

Gerry walks back to his seat and the chapter applauds him.

"We want to see *your* timeline," someone says from the back of the room.

"Excuse me?" I ask.

"Yours. Show us yours."

"My Alcohol Timeline?"

"Yeah, dawg. You said you did one."

"No, no," I say. "That's private."

"We're showing our, like, deepest and most personal moments, bro!" It's someone in the back of the room, and he's got a milk jug full of water. He unscrews the cap and takes a swig, swirling it around in his mouth. Has thick arms, a 20-inch neck, probably training for some athletic competition or another. "But *yours* is personal? How we s'posed to trust you?"

"Yeah," someone else says. "How about just, like, the biggest spike?"

"Not a chance," I say. "Let's get back on task."

"Come on!" Water Jug says. "Don't even need to show us everything."

The room is grumbling now, kids nudging each other, a bubbling collection of side conversations and under-their-breath jokes and comments threatening to turn to full boil.

*Do you want to be a leader or a punchline?* Headquarters doesn't want us to discuss our own negative experiences with alcohol because Headquarters wants us to be the living embodiment of social responsibility. We are not cautionary tales. I'm picturing our Educational Consultant Code of Conduct: "While you're a representative of the fraternity, the four D's are off-limits," the Marathon Man tells us. "No dating, no drinking, no drugs, and no digital footprint." Consultants cannot accept a drink at a fraternity house, cannot accompany undergraduates to a bar, cannot purchase drinks for (or accept drinks from) alumni, cannot purchase a drink for an undergraduate female, cannot…Well, there are dozens of scenarios. And failure to meet these guidelines results in immediate termination as an Education Consultant. "You're not 'one of the guys,'" LaFaber told us. "Watch what you do, watch what you say. Everywhere." We had a consultant two years ago who talked about his DUI during college. A great story. Very compelling. Guess the chapter's response. "Our consultant got a DUI. Fucking hypocrite." A three-day chapter visit, and they were posting that on *comment boards*, as if it was the only thing they'd heard.

"It's...I don't even have my timeline anymore," I say.

"Bullshit, you don't have it. You can't remember it?"

"After I went through the workshop training, I tossed the paper."

Water Jug shakes his head, disappointed. "Tossed the paper? Come on. This guy's bullshit. We're listening to this?"

"I'm a traveling consultant. I don't have a bedroom anymore," I say, leaning forward from the couch to project my voice, "so I can't pin it to my wall like a poster, if that's what you expected. Not like it would make a great interior decorating choice anyway."

The room breaks into choppy chuckles, amused but hesitant, as if this room of frat stars never expected me to crack a joke myself, and now they're unsure how to treat it.

"And when you're driving across country," I say, "the last thing you want is for a cop to pull you over and find a giant timeline of your lifetime of alcohol abuse."

Water Jug laughs, nods finally. "All right, all right. Fun Nazi is a fucking smart-ass."

The room joins him in subdued laughter, then settles.

"Back on task," I say. "Who's next?"

Again, the stifling silence.

"One more timeline," I say. "Anyone else? Please."

"Yeah, I'll go," someone says, and it's James (or Joe, or Jason). The one who smells like gym clothes and basketball courts. The one who hates "Nationals" but loves his fraternity brothers. He walks to the center of the Chapter Room, presses his timeline against the wall, smooths it so we can all follow the Sharpie-drawn milestones. And I can almost feel the room pulsing with electricity now, hairs standing on end, as though we're all waiting for lightning to strike and sizzle the house from the inside out, reduce everything—the rotting boards and the broken toilets and the broken members—to a pile of post-disaster rubble, a scene of destruction like the one the cable news stations played after the fraternity house fire at Georgia two years ago. Everyone in the room is buzzing, ready to be reduced, ready for the lightning strike breakthrough so we can clean up the rubble, clean up this mess of a chapter.

*Develop our members into the socially-responsible leaders of the next generation.*

One more timeline.

"All right," James (or Joe, or Jason) says, and his timeline is mostly empty. "Here goes. This is when I took my first drink," and he points to a scribbled date at one side of his sheet, "and this is when I learned that I'm a huge fucking alcoholic," and he points to the other side, where the word "TODAY" is drawn in all-caps. "Big fucking deal," he says. "The end."

The entire room seems to burp one quick uncontainable laugh, then swallow and fall silent. Silent as the inside of a coffin. Heads turn. All eyes on me. Staring at me like I'm supposed to be offended, and I try to rewind the moment and figure out what was said, the words, the tone, did I hear correctly? "Um," I say, and all I can think about are those moments when a sports broadcaster accidentally says "Jesus Christ!" while watching a tackle, a slip-up swear word, and you don't even realize it until the commercial break when one of your friends says, "Wait, did he just say 'Jesus Christ' on the air?" and then you're not sure what has actually been said and what you've imagined. And now it's twenty seconds later, and I know it happened and I'm trying to think of the reaction a role model *should* have. Anger? Surprise? Disgust? To say the wrong thing can be more damaging than saying nothing at all.

But then someone laughs…cackles…And then someone else.

And someone claps with great enthusiasm, and then someone else says, "There you go, Jay, you alcoholic bastard!" and the room descends into a growing cheer chorus, everyone laughing clapping hollering. And then someone pushes someone else off a couch and guys are throwing paper.

Disgust, right?

And right there—fifteen seconds ago—was when I was supposed to have said something, grabbing hold of this slippery moment and forcing it to stay still in my hands and straightening it and making it look meaningful. And I missed it, and once again I'm forcing myself to cough out a chuckle, and all I can do is try to look like I'm supposed to look the way I do, however I do, and I'm clapping and telling everyone that I hope they had a good time and that they got something out of the workshop. "We'll end here," I say, forcing a smile.

"You're all right," Jay tells me. "You're all right with us, man."

The chapter gives a polite but disinterested applause, the sort one expects for the unknown opening act of a small rock concert, and they thank me for coming; mostly, their backs are turned as they clap, eyes already focused on whatever destination—bedrooms, bathrooms—has already been on their minds for the last forty minutes of this workshop. They shuffle out of the Chapter Room, pushing couches back into bedrooms and folding and stacking metal chairs.

*

The President—another semi-familiar face, another forgotten name— walks up to me a short while later, tells me that I was better than the Educational Consultant who came to Pittsburgh last Spring, that I know how to take a joke, and he invites me to come out with the chapter tonight, to hit up a place called "The Mill."

"It'll be a damned good time," he says. He's wearing a tank top with a crackling Steelers logo in the center, and he keeps scratching at the flaking screen-print paint. Yesterday, it was a Pitt Panthers tank top. Both days, he's smelled like beer. "We can talk and shit."

"The Mill. Is this a restaurant? Or a bar?"

"Little bit of both," he says.

"What kind of food do they serve?"

"I don't know. Burgers? Nobody ever eats there, know what I'm saying?"

"Just drinking, then?"

"I guess," he says, scratches again, and a white chip of the Steelers logo flutters to the floor. "We get some tables, chill for the night. Nothing formal. But the guys, they'll listen to what you have to say. If you want to talk. You made an impression, man."

"An impression," I say.

"They usually don't listen to a single word that someone from Nationals says."

"Well," I say. "It's been awhile since I've kicked back."

I *had* reached them, hadn't I? And what would be the harm in going out...in modeling responsible behavior, responsible drinking?

"Yeah, bro," he says, burps. "Think of the Facebook updates you can write. How jealous your buddies will be when they see you're out on the town, different place every night."

"Ha," I say.

But ever since I shut down my Facebook account, Jenn has told me that she has no idea what I'm thinking. "You sound more distant," she told me over the phone. I'm a thousand miles away, I said. Of course I'm distant. "No," she said. "I never know what you're doing. I can't even picture you, sometimes. Where you are." You hear my voice, I said. Isn't that better than silly little comments on Facebook? But she only said: "I feel like we're drifting." But I do find myself still thinking in status updates. Every day, all the things I could tell the world. All night long, what I *could* be doing.

"Charles is...out at the mill with the brothers at Pittsburgh!"

"Charles is...loosening his tie, rolling up his sleeves, and blowing off some steam."

"Charles is...knocking back Yuenglings beneath the Cathedral of Learning."

I think of the comments I might receive. "Keep up the good fight!" "Drink one for me!" "Stay safe out there, Charles!" From friends, from old classmates, from Jenn. The alternative?

"Charles is...alone in the guest room. On a Friday night."

"Charles is...waiting for tomorrow."

"Charles is...a beacon for leadership."

Because, yes, there's the idea of the Marathon Man, that fraternity man I'm supposed to be, and there's this image of Walter LaFaber, also, Windsor-knotted tie under his blazer; LaFaber, sitting behind his metal desk at the Headquarters building, rows of higher education journals in his bookshelf; LaFaber, my boss, who saw someone different in me, a professional with an Organizational Communications degree rather than just a clueless college kid who couldn't decide on a better major. And yes, there's this image of my father, also, standing on his front porch back in Cypress Falls, Florida, on his Saturday mornings, coffee mug in one hand and the other hand slipped into the pocket of his pleated khaki shorts. Hair combed, polo shirt tucked into shorts. Business-world poise as he waits for me to come crawling home a failure.

"You'll come out?" the President asks me.

"I'm sorry," I say. "I can't."

"You got somewhere better to be?" He laughs. "This empty house?"

"No, no. It's just that a bar isn't professional."

"What do you mean?"

"I'm not a college student."

"Bro, you're only, like, a year older than most of the guys here."

"No, really. I wish I could, but I can't."

"Come on. It'll be good for you. It's Friday night, man." He slaps my back.

I tell him that I appreciate the invitation, but no. He narrows his eyes.

"Bro. This is a fraternity. A *frat*-er-nity. Just come out for one beer."

"No," I say. "It's more than that."

"You don't got to drink if you don't want to."

"We're trying to build socially responsible leaders," I say. "We're trying to change the culture of alcoholism. I can't do that at a bar."

He sighs, holds his hands up in surrender, backs away. "Whatever. Suit yourself, man."

And that's it. I've made my responsible decision. And so it's Friday night and these guys will head to the University of Pittsburgh bars and enjoy the night, but I'll creak back down the hall to the guest room to sleep and to model good behavior. Wait until morning. Pack up and drive to a hotel for Saturday night. Take the day off to figure out what I'm doing wrong out here. One day off. Then pack up and drive to Shippensburg University. Pittsburgh to Shippensburg, yes. Other schools where I can still accomplish the mission. Cover the proper material for the Alcohol Responsibility Workshop. Shippensburg to St. Joseph's to New Mexico State. To Texas Tech. To Fresno State. Fourteen more weeks of travel for the Fall Semester. "Visit Reports Completed / 3 Days After Visit." "No Fried Food/ EVER." "Email Chapter Presidents/ Weekly." "No Alcohol with Chapter/ EVER."

But as the President walks away, shaking his head and already calling someone else's name—"I invited him, but he's being a pussy"—I'm thinking about the Mill, the slick countertops with drops of beer spilled across the lacquer, loud '80s rock from the jukebox, "Don't Stop Believing" and "You Shook Me All Night Long" and pitchers of Miller Lite until Semi-sonic's "Closing Time."

*

Late at night I call Jenn, but, of course, it's a Friday night. So—

"Whoooo!" she screams when she answers the phone.

"Jenn?"

"Whoooo!" Voice like a child on a roller-coaster.

"Are you out at the bars right now?"

"Whoooo! Charlie!" Car honking in the background. Chatter and laughter. "The girls say hi, Charles! But we've got to go!"

"Are you—"

"We're coming! Hold on!"

A male voice in the background: "I got your nose, I got your nose!"

"Um," I say. "What?"

"The girls say hi, Charles!" she says again. "Call tomorrow!"

When I hang up, I hear similar noises coming from the rest of the fraternity house: the hallway outside the guest room, the upstairs bedrooms, the kitchen, the chapter room. Cans crunching, girls giggling, *whoooo!* and high-fives and clanking bottles and someone saying "But it doesn't *look* like a cauliflower!" I stare at my laptop screen and think again of the status updates I could write if only I clicked a few buttons, restarted my Facebook profile, re-joined that world.

But after a few minutes, I close the computer and try to settle into the disturbed guest room futon. Because there are two unthinkable spikes in my timeline, snapshots that keep developing in my head throughout the night, photos tagged as "Charles Washington" just waiting for me to reactivate my account to be republished online for all the world to see. And I can't go back to that.

# The Grand Tradition
## CHAPTER TEN

This was my original plan for Saturday: after two straight weeks of fraternity house-hopping, I'd take a "free day." Time off. A hotel stay. A day that wouldn't smell like spilled beer and McDonalds wrappers, a day when I wouldn't have to explain to anyone why binge-drinking was not an "extreme sport," a chance to sleep in a comfortable bed and take a shower without wearing flip-flops on mildewy floors, a chance to get outside and fulfill my goal of "Jog three times/weekly," maybe sit at the pool, watch college football on TV, have a drink at the bar without worrying whether anyone was watching. At the very least, a chance to sleep comfortably, no frat stars crashing into my bedroom unexpectedly. Forget the failed workshop. Remind myself why I'm out here.

That was the plan. But this is what happened:

Early this morning. Everything still pre-dawn peaceful in the Pittsburgh chapter house. So quiet that I could hear the low hum of the outdated refrigerator in the kitchen down the hall, the scattered snores of fraternity brothers in their upstairs bedrooms. I was ten minutes away from sneaking out of the house and driving away and enjoying my Saturday off. But at 8:04 AM, my cell phone ring-tone blared through the entire first floor, the metal and plastic of the phone vibrating against the wood floor of the guest room so loud that I could hear the noise all the way down the hall in the bathroom. Without even dropping my toothbrush, I darted down the hall and found the phone and flipped it open and said something with a mouthful of Colgate that almost passed for "hello."

"Charles," said a familiar voice on the other end. "Good morning." Crisp voice, starched. The kind of voice impossible to catch off-guard, the kind of voice that would never answer a phone with a full mouth: Walter LaFaber, back at Headquarters.

"Eyyy," I said, trying not to swallow, and I hurried back to the bathroom, a glob of toothpaste slipping down my throat.

"You weren't asleep, were you?"

"Mmmm?" I said. "Mmm-mmm."

"Good. I'd hoped not. Where are you right now, Charles?"

I attempted the word "Pittsburgh," but it probably sounded more like "Riisssrrruhrr." The question was a mere formality, though; LaFaber *knows* where I'm at. He drafted the consultant travel schedules before I even arrived for orientation. He mapped the distances between chapters, divided the three consultants into travel territories. Brock London travels Texas and the Gulf States; Nick Bennett travels the South. And I drive everything beyond.

I covered the phone's mouthpiece, spit into the sink.

"What are your plans for the day?" LaFaber asked.

"Driving. I have a hotel reserved for tonight."

"Travel day?" he said.

"I need to stretch out in a real bed, get a good night's sleep." I looked around the Pittsburgh bathroom that I'd been using for the past three days, the once-white floor tiles that had taken on urine tones, the limp shower head, the thick black-orange mildew trail that slinked from the sink's rim to its drain. I'd slept on a broken futon, had misplaced my shampoo and a folder full of print-outs, and as I'd searched for them this morning I'd knocked the stack of "Fun Nazi" business cards into the depths of my suitcase; they fell under shirts, inside shoes. "I need to recharge my batteries."

"So you've got no plans, then," LaFaber said.

"Well," I said, but I knew immediately that I'd walked into a trap: LaFaber never asks a question if he doesn't already know the answer. Not only does he have the energy and hard-hitting presence of a linebackers coach, but he also has a full shelf lined with leadership books and biographies of Great Men, each flagged with dozens of post-it stickers. He knows exactly how to get his employees to do what he needs. Stares you down, silent, brown eyes growing darker by the moment, the scar on his forehead shining brighter like it's watching you, too, and you'll eventually cave. Doesn't matter what he's asking ("Could you pick up the sandwiches for the luncheon this afternoon?" or "I need you to run up to West Lafayette tonight to deliver a package"); when he's done, you're convinced it was your idea. And every time we talk over the phone, I picture him rigid with the same discipline I remember from the office. Perfect posture, puttied hair, unwrinkled pants, standing—never reclining—while on the phone. Walter LaFaber, staring into his office walls as though he can actually see past the trees outside, past the Indianapolis office buildings, as if he can see for miles and miles and he can actually stare me down from hours away. "No," I said. "No, not like...*plans* plans."

"So can you cancel the hotel tonight?"

"I don't know," I said. I leaned into the mirror. Flesh around my eyes looked worn. I could probably have slept for another five hours. Sometime after 2 AM last night, after the Mill closed, the first wave of drunk brothers crashed back into the house and raided the kitchen. Every fifteen minutes after, another carload banged through the front doors all at once, and they swore and shouted and drank in the main foyer for what seemed like hours, and as I lay on the guest room futon, I watched the door, afraid that someone might burst in to play Beer Pong or to have privacy with a girl. And now that the entire house had likely been woken by my cell phone, I knew I'd never even get out of here. The President would soon come stumbling downstairs with questions about the house air-conditioner, who to contact if it keeps freezing over, or maybe the Treasurer would stop me with questions about fire insurance, or some other gruff and angry frat star would want to argue with me about the benefits of hazing, of Hell Week, of making pledges drink piss. "There might be a cancellation fee," I tried.

"Most hotels won't charge cancellation fees," he said.

"Oh."

"I've got a treat for you, Charles."

"Really."

"I spoke to Dr. Wigginton, and he'd like to meet you."

"Dr. Wigginton? Like, *the* Dr. Wigginton?"

"*The* Dr. Wigginton."

Dr. Wigginton: one of only five living alumni awarded the title of "District Magistrate." The sort of man for whom I was given a prep file, should our paths ever cross: made his career in business and politics in Philadelphia, initiated a charitable not-for-profit in Chester, supported Penn State substantially enough for the university to name a fundraising office after him (and is rumored to have made the "anonymous" financial contribution to the Nu Kappa Epsilon Headquarters that directly funded the fraternity's award-winning "DO IT!" social responsibility program, the backbone of our leadership development mission and our workshops). Has a portrait hanging in the lobby of the headquarters building, awards named after him, wears embroidered sashes at conventions, and when he clears his throat everyone shuts up. *The* Dr. Wigginton. "Meet me today?" I asked.

"Today," LaFaber said, and I could tell from his voice that he was smiling. On the one hand, he's a supervisor dedicated to employee morale, slapping backs and issuing compliments, gripping shoulders, clapping high-fives, making you feel like he's just done you a favor or given you a hook-up ("I've got a treat for you"). But on the other hand, he also revels in maximizing his staff's every free second. "This isn't a problem, is it?"

Last weekend, he questioned my dedication because I'd told him I was unable to drive 300 miles to Virginia Tech to investigate complaints of an unsanctioned party. "I'm all the way in Pittsburgh already," I said. "Can the school investigate?" But LaFaber told me that the National Fraternity needs standards, that if we don't hold ourselves accountable, we might as well become Animal House. "We'll see what becomes of the situation," he said sadly. "We could have handled things ourselves, kept the school out of it. I just hope this isn't a recurring issue with you, Charles. You *are* in this for the right reasons, correct?"

"I can make it to visit Dr. Wigginton," I said this morning. "I can do it."

"Excellent. Smart decision, Charles." He cleared his throat. "You'll need to be on your best behavior, of course."

"Of course."

"Spotless in appearance. You are our representative."

I rubbed my eyes, looked at myself in the mirror once again. "Don't worry. I'll finish up here, and...I spent the last three days with a bunch of frat stars. I'm sure they were a bigger challenge." I was hoping for a laugh, but I heard only the tapping of his keyboard.

"He's the type of person who makes things happen, Charles."

"I understand. This is the sort of networking opportunity I signed up for."

"He's a tough man to impress," LaFaber said.

"I can do it."

"Yes, well," LaFaber said. "It's a bit of a drive, of course. So you better get started."

So. New plan.

**TRAVEL SCHEDULE – CHARLES WASHINGTON**

~~Summer Training in Indianapolis~~

~~University of Kentucky~~
~~East Tennessee State University~~
~~University of Virginia — Green Valley~~ ///
~~[redacted] Airport~~ /// [redacted] alumni weekend
Shippensburg University
St. Joseph's University
New Mexico State University
Texas Tech
California State University—Fresno
California State University—Highland
California State University—Long Beach
California State University—San Francisco
University of Delaware
Marshall University
Miami University (Ohio)
University of Toledo
Central Michigan University
University of Michigan
Bowling Green State University
Purdue University
Indiana University

Headquarters – Mid-Semester Debrief (Indianapolis)

University of Oklahoma
University of Kansas
University of Missouri—Columbia
University of Nebraska
Iowa State University

Thanksgiving Vacation

Bradley University
University of Iowa

Headquarters (Indianapolis)

Christmas Vacation

I packed myself into my car, began driving Interstate 79 north even though I have to drive to Shippensburg University tomorrow, which sits squarely in the center of the state. The opposite direction.

*

This is what *should* happen on an alumni visit: No forms or spreadsheets. Just a few hours to (as LaFaber says) "show some love for the men who made this fraternity possible. Chat 'em up. Make 'em feel appreciated." A few hours with a man who has authored books on investing, or who runs his own Foundation, whose name I can casually mention when I return home after my year on the road. "That reminds me," I can say, "of the time I met Dr. Wigginton, and he told me..." and, of course, it won't even matter *what* he tells me, only that we'd spoken. Full afternoons to experience a small part of the greatest social network in America, the Grand Tradition, and Dr. Wigginton—whom I visit today—knows everyone worth knowing.

When I visit the fraternity houses, I'm there to help the students. But when I visit the alumni, they're supposed to help the *consultant*: this is what redeems a life on broken futons.

*

Dr. Wigginton lives in Kinston, Pennsylvania, a quiet mountain town far removed from the commerce and industry of Pittsburgh, from the sprawl of the suburbs. Far removed from the convenience of the interstate, too. I rumble off the highway sometime before 11 AM, slow onto a two-lane country road bordered by overgrown grass and cut with deep potholes. Soon the towns disappear, the scenery melting into an endless expanse of cattle-grazing land.

I scroll through my cell phone, leave a voicemail with Jenn. Call a few old fraternity brothers who have graduated and moved on to office jobs; call a few young fraternity brothers probably enjoying their Saturday at the pool or at a football game; call the other two NKE consultants, Brock and Nick, who are probably enjoying hotel days in Memphis or Austin or wherever their travel schedules have deposited them. Nobody answers. For fifteen minutes, I leave voicemails and stare at the empty landscape.

Later, I try to text Jenn to tell her about an edge-of-the-highway t-shirt store I drove past called Hooliganz. Apparently, it's dedicated entirely to slogan t-shirts, most of them offensive, hanging in the windows: "Sex: do it for the kids!" and "Sweatshops...another day, another dollar." We've always disagreed about the novelty of these shirts; I think they're annoyingly over-clever, a waste of money ("You can only wear them once," I said, "and then you've used up the joke"), but Jenn insistd that, on the right body, they're timeless. Carefree youth. As long as you're smiling, who cares what anyone else thinks?

The Jenn Outlook.

But today, she doesn't respond to my text message.

*

Sometime after noon, after an hour of driving that feels like a full day, I finally arrive in Kinston, a town seemingly built along a single road. Old men sitting outside downtown diners so quaint that they were probably built before quaintness was ever an aesthetic consideration, every store and every business built into old houses, every wooden store-front sign hand-painted or hand-carved and marking the houses as "Family Dentistry" or "Attorneys at Law." In the distance, the blue outlines of modest mountains zig-zagging across the horizon.

The air feels different in Pennsylvania, too, sun farther away. Rural Florida is all swampland: thick briars and low palmetto scrubs. Hot, dark places where things slither and snap and burrow. Rural Pennsylvania doesn't feel as if it is packed so tight.

When I pull into Dr. Wigginton's brick driveway just past downtown Kinston, everything seems so promising. He sits on his front porch reading the newspaper and drinking from a dark brown coffee mug, same thing my father does every Saturday morning, and as soon as he sees me, he stands and buries one hand in his slacks pocket, lifts his mug gently in my direction. I've seen his portrait at the Headquarters along our Hall of Fame wall; I've seen him at conferences; Dr. Wigginton is the kind of man who still dresses like a gentleman from a bygone era, like a character in a *Godfather* flashback. Button-down white shirt, brown jacket, dark pants. He is sixty-five, probably, with the happy-smooth skin of a man who's never known failure. Wears glasses, but seems in such good health that his eyesight might be his only deficiency: stands tall, slender, doesn't hold his back as he walks, doesn't creak with rusty joints. He approaches the car, shakes my hand as soon as I clear my door, and before he says a word or gives even a hint of an introduction, he laughs with an intellectual huff, then looks at me like I should be laughing, like we shared some inside joke.

"So *you're* the one," he says, voice rich with network news anchor gravitas.

"Charles Washington," I say.

"You're the lucky traveler, are you? You took the Headquarters bait this year?" And then another round of huffing laughter.

"Bait? No, no." I force a smile. "This job is a dream come true."

"Mmm," he says.

"The fraternity had an incredible impact on me as an undergraduate," I say. "I want to share that with others. Help them achieve all they can."

"Yes, yes, no need for explanation." He sips his coffee, and I stand still for a moment while he tips his mug back and makes a straw-at-the-bottom-of-a-milkshake slurping noise for five or ten seconds, the slurping growing so loud at one point that it scares some birds from his porch railing. "The Explorer," he says and pointes.

"My car," I say, "my best friend these days."

"Mmm. Seen better days, by the look of it."

I look back over my shoulder. Big-city grime on the wheels, dust from the country roads all over the body. And I washed it last Saturday. "It's dirty, I guess. And packed pretty tight. But I spend most of my time in there. I try to keep it clean."

"Take care of the car." He jabs the mug at me. "Don't let the car take care of you."

"Ha. Right."

"I don't particularly approve of sports utility vehicles."

"Oh, I—"

"Yes," he says. "You travel. Quite a load to carry. I've heard it before."

"That's right," I say.

"What year is it?"

"Three years old."

"Warranty expired, I assume."

"Just expired, yeah."

"Bad news for a man who travels."

"Well."

"Did you purchase the car yourself?"

"Um. My father helped me with the down payment, but I—"

"Your father?"

"It's just a car," I blurt finally and hold my hands up, then remember to attempt a good-natured smile, just the same as when I was a freshman in high school and the juniors on the JV team would toss sunflower seeds at all the newbies, tell us that our shoes were untied. *Just pretend you're in on the joke*, the sophomores would say. *Just laugh and check your shoes.*

"Two things can tell you all that you'll ever need to know about a man," Dr. Wigginton says. "His shoes, and his car." He looks me up and down. I'm wearing brown dress shoes, no laces (so at least they aren't untied...), but they too are coated in big-city grime and country dust. I've never polished them.

"It's a Saturday," I say. "A little more casual today."

"Well. Come inside," he says. "Have you had lunch yet?"

I scratch the back of my neck. "No, I guess not."

"I've got chili on the stove."

"Chili. That's..." Going to give me terrible gas. "That sounds good."

"I've got a lot on my mind, Mr. Washington. I hope you don't mind if I pick your brain a bit. So much to talk about with these Pennsylvania chapters."

"I don't mind at all."

"That's what you're here for, of course. To answer questions."

"That's what I'm here for."

But when I begin walking up the steps to his porch, he stops me. "Don't you want to bring your bags inside?"

"Oh?" So I open the Explorer's passenger-side door, grab my laptop case. "Got it."

"That's it?" He's looking at me with a puzzled expression, as if I told him that this is the only bag that I carry in my car, as if I told him that I pack all of my clothes and all of my toiletries into a single laptop case.

"Sure." I shut the door. "I don't think I'll need anything else, right?"

He shrugs. "All right? Follow me."

117

Predictably, Dr. Wigginton's house is old, the type that makes haunted creaking noises. And instead of the steep odor of rotten beer-urine-demon-piss to which I've become accustomed, everything smells of coffee beans and toast, the faint tomato aroma of chili wafting from the kitchen. Not the sort of house you'd find in Florida, though. It's tall off the ground, has a deep basement and high ceilings, is so roomy that it'd cost a Florida fortune to air condition in the summer. And inside, it's brown, the color of bad 1970s leisure suits or Midwestern flannel, the clothing you might see in *The Deer Hunter* or *Amityville Horror.* Brown and yellow carpeting. Brown and white walls.

"You can leave your bag in the guest room," he says.

"Is your wife home?"

"No wife, no wife. Right this way, Mr. Washington." And as we walk past the office on the way to the guest room, I notice that it, too, is drowning in brown. A dark brown desk so gargantuan that it looks like a piece of construction equipment ready to grind to life. The room itself is like a church sanctuary washed in the colors of its stained-glass windows, aglow under the illumination of fraternity shrines and relics: a maroon-and-blue NKE flag hanging on the wall, a gigantic framed portrait of Dr. Wigginton standing against a mantle (pressed white carnation under the frame), a framed oil painting of the Penn State chapter house. The sort of display—plaques, composites, awards, banners—most fraternity men dream about and try to build during college. Dr. Wigginton has done it: he's created a house dedicated to NKE. And no, this certainly would not have been possible had a woman taken residence here.

*

This was the plan: on my "free day," I'd not only get some R&R, but I'd also choose my meals carefully, try to get back into a normal digestive rhythm. I was healthy in college, jogged regularly and lifted weights three times a week. Now, living on the road, I needed a free day, where I could order Subway or Chick-Fil-A, a garden salad or a turkey wrap, anything to offset the sausages and cheesesteaks and French fries I've been eating with the fraternity brothers. That was the plan. But this is what I get: bacon-and-beef-heavy chili. And you don't refuse home-cooking from a millionaire.

We sit on the porch together, Dr. Wigginton in a rocking chair and me in a matching wooden porch chair.

The chili is the same brown as the house, a lumpy mass of tomatoes and ground beef and kidney beans so thick and over-boiled that bean is indistinguishable from beef. I crumble a palmful of crackers and rain the crumbs throughout my bowl. The color doesn't change.

"If I was part of the original chapter of Nu Kappa Epsilon Fraternity," he says solemnly, rocking, "I would offer you a glass of sweet tea. As a common Yankee, however, I hope artificially *sweetened* iced tea does not offend."

On a small table between us, he's left a pitcher of tea and two rocks glasses. It's an incredible pitcher, too, an ornate metal top and spicket, sliced lemons floating throughout. Any man that can put so much money and effort

118

into his iced tea, I think, has a great deal of both to spare. "I like artificial sweetener better, anyway," I say. "Love the pitcher, too."

"Mmm," he says disappointedly, looking away as if I've failed some sort of test. "So you're from Florida, I'm told."

"I am."

"Have you been to any of the original South Carolina chapters?"

"No, I never got the chance."

"You work for the Headquarters and you've never been?"

"I graduated from Edison University. A private school on the Gulf Coast? Probably ten or twelve hours away from South Carolina."

Dr. Wigginton shakes his head sadly. "The Alpha Chapter at Carolina Baptist is a thing of true historical beauty. Cobblestone roads throughout campus. Sycamore trees. Wrap-around porch at the fraternity house." He closes his eyes. "It's a tiny school, but the house is magnificent. Mag-*nif*-icent. If you call yourself a Nike Man"—and he smacks my knee and leaves his hand there too long—"you are incomplete for never having been."

"I'll, um, have to get down there."

"This is what makes fraternity so endearing," he says. "The tradition."

I think of several different responses. Maybe "You bet" or "Absolutely!" or "I love tradition, too," a full thesaurus of affirming comments. But eventually I just settle with, "My travels have been great so far. I've seen quite a bit."

I take another bite of the chili, thinking as I swallow that the calorie count probably exceeds the daily allotment I've set in my personal goals, thinking that my stomach is going to start gurgling at any moment, thinking that—just as I work myself into a conversational groove and Dr. Wigginton finally warms to me, just as he's about to say "You, sir, are indeed a Diamond Candidate"...at that precise moment, I will be unable to hold back an earthquake-strength chili-fart. And from that, there can be no recovery.

"You've seen quite a bit?" Dr. Wigginton asks, and for the briefest moment he seems interested. But then: "It's nothing compared to the things *I've* seen, I can assure you."

"Sure. I wasn't saying—"

And then he tells me that he's seen every East Coast chapter house. He and several other Penn State alumni, he says, took a summer retirement trip along the coast several years ago, stopping at every school at which a Nu Kappa Epsilon chapter house had been erected. "When we walked into the houses," he says, "the first reaction was confusion." He makes a face of mock perplexity, and suddenly a system of wrinkles ravages his once-smooth cheeks and forehead. "Who's the old man, they asked. But when they found out who we were..." Burly laugh. "The reaction turned to terror."

While I was an undergraduate back at EU, alumni would sometimes stop by the house wearing faded NKE polos tucked into pleated khaki shorts, and they'd walk the hallways pointing out tiny defects in the crown molding or paint. Lou Forester, a Board member for our Housing Corporation, stopped by each Spring with his wife and—as he led her to each room of the house—

119

asked her if *she* would ever live here, if she would allow her son to live here. "You're an alumni," I remember telling Lou, "and we're just kids. Of course you can live better than this." I thought it was a clever response. "First of all," Lou said without even turning from a small scratch on one of the built-in bookshelves, "I am a single alumnus. The word 'alumni' refers to a group, the word 'alumnus' refers to an individual. Until we can make that distinction, we can never have a productive dialogue. Second, my name is on the wall of this fraternity house. Under 'Diamond Donors.' Until your name is listed anywhere on the Donor Roll, your input is not taken seriously." I was just a sophomore when I questioned Lou, and so I quickly learned to shut up and let him make his inspections. But still, from that moment, the word "alumni" burned in my mind. Alumni…donor…the pinnacle of fraternal and professional excellence. Never once did we have an alumnus stop by the house wearing a torn AC/DC shirt and cut-off jean shorts, smelling of fish bait and rum: every single alumnus seemed wealthy and powerful, confident and comfortable, so much that we undergraduates felt like their subordinates, like we were interning in *their* fraternity. I've always pictured the day when I could finally sit with them, talk with them, compare careers and cars and clothes and wives and sons. I've always pictured the day when that word "alumnus" would be bestowed upon me.

*

Nu Kappa Epsilon distributes to every new pledge a 250-page hardcover manual called *The Marathon*, the most recent edition filled with information on the "DO IT!" program, filled with diagrams and hierarchical charts of the National Fraternity, and—most important—filled with the rich and graphic-intensive history of the Fraternity. The manual tells us that Nu Kappa Epsilon Fraternity was founded in 1910 at Carolina Baptist College, the dream of eight young men scattered far from their birthplaces of Charleston, Columbia, and Charlotte. As was typical in those days, none of these students was older than eighteen; five of the eight men were boys, just seventeen, and one was *sixteen*.

A tiny liberal arts college in the northern sand hill country of South Carolina, Carolina Baptist prided itself on its literature and history departments, and the rigorous curriculum was designed to ensure that each male graduate (there were no female students in those days) could converse extensively on the subject of the classics, could speak admirable Latin, and could call-and-respond for hours with Biblical quotations and British poetry.

Carolina Baptist: fertile soil in which would grow many future lawyers, politicians, professors, and pastors. The college at which these eight students studied was the quintessence of Bible Belt Academia. Not just "fertile soil"… no, bigger…a full nursery of sturdy trees. Yes, plant wealthy-but-rough Southern boys in the tilled dirt of Carolina Baptist, there in the sunshine, and after four years of study, watch them emerge with a newfound sense of culture, etiquette, a firm connection to the strong roots of Deep South Power necessary to earn quick trips into esteemed law firms, into graduate school at the University of Virginia or Duke or Vanderbilt. In 1910, a degree from Carolina Baptist College was a golden ticket born of four solid years of scholarship, of study late at night in the humid dorm rooms, reading thick textbooks by the light of the student's lamp.

The campus community at Carolina Baptist, also, featured enough extracurricular activities for these young men to remain constantly and thoroughly immersed in those Deep South roots of power, that branching underworld of connections which their rich politician-fathers had secured for them at such great expense. The most distinguished of these activities was the campus literary society, The American Men of Letters, and it inducted just three new men each semester and published annually a 50-page book of poetry and of criticism on the contemporary classics of Southern literature. Held in equal esteem was the Carolina Baptist baseball team, which played against nearby Furman, the University of South Carolina, the College of Charleston, and Emory and Oglethorpe down in Atlanta; years later, alumni would claim that the baseball team's overwhelming Southern dominance so scared other universities that the Southeastern Conference passed over Carolina Baptist in the early years of the sports conference's formation. This legend, of course, ignores the obvious fact that Carolina Baptist had no football team, which, as the years passed and the SEC universities grew larger and more prominent and football became more and more important, sealed Carolina Baptist's current reputation as a tiny, quaint, and mostly irrelevant campus. That soil hasn't gone infertile in the last century, but the tree nursery now seems more like a hobbyist's garden.

Three fraternities also met regularly on campus, though in the years immediately following the turn of the century, they didn't yet live together in fraternity houses. Alumni would wait until after the Great War to petition the college for land on which to build the current Greek Row, a block of column-adorned, plantation-style mansions, each complete with porch swings and weeping willow trees. In 1910, these fraternities admitted just three or four new members each term, and as their rites of passage, they didn't haze their pledges (many fraternity historians insist that hazing originated as the soldiers of WWI and WWII returned to college and introduced boot camp tactics into the houses). Instead, each fraternity steeped itself heavily in a specific academic subject, one studying Roman history and another studying Romantic poetry. Professors and dignitaries at Carolina Baptist sat in honorary positions with these fraternities, giving them extra reading assignments as though fraternity life was another class, helping them to organize academic banquets at which poetry was recited and grades celebrated. And, of course, the greater the passion that students, alumni, and faculty developed for these fraternities, the greater the number of annual traditions and friendly rivalries that developed. Today, Carolina Baptist still holds its Fraternity Wheelbarrow Pull (though the winning fraternity is no longer made to wear dresses and cook dinner for the losers).

An invitation into any campus group, society, sports team, or fraternity, was seen as an instant invitation into that larger network of Southern

Somebodies. Admission into Carolina Baptist College was special, certainly, but it was only the first step; membership in a fraternity or a literary society meant that you had *made it*, no worries. You'd latched onto those roots, and now your future could become warmly intertwined within them, could grow along with them.

The only problem, though, was that the very exclusivity that seemed essential for these campus groups to exist soon worked to their detriment. Carolina Baptist had been slowly increasing enrollment in the early 1900s, and by 1910 reached a staggering 220 students. But the fraternities, comfortable with their membership numbers, refused to adapt and grow. Exclusivity became *even more* exclusive, as more potential suitors—from which the fraternities could select at will—appeared on campus, and were rejected and discarded like invasive weeds.

But thankfully…two blood brothers, Lesley and Jackson Cohen, separated in age by only a year but electing to enroll at Carolina Baptist at the same time, both found themselves in Fall of 1910 among the large number of disappointed freshmen not selected by any fraternity as pledges. Lesley and Jackson soon made friends with a student named C. Anthony Croke, and (as legend goes) the three began to dine together every evening, began to watch with hawkish interest the interactions of the other campus fraternities.

So infatuated with their own traditions were these fraternities, said Jackson Cohen (the most assertive of the three youths), that they had forsaken all that was meaningful about the fraternity experience. He claimed that fraternity brothers were neither "brotherly" to one another, nor interested in working together for any common good; they seemed devoted only to exploiting that life of power that they had entered. Essentially, he said, *fraternity* at Carolina Baptist had died. From *The Marathon*, a famous NKE quote: "We shall have a brotherhood of our own," said Jackson Cohen. "We shall have a selfless fraternity of gentlemen more distinguished than they."

And out of this desire for fraternal bonds came Nu Kappa Epsilon, officially established in November of 1910. And the fraternity bloomed first on that Carolina Baptist campus, as the neglected suitors from all other campus fraternities jumped at the opportunity to start something new and different, to start something *living*, to find their place, to secure the companionship that they so desperately craved. To found a fraternity, they believed, *the right way*. Then the fraternity spread its seed throughout the entire Deep South, where many similar colleges and universities experienced the same phenomenon: growing in enrollment but under-served by the over-exclusive campus fraternities.

Nu Kappa Epsilon first received petitions from students at those schools closest, from Furman and South Carolina and Chapel Hill, and then from schools as far south as Stetson University, and as far west as Ole Miss. Growth slowed during the Great War, but the Roaring Twenties brought a fresh crop of young men to college, and from coast to coast, these men looked to join brotherhoods as strong as those that they had left in the military, and NKE soon found itself with chapters at UCLA and Washington and Penn State and Pittsburgh and Illinois. The Grand Tradition of Nu Kappa Epsilon had begun.

It's a fun story to tell, a fun history lesson for any chapter that doesn't "get it." They are part of something larger than themselves, a century of tradition that began with young men just like them.

So that's the official history. And when we tell the story, we make the intentions seem so pure. But I'm quickly learning that history is never so neat as we'd like to believe.

*

This is Dr. Wigginton's version of the history:

"Have you been to State College yet?" Dr. Wigginton asks me, still on the porch after more than an hour of one-sided conversation. He's already refilled my chili bowl, and once again I couldn't refuse his hospitality.

I tell him that I've been in Pennsylvania only three or four days.

"Mmm," he says, and shakes his head again. "I visited two weeks ago for a coach's brunch. Only a few old-timers came by. You have seen the house, correct?"

I tell him that I don't think so.

"You don't know the story of the Penn State house fire? 1985?"

The gas is starting to build from the chili. I take a deep breath and will it away. "The Penn State house fire?" I say. Does *every* chapter have a house-fire story?

"I'll have to refresh your history at another time. In any case, it's an impressive mess those young men have made of that home! More than a hundred members, and they seem incapable even of wiping the sprayed beer from the glass frame of the charter."

I picture the ceiling fan at Pittsburgh, the beer, the paint.

"They cannot empty trash cans," he says. "Even on gameday, they cannot just pretend that they appreciate tradition. And this is a four-million dollar house." So far, I've been his audience but not his conversational equal, and I fear that I might spend the entire afternoon listening to him relive his fraternity memories. A wasted alumni visit. So I tell him that I understand, that I appreciate tradition, that this was the reason I took the job.

Dr. Wigginton stops, considers me from an angle, eyes squinted. "Do you?"

"Most definitely. When you become an alumnus"—I savor the word— "that's, like, the most important thing. Tradition. How everything, everyone, fits together."

He reaches into his pants pocket, digs around for a moment, and then his hand re-emerges with a thick gold coin the same size as the rim of his coffee mug. He holds it up for me, lets the sunlight catch its side to shadow the embossed script across its polished surface: "A New Beginning," it reads, with the voluptuous outline of a white carnation below these words.

"Do you know what this is?" he asks, voice dramatically low, as if he's looking into the lens of a camera, prepared to inform the world about the death toll from a South Pacific tsunami.

123

"It's a coin?"

He shakes his head. "This...*this* is tradition. One of just fifty alumni medallions produced to commemorate my chapter's founding. You've never seen an alumni medallion?"

"I don't think so."

"You appreciate tradition, Mr. Washington, but you don't seem to know very much."

"I, um. I try to learn."

"Experience is the best teacher," he says and points his spoon at me. "It was an all-Southern fraternity in the early century, that's what you can't learn from reading those manuals. And Penn State was *vital*." He clears his throat and lets out another "Mmm, mmm," like the low motor hum of a failing weed whacker. "You see, you'll learn a bit when you visit my boys at Penn State next week." He smacks my knee again. A moment, this knee-slapping, that I can't figure out. An old-man quirk, the same as when my grandmother used to call the ladies at her church "her girlfriends" and the kids on my block "my boyfriends?" Or an awkward attempt at youthful masculinity, like when my father wears a Red Sox hat on company picnics?

"I don't visit Penn State this semester," I say.

"Mmm," he says. "Well. We were the first chapter established north of Mason-Dixon's line. The *first*. The original founders at Carolina Baptist were hesitant about expanding northward, you understand. In those days, young men still had grandfathers who'd served in the Civil War. Try to tell some Confederate soldier that you're now *brothers* with a young man in Pennsylvania." I shift in my chair, open my mouth, gas building again. Close my mouth, sit still, hope he won't smack my knee again. "It was Lesley Cohen, more than the others. The manuals praise him, but he didn't want to colonize outside the Carolinas." Dr. Wigginton sits back, looks at the porch railing and shakes his head. Laughs. "He died early, that's something else the manuals don't say. The joke is that he visited the University of Illinois, saw that they had a Negro brother in their fraternity, and had a heart attack on the spot!" Laughing harder now, but still with that newscaster look, like he's watching video of a squirrel water-skiing.

"Are you joking?" I ask.

"Oh, no no. You should read Cohen's early speeches at conventions." He stops, looks at me, trying to decide if he can trust me with a secret. "The number of times he uses the word 'nigger,' a Klansmen would be embarrassed." Closes his eyes and chuckles again, face overtaken by wrinkles. "Had an alcohol problem, too, did Lesley Cohen. Fell from a bridge in his early thirties, and"—now Dr. Wigginton is wagging his finger, laughter subsiding—"probably a good thing, too, for the national fraternity!"

"This is all true?" I ask. "Where is this..."

But Dr. Wigginton still isn't listening to me. "Truth be told, we only started at Penn State because...Roger 'the Rooster' Redding, they called him, a Nike from Charlottesville...fled the University of Virginia because, it's rumored, he impregnated the daughter of the local sheriff! Rode out of town with a shotgun firing at his heels! Enrolled in Penn State, found five other men who would form a new chapter of Nu Kappa Epsilon with him, and the rest is history. First chapter in the North."

"He got her pregnant and just left town? That's the story behind Penn State?"

"It's legend, young man," he says and waves away my question. "Don't question it too much. This was, oh, 1913, 1914, I believe, and once the Penn State chapter was going, they spoke with friends at Penn, Cornell, Pittsburgh, Delaware. The schools, in those days, they all played one another in baseball, see, so our brothers—all of whom played for State—knew the outfielders at Pennsylvania. And the brothers, they just started all of these chapters across Pennsylvania and even as far west as Miami University in Oxford."

"But a sheriff? A shotgun? Lesley Cohen on the bridge? It just seems so...not right."

"That's why they can't write it in the pledge manuals," he says. "But we're the reason—Penn State is the reason—that this fraternity flourishes from coast to coast. Oh, certainly, certainly. This is the reason that these medallions were issued: to honor the first decade of Penn State brothers, those who made this a truly *national* fraternity. We'd have been a strictly Carolina fraternity, otherwise. And can you imagine that?" He pats my knee again.

I remember talking with Walter LaFaber a month or two ago, back at Headquarters, when he first discussed the esteemed Dr. Wigginton. LaFaber had a general's look in his eyes, the sort of sharp edge that says, "When we speak of Dr. Wigginton, we speak with reverence." But was there something else in that look?

"So how did *you* get one of the medallions?" I ask.

"An interesting story," he says. "Long. But very interesting."

Shit. So quickly I try to steer the conversation away from odd fraternity legends, guide it back toward *me*. Only a short while left before I take off to find a hotel somewhere, and I need to make an impression. "I bet," I say. "You know, it's going to be tough to leave Nike when my contract expires in May. I don't even know where to start looking for jobs."

"Mmm," he says. And thankfully he deposits the coin back into his pants pocket. "A common enough problem. What's your degree?"

"Organizational communications."

"Vague field." He stares into the clouds. "Difficult to find quality careers."

"That's what my father said. But my advisors told me that vague was better."

"I would have advised you toward a different major."

"I can't go back now."

"You graduated in Spring? You're fortunate to have found a job so quickly."

"I worked hard in college. I'm, you know, confident about the future."

"Organizational communications." He inhales and seems to taste the afternoon air. "My colleagues have grown fond of filtering resumes, you see. They receive large stacks, hundreds, and so they try to make candidate selections more efficient. There are some degrees that…due to the reputation of a program's difficulty…they discard the resume if they see these degrees."

"They do that? Filtering?"

"Mmm," he says, shrugs. "But there's hope with the path you've begun. Continue to wedge yourself into the world of college administration. Most of these consultants I meet, they're climbers. They use this position to get something better. That's what you should do."

"Well. That's not why I took this position, to be a 'climber,'" I say.

"No? That's not why you're on my porch right now?" he asks. "Ahh, that reminds me! Walter told me about the…Wait, have you visited Illinois?"

"Not yet."

"Have you at least heard about the problems at Illinois, then?"

"No," I say. "Something serious?"

"Yes. But if Walter hasn't told you yet, I shouldn't elaborate. I can only say that you might be enlisted to avert catastrophe at that university."

"Oh," I say, the bowl of chili gone cold in my hands, and now he's talking about something else, and I consider trying to redirect the discussion back to my career, but it seems futile. Afternoon in Kinston, Pennsylvania, and I have nowhere to go but the porch, with a smiling old man who still takes tiny bites long after the food is no longer worth eating.

"So you'll be staying with me tonight, I've been told?"

"What?" I say, and the comment is so sudden that I can't stop the next run of gas, and here on the porch in a world so silent that I can hear a car door shutting from some anonymous corner of town, I rip a fart.

Dr. Wigginton swirls his chili.

Maybe didn't notice? "Walter LaFaber told me that you'd canceled your hotel. That you wanted to stay here."

"He told you…" What *had* LaFaber told him?

"It is short notice, but I suppose I can make the accommodations."

I just farted on the front porch of a multimillionaire Pennsylvania icon, but worse: he now think *I* am imposing on his summer home, that I just *happened* to drive four hours out of my way, that I'm some uncouth road-weary drifter who needs food and shelter before returning to a sun-beaten life of hitchhiking and odd jobs on old farms. Alumni visits are supposed to be opportunities to impress important people; I'm supposed to hand him my resume, talk to him about his connections, and he's supposed to call me a Diamond Candidate and tell me that he'll find me the best damn job he can when my NKE contract expires. "Well," I say. "If that's all right that I stay here?"

"Mmm," he says.

"If you've got an extra bedroom, I mean."

He swirls the chili. "You've seen the guest room. No trouble at all. Easy access to the bathroom, as well, if you need it."

I rise from the chair. "I suppose I should grab my suitcase."

"Ahh, there *is* another one," he says. "I didn't think it possible that you could stuff so much into a laptop case."

126

"Oh. Right. Ha."

"Might want to take a walk, too, Mr. Washington. Let it all out."

"What?"

"When you come back, I'll add a little vodka to the iced tea," he says.

"No, no, I couldn't—"

"It's Saturday, Mr. Washington. Don't tell me you've made other plans."

Another new plan, then: stay the night with the creepy old man. But how would Jenn look at it? Maybe I can avoid the iced tea and the vodka? Pretend to go to sleep early, and maybe even sleep well, batteries re-charging, before I drive to Shippensburg tomorrow and start over again?

I pull my monstrous suitcase through the living room, its wheels leaving espresso-colored trails in the high carpeting, and I unpack on a tiny, twin-sized bed, its comforter smelling of a back-of-the-attic stack of sweaters. When I pull my toiletry bag out of the suitcase, a "Fun Nazi" business card flutters to the bed's brown sheets.

"Tell me about this Facebook," Dr. Wigginton says from the other room.

I scoop up the Fun Nazi card. "What?"

"The Facebook. The thing that the kids are all doing."

I meet him back in the living room where he's set up a surprisingly sleek laptop on the breakfast table. "You want to know what it is?" I ask. "Or you want to set up an account?"

"Both," he says. "Come. Sit. Are you on the Facebook?"

"Not anymore."

"Why not, Mr. Washington? From the articles I've seen, it looks delightful. All the youth and excitement, the photos."

"Um."

"Tell me. Sit, sit."

And so I sit at the table with him, tell him about how it all started, a whisper of an idea as we EU students were spilling our lives into AIM messages, into daily quotes and photo albums and profile-page mp3 anthems on MySpace. It was something up north, "the Facebook," an online yearbook at Harvard or Yale or somewhere, and it would never be as cool as MySpace. I mean, seriously. On MySpace, you could be friends with the Carver from *Nip/Tuck*; you could organize your top eight friends, give out the best spaces to the highest bidders, beers from bros and hook-ups from the ladies; you could be friends with Obie Trice, and you could hear the new T.I. joint via bulletin, the very second he released it. Facebook was just…it looked like a high school project. Just white and blue, no flexibility to the way you designed your page, no embedded songs to play as your profile's soundtrack. And you could only be friends with *other students at your school?* Lame. What about your twenty-something friends without .edu emails? Facebook: kids' stuff. But then, maybe 2004 or 2005, just like the national fraternities of years past, it spread from the Ivy Leagues to the state universities, and soon it was moving from computer to computer at Edison University, inescapable as a virus, and you started to realize that the things that had made MySpace so cool—the songs, users of all ages—actually made it extremely uncool. You didn't want friend requests from 13-year-olds, from gay 40-year-old men; you didn't want your computer to freeze from loading so many advertisements; you didn't want to listen to someone's profile song every time you clicked on their page to see if anyone had posted a new comment; for that matter, you didn't want to *have* to click on someone's profile to see if they'd written anything new. You wanted the status updates delivered to your screen. "Charles is…heading to the football game!" Boom: now everyone knew. "Charles is…pissed that we lost again!" Boom: now everyone knew. Okay, so "poking" was pretty lame, but Facebook was suddenly *the thing*, everywhere, a way of life. You organized your day around Facebook, kept track of silly observations throughout the day so that you could write funny status updates when you got home. You read more online articles now, simply because you wanted to share what you were reading. You saw yourself tagged in another girl's photo album and you thought, "Damn. She *knows* me. She *tagged* me!" And you thought that meant something.

But then it had to go. Had to, because Facebook said more about me than even the most intense and introspective autobiography ever could.

This is not *exactly* what I tell Dr. Wigginton, my quick summary more of a generalized "This is how people felt about it," nothing personal about myself, but he's barely listening because he's already setting up an account, off and running. Searching for and finding Nu Kappa Epsilon brothers throughout the state of Pennsylvania. "Oh, spectacular, what a fantastic way to maintain the bonds of brotherhood," he says, and he clicks on their pictures and then it's, "Oh, why can't I leave a *comment*?" and he sips his vodka and iced tea and the boys in the pictures are shirtless at the pool and I say, "Looks like you got the hang of this" and slip away.

*

Later, I sit in my guest bedroom, laptop open on the brown desk, finishing reports while in the living room Dr. Wigginton sits remarkably upright in his recliner with the laptop open and his eyes wide, USA or TBS or some basic cable network in the background, the deep chimes of *Law & Order* scene transitions ringing as loud as a grandfather clock, a tall glass of iced tea and vodka on the end-table beside him.

Again and again, I tell him that I'll join him once my work is finished.

Cell phone pressed to my ear, and—as usual—no one answering.

Four times I call Jenn. Voicemail, every time.

We have basic cell phones, a shared office plan for the three Educational Consultants that includes only limited text messaging (additional charges deducted straight from our paychecks). Unlimited anytime minutes, LaFaber told us, but our business is to be conducted over official emails on our provided laptops, and our cell phones are not to be all-purpose Batman-esque utility tools capable of full internet usage, GPS navigation, music storage, stereo-quality sound, or full-color movie and photo recording. We're a non-profit, after all. So my personal cell phone sits back at the Lodge in Indianapolis, disconnected and useless.

"This is Jenn," her voicemail recording goes, her voice sad-happy depending on the syllable, a mix of highs and lows: "I'm out right now, busy busy, so leave me a message and I'll get right back to you. Love ya."

Beep.

"Jenn," I say, "it's me again. It's sometime around four, I think. You're probably out at the pool? Or, wait. There was a football game today, wasn't there? Anyhow. Made it safe to Kinston." I whisper: "I need someone to talk to. *Please.*"

Hang up.

We've talked only three times in the past week, despite my goal to call her twice daily. And for some reason, we now scrape for conversation, painful silences after she tells me about parties she's been to, sorority events she's helping out with. "Jackie got engaged, so we went out to celebrate," she told me a week ago, and I pictured these five or six girls, seniors and best friends, going out to Macaroni Grill and ordering Caesar salads and chardonnay, all of them wearing skirts or dresses suitable for a wedding rehearsal dinner, but she said, "We got retarded down at Central. All I remember is dancing. I smelled like tequila this morning."

I imagine Jenn in her short jean skirt, highlighted blonde hair wet with the sweat of close dancing, close bodies packed into Night Lights. And I wonder if the "Jenn Outlook" is now allowing her to see the bright side of a life without me.

This is our text-message conversation over the past week. I've got only 100 messages per month; that's approximately 25 per week. Notice how the conversation abruptly ends:

Charles: Just saw the KD house at Pitt. Pretty spectacular.
Jenn: Thats cool.
Charles: Did I wake you up?
Jenn: Sort of.
Charles: Sorry. Will call later.
(later)
Charles: U there? I called twice.
Jenn: At the mall with Tonya.
Charles: Awesome. Big sale at Express this week.
Jenn: ???
Charles: I keep getting emails about it. Buy 1 get 1 free stuff.
Jenn: Sometimes I wonder about you.
Charles: At least Im not getting emails from bed bath and beyond!
Jenn: Gotta love discounted cookware.
Charles: Will u call me when u leave?
(later)
Charles: Eating promanti bros sandwich. U would love it.
Jenn: ???
Charles: I left u a voicemail.

Jenn: At the movies.
Charles: Im using up all my texts. Call when u get out. Any time.

I hide awhile longer in the brown guest bedroom, thinking about Jenn and Night Lights and short skirts and all of those bodies, all of that energy. But I can't hide forever: Dr. Wigginton pokes his head through the guest bedroom doorway sometime after 6 PM, still wearing his blazer and looking so over-layered with clothing, so hot and stuffy that I feel uncomfortable in my khakis and polo.

"I get the feeling you're avoiding me." Voice sounding as if he's finished three vodka-iced teas, even took a short nap. He knocks on the wall with his knuckles. Then traces the door handle with his index finger, round and round and finally pushing in the latch on the door's side.

"I just thought that you fell asleep," I say.

"Well. Maybe." He laughs his burly laugh. "In any case, it's dinner time, young man."

"Okay. Give me a second to save my reports." I close my laptop, but he doesn't move away, just watches as I unplug and slide the computer back into its leather case.

"We're meeting a few other alumni," he says.

"We're going out?"

"Oh certainly, certainly. It *is* a Saturday night, Charles. Could be a late night, too. And you didn't join me for a drink this afternoon, so…"

"Oh, I just thought…I don't know what I thought."

"If you can handle an older crowd, that is. If you can keep up."

"No problem."

"There will be a few State College alumni, like myself, and a few who drive from Pittsburgh. We have alumni outings once a month, you understand, to stay fresh as advisors, to renew those bonds"—he clasps his hands together like links in a chain—"those bonds of fraternal friendship. You can give us the updates from Headquarters, let us know what we—ahem—we distinguished alumni can do for the National Fraternity." Something about the way he says all of this…his over-emphasized grandeur, his Charlton Heston voice, like he's in a 1960s Biblical Epic…so dramatic that it feels staged…but thankfully, the drinks have at least smoothed away any unfriendliness. "We meet at a restaurant down the road called The River Bend. It's not Florida, but they have some great seafood. Some great lake trout."

"I can give it a shot."

So new plan, again: dinner with alumni. No sleep till…when? But maybe there is some promise for my day once again? Maybe this visit will go the way I'd hoped? Maybe the others will be better than Wigginton.

*

After Dr. Wigginton tells me that we're going to dinner, I spend thirty minutes in the bathroom getting ready, as much time alone as I possibly can. I close my eyes in the shower, press my head against the slippery wall, and…I

130

think I fall asleep for a moment, standing up. "Everything all right in there?" Dr. Wigginton asks from the hallway.

"Huh? Oh, yeah, perfect."

"Do you need towels?"

"No, I've got my own."

"Soap?"

"I'm—" does he really think I'd take a shower without soap?—"I'm fine."

"I have extra socks if you need them," he says, and when I don't answer, I assume he'll walk away. But when I step out of the bathroom, dressed once again in khakis and a Nu Kappa Epsilon polo, the standard business casual we're required to wear during alumni visits, Dr. Wigginton stands there, stares me up and down. "Is this the shirt you're wearing?" he asks.

"Just a Headquarters polo," I say.

"Mmm."

"Why? What's wrong?"

"We're going out to dinner, Charles. Not one of your alcohol workshops."

"You think I should change?"

"I would suggest it," Dr. Wigginton says. "Strongly suggest it."

"Most of my shirts are dirty. It's not always easy to find a laundromat."

"Find something. You'll make everyone uncomfortable, dressed like a damn Fun Nazi."

*

Twenty minutes later, we're driving. Or, rather, *he* is driving. Buckled back in a passenger seat for the first time in weeks, helpless, I silently criticize Dr. Wigginton's every maneuver, every decision, pressing my foot against a phantom brake pedal, grabbing the "oh shit" handles and bracing myself when the car jerks unexpectedly, leaning far to the left as though my weight disbursement might effect a smoother turn. You stopped too long at a stoplight, I think. Use your turn signal, I think. Conversation rarely veers from fraternity life, from discussion of national policies or my observations of student behavior, and only once do I manage to squirm out of that subject to ask: "So what sort of work do you do now? Are you, like, *fully* retired?"

"Oh certainly, certainly." He turns the heat higher.

"So you have no responsibilities with Morton & Sons, anymore?" I ask. "Do you still talk to anyone there?"

"I've rid my life of the stress, young man. Now, I work for the fraternity. I'm doing that which has always been closest to my heart."

Sky fades from blue to orange to post-sunset purple. Car snaking through thirty or forty minutes of winding 25-mile-per-hour backroads, finally winding up at a hilltop restaurant overlooking the same interstate I traveled earlier today. Beyond the interstate, in the distance: a dark circular lake, broken in the center by shimmering, white-capped rapids, thin and barely-visible branches of a river shooting off in several directions. We pull into the chunky dirt parking lot, Wigginton's car bouncing high and low in the potholes. The restaurant, The River Bend, is the type of place that screams "corporate," the type of restaurant with a gigantic sign and bright, flashing neon logo so extravagant that it simply can*not* have been produced by some Mom and Pop with entrepreneurial ambitions. Mountain-home façade, piles of firewood on either side of a stone walkway leading to heavy oak doors. The River Bend could be a repainted Cracker Barrel or Smokey Bones.

Inside the restaurant, a plump teenaged hostess in corduroys and maroon polo leads us to a back-corner table so ultra-lacquered that my drink (water with lemon) slides across in a collected puddle of condensation, as if pulled by an under-the-table magnet. We sit alone for fifteen minutes, Dr. Wigginton asking me if this isn't just the most *fantastic* restaurant ever, and I try not to answer honestly. "Try some homemade apple pie," read the placemats. "Try a Smirnoff and Tonic with Coke and Lime!" read the table-tents.

Eventually, after we finish a basket of cornbread, two other alumni join us. They walk together, these two, but one clearly leads and the other follows sheepishly.

Ben Jameson, the leader, is in his mid-thirties, wears cargo shorts and an "Ed-Tex" polo with no undershirt (nipples poking out in the restaurant's A/C), and hails from the University of Pittsburgh. He speaks in frustrated tones about his wife and kids back home. "Little Matt's been reading Dr. Seuss lately," Ben says. Amazingly, despite his age, despite his degree and his ten years of work experience following graduation, despite the fact that his hair is thinning and his muscle has softened to a fatherly flab, he has the same *fuck the world* tone to his voice as the undergraduates at Pittsburgh. "Kid walks around the house *constantly*, reading out loud," he says. "One fish, two fish. Go dog go. Whatever. Drives you *cra-zy*. Trying to watch *Sportscenter*, and the kid's standing in front of the TV saying *Go! Dog! Go!*, listen to me, listen to me, and what am I supposed to do? I can't *ignore* him."

The other alumnus, the follower, is skinnier, bald with hairy arms, smiles nervously in agreement with everything Ben says. His name is Anthony, also a graduate of the University of Pittsburgh. Both men serve as alumni advisors for Pittsburgh, and both—as advisors—are responsible for helping the Pittsburgh undergrads to enforce financial policies and chapter bylaws.

"I need to get fucking hammered tonight," Ben says. "Hammered."

Anthony looks down at the table and coughs a chuckle.

"Don't worry, doc," Ben says to Dr. Wigginton. "Anthony drove us. He's my DD."

"Oh certainly, certainly," Dr. Wigginton says.

"Where'd our waitress go?" Ben asks. "Little cutie, wasn't she?"

But who knows? Maybe they just go to the chapter house to play pool, drink Rolling Rock, and watch football.

\*

I'm still dressed in flat-front khaki pants, but I traded my NKE polo for a striped button-down that I pulled from my dirty-clothes bag, sprayed with deodorant, ironed. Already, I'm searching the shirt for wrinkles or dirt splotches or stains, and every time Ben speaks, my dirty shirt is my excuse to smooth my pants and my sleeves, to stare at my chest or my lap so that I don't have to respond.

"I love these nights out," Ben says. "Makes me feel young again."

Several minutes later, two older Penn State alumni arrive and exchange excited pleasantries with Dr. Wigginton. One, Henry Guffman, looks like an older, swollen Don Johnson (with the addition of an untrimmed moustache); he "owns a little construction company in Barlow, just down the road." The other alumnus, Clyde Hampshire, is just as old and wealthy as the Doctor, and also occupies several ceremonial positions in the fraternity. He tells me that he served for eight years as the Housing Board President for Penn State. It was great, he says. That does sound great, I say.

"Our monthly alumni gatherings are always in flux," Dr. Wigginton says. "Some months, we have more than fifteen. Other months, as few as four or five. Either way, small or large, these reunions are the perfect nourishment for the fraternal hunger."

"So what about it, gentlemen?" Ben says. "Split some pitchers?"

"Mr. Hampshire?" Dr. Wigginton asks, looking at Clyde. "Shall we?"

"I might as well," Clyde says. "I'm already up past my bedtime."

Dr. Wigginton and Clyde Hampshire laugh the same huffing, deep-throated laughs, hands on one another's knees.

"All right, then," Ben says. "Where's our girl? Where is that little thing?"

I lower my head, smooth my pants.

"Hey, cutie. We're gonna need some service. Let's go." Ben claps.

Scattered laughter around the table. I keep my head down.

Our waitress arrives and introduces herself, and someone—Clyde Hampshire?—cuts her off to say, "Thank God we have *you* tonight. I don't know what we would have done, had we been waited on by that fat gentleman." Laughter. "A wasted night," someone else says. Hearty man-laughter. Some nervous 20-year-old female laughter, too.

When I look up, Ben is very obviously staring into her chest.

She is blonde—no, brunette, with clearly visible roots—and has the athletic build of a volleyball player. Almost looks like Jenn, except that Jenn is leaner and *never* allows her roots to show. (And Jenn doesn't wear choker necklaces as this girl does; the farther I travel from Florida, strangely, the more popular that surfer accessories become. The undergraduates at Pittsburgh wore board shorts and "Rusty" t-shirts, as if they live only a few blocks from the beach and are ready to load up their Jeeps each morning to see what fortune the waves hold for them.) Ben leans into her, lets his voice descend into an *older is sexier* tone, and says, "Need a pitcher of Yuengling and six glasses."

"That it for now?" she says.

Six glasses. Six of us. Five alumni, and myself.

And that sounds fantastic. A way to redeem the day. Yuengling. Splitting pitchers with the big boys. Again, I savor the word *alumni.* On Homecoming weekends back at EU, when the alumni came back to the house en masse, we'd buy a couple cases of Heineken and let them have the house to themselves. Loosen up, enjoy yourself, we said. (Then cut us a check for our scholarship fund!) A couple brews with the big boys, I'm thinking, with the *alumni*, with a *District Magistrate*, and I am picturing myself on the edge of my seat, beer in my hand recounting stories from my first two weeks of travel to an alumni audience enthralled, laughing, beers in their hands, too. Stories. Jokes with alumni. Dr. Wigginton telling me that he will hand my resume to his friends, certainly, that it will not be filtered, that he has my back and that this is what fraternity is all about. I'm smelling the beer, tasting it. Yuengling. Crisp and cold, light carbonation.

Six glasses.

But the Code of Conduct: "While you're a representative of the fraternity, the four D's are off-limits. No dating, no drinking, no drugs, and no digital footprint."

So I say to the waitress, "None for me. Just five glasses is fine."

"None for you?" Ben asks.

"Mmm?" Dr. Wigginton asks.

"What are you, the sober driver?" Henry Guffman asks in his deep, phlegmy voice.

"No, no," I say. "It's just—I can't drink with students or alumni."

"Oh, the Headquarters," Dr. Wigginton says, shakes his head. "Silly little *rules*. Come now, Mr. Washington. I'm certain a glass of beer at a *restaurant* will not get you fired. We're tight-lipped. We aren't a bunch of rambunctious college students, after all."

"No, it's not that. I should just stay clearheaded."

"You got to be kidding me, right?" Ben asks. "Some of us are twice your age, and *we* don't care about clear heads. Do we care about clear heads?" he asks the waitress, who still stands by nervously, attempting a smile, shifting her weight from foot to foot.

"I guess not," she says. "No clear heads tonight."

"Fuckin' A," Ben says. "This is a *fraternity* gathering, for crying out loud."

I'm silent for a moment. "It's a personal decision, is all. Nothing against you all."

"Is it your gas?" Dr. Wigginton asks.

"Gas?" Clyde Hampshire says.

"Chili for lunch," Dr. Wigginton says. "He had very bad gas."

The waitress still looks nervous, but now she no longer needs to fake her smile.

"No. Come on," I say. "I just can't do it. It's the *rule*."

"Fine. Just five glasses," Dr. Wigginton tells the waitress, touching her hand.

"Well, fuck," Ben says. "Not going to twist your arm."

I want to tell the waitress that I *would* drink if I were with my friends, that everything would be different if I was back home, but these are alumni and I'm an Educational Consultant, and the mission, and the National Fraternity and its leadership development programs, and the Code of Conduct I have to follow, and tough choices and goals, and I know that a beer—just one—would show the whole table that I am one of them, that I am *alumni*, part of the Grand Tradition, and *no drink* draws a line between them and me, forever segregates me from their ranks, their club, their favors…I stay silent for several minutes, then, as the five resume or finish bits of conversations from previous gatherings, knowing that I've followed guidelines and the New Charles Washington is preserved, but that this is a failed outing nonetheless.

Soon, I start to catch vital information: I learn that the quiet one, Anthony Simmons, is the District Representative for Western Pennsylvania, an important advisor position. I should have known, but sometimes the names and districts and regions blur together.

They talk fraternity. The state of their chapters, the state of students today. Beer sparkling in pitchers, while I drink water.

*

And then: so much for sober drivers. Ben drinks his beer in massive gulps and Anthony tries to keep up, taking long and labored sips each time he sees Ben drink. Clyde Hampshire and Dr. Wigginton appear to drink conservatively, small old-man-sips, but by the time the waitress arrives again, both have finished their beers and are ready for a new pitcher. The night doesn't feel like it'll be a quick affair, either: these alumni have driven a fair distance to be here, and damned if they aren't going to suck the night dry.

"Sure you don't want a drink, Charlie?" Ben asks me. "C'mon!"

"I've got my water."

"Just a sip. Just a little siplet. No need to be a pussy, Charlie. You're among men."

Anthony snickers soundlessly, tries to chug but spills beer on his shirt.

Back at EU, we never really saw the alumni get drunk. Yes, we bought them alcohol, and yes, we came home to trash-bagged beer bottles and flattened cardboard boxes, but we always left them alone at their reunions. That's the way they wanted it. Much like my grade school teachers, who guarded the door to the faculty lounge ferociously and who always looked just a little uncomfortable when we saw them at the gas station or the grocery store, blocking our view of their carts, their M&M snack packs, their chewing gum, their tampons or toilet paper or condoms or laxatives, the chinks in their adult armor.

*

And then it's Ben saying that he wishes kegs were legal in fraternity houses. "We were allowed to have them when I was an undergrad, and we never sent anyone to the hospital," he says. "That's the worst thing about Nationals"—and he points at me, as if I wrote the alcohol policies—"they banned kegs. And why? 'Cause, like, one kid gets alcohol poisoning. Bullshit."

And then it's Clyde Hampshire telling us that things went downhill when *they*—"they," again meaning "The National Headquarters," or maybe parents, or lawyers, or university administrators, or everyone—outlawed hazing. "We

135

knew how to keep it under control," Clyde says. "It made boys into men. It made all of us into brothers."

"The Terror Machine," Dr. Wigginton says, eyes shut.

"The Terror Machines," Clyde Hampshire repeats.

The table falls into silent reverence.

"What's that?" I ask. "What's the Terror Machine?"

"Historically, during Week Seven of the pledge semester at Penn State," Dr. Wigginton says. "Utter humiliation. A contraption that was so physically and emotionally demeaning that pledges sometimes could not speak for days afterward." He closes his eyes again, shakes his head. But I can't tell if he's upset by the memory, or if this is nostalgia for a beloved tradition that has now been outlawed.

"What did it do?" I ask.

"That is something we do no talk about," Clyde Hampshire says.

"Part of the mystique of the Penn State chapter," Dr. Wigginton says.

"The Terror Machine," Hampshire says, and everyone raises glasses high and drinks.

*

Sometime after Anthony spills a beer across the table and into the onion ring basket, Henry Guffman launches into a hearty diatribe about all the things he can't understand about young people: the tattoos, the piercings, the torn jeans, the baseball caps turned backwards, each new item stated incredulously—"I saw this kid wearing headphones! While he was on his skateboard!"—and with the anticipation of laughter, as if he is a stand-up comic in the middle of his routine. "You know, I read this thing," he says when the comedian thing is clearly not working, and now he speaks like a researcher with some incredible new finding. "It's called the Beloit College Mindset. They put it out for teachers and professionals that work with college kids, and it's this giant list of factoids. Shit that kids don't know. Like, for kids coming into college right now, it says that Paul Newman is a salad dressing, not an actor."

"Intriguing," Dr. Wigginton says.

"And, like, rap music has always been mainstream," Henry says. He sits back in his chair, gulps his beer. "And the Facebook!"

"The what?" Clyde Hampshire asks.

"The Facebook!" Guffman repeats.

"Oh, delightful!" Dr. Wigginton says. "Yes, the Facebook. Mr. Washington here introduced me to it today. How wonderful."

"Got me an account," Ben says. "Who needs porn when you got an endless supply of Spring Break photos, am I right?"

"You too?" I ask.

"I couldn't, not up until recently. Needed a school email. But I was first in line when they dropped that restriction."

"I don't know," Guffman says. "Maybe I'm starting to sound like my grandfather, but I just want to go back to the good old days, you know? These kids. So different."

Soon, the pitcher is finished. And another, before our food arrives.

"What about this Obama?" Dr. Wigginton asks me. "Does he have a chance?"

The whole table staring me down. "Gosh, I don't…I don't know," I say.

"They say he won the nomination because of the social media," Hampshire says. "Is that true?"

"Maybe?"

"You don't want him in office, I'll tell you that," Guffman says and jabs his finger into the table. "He'll put a tax on fraternity houses. Guaranteed. Easy money for his socialist agendas, just taxing fraternities, cause who's gonna complain? Whole world thinks fraternities are a bunch of rich snobs, so get ready, *whoo*."

And another pitcher.

"How is the chapter at Pittsburgh, these days?" Dr. Wigginton asks Ben, a question he must have asked me four times while we ate chili on his porch, but Dr. Wigginton never seems to tire of fraternity discussion. And I'm now starting to ache for some other conversation topic: the NFL maybe. College football. Even Brad and Angelina. Whatever. How can anyone keep saying some of these words and not feel a dull throb in their skulls? Fraternity fraternity fraternity fraternity fraternity fraternity. After awhile, it even sounds strange on your lips, and when you stop to listen to yourself speak, you wonder what the hell you're talking about. Fraternity fraternity fraternity fraternity.

"Delta Beta's doing good," Ben says, slicing his steak. He sticks his fork into a thick, fatty cut, holds it up in admiration, and crams it into his mouth. Delta Beta is Pittsburgh's "chapter designation"; each of our fraternity chapters has a one or two-letter designation (Carolina Baptist is "Alpha" chapter, South Carolina is "Beta," etc.) used forever to identify that school as part of Nu Kappa Epsilon. "Never better, actually," Ben says after he swallows. "Kicking ass. I went to their last party, and I was fucking shocked. We never got girls like that when we were in school. We had fun, yeah, but this was ri-*dic*-ulous. How's Delta Alpha?"

"You went to an undergrad party?" I ask, but softly, and because they are drunk, loud, overpowering, my words are lost.

"We have a few problems with Delta Alpha," Dr. Wigginton says.

"Anyone hear about Delta Delta?" Henry asks.

"Delta Delta," Clyde Hampshire says, shaking his head.

"Are you going to visit Delta Delta?" Henry asks me. "There's a problem chapter, right there. I tried advising them. Too difficult. But I hear good things about Gamma Alpha. Rough campus, but really good group of guys, I hear."

"Those Gamma chapters," Dr. Wigginton says. "In such a tough spot."

"Fuck the Gamma chapters," Ben says, and he is now craning his neck, looking around for the waitress. "I fucking hate upstate New York. Where's our waitress?"

An evening with five successful alumni, and we are talking in Greek letters. All of them are talking now, in fact, speaking over one another, saying

Gamma Alpha and Gamma Zeta and Delta Beta and Chapter House and Pittsburgh and Penn State and Hey Babe, Let's Go, and Delta Delta and Fill It Up, Baby, and Do Not Want to Go Home, What a Fucking Headache and Delta Delta and We've Gotta Do Something to Help Those Guys and Illinois is a Financial Nightmare, Can You Believe It? and What's Up With the Sandor Lawsuit?, and Delta Beta and Alpha and Beta and Gamma and—

"We're starting a new program at the Headquarters," I say suddenly, loudly, and maybe I cut someone off, cut everyone off. But this is my opportunity to break out of the irrelevant *not one of us* shell in which I've been cast ever since I refused the beer. "A mentor program."

The table goes quiet. Five men all turning to me, necks moving so slowly that I expect them to squeak like old wheels on rusty axles, and they stare. Henry Guffman's bloated face and cheeks seemingly changing shape as he breathes, his overgrown mustache rustling as the air enters and leaves his nose. Anthony's skeletal face has now taken on cherry tones from all the drinking, his pale bald scalp now contrasting more heavily. They stare, all five of them.

"Mentors?" Ben asks. "What the fuck for?"

"Teach them how to hold their liquor!" Anthony shouts, and his red face stretches into a hysterical smile that looks more like the scream of a dying man. He slaps the table, nearly spills his beer again, and begins a laugh that sounds too demented to really be happening. "Drinking mentors, ha! We could teach them a thing or two!" Smiles around the table, too, expressions that suggest that such an explosion was inevitable from Anthony, that they've been waiting for his quiet to crack and the loud drunk man underneath to pop out.

"Breathe, buddy, breathe," Ben says and pats Anthony on the back.

"You may continue, Mr. Washington," Dr. Wigginton says.

"Well, we just realized, you know, that a lot of students are joining campus organizations for the purpose of networking," I say. "And since our mission is leadership development, we decided that *we*—the National Fraternity, with all our alumni—could provide more opportunities for our members. We're trying to organize groups of alumni in some of our major cluster areas, and we're building a database, compiling names and careers and we'll have these roundtables—"

"Sounds like a lot of effort," Anthony says, thin face still caught in the grip of that deathly smile as he speaks, but he is no longer laughing.

"Sure," I say. "But worth the effort. We're redefining fraternity life—"

"You see all these movies," Anthony says. "Like that one. What's it called? *The Skulls*. Where fraternities are these, like, highly-organized secret societies that run the world, and new pledges get convertibles and 100-grand jobs when they graduate."

His smile has vanished.

"Well," I say, "the idea of the mentoring program isn't—"

"Already doing it. I hired this Nike kid from Delaware," Henry says, and tiny beads of beer line his mustache. "Straight out of college, I hired him.

He tells me, this fucking kid, he tells me he was President of the chapter there, that he was House Manager, that he was this and he was that. This kid doesn't even have, like, the most basic knowledge…I mean, I guess I can only blame the school, not the fraternity…but this kid couldn't do shit for research without google. Had the toughest time actually calling people. You got to hire a Nike, though, you know? He's learning, this kid. He might be all right. You got to hire a Nike, is all I know."

"I give my money," says Clyde Hampshire. "I simply cannot give my time, too."

"Only retirees can afford to give time!" Dr. Wigginton says, slaps Clyde Hampshire's knee. "You're still a year away, sir!"

"Tell you what, doc," Ben says, "I win the powerball and the first thing I do…well, second thing I do…first thing is, I dump the wife and pick up a little piece of ass with *college girl* written all over her…But the second thing I do is I put a couple hundred grand into this fraternity. You match me, we invest that shit, and you see what we can come up with. You and me, we'll make that Pittsburgh house into something special. Hell, build myself a guest house."

"It wouldn't take much time," I say. "It's just that college kids *need* mentors in the business world. They need someone to help them figure things out."

"Bah," Clyde Hampshire says. "Millennials."

"What does that mean?" I say.

"Millennials," he says again, and I notice now how massive his gray eyebrows are, hairs curling outward. Nose hairs descending, also, and he's missed a few spots shaving on his neck and on his left cheek; the hair is long, looks as though he's missed those spots for days. I expected a man with so many business-world accolades, such wealth and prestige, to appear careful and orderly, but Clyde Hampshire shakes, jitters, slurs under the influence of alcohol. "The Mil-*len*-nial Generation," he says, "that's what they're calling kids today. Kids born now, kids going to school. It's the next generation after Generation X. Kids who don't know their ass from a hole in the ground."

Dr. Wigginton laughs hard, but no sound comes out; he holds his belly.

"Of course they need mentors! They know all about the *Simpsons* and Britney Spears," Clyde Hampshire says, "but they can't tie their own shoes. Of course they can't figure anything out! Everything has been handed to them."

"Here, here!" Ben Jameson says, pounding his glass on the table.

"You want me to waste my time mentoring kids who should have their act together anyway?" Henry asks. "That's the idea here?"

"No, I'm not saying that."

"Everything has been handed to them," Hampshire says. "Everything."

"It's not that they're lazy or sloppy," I say, and I struggle to say "they" and not "we." "It's just that some of them, some students, they're lost, you know? We're a leadership development organization, so—"

"What about the parents?" Henry asks.

"What about them?"

"Shouldn't parents be the mentors? Teach them all this stuff?"

"But the fraternity should *bolster* that," I say. "Not everyone's born into the same family, but joining the fraternity should be like joining a *new* family, a perfect support network that's never going to fall apart. It's...it's the *Millennial* Family."

"A family," Henry says. "Already got one of those, thanks."

"And what do your parents do for a living, Mr. Washington?" Dr. Wigginton asks.

"My parents?"

"Yours."

"My father is in real estate."

"Your mother?"

"She was an administrator at a doctor's office," I say. "But my father made enough that she resigned a few years back."

"Ahh, they're still together?" Clyde Hampshire asks. "That's all the support network a young man should need. A stable family."

"That's not what we were talking about."

"But here you are, Mr. Washington," Wigginton says, and he scratches behind his ear with a professorial pretentiousness, as if settling the matter. "A self-sufficient young man who's clearly benefitted from the mentoring of your father. A strong work ethic instilled by successful parents."

"Unlike most of this generation." Henry Guffman gulps his beer. "They just use and abuse it, know what I mean?"

"Millennials," Hampshire says one last time. "Dependent. The Entitlement Generation."

"Indeed," Wigginton says, eyes half-closed, head swaying. "If it weren't for *us*, many of these undergraduate chapters would be headed down that dreary road to closure. They *need* us." He places his cold hand on my wrist and I try not to flinch. "Why, Mr. Washington, just last Spring, we had to step in at Penn State. The administrators, you see, they attempted to shut down the house. Claimed to have evidence of some indiscretion, hazing or sleep deprivation or some such nonsense. We'd warned the undergraduates before, of course. The culture has changed, we told them: these things are no longer allowed." He releases my wrist. "I had to organize the alumni, men whose combined contributions to that university exceed seven digits. We had to threaten the administration, Mr. Washington: punish the undergraduates, and we will withhold future donations!" His eyes are open now, face smooth but volcanic red. "What Mr. Hampshire says is God's honest truth. These children are handed everything. What more should we be expected to give them?"

"I don't know," I say. "I don't know. Nothing."

A grand tradition stretching back more than a century.

*We are leaders.*

A mission to build young men into socially responsible citizens.

"Noble," Jenn said when we talked about my career. *Noble.*

And then it is Pitcher Number Seven, and I hang my head each time the waitress stops by the table, and every other word out of anyone's mouth is slurred, swears speckling every sentence as if they are trying to fulfill the criteria for a Good Ole Boys Club caricature, *titties* from Guffman and *for fuck's sake* from Hampshire, *buncha cunts* from Ben Jameson, *so very faggy* from Wigginton...

The dinner bill comes—I reach for my wallet, but Dr. Wigginton is a king, a provider for his people, and he covers everyone, the alumni all ho-hum like they expect it but I am jubilant because this meal cost more than my daily budget allows. Ben makes one last attempt at the waitress, but she looks beyond patience and so he says "fuck it" (loudly), and I help the Doctor out the front door, take the keys and help him into his passenger seat, and then I am driving us back through dark roads and twisting mountain setbacks, back to Kinston and to his home, but he falls asleep and I make a wrong turn and at one point the road ends and I have to turn around and drive fifteen minutes back to the last intersection and he wakes up briefly and says, "Oh, left here," then closes his eyes again.

And when we grumble into Kinston and park in his brick driveway, he opens the passenger-seat door and tries to get out without taking off his seatbelt, then unlatches and tumbles onto the ground. Stands and wobbles, sloshes past his front door, through his living room, falls into his bed in his blazer and dress pants. "No fun-time tonight, young man," he says, but then goes silent.

I turn off his bedroom lights. Leave him. Decide to take a late-night shower, since Henry Guffman knocked over a glass and coated my entire upper torso with Yuengling. A late-night shower, so I can sneak out of here early in the morning.

The tub and shower curtains have a musty old man odor to them, like vinegar and Dial bar soap and orange Bic razors. For awhile, I think about how funny it would be to snap a photo of the good doctor, passed out like that on his bed. Snap a photo and share it with the other consultants. So pathetic, this old, drunk man. This fraternity figurehead, this Nike Hall-of-Famer. This man who has been built into an Alumni Legend...look and see the grand tradition of the fraternity! Legs hanging off the bed, slacks going wrinkled, face mashed into the headboard, glasses sideways and ready to snap.

I think about taking the photo.

Uploading it online: *I'm* the one who needs to worry about a digital footprint?

Charles is...just showing it like it is.

Dr. Wigginton is...going to be surprised when he finds himself on Facebook!

But I leave the camera in my bag.

This night wasn't supposed to happen like this, but I still need Dr. Wigginton to be who he should be. Maybe everyone does. What good is it to destroy the legend, the history? I still need Walter LaFaber to be who *he's* supposed to be, also, can't let myself think that this was a joke, or worse, that he's just funneling exuberant young men into the gleeful open arms of a lonely old pervert in the no-one-can-hear-you-scream mountains. Those things can't be true.

Late at night I call Jenn again, and when she answers, all I hear is the static-loud noise of a party, a bar, a DJ, whatever, and she just keeps saying, "I can't *hear* you!" Two nights in a row. And so I hang up and turn off my phone. I sit on the brown sheets and a sharp glint of white catches my eye, something poking out under the pillow; it's that fucking Fun Nazi business card again. I turn it over in my hands, over to the white, blank back, over to the front, to "Fun Nazi." I should toss it in the trash, just forget about it because it was a meaningless gag, but this is the thing that I won't let go, this is the thing that I'll latch onto.

I place it atop my laptop case so I can stare at it. I'm the Fun Nazi? I'm the one who doesn't get it? I wander Dr. Wigginton's kitchen, floorboards creaking, find a bottle of Gentleman Jack in a high cabinet, floorboards creaking from somewhere else but his bedroom door is still shut, it's just the old wood and ghosts of this house, and I take a quick shot and put the bottle back, then grab the bottle again and sit outside on the porch and all is black and sounds like crickets or birds or wind, branches snapping, and I pour another shot, kick it back, then another. *I'm* the Fun Nazi?

*

Early in the morning, I wake up to a cup of coffee, toast, and oatmeal on the breakfast table. But I leave as quickly as I can, thanking and thanking Dr. Wigginton until I've said "thanks" so many times that—like "fraternity"—it doesn't even sound like a real word anymore. "You are welcome back any time, my brother, *any* time," he says, and I say, "It's a little out of the way," and he just says again, "Any time, Mr. Washington, that bedroom is yours. I am indeed impressed by your professionalism, sir. I'd love to catch up at greater length." Smile. "Enjoy Illinois."

"I'm not going to Illinois," I say.

"No?"

"I'm going to Shippensburg."

"A fine mess, Shippensburg," he says. "But I have a feeling you'll be headed to Illinois soon enough. Soon enough. There are fires that need putting out."

"Okay."

"Stay safe," he says. "Stay alert."

"Right. Thanks for putting me up."

Pack up and drive. From Kinston, back to Pittsburgh. Then Pittsburgh to Shippensburg.

A long drive today. Barely slept, and if I was tired yesterday, today I feel like I could collapse at any moment. Clothes are wrinkled, but no time to iron. Suitcase is a disorganized mess of dirty and clean clothes. Didn't have time to do laundry. Hair feels long. Fingernails. I didn't shave, didn't brush my teeth. Pack up and drive and arrive at Shippensburg and stay professional, that's the goal. Forget about the last workshop, forget about the alumni visit.

Three days at Shippensburg. Three days. Then I pack up and drive again. Then: St. Joseph's. Then, a week from now, a night at a hotel, and sleep, and time to re-energize. Then…well…yes, then then then.

# The Ship

CHAPTER ELEVEN

**TRAVEL SCHEDULE – CHARLES WASHINGTON**

*✈ Shippensburg University ✈*
St. Joseph's University
New Mexico State University
Texas Tech
California State University—Fresno
California State University—Highland
California State University—Long Beach
California State University—San Francisco
University of Delaware
Marshall University
Miami University (Ohio)
University of Toledo
Central Michigan University
University of Michigan
Bowling Green State University
Purdue University
Indiana University

Headquarters – Mid-Semester Debrief (Indianapolis)

University of Oklahoma
University of Kansas
University of Missouri—Columbia
University of Nebraska
Iowa State University

Thanksgiving Vacation

Bradley University
University of Iowa

Headquarters (Indianapolis)

Christmas Vacation

"Be on the look-out," LaFaber said to me in our one-on-one phone-call debrief last Monday, just after I'd facilitated a recruitment workshop at the University of Virginia-Green Valley (the students still call it "Green Valley College," the school's name before its absorption into the UVA system). "Be on the look-out for anything and everything, Charles," he said in that meat-grinder voice of his, and—as always—I pictured him standing in his cold office, fingers touching the spine of some leadership journal in his metal bookshelf, looking out the window and searching for me. "It's *Rush* season. An exciting time, but a dangerous time."

"Don't worry," I said. "I remember Rush. I'll be ready."

"You've never been to these Northeast schools," LaFaber replied tiredly, as if I couldn't possibly understand what he was preparing me for. "We can't afford another Sandor lawsuit."

"I know. Trust me, Walter."

"Be on the look-out. Anything suspicious, you report it. Right away."

That was a week ago. Now it's Sunday morning, and after a long drive from Kinston in the western mountains of Pennsylvania, I pull into the choppy gravel parking lot for the Shippensburg University fraternity row, tiny stones kicking up from the ground and *tink*-ing against my Explorer's underbelly. A headache pounds under my skull in an inconsistent rhythm, eyes crusty no matter how many times I rub them, back aches from all the packing-up-and-driving, the poor sleep, the detour to Wigginton's house. I park between two Jeeps, as far away from the seven fraternity houses as possible, crunching over empty beer cans on my way to the curb. Nu Kappa Epsilon has the very first house on the row, and like the seven other houses situated around this gravel parking lot, it's a block of a building, two-story, sandy-yellow with a sagging wrap-around porch.

Each house has the shell-shocked look of having been party-bombed last night. Red cups and Rolling Rock beer bottles litter the yards, along with Taco Bell wrappers and deflated basketballs and volleyballs and dirty socks and underwear, all of it existing together in a muddy marshland of trampled grass. Looks like all of the famous photos of Woodstock's aftermath. It's almost noon here in Shippensburg, but the row whistles with a Ghost Town emptiness, full parking lots, sure, but the middle of the day feels like the dead of night.

Be on the look-out? Not very difficult.

Shippensburg appears to be smack-dab in the middle of "Rush Season," starting its fraternity "Rush Week." Across the country, in the early weeks and months of the Fall semester, fraternity chapters scrape together thousands of dollars from their budgets—*tens* of thousands, sometimes, at schools like Florida, Alabama, Ole Miss, the Big Ten, the Ivy League, where big money is on the line—to repaint the scratched and stained exteriors of their houses, to replace broken hinges and door knobs, broken doors, to purchase two-story-tall banners with bright Photoshop-designed lions and tigers and "star shields" and Vikings and dragons and larger-than-life Greek letters,

ΣAE in italicized purple, ATΩ in gold and navy blue, ΘX in thick muscular letters. Rush Season, forty or fifty testosterone-fueled 20-year-olds re-converging and shattering the long dormant summer at the fraternity house, the long dormant summer of the college campus likewise shattered by new freshmen moving into dorms, attending their first lectures in centuries-old college halls, allowing themselves to be pulled in every direction by their new independence. An explosive mixture, this population of young people, thousands and thousands of 18- to 22-year-olds arriving all at *once*, these kids in Abercrombie t-shirts, Gap jeans, thinking about youth and friends and MTV and parties and *Van Wilder* and *Road Trip* and every other college movie ever created, thinking Spring Break, ESPN College Gameday, *all at once*…and the fraternities are there with their Rush budgets funneled into renovated and redecorated houses, doors flung open, kitchen tables topped with barbecue and brownies. Rush Season. Doors open, arms wide open to take in the young and eager masses aching for activity.

At the National Headquarters, we get daily updates on "pledge number tallies" from our chapters, hard data assuring us that chapter houses will now be filled for another year, that the torch will be passed and the Grand Tradition can continue. But while Rush Season is cause for optimism and excitement, it's also cause for extreme worry. At most schools, Rush is informal, a single week set aside by the university for fraternities to *recruit recruit recruit* and replenish their ranks with freshman men, the fraternities holding informational sessions and social events—cook-outs, lobster bakes— and voting late-night on potential new members, issuing bids to those desired for membership. A whirlwind week of hard work, long nights, new faces. And a mandate—real or imagined—that the fraternity must do *whatever it takes* to achieve the highest pledge tally on campus. Last year, one fraternity chapter at Moo University received 200 underage drinking citations at a party. Members *and* guests. And on the same weekend, at the Delta Pi Beta house at DuPont, a fraternity brother was giving a tour of his chapter house when he discovered a *dead girl* in the basement from a wild party the night before. She'd crawled into a closet, drunk. Alcohol poisoning.

Rush Season. The things I learned during training. The scope.

Back at Edison University, Rush was formal. Male students dressed in shirt and tie and paid an entry fee to be escorted from house to house by a Rush Guide for a full week. At the end of this week, the student decided which fraternity he'd pledge by filling out a scantron with his top choices. I was usually responsible for giving the Rush presentation to the assembled freshmen at our house, listing our intramural championships, our academic accolades; during the presentation, another fraternity brother would pull several freshmen from their seats, offer them a "house tour," lead them upstairs to his bedroom, tell them to close the door, shh shh, this is against the rules, and he'd open a large blue cooler in the center of his room, revealing plastic milk jugs filled with Hunch Punch. "Enough of the presentations and trophies," he'd say. "This is what it's all about."

Just one harmless cup. I'd like to think—now, as a consultant—that we didn't do this, that I didn't know about it. But as a freshman, I drank from those jugs.

Be on the look-out, LaFaber told me. Anything suspicious, report it. Charles is…going to do things right this time, damn it.

*

Earlier this morning, over the bottom right corner of the plexiglass covering my speedometer and odometer, I taped the Fun Nazi business card. It seems to keep reappearing no matter how I try to dispose of it, so I figured, why not just keep it around as a reminder? Let it be my daily motivation. The only problem, though, is that it didn't *mean* the same thing this morning as it did last night. Last night, I saw this card and thought, "You don't have to be a Fun Nazi. Loosen up." Now I'm thinking the opposite: "You don't want to be the same as those guys last night."

LaFaber warned me about Shippensburg University. Last Spring, they told the Educational Consultant that he couldn't stay in the chapter house; they locked their front doors, wouldn't let him inside. The undergraduates were placed on suspension for this, but out here in rural Pennsylvania…so far from the Headquarters in Indianapolis…what does *suspension* mean?

A Jeep grumbles into the gravel space beside my Explorer, and I pretend to look through my center console for something important. Don't mind the guy with the out-of-state license plates, the guy in shirt and tie with a full wardrobe hanging from a rod stretched across his backseat, the guy who's going to *spy* for *anything suspicious* over the next three days. The Jeep's doors open and two guys hop out, one wearing a Penn State shirt with blue gym shorts and carrying a Burger King bag and a Gatorade bottle, the other wearing a red TKE shirt with an illegible slogan along the bottom.

"—on his fucking *couch*," TKE-shirt shouts as he slams shut his door.

"With that girl?" the other one asks. "Holy shit."

They both laugh, their voices fading as they hop-scotch the yard trash and pass the NKE house before finally disappearing through the open doorway of the Tau Kappa Epsilon house.

I didn't plan it this way; I didn't *want* to sneak in unannounced. I called the Shippensburg chapter president, James Neagle, seven times this past week. Daily emails. No response.

Sitting in my Explorer, and Jenn's "Remember Me" mixtape CD of late '90s/early 2000s pop hits settles on a Britney Spears song. Earlier, it was N'Sync's "It Makes Me Ill," and before that Kandi's "Don't Think I'm Not," each song by now memorized from dozens of listens, and each new listen a reminder of how many miles I've traveled. Here I am, past noon on a Sunday, tired from an all-morning drive, tie hanging loose and sloppy over my light blue button-down like a dog's tongue after a long run. Head pounding. "Toxic," Britney's singing. "Don't you know that you're toxic?"

I think of walking inside, just walking straight up to the fraternity house and opening the door and finding Neagle. Rustling him out of bed, the

same as LaFaber might do. Just walk straight up there, right into that mess.
Confront it.

I think of Fall Rush back at Edison, of the four years' experience I've got.
The jugs of alcohol, the drunk freshmen. This is something that I should've
done a long time ago. I think of calling Jenn, too. I've got a minute. I think of
her happy, high-low voice. I think of her blonde highlighted hair falling over
a powder-blue sorority t-shirt. I think of the party, the bar she went to last
night. I think of her dancing.

"Toxic," Britney's singing. "Don't you know that you're toxic?"

I adjust my tie, check myself in the mirror, step out of my vehicle. I tiptoe through the wasteland yard of fraternity row, plastic wrappers and beer
bottle labels sticking to my shoes, and I knock on the front door hesitantly,
off-and-on for a minute, before I finally check the handle—*unlocked*—and
step inside.

*

If the main foyer at the University of Pittsburgh felt like it was on life
support, the Shippensburg living room feels like a corpse left in a boiling
dumpster for a Florida summer. The room is a square space, a long hallway
stretching tail-like out of the back and leading into parts unknown, a sickly
staircase at the front leading down to a basement and up to the bedrooms.
There's evidence of a strong history here: a glass-encased trophy shelf
(spattered, of course, with something brown), an NKE flag along the back
wall, and several oil-painted portraits of gray-haired alumni. But there's also
evidence of the worst of Rush Season: display boards broken in half and color
photos that had been glued to the foam boards now scattered throughout the
room, sofas standing on-end, burnt or soaked cushions stashed in corners or
in the fireplace.

Industrial-sized trashcans overflow with bottles and cans; cigarette
butts are smashed into the scuffed flooring; muddy footprints lead in every
direction, keg-dragging scrape marks in the hallway. No residents lurking
about, but still I stay quiet.

Despite this lifeless emptiness on the Sunday morning after the first wave
of Rush parties, there *is* life here on Greek Row. It hasn't been awakened yet,
but the house is alive, and it's going to be every bit as antagonistic as it was
for the last consultant. Wouldn't let him sleep in the house? Didn't care about
suspension? That's how it goes at the Ship. "Small school in a dead-end town,"
LaFaber said. "Kids that wind up at the Ship? When they join fraternities and
sororities, forget about leadership development. At best, these are drinking
clubs." At worst? LaFaber told me about one of our SUNY chapters, Rochester
or Buffalo, one of those cold campuses in rusty upstate New York that the
National Headquarters closed several years ago. The fraternities had become
gangs there. The administration forbade wearing Greek letters on any clothing.
And after an altercation at a football game, our NKE chapter "fire-bombed"
another fraternity house with flaming bottles of Everclear. "You've got to be
tough, Charles," LaFaber told me. "Pennsylvania is not Gulf Coast Florida."

147

I follow the scrape marks down the first-floor hallway into the darkness, tip-toeing across the floor with careful steps. "Oh shit," I say, feet clicking and snapping as I enter the remains of a once-industrial kitchen at the end of the hallway. How many NKE Sacred Law infractions can I find here, without meeting even a single undergraduate, that would push our National Alumni Council to revoke this chapter's charter? Have these guys ever looked at, ever *heard of* the Sacred Law of Nu Kappa Epsilon? Keg over there, by the sink ("Law XVI: No chapter shall store kegs on fraternity premises, nor purchase kegs with chapter funds."). Empty bottles of 180-proof Diesel near the trash can, probably the ingredients to a batch of Hunch Punch or Jungle Juice ("Law XVI, Section 3: No chapter shall make available free-flowing sources of alcohol to members or guests. This includes, but is not limited to, mass-packaged beer (cans or bottles), kegs, open bars, and mixed-drink 'punches.'"). All of this during Rush Season, too, doubling-down on the rules infractions ("No chapter shall use alcohol in the recruitment of members."). Could I find drugs, too, if I searched? Criminal activity? And if I found it...what would these guys do to me? If I'd been sent to investigate the fire-bombing at that SUNY campus, what would *those* brothers have done to me?

Above me the ceiling creaks with activity, and I jump. The bedrooms. They're waking up. Tumbling out of beds, tossing sheets to the floor, stumbling to the showers, sliding into board shorts or blue jeans, preparing to clean the crime scene before the Fun Nazi arrives. James Neagle has received my voicemails, sure he has, he just didn't feel like calling back, and now he probably thinks he's got time before I arrive...an Educational Consultant wouldn't dare enter the house without his invitation, after all. That would be breaking and entering, trespassing.

The stairs creak, wooden boards under the stress of sneakers.

Someone coming down...

I should never have stepped inside.

I retrace my steps through the hallway, quietly as I can. Ceiling creaks. In the stairwell, someone says "lunch." Shit, shit. I retrace my steps back to the front door, manage it open gently, walk onto the porch so softly that it feels like I'm floating, down each of the cracked stairs, out to the lawn, turn my back on the house, hope no one is watching me from an upstairs window. Back into the gravel parking lot, back to my Explorer. I picture the first floor now filling with frat stars while I sit in my front seat and stare at the house from a distance.

*

The Fun Nazi card stares back at me from its spot below the speedometer. Sharp corners, crisp type, just like a real business card: someone took great care in constructing this joke.

To the brothers of this chapter, this was just a mindless college party in rural Pennsylvania, but it's a *fraternity* party during *Rush Season*...I'll have to ask questions. Document this. All of the proper forms and the proper signatures. No running away, no hiding in the guest room after the workshop ends. I chose this, all of it. To be the Fun Nazi. To confront the fraternity stereotype.

From the seat of my Explorer, I dial James Neagle once more, and finally someone answers. "Who's this?" Rough big-city voice.

"Charles Washington." Assertive.

"Who?"

"This is Charles Washington. The Educational Consultant."

"The what?"

"From Nu Kappa Epsilon Headquarters. I *am* speaking to James Neagle, correct?"

"Yeah, this is him."

"James," I say, "I left you several messages about my visit. Emails, too."

"Huh? Oh. Must not've gotten them. Haven't checked my email in awhile."

"What about your voicemail?"

"Huh? Should have Facebooked me."

"I don't have Facebook. I'm not a college student."

"Don't have Facebook? What'd you say your name was?"

"Charles *Washington*," I say. "The EC? From the Nike HQ? I'm going to be in town for the next three days. To meet with your advisors and officers, to inspect your house?"

"From Nationals?" James asks. "Whoa. First *I* heard about this."

"James, listen," I say and I want to swear, want to tell him that I know he's bull-shitting, but this is my chance to do everything right, to prove that I *can* do it right. "I'm going to be here until Wednesday," I say. "We need to sit down and make a schedule for my visit. Today."

"Bob," James says, but it's hand-over-the-phone muffled. "Fucking guy from *Nationals* is coming into town. Now."

Another voice, distant: "The fuck *they* want?"

Then, James again, to me: "Are we in trouble or something?"

"No," I say. "No. Every chapter gets a visit from a consultant at least once a year. This is standard. I meet with your officers, help you plan your budget, and...Have you never met with a consultant before? You *are* the president, right?"

"Yeah," James says. "No consultant's ever been to Ship before."

Head pounding.

"We got Rush, man," James says. "We're too busy for a visit or whatever."

Head pounding. "Well. I'm here in your parking lot."

"You're *here*, already?"

"Parked," I say.

"Everyone's asleep. You know...it's fucking *Sun*-day. Day of rest. You can't come in here all unannounced and shit."

"It's noon," I say, check my clock. "It's almost one, actually."

"Yo, what the fuck? Let us clean the place up a little, man."

"I'm..." I say. Head pounding. "I'm walking up to your house right now."

And now I'm ready. I leave my Explorer and walk the same path through the garbage-yard, knock on the door, and when it opens I make myself look surprised at the inside of the house. "Oh, hello," I say when a young man enters the doorframe. He is grogginess personified, a lumbering bear ripped from sweet hibernation, the body of a rugby player and the face of a mangled boxer, cigarette wedged behind his ear; he stands in the doorway for ten seconds or so, staring in the distance without any indication that he has control of his muscles, and he is a billboard—a *billboard*—for our fraternity. Sleeveless blue NKE shirt with letters so large that I could've read them from the parking lot. I can picture him chugging cans of Coors in ten seconds flat, then crunching the can in his palm.

"You the guy from Nationals?" he asks.

"That's me." I extend my hand. "Charles Washington."

He bumbles forward, pulls the front door closed behind him, and accepts my hand in a bone-crushingly powerful handshake. Reminds me, strangely, of Walter LaFaber's grip. He pulls the cigarette from behind his ear, sticks one hand down his black track pants, fishes around, and a moment later retracts his hand and he's holding a lighter. "House is a little messed up right now," the rugby player says.

"Looks like the whole Row is. What happened here last night?"

"Had a couple people over," he says, sucking on his cigarette until the end turns to ember and ash. He blows smoke into the light September breeze.

"Looks like a *lot* of people were here."

"Maybe," he says. "I'm James Neagle, by the way. Chapter president."

"Very nice to meet you."

His eyes seem to regain life and energy with each smoky inhalation, and his zombified glaze is starting to melt; underneath, however, is suspicion and anger. Two types of chapters: *those who get it* and *those who don't*. If this is a drinking club, then our mission of leadership development stands counter to everything that Neagle believes his fraternity should be.

"Got my room cleaned up," he says. "You can stay on my couch."

"Um," I say, "excellent."

"You probably want to look through our house. Don't you?"

"I'll, you know, need to document some things."

"Phhh," he says, blowing smoke everywhere. "Figured."

Neagle stands a full six inches taller than me. His traps are large enough to make him look like he's wearing granite shoulder-pads.

"Lot of guys still sleeping?" I ask.

"Some."

"Well."

"Well."

"I suppose I'm a little hungry right now. Have you had lunch?"

"Naw."

"Are you hungry?"

"Phhh," he says, flicks his cigarette. "I could eat."

"We could take a ride, then. Give your guys a chance to wake up."

150

"I'll drive," he says. "I know a place."

And I stare at the closed door for a moment, wondering why I need lunch and why *I* suggested it and knowing I should be inside the house, but I follow him down the rickety porch steps and slide into the passenger seat of his mud-splashed pickup, and I think, *there's still time.* The pickup gives a healthy cough and a deep *vroom*-ing grumble as he gases it and drives us out of the gravel parking lot. The conversation is one-sided for most of the drive: I ask him how he likes Shippensburg, why he joined the fraternity, why he decided to become president, what's his major and what are his career aspirations, and his answers crackle with disinterest. Quick sentences. Youngest of four children, the first to go to college. Others went into the military. He's a business major, wants to work in Philly. Bank, maybe. Deeper probes—do your parents like the idea of the fraternity? what do they think about you as president?—elicit shrugs.

I imagine his fraternity brothers cleaning the house at this very moment, disposing of evidence while I'm gone. I imagine that LaFaber would've muscled his way into the house, said "We've got a problem," and would've immediately set about recording the damages while Neagle stood watching. I wonder why I couldn't do that.

*

Only two roads in Shippensburg, and their intersection forms the center of town. Along one road is the university, but along the other are little one-and-two-story houses and shops smashed up against one another, white and baby-blue paint peeling from the exteriors. House after house, it's all the same: gift shop, antique store, gift shop, antique store, like the repeating background of an old *Tom & Jerry* cartoon.

Neagle takes me to a downtown restaurant called Little Philly Bagel, and it's one of those order-at-the-counter-and-get-a-number-and-then-a-waitress-comes-to-your-table-and-delivers-your-food sort of places. The kind where I always wonder whether or not to leave a tip. It bothers me because it's impossible to budget; I leave 17% at restaurants, always, and I need to know what I'm supposed to do at a place like this. We sit in silence and wait for the waitress to deliver our lunches. When she comes, it feels as if the bitterness lifts, even if only slightly.

"Your house," I say, "is a real mess."

The waitress places my ham sandwich on the table, smiles.

Neagle makes a clicking noise with his jaw. "Sure is."

"Is that just because it's the start of the semester?"

No response. The waitress slides something deep-fried before him.

"Were there things in your house that would violate rules?"

—and then the waitress is gone. And the bitterness resettles.

"Phhh," he says, as if still blowing smoke. "What rules?"

"*Rules* rules. University rules? IFC rules? City ordinances, laws?"

"Phhh," he says again. "Listen. Thing you got to understand is we don't worry about that. Our house is off-campus. The land is in dispute between city and county, so police don't come by. They don't want the hassle. We're golden: anything goes on the Row."

Satisfied, face chiseled into a case-closed expression, he bites into his fried sandwich and an oozing glob of orange-white sauce splashes onto the wax paper. His mouth is so full, chewing so strenuous, that he looks like a predator, a tiger tearing into a tackled zebra.

"We've got Headquarters rules, you know?" I say. "No matter where you are."

I open my portfolio notebook, show him the Circles of Danger diagram:

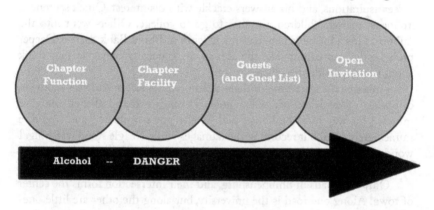

"You're in the most dangerous circle," I say. "You guys could get in a lot of trouble for this stuff. Haven't you read the alcohol policies in our Sacred Laws?"

"Do what you got to," he says. Stares me in the eyes.

I look down, look into my notebook and shuffle through papers. Anything suspicious, report it, LaFaber said. A well-meaning mandate, but LaFaber doesn't have to sleep on the couch in James Neagle's bedroom for three nights, down the hallway from forty alpha males without mercy for guys in shirt and tie, smarmy "Nationals" consultants "out to get them."

"Let's go over the schedule for my visit."

He shrug-nods, continues chewing.

"Did you complete the scheduling worksheet?"

He raises his head, eyes zero in on mine, and it looks like he's got rocks behind his cheeks. Doesn't nod, doesn't swallow, doesn't move. "You mean, you're not here just to count our kegs?"

"The visit schedule was in one of the emails I sent you." I look for an acknowledgment that I spoke, but when he doesn't respond I keep going: "I guess you didn't check it?" No response. "Well. I mean. I've got some workshops that I *need* to facilitate, and some paperwork that's essential." No response. "So I guess the thing is, you know, what's most important is to figure out times," no response, "and sort of find the best time to meet and get these things done and to talk with everyone?"

He swallows. "Don't got a chapter meeting till next Sunday. Till after Rush is over."

"Right. Rush."

"We're busy. This is a bad time for a visit."

"This is my scheduled visit. I can't just leave town."

He swipes a French fry through a patch of collected orange-white sauce. "I'll do what I can for you," he says, and he pops his last bite of fried matter into his mouth.

And I realize that I've been speaking so much that I've barely touched my sandwich; when I attempt to scarf it down in one quick minute, he looks at me as if I'm uncivilized, so I only finish half of it and throw the rest out, pretending I wasn't hungry. And then we're back in his pickup, dented Coke cans and plastic water bottles at my feet, swishing with chewing tobacco spit. When we arrive back at the house, the yard is still garbage and party pollution, but several fraternity brothers lean against the unsure railings of the wrap-around porch, the nearby dumpster overflowing with black trash bags.

"I'll get the schedule together," he says and jerks the gearshift into park.

I ask him if I can maybe take a look around the house, and he steers me to a fire-hydrant-shaped guy on the porch named Chris, who wears plaid golfer shorts and a white polo and has a hat that says simply, "SHIP." Neagle tells me that Christopher here will show me around while the officers are gathered in the chapter library for our meeting. "Show him the sights," Neagle says. "Take care of the big guy," and he slaps me on the back.

*

We wander the muddy lawn, and Chris—shorter than Neagle, but much thicker—tells me how *bad* Teke is, how *dorky* the Kappa Sigs are, how Pi Kapp just got booted from campus, how every sorority just *loves* Nu Kappa Epsilon and this is the best fraternity in the world and they're going to kick ass during Rush. He's looking down Greek Row as he talks, looking at the other houses not as neighbors, but as enemies, and he goes into maniacal blinking spasms every minute or so, laughing non-sensibly. Each fraternity house has a bright two-color banner hanging from its second-floor window, strung up with bungee cords, which says "Rush Kappa Sigma" or "Associate with the BEST!"

"I spray-painted a penis on Fiji's front door last Fall," Chris says. He laughs, blinks rapidly, and as we walk to the back side of the house, he points at the sloping roof of the NKE chapter house and says, "This is balls to the wall, man."

And *holy shit* the *roof!* And suddenly I feel like I'm in a demented carnival funhouse, and he's blinking and laughing and saying, "Gonna get at least twenty pledges this Fall, maybe thirty," and someone has painted the words "Fuck the Bullshit: See *NIKE* City" across the shingles in bright red paint.

Chris laughs, blinks, laughs. "We had the biggest party last night!" he says. "Ha!"

153

And the words on the roof, *Fuck the Bullshit*, each as tall as a basketball player…a rusty red…and I could never have imagined anything like this…

"At *least* twenty pledges," he repeats.

"Is that…" I start. "I mean, shit. Is that *perm*-anent?"

"Oh, it's so fucking tight, yo," he says. "Everybody loves it. It's like those old Rock City barns, you know what I'm saying? See Rock City? Ha! It's throw-back, like, *Mad Men* style."

"I mean, shit," I say. "You do know who I am, right?"

"The guy from Nationals," Chris says.

"Yes."

"We should win some kind of award for Rush this year," he says. Blinks, laughs. "Like, you guys have awards at the conferences every year, right? Most pledges Rushed? That kind of stuff? We should win some of that shit this year."

"Do your alumni know that you've defaced your roof?" I unbutton my shirt's cuffs. Alumni disapprove when pool tables fall to three legs or when bedrooms go into disrepair, but as long as the house is spick 'n span during Fall football season, little bits of destruction are fine. Hell, alumni like Ben Jameson probably *contribute* to the minor destruction. But the house is a representation of the past, present, and future of the fraternity chapter, there for everyone to see: "Fuck the bullshit," the graffiti says.

"Alumni," Chris says. "What do *they* care? Not like they do anything for us."

"They bought the house."

"They never fix anything. Never donate money."

I could lecture him. I could spout off the Top 100 Reasons Why Alumni Don't Donate Money (house irresponsibility topping the list), attempt to do missionary work on Chris, this gruff ball of muscle. Help him *get it*. But he's already pointing to some other features of the house, laughing, flexing his biceps as he points to a few broken posts below the porch.

"Fuck the bullshit," he says to me. "Oh, we're fan-fucking-tastic!"

*

There are three toilets in the upstairs bathroom. One doesn't have a seat. The other two don't have doors. None of the stalls has toilet paper. And where else can I go? A gas station down the road? An antique shop? It occurs to me that I haven't used a bathroom that I would call "my own" in several months, that I never know what to expect, and that I've been holding my breath before opening bathroom doors in fraternity houses because I've been harboring the fear that one will eventually look and feel like the Shippensburg bathroom.

*

Hours later, I'm in the Shippensburg basement for an Executive Board meeting, surrounded by eight pissed-off fraternity officers.

Maybe I didn't expect boardroom professionalism—conference tables and TV/VCR combos and dry erase boards and padded gray chairs and suits and ties and absolute attention when someone speaks—but when Educational

154

Consultants came to visit Edison University, our house was spotless, the books in our chapter library laser-lined on the shelves. Even Pittsburgh attempted an orderly meeting area. But this is what I'm given here: a dark basement that feels like a medieval dungeon, complete with a distant dripping noise, the vents opening into the bedrooms upstairs so that the basement echoes with 50 Cent's "Many Men" over and over again, interspersed with grunts and clanks like someone upstairs is working out with free-weights and this is his *get pumped* song. In the corner is a warped ping-pong table covered and stacked high with yellow and red plastic cups. The smell of urine-soaked burlap hanging over all of this. And the officers all wear board shorts and stained wife-beaters and make such productive comments as, "When is this gonna be over, yo? Told Jess I'd meet her at the pool."

"First," I say and open my portfolio notebook, "a couple housekeeping details that I'm required to go through. No pun intended. About, um, housekeeping?" Blank stares, angry stares. "Okay," I say. "I'm going to pass out the Officer Update Form. I need you all to update your contact info and return it to me by the end of this meeting."

And now they're not even looking at me. Eight officers, staring at the vent, probably wishing they were behind their own stereos, under their own dumbbells.

"Blood in my eye, dog, and I can't see," 50 Cent blares through the vent.

James Neagle, chapter president, makes no attempt to sustain everyone's focus.

"And I'm try'n to be what I'm destined to be," 50 Cent raps.

"Next," I say, speaking louder, "I need to schedule one-on-one meetings with each of you. I've got a list of visit responsibilities while I'm here, items I need to collect and things I need to talk about with every officer."

"And niggas try'n to take my life away," 50 Cent raps.

I stare at the vent, willing it to shut, but there's no chance of that.

"I put a hole in a nigga for fuckin' with me," 50 Cent raps.

I speak even louder, running my finger down a "Chapter Efficiency" checklist on my laptop. "How many active members are currently in your chapter?" and "Does each officer have an operations manual?" and the answers thud like thick, dusty library books dropped on a table. The eight officers have melted into one dark clump, a mass of antagonism, crossed arms and squinted eyes, sighs and shaking heads, as I continue with the questions:

| Does your chapter have a written budget? | No |
|---|---|
| Semester Dues, Per Brother? | $415 |
| Housing Corporation Dues, Per Alumnus? | ? |
| Does your chapter have a savings account? | ? |

And then: "How many new members has your chapter recruited in the past year?"

"Recruited?" one of them asks. Danny is his name. Danny DeKalb. Kid with hair so perfect he doesn't seem to want to mash it down and spoil it with a baseball cap like everyone else. The only blonde in a room full of soot-colored scalps. He's the Vice President of *Recruitment*, but his James-Franco-face is cocked into a sucker-punched scowl. "What do you mean by *recruited*?"

"Recruited," I say. "New members. Like, through Rush."

"Why not say *Rushed*, then?" he asks. "Why this technical word? Makes us sound like we're a business or something, not a fraternity."

"Rush and recruitment," I say, "they're not the same." Minor difference in word choice, but major difference in attitude, I tell them. If we can change the word choice, that's the first step to changing the culture. I tell them that "Rush" is just a week out of the year set aside by the university, advertised to students, and then all of the fraternities and sororities use this *single week* for *new member recruitment*. But at the Headquarters, we found that it's better to say *recruited*, because that way we can understand that recruitment is a year-round responsibility. It's anytime that you're selling your fraternity to non-members. Fraternity recruitment is 24/7/365. We're always selling ourselves, that's the point. Always abiding by recruitment guidelines when speaking to non-members, always beacons of leadership, Marathon Men:

Blank stares from the eight of them.

"Thirty," Danny says. "Fucking shit. Didn't need a dissertation. Thirty pledges."

I nod, exhale, input the number into the worksheet: 30.

"Next question. Do you use alcohol in recruitment?"

And the answer is obvious by the condition of the house. Alcohol? Kegs, hunch punch, jell-o shots, ice slides, jager bombs, frozen margaritas, shotguns, Irish car bombs? Hell, if it's *in*, and it's cheap, and it'll rock the Row, these guys probably did it last night. Shit I've never even heard of.

"That's against the rules," Danny says.

The others nod, their faces aglow with deceit.

I wait a moment, unsure if I should force the subject, unsure how I can do it tactfully and intelligently, but I finally just blurt, "But you had a party last night."

"Rush starts on Wednesday night," Neagle says. "After you leave. Since you wanna get all technical and shit."

"But it was a *recruitment* party. Didn't you just hear what I said? Recruitment is year-round."

"Rush starts on Wednesday," Neagle repeats.

"You had a party. An open party? Free alcohol? To *recruit* new pledges?"

"Can't be a Rush party if it's not during Rush Week," Danny says, shaking his head. "Everybody gets crazy the start of the semester. Whole Row blows up. We drank some beer, had people over. No different than anyone else."

"But it doesn't matter," I say, thinking of all those drunk driving accidents, porch collapses, blood alcohol poisoning, all the ways that fraternity members and their guests have died over the years, have fed the Frat Guy stereotype. I'm thinking of the Sandor lawsuit, those parents who want to sue Nu Kappa Epsilon into oblivion. Head pounding, and I'm thinking of marijuana and ecstacy, beer and GHB, 16-year-old girls in the bedrooms of 25-year-old males, drunks drowning in bathtubs, young men crushed under tumbling dressers. Rush is a full season at universities, and when something goes wrong, *the specific day of week doesn't matter.*

All the workshops and manuals. But it's blank stares because they don't care.

"What the fuck do *you* know, anyway?" Danny says finally.

"I know that you guys are not in good shape, financially," I say, because it's the only thing I can say that won't cause them to erupt. I can't tell them that their house is a disgrace and that they're a disgrace. No. My comment is safe because it's just numbers, inarguable numbers, and no one can deny numbers: "You don't have enough members to afford this house," I say. "Your dues are too low. You're spending more money on Rush than a full semester of pledge dues will generate for your chapter. These numbers don't indicate a very promising future."

"Phhh," Neagle says. "Thanks for the update. You're a real Positive Pat."

*

At night I try to sleep on Neagle's couch; I stare at his empty unmade bed and wait for him to walk upstairs from whatever they're all doing on a Sunday night, down in the main foyer and in the basement. Stereo-speaker bass rattling the cob-webbed vents. Stayed out too late with the alumni last night. Wait, that was *last night*? Need sleep. Can't allow myself to wake up later and later each day.

But I can't sleep. I keep thinking about what might happen if I let my guard down. I keep thinking about those Fun Nazi business cards, the craftsmanship. I imagine a permanent-marker mustache on my face, a fake plastic snake on my chest, my hand submerged in warm water and my pants soaked with urine. I imagine Facebook status updates, too, all of my thoughts squeezed into 160 characters or less: "Charles is…at Shippensburg, and can't sleep."

"Charles…can smell fifty different types of beer soaked into the carpet."

"Charles…would rather be sleeping on the floor."

157

And I'm awake. For hours, it seems. But Neagle's bed remains empty.

The bedroom is hot, dark, full of angry angular shapes.

Before tonight, sleeping accommodations were below expectations, but still manageable. At the University of Kentucky, I stayed with the Alumni Advisor in the former bedroom of his 22-year-old son. Clean bed, clean sheets. At East Tennessee State, the chapter cleared out an unoccupied room for me. Even at Pittsburgh, I received the guest room. At the time, that house felt like a melting house of wax, but now...a fucking *couch*? I'd kill for Pittsburgh again.

The cushions are hard, too. No. Just one is hard: the middle cushion.

Sometime after 2 AM, my eyes adjusted to darkness now, head pounding and still no Neagle, I roll off the couch, kneel beside it, inspect the three cushions. And I knew it. Different patterns! All three cushions have come from different couches! I move the hard cushion to the end, to my feet. Head pounding.

But now the "head" cushion is too soft, and every time I hear any noise in the hallway, my eyes open and I tense up. And something is poking me in the back, and it's probably something they left in the couch, like a fork or something, just to fuck with me, but after awhile I check it out, and it's just a spring: a spring has popped through the cushion fabric. I feel an open wound on my back.

"Charles is...bleeding, and itches."

"Charles...just wants to fucking sleep! Is that really too much to ask?"

Head pounding, and this is tomorrow's schedule:

| Monday | |
|---|---|
| 9 AM | One-on-One w/ House Manager |
| 11 AM | One-on-One w/ Treasurer |
| 12 PM | Lunch w/ Alumnus, Rick Hall |
| 1:30 PM | Workshop |
| 4 PM | One-on-One w/ Historian |
| 5 PM | Dinner at Meal Hall w/ Treasurer |

And I just keep picturing it behind shut eyes, arguing with myself that I have to be ready by 9 AM, not 10 AM, not 8 AM, arguing with myself that I'm remembering the right schedule.

"Charles is...hearing someone having sex down the hall. Really?"

Sometime after 3 AM, head pounding and still no Neagle, and I stare at the cigarette-smelling pillow that Neagle gave me, and it's covered in hair. Short hair. Clipped. Curly. Cat hair, I want to think, but no. Shavings from someone. Head, neck shavings? Chest shavings? Scrotum shavings. I throw the pillow on the floor, use the armrest for my head. Roar because Neagle isn't here, that fucker, and if he was...if he was...

And then I spend the night staring at Neagle's bed, coughing loudly, swearing every now and then, hoping to wake him. But the bed remains empty, I know that. Even when I awake in the morning, more tired than when I'd first slipped under this rough blanket, Neagle isn't there. Empty bed. Empty fucking bed, and my back hurts from the couch.

Anything suspicious, report it, LaFaber said.

And that's it, now. Fun Nazi, it's not so difficult.

Sometime after 11 AM, as I sit in the foyer talking with the Treasurer, Neagle bumbles in through the front door. "Spent the night at my girl's place," he says. "Thought I'd give you some privacy. You sleep well?"

"Hmm?" I ask, and I could waste my energy on being mad at him—you *fucker!* I needed a good fucking night of *sleep*, and you gave me your *couch* when I could have had your *bed*, you lousy *piece of shit!*—but I keep it in check, say, "Oh yeah, fine."

Can a group of frat stars be rehabilitated, transformed into a leadership group? Three weeks ago, I believed I could accomplish the impossible. But now? The only realistic rehabilitation is elimination. Pull the weeds from the garden.

Anything suspicious, report it.

Yes, that's it. Charles is on a mission.

*

I find all the materials I'll need in my Explorer. I keep a plastic snap-shut box on the passenger-side floor, and inside the box I've assembled a file-system for each of the universities I'll visit: manila folders stuffed with membership reports, financial data, chapter histories, disciplinary records, names, addresses, phone numbers, alumni contact info, fraternity house floor plans.

I take the Fun Nazi business card from its spot below the speedometer, tuck it into my shirt pocket. Pull the digital camera and the Housing Damage forms from the "office supplies" case in the back seat, red pen from the center console—and it's the hyperbolic red of the fake blood from the original *Dawn of the Dead*—and I head back inside the house, snap pictures everywhere, waiting until rooms are empty and brothers are in class so I'm not caught. Snap photos of the leaks in the basement, the keg taps in the cupboard, the over-filled dumpster, the unstable porch, bottles of Absinthe in one bedroom, marijuana posters, bongs under beds, anything, everything, more than 250 pictures, until I'm deleting the tame photos to make room for extra pictures of destroyed walls and—*jackpot*—a receipt on Neagle's desk for two kegs.

I fill out all the forms with my red pen. Sign them, date them.

Rush Season, LaFaber said. And yes, here I am, working so quietly that Special Ops would be proud. Forms, forms, forms, until I've got a stack so thick that it bends the paperclip binding it together. This is how I spend my Monday, often retreating into my Explorer, an orderly place where no one will find me, and I sort through the evidence.

At dinner, Neagle sees me walking to my car, shouts from the porch: "Dinner?"

"Got a couple things to finish," I say. And I'm back in the Explorer.

And even though he tells me later in the night that I can take his bed because he's going to sleep at his girl's place, I stay on the stiff couch.

*

Tuesday evening. Lists and lists of infractions. Digital photos of kegs stored in bedrooms, in closets, dirty shirts thrown sloppily over the taps. Bongs beside x-boxes. I've got it all. Written infractions like police reports, on the NKE standardized forms, the letterhead, official, signed, authenticated by the Educational Consultant, the Fun Nazi, *my name* fucking them:

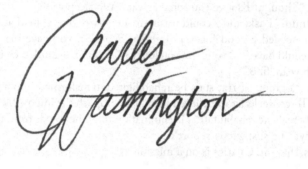

This is a drinking club about to lose its charter. About to get evicted from its house.

Tuesday evening, safe in my Explorer, I dial LaFaber at the National Headquarters, the final minutes of HQ business hours. He answers after one ring, knows it's me from the Caller ID and says, "Charles, it is *great* to hear from you," so quickly that I think he might have been speaking before he even picked up the phone.

"Why is it good to hear from me?" I ask.

"It's always good to hear from you," he says.

"Oh. Well," I say, "thank you?"

"Anytime. What's up?"

"I'm at Shippensburg right now, but you probably already knew that?"

"The reason for my good mood."

"Shippensburg? You said this chapter was worthless."

"It was," LaFaber says. "Until *you* got there."

"What do you mean?"

"You've done a hell of a job in two days, Charles. A hell of a job."

"But I haven't told you what I've done."

"I just spoke with Donald Annbloom, their Housing Corporation President? We're on the verge of some good things out there."

"I don't...know about this," I say.

"Sometimes," LaFaber says in his gritty halftime-speech voice, "when you're on the ground, in the middle of combat, enemy fire all around you, it's difficult to see that you're actually winning the battle. That you're winning the *war*."

"I'm not sure that's the case. I've got to tell you about some of the things I found here. I mean, this chapter is about as bad as it gets."

"Okay, okay," LaFaber says, and I think he sighs. "Don't say this over the phone."

"Why not?"

"Liability, Charles. Did you write any of this information down? The bad stuff?"

"Yes," I say. "*Yes*. I've got photos. I've got descriptions, forms. I've got everything but their charter."

"Hmm," LaFaber says.

"This place is a risk management *night*mare."

"All written down?"

"Yes," I say. Proudly, because I've done it. I've shed those old college clothes, the t-shirts and jeans, stepped one leg at a time into the pressed pants of professionalism. I am *exhausted*, but I did everything I could to fulfill our national mission. To the fucking letter.

"Okay, okay," LaFaber says. "Let me tell you what Donald Annbloom told me. Our conversation. You realize the sacrifices that Housing Corporation has made the last few years?"

"They're in debt. Finances look bad."

"The Housing Corp—it's just five alumni—they still have more than half a million to pay on the mortgage, Charles. This is big-time, you know. And that Ship chapter hasn't had their house filled to capacity in ten years. That Housing Corp has accumulated so much debt...the alumni have sunk their personal finances into that structure."

"They *can* sell the house," I say.

"Charles. You've been staying in that disaster for two days—"

"Three."

"Three days. Do you really think anyone would buy it? Especially in this economy?"

"Maybe. Another fraternity? One without a house."

"That's a dying Greek Community, Charles. Ship has closed five fraternity chapters in the past three years. There's nobody *left* to buy it. And no National Fraternity is going to start a new chapter there. It's not safe. It's a financial sinkhole."

"So are you saying that...Wait, what are you saying?"

"This looks like the first good Rush the chapter has had in ten years," LaFaber says. "Thirty new pledges, they're saying. They can *fill* that house. Their president—this James Neagle—actually set up a payment plan with Annbloom to start chipping away at the debt. That's *your* influence, Charles."

"I found kegs in the house," I say. "Kegs!"

"Yes. That is a serious infraction."

"You should *see* some of the things I've documented. I'll send you the photos."

"Listen, Charles," LaFaber says. "This is great. This work you did is great. I don't want to understate that. But you've got to understand when I say that we can *mold* this chapter. Our business is to *develop* socially responsible leaders, not just cut our ties when things are tough. They're with us. They're on the verge. What we've done is shift their attitude. That's the tough part for a higher-ed professional."

"Kegs," I say. "Their attitude?"

"You haven't sent me any of those photos or documents yet, have you?"

"No."

"I need you to delete them, Charles."

"Delete…you're kidding me."

"We can work with them, Charles. They're with us."

"All the work I did," I say. "Work with *them*?"

Silence from the other end; Walter LaFaber can be as excruciatingly patient as a first-grade teacher, holding his thoughts, thinking or waiting for someone else to speak, but silence makes me uneasy. So much blank space, and I want to fill it. While driving the highway the past few weeks, past open fields extending so far into the distance that they go hazy, I kept picturing some sort of commercial development, progress, in all of that blank space. Right now, it's just grass. Just tree stumps. Certainly something must be better than *blank space*! And so I keep talking, telling LaFaber how I had to sneak around to take pictures, how I had to investigate, spy, and this was such a dangerous operation because *what if they found out?* And we can't just give up now. It's not fair to anyone, not fair to me.

"You have to realize," LaFaber says, so patient, "that this isn't about you."

"I know that."

"This is about something much larger than you."

"I know. It's just that we've got all of this evidence."

Silence again.

"This is about a national organization," LaFaber says. "This is a business. Millions of dollars are on the line, Charles."

"What these guys are doing is *not* good, though. It's dangerous. We're trying to prevent another Sandor lawsuit, right?"

"I appreciate the work you've done, Charles. But I need you to keep something in mind. Nu Kappa Epsilon isn't your run-of-the-mill business, your FedEx or Starbucks."

"I know that," I say. "We're *values*-based."

"Yes. And tell me again where our money comes from?"

"Alumni. Our foundation. Student dues."

"Correct. Our money comes directly from those we are supposed to discipline. When we close our chapters, we shut off our income. We have no money for the programs, the workshops, the consultants, the Headquarters, all that helps us to keep our focus on values and leadership development. We live and die with the students."

162

Silence, and I'm supposed to be understanding and accepting Walter LaFaber's viewpoint, but I fill the blank space by saying, "This just doesn't *feel* right."

"This isn't about you," he says again.

*

Here in Neagle's bedroom on Tuesday night, as I twirl the Fun Nazi card around and around in my hands, I'm surrounded by tacked-up *Maxim* centerfolds and covers. During dinner last night, Neagle told me that *Maxim* just started shipping magazines to the house a few months ago. More subscriptions than there were members in the house. So many magazines. So the guys cut them apart, plastered them to walls. In the bathrooms here at Shippensburg, there are tall stacks of sticky magazines. Wet pages, ink-smeared covers. In Neagle's bedroom, Christina Aguilera receives a full wall. The same photos, over and over again. Christina in a thong. Christina in the pool, with a beach ball.

Fun Nazi card twirling, twirling, corners bent now.

I'm trying to think of Jenn, but I'm afraid to call her. We keep missing one another, and I'm afraid that another phone call will mean another message. Here in Neagle's bedroom, alone, models staring at me from every wall, liquor bottles staring at me from the top shelf of his door-less closet. Neagle's room is the prototype for frat star bedrooms…*Neagle* is the prototype frat star. And now a new generation of frat stars will assimilate into Ship after Rush.

At Edison, the university co-owned the fraternity houses with our alumni donors; we obeyed the rules, feared the reach of the National Headquarters. But there is no reach, is there? Flipping the Fun Nazi card, staring at the typed title, flipping it again, staring at the blank back.

Two doorways down, 50 Cent is playing again. "You can find me in the club," 50 is spitting, lazy-hip, "I'm into havin' sex, I ain't into makin' love—"

And I don't hear barbells this time. Only laughter. Conversation. *There is no reach*, I'm thinking, and I know they're drinking over in that bedroom, clinking Bud Lite bottles, talking about college football and some sorority girl's Facebook photos, and I want to change out of my khakis—in college, I *never* wore khaki pants, how fucking *old* they make you feel—and over there, the song changes from 50 Cent to Miley Cyrus, and she's telling them that there's a Party in the USA, and she's nodding her head like yeah, and they're laughing cause they're listening to Miley Cyrus and why not?, it's funny, and Miley is talking about how the Britney song was on, the Britney song was on, and I'm thinking of the CD in my car, Britney asking me, "Don't you know that you're *toxic*?" and I'm thinking, yeah, if this isn't about *me*, then I don't have to model some strict Code of Conduct, and I'm standing up, stretching, tossing the business card onto my suitcase, creeping to Neagle's bedroom door, entering the hallway—

—but suddenly someone is in the doorway.

—Danny, the Vice President of Recruitment. "Time for our one-on-one meeting, right?" And he's shutting the door halfway, just halfway, and it's the two of us in the bedroom and I can barely hear the music now, and Danny's saying, "I been thinking, you know, and I got a lot of things I want your opinion on. A lot of different ideas for Rush."

And I'm saying, "Yes," and now it's business as usual.

*

Wednesday morning. Late. I haven't talked to any of the brothers this morning because it's pack-up-and-drive time. It's rearrange-my-items-in-my-suitcase time. It's straighten-up-my-Explorer time. Pittsburgh to Kinston. Kinston to Shippensburg. Shippensburg to Saint Joseph's.

I shove my suitcase into the back-hatch of my Explorer, carefully removing stray items and finding new homes for papers and materials that have somehow come loose from their previous positions. Replace several shirts on the backseat rod. And, packed up tight, I drive, making sure to tear out of the Greek Row parking lot, making sure to leave a heavy cloud of dust to coat the parked cars.

"Charles is…excited to get out of this shitty little town. Fuck Shippensburg."

"Charles is…driving to Philadelphia!"

"Charles is…driving, driving, driving."

"Charles is…!!!!!!!!!!!!!!!!!!!"

But sometime around noon, the green Central Pennsylvania countryside slowly morphing into the gray outskirts of big-city urbanization, my cell phone rings. I turn down the stereo volume, diminishing Britney Spears' voice, and I answer the phone without checking Caller ID.

"Charles," says an urgent voice on the other end.

"Walter LaFaber. So good to hear from you again."

"Yes," he says. "Listen, Charles…"

"Good news again, I hope. Good news because it's me?"

"Not quite, this time. Unfortunately. Where are you, Charles?"

"Driving east to Philly."

"You're already on the road?"

"Yeah."

"Get off on the next exit, Charles," he says. "Get off on the next exit and turn right back around, just the way you came."

"What—" I say. "What are you talking about?"

"Emergency. Extreme emergency at the University of Illinois."

"Um," I say. "So?"

"You've got to get to Illinois by tomorrow morning, Charles."

"I'm in Phila-*del*-phia."

"You've got to get to Illinois, Charles," he says again. "You are a *traveling consultant*. This is the job. This is what you live for."

"That's…how far is that? I can't just turn around!"

"You can," LaFaber says. "Nobody plans emergencies, Charles. Nobody plans on a kid going to the hospital for blood alcohol poisoning."

"That's terrible," I say, "but what am I supposed to do about that?"

"That's not all of it. We found a Facebook event page. Open keg party at the Nike fraternity house: six bands, Jell-O shots, water slides, a *Girls Gone Wild* camera crew. This Thursday, the page says. We need you there before this happens. *Need* you. It's rough, I know, but it's something every consultant has to do at some point."

"*You* stumbled across a Facebook page?"

"We're lucky we caught this when we did."

"You're kidding, right? This is all a big fucking joke, right?"

"Charles," he says, voice rigid again. "Show some professionalism."

Drive. Turn around and drive. Shippensburg to Philadelphia, u-turn, Philadelphia to Illinois. To fucking *Illinois*. To Champaign-Urbana, Central Illinois. Approximately 147 miles between Shippensburg and Philadelphia, according to the Yahoo! Maps directions I printed and store in my snap-shut plastic case on my passenger-side floor. One set of directions for each trip, from university to university, chapter house to chapter house: Pittsburgh to Shippensburg, Shippensburg to St. Joseph's, St. Joe's to Delaware? Or is it Marshall? All the way through December at the University of Iowa. But no directions from Philadelphia to Champaign-Urbana. No mileage. No telling how long this drive will take.

Three days at Illinois, an emergency visit.

Rush Season. Anything suspicious, report it.

*Why bother?* I'm thinking, but I set my Explorer to cruise control.

# Emergency Visit

## CHAPTER TWELVE

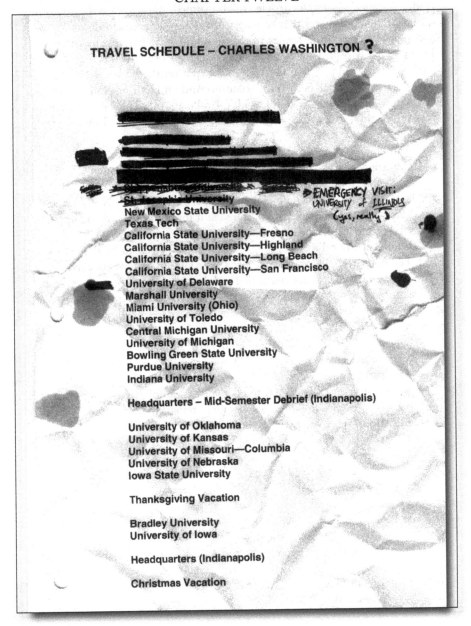

TRAVEL SCHEDULE – CHARLES WASHINGTON **?**

St. Joseph's University
New Mexico State University
Texas Tech
California State University—Fresno
California State University—Highland
California State University—Long Beach
California State University—San Francisco
University of Delaware
Marshall University
Miami University (Ohio)
University of Toledo
Central Michigan University
University of Michigan
Bowling Green State University
Purdue University
Indiana University

Headquarters – Mid-Semester Debrief (Indianapolis)

University of Oklahoma
University of Kansas
University of Missouri—Columbia
University of Nebraska
Iowa State University

Thanksgiving Vacation

Bradley University
University of Iowa

Headquarters (Indianapolis)

Christmas Vacation

▷ EMERGENCY VISIT:
UNIVERSITY of ILLINOIS
(yes, really)

Thursday morning. Early afternoon of my second day of travel toward the University of Illinois. Shaky from caffeine and sugar. Coffee, a sausage biscuit, orange juice, coffee again, Mountain Dew, a glazed donut, all the things I swore I would *not* eat while I traveled. My hands shake on the steering wheel as I drive. Past noon, but a giant styrofoam cup of cold coffee still sits in my cupholder, the liquid muddy brown from powder creamer. One of my goals for this Fall Semester was "No Coffee in Mornings," because I read a *National Geographic* article which claimed that apples wake you up quicker than coffee, and they're more nutritious, but comparing apples to coffee is like comparing apples to oranges: a fucking *apple* while driving? Holding the core in your hand, fingers sticky all over the steering wheel and the stereo volume, waiting for a clear spot on the highway to toss it. No, on the road coffee is the only solution. And on Hour Four of my drive last night, I even drank a couple sodas. Broke another Fall Goal, stopped at McDonald's, ate a 20-piece Chicken McNugget as I drove. Every fucking nugget.

And now I've stopped at another gas station, a 7-Eleven on the outskirts of Champaign-Urbana, home of the university. More soda, a bag of Cheeto's, a prepackaged turkey sandwich with squeeze-on mayonnaise. I sit in my Explorer, chewing, headache growing, and I stare at the Fun Nazi business card stuck below my odometer. I've stared at it for hours, off and on, flipping it around to the blank side sometimes.

I pull out my cell phone, inhale, and I force myself to be patient like LaFaber. Aside from voicemails and texts, Jenn and I have now gone five days without meaningful conversation. I dial and the phone rings three times; I flip the business card to the blank side, and I'm already thinking that she won't answer. Maybe I *should* just hang up, pretend she isn't—

"Hello?" she asks suddenly.

"Jenn," I say. Smooth my pants. "Jenn. Hey."

"Charles," she says.

"How, um, how are you?"

"I'm good, Charles," she says, and her voice is not high-low, not sorority-girl happy. A silence follows our opening remarks, the type I've been encountering so much lately, where both parties in the conversation seem to realize that there is much to be said but where to start, where to start? "Too busy to call me lately?" she asks finally.

"Yeah," I say. "I'm sorry. It's been pretty bad. A lot of phone tag."

"I've been pretty busy, too."

"Oh yeah?"

"It is possible for me to be busy, too, you know."

"Yeah. Of course. I just…you know?"

"A lot of sorority stuff. Senior year stuff. I got nominated for Homecoming Chair, so things have been crazy."

"Oh, cool. I didn't know about that."

"We haven't talked."

168

"Right."

"We're doing Homecoming with Kappa Sigma," she says. "Did I tell you?"

"Kappa Sigma. Good stuff."

"We like those guys," she says. "They came to our house and made us breakfast the other day. We came up with a great idea for the Homecoming float."

"Breakfast."

"Breakfast," she says. "And a rose for every girl."

"Interesting. Breakfast and roses. Real gentlemen, those guys."

"Charles, I hate to do this."

"Do what?"

"Cut us off. But I'm supposed to go to lunch with some of the girls."

"You can't talk for a couple minutes?"

"Things are hectic. Homecoming. You remember. You *are* flying back for the weekend, right?"

"Plane tickets are so expensive," I say.

"You have a job, a salary. You haven't been back here in more than a month."

"This job is non-profit. I can barely afford my car payments."

"You promised you'd come back," she says. "Next weekend. Homecoming is a big deal, Charles. You can get a *weekend* off, for crying out loud. You want me to call your parents, see if they can come into town to see you, too?"

"No. Don't call them. I'll look into the tickets." How else can I give her my NKE letters, clasp the charm around her necklace and confirm once and for all the seriousness with which I've burdened my life? Of course, how can I plan ahead to make it down to Florida when I'm being shuffled around, when I don't know where I'm going on any given weekend? I'll check ticket prices later, when things slow down.

"Okay. They're calling my name," she says. "Text me later."

"I'm almost out of text messages."

"God, you've become a difficult guy to communicate with."

*

I pull out of the gas station, grumble along the interstate toward the university.

Six hours of driving last night before a sharp detour into northern Ohio to find an alumnus who, LaFaber told me, had a guest bedroom where I could stay for the night. LaFaber gave me this guy's number yesterday afternoon, told me there was no need to blow $80 of Headquarters funds on a hotel when he'd found a place I could stay for free. "Life in a non-profit is *never* easy," LaFaber said. "It's a labor of love." So he hooked me up with this alumnus, Paul Bennett, a former Educational Consultant now studying Student Personnel at Toledo. Six hours of driving...plus two more hours to get to Toledo. At one point, I missed an exit, drove twenty minutes out of my way. When I finally realized that I was heading in the wrong direction, I also realized that I couldn't remember the last hour of driving. Not a single second. The last hour of my drive had become a blank.

169

"How's the road treating you?" Bennett kept asking last night while I tried to fall asleep. "What's been your favorite visit? Your favorite school?" And then he asked about the National Fraternity, about any big news, about his alma mater, the University of Kansas, because "I can't get back there as often as I'd like." Eight hours of driving last night and another seven hours of driving this morning.

So much caffeine, my head pounding all the way. Shirts on the hanging rod in my backseat swaying on their plastic hangers, like they could slip off if I hit a bump. Last thing before we left Indianapolis, LaFaber drew this on the dry erase board:

Told us to face the hangers the same way, just like the drawing, and if we placed them the wrong way, they'd twist around and shoot off the hanging rod if we braked too suddenly and then our backseats would be a mess, utter disorder. Even if just two or three hangers slip off, I'll lose count of my shirts and the days on which I wore them (some can be worn twice before washing) and I won't be right, no, and I'm wondering if I placed the hangers in the right direction, even, if I mixed up the drawing in my head, if I'm arranging my life under the wrong system. This Explorer is packed so tight that it's hard to move, hard to breathe.

After seven hours of driving, I arrive in Champaign-Urbana. And I coast through the obligatory "campus town" district, down a road called Green Street; students seem to skip from corner to corner with an in-your-face happiness, as though they know and don't care how grimy I feel from the foreign showers I've been using, how envious I am of their t-shirts and shorts. They sit outside internet cafes at metal tables and they type on wireless laptops. They sit outside the Starbuck's across the road, outside Panera Bread, outside a "Used Books" shop with a heavy black door. They sit in a carefree September happiness, class syllabi still fresh from their professors' copy machines, the spines of their textbooks still un-creased from lack of use, quizzes and midterms and final exams still months away. Oh, they're happy here at Illinois. It's Rush Season, but not just for fraternities; the season is a state of mind, and everyone on this campus is living it, flaunting it, sorority girls walking in packs from Smoothie King or Jimmy John's, wearing cheerleader-skimpy gym shorts with ΠΒΦ or ΚΚΓ across perfectly round asses. Two black kids, one in an Omega tank-top and the other in a stark white undershirt, hop out of a Honda parked at the curb, and they saunter into Subway. Several students rush out of the two-story bookstore on the corner and scurry across busy Green Street, avoiding bicycles and cars, avoiding campus shuttle-buses so large that they're actually *two* buses joined in the center by some accordion-like connector. Blue shirts, orange shirts everywhere, shirts with "CHIEF" or "Fighting Illini" splashed across the front. They're all so satisfied, these kids, that they could be coming from the pool, not from class, that they could be wrapping up their week, but it's only *Thursday*, 3 PM! Yes, Rush Season for everyone at the University of Illinois. Everywhere. Every intersection, every sidewalk. I take another sip of my coffee; it's cold and tastes like dog breath.

The local bars, on the other hand, look worn-out from the early semester. Bartenders stand outside the doors, slapping dirt from filthy mats. In the back of a bar called Legends, a bartender hoses out a trash can, a thick goo bubbling out the bottom. Mid-shift servers and cashiers file into Murphy's, into Brothers, into Zorba's.

I spend ten minutes, fifteen minutes, turning down one-way roads, backtracking, making wrong turns that I can't correct, ending up in places I've been five times already. Head pounding. Shirts swaying on their hangers. I pass fraternity house after fraternity house, sorority houses, left and right, all around me, but they are scattered between classroom buildings and dorms and bus stops and the campus YMCA and the Armory, and there's no central Greek Row so there's no pattern and no way to know exactly how to find the Nu Kappa Epsilon house. Fifteen minutes, *twenty*, but finally I find West Chalmers, another street over-populated with historic fraternity houses: tudor-style mansions under the shade of maple trees, directly next door to limestone castles with every decadent Gothic feature save for gargoyles, "RUSH" banners hanging from nearly every roof. Five fraternity houses in a row on Chalmers, and another seven or eight down Armory Avenue. Shippensburg's Rush Season was dangerous, but at Illinois, a school of 40,000 students where more than 5,000 affiliate with fraternities and sororities—largest Greek community in the country—the possibilities are even scarier.

Moments after I turn onto Chalmers, I find the NKE fraternity house and pull into the parking lot, a tiny dirt pen in the shadow of a magnificent structure that, were it not in a college town, were it not surrounded by similar houses, were it not occupied by 75 fraternity brothers, could be serviceable with some paint touch-ups as a celebrity mansion on *Cribs*.

I have trouble negotiating my Explorer into a parking spot, almost scrape an Oldsmobile. Shirts sway in the backseat, and I can't see out my back window.

The tall, wooden lamp post outside the house is covered in flyers, top to bottom. Fifty or sixty fluorescent-papered flyers stapled to the crackling wood. "Where do YOU want to live?" the flyer asks in large type, a picture of John Belushi in his iconic "COLLEGE" sweater slapped below the text. Then, clear as a court summons, the words: "NKE House, 10:00 PM, Thursday Night. Beer, Beer, Beer, Beer, Jell-O Shots, Beer, Girls, *Girls Gone Wild* Camera Crew. Any questions? Be there."

And this flyer is probably posted all over campus.

This is it. Illinois. An historic chapter with more than 2,000 alumni since 1921, smack-dab in the middle of Big Ten Country. If I can't make a difference here, save *this* ship, I'm just painting over a stain.

171

*

The porch of the Nu Kappa Epsilon chapter house is modest, stretching only the length of one side, but the front door is an intimidating wooden block, the letters "NKE" carved into its surface along with elaborate expressionist white carnations and the date of the chapter's founding. There is an electronic button-pad lock above the door handle...but someone has wedged a rock the size of a football (the words "Go Away!" scrawled in black marker) between the door and the frame, rendering the lock irrelevant. I push open the door, hold my breath, expect the chaos of Shippensburg.

But here at Illinois, after I pass through a small foyer and walk up a half-dozen stairs into the living room, there is...*nothing*. Just an open room, wood-paneled walls and floors that make it feel like a colonial library, but no furniture, no posters, no framed portraits, no stitched NKE banners or flags. Just an empty room, a fireplace and empty mantle and several thick rolls of industrial-strength black sheeting pushed up against the wall like smooth black bails of hay.

The living room is dark and hollow, and I wonder if this is an encouraging development. If this chapter cleared out the room to preserve all furniture from the inevitable damage it would sustain during a house party, I almost admire their forethought. Don't want any freshmen puking on the rugs, after all.

Eventually I locate two stairwells on opposite ends of the room, each shrouded in shadow. I pick a stairwell, my every step leaving deep booming thumps, a pretentious academic sound, the kind of thoughtful clanging I imagine whenever someone says "hallowed halls."

When I descend into the gigantic basement of the fraternity house, the hallway branches off into several clearly labeled rooms: a kitchen, a mess-hall-style cafeteria, and a library. I open the first door, "Chapter Library," hoping I can find someone in all this emptiness, and sitting inside is a clean-complexioned young man in a white polo. He's got messy-stylish frat-star hair, but he's holding three thick library books under his arm, one of which says, *A Critical Approach to the U.S. Tariff.* "You must be Charles Washington," he says, and it's a mild voice, a Rob Lowe or James Spader voice.

"That's me."

"Adam Duke," he says. "Chapter President. I was just about to give you a call, see when you were getting into town."

"Were you?" I ask.

"Please come in. Have a seat."

I follow him into the Chapter Library, a room with its own fireplace. Above the fireplace hangs a golden-framed charter, the original 1921 document preserving the signatures of the chapter's founding members and the edict of the National Fraternity, establishing the group as the "Iota Alpha" chapter of Nu Kappa Epsilon. Everything appears clean and polished; no fingerprints, no stains, no dust, no burn marks. This isn't what I expected from an "emergency visit." Adam Duke is about my size, nothing special, but his voice is calming, not antagonistic; I expected someone who would act like an enemy.

"I wish I had more time to talk to you on a one-on-one basis," I say. "But I've got a strict schedule for the rest of the day. I just got here, and I've already got a meeting in a couple minutes with your campus Greek Advisor. Then a dinner meeting with a bunch of your alumni."

He nods, reassumes his seat in a leather chair behind the desk. Motions for me to sit down on a wooden chair on the desk's opposite side. "Have a seat," he says again. "Please. I've got class in about twenty minutes, anyway. I'm supposed to lead discussion today. But ask me anything you want to know."

"Oh." I scratch the back of my neck. Nobody's ever given me that prompt before. I think I actually *wanted* him to be an asshole, just so I could be an asshole, too. Give my frustration some outlet. "Okay, then," I say. "First thing's first. This freshman…the blood alcohol poisoning thing. This thing is big."

"Josh Martin is his name," Adam says and nods. The confident nod of a scholar on a History Channel special. "Honestly, I don't know how this was inflated into such a big story. It's not a big deal. Josh barely drank anything in the house."

"It was a party, right?" I ask. "He had *something* to drink?"

"No party. Most of our brothers were out on Green Street, actually. Josh Martin is a high school friend of one of our brothers. In town for the football game last weekend. But they both drank so much beforehand that neither wanted to go out. Josh passed out here in the basement sometime after midnight. Actually, we were lucky that someone found him and called 9-1-1. They said he was barely breathing."

"And he's fine, now?"

"Physically, yes," Adam says. "If he hadn't been here at the fraternity house when he passed out, with so many people nearby, he might have died. But still, his parents…can you believe this? They keep calling for an investigation, calling for suspensions, throwing out the word 'lawsuit.' Like *we* gave him all that alcohol. We saved the kid's life."

"I see."

"So that's currently where we stand," Adam says, nods again.

"Okay," I say, head pounding, swaying, but I need to focus. "Then there's the other big problem. This blood alcohol poisoning thing…we can deal with it, since it doesn't really seem, you know, according to what you just said, that you've done anything wrong. But this party. We need…we need to deal with this issue, too."

"Certainly. What would you like to know?"

"This doesn't sound good," I say. "There's so much wrong here."

"Truthfully, I think this is the best decision we've ever made."

"Explain?"

"Things have been rough around here for a few years, ever since the rape accusations. We need something to really get our heads above water."

"Rape," I say. "That doesn't sound good, either."

"No, no, *two years* ago," he says. "When I was a freshman. I don't know all the details because I was just a pledge at the time. Not really privy to the inner workings of the house. But something happened in the basement. Without getting graphic, I'll just say that there were four girls and seven guys, total. All consensual. Next day, though, one of the girls goes to the police, says she didn't want to do it, she was forced, etcetera, etcetera."

"Four girls and seven...what does this have to do with your party?"

"We were a strong chapter then, back when I joined." He's still nodding as he talks, nodding constantly, as if it's all so simple, so cut-and-dry: they had 110 members, he says. Best GPA on campus, intense campus involvement. One of the top houses at Illinois. But with the accusations of rape came the impending threat of lawsuits. Despite the accusing female dropping her case and apologizing, the National Fraternity still arrived on campus and conducted a hasty "Formal Review" of the chapter, expelling all seven of the "offenders" and initiating a rigorous re-organization, suspending fifteen other members who didn't meet some standard or another, and placing the chapter on a year's probation. Frustrated and confused by this odd turn of events, nearly a quarter of the chapter (and almost the entire pledge class) protested these national decisions by relinquishing their pins and moving out of the house.

I let Adam go on for awhile; he makes honest eye contact as he speaks (if this was a job interview, he'd be hired on the spot), but my focus keeps drifting to his styled brown hair and to the history books that rest on the desk before him. To his white polo, which I realize is Burberry, his thick silver watch. Adam Duke is wearing clothing and accessories straight from the front-matter advertisements of *GQ* or *Esquire*. He's 20 years old, probably doesn't have a job, and while I smell of old coffee and McDonalds and have the frumpy look of a DMV or Post Office employee, he has the carefree look of young money, born into a swollen bank account.

"I don't get it," I say finally. "What's the relevance of all of this?"

"The entire year after the accusation," Adam says, "even though the case was dropped, everyone on campus was talking about it. Calling us rapists. And who wants to be associated with that? Guys couldn't even wear their Nike shirts on campus, couldn't bring girls back to the house. If you haven't noticed, there are plenty of empty bedrooms upstairs. Economically speaking, it costs more to maintain this place—internet, meal plan, electric—than the money we generate through rent. Things have fallen apart since those accusations."

"It's been two years."

"Exactly. This year's Rush, this is our last chance. Incoming freshmen don't know about the incident. Campus is starting to forget. If we have a good party, a real blow-out, we'll have a good Rush and things will be normal again. There won't be a cloud over our house."

And this is the same type of thing we used to say back at Edison at the end of every Fall semester, when we had one "blow-out" party at the beach out in Captiva. The final weekend of warm Gulf water before Florida's quick winter blew in. Jugs and jugs of margaritas, coolers crammed with Coronas. "Wasted on the Water," the party was called, and because we kept such a sterling reputation throughout the school year, we figured that we were less likely to get into any serious trouble for this one party we had. This *one* little party, where we usually booked three bands, hired four security guards, and set up a basketball-court-sized tent in the sand. We deserved to cut loose, we thought. This party saves our sanity.

(Just like that cooler of Jungle Juice during Rush. Shh, shh.)

I close my eyes, rub them. Smooth my pants. But I'm still shaking.

"Listen, Adam," I say. "I understand your position. But flyers? A Facebook page? A fifteen-kegger? This breaks so many rules that I don't even know where to begin. I'm tired. I've been driving so much, and I'm…I've got to explain to your Greek Advisor why the university shouldn't take immediate action. You see how this is tough for me?"

"Other houses are having parties. This is nothing out of the ordinary."

"I just…" Close my eyes, rub them. When I open them, the room is blurry, Adam is blurry, swaying, and I'm picturing my Explorer grumbling over rough roads, the shirts in my backseat swaying on their hangers, door handles rattling, bags and suitcases rustling, everything so tight and feeling like it is going to collapse around me. "*Please*, Adam. Just cancel the party." Slipping out of my mouth: "Just *cancel* the thing, all right? This is a *big* offense. Big." And, I'm thinking, do I even have the energy to be the Fun Nazi right now, to document everything like I did at Shippensburg and then have it all mean nothing?

"How big of an offense?" Adam asks.

"Big," I say. "*Big* big," but I don't know. Two days ago, I thought I knew, but now? I only know that I want to sleep, that a company credit card means *shit* when you can't use it for a hotel room, that my head is pounding, that my hands are shaking. "You seem like a nice guy," I say. "Intelligent. Really you do. So I'm not going to lie to you or anything. I'm a straight shooter. I don't beat around the bush. You know what I'm talking about, Adam? Honesty, you know? Honesty's the best thing. What's it do for anyone to be deceptive? To lie to someone? To themselves? You know?"

He nods politely. But he's wearing Burberry. And I don't even know what I just said.

"I'm frustrated, Adam. I'm frustrated with the things I've seen, and I don't have the energy to deal with more of this shit. I want things to work out. I need you to work with me, Adam. You're going to *cancel* this, Adam."

He nods.

I'm silent for a moment, trying to replay my words.

"So they sent you all this way just for our little party?" he asks and smiles mercifully. "You weren't supposed to be at Illinois until late October, right?"

"That's right. That's exactly right."

"We have your visit listed on our semester calendar. We'd planned around it. Even found an alumnus off-campus who has a guest room. For tonight, we just cleared out one of the empty bedrooms and set up an air mattress for you."

"Well," I say, "that's good."

"I do feel bad. Right now, you were supposed to be at—" and he holds up his finger, closes his eyes, gives me the "don't help me out" head shake, and finally says, "Saint Joseph's, right? That's quite the drive you had to make. I apologize for that."

"Yeah," I say. "Quite the drive."

"Where are you headed next?"

"Delaware? No. I don't know. I'm mixed up right now."

Details are swaying, shaking loose.

"This is quite the job you've got," he says. "Driving back and forth. We really don't want to make things difficult for you."

"Thank you. Just do what needs to be done."

"I'll call the Executive Board together. Don't worry. By the time you get back here tonight, we'll have this sorted out."

"Good," I say. "Good, good. I mean, I wish I could stick around here, help you out with this, but I've got to meet with the Greek Advisor. Try to prevent the university from going crazy. You…take care of this, Adam. I'll be back after dinner." And he shakes my hand, actually *shakes* my hand with real feeling and I look into his eyes, these crisp, green eyes, absolutely clear like he's paid good money to ensure they will never go bloodshot, and he heads to his class and leaves me in the library.

I want to feel relieved. Like I've just had a breakthrough moment, like I've made a difference and I've ensured that Adam and Illinois are "with us" and that the party will be canceled. Like I can call LaFaber tonight, and I can call my father and I can say, *look*, look what I did, I just *saved* a chapter and a house and so much money and maybe even some *lives*.

Before I leave the house to meet with the Illinois Greek Advisor, I walk up the stairwell from the basement to the first floor, but I don't stop in the main foyer. I travel another floor and wind up at a hallway lined on both sides with bedroom doors, many of which are closed, posters for the Fighting Illini or Fallout Boy or the Chicago White Sox taped to their surfaces. The first door on this floor, however, remains open, and a small nameplate beside the doorframe indicates that this is the "President's Room." Adam Duke forgot to shut his door before he left. I resist the urge to creep inside and document receipts and illegal paraphernalia as I did at Shippensburg because, if Adam cancels this party, nothing else matters. But I do walk as far as the door, peek around the corner and into the room. The walls are painted in icy blue. A flat-panel HDTV—50 inches, at least—is bolted into the wall like a mounted portrait, tall and thin silver speakers fastened to the wall on either side of the television. At the far end of the room is a frosted glass shelf, held by several platinum brackets, and along the shelf are no less than ten full bottles of liquor: the only brand that I can see from where I stand is Grey Goose. This kid is in college and his bedroom feels like a penthouse.

Down the hallway a door opens, so I hustle back to the stairwell.

*

I stuff myself back into my Explorer, back out from the tight NKE parking lot and pull out onto the pot-holed road, but I'm facing oncoming traffic, driving the wrong way on a one-way street and someone is honking and I turn onto another street the first chance I get. The roads in Champaign-Urbana…I could've walked from Chalmers to Turner Hall—the historic building housing the Office of Greek Affairs—but the Illinois campus map makes the school look so sprawling that it's exhausting, attempting to measure distances in my head, the inches of the map converted to miles to quarter-miles to footsteps to sweat on my forehead and sweat under my arms and a soggy dress shirt and soggy socks and I'm not unpacked so I can't just change clothes when I get back from my meetings, and so I drive. Twist up hills and down hills, past construction, past granite and limestone and crowds of blue-shirted students waiting for shuttle buses to pack them up and shoot them back to their dorms, until I finally find meter parking outside a Panera Bread equidistant from both the NKE house and Turner Hall.

So I drove ten minutes just to spare myself five minutes of walking. And *meter* parking! I'll have no receipt when I fill out my expense report.

When I enter the over-air-conditioned lobby of Turner Hall, an Asian girl in a "Math Nerd" shirt directs me to the elevators. Upstairs, I pop out into another lobby, this one swarming with students in orange, blue, white, "Chief" shirts and "Illinois Basketball" shirts and they all love this school, *love it*, and once again I'm the easily identifiable Fun Nazi—shirt and tie, sweating, scowling.

I follow a sign that says "Greek Life," and soon find myself in another lobby.

"You must be from Nu Kappa Epsilon fraternity," says a pineapple-haired young woman in a pant-suit. She rises from her computer desk with her hand outstretched, smiling with such force that she looks like Jack Nicholson's Joker, and she sounds unbearably energetic, happy, too happy, *orientation* happy. "I'm Sandra Worth," she says, "the Graduate Assistant for Greek Life. You're Charles Washington, correct? The consultant from EU?"

"That's me. How'd you know?"

"You've got the consultant *look*." She giggles in an insider way. She's the model of Student Affairs enthusiasm, this Sandra Worth, likely a 23- or 24-year-old grad student straight from four undergraduate years as an RA or Orientation Leader, now funneled into 60-hour work weeks as a Graduate Assistant in whatever department her College Student Personnel program sees fit. In this case, she works under Dr. Lynn Jacobs, the university Greek Advisor.

"The consultant look?"

"Tired," she says, giggling again like it's something she can't help, hiccups or a coughing fit. "You look tired."

"Thanks," I say. "I try hard for this look."

"Not in a bad way. I've been the Assistant here for the past year and a half, so I've seen a lot of consultants, and I've seen the whole cycle."

"There's a cycle, is there?"

"Oh yes. You start off looking like you're going to conquer the world and then you start looking tired. A couple weeks in bad beds with no sleep. Am I right?"

"Something like that," I say.

"How long are you on the road for?"

"One year."

"You're lucky. Some of the fraternities employ their consultants on two-year contracts. They have junior and senior consultants so that the younger guys have a support network. You don't want to fall back into the trappings of college life, you know?"

"The trappings of college life."

"Yeah," she says, giggles. "We try to put consultants in contact with one another when they're here, just so you have some interaction with other professionals. Or, you know, us grad students can take you out. We like to have fun, too."

All that Sandra says, even the tone of her high, caffeine-pricked voice, reminds me of a girl I knew back at EU, an ADPi named Elizabeth Westfield, and I'd known her all four years of college. In social settings, she seemed to always relate her career progress, telling everyone her grade point average, her completed coursework, her interactions with businesspeople of note. During our senior year at EU, she landed a decent internship and, a couple weeks before graduation, while we celebrated the start of Dead Week at a bar called Gulf Breeze, she told me she'd lined up a job with Coleman-Harris Advertising. "We're too old to even be at this bar," she said, peering around as if someone was watching her, judging her. "It's a college place. We're graduating." I can almost hear a conversation between Elizabeth and Sandra, both of them discussing with disdain the "trappings of college life." But Elizabeth is in a cubicle now, learning the programs her bosses told her will best economize her time; she's learning how to fill in forms, busy work, just as she did when she colored paint-by-numbers in kindergarten, just as *I* did at my internship at Gulf Coast Communications. Sandra probably stays inside on weeknights to watch bad sitcoms, only goes out on Friday and Saturday nights to bars that serve Blue Moon with orange slices and charge too much, to bars that serve thirty different kinds of designer martinis, to bars where balding 35-year-old men in sweat-necked white dress shirts are post-college frat stars.

"Spring will be different for you," she says. "There's a whole new cycle for Spring. But I can't spoil it, you know? The *experience* of consulting is the main reason to do it."

"Yeah, the experience. Did you do it?"

"No," she says. Shakes her head sadly, short blonde hair rustling like there's something living inside. Her pant suit is tight on her skin, but she doesn't look like she minds. "I wanted to," she says. "I really did. It's just...I wanted to go to grad school, not put it off. I figured if I put off grad school, I might never come back. Life's so short, you know? And I just wanted to get on with it, and—"

178

I nod, thinking of our party, Wasted on the Water, the time that I spilled daiquiri all over Jenn and her shoulders were stained red for the rest of the day, and her white bikini top was stained, but we were so drunk that we just laughed and she dumped a daiquiri over my head.

"—and it's absolutely everything I expected," she says. "Wait. Wait a second! Don't you want to know what sorority I'm in?"

Head pounding, and I'm not sure I heard anything she just said.

"Sorry," I say. "What sorority were you in?"

"Don't use the past tense. We're members for life, remember."

"Right. What sorority *are* you in?"

"I'm a Delta Zeta," she says. "From Miami University."

"Oh."

"We were founded there at Miami. Very exciting."

"Oh."

"Miami *University*. In Oxford, Ohio. Not 'The U,' in Florida. I'm sure you were wondering that. Miami University was a school before Florida was even a state. No offense."

"None taken."

"Don't you want to know about your chapter here?"

"I figured that when I talk to Dr. Jacobs, she'd—"

"Quick objective viewpoint on Nu Kappa Epsilon," Sandra says. "I know the chapter president, Adam, because I've communicated with him so much the past week about the alcohol poisoning. You know the details?" I nearly interject, but she doesn't give me a chance. "He's a nice guy, and the brothers are all nice guys. Great GPA. But we have a term in our program, and that's 'All-Star Squad.' You know how some sports franchises will go out and spend money on the best free agents, and they'll have a group of great individual athletes, but the team itself doesn't win? That's Nike! Nice individuals, but not a good team."

"Thank you, Sandra," I say. "I appreciate you telling me that. But I've got a few meetings later this evening, also. Is Dr. Jacobs ready for me?"

"She's meeting with the Dean," she says. "I updated her appointments on Outlook to clear time for your meeting, but you know how it goes? The Dean comes first. It's hard to cut it short when you're eating cobb salad with the woman who controls your job."

"I've got to wait, then?" I say.

"I'll keep you company!" Sandra says and pats a padded chair beside her desk.

I can't tell if she's flirting or if she's just unceasingly cheerful. This is my first extended contact with a college-age girl in several weeks, but I consider briefly how many college guys Jenn talks with everyday, back at EU. How many other fraternity guys.

Sandra asks me what my favorite campus has been. I start to answer, but then she asks me if I've ever been to Indiana University. I start to answer, but then she tells me that MGCA was one of the best weeks of her life. I start to speak, but then she tells me about all of the chapters at Illinois, about how this Greek community is great, the largest in the country. It's tough work to be a fraternity or sorority member here, she says, but it's so rewarding, and I'm thinking that Jenn wouldn't screw around on me, that she's probably just busy, like me. Such an incredible community, Sandra says, and the percentage of the student population in fraternities and sororities is unbelievable. Every now and then, there's a small problem, but the chapters are all so old and established that it only takes a call to the alumni and they stop in and have a come-to-Jesus meeting with the undergrads, and the problem goes away.

Jenn has this way of putting her fingers (just the tips) along the upper portion of your chest as she talks, on every guy's chest, and I never thought about it because I was always around, and it was usually *my* chest.

Sandra is now talking about Miami, about how—at Miami—the sororities don't have houses and one sorority wanted to build a house but the other national sororities *blocked* it because that would hurt *their* recruitment numbers and then *they'd* be forced to build houses also and there's so much *money* at stake. And there's just as much money at stake here at Illinois, she says, much more than at Miami. Million-dollar houses. Millions of dollars in alumni contributions to the university. She talks about how impressive the new Pi Kappa Alpha house is—have I *seen* it?—and she's telling me that we have a great responsibility in higher-ed, that we need to ensure that the organizations don't slip up, and it's *totally under our control*, she says, but I'm not sure anything is under my control and my vision is shaky and I'm picturing the shirts swaying in my backseat again, and I'm picturing myself packed into my Explorer, surrounded by suitcases and snap-shut cases and boxes of supplies and I can't even move my arms or turn the steering wheel or reach the emergency brake, and it's like getting strapped into a rollercoaster and knowing that I'm stuck going wherever this machine wants to take me, up up up, dowwwwwwwnnnn, and I'm thousands of miles from Jenn and I have no control.

"I think..." I say.

Sandra's voice, her giggles...they're somehow inside my head, cutting into my brain...they're behind my eyes, pulling my eyes back into my skull... it feels like my face is puckering into an implosion.

"I think I need to make a phone call," I say, and stand up while she's talking.

*

Outside Turner Hall, I call Jenn.

I stand on the building's concrete steps, a half-block from the long grass expanse of the school's quad where students lay out on towels and fling Frisbees, something I rarely saw back at Edison University. Our students didn't sport long hair or tattoos, our girls didn't wear hemp dresses. There were no protests, and there was no literary magazine, no poetry readings. When we wanted a tan, we went to the pool or the tanning beds, not the campus greens.

180

"How was lunch?" I ask when Jenn answers the phone. I try to sound like I'm interested, but I think my question comes out sounding condescending.

"Fine," she says. "It was just Applebee's."

I try to lighten my tone. "Applebee's sounds good. I had gas station food for lunch."

"That doesn't sound like a very good choice for lunch."

"Ha ha. I wish I *could* choose. But it's hectic out on the road."

"You could have had something else, I'm sure."

"Well, yeah," I say. "I didn't mean, you know, that I definitely couldn't have."

This isn't how I imagined our first conversation in forever would go.

"You look up plane tickets?" she asks. "For Homecoming?"

"I haven't been in front of a computer."

"So...*no*, then?"

"Yes," I say.

"Yes, no? Or yes, yes?"

"Um," I say. "Yes, no?"

"Yes, no, you haven't looked up plane tickets?"

"I just—" I say. "I haven't been in front of a computer, I said."

"You're being difficult on purpose, aren't you?"

"Me? I didn't mean to be. *I'm* being difficult?"

"Homecoming is a week and a half away. You know that." And her voice is low and disaffected, not at all the high-low syllables of her voicemail recording, the intonation of some happier time. Where has the Jenn Outlook gone?

"I know that, I know that," I say. "You told me. Things are just difficult for me."

"You've got a laptop. I don't understand why you can't just book tickets."

"This laptop doesn't have wireless. It's ancient, Jenn, I've told you that. Every time I want to go on the internet, I have to unpack that gigantic fucking ethernet cord and hope to God that there's a place to plug it, and that I don't need some obscure password."

"You could use someone else's computer, right?"

"I'm not at the house. I'm...God, I don't even know where I'm at."

"You're at the University of Illinois," she says.

"I know *that*. I mean, it's all maps and...I don't even know where I'll *be* next week. I have to check my schedule. Like, really."

"I thought you had your schedule memorized. Pittsburgh to Shippensburg, Shippensburg to Saint Joseph's, all that. You should have just put it all on Facebook."

"No longer an option."

"Which is too bad."

"Things have changed," I say. "It's...getting harder to stay organized."

She sighs. "What's the point of having a boyfriend I never get to see?"

"I just—" I say. "Wait, what?"

"Listen, Charles," she says. "I'll, you know, have to call you later tonight. This probably isn't a good time. We're supposed to have an Executive Board meeting in a couple minutes." Someone is laughing in the background. A girl's laugh, light and innocent, but I can't help thinking that it's *me* that this girl is laughing at.

"Sure," I say. "Oh, sure. I understand."

"What?" she says, not to me. "Oh, God."

"Hello?" I say.

"Charles, hold on." And suddenly the phone grows louder with laughter, and Jenn tries to say something else but her voice breaks up a little and she says, "I've got to go, Charles. Why don't you just give me a call tonight, could you? Or tomorrow."

"I wanted to talk now," I say.

"Call me when you get the tickets," she says, and she hangs up without saying goodbye.

Slipping. Things are slipping. We had a way that we always ended phone conversations back at EU, a cute couple words (*not* "I love you," but something just as routine, a little inside joke), and I'm thinking but can't remember, and I'm holding the phone so tightly I'm surprised I'm not cracking the plastic. I run my hands through my hair and shiver violently, like it's cold out but it's still oven-hot.

*

Ten minutes later I'm ushered into Dr. Jacobs' office, past stacked boxes of three-ring binders that spill from her doorway into the hall. Her degrees are posted prominently on the far wall of the office: Bachelor's from Nebraska, Master's from Bowling Green, Doctorate from Penn. But there are other certifications scattered about, mixed with group photos from dozens of conferences, fake smiles, none of it actually hung on any wall, the photos and certificates resting in random spots as if still waiting for someone to pound a nail into the drywall and affix them permanently. Bookshelves wrap around the room, and the reading material all feels predictable—notebooks labeled as ASB Manual or Operations or Conference 1999, and probably ten different books called "Leadership"—but it, too, is stacked haphazardly, as if just unpacked and life is too busy to organize.

Dr. Jacobs is a gaunt woman in her early 50s, with frighteningly jagged black hair and crackling wrinkle lines that make her smile look more like a teeth-gritting gasp. At many schools, I've learned, the Greek Advisor position is seen only as an administrative starting point for new Master's degree holders, with most advisors remaining in this position for only a year or two before rising to something sexier (Assistant Dean, perhaps, or Director of Campus Housing). It's the climbers who are responsible for so many Greek Communities falling into administrative disarray, thus allowing so many "drinking clubs" to grow without the university's knowledge. Dr. Jacobs, I've been warned by LaFaber, has decades of experience in university administration, but was demoted to Greek Advisor for conduct issues. Foul language, comments that sounded threatening, but nothing ever extreme enough for firing. She is not a "climber," but instead a "lander." Perhaps by leaving packed boxes on her floor, she's registering her disappointment with the Greek Affairs position, still holding out hope for a softer landing in a new department.

"Nu Kappa Epsilon," Dr. Jacobs says. "I wish I knew more about your fraternity."

"Nationally?" I ask. "Or here at Illinois?"

"Both," she says and holds up her palms. "We have more than 50 fraternity chapters on campus, Mr. Washington, more than 25 sorority chapters. That's as many groups as most national organizations have across the *country*. By and large, many tend to be complacent, living in the bubble of their houses, sectioned off from the rest of the student body as though their house is just a dorm. *House-Centrism*, I call it."

"Hmm. Well, I've got quite a few meetings today, so—"

"An inability to see beyond the front porch of the individual house." She points her finger into her desk. "And it extends to the community lexis. Students don't say 'fraternity' or 'brotherhood,' here. More often they ask, 'What *house* do you belong to?' The fraternity reduced to real estate, binding the members, holding them hostage, depriving them of opportunity."

"Um," I say. I haven't even sat down yet, but this is standard practice for Greek Advisors and higher-ed administrators: a recited speech detailing their theories. "Can I sit?"

"And this, in turn, breeds a revolving door feel for the Greek Community. When a group huddles into itself, it doesn't feel responsible for others. Last Spring, Sigma Nu couldn't maintain the membership numbers necessary for keeping up with housing costs. So the National Headquarters dissolved the group and agreed to re-start the chapter in four years, once the current members graduate. Standard practice. But what's interesting at Illinois is that nobody notices. It's just another house. Here today, gone tomorrow, back in four years. I've been fine-tuning my article on this theory for two years."

"Sounds like it," I say.

She is silent. Stares into my eyes as if gauging whether I'm worthy to be taken seriously in her field. Maybe I was wrong. Perhaps she loves her role as Greek Advisor. She hasn't unpacked her office, but she's obviously been using her position to further her research.

"And, of course," she says, "you can't ignore the Millennial impact."

"Millennials," I say. "That's the second time I've heard that term in the last week."

"Millennials," she says and gives her teeth-gritting smile. "Start with Strauss and Howe's work on the subject. Seminal, if superficial. And extremely self-congratulatory that they invented the term. Harold Vernon, a man I know personally, has written extensively on the Millennial Generation. Much more rigorous."

"Interesting. But I was wondering if we could talk about the—"

"What we've found about Millennials, kids in college now," she says, "is that they're community-oriented. Nurtured by parents, involved in team sports and after-school programs all their lives. Unlike Baby Boomers or Gen-Xers, both of whom fought against the establishment, Millennials have been brought up to believe they *are* the establishment. Just like the old G.I. Generation who fought World War II. It's a return to conformity, with social activism only acceptable if it's mainstream: an anti-war Facebook group, for instance."

"Listen," I say. "I'm in a bind for time. How does this—"

"House-Centrism," she says. "Two hundred years of tradition in some of these houses. Alumni, money. Each fraternity believes it is the only community that matters, and their behavior becomes arrogant. Those who don't join fraternities are branded outcasts. But on a campus as large as this, that means that we've got *35,000* outcasts! So we've got two groups opposed to one another, all conformist Millennials who believe that *their* way is the *right* way. Really, we could be looking at a destructive backlash against Greek life in the immediate future."

"Well, it's a good thing we've got a noble purpose, then," I say. "We can change the culture. Keep it focused on leadership. But the reason I'm here has nothing to do with a—"

"The Millennials have *no* sense of purpose, that's the real problem." She shakes her head. "The G.I. Generation had a quote-unquote good war, and the space program, and a new information age. They were saving the world. The Baby Boomers were speaking out against Vietnam, against old social constraints. A sexual revolution! Even Generation X was lashing out against the hypocrisy of their parents, the failed idealism of the Baby Boomers. But the Millennials strive toward no true goal. A nationwide recession that in no way resembles the hardships of the Great Depression? A world where kids think they've got it rough if their iPhone is too slow? Ha! They have only a sense of entitlement, a feeling that all the world should be perfect, 'noble' as you say, and their perfect lives should never be disrupted. That, of course, is off-topic: a completely different article I've only just begun to draft."

"Off-topic?" I ask, and suddenly I can no longer even remember why I'm here in this woman's office, what questions I was actually supposed to ask. *Would you consider Nu Kappa Epsilon to be in the top third of chapters on campus?* Why am I here? "Can we," I say, and rub my eyes, "can we talk about Nike?"

She wipes her forehead, bends down to a file cabinet, opens the squeaky-clean door. She's ruffling through a stack of papers inside a manila envelope, all of them heavy cardstock with a blue "I" in the middle of the letterhead. She licks her finger, turns a sheet, scans some sentences, licks her finger, turns another page. Finally says: "Here we are. A houseguest in the hospital for blood alcohol poisoning, advertisements for an open keg party. I know only what I've read, so you can imagine how that colors my perception of the fraternity you represent? The better question is: what can *you* tell me about your fraternity, Mr. Washington?"

"What can I..." I open my portfolio notebook, searching for a response. Shirts swaying, details slipping. "How long have you been Greek Advisor?" I ask.

"Four years," she says, eyes narrowed as though I've challenged her on some key issue of her research.

"And you don't know anything about Nu Kappa Epsilon? They're on your campus, and you don't know anything about this fraternity?"

"Like I said," she says, still scanning papers, "it is very easy to lose yourself in a Greek community so large. While we've compiled ground-breaking research, many of us in these administrative positions simply cannot make the time to get hands-on with the groups. The sheer number of organizations, and the constant student turn-over, all of these things work against us. So we leave the hands-on work to the practitioners in the field, such as yourself. For us, Mr. Washington, these groups remain—" and she tears a sheet from the manila envelope, presents it on her slick desk for me to gaze upon:

| Chapter | GPA - Chapter | GPA - New Members |
|---|---|---|
| Sigma Alpha Mu | 3.394 | 3.291 |
| Delta Tau Delta | 3.390 | 3.010 |
| Alpha Tau Omega | 3.284 | 3.201 |
| Delta Upsilon | 3.275 | 2.998 |

"Numbers," she says. "Numbers and letters on a page."

"But in four years," I say. "*Four* years, you've been here. You know nothing?"

"It is im-*poss*-ible," she says coldly, leans back in her desk chair, and now turns her attention to her computer and scrolls through whatever Internet Explorer window is stretched across her screen, "to meet everyone. If a chapter is unwilling to actively involve itself in the campus community, and is unwilling to take that first step and ask for guidance from Greek Affairs..." She holds up her hands again. "If that is the case, as it is with Nu Kappa Epsilon, we can only do so much."

I've been to five states in three weeks, sleeping on couches. She has them all at her doorstep, and she knows them only by Excel spreadsheets? I rub my eyes, and my head pounds harder. Her neck is so thin, the size of my wrist but covered in loose flesh.

"I can tell you this," she says. "We need to get this situation—this party—worked out as quickly as possible. Illinois does not need an incident to start its semester."

"I agree," I say. "Definitely. We need to do something."

"We need to get this squashed. These parties are the trappings of a bygone era. This is not acceptable in the *Here* and *Now*. We need to get this taken care of, this situation."

"Oh, I agree," I say. The trappings.

"Then call me in the morning. I look forward to an update. Good luck, Mr. Washington."

"Wait, that's it?" But she motions for me to stand and so I do, force my hands in my pockets, stop myself from telling Dr. Jacobs that she's got too much skin for her skeleton, that she needs to leave her office and walk her ass to the NKE house and see how well her theories hold up. I say nothing. Because of all things in my life, I do have control of this party tonight; I can stop it with or without her; I can change the culture. This is it. Illinois. I am a leader.

*

After I leave Turner Hall, I meet up with three alumni at a pizzeria called Garcia's, where one has assured me over the phone that we will find "dee-lish deep dish." But there's a problem with how he speaks, how jovial he sounds. "There are *real* concerns here, and we've got to intervene," I say when we sit down together around a pizza that takes up most of the table...my head pounds, and I drink Diet Coke after Diet Coke instead of devouring the pizza as the three alumni do. I look for fear on their faces, for anger or hope, but these guys—all thirty-somethings in town for the first time in years—talk as if they haven't thought about the fraternity since college. They're more focused on Garcia's, on Champaign-Urbana, on the university, than they are on the party later in the night that could forever alter their fraternity.

"Illinois has a chance to go deep in the tournament," one of them—Ed Huggins—says.

I try to refocus his comment, force the issue. "You'll have nowhere to come back to if the chapter closes."

"I'll be honest," Huggins says. "This group is..." He lifts his hands in the air, shakes them around a little, closes his eyes and makes an I-just-swallowed-piss face. "They're just...*eh*-hh? So-so. I walked around with them during Homecoming last year, and I was embarrassed. It'll be good to close them down. Get rid of that rape reputation. Start from scratch."

"Closure isn't a foregone conclusion," I say. "We need to think about this chapter as if it's still the brotherhood that you were a part of. Present-tense."

"It's a different house," Huggins says. "Different than when I went to school."

"You have to care," I say. "*Have* to."

"Why? What can I do? They're kids. Kids party."

"You don't see what's wrong with this? Flyers? Kegs? The liability?"

"We're losing a ton of money keeping that house open," Huggins says. "I see what's wrong with the Housing Corp's bank account. If they have the party, you'll shut 'em down on the spot, right?"

It becomes difficult to eat, to cut my deep-dish pizza into manageable pieces. Time is running out before the party, and I wasted my afternoon with Greek Affairs and my evening with alumni who have no intention of helping me. As I carry a bite of pizza to my mouth, a chunk of tomato and cheese slips from my fork and lands on my shirt.

"Watch out, buddy!" Huggins says.

186

*

At some point in the evening, my mother called and left me a voicemail. After I spend fifteen minutes in the bathroom dabbing the tomato splotch on my shirt, I check the message.

"Charles," she says. "You aren't calling me back. We haven't talked in weeks. You can't still be upset? This is life, Charles. Don't shut us out." I delete the voicemail.

*

When I get back to the Nu Kappa Epsilon chapter house after dinner, all has gone late-summer dark, a color that warns of a coming cold.

Perhaps a dozen fraternity brothers have gathered on the porch, two of whom stand cross-armed and wearing imposing black "Security" t-shirts, many others arranging fold-out tables into rows, blockades. On one of the tables is a tall cardboard box, inside of which appears to be a stack of neon orange "21 & Up" wrist bands, and beside the box rests a black Sharpie and several folders stuffed with printer paper. From somewhere inside the house comes a drummer's *thump*, then a ba-*dump*, then a *thump*, ba-*dump*-a-*dump*-a-*dump*, then crashing cymbals, then a strum of guitar strings and microphone feedback and someone saying in a deep voice, "Check the levels, man, it's fucking crazy distortion." Nothing has changed; the party will still happen.

"You've got to be kidding," I say, then louder so the brothers on the porch can hear me, "You've got to be *fucking* kidding me!" No one turns to look. Inside, someone is beat-boxing into the microphone, freestyle rapping.

Our spiral-bound "Educational Consultant Resource Guide" says something about this, something about the recommended procedure for handling social events. Different than a run-of-the-mill investigation. Phone call to Headquarters? Or make every attempt to end party, *then* phone call to Headquarters? I remember every word of the "Code of Conduct," Page 12, all of it, from "Model the behavior of the ideal Nu Kappa Epsilon brother, the Marathon Man," to "Safeguard the National Fraternity's good name," to "No dating, drinking, drugs, or digital footprint." I remember these, but I can't picture the proper procedure for stopping this party, which page of the resource guide, how many bullet-points, in which order...where did I even leave the resource guide? I can only picture the hangers in the backseat swaying, clothes slipping off, scattered on my backseat. Explorer bumping, shooting downhill and I can't stop it. Slipping, details, everything. I run my hand through my hair, across the stubble on my chin; my hand still shakes from the caffeine, so I stuff it in my pocket. And there in my pocket, I feel something rectangular with soft corners: the Fun Nazi business card again. At some point, I pulled it from my dashboard and dropped it in my pocket. I flip it over and over before me, staring first at the "Fun Nazi" side, then at the blank back.

There is opportunity here in this moment. A weaker consultant would turn away. So I walk up the steps to the front porch, and I don't know what I have in mind, but I need to do something. I am a leader, a role model.

In the far corner of the porch, beyond the tables and the scurrying brothers, I spot a shiny row of kegs, maybe fifteen in all, grouped together as though just delivered, silver surfaces glistening with condensation. One of the fraternity brothers stands behind them, the handles of a rolling dolly in his grip, and he's looking at all of the kegs with an expression that says, "where do I start?" Someone else points to the door, says, "We need to get five of them into the freezer downstairs. The rest, you can take into the library and the backyard and start icing."

"We need one of them up front," someone says. "For the guys working the table."

"A full keg up front?"

"Why not?"

I walk up the stairs and one of the brothers says to me, "Party's not until 10, bro." He tears open a bag of ice, dumps it into one of the half-trash-cans.

"I need to speak with Adam," I say.

"Oh," the brother says, voice dropping. "You're *that* guy, aren't you?"

And these guys are bigger than I thought they'd be. Bigger than Adam, bigger than me. Thick, defined torsos under Abercrombie polos. Sleeves barely covering their biceps. I don't know why, but perhaps because this is a dying fraternity chapter, I expected them to be smaller. Maybe they'd all be pale suburban kids with freckles and flabby stomachs. Five-six, five-seven. Scared. Insecure. Easy for me to handle. But these guys are tall, built, GNC regulars, the type who wouldn't be caught dead using Cybex machines, only free weights.

"Yes. *That* guy," I say. "That's who I am."

"He's in there somewhere. Just hold your breath in the foyer. They just spray-painted the visqueene."

"Right," I say, but they aren't even paying attention to me anymore.

I stand tall, walk past them and into the house, into a club-dark room where the walls are now covered in black sheeting, and the sheeting is gang-style graffitied with glow-in-the-dark words—"NIKE, BITCHES!" and "Cum on over, baby, Cum on over" and "Make your mom happy, Sleep with a NKE"—and neon pink renderings of the Nike swoosh and slippery red Rolling-Stones-style tongues and it's all glowing under this flickering black light, all around me, and a DJ booth occupies one distant corner like a wasp's nest, some guy in all-black—black sunglasses, black headphones— sorting with flickering insect-fingers through a crate of records, and the black light reveals lint clinging to my pants and detergent stains across the front of my dress shirt, and the tomato stain from the pizzeria seems to stand out even brighter, and someone has spray-painted "YOUR MOM!" in electric yellow and I stumble a moment—all around me—and find the stairwell and it's dark, too, and I keep stumbling, trip down some stairs and then I'm opening a door and I'm walking into some other room, and it's not the basement, it's another open room and I haven't been here before, and the band—four guys in grungy indie-rock clothing, torn jeans and vintage

188

Spaghetti-O's T-shirts—is tuning its instruments and they all see me enter the room and they look at me and the lead singer says, into the microphone, "You need something, bro?" A wave of feedback pierces the room and I shake my head and I see a doorway to the backyard and I lurch past the band and outside.

Out here, out where the sky is darkening, the air should be fresh but instead smells like cigarettes. I spot Adam, wearing a pair of jeans so destructed that I can see the insides of his pockets poking out at his thighs; his hair is even spikier now, his polo replaced by a tight black graphic tee. The sort of shirt Ultimate Fighting fans wear. He stands here in the backyard, supervising two guys as they hammer stakes into the ground, wrap orange construction-site netting from stake to stake and create a compound out of the yard to perhaps give the impression that they are keeping people from entering the party from the back.

This is it. This party is minutes from becoming a reality.

"Don't, please don't," I tell Adam.

"The fuck do you care?" he asks, and the words sound so different. Voice edgy and unsympathetic. This isn't the same Adam.

"You didn't get the Executive Board together?" I ask. "You didn't get this sorted out?"

"Over there, over there," Adam says to one of the brothers, who carries a dirty cinderblock. "We got it sorted out, sure. And it's looking pretty good."

"You never had any intentions of canceling this party, did you?"

Adam reaches into a cooler, picks out an ice cube, clenches it in his closed fist until water seeps out from between his fingers. In his other hand, he holds a full bottle of Goose Island 312. Fifteen kegs, and this kid's bought his own craft-brew six-pack.

Guitar strings from inside the house. Then: "Check, one, two."

"All this time," I say. "I go to your Greek Advisor, to your alumni, try to work through this. All this time, it doesn't matter. You weren't going to cancel this party."

"Yo, yo," someone says over the microphone inside, and it blasts out of the speakers, static-saturated. He sings: "Summer-*tii*-iiime, and the livin's easy."

"You could get arrested," I say. "What if someone dies this time? Not just alcohol poisoning. What if some freshman chugs a bottle of vodka and falls face-first into the toilet?"

"Won't happen," he says.

"You don't know all of the things that could go wrong at an open party. And you're responsible, Adam. *You.* The chapter president. The national fraternity would get sued into oblivion, but *you're* the president and *you're* responsible for the party: you'd get thrown in jail."

He shakes his head. "You have to take chances."

"Chances. What are you talking about? You're such a smart guy."

"Yes. Yes, I am."

I start to say something, a sound.

"Right now, I'm at home," Adam says. "I'm at my fraternity house. Don't you realize that? You people at Nationals keep talking about risk management and circles of danger, all this bullshit. But don't you realize that this is fucking *college?*"

"It's college, but there are real consequences for your actions."

"It's college, and everybody parties," he says. "That's what I meant."

"You said you'd make an effort to stop this."

"I never said that. You said that."

"I just...what are you hoping to accomplish, Adam? Come on."

"A party. A good party. What does it look like?"

"You could lose your house over this, even if nothing goes wrong," I say. Straining, not sure if I believe that. Head pounding. "Headquarters could shut you down."

He shrugs. "You make the rules, not me."

Microphone feedback inside.

"Let's go somewhere to talk about this," I say. "Somewhere else."

"Talk about what?"

"Talk about how to work through this."

"Not interested in that conversation," he says. "We're not canceling the party."

"Just tell me," I say, fingers at my temples, "what you're hoping to get out of this. You could get evicted, thrown in jail. What's the risk/ reward?"

"You went through Rush. Shit, look at you. You only graduated four, five months ago? Without a Rush party, you might as well order pizza and play chess and jerk one another off. This is how it's done. *You* know. I know you know."

"We've got specific rules, though," I say.

He tilts his Goose Island back, chugs, wipes his lips with the back of his hand. "Fuck your rules," he says.

"Fuck *my* rules?"

"Fuck your rules. This house has been absolutely pathetic for the past two years. Who visits the *rapist* house, huh? What have your rules gotten us? More pledges? More girls? You kicked out half our house and left us for dead. This is it for us. I don't want to go through all of college paying the price for what some girl said *before* I was even a brother. This party will keep the house alive, change things."

"Fuck *my* rules?"

"This is it. For us, this is it."

"I don't..." I say, shaking, and I swear it's cold outside now.

Slipping, everything, because I'm thinking about Wasted on the Water, our annual party at EU. Had we been confronted just minutes before the party started (hell, even days or weeks before) and told to pack up, dump out the booze, go to sleep, we would have revolted. It was *our* social event, our chance to unwind and play drunk volleyball and sit in hot tubs with beautiful girls and enjoy our own youthful recklessness...no one could take it away from us.

190

"Nationals has been trying to shut us down for the last two years, anyway," he says. "We're a poor investment on a great campus, they say. We're dead, one way or the other. Have the party, we get shut down. Don't have the party, we have a shitty Rush and don't fill the house and we get shut down. If this house is going to get shut down no matter what, we might as well go crazy, right? We might as well have *one* good night as a fraternity."

Microphone feedback.

"You're not right," I say.

"Then tell me what's right."

"This is about more than you, Adam. This is about *me*, too."

"Unless your house is a hundred grand in debt, I doubt that," he says, tosses his empty beer bottle onto the ground and turns his back on me. "But stick around if you want. You look like you need to unwind. Still have the room upstairs cleared out for you. Air mattress and everything."

*

Minutes later, after stumbling back through the dark house, feedback pounding everywhere, I sit behind the wheel of my Explorer in the NKE house parking lot and I dial LaFaber at his home number. My tie is tight, and I grab and claw at it, making it looser and looser until my entire neck and collar look vampire-mangled.

A group of girls—all of them wearing second-skin white pants and bright tube tops that keep slipping down their breasts, and they keep pulling the tops back up, *slipping down*, pulling up, over and over—walk to the front door of the NKE house, and one of the brothers hands them wrist bands and plastic cups, and the girls giggle and walk inside, all bouncing tits and airbrushed asses and this is it, then. It's started. LaFaber will tell me to be resourceful, no doubt, that this is the challenge that consultants live for, that I should cut the power or block the front door or who knows what?, but this is impossible; this is like trying to witness to a non-believer while he's black-out drunk.

As soon as LaFaber answers his phone, I spill the story of my entire day without pausing for breath. "Charles," he responds. "It's past 10 PM. Where are you right now?"

"In their parking lot," I say. "And shit! Another group of girls just walked in. The party is starting. It's *starting!*"

"Charles. You're still at the house?"

"I should go back inside, try to stop it—"

"You need to get out of there. If they are determined to have this party, we can*not* have you at that house."

"What do you mean? Where do I go?"

"It would be bad news if anything happened at that party, and a national consultant was present. Bad news. You need to get out of there. Get a hotel."

"What, like lawsuits? Like I'd be involved?"

"We don't want it to come to that. You need to get out of there. Get a hotel."

"Where? I don't—"

191

"Wherever," he says and yawns audibly. "Be resourceful."

A hotel? Past 10 PM? "I don't have an internet connection to look…" I start. Ordinarily, I'm only allowed to book hotels on Saturday nights, but now suddenly…"I don't know where the hotels are. I don't know where anything is. I just got here this afternoon!"

"We didn't even have internet when I was a consultant," LaFaber says. "Be resourceful."

"I just…*fuck*."

"Charles."

"Damn it. I'm *stuck* here. What do you want—"

"*Charles*," he says. "Hold yourself together. This is not the time to implode."

"Not the…what?"

"Get a hotel," he says. And usually, I imagine LaFaber at the window of his office, parting his blinds with his fingers and leaning close to the glass, staring out across the country, over thousands of miles of cornfields and highways and high-rises, seeing me and keeping me in line with his serious eyes. Now, though, I imagine him in the bedroom of his condo, sitting at the edge of his bed, eyes like slits, eager to hang up and go back to sleep. "Relax for the rest of the night," he says. "Get some sleep. You're no use to anyone if you're…wound up. I signed the paperwork this evening that effectively closed the Illinois chapter."

"This evening?"

"This evening," he says. "They're finished."

"Then why am I still *here*? Why did I spend all day trying to stop this? Why didn't you tell me?"

"Standard operating procedure, Charles," he says. "You know all about this, I trust. We immediately suspend a chapter whenever we hear of major risk management issues, just to cover our bases. That happened yesterday. Pending investigation, our suspension process allows us to close a chapter within twenty-four hours of the initial suspension, which we did. Strictly a paperwork closure to limit our liability, should there be trouble tonight. It puts the responsibility for any…damages…onto the chapter, and relieves us as much as possible. We can always reinstate Illinois, but from the looks of the situation, what's worth saving? Depending on what happens in that house tonight, we might've just dodged a bullet."

"They're still having the party," I say. "We didn't dodge anything."

"They're no longer part of our fraternity, though. Not anymore."

"What does that mean?"

"They can do whatever they want," LaFaber says. "They aren't part of the National Fraternity anymore. We've cut them loose."

"This seems so quick. Too easy."

"Listen, Charles," LaFaber says. "It's *Illinois*. A big university. We uphold our values, close the chapter, then re-organize later. Standard."

Standard. And I'm thinking of my goals, of the "Healthy Eating" section of my goals. No fried food. No KFC or Hardees. No breakfast buffets. No danishes or cinnamon buns or Krispy Kremes. No elephant ears. So many ways I could get fat, waste money, so many ways. No beer, I wrote in those goals. No hamburgers and no French fries. No milkshakes and no ice cream. No pork rinds or onion rings. Standard, I'm thinking, but *look at me*, I'm already softer and pudgier. I never had control of this chapter, could never change anything even if I operated flawlessly; they've been closed all day and I didn't even know it.

"I have to go," I say. "I have to find somewhere to sleep."

"Great," LaFaber says. "Just get away from that house. Get out of that city, even. Hotels are out by the interstate. The second they find out they've been closed, you *don't* want to be around. Nothing you can say or do will make things right for them."

*

By the time I find a hotel, check in, unpack, and flop into bed, it's past 11 PM. My head is pounding so hard and with such steady rhythm that I find myself taking deep methodical breaths as if I'm jogging. Pounding so hard that my head actually feels like it's shaking. Deep breaths.

I tug my heavy-weight suitcase to the far end of the room, drop it onto the floor, pop the top and swing it open. The opened suitcase looks like some dissected creature from a high school biology lab, a cut-open cross-section of my life, but it looks different than usual, disheveled and scattered. This is a creature dissected by the classroom rebel, and he's stabbed everything with his scalpel, and I don't know what's dirty, what's clean; my boxers are bunched up, wedged between mismatched socks and crumpled shirts, my bottle of vitamins opened and spilled out.

The room is hot. I'm tired, but I want to move. I'm suffocating.

I step outside the hotel, unlock my Explorer, open the center console. On the left side, I keep a package of black pens, a stack of notecards, and a flashlight. Each of these supports the next, fits so snug that removing anything would cause the infrastructure to collapse like a burning house. On the right side of the console, I keep the bound Sacred Laws of Nu Kappa Epsilon, and, under a pair of gloves, a flask filled with Jack Daniels left over from the Senior Send-Off. For an emergency. I remove the flask, lock the car, re-enter my hellishly hot room.

I drink from the flask until my headache subsides, and I'm thinking that I could walk back down to the front desk, talk to the cute girl at the counter in the red Ramada polo and khaki pants, maybe get her number, invite her to the NKE party, why not?, but I can barely remember what she looks like, and I finish the flask and I'm calling Jenn, leaving her a message, and I'm not even sure what I'm saying, but it has something to do with how I need her to be there for me and *where is she* and when I look at the clock, I see that it's midnight, and I'm thinking, *where am I going tomorrow?*, thinking *one stack clean shirts, plastic bottle of vitamins, one stack clean boxer short*s, thinking tube tops and tight white pants, and I flop onto the bed, and I'm tired and my head is pounding again.

193

*

Internet access at the hotel runs $15 a day, and even though it's the middle of the night and I'll be gone in just a few hours, I open my laptop and enter my credit card and head straight to the Facebook home page.

"Charles...hasn't been back to this page in months."

"Charles...wonders what's on the other side of this login page. How has the world changed? Check it out. Just a peek, just a peek. Sign up, Charles. Reactivate yourself."

But I don't. I erase the **cwashington@edisonu.edu** username, the •••••• password, because I've come too far and I won't slip back into the old me, and I simply type "Nu Kappa Epsilon, Rush Party, Illinois" into the search box, because—now that I'm here—I want to find the event page that this chapter created, the event page that alerted the Headquarters to this nightmare and brought me here. Not too tough. It's the first search result listed:

| **event** | **Time** | Thursday Night. Come whenever. |
|-----------|----------|-------------------------------|
| **31** | **Location** | Nu Kappa Epsilon House |
| 3,245 attending | **Created By** | Adam Duke |
| | **More Info** | |

| I'm Attending | Maybe | No |
|---------------|-------|-----|

"Charles...is shocked that it's so blatant."

"Charles...is actually impressed that there are 3,245 RSVPs. That's a hell of a party." And the girls...so many girls attending...picture after picture of young women in short jean skirts, in tight black shorts that end just south of their asses, so many swooping necklines, so many breasts and so much exposed skin that—as I'm scrolling through the attendees—I look back over my shoulder here in the hotel room to make sure no one's watching me.

It's just me and this hideous bedspread, of course, and this laptop, and this event page, and all of these sexy profile pictures, but before I know what I'm doing, I'm clicking onto their profiles and searching whatever half-pornographic pictures these girls have made public for all the world to see.

Snapshots of a 21-year-old female standing/crawling on bartop, t-shirt soaked from spilled tequila. Another photo: her tits perked out like this is part of a portfolio she sent to *Maxim*. Panoramic shot of seven sorority girls in bikinis so tiny, so precariously adjusted over the choice sections of their anatomy, that it seems any movement at all—a single step, a slightly raised arm—might tear the fabric, might rip the whole top free.

"Charles...shouldn't be doing this."

"Charles...is staring directly at Jenn, now."

And yes, at some point, I typed "Jenn Barry" into the search field, and now I'm lurking on *her* profile page, but she's set it to "Private"—viewable only by friends—and I no longer have a Facebook page myself and thus am not her friend and thus can see only her profile pic (Jenn on a beach chair, wearing a pink tank top and a pair of white shorts, sipping a margarita, and you can barely see another arm on the photo's left side, and it's *my* arm because I'm in the next beach chair over, and have I been cropped out of the picture?) and her most basic information ("School: Edison University," "Hometown: Tampa, FL," "Relationship Status: It's Complicated"), and that's all I can view as I scroll through her page as a stranger, and I rub my eyes and close the Facebook page, and "It's Complicated?" Did I just see that? I shut my laptop and look over my shoulder again. Alone. This is what I've become?

Six months ago, I *was* Adam Duke. Senior in the fraternity house. President. In charge, directing a two-hundred-thousand-dollar budget, honored at the Alumni Ball, ready to graduate and assume some important job. "Man on campus," people joked. I wasn't just sitting on a beach chair nearby; *I was in the Facebook photo*, not an empty hotel room drinking Jack Daniels.

Blank side of the business card, all that white space.

And minutes later, I'm back in my Explorer and I'm driving toward the Nu Kappa Epsilon fraternity house, toward the party, ready to do something, who knows what?

*

Erratic, shaky, my driving, and I pass a police car parked at a gas station and I grip the steering wheel harder and try to drive straight but I slip over the center line in the street and have to correct myself. I watch out my rearview mirror, slow down, but the cop doesn't follow.

When I finally arrive at the house, the parking lot is packed, bumper to bumper, and so many kids are standing in the front yard in a winding line from the curb to the porch and the door, that I park around the corner and watch the party from a distance. One of the fraternity brothers—could be Adam, for all I can see—stands atop a keg on the porch and points to someone in the line and shouts and laughs. Another pack of girls, white pants and tube tops, saunters past my Explorer and joins the slow-moving line into the party. From inside the house, the microphone feedback has been replaced by the steady bass-thump of party hip-hop. I can only imagine what's happening in there. Hundreds of students holding plastic cups full of keg beer, guys pressed against girls, strobe lights and smoke in the air, so loud with the combined noise of a thousand conversations and a band and a DJ that you can say anything you want, move anyway you want. My hand is on my door handle, shaking on the door handle.

And suddenly there is a knock on the window of my car, the sound of fingernails or jewelry tapping against glass.

I jump back, nearly bang my head against the ceiling, and there is a girl at my door. Dark hair and makeup so bold that—under the strange glow of the streetlights—her face carries an exotic tone, indigo on bronze. But even with the alien lighting, she is stunning, and she is only two feet away from me, and we are separated only by my window. She wears a bright pink club top, cut so high at the bottom that I can see her flat 19-year-old abs, so sparing at the top that her bra straps are visible under the thin straps that crest her shoulders.

Her fingers still touch the glass and she says something, but I can't hear. "Roll down your window," she mouths.

I realize that I've been pressing back against my center console for five seconds, ten, eyes looking shocked or scared and hand still gripping the handle tightly, so I loosen up, comply.

"Hello," I say when the window is down.

"Hey. What are you doing in there?" she asks.

"I'm just, you know, sitting?"

"Sitting outside? While your party's going on?"

"Sure?"

"Must be a crazy-good time in your car to keep you from the party," she says, and she peers inside, scans the dark interior. I wonder what she sees, if these folders and snap-shut cases and hanging rods disturb her, if they tip her off that I am not whoever she imagines me to be. "No. Definitely doesn't look very fun in here."

"It isn't," I say, and wish I could have said something flirty, the sort of mindless boy-girl banter I was able to spin off without a second's thought back at EU.

"So why are you out here?"

I open my mouth, but I can't stop staring at the bare skin of her shoulders.

"Are you smoking?" she asks with a smile. "Are you about to light up?"

"I don't..." I start, but I don't want to let her down, this girl who approached my Explorer. "Not now. Um. Not yet."

She licks her lips. "Well. Come get me when you do."

"I will. Are you," and I swallow, "are you going to be inside there? In the house?"

"Please," she says. "Free beer."

"Right. Dumb question."

"Your car's pretty full," she says. "Why?"

"I had a long drive. I'm packed up."

"You just got into town? Classes started a week ago."

"Oh, it's...I've been busy."

"You really should unpack. You don't want someone breaking into your car, messing with your stuff."

"No. No, I don't want that."

"You sure there's going to be room for me in there?"

"I'll make room."

"Why don't you come inside *now*, Adam?" she asks. "Fill up at the keg, then we'll come back out later and, you know, take care of business. Light up."

Head pounding, but finally in a good way. Pounds with possibilities: follow this girl, this sorority girl tanning lotion model with the tight body, follow her across the street and up the stairs of the front porch, in full view of the Nikes on the porch. And they'll ask, "Is that the fucking *consultant*?" and I'll laugh and shrug and follow her inside and we'll stand in line for the keg and we'll drink up, and in the hot, close crowd of the packed living room, I'll be pressed up against her and we'll drink, our bodies on top of one another, and later, hell, she could come back with me to my car, come back with me to my hotel.

"Tania!" someone screams from a distance.

"Oh my God!" my girl shrieks, and turns. "I didn't think you were coming!"

"I told him I had to take care of something," says the other girl, ten feet away, five, closing the gap, and now my single girl has become a group of five girls, all dressed to party, and they're all hugging and making shrill noises, greeting one another, and one of them looks at my window and asks, "Who is that?" and my girl says, "That's Adam," and then, "What's he doing in there?" and they all think I'm someone else, and I don't make any noise, and suddenly I just want all of this to go away so that I won't have to explain that I'm not who they think I am, that I am instead some creepy guy in a dark SUV hovering outside the party, and now Tania asks me, "So are you coming inside, creepster? Or you just going to sit out here all night?"

"I have to make a call," I say. "Be inside in a second."

"All right," she says. "Find me."

And they're gone, across the street and into the line without me, up the front porch without me, wrist bands and red cups, disappearing into the strobe lights of the party. One by one, new packs of girls stream into the house, new groups of guys, and I'm still alone, and the way the night continues to move, so quickly, it feels as if the previous five minutes never even happened.

And, I realize after awhile, my hand remains on the door handle. And I stay that way until the long line outside the house dwindles, until the party's energy has been sucked inside, until there are only a few people left on the porch, drinking beer and chatting casually. One of them looks like Adam Duke, could be, and he stares directly at my Explorer with such a concrete-hard expression that he might as well be shaking his head.

I watch the party awhile longer, but eventually I return to the hotel.

*

Sometime after 3 AM, I wake up because I've got to piss. I'm still fully-clothed, my head hurts, and I walk into the bathroom and pee for two full minutes. I think I dreamt about urinals for the past few hours. Urinals and college bars.

As I piss, I'm thinking: *where am I going tomorrow?* And when I come out of the bathroom, I rummage through my papers because my head is mixed up and I forgot what school I'm supposed to be at next after ~~St. Joseph's~~, details slipping, and I discover—*holy shit*—that I'm supposed to be in New Mexico next, in Las Fucking Cruces, and my flight leaves out of Philadelphia on Saturday morning. I booked that flight because I was supposed to be at St. Joseph's, so now I've got to drive all the way back to where I came from, Philadelphia, all twelve hours, and my head still pounds and I'm dizzy and still drunk.

First thing tomorrow morning. Drive.

Illinois to Philadelphia.

Flight out of Philadelphia. Flight to New Mexico.

I'm supposed to pretend that this day never happened?

# Vacation Visit
## CHAPTER THIRTEEN

"Consultants have a tendency to feel broken-down at the halfway point of the semester," LaFaber told us in our summer training as we all sat in the conference room at the National Fraternity Headquarters building. He'd just handed us—Brock, Nick, and me—our travel schedules. "Right now, I know that you're all ready to take on the world, but this can be a rough job. You visit places that aren't exactly tourist destinations."

Nick and Brock pored over their own schedules with curiosity, nodding and pointing to various destinations as if discovering the names for the first time. "The Deep South Territory," Nick read from his sheet. "North and South Carolina, Alabama, Tennessee, Virginia, Florida, Georgia..." Nick had graduated from UCLA with a tan as deep as mine, and so it seemed only natural that he'd be assigned a travel region that included schools where real "winter" remains forever a state away.

"A great territory," LaFaber said. "The Deep South. The fraternity's most historic and influential chapters. Quite the honor."

Brock, a graduate of Central Texas, received the "Gulf Coast Territory," a wide-stretching and amorphous territory including chapters in Mississippi, Texas, Arkansas, and bits and pieces of the Rocky Mountain states. Perfect for a boy built like a tractor. A cowboy consultant for cowboy fraternity chapters.

"The Great Midwest," I read from my own sheet, confused. "New Jersey, New York, Pennsylvania? That doesn't sound like the Midwest."

"A geographically misleading title, certainly," LaFaber said, "but it's the most challenging territory, without a doubt. States where fraternity life hangs by a thread. Some tough schools, tough chapters. I thought you'd want a challenge, Charles."

"Oh. Definitely, definitely," I said.

Of course, this was the moment when I should have realized I'd never be able to drive home to Florida on weekends, and any promises I'd made to Jenn would go unfulfilled. Maybe I could have been realistic, and that night called her and told her that I'd work something out for Thanksgiving, but a quick jaunt from Delaware to Florida was not in the cards. But I'd written my goals, and I wasn't about to abandon any of them to something so silly as reality.

"Each of you will also notice that we've given you *vacation visits*," LaFaber told the three of us as we ran our fingers down our travel schedules, coming inevitably to a series of California or Washington or Arizona colleges. "Costs way too much to have you *drive* all the way out to the West Coast. The gas, the hotels, the man-hours spent driving cross-country, back and forth. That's pure fantasy when you're working for a non-profit, gentlemen."

"So," Brock said, squinting at his paper, "you divide the West Coast between us?"

"Correct. We want you to get a breather," LaFaber said. "Enjoy the sunshine. Enjoy traveling by air, leaving the highways behind for a couple weeks, accumulating frequent flyer miles. Vacation visits. Perk of the job."

So the National Headquarters books flights to Los Angeles or Phoenix or Seattle, and when we arrive, the chapter brothers drive us around for the duration of our visit. Stress-free, he said, but we'll have no cars. No rentals. Our lives in the hands of fraternity boys to whom we have not yet even been introduced.

*

Late Friday afternoon and I'm standing on the side of the highway waiting for AAA. Sun high over the horizon. Ninety degrees, no shade. Been parked here along I-70, somewhere south of Pittsburgh, for hours. Behind schedule to make it back to Philadelphia by tomorrow morning for my cross-country "vacation visit" flight, my front tire a gashed rubber mess torn apart by a deep pothole several hundred feet back.

A semi-truck roars past me on the interstate, eighty miles per hour, its windy wake rattling my parked Explorer on the road's gravel shoulder. Each passing semi (and there have been hundreds so far) feels deadlier than the last, faster, closer, each rumbling along so effortlessly to its destination...

Earlier today, I left Illinois in a hung-over haze: the Midwestern landscape rolled with anonymous hills, receded to jagged strip-mining, then became green and lush again; mile after mile, landscape shrinking, growing, rising, falling, flooding, emptying, melting, as though I was watching millions of years of Earth-change in minutes, hours. Making good time, ready to forget the past week, thinking I could stop soon for lunch. Then—

Potholes. Until today, they'd been nothing more than a minor frustration, weather-induced stretch marks on the smooth paved skin of Indiana and Ohio. But as I entered Western Pennsylvania two hours ago, a series of ever-sharper and deeper cuts opened in the highway, and suddenly the car in front of me switched lanes, and there—before me—coming at me quickly, unavoidably—no chance to switch lanes—a dark hole in the pavement, and my first thought was that all of those images I've been picturing—stuffed in my Explorer, topping a hill, speeding downward toward something black and unknown—had come true. Front tire fell first, fell hard like a ballet dancer misjudging her steps and tumbling into the orchestra pit. Then the back tire, a crunching metal noise, Explorer tilting. Steering wheel slipping from my hands, assuming control of itself, and I swerved into the center lane, then into the shoulder, where my lopsided SUV finally slowed, kicking up dust and gravel as it came to a rest.

It took me a moment to realize what had happened. Adrenaline was animating my every tired muscle, but still I couldn't move because I didn't know where to start. Hanging rod in my backseat had come loose, sending shirts and pants into the shadowy corners of my floor; Atlas and CD case had disappeared from the seat, bags and suitcases rearranged throughout my car, under or on top of one another. Smoke rising from the front of the car, from the back, a combination of hot rubber and disturbed dust, and I worried what else might have happened in that dark pit. Severe damage to the undercarriage of my car, some one-in-a-million gas tank puncture? It took me five minutes to finally open my car door...clumsily, head pounding...I stayed close to my car, shivering or flinching each time a semi passed.

A little over five hours of driving left to Philadelphia for tomorrow morning's flight, and I'd been hoping for a hotel room tonight. Just outside Philly. A place to stretch, to sleep, to beat this headache before I hop on a plane and fly across the country.

And now another semi passes, its accompanying wind gust shaking me so vigorously that I wonder if any of these drivers are coming *closer* just to scare me.

Philadelphia to Champaign-Urbana. Champaign-Urbana to...here, somewhere in southwestern Pennsylvania, some grassy spot without mile markers, no distinguishing landmarks that I could list for the AAA call center. "Might take longer than usual," dispatch told me when I called. "Are you in a safe place?"

"I'm fine," I said, but that was a mistake which put me at the bottom of his list.

But there—out in the distance—a single willow tree far out in the valley, a pack of cows huddling together under the only shade for miles in this hot September field. So I called back AAA and told the dispatch operator that *yes*, there is a landmark here. There is. A single tree and a group of cows. She sighed, told me she'll make a note of it.

I thought about calling LaFaber, too, but what would he say? Maybe he'd tell me that the National Headquarters still believes in me, that they'll pay for any damages to my vehicle, that they can change the time of the flight? No. He'd tell me to "tough it out," to get to Philadelphia by any means necessary. That he's disappointed in my driving, that I sound hung-over (I brushed my teeth twice this morning at the hotel and still my mouth tastes like Jack Daniels; I stopped for gas station coffee and a package of powdered donuts, but the alcohol aftertaste still festers). LaFaber would know this, can stare out his window and see my hangover. Maybe he even saw me lurking on Facebook last night, lurking outside the NKE house.

I think about straightening the mess in my car, but I still don't know where to start.

*

There is something else, too. Something else I did this morning. When I pulled out of the hotel's parking lot, I made a wrong turn but didn't realize where I was headed until I was almost there: the Nu Kappa Epsilon house. Yes. It was 7:00 AM when I parked at the same curb where I'd watched the party from afar last night. A lingering morning mist wrapped around the wet exterior like a moth-eaten shawl; and the Pepto-colored sunrise made the house feel sickly, as if it was ready to puke all the empty kegs and cups and snoring frat stars out that heavy oak door.

And I don't know why I did it, either. I don't know why I left my car and walked the front porch, shoes crunching over wrist bands and flyers. I don't know why I walked through the open front door and into that humid foyer, that dark, visqueene-covered living room. Who was I hoping to find? There was indeed a couch in the living room now, and there were two young men sleeping on that couch, but I didn't wake them...I headed for the stairwell instead, for the basement, for the library, and I pulled the fraternity's original 1921 charter from the wall, and walked back the way I came...up the stairs, out the front door, back to my car.

The charter is wedged in my back seat now, the glass splintered from the impact of the pothole, and still I have no idea why I needed to take it. But I did. I have it.

*

Charles Washington...never learned how to change a tire. Is this strange?

Charles Washington is...checking the pressure on his other tire, and it's dropping.

Charles Washington is...noticing that his WHEELS are also dented and mangled!

Charles Washington is...wearing a clean dress shirt and a pair of khakis, and wants to change clothes PRONTO. Too fucking hot. Is it unprofessional to change clothes in front of all these passing vehicles?

Charles Washington...wishes someone would have taught him how to do this.

Charles Washington is...pissing on the side of a highway for the first time EVER.

Charles Washington is...still waiting for that tow truck.

At 8 AM tomorrow, I board a flight to El Paso. Then: three weeks without my Explorer, plane-and-school-hopping on my "vacation visits" as I fly to El Paso (en route to New Mexico State University in nearby Las Cruces), then Lubbock (Texas Tech), then Fresno and Highland and Long Beach, then finally San Francisco before my final flight back to Philadelphia to reclaim my Explorer, which I will then drive to the University of Delaware.

At some point I call Nick, who is somewhere in South Carolina right now, likely nearing the "vacation visit" portion of his schedule also. We've been labeled, the two of us, as mirror images. Same height (just a hair under six feet tall), same weight and build, same brown hair and smooth faces and coastal complexions. Same face, different ends of the country. But while I've tried since taking this job to dress in pressed slacks and crisp button-downs, Nick dresses in short-sleeved shirts left untucked, slip-on Steve Madden shoes without laces; he styles his hair with greater flair; all summer, during our training, he'd wake up later in the mornings (slapping the snooze button for 45 minutes), would go out to bars on Tuesday or Wednesday nights when we had to be in the office by 9 AM the next morning. I withheld my comments about how he shouldn't still behave like a college student, particularly because Nick and Brock were my only two friends during this past summer in Indianapolis. Twin brothers in appearance, Nick and me, but we're nothing alike: I have a long-term girlfriend in Florida, and Nick is gay, single, cares only about the moment. Even bragged after our first week on the road that he'd hooked up with a consultant from Sigma Alpha Epsilon at the University of Georgia, that he'd spent the night in the SAE guest room and *ooh boy*, can you imagine what some of those Deep-South Bubbas would do if they found out about that? *You should probably keep that to yourself*, I told him. *Forget about the Bubbas. What would* LaFaber *think?*

Still, we three consultants understand one another. Changing the culture together.

"Broke down in Pennsylvania?" Nick asks after I explain my situation. "Sounds like a bad Lifetime movie about drug addiction."

"Ha, right," I say.

"I got stuck in some mud a week ago. If that's any consolation."

"I guess," I say. And then there is silence. "Nick, have you had any… situations yet?"

"Situations?"

"Alcohol infractions? That sort of thing?"

"Shit, no," he says and I can picture him surprised at the question, glaring at the phone as if it's just farted. "These South Carolina chapters, they're pretty chill."

"No kegs? No parties?"

"A little of that, nothing major," he says. "But I told myself from the start that I wasn't going to be a Fun Nazi. I wasn't going to take this more seriously than it is."

"Yeah," I say. "You're definitely living it up, aren't you?"

"I heard you ran into some problems at Illinois. An emergency visit?"

"Pretty intense, yeah."

"You're out of there now?" Nick asks, voice—as always—interested but never fazed. "That's the great part about this job. No matter what the problem is, it never lasts longer than three days. You're there, you're gone. Boom. Clean slate."

"Exactly," I say, but is that really the way of it? My head still hurts, my eye twitches, one of my dress shirts is ruined by pizza stain. I have a cut in my back, stiffness in my joints from the Shippensburg couch. My suitcase is slimy from fraternity house floors. And my Explorer might be fucked. Everywhere I've been, all of these places are following me.

"Take a nap or something," Nick says. "Read a book."

"I wish."

"Don't wish. Just do it. Relax."

"I'll try," I say, but I'm inspecting each car that materializes on the horizon, checking to see if it could be AAA.

*

The tow truck arrives after 8:00 PM, and the muddy driver-side door opens to reveal a wiry man with a rusty moustache and reddish facial growth that creeps invasively across his cheeks. Arms so hairy that I can't tell if the skin underneath is freckled or just dirty. He shakes my hand, but greets my situation and personal appearance with disinterest. "Florida," he gurgles, spits, when he looks at my license. "Ya'll better watch out on these Pennsylvania highways. Weather damage on the pavement, and all that."

"Nobody fixes the potholes?"

He shrugs. "Sometimes. If someone actually hits one and complains."

"That's what it takes? That thing was huge."

"No blame or nothing. People just get used to the holes out here."

"You've got to be kidding me."

"Well. Let's take a look at the tires," he says, and he shuffles to the front tire. The verdict, he tells me after careful examination, after he rubs his oil-darkened fingers over his hairy chin, is that not only is my front tire destroyed and my back tire severely damaged (still driveable, he assures me, but...*whoo*, he says...I'm going to want to get it looked at, quick), but both wheels are also damaged. Even with new tires, he says, the sharp, stray metal from the dented wheel could puncture my tires at any moment. Looks like a fork with two of the prongs bent in the wrong direction.

"I can change your front tire," he says, "but I might scrape up the spare as I'm doing it."

"It's just a rim, right? Can't you just, like, replace the rims real quick?"

"Rim's part of the wheel, just the outer edge. It's not as easy as changing a hubcap."

"How long does a spare hold together?"

"One of them little donuts? Couple hundred miles."

"I've got to get all the way to Philadelphia," I say.

"*Whoo*," he says. "Philly. Can't say that's a smart idea, what with them wheels all fucked up. You'd be looking for trouble, you do that."

"I've got a flight."

He shakes his head. "I'll change the tire. But I'm telling you this, man," he says. "Them donuts are quick to burn out. You don't want to drive on it for more than an hour at a time. Heat it up too much, and your spare'll be toast."

My Explorer—my office—my bedroom—my entire life in that vehicle... And I'm only able to stretch my salary to cover car payments and insurance and food and student loans. I can't cover the cost of repairs, even just the deductible.

"Does insurance usually cover something like this?" I ask.

"Depends. Everyone's insurance is different."

"Well, should I call highway patrol? Fill out a report?"

"Naw," he says. "That pothole don't have insurance. Ain't gonna sue you."

"Right," I say. "Wait, what?"

"I'd just take yourself up to Bethel. Get new wheels and new tires. They'll

204

have to put a special order in, you know. Might take awhile, but…this ain't safe, what you got."

But there's no doubt in my mind as the tow truck driver talks, no doubt. My plane leaves early in the morning, and I'm not leaving my car anywhere except the Philadelphia International Airport parking lot. What are the chances that a mechanic's shop would even remain open on a Friday night? So I watch the driver shake his head one more time, then climb back into his clanking truck, and I wait until he's pulled back onto the highway and he's out of sight, and then I drive in the slow lane, my spare tire heating beneath me, catching tiny potholes and bumps in the road and every one of them feels greatly magnified with this weak tire. I turn my radio louder to drown out the high-pitched squealing sounds made by the spare, try not to think long-term right now, only short-term. Airport, I think. Airport. The national fraternity's "DO IT!" time management program suggests that life is a checkerboard of short and long-term goals, that a successful leader must integrate both. I'm picturing the diagram in *The Marathon* pledge book, where white is long-term and gray is short-term:

| Marriage | Practice for Intramurals | Children | Study for Test |
|---|---|---|---|
| History Paper | Career | Jog | House |
| MBA | Date on Friday | Health | Cash Check |

But I've discarded or abandoned so many of my goals, and so much has gone wrong, and it feels like I've painted over all of it and have a new checkerboard that looks nothing like the original:

| Jenn? | Get to Airport | Health? | Don't hit another pothole |
|---|---|---|---|
| Find Mechanic | Career? | Buy new tires, wheels | Goals? |
| My Expolorer is FUCKED | Paycheck won't cover this | None of this is working. | Spare is overheating, pull over |

*

The drive to Philadelphia should take only five hours, but it's so bumpy that I'm haunted with visions of my spare tire melting and spinning apart and so I stop every thirty minutes or so. Let it cool. I stop at a Denny's along the interstate, order a fried chicken sandwich because my head still pounds. Greasy fried chicken with greasy French fries and a small tub of ranch dressing. I sit alone in a booth, still dressed in shirt and tie, and I think my waitress feels sorry for me. Later, I stop at a Super Wal-Mart and wander the aisles and end up in the pharmaceutical section, scanning all the different pain relievers: aspirin, non-aspirin, acetaminophen, ibuprofen, chewable tablets, gel capsules, 24-hour relief, instant relief.

I stop at a rest area, find it difficult to simply sit at a dark picnic table making random phone calls to friends who don't answer, and so I stop at another Super Wal-Mart because it's the only store open so late, here in the middle of Nowhere, Pennsylvania.

\*

I sleep for four hours in a smoky Sleep Inn, knowing I've wasted money from my slim hotel account, knowing I don't have time to unpack and relax and take anything more than a quick shower, knowing I don't even have time to shave and iron a new dress shirt...so I wear the same khaki pants and a wrinkled NKE polo when I leave the hotel at 5 AM.

Early Saturday morning, I drive the remaining hour into Philadelphia, the countryside finally crackling into industry and urbanization, cement and steel and glass, blinking intersection lights and car exhaust, thousands upon thousands of cigarette butts tossed from open windows and collecting alongside the curbs, discarded newspaper pages caught in the sweep of wind and fluttering across the highways. Finally I arrive in Philadelphia, at the airport's long-term parking.

When I find a parking space, though, I don't want to leave my Explorer.

For three weeks, my damaged car will sit in this lonely spot here at Philadelphia International, naked to thunderstorms and heavy wind gusts, splotches of mud spun from truck tires; children will bump my hood; neighboring car doors will open too far and too quickly, scratching and gashing my paint. My tire will leak, go flat.

My Explorer is packed so tight that sometimes I can feel the engine straining to start; I can feel the slow acceleration, everything sliding on the seats when I brake, my blood-red suitcase knocking gently into my back door or catching in the carpet. I know all the sounds. And after three weeks of nonstop travel, I don't want to leave it behind. It shouldn't be this way, that my only functional relationship is with my car, but somehow that's where I am.

I gather what I need for the next three weeks. Suitcase, garment bag, laptop case.

Three bags: one over my shoulder, one in each hand. That's all.

The Fun Nazi business card is wedged into the space below my odometer.

Three weeks, I'm thinking, and I could bring it along, pull it out during the inevitable late-night moments when the houses are all screams and club music and sticky liquor residue on my guest-room pillow, and the card can remind me of my purpose, whip me into shape, send me back out to the living room to stop the—

But I flip the card over, look into all that white space, and leave it.

# Insiders In, Outsiders Out

CHAPTER FOURTEEN

At the National Airlines ticket counter just inside Philadelphia International, the e-ticket terminal spits out my credit card without reading it. "Insert a VALID credit card," it says, the word "valid" capitalized and flashing like I wouldn't have noticed it otherwise. I re-insert the NKE company credit card and the terminal spits it out once again, repeats the same message.

Wipe my neck and forehead and try to smile for the long line of travelers switching back and forth behind me, and they all stare impatiently, like I'm the guy at McDonalds who's never seen the menu and can't decide between a regular cheeseburger and a Quarter-Pounder. I look around for someone at the nearby ticket counter, smile again, expect some burly Pennsylvania security guard to grab me by the neck and grumble into my ear, "Back of the line, buddy," in the same voice he'd use if I was just some punk fucking with the machine. When I re-insert the credit card, the message changes: "Your credit card cannot be read. Please see a Ticket Agent." I fumble through my wallet, searching for my debit card instead, and I find it and jam it into the machine but the message won't disappear, just jeers back at me like I've committed a crime. "Fuck," I say. "Fuck fuck fuck." Then realize I've sworn aloud. Around this crowd, businessmen, families, and I'm wearing this NKE polo, this billboard.

"Sir," I hear from somewhere distant, and behind the ticket counter someone has materialized. Brown-haired woman in her 40s, tired eyes like she's seen it all and has no time for this shit. "Sir, you need to come here," she says, voice burdened by decades of two-pack-a-day cigarette addiction. "We'll need to input your information manually." She motions with one old-beyond-its-years hand, then smoothes her frizzy hair back into her ponytail.

I lug my suitcase, my garment bag, my carry-on laptop case to the counter.

Sixteen weeks, I'm thinking. Philadelphia to New Mexico State. New Mexico State to Texas Tech. To Fresno State.

"Sorry," I say. "Airport travel isn't really my thing. I mostly drive everywhere."

"Name," she says. "ID?"

"I mean, I travel a *lot*, you know? For my company. Just not on planes."

"*Name*. ID."

"Washington." Hand her my license. "Sorry."

"Flight number," she says. Then: "Number of bags you'll be checking today?" Then: "Siiiiighhhhhh." She hands me my tickets, fastens stickers around the handles of my luggage, points to the security line fifty feet away.

Then it hits me: she didn't comment on my Florida driver's license. For the first time in over a month, someone was uninterested in the distance I've traveled. I could tell her that I've traveled from Fort Myers, Florida, to Indianapolis, to Kentucky, to East Tennessee, to the mountains of Virginia, to the big cities of Pennsylvania, to the heart of Illinois and back again, and now I'm headed out West...but surrounded by this crowd of middle-aged men in navy blazers and hastily ironed barley-colored dress pants, each of them smelling of hotel rooms and travel-sized bottles of facial lotion, each of them packing the same Jos A Banks travel toiletry bag, each of them representing a different state/ different business...to her, I'm like a junior version of *them*.

"Ugh," I say. Sharp pain in my stomach. "Could you, um...closest bathroom?"

She sighs, and it occurs to me that even her sigh—her indication to the world that she is weary—sounds as though it drains her of energy. "Right next to the checkpoint," she says.

"Thanks. It's just...too much fast food."

"Sure," she says.

Rush to the men's room, enter the first stall and gag because someone has left sopping brown towels bunched up on the toilet seat, and so I back out and rush to the handicapped stall where I spend the next ten minutes gripping the cold toilet seat, stomach pains persisting. Just dry heaving, though. Nothing more. So look on the bright side, Charlie: now you don't have to dig through your bags for your toothbrush.

When I drop my suitcase and garment bag off at the security center, two men in white dress shirts and black ties fling my bags onto a clinical table, open them—everyone in the airport now looking, suddenly—and with latex gloves they sift through my boxer shorts, open my toiletry bag, hold up my razor, and it's Charles Washington on display for everyone. And I smile and cough and pretend everything is ordinary, ordinary, but my suitcase was already disheveled before this inspection and now it's worse. They sift through several pairs of dirty boxers (which I forgot to toss into my dirty clothes bag...and shit, I forgot my dirty clothes bag, and now how will I keep the dirty clothes separate from the clean?) and then find my other NKE polo and it registers to them that I'm wearing an identical shirt and they laugh.

I don't see my goal sheets. I thought I'd packed my goal sheets into my suitcase.

My bags—me, my things, my life—are zipped back up, dropped onto the conveyor belt, and they disappear into darkness.

*

At the gate, I learn that my flight has been delayed for mechanical reasons, that the next plane in line will not be ready for at least two hours, so I won't leave Philadelphia until noon. I could try to spread out and sleep, but I refuse to allow myself to be perceived as a fraternity stereotype, so I find a seat and sit with remarkable posture, no slouching, open my laptop and nod at the Excel spreadsheets on the screen and read through old reports and type and save documents, and this feels good.

Two seats down, a man shouts into his cell phone, "I don't *care* what Anderson told you. Is *he* the General Manager? Listen to me. Cancel that order. Hear me? We'd lose our *ass*-es."

Actually, several other blazer-wearing travelers are doing the same. "Friedman, ha!" one yells into his cell phone. Tall, overweight, spilling out of his seat. Looks like he hasn't paid attention to health or fashion since the day he took his first big job, just keeps shopping at the same men's store, buying new navy blazers when the old ones go into disrepair, only trims his moustache after he realizes it's dangling into his coffee. "Ha ha!" he says. "That guy doesn't know his ass from a hole in the ground! Wait till December, I'm telling you."

And I'm typing a report that says, "My meeting with the Greek Advisor at Illinois yielded little insight into their chapter operations. She seemed unfamiliar with both the local chapter and the National Fraternity. Sadly, she didn't seem to take the entire party situation seriously." And it doesn't feel like something that any of these men—these Blazers—would be writing.

"No, we had a conference here in Philadelphia," one of the men says into his phone. "Yep. Looks like the whole airport was there, couldn't wait to get out. Ha!"

Indeed, some of the men around me are still wearing nametags over their blazers, the conference logo—"Business 2.0"—in heavy letters.

"Sure," another one of them says. A different man, but it feels like he's continuing the exact same phone conversation. "Wave of the future, my friend. Talked to someone whose business doubled after he integrated a social media page. Don't laugh."

Still more than two hours until boarding, the woman at the gate tells me, and I'm tempted to shop in Philly's "Air Mall," tempted to find a new shirt or new shoes, but I've got nowhere to put any of it. Stuff it in my suitcase, my garment bag? No room. I've got a pre-assigned shirt for every day of the week, and any new additions would fuck up my system.

Sit in silence. Grab a discarded newspaper so it looks like I keep up with current events.

In less than two months there is a presidential election, but ever since I shut down Facebook, I've barely followed. Don't know what anyone's thinking, which Sarah Palin videos are being posted and shared, which anti-Obama commentaries are being linked, which friends support which candidate, which issue, who "likes" whose status updates, who is fear-mongering and engaging in comment wars over Obama's "socialist plans for America," or McCain's secret desire to start a war with Iran. I don't know anything, and I don't even know how I'd *start* to know things again.

*

After awhile I relocate to the Sports Nation Restaurant & Bar a few gates away. I can't tell if I'm hungry, don't remember the last time I had a meal "on schedule."

Fall heavy onto a stool far removed from any other travelers. Slick brown bar-top, and underneath the lacquer are zany cartoon drawings of airplanes taking off and soaring, like the airport has to reassure us—even as we order drinks to calm our nerves—that we have nothing to worry about when we board our planes: no twisted landing gear, no ice on the wings, no terrorists brandishing box-cutters.

The bartender, a late forty-something woman, has the same tired look as the woman at the ticket terminal, the look that says, "I've worked in too many different places to even pretend that I enjoy working anymore." When do you first develop such a look? And once it takes over your body and your face, can you ever shake it? Have I developed it? She punches numbers on a computer screen, scribbles something into a calculator-sized notepad, glances back and forth between the computer and the rows of liquor bottles against the wall-length mirror at the back of the bar. It's barely 10:30 AM, the slow hours, and she's taking inventory.

I clear my throat, squeak my stool, and the bartender turns around. She's wearing a gold nametag on her maroon polo shirt, and it says, "Mindy."

"Hello, Mindy," I say.

"Give me two seconds."

A lone man in a gray suit sits at a six-top table in the Sports Nation dining area, has his laptop open on the tabletop, an extension cord dropping from the computer to the floor and extending twelve feet—under several other tables—to a wall outlet. Like so many of the other Blazers, he's holding a cell phone to his ear and speaking loud enough for everyone in the airport to hear: "You don't do that in this business," he says. "At the end of the day, we've got to make a decision, don't we? It's like comparing apples and oranges, so I don't even know why we're having this discussion." His waitress, the only waitress working, steps carefully over his extension cord, smiles at him even as he turns away and speaks *louder* into his phone, and she points to his empty glass and mouths "another?" and he nods, disinterested.

Mindy is still taking inventory.

I clear my throat, but she doesn't look my way.

So I think, *fuck it*, who's this guy talking to, anyway? Could be anyone. His brother, his father, his mother, his wife. Could be anyone, but he's got the Look, like He Matters, so I open my own cell phone, scroll through my call log for someone to dial. LaFaber? No. I haven't even told him about my flat tire, and that's a conversation I don't want to have. Brock? No. He never shuts up; that's a conversation that would be too one-sided. Jenn? And before I know it, I'm dialing Jenn, dialing her from a Philadelphia airport, and she's answering the phone, *actually answering* for the first time since the Greek Life Office in Illinois —

"I was wondering when you'd call me," she says.

"Oh," I say. "Is that a good thing or a bad thing?"

"Both."

"Okay? Did I just wake you up or something?"

"No," Jenn says and there's a rustling noise. "I was getting up. Where are you? It's loud. What's that beeping noise?"

"I'm at the airport. One of those golf cart things is driving by."

"What are you doing in the airport?"

"I told you in July," I say, "back when I emailed you my travel schedule. I told you I'd be flying out West."

"Whoa, sorry. I didn't memorize your schedule."

"You should at least look at it."

"I do," she says. "Every now and then."

"I'm flying to New Mexico."

"Cool," she says, yawns.

"I called you yesterday. Several times, in fact."

"Oh, don't worry. I got your texts about the truck drivers."

Out there on the side of the highway, no response from Jenn as I called, no response from Jenn when I texted, but I realize now that it's probably because of the texts I sent: "Fucking call me back! This is important!" And later: "I fucking hate truck drivers! Do they drive like assholes on purpose?" I thought she might read this last text, look away and shake her head and rub her eyes, then examine the words again to make sure she'd read correctly. Did Charles just write that he fucking hates *truck drivers*? Does Charles remember a single fucking thing about me? And I thought that she might then—so upset by my texts—hit "talk," and then my phone would ring, and she'd be mad, but we'd be talking again. I'd have her on the phone.

Charles is…trying.

Charles is…is he?

"Oh yeah. The texts. Well, a lot happened yesterday—"

"My battery ran out. Phone's been acting retarded, so I couldn't call you back."

"It was a rough day."

"A flat tire?" she asks. "Did you change it yourself?"

"Um. I don't really want to get into it right now. It's...I'm tired of thinking about it. So what's going on at the house today?" I ask, then look around Sports Nation at the other Blazers on their cell phones. I could be talking to anyone, a business associate, but I'm asking about her *sorority house*? And I wonder why the bartender doesn't take me seriously? "Good stuff, good stuff," I say when Jenn doesn't immediately answer. "What's in store for your Saturday?"

"What's 'in store' for my...who talks like that?"

"Anything big happening down in Fort Myers?"

"Charles," she says. "Are you still talking to me? Why did your voice just change?"

"Ha ha!" I say. "I don't know what would make you say that. But I can't wait to get down there soon. It's been awhile since I've been to that part of the country."

"I don't..." she says. "Did you book your tickets for Homecoming?"

"Send me an email," I say and look around. "Remind me of the specific dates again. I'll have to input it into my Outlook calendar. I've got my laptop with me."

"Charles, really," she says. "Next weekend. Did you book the tickets?"

"Oh, I'm fantastic. Absolutely fantastic."

"What are you *talking* about? We're talking about Homecoming."

"Things are going so great with the consulting."

"Okay? What does that have to do with anything? You can't get away?"

"Ha ha!"

A pause.

"Ha ha!" I say.

"This is fucking frustrating," she says. "Are you even talking to me?"

I smooth my pants, try to laugh again, look around the bar and no one is looking at me, and so I say, "What's the weather going to be like next weekend?"

"It's Florida. September in Florida. Same as always, Charles."

"Ahh, yes," I say. "Truth be told, I haven't actually...*purchased*...the tickets."

"I knew it. I knew it."

"I'm just not sure which airport I'll be at. I have to look into it."

"Do you remember when you told me you wanted to be a consultant?"

"Yes, I do," I say. "A noble career. So here I am."

"What else?" she asks.

"What else?"

"What else?"

"I don't know. I mean. I can't remember. Not off-hand."

"I said that I supported your decision. Do what's in your heart, all that."

"Correct."

"But I also said that the only way we'd be together is if you got some weekends off—not all of them, just some—so you could come back to Florida. That's what we agreed."

"Well," I say.

"Even my father was able to live up to that sort of arrangement."

Wait, *she's* lecturing *me*? This is my job, I want to tell her. I just got a flat tire and did more than $1000 worth in damage to my Explorer for a job that pays nothing, and you're out in Fort Myers, waking up at 10:30, en route to the EU pool, en route to pre-parties and drink specials and post-parties at the Kappa Sigma house and alcohol and *good times* and black mini-mini-skirts and those 1980s turquoise t-shirts you love, the ones with the gigantic necklines where one bare shoulder hangs out and the collar circumference is hula-hoop-large and so it seems like the whole shirt is slipping down your body and *I loved it when you stopped by the house wearing one of those shirts,* because—if I hugged you just right, let my hand slip over your shoulder, gave the shirt a tug—it would be a puddle of fabric at your feet and I'd say "whoops" and we'd have to fuck right there, wouldn't we? Back in the house, back in my president's room, back where there wasn't a blazer in sight. And that's what you're wearing right now, without me, that's the carefree joy of your life, and you can't understand where I am now, you just want to *lecture me*? So I say, "All right then, yep, I'll get back to you!"

"What the *fuck* does that mean?"

"Okay, ha! Talk to you when I land," I say, end the call and turn off the phone. Clench my fist, my stomach. But strangely, Mindy the bartender is now standing directly in front of me.

"Jack and Coke," I say. "Rough day. You wouldn't believe."

"I'd believe," Mindy says, and seconds later slides me a Jack and Coke. It's getting later now, more Blazers arriving from their conference and huddling at tables for early lunches. Sip. Smile every now and then, just in case anyone wants to know whether or not I'm happy.

*

The crowds outside Sports Nation grow as the airport traffic increases in the late hours of the morning—planes skidding to a stop, planes blazing off, mothers and fathers reigning in families of five or six and toys dropped across the tile floors, Blazer after Blazer grunting past with thick-shelled briefcases. Crowds form long lines into Starbucks. Couples—young couples on their first vacations, maybe—hold ice cream cones, the mint chocolate chip dripping down the waffle cones, and they laugh as they race to lick it up. 11 AM, a transition hour. Coffee. Hamburgers. Ice cream. Jack and Coke. The airport a random collection of displaced or re-placed travelers. Gray hair, blonde hair, brown hair, highlights, buzz-cut, mullet, and—what's this?—from the crowd outside Sports Nation, someone stares back at me. Directly at me, as though my "people watching" is a crime. Someone familiar. A 35-year-old man with hair so thin that he shouldn't be using gel. Stares at me and laughs. 35-year-old man carrying a laptop case and wearing a short-sleeve blue dress shirt with loosened tie. Clean-shaven, except somehow still rough, looking like he was just involved in gritty combat with a copy machine.

And he takes a step in my direction.

I slide the Jack and Coke across the bar-top so that it might possibly have been left behind by some now-departed patron at the barstool beside mine. Is it bad to drink before noon? I touch my hair briefly: it's a mess, an ugly smattering of slopped hair. When I stepped out of the shower, I squeezed a glob of hair gel into my hand, plopped it onto my scalp, tussled my hair without even looking to ensure that it had a semi-intentional appearance.

He walks closer, his brown eyes growing darker as he approaches, still smiling like he just got away with something, like he's the poster-boy for corporate scandal.

My eye twitches, and he's ten feet away, and just as I catch a whiff of starch from his dress shirt, I place him: *Ben Jameson.* Ben, who I met back in Kinston, Pennsylvania, when I stayed with Dr. Wigginton; Ben from the University of Pittsburgh; Ben the drunk alumnus with a wife and the two kids who never stop reciting Dr. Seuss. Ben Jameson is in the Philadelphia International Airport, standing beside me, breathing hard, laptop case heavy in his hand.

"Well, howdy," Ben says, looking down at me.

"My God," I say. "I never expected…"

"Damndest things happen at airports," he says. "Crazy fucking places."

"I guess."

"No one's sitting here, right?" he says and drops his bag on the floor, taking the barstool beside mine. "Long fucking week. I need a drink. Spending the whole damned day in airports."

I don't know what to say, so I nod.

"There was this one time," he starts, then yells "BARTENDER," then continues: "Out at this airport in Spartanburg, South Carolina? Little shit-hole, honestly. Sunday afternoon, and I'm at the airport wearing this Nike shirt from college. Casual day. This old guy, seventy years old, a Dr. Wigginton type, except with this thick Southern accent, talks all slow like. And he sees my shirt and tells me about his pledge days at the University of North Carolina. Tells me about how they used to—back in the '50s, I guess—cover these kids with honey and drop feathers all over them and then drive them out to the middle of nowhere and just leave them there. Crazy stuff. Old School. And those guys from North Carolina are, like, *distinguished* now. Senators and CEOs and shit. This guy just tells me this stuff, right out of the blue."

"Crazy," I say.

"Fucking airports. So where you headed now?"

"New Mexico."

Mindy arrives and there's a glimmer of recognition in her eyes, too.

Ben laughs. "Hey there, Mindy. I need a Jack and Coke, but mostly Jack. That's what you're drinking, right, kid? So make it two," and I start to raise an objection because this is an alumnus and I promised the organization—I promised myself—that I would follow a Code of Conduct, I would be a Marathon Man and not a Frat Star and I would elevate the image of fraternities to their rightful place, but Ben just points at my glass as if to say, "too late, busted," and then he's talking again: "No shit, New Mexico. There are schools out there?"

"I'm visiting New Mexico State University. So…yeah."

"Probably all they do is teach English, am I right?" He laughs. "Southwest states, I'm telling you. Over-run by Mexicans. Shit. Schools probably are, too. Not that I'm prejudiced or anything. But they're taking over down there. Pretty soon, they'll be spreading all over."

And all around Sports Nation, the tables are filling. A woman in a black pant-suit sits and opens a trashy-looking airport novel, one with a pink cover and glistening torsos. Two fat men in navy suits pull out chairs at different tables, debating which has the best view of their gate, before finally settling on a booth. And I'm wearing a polo and sitting with a man in a short-sleeved button-down whose every foul-mouthed comment makes me flinch, and I find myself constantly glancing around to see if we are causing a scene. When he says "Mexican," one of the fat men in the navy suits raises his head, but it might have been a coincidence.

"Well," I say. "It's New Mexico. I think it's always been…Hispanic."

"The fraternities there. Shit. Probably all Mexicans, too, huh? Saying our oath in Spanish. Can you imagine being a *brother* to someone who doesn't even speak English?"

Mercifully, the drinks come and the bartender asks Ben for his credit card. He tells her to start a tab because we've both got some time to kill before boarding. Then he tells Mindy that the University of Pittsburgh game is on ESPN2, so if she wants a tip she should probably change the channel. Amazingly, she does so happily.

"Mindy's the best," Ben says.

"You know her?"

"Been here a thousand times. You take care of Mindy and you're in good shape. Ain't that right, sweetie?"

"I don't know what you're talking about," she says without looking at him.

"Course you don't. Eagles fans. Fucking clueless."

"So," I interrupt, trying to prevent more obscenity, "there's a Pittsburgh game on today?"

"Fuckin' A. It's Saturday. College fucking football, brother."

I look around. "Right."

"I forgot. You went to some small school, didn't you?"

He gulps his Jack and Coke, so I take a sip of mine.

"Who do you play?" I ask.

"Some sucker school," he says and chokes on his drink, coughs, then laughs. "Every year, they bring some poor cupcake school to start the season, televise the game, give our team a victory. This year I think it's some Florida school. Probably *your* school, for all I know."

"Heh," I say and suddenly I hope I don't have to watch EU get creamed on television in this bar. I take a larger sip. "So where are *you* headed, Ben?"

215

"Same shit, different day. Out to Boston this afternoon, then Hartford for most of next week. Back to Pittsburgh next Friday."

"I didn't know you traveled so much."

"Not that much. But it gets me away from everything."

"Everything?"

"The wife, the kids. Everything."

"Oh, right. I forgot."

"Forgot what?"

"Nothing. I thought…Isn't it nice to just slow down, though? Settle in one place?"

"Are you smoking crack?"

"Am I smoking crack?"

"I got these friends, they spend every night at home. They're dying, brother."

"Dying?" Sounds like a rough word.

"Life is all about moving. You stay still, you're fucking dying. Sharks, they don't ever stop, don't even sleep. The second they stop, they drown. Sharks got it right."

"For some reason, I thought you said you worked a desk job."

"Nope," he says. "All the chumps work behind desks, am I right? No, listen. Really. Desks are entry-level work. A fucking monkey could do half the work that they have college graduates doing."

"Down economy, though."

"Fuck that. There's jobs out there. I don't give a fuck what anyone says. Recession, economic downturn, blah blah blah. Look at me. Senior year of college, my parents both died within a year of one another, so I had to find a job. Quick. Take care of my younger sister. I just made sure to take the best one, best money, instead of settling like so many of these kids are doing today. Just a BA and I started off at 45 grand. My advice: don't settle. Be fucking aggressive. That's how you got *this* job, right?"

"Sure," I say. "No settling."

"Sweet job. You're not cooped up in a cubicle. You know what I'm sayin'?"

"But traveling, you've got no time at home to, you know, see the people you love."

"Ha, good one. My other advice. Don't get married."

Silence as we both stare at the television.

"Are you satisfied, then?" I ask.

"What the fuck are you talking about?"

I look behind me. No one has moved, no one has registered his comment.

"With your career, I mean," I say. "Are you satisfied with who you work for?"

"The fuck are you asking that for, all of a sudden?"

I look around again.

"Stop that," he says. "These fuckers…what do they care about what I say?"

"It's just, I try to be professional."

"Professional. Professional," he says and shakes his head.

216

"There's a certain way that I try to present myself."

"Do I look satisfied? Shit. I'm just like you. Just like any of these pricks around here, all lying to each other. Nobody likes doing clean-up work for some executive making twice their salary. But it's a job. You're not supposed to *like* your job. You just shouldn't hate it."

"Interesting perspective."

"*Mindy,*" Ben says. "One more Jack and Coke for both of us. And a little extra pour pour, if you know what I mean."

"That might be a bit much," I say.

Mindy smiles, and it's the first time I've seen her smile. Doesn't seem right. It's like watching a former linebacker—one of those guys with jutting chins and rock-solid jaw lines and angry black eyes and countless scars and blood blood blood constantly on his mind—sitting in shirt and tie on a morning talk show and talking about his crème brulee recipe.

"We have a tradition back at the frat house," Ben says. "Game day tradition that's been going on for years. We call it Big East Bellybuster."

"Big East Bellybuster?"

"Yessir. We give a toast to every team in the Big East. Well. A toast to their opponents, whoever we need to win. The conference has changed a little in the past couple years, but it's the number one reason to look forward to game day."

"That could be seven drinks," I say.

"Start of the year is always rough, out-of-conference play," he says. "God, I miss college. *Mindy.*" Mindy returns and Ben slips her a twenty. He mouths something to her. "They don't like you getting rip-roaring drunk before your flight," he says when she walks away. "So it's good to know people." A moment later, as we watch the college football scores scroll across the bottom of the television screen, he pushes a plastic Starbucks cup—the kind usually used for Frappuccino—in my direction. At the bottom is something light yellow, like watered-down honey, and he says, "Isn't too strong. Drink it, but don't make a scene." He's got his own Starbucks cup, and when he sees the score for the Temple-UConn game, he says, "Godspeed to you, Temple," and we drink the shot.

*

"I got held off a flight at Dayton Airport because I got so drunk, but that place is small potatoes," Ben says. We take a shot to East Carolina, playing West Virginia. Then another to UCF, playing South Florida. Then another to Oklahoma, playing Cincinnati. I realize that I'm slouching in my seat, totally unprofessional, so I straighten up, look around, and as always no one pays any attention to me because they're all absorbed in their laptops, and Ben's pushing another shot in my direction, and we're toasting to Tennessee Tech, I think, and Ben tells me to be quiet when the ESPN Gameday crew discusses the Pittsburgh game, which is coming later in the day, and I nod along with the commentators even though I've never watched a Pitt game and things are starting to get loud and hazy.

"Kicked out of an airport?" I say, and Ben just nods. "I actually got kicked out of an American Cancer Society fundraiser during my junior year."

"Killer," Ben says, sips his Jack and Coke and stares at the television and squirms in his seat when ESPN replays a bone-jarring tackle from last week's Rutgers University football game. The program cuts to a shot of a football player on a stretcher, then to another shot of the coach near tears at a press conference.

"This could be his career," the coach says. "He could be done."

"We bought tickets for fifty bucks," I say, "and it was all-you-can-eat grouper and an open bar. I went with a couple of my fraternity brothers. Bad idea, right? We made t-shirts that said, 'Drinking for charity,' and we each finished off seven or eight vodka tonics before some guy in a tuxedo came up to us and said we'd had enough."

Somewhere a child screams about G.I. Joe., and I don't bother turning around.

"This is the right idea," Ben says, pointing emphatically at his drink with his cocktail straw. "You've got the right idea now, kid."

"What do you mean?"

"Just a couple drinks, you know?"

"I've never had anything against drinking," I say.

"No?"

"It's just our consultant Code of Conduct."

"You take that shit too seriously, brother. You loosen up, you'll get somewhere."

"But," I say and pause and my head sways and I have to steady myself, "I've got, you know, a job to do. I can't be a role model if I'm drunk. I can't."

"And you'll never get anything accomplished, either, if you're so fucking uptight." He taps the cocktail straw against the rim of the glass, silent for a moment, staring down into the ice cubes. "One thing I've learned: in a circle of smokers, nobody trusts the asshole who won't light up. You actually care about your job, kid? The fraternity?"

"Of course. I'm on the road. I've given up everything to—"

"Then you do what you need to do in order to see results."

"I can make a difference without..." and my head is swaying again and I forget what I—

"In a fraternity house, nobody ever listens to the guy without a drink," he says. "You want to look back and say that all this was for nothing, this whole year you're spending in this job, that you couldn't make a difference because you refused to drink a goddamned beer?"

Charles is...thinking he has a point.

Charles...should have gone into the Illinois party, unpacked in the guest room.

Charles...will not make that mistake again.

How different would it have been, I wonder. Pittsburgh, the alumni dinner, Shippensburg, even Illinois. If I'd rolled up my sleeves, if I'd sat down with a drink. Would it have hurt? Would they have been more willing to listen when I talked about the mission?

"You can have some fun," Ben says, "and still do your job."

I see what you're saying, I say, or maybe I don't.

"Just loosen up, you know? Good things will happen."

I'm picturing those hangers in the backseat of my Explorer, those hangers swaying as I grumbled over potholes, the entire Explorer thrown into chaos when I fell into that final, deep gash, hangers shooting from the backseat rod. I never cleaned it all up, not completely. I never cleaned *myself* up today, but suddenly there's something reassuring and fresh about letting it all slip away just as easily as those hangers. About *not* cleaning up. About falling into darkness.

We take a shot to Akron. I think?

*

And Ben is telling me about a room in the basement of the Pittsburgh house, a secret room whose door is hidden behind a bookshelf like in some old *Batman* cartoon, and I say that he's got to be shitting me, the brothers never showed me any "secret room." And he says that I'd be surprised the things they wouldn't tell me, and in this secret room is where they hold "formal chapter meetings" once a month, everyone in shirt and tie and brotherhood pins and full fraternity ritual regalia, and they take it so seriously, don't allow anyone to even bring a cell phone or a Gatorade into the meeting. *Pittsburgh?* I ask. Can't get into the secret room unless you've been initiated, he says. Part of the Pittsburgh family. Insiders in, outsiders out.

*

And I've forgotten where I am, and I look around and spy all the Blazers and everything, and I swirl around on my stool and knock my laptop case onto the floor and Ben Jameson beside me is laughing as I stoop to collect the bag, and I search through the side pouch and check my ticket and the clock on the wall and it's blurry, not just swaying but blurry. I've only got a couple minutes until boarding time.

"Thank you so much for the drinks, man," I say, standing. I shake my head. "*Sir.* I mean *sir*, not *man*. Sorry. You know how it goes? Talking with undergrads all day, and shit, I start speaking like them. But seriously. Thanks for the drinks. I mean…I shouldn't have, you know? But it is cool to let loose, I'll admit it."

"No problem," he says, and he sips a water now, and I never even saw Mindy drop it off. "I'll tell you what. You coming back to Pittsburgh anytime soon?"

"Not this semester," I say, and I grab his water and take a gulp, place it back in front of him, stumble a little, and he laughs. "Maybe in the Spring."

"Tell you what. Here's my card."

He hands me a silver business card, foil-etched name and position below a bright red logo: "ED-TEX INDUSTRIES." Ambiguous but sleek, like a high-tech defense contractor, a company deciding the future of the planet, and I'm downing shots with this guy, this alumnus, in a Philadelphia airport. And isn't this better than if I'd just declined the drinks?

"You're all right, kid," he says. "Good head on your shoulders. Drop me an email when you come for Spring. I'll get some basketball tickets, gather some alumni in town."

"Alumni," I say. "I can't drink in front of alumni."

"News flash," he whispers. "You're wrecked right now."

"No-oooo," I say.

"I'm an alumnus," he whispers.

"No-oooo," I say.

"I'll sweeten the deal," he says. "Barbecue at the house before the game. I buy the kegs. We'll stack 'em high in your honor. Show you how we do things in Pittsburgh."

"Hmmm."

Then Ben Jameson pats me on the back. "In the meantime, live it up. All this you got in front of you. Young and shit. Probably got a hot little thing back home, too, don't you?"

"I have a girlfriend," I say. "Jenn."

"Piece of ass with 'bend me over' written all over her, am I right? Live it up."

"Sure," I say. "No doubt."

"Everything changes, is my point," he says. "You get a job. Wifey gets fat. You get a couple brats running around the house, never see your friends anymore. You lose your goddamn hair. You wonder how all this happened, you know? So all I'm saying is, live it up. You're young right now. You come to Pittsburgh, you're going to live it up. What do you say?"

"Yes," I say.

"We can show you the room, even. I vouch for you, brother." He pats me on the back again. "We'll make it happen."

"Yes. I'm there. I'm sold." And we shake hands. I thank him again for the shots, tell him this was a great time, and I speed-walk to my terminal, not thinking about where I'm going or the steps I'm taking.

*

I remember when the Educational Consultant visited Edison University during my junior year, his tiny Hyundai Accent occupying the chapter's "Reserved – President" parking spot for four days. Wore the same Nu Kappa Epsilon polos that I wear now, same blue dress shirts, same backseat rod. At the time, just as with LaFaber, there was something otherworldly about this guy: how he spoke of his pristine chapter house back at the University of Washington, how he looked at our budget and within seconds had found a massive error in our Treasurer's spreadsheet, how he spoke of the National Headquarters as if it was the Emerald City. His posture, his carefully chosen words in each workshop he facilitated, his perfect responses to even the most inane questions that my chapter brothers asked ("How can we amend Sacred Laws to, like, make it legal to have kegs at the chapter house?" "What's your name?" "Jonathan." "Okay, Jonathan. Well, first of all, it is *legal* to have kegs at your house. But as members of Nu Kappa Epsilon, we believe that it's our responsibility to battle the fraternity stereotype of binge drinking, and a regulation prohibiting kegs is one way that we strive toward this goal. On a different note, though, it's important to understand that the fraternity supports your right to *drink responsibly*. Along with several other fraternities, we actively fight any college or university that forces campus housing to go dry. In fact, studies have shown that students are safer when…"). And yes, I was transfixed, amazed that someone could have his life so neatly ironed.

But after the consultant left: "Homeboy needs to pull his pants down a little," my friend Gavin said. "His belt was at his fucking nipples. Looked like my grandfather."

And: "You hear what he said about our guest room? That it was unacceptable?"

And: "Saw me drinking in the foyer and asked if I was underage. You believe that?"

And: "Guy was a fucking douche bag. The fuck does he know?"

And for all the perfection, maybe I was the only one impressed?

# Flight to El Paso
## CHAPTER FIFTEEN

Walking in a single-file line behind ten or fifteen Blazers, each of them processed by the attendant. On the plane, each Blazer navigates the center aisle to his seat, deposits carry-on bag in overhead compartment in one swift motion. Scattered families/vacationers stall the overall progress, but the Blazers stream inside like high-speed internet, and I'm so drunk and bumbling that I feel like outdated dial-up.

I knock into someone. Try to apologize but can't enunciate. Plop down into Seat 13.

I think about the Marathon Man diagrams, that—sloshing into a plane—this isn't the drawing the National Fraternity had in mind when they hired me:

Beside me is a Blazer, smells like cardboard and cologne. Trimmed beard so wooly that I almost feel like itching it for him. He's packed a light lunch, Ziploc baggies with slices of cheese, crackers, strawberries…Has a copy of Stephen Covey's *The 8ᵗʰ Habit* on his tray table.

All around the plane, Blazers find their seats, drape their jackets over their legs. One frustrated man with curly black hair has trouble folding his *Wall Street Journal* in such a way that he can read while still giving the wide woman beside him room enough to position her laptop on her tray table. Shorter man in a green blazer opens a Cinnabun to-go bag, passengers around him bursting with envious "Ooh, that looks good" commentary.

And then they all stare at me, these men and women. Noticing the embroidered letters on my polo, NKE.

Time passes. Shuffling noises from everywhere, laughter.

And then the captain's voice crackles from overhead and people are buckling seatbelts and I close my eyes and I'm not this—

—but instead this—

224

And soon the world is moving fast around me. Won't stop.

—and then the plane is moving down the runway, moving-bumping—

—and the Blazer is in the window seat and he barely looks out but the runway is whipping past like a gray smear and the buildings, trees, towers, here, gone—

—plane lifting up, *breathless*, everyone, for the requisite fifteen seconds—

Lifting.

Lifting.

Turning on its side.

And I'm still holding my breath, thinking: if the plane crashed right now, would any of this have been worth it? High school, college, the clubs, the honor societies, the officer positions, the National Fraternity Headquarters, the "sacrifice in salary" and Pittsburgh and Shippensburg and Illinois, no life insurance, no will, no real possessions, an entire lifetime leading to *this point*, and viewed from this perspective, my God—

Plane straightens out, but my fingers still clutch my thighs.

Fingers pried from pants, forced toward armrests.

—cabin pressure so fucking tight that it feels like I'm back in my Explorer, surrounded by all of my notebooks and snapshut cases and binders and forms and the Explorer is collapsing and I can't breathe.

And I sit. Sit. Sit. Fingers clenched on my pants again.

And how can everyone else just sit there, I want to know, so content and so trusting that all will work out? What have *they* accomplished that makes them so carefree? Confined space, heads close to implosion, the rooftops of one of America's oldest and greatest metropolises shrinking beneath us, and they all just go about their business, continue reading newspaper articles and snacking on cheese cubes?

I breathe deep. Thumb through the pocket on the seat-back in front of me, past *Sky Mall*, past an old granola bar wrapper, past the instructions for emergency landings, my fingers finally stopping at the barf bag—and oh God, what would I look like, if it came to that? How would the Marathon Man handle turbulence, a sudden and uncontrollable rumbling in his gut?

Is that how he would handle adversity?

Is that it? Is that me? That slick Marathon Man who always has the proper response to any question, any situation. Or is this more accurate?

My final moments: that about sums it up.

Plane feels *tighter* than my Explorer suddenly, more suitcases and more duffel bags and more seats and more garment bags and jackets and blazers and men/ women/ children/ noise and I can't breathe, can't breathe, no control, and I think of my goals and try to settle myself, but they're back in the Explorer, aren't they?

So I think of any numbers that I can, anything tangible, like how much money it must cost to fly Flight 183 from Philadelphia to Dallas, how many miles, how much gas is expended to move this hunk of metal and people and Samsonite from Point A to Point B. 150 passengers? $200 tickets? Staff costs, gas costs, marketing costs, web site costs, on-board snacks and drinks, plane maintenance, cost of the *plane* itself, in-flight movie and magazines and headphones.

To move my Explorer from Champaign-Urbana to Philadelphia (760 miles), it costs the National Headquarters $266, which is 35 cents per mile travel reimbursement, but then we've got to add staff salary, right? so we add the fixed staff salary of $12,000 per year (which equates to roughly $33 per day) and a dining allowance of $5/$10/$15—breakfast lunch dinner per diem— which I cannot exceed but which must be paid with credit card (receipts must be included on my expense report, stapled, mailed to Walter LaFaber, Director of Chapter Operations, who gives them to our Headquarters Financials Director) and of which I do not receive the remainder if I do not spend in its entirety, meaning that the maximum Headquarters per diem payout would be $30 a day and the minimum could be $0 (but I generally hover around $20 each day), but I'll add all this up, and I'm breathing easier now, and let's see, if it's 760 times 0.35, plus $33, plus $30, and that's about how much the Headquarters is willing to pay for a Consultant's travel day (and, of course, to achieve this number, student dues—and that's the amount of money we charge to each initiated student member of NKE, payable by September 15 of each Fall semester and February 1 of each Spring semester—are fixed at $50 per man per semester, and alumni contributions to the *Headquarters*, not the Foundation or the Brothers Assisting Brothers program, must exceed $200,000 after cost, which is tricky since our giving campaign nets millions for the Foundation and BAB scholarship program but very little for the Headquarters, because who wants to donate non-tax-deductible money to the *business* end of fraternity life?), so that works out to $330 for today, and if you take that as an average amount, multiply it by 32 (the approximate number of schools I'll visit in a semester), then I cost about $10,560 each semester, and even if there's something wrong with that number, with my math, I know that all of this is calculated carefully at Headquarters. The amount of money I can spend at hotels, the number of chapters I can visit, the alumni dinners I attend, the emergency visits I make, the chapters I keep open, the chapters I close, all of this is part of some pored-over budget that has nothing to do with a mission statement, and after everything, I cost so little, I'm worth so little.

But I'm breathing again. Still tight, but I'm breathing again. Just numbers. With numbers, at least I know.

My Blazer-Neighbor munches on crackers, makes "hmm" noises as he reads Covey. Dog-ears a page, and now he's looking at a diagram of something, some "success model" or something. Quadrants to divide his workday goals.

Overhead bell dings. Captain tells us that it's safe to move about the cabin, and all around me Blazers unbuckle their seatbelts and stand and stretch as though this—the take-off, the flight—is some task they've completed and can now scratch off their daily task list. They stare at me, these Blazers, and I loosen my grip on my pants and stretch out and breathe easy, because it's Saturday, *Saturday*, and I'm not opening my laptop case again.

High above a patchwork system of interstate-farm-community, and I'm picturing all the universities in the distance, all the white-columned houses, all the students and alumni and administrators. Up here, it's all so distant.

*

Somewhere over Oklahoma, it finally happens: I wake with a violent stomach-clenching. All those Big East shots, whatever they were, have been gathering in my stomach like a drafted army, training while I've been complacent, waiting until we're over the most sickeningly bland section of the country to really charge and baton-thrust my stomach, and it's sharp pains and —

I unbuckle my seatbelt, push myself up, stumble through the aisle, bump into Blazers on their laptops, mutter "sorry sorry," bump into sleeping women and children, bump hard into a Blazer writing on a yellow legal pad and think briefly that he's looking *very* productive right now and *look at me* and what's everyone going to think if I just yack across the aisle, all over their pleated dress pants. Will they think I'm airsick? Just something I ate? Will I be forgiven, or will they only see the fraternity letters on my shirt? What's the airline procedure for *that*? Do they draw this in the airline pamphlets in the seat-backs: what to do when frat boys are puking on flights?

Slither into the cramped bathroom, shut the door. Hang my head over the sink and try to focus on my blurry reflection in the mirror.

Low rumble of the engine. Smooth out my polo shirt, smooth my pants.

The engines…head feeling lighter…stomach pains passing…just want to sit on the toilet, just in case…hang out here…close my eyes…just in case, just in case…

228

\*

A knock at the door.

I lift my head from my hands. World refocusing. With weak knees, I stand; limbs fuzzy, but I've purged something awful, something toxic, more than just the alcohol. When I open the collapsible door and clunk out, two men in shirt and tie stand in the aisle outside the bathroom. "Oh," one of them says. "Sorry. I didn't know if anyone was in there."

"No problem," I say, but there's a gurgle in my voice.

"You all right?"

"Fine," I say. Fingertips sliding down the door. Trying to steady myself.

"Are you drunk?"

"What?"

"Are you drunk? Were you puking in there?"

"No, it's…" I say. "Airport food."

"You smell like liquor."

"That's, like, the toilet. Just wait a minute before you go in there. Wait for it to clear up."

"You're drunk. We should tell the flight attendant."

"Please. I just had to shit."

"A twenty-minute shit?"

"Nu Kappa Epsilon?" one of the men says, deciphering the letters on my polo. "You're in a fraternity, huh? Big surprise."

"You want to let me by?"

"I was in a fraternity," he says. "Thought I was tough shit. Then I grew up."

"I'm not in a fraternity," I say, and stumble forward a step. "I *work* for a fraternity."

"Can't even stand up straight."

"The plane turned," I say.

"We never used to drink in our letters," the man says, leaning into my face. His breath smells of onion. Face is clean-shaven, but he's so close I can make out the nicks, the long red marks where his razor scraped his flesh too deeply. "You wear your letters, and the whole world's watching you. You're a fucking disgrace."

"I'm on my day off," I say. "I work for a fraternity, and I'm on my day off."

"Right," the man says, shaking his head, and then he turns to his partner. "You're first, buddy. You got hand sanitizer, right?"

"Fuck you both," I say.

"Just walk," the man says, and he doesn't turn to face me. "Just walk."

When I return to my seat, my Blazer-Neighbor is sleeping, his Stephen Covey book wedged into the seat pocket below his tray table. He looks like a bad sleeper, like he's going to burst out in a series of booming snores to rival the plane's engines. I sit down, struggle to stretch out, wish I could turn on my cell phone to check the time; I hail the flight attendant, wondering how much a Jack and Coke runs. Five dollars?

Outside, past my neighbor, Oklahoma continues. Or maybe it's Texas by now. Maybe we're about to head into our final descent. Reddish green land, the hair-thin gray stripes of two-lane country roads sectioning it off. Vast. Red, green. And suddenly, I don't want this flight to end. "Fuck them," I say, louder than I should.

*

Connection in Dallas. Four hours until departure. Hungry, thirsty.

I find a Chili's in the airport, one of those miniature versions sized to fit in whatever open space the airport had available, and I grab a stool at the bar, order a cheeseburger and fries. Then check my messages. Jenn left several, and I listen to her tell me that she doesn't know if this is working out but she wants to try, really, she sees her future and she sees that I'm in it and she wants to keep this thing going but she needs something from me, and I smile and laugh because what does it matter? She's back at EU. Parties every night. Homecoming week.

I scoot a couple barstools down, next to a middle-aged woman who looks to be chain-smoking but doesn't even seem like she's inhaling, just holding the cigarette between her fingers, smoke tendrils climbing from a collection of stubbed-out butts in the ashtray inches away.

The bartender returns, asks what she can get me. "Jack and Coke," I say. "ID?"

I'm happy she asked, and I'm happy to show her.

The woman beside me is drinking a light beer, one amber shade removed from clear. No foam, no carbonation, no condensation. Might as well be a lukewarm last-night left-over.

I sip my drink and watch the *Sportscenter* college football highlights on the television at the back of the bar, and I'm thinking that I could talk to this woman next to me, listen to her old-woman problems or whatever. Sip after sip of my drink, my pounding headache loosening with each sip and almost *gone* now, I'm thinking that Jenn would talk to another man on the next barstool, would place her hand on his chest and laugh at his jokes. So finally I grab the bartender's attention, and I say, "Two Jack and Cokes, please. One for me, and one for my friend here." And the old woman looks at me through squinted eyes and shakes her head and the bartender says something to her, followed by "frat boy," and I laugh and ask the woman if she's sure. No drink? It's on mee-eeee. She tells me that I've *got* to be kidding her.

"Fine, I'm kidding," I say. "Ha ha."

Retreat to my original seat. Remind the bartender that *I*, at least, want another.

*

There are text messages from Jenn, also, but they're blurry, and there are so many abbreviations—"u" and "2nite" and "4tunately" and "gr8"— and I don't know what I'm looking at anymore. I type something, but the auto-complete feature keeps placing the wrong words in the wrong spots. "Mission," when I tried to type "miss you." "Workshop" when I tried to type "waiting." Eventually, there's a text message finished, but when I try to send, my signal is lost and the text drowns in a quicksand of error messages and circular "try sending again?" notices.

*

Flight to El Paso: red-brown West Texas desert rising and falling, collecting and crumbling, a giant sandbox of bucket-shaped hills and shoveled-out holes, and I don't know our altitude but this is the first time I can actually see *tiny* details from the windows. Individual stones on the ground. Footprints. Scratch marks on the rocky walls of steep mountains. Tumbleweed. No neighbor in the seat beside me—this connection flight is a smaller plane, two seats on the right and just one on the left—and at one point I press my face to the glass for a good five minutes.

Sleep for a bit, wake up re-energized on final descent, and devour the bag of peanuts left for me. When we land, I buy a pack of Trident to cover the alcohol smell sizzling on my breath. At the baggage claim, I wait for my two checked bags to spin around the dizzying conveyor belt, wait with all the same people whose heads I saw on the plane but who all look so different now that they're standing.

Black bag spins around, not mine. Blue bag, not mine.

But *there*...my red monstrosity!

After I grab my suitcase—and I'm not sober yet, and I don't want to *be* sober, either, I want to go out on Saturday night at New Mexico State, keep this up—someone confronts me. Wearing a red t-shirt with "NKE" across the front, a slogan that says, "When it comes to JUST DOING IT, accept no substitutes," and he says to me:

"Hey, is your name Charles Washington?"

"Huh?" I say.

"Your shirt. Are you the Educational Consultant?"

And I imagine saying *no*, walking away...four days to myself... wear jeans and roll up my sleeves, escape the workshops, the mission statements, the sweat and the energy that has led to nothing, maybe just grab a hotel room and fudge some reports and find a college bar and saunter past the dance floor, the bodies pressed against one another, the smell of department-store perfumes and colognes and keg beer, the dim lights and Flo Rida and "apple bottom jeeee-ans, boots with the furrr-rrr, got the whole club lookin' at her-rrr" and girls in tight pants getting low low low low, and another drink in my hand, standing at the bar and no cigarette-smoking old woman muttering "frat boy" disdainfully under her breath, no blazers or ties, no talk of leadership or stereotypes, only head-nods and high-fives, fist-pounds...

It's a fantasy. I know that. But this is a college kid standing in front of me, and I also know that I've been going about this all wrong. *Loosen up*, Benjamin said. *In a fraternity house, nobody ever listens to the guy without a drink.*

"That's me. Charles Washington."

"I'm Sam," he says. "Sam Anderson."

"Nice to meet you, Sam," I say.

231

"I'm the New Member Educator."

"That's great, Sam."

"How was your flight?"

"Oh, super," I say. "A little short, but…super."

"You got your bags, right?" he asks. "We've got dinner plans."

"Dinner," I say. "Super. I could use a drink."

# Las Cruces
CHAPTER SIXTEEN

It's Saturday evening, about the time my parents are sitting down for dinner back on the Gulf Coast, about the time my fraternity brothers back at EU are just starting to make plans for their night, about the time Jenn usually steps into the shower for her hour-long "going out" makeover, and I'm sitting in the passenger seat of a styrofoam-smelling Toyota Corolla, riding the dry highways of southern New Mexico.

"Whole lot of *nothing* out there, isn't there?" Sam asks from the backseat of the car.

For the entirety of our drive, I've been staring out the passenger-side window.

Sam Anderson, who met me at the El Paso baggage claim and escorted me to this car, knows that I'm from Florida, that this is my first time in the deserts of the Southwest, but he doesn't know that my head still swims in a pleasant half-drunk buzz, that I keep blanking out, snapping back to consciousness.

I rub the back of my neck. "It's very big."

Sam is the New Member Educator for Nu Kappa Epsilon at New Mexico State University, and he's stuffed in the backseat between my suitcase and a pile of backpacks and orange vests and camo hats and hooks and poles.

Jose Rodriguez, the driver, is this NKE chapter's president, and this Corolla—its paint dulled under what feels like an inch-thick layer of desert dust—is his vehicle; he drives the three of us from the El Paso International Airport to Las Cruces, New Mexico, rarely looking away from the road, holding the steering wheel and commanding the car with remarkable discipline.

Headache is gone now, eye has stopped twitching, but I chug a bottled water because I've never felt so parched in my life...out here, the entire world feels like a dehydrated snow globe, the snow replaced by dirt and dried-out vegetation, and it seems as if—every time I think the dust has finally settled—someone is shaking the dust globe again. Just thirty minutes ago, when Sam and I stepped out of the airport and into the early evening to find Jose's idling car, we were blasted by the sort of hot air I'd expect when opening the oven door to check on a pizza. This isn't stifling Florida heat, where every minute of summer feels as if you're trapped in a boiling high school locker room. It isn't Pennsylvania or Illinois either, where September feels like a transition to a violently cold season, and all of the American Eagle advertisements are already showcasing sweaters in dark browns and oranges. A "dry heat," they call this, but until now I've never felt it before. I've never been to the Rocky Mountains, to the deserts of Arizona or West Texas. Born and raised in humid Florida, my farthest trips west came when my parents took me to see cousins in Houston, another Gulf Coast city where a day's bear-ability is measured by the humidity.

And the idea of "dry heat," of deserts, of a "vacation visit"—even if I'm only going to the small town of Las Cruces—feels exhilarating, suddenly. *Vacation visit.* The business card back in my car, flipped.

All that blank space.

"Las Cruces is right past this mountain," says Jose as we near the university. Jose is a muscular Mexican with a well-maintained fade; he wears all white (white polo with khakis either sun-bleached or washer-faded), and he speaks a slow and thoughtful English, traces of an accent rising and falling with the rhythm of his sentences. Maybe his tight haircut means he is conservative, a strict Catholic, a committed ROTC student...or maybe, on the other hand, his back-seat collection of hunting equipment means he is instead adventurous, reckless even, a Generation Kill type. I can't tell. "From Las Cruces to El Paso, it is only thirty minutes," he says, "so this is not a bad drive. And Mexico is just beyond the river in El Paso, so it is a quick drive from our school to Mexico."

"Your school's only half an hour from Mexico?" I ask.

"Always interesting," Sam says, "but a little wild, a little dangerous."

"I've never been," I say.

"No?"

"But I definitely want to check it out."

"If you go," Sam says, "just make sure you order bottled water. Otherwise, you're going home with a different sort of vacation souvenir."

"Noted," I say.

"Mexico is so close," Jose says. "A popular spot for underage drinkers." He drives barely a mile per hour over the speed limit, rarely passes any of the slow right-lane traffic on the highway. Conservative? After all, he sits with an upright driver's ed discipline, even adjusts his rearview regularly. Or reckless? Perhaps this plodding is the result of a car worn weak from years of irresponsible driving, a man forced to change his ways after too many street races gone sour...

"My eight-year-old sister could drink in Juarez," Sam says from the back seat.

"Hmm," I say. Conservative, disapproving?

"Shit," Sam adds. "I even took my sister out there, once."

Or reckless?

"Get her wasted?" I ask, cracking the joke without—*shit*—considering reactions.

Silence for a moment, the car a tomb of judgment.

"She's eight," Sam says severely. "No, I didn't get her *wasted*."

"I was only playing. Just...you know?"

He stares at me with angry eyes, cheeks hard, hat so tight on his scalp that it looks like the fabric might splinter. Then his face opens into a wide smile. "I know, bro. Just fucking with you."

I exhale.

"I'll wait until she's thirteen to get her drunk," Sam says.

"Ha!" I say.

He's a joker, I learn, the type of loud, crude, baseball-cap-clad *bro* who might as well have been plucked from Pitt or Shippensburg and deposited here in the desert.

I turn to Jose beside me. "Are you from Mexico? Juarez?"

"Oklahoma," he says.

"Oh. Sorry. I didn't mean to assume…"

"My *parents*. They are from Mexico. They live in Las Cruces. They own a pecan farm." And he points out the window, past dark and dry and unending New Mexico and West Texas desert, and in the distance stand rows and rows—thousands—of scraggly trees, thirsty-looking like they hate that someone has planted them out here, and Jose says: "Just like those. Pecan trees. Those are owned by the university, I think. Our school is very agricultural."

"Didn't know that."

"This is why we are called the Aggies."

"I see. I get it."

"Most people don't. They always ask, 'What is an Aggie?' It gets old."

"Did you have a football game today?"

"We play at Utah State," Sam says from the backseat. "Night game."

"You do anything special for road games? Get together for drinks?"

"We tailgate for home games," Sam says. "Away games aren't usually televised."

"Too bad," I say and shake my head. "Well, there's plenty of other games tonight. We should stake out a spot at a bar, get some pitchers, watch some football."

"Um," Sam says and meets Jose's eyes in the rearview and they both have this look like *This guy's coming along? Not gonna happen*…And it's something I hadn't anticipated, that at the moment I'd like to actually join them for a drink, I might be rejected.

So I try to change the subject before they shut me out altogether.

"Did you happen to see who won the Pittsburgh game?" I ask. "Earlier today?"

"Pittsburgh?" Sam asks. "The Steelers had a Saturday game?"

"No, no. The University of Pittsburgh."

"There's a university in Pittsburgh?"

"Yep."

"You *sure*?"

"It's a large school," I say. "Probably bigger than NMSU."

"I doubt that," Sam says.

A silence falls upon the car for a few moments, conversational doldrums from which it might be impossible to escape. For most college-aged men, all of life is a competition. What we order for dinner, how many beers we drink, our shoes, our shirts, our cars, our haircuts, our jokes, our jobs, our girlfriends. The size of our fraternity houses, or the size of our alumni contributions. And it occurs to me that even my statistic—the reliable statistic, the number of students enrolled at a university—has now become the object of competition. For four years, Sam's entire world has been New Mexico State University, the restaurants and the dorms and the classrooms and the bars and the football team. To admit defeat in this particular competition, to admit any sort of deficiency in the university is, perhaps, to admit personal flaws.

"So, like, are there cool things to do in Mexico?" I ask finally.

"Many things, yes," Jose says. "You just need to know what they are."

"Okay," I say, and I wait for more but there is no further response.

*Loosen up*, Ben said, but already it seems I've fucked up the vacation visit.

*

The landscape doesn't change much, looks like we're going nowhere, but at some point we circumvent the looming mountain—it really just looks like a pile of soil and rocks that someone dumped on the horizon—and a messy bit of civilization is scattered over the rolling dust-scape ahead: Las Cruces. As we near the city and the university, I see that the open fields of dirt surrounding the city are littered with discarded plastic bottles, orange juice bottles and milk cartons and water bottles, all empty, grocery bags dancing across tipped-over shopping carts. In the city itself, adobe-style houses stand next-door to dumpy lots, abandoned storefronts. Pittsburgh and Philadelphia, despite the exhaust and the cracking highways, felt like *finished* cities beneath the grime, places populated purposefully and now pulsing with activity, but here, all the world looks forgotten-about, as if the unbroken desert winds have toppled and scattered a once-stable city and no one has come to pick up the mess.

And, it seems, this is barely a "college town." Not like the University of Illinois, where every house was a fraternity house and every building bore the "I" logo. No. Here, there are standard four-lane streets with standard names (Stewart Street and Payne Street, and even as we pass the stadium—a tall, grassy mound, cut in the center with bleachers—there is no "Stadium Avenue"), standard two-story commercial buildings, standard fast-food locales like McDonald's and Carl's Jr, none of it even painted in the colors of the school. It is a sprawl of urbanization effected by a state university, but not a college town. No strip of college bars, no swarms of students in NMSU t-shirts, no Rush Season excitement. Through my car window, I watch a mother herd her three children up the stairs of their apartment building. A mother? A family? In a college town apartment complex?

As we drive to Jose's apartment where I'm told I will stay for this visit, we pass short hunkered-down classroom buildings that have the look of a budget-crunch high school campus. New Mexico State University, unlike the historic schools of the Northeast (even Shippensburg), probably had the misfortune

236

of being built in the 1960s, and instead of century-old brick decadence, it looks like a functional campus built to absorb a population boom.

"Are you all right?" Jose asks.

"I'm great," I say. "I've just never been anywhere like this."

"This?" he says. "This is Las Cruces. That's all it is."

"I'm sure you'll be happy to leave this shithole by Wednesday," Sam says from the backseat, removing his hat and running his hands through his haphazard brown hair. And where is the competition now? He is a man, a fraternity man, a *college man*: he's supposed to be *excited* about New Mexico; he's supposed to talk about the NMSU football team, about concerts and restaurants and bars and festivals; he's supposed to boast of this town's college-ness, how happenin' it is, how hard they party; he's supposed to cheer for his school like an SEC football fan in the swollen mobs on ESPN's "College Gameday."

"Okay, so what are the plans for tonight?" I try again. I'm on the edge of my seat, have unbuckled my seatbelt without realizing it, and I try to make eye contact with both Sam and Jose. My buzz is wearing off, and I feel somehow like time is running out on my Saturday. "Cool stuff to do in Las Cruces, right?"

"Cool stuff?" Jose says.

"Like, going out?"

"We never talked about these things with our last consultant."

"Who was your consultant last year?"

"He was short," Jose says. "Very serious."

"Hopefully I'll be different. I'm serious, but not *that* serious."

"He glared a lot," Sam says from the backseat. "Never seemed happy."

"He yelled at one of our pledges about his t-shirt," Jose says.

"Yelled about a t-shirt?" I ask.

"Did not like the slogan. I forget what it said. Made him turn his t-shirt inside-out."

"Oh," I say. "That's not cool."

"He had very shiny shoes, too. Polished them each night."

"Well," I say. "Not me. My shoes are, you know, dusty already."

"It'll get worse," Sam says. "Can't keep anything clean out here."

"So what about the bar scene, then? Does it make up for the...dust?"

"Some killer army bars, if you're into that," Sam says.

"Army bars," I say, and no...I'm not into that.

"Our last consultant," Jose says, flipping his turn signal a full 200 feet before he makes his turn, and completing a magnificent hand-over-hand rotation of the steering wheel, "he told us that the best thing to do for a traveling consultant was to make sure you had time to rest, and that you had time to yourself."

"Time to rest?" I say. And I suddenly realize with depressing certainty that, because I have no car, I can't go anywhere on my own; if I want to go to a bar, I actually have to *convince* them to drive me to a bar.

Sam brushes sweat from his forehead, knocks his baseball cap sideways, leaves it like that. "Yeah. The guy kept saying he was tired. Exhausted from all the traveling."

I chug my water, still thirsty. "Well, that's not—"

"So we thought it would be nice," Jose says, "if you had some privacy tonight. We have some things to take care of, so we will leave you at my apartment to relax."

"Leave me at your apartment?"

I can watch his DVDs, he says. They know a great taco-burrito delivery place and they'll order me some dinner. I can watch TV, read a book. I can play X-box, fool around on the internet, get caught up on reports. I can go to sleep early, he says. The place is all mine, and I can sleep as late as I want tomorrow. Wake up refreshed.

"I don't..." I say. "It's Saturday night."

"Don't worry about us," Jose says. "We have many things to take care of."

Sam's baseball cap is sideways still, and he doesn't care, still hasn't fixed it, *hasn't fixed it*, and it is a certainty now, isn't it? I couldn't get a read on these guys before, but I know now that Sam is not just a joker but a full-fledged *frat star* who had this whole abandon-the-consultant thing planned... But there are different types of frat stars, I decide: those at Pittsburgh and Shippensburg whose every movement bespoke the "drinking club" lifestyle, those at Illinois who had money and power and didn't give a damn about the world outside their house, and now...this. Someone who hates not just the National Fraternity and its consultants, but also his own school, his town, perhaps his entire state.

Sam's hat is sideways, and he is really, really fratty, frat-tastic even. I see this now. The hat, the jokes, the planned attempt to drop me off: there was never a question how to categorize the chapter at New Mexico State University.

"So what are *you* guys doing, then?" I ask. "While I'm, you know, resting?"

Silence in the car. Sam scratching the hair under his hat.

A week ago, I would have appreciated silence and sleep, a welcome retreat from the madness of my daily schedule, time to—yes—recharge for the next grueling week, but now I'm thinking, You two are going out on the town tonight, aren't you? Hitting up that one hidden college bar in this entire dusty town, some shack-in-the-woods dive with plank floors and two-by-fours for walls, but giant beer tubs lining the interior, and 20-year-old college girls in short black skirts and low-cut sex tops, and Kanye's "See You in My Nightmare" bumping loud enough to shake the neon Budweiser signs on the walls.

"Tonight," I say. "What are you guys doing?"

"Nothing exciting," Jose says. "We have some planning and details and things. I think that I would probably rather stay at home if I had the choice."

"Yeah," Sam says. "Whoo. I'm exhausted."

"No, really," I say. "I'm *not* tired. I'm *not* sitting at home."

"Um," Sam says, and now he corrects his hat.

"We *do* have an event for our pledges tonight," Jose says. "That is where we will be."

"An event for your pledges?"

"It's not a big deal. It's just a stupid little thing," Sam says.

"It is nothing that we were trying to keep secret," Jose says, his slight accent giving the words a strange foreign appeal, as though New Mexico State's pledge event is special because it is unlike anything I have ever experienced before in the States. "It is nothing bad. It is actually an educational event. An Etiquette Dinner. We got the idea from National Convention."

"And I can't come?"

"Naw, it isn't that," Sam says. "Naw, we just..."

"It would probably be very *boring* for you," Jose says and then laughs humorlessly, face like a mob-movie background goon who wants to convince the boss that he didn't fuck up. "We use the *Marathon* as a guide for the etiquette lesson. Conduct of a gentleman. We talk of things like pulling out chairs for ladies, working from the outside in when using silverware."

"Yeah," I say, measuring their expressions, gauging their fear. I *am* still the Educational Consultant, the Fun Nazi who can make misery of their happy fraternity functions. "We had pledges who'd eaten TV dinners their whole lives. Sure, they need these sorts of events."

"Right," Sam says from the back. "They come to college *so* rough. We got guys who grew up in military families. Love hunting, hiking, but no indoor manners."

"Most of our brothers," Jose says in his slow English, and he turns the steering wheel—hand over hand, absolutely textbook again (*but only to the untrained eye*, for the Fun Nazi can see his reluctance to speak too quickly, to look me in the eyes as he speaks) and we pull down a choppy road that leads to a mud-colored apartment building, "most have grown up in either the military or as first-generation immigrants. Homes without fathers. Very poor."

"It's an awesome event, really," Sam says, maybe excited because—as New Member Educator—the Etiquette Dinner is *his* event to organize. Maybe he thinks the Authority Figure in the front seat is enthralled by his creation. Maybe he's willing to say more than the tight-lipped chapter president.

"What makes it so awesome?" I ask.

"We get them together, our pledges, and they're all dressed up in shirt and tie and everything," Sam says, "and we invite a sorority to come over as their dates—"

"A sorority?" I ask.

"Right. They, um...they come to the house..."

And now he's gripping the bill of his baseball cap, wondering if he's said too much.

Etiquette Dinner, I think, still turning the words over in my head, and attempting through a waning state of inebriation to process images of the night. Sorority girls. The bodies in their tight white pants waiting to enter the front door of the fraternity house. When I close my eyes, though, I see only numbers and spreadsheets and then the Code of Conduct and "three times/weekly" and "No Dating, Drinking, Drugs, or Digital Footprints" and "NEVER," and I rub my eyes, smooth my pants, try to make it all go away.

"This sounds like fun," I say. "I think I want to do this."

"You want to..." Sam says. "You want to watch?"

"I want to *do* this."

"You want to participate?"

"Definitely."

"Well. Like. This is for our pledges?"

"Etiquette dinner," I say again. "This sounds fun. So what's the deal? When's it start?"

"You really want to do it?" Sam asks, voice sinking. "No joking?"

"Of course, of course."

"Hmm," Sam says. "'Kay. Well. Guess we can..." He looks to Jose.

"It is..."

"There's a few..."

"...a detail that needs..."

"...but, shit..."

"I did not think that..."

"I hope this isn't going to be a problem," I say. "I don't want my visit to be *too* serious. I can get serious, if you prefer?"

"No. Of course. We change things," Jose says. "This will work."

"All right," Sam says, not visibly upset, not displaying the look of a man in the heat of competition whose best-laid plans have been spoiled, just continuing to run his fingers over the bill of his hat, staring at the ceiling of the car in strong contemplation, morphing from *Man With the World's Greatest Event* to *Man Who Must Fix Now-Flawed Event*.

"I've never done anything like this during a chapter visit," I say. "Usually it's just meetings. I like to have fun, though. Really. I'm a consultant, but I'm still *your* age. Still young."

"I guess you are," Sam says.

\*

At Jose's off-campus apartment, I drag my bags to his living room and then scarf a bag of his potato chips and watch the USC game while he's in the shower and, mostly sober now, I open my suitcase and stare at the inside, at the shirts, the socks, the shoes, the belts, the toiletry bag. Just as when I stared into it at a hotel in Illinois, nothing is where it should be. And after a careful inspection, I realize that—yes—I definitely left my goal sheets behind in my Explorer. They're nowhere to be found. And I'm thinking that these black shoes in this corner of the suitcase could be easily moved a couple inches, and this stack of undershirts could be easily straightened, this bottle of vitamins lifted, shifted to a better location.

240

But I grab only what I need from the suitcase, from my garment bag, shut both of them and try—eyes closed, straining—not to think about how I will organize them later.

Before I shower, I check my cell phone's voicemail and discover that Jenn has left three more messages since this afternoon. The first message is confused, cryptic, sounds like she called for a reason and then forgot ("I, uh... listen, I called Charles, because...I've had these weird feelings lately"), and it's all rambling build-up with no payoff. The second message is more focused, but still Jenn doesn't seem to say much; she tells me that she wants to make plans *now*; am I getting a hotel room, because I know I can't stay at the sorority house, right? And what was I thinking about for Thanksgiving? I get the whole week off, right? She'll call my parents, is that okay? This second message is all questions, a feeling-out, but underneath I hear a tremble of emotion that finally surfaces in the third message: "Charles," she says, no accompanying happy high tone in her voice to counter the upset low, "we need to talk. Really. Where are you? Things are not good, Charles. Where are you?" She sounds drunk. Bravery fueled by alcohol. The middle of the afternoon and a gameday six-pack helped her to find the words that she hasn't been able to speak in the last month.

"Where am I?" I ask. "Where *am* I?"

I call her back, not even willing to stifle the rising anger because I want it to match—no, *exceed*—that sharpness I sensed in her messages. *Where am I? Things are not good?* I'm working. Out in New Mexico. *Working* while she's drinking.

"I was in an airplane, Jenn," I say as soon as she answers. "I was in the *air*."

"What are you..." she starts, then switches to, "Charles, why are you yelling?"

"Why am I *yelling*? I'm not yelling."

"You're shouting."

"I was in an airplane, Jenn," I say again. "That's where I was."

"Okay? What are you *talking* about?"

"You kept asking where I was. In your messages. I was in an airplane."

"All you had to do was tell me—"

"I'm trying to tell you."

"All you had to do was tell me what you were *talking about*. You just call me and start saying these random things. How am I supposed to know what you're talking about?"

"Why leave the message, then?" I ask. "Why leave a message like that if you don't want an answer?"

"How..." she says. "What's going on here?"

"I'm answering your question, that's what's going on."

"You're yelling again."

"I'm not."

"You're yelling. And you make no sense."

"I make sense, Jenn. *You're* the one..."

"You call me and you start yelling?"

"I was calling you back because *you*—"

"I got emotional today," she says. "What do you expect? The way you've been talking to me? Texting me? You told me you'd call me, and I didn't know you were flying all day."

"I told you this morning."

"No," she says. "I knew you were flying, but not all day."

"You were preoccupied. You didn't care."

"Charles," she says. "Please. *I'm* preoccupied?"

"You're always preoccupied."

"I texted you, like, ten times today. Did you check your texts, or did you forget to even turn your phone on when you landed? This fraternity has become your life."

"You're preoccupied," I say again. "You've got your socials. You were at a football game all day, weren't you? Tailgating? What do you need a phone relationship for? You're just doing me a favor by staying with me. Humoring me. Don't do me favors."

"Charles. You misunderstood me."

"Were you at the tailgates today? With another fraternity, right?"

"What does that have to do with anything?"

"You were."

"Fine. So what?"

So what? And a list of answers occurs to me. So what? So you were in those grassy parking lots outside the stadium, standing beside beer troughs and flirting with other guys for free cans of Bud Lite. So you put your hand on some frat guy's bicep and asked him to help you up onto his tailgate. So you asked another guy, bigger, drunker, to hold your legs while you climbed up onto a keg and did a keg stand. He held your legs and you were wearing a jean skirt probably, and he helped you down and with a towel wiped off the beer from your wet t-shirt. So it sounds good when you say you care about "doing the right thing," when you tell someone their plans are "noble," but all you're really thinking is that it's cute and charming…for now.

"I don't need this, you know?" I say.

"Don't need what?" she asks.

"This. You, on the fence like this. I want a girlfriend who's either with me or is not."

She sighs. "What do you want me to say, Charles? I was emotional today. I missed you, is that what you want to hear? I was sad, then I was angry, then I was just drunk and everything kind of boiled. I don't know what else to say. I said too much already."

"Well, then. It's all settled. Life's perfect."

"Don't be an asshole."

"I've got to get a shower," I say. "Work never ends around here. 24/7, you know? It's my life, like you said. So I'll have to talk to you tomorrow."

She protests a bit, tells me that I should call her again tonight, but there's no point in that. I don't want to pencil in another goal for the evening—"Call

Jenn/ 9:00 PM," or "Devise strategy for reconciliation/ 10:00 PM"—while she enjoys her night. No, instead I hang up my clothes on the towel rack in Jose's bathroom, and I shave, and I arrange my hair gel and my comb and my toothbrush along a clean countertop, and I step under the showerhead and hot water hits me and I watch the layers of desert grime on my skin come loose and wash away.

*

Afterward I'm driven to the NKE chapter house, which is located in a neighborhood directly across the street from the university. Out in the paved parking lot of the house, Sam tells me, "Just wait outside here with the pledges while we finish getting set up inside, 'kay? We'll be back in a second."

The fraternity house is sand-colored, would probably blend into the dusty landscape in the daytime, but now darkness is taking control of the evening, the wide-open sky deepening to navy and the moon growing crisp, high-definition white clarity. It's mid-September and the sun is starting to set sooner.

Surrounding me in the parking lot are the fifteen pledges for this chapter's new member class. Rush concluded two weeks ago, Sam said, so the world of fraternity life is still new to these kids; they're living the denouement of Rush Season, the final still-clueless days before the definition of "fraternity" balloons to include a national organization with 120 chapters and Educational Consultants and a hundred-year history stretching back to a place called Carolina Baptist: they are living the days when "fraternity" is a happy ending to a tumultuous first few weeks of college, when "fraternity" is a cozy college family and "family" never needs to mean more than family.

Among these fifteen freshman students, I alone wear a full suit and tie, just unpacked from my garment bag. The others wear a mix-and-match, borrowed-from-here-and-there, whatever-I-could-get-my-hands-on ensemble; they wear awkward-sized dress shirts with ties poorly tied, torn cargo khakis, scuffed and dusty dress shoes. Impoverished backgrounds, Jose said: for some of these kids, 17- and 18-year-olds, this might be the first time they've ever had to wear a tie. But we are all together, fifteen freshman men and a single college graduate, waiting outside the house for the new pledge sisters of Alpha Alpha Sorority to arrive.

I consider introducing myself as the Consultant, listing off my job responsibilities and speaking of the national mission, modeling the correct social behaviors of the Marathon Man.

"—this fucking girl, *Maria*," one of these kids says, "body like it was *built* for fucking."

Uproarious laughter from the rest of the pledges. A group of young men whose experience with sex largely consists of a few hectic afternoons at their girlfriend's homes back in high school, trying to slap on a condom and find the right spot and grope without seeming like they'd never seen a naked female before, trying not to come too quickly but at the same time trying to finish before her parents came home from work, and oh shit, I put the condom on wrong and it pinches, it pinches, *oh my God!* But they're laughing over there at the sex-talk, the whole group of freshmen.

Except one. Because he's wandered over to me, has a cigarette in hand. Spiky black hair that shoots in every direction, wearing a violent red shirt with black pants. Looks like he wants to join the cast of *Jersey Shore*, but he's too short, too tiny, has no muscle mass on his frame.

"Got a light?" he asks, lifting his chin in a "'sup" motion, brandishing the cigarette.

"No lighter," I say. "Sorry."

"Have I met you?" He lifts his chin higher, squints hard.

I open my mouth to answer, then stop.

This early in the semester, all the pledges are still learning one another's names. They're all strangers. So I could introduce myself as the Consultant, the Fun Nazi, but I have a choice.

Blank white space. Possibility.

"Yeah," I say. "You've met me. I'm Charles."

"I don't remember you." His squint has gone suspicious, the unlit cigarette now dangling from his mouth. Solid spikes of hair under the fading light looking somehow *more* solid and dangerous than hair should, as if they are not simply a glued-together collection of strands but rubber or hard plastic to the core. "You don't look familiar."

"I've been busy. With classes."

"You look nice. Nice suit." He takes the cigarette from his mouth, stares me up and down, motioning with his hand to let me know that he's taking in the visual of my professional-wear, that he sees the crease in my pants, the straight collar points of my shirt.

"Thanks."

"You look a little old to be a pledge. How old are you?"

"Ouch. I look old?"

"How old are you?"

"Freshman," I say. "But I took a couple years off after high school."

He sucks on his cigarette, then realizes it's still unlit. "True," he says. "True."

And then he's off, asking someone else for a light, is successful in his request, but still stands nearby as if keeping an eye on me, all the while smoking his cigarette with forced displays of adulthood, taking long and dramatic drags to bluff the world into thinking he's an old pro.

Nearby, another pledge has a plastic flask tucked into his sock, takes quick sips while no one looks.

"—so drunk that I passed out under the coffee table!" another shouts.

More of the uproarious laughter.

"Fuck that shit, bitch!"

Laughter, and I try to smile.

*

Sometime after 8:30, after thirty minutes of waiting in the growing darkness of the September evening, after all the pledges have let their shoulders slump and have gone from stories of raucous drunken debauchery to muffled complaints about "when this shit's going to start," five modest sedans—pink lays hanging from rearview mirrors, Alpha Alpha bumper-stickers on back windows—pull into the gravel driveway. The pledges organize themselves into an excited clump, like paparazzi on the red carpet at a premiere, in anticipation for the arrival of the females who will be forced to listen and talk with them for the duration of this event. This Etiquette Dinner, while supposedly "educational," doubles as a fraternity-sorority "mixer," a blind date between fifteen guys and fifteen girls.

I stand behind the Pledge Clump, shoulders hunched, trying to stay inconspicuous.

The car doors open, so many at once that it just sounds like microwave popcorn—tump tump tump tump tump tump—and the sorority girls step out of the cars and form a single-file line behind an older, assertive brunette.

"All right," one of the pledges says softly. "This is it, boys."

"I get the one in the red," says another.

The NKE pledges whistle with delight as they check the sorority girls out. Like the young men, these freshman girls are also dressed with uncertainty of purpose, unsure if they're going out to a club or going to an internship: they remind me of Paris Hilton from *The Simple Life*, wearing Gucci as she corrals a group of pigs on the farm. Some girls wear brilliant knee-length red skirts with black halter-tops, and others wear tan or black pants so tight I could see their goosebumps poke out if the temperature dropped ten degrees. The clothes glimmer with newness, perhaps purchased from the mall earlier today, acquired for this occasion just as the NKE pledges borrowed ties from roommates earlier today. They're mostly Hispanic, the girls, just like all of the guys, and each moves with side-to-side hip sways copied from Beyonce or Rihanna videos, attempting to milk the motion for all the sexiness it's worth.

Several girls wear shimmering silver or gold necklaces with gigantic cursive charms reading "Rachel" or "Tamara," and twinkling hoop earrings and purses purchased from Clare's or Rave or whatever celeb knock-off store is in the Las Cruces Mall. Items that were undoubtedly hip in high school, and that have yet to be phased from their wardrobes. It is a crowd of young people who have just crossed the borderlands into adulthood and who are still trying to imitate what they see in this new world. Some are good at it, but most are just obvious.

My suit is Ralph Lauren, silver-black (the salesman described this color and style as the *new*-new black, "a suit for men who know that there are just *so* many possibilities for black"), black fabric coursing with veins of silver, "a look that says both business and pleasure." I spent most of my graduation gift money on this suit, but it's an outfit I never intended for a New Mexico State pledge function. In fact, I'm the only one whose tie looks tight, confident.

A desert wind cuts through the parking lot, and we all get sand in our eyes.

For the second time today, I think: this is all a bad idea.

*

During my freshman year at EU, I was probably no different than any of these NMSU pledges, still learning how to act with social grace. Failing as often as I was succeeding. Waking up in my own puke, my father standing over me. That sort of thing.

In fact, there is perhaps no single year in any human lifetime where the gulf between *What I Know* and *What I Want Everyone to Think I Know* is as deep as it is for freshman men at American universities. You've never filed your own taxes, never worried about your own insurance, never even tried any beer besides Bud Lite, but you've officially hit *legal adulthood*, which you equate immediately with Manhood, capital M, so you think you should never admit any shortcomings.

Freshman sorority girls, though, are a different species entirely.

No responsibility, but also no social pressure to be "the man," either.

If I drew it out in one of our alcohol workshops, this is what a sorority girl's social progression through college would look like:

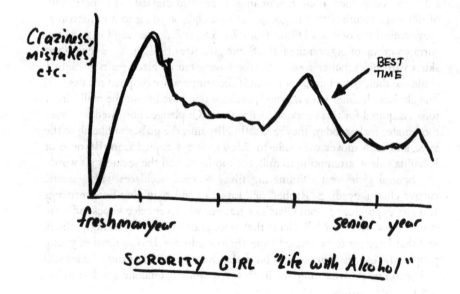

246

Freshman year, while fraternity guys are still rough and unrefined, sorority girls at EU are a boiling witch's brew of wild and uninhibited freedom, of first real experiences with excessive alcohol consumption, of their first sex in bedrooms where parents do not lurk a bedroom away, their first one-night stands, their first one-night stand-ups, of boom-boom-boom hook-ups; untamed, everywhere, out of control; if you want a relationship more serious than a drunken at-the-bar make-out, you avoid them. Sophomore year, they settle down, but they're *pissed off* because the upperclassmen (interested in them the year before) are now turning their attention to the new class of incoming freshmen girls, who are untamed, everywhere, out of control, etc. Junior year, though, EU girls were most comfortable in their skin: 21 and unintimidated. As seniors, they know who they are, and they know how to have a good time without getting stupid or jealous; they are at their most reasonable.

A freshman girl, though? Wild. Untamed. It's a matter of years, but it's a different lifetime entirely. And hell if I even know how to talk to a girl like that anymore.

*

"*Gentle*-men," Sam bellows from the front doors of the fraternity house, his ensemble now switched from faded-baseball-cap-and-frat-shirt to dress-shirt-and-khaki-pants; he walks down the stone steps of the house with the authority and importance of an old Roman general, surveying the massive crowd of freshmen. This is a new Sam. Not the same kid that met me at the baggage claim. This is *New Member Educator* Sam, the old and mature fraternity brother, the man elected each semester to teach and test the young pledges on fraternity history, on traditions and customs. He walks chest-out toward our clump, passes us without so much as a glance in my direction, and shakes the brunette's hand.

They give one another soft smiles that seem to hide secrets.

"The kids are going to have a good time tonight," Sam says in a low voice.

"I hope so," she says. "They got all dressed up."

"Don't worry, Nicole. I'll have them home at a reasonable hour."

They give those conspiratorial smiles again, Sam whispering something inaudible. And then he turns and looks back at our Pledge Clump. "All right, guys, you know the drill. Form a single-file line and then we'll pair off with the ladies. 'Kay? Once you get a partner, walk to the front doors of the house and someone will seat you in the dining room."

"Dining room?" one of the pledges yells. "Ha! That's what you call it?"

Sam shakes his head. "Thousands of comedians out of jobs," he says, "and you got the nerve to try to be funny? Come on. Any other jokers out there?"

Silence from the Pledge Clump. Most look down at the dirt, spirits momentarily crushed.

The spiky-haired pledge is twirling a cigarette in his fingers, lip trembling.

"We've cleaned up the house," Sam says, "made it into a first-class restaurant for the night. Remember everything we taught you. Act like

respectable Nu Kappa Epsilon gentlemen tonight—do *not* embarrass me—
and I'll see you again after your dinner."

My stomach clenches again, the same no-turning-back sensation as
when I first stepped out of my car at orientation.

Nicole motions with one long and elegant arm for the guys and the girls
to begin pairing. Likely, she's the sorority New Member Educator, Sam's
female counterpart, the initiated sister responsible for her sorority's young
pledges. I hear her say something like, "Aww, my babies are growing up,"
and then she's digging a digital camera from her purse, scrolling through
previously captured photos, raising the camera, pointing it at the crowd as we
pair.

Pictures. Likely to post online somewhere.

"Shit," I say, and I turn away and see the flash all around me.

Just my back. No one will recognize that.

"Shit," I say again when I turn around and Nicole snaps another photo
and I am suddenly, unavoidably, front and center in the shot.

"Fantastic photo," Nicole says happily. "That's going online, definitely.
Good luck, girls. You look great."

Even if I'm never tagged, my likeness—best suit, best hair, best posture—
is going to wind up on the front page of the event's permanent history. I am
the cover of a Rush brochure, I am a Facebook photo album cover.

The other pledges are rushing forward now, shaking hands and speaking
in shaky voices (camera's bright flash continuing to illuminate the parking lot
in periodic bursts), and a few have tried to lift their partner's hands to kiss the
tops, but it's such a forced attempt at chivalry that it's laughable: they're about
to have dinner in a frat house, not take a romantic carriage ride.

Another camera flash, and I turn to escape it, then another flash, and I
shift away and now stand before a beautiful dark-skinned girl with electric
highlights in light brown hair, and when the next camera flash strikes they
glow with Hollywood brilliance, and as I stare at her, this gorgeous girl who—
like me—looks too confident to be a pledge, too mature in every sense of the
word, mental-physical-spiritual, the camera and the photos and the digital
footprints no longer matter. She wears dark blue eyeliner and a black cocktail
dress that makes the curves of her breasts and her hips shimmer, every subtle
movement a revelation begging that you follow the curves to see what will
happen next, and she tells me her name is Maria; and I wonder if this is the
girl who, as someone noted earlier, has a body built for fucking.

"Nice to meet you," she says in a pillow-soft voice.

"No, no," I say. "It's nice to meet *you*."

"Do I know you?" She looks at me with real curiosity, hand on her hip.
And if only she could stand here like this, maintain this pose forever, I would
be a happy man until I died.

"Maybe. I'm around the house a lot."

"I swear I've met you."

"Sure, sure." Straight-faced. Just another pledge. "Probably."

All of us walk inside the house, pair by pair; somewhere behind me in the parking lot, Sam Anderson argues with a pledge who claims that there aren't enough girls to pair up with. "We're one girl short, Brother Sam," the kid says. "What am I supposed to do? I don't have a partner." I turn around and—just as I pass through the front doorway—accidentally make eye contact with Sam, who has his hand on this kid's shoulder and is telling him that he's sorry, that we must have miscounted, that he'll have to sit this one out, and I'm responsible, I'm Guy Number Sixteen and I ruined this kid's night, but I try not to think about it.

*

Maria and I enter the fraternity house, and because I wasn't able to see the interior earlier I have no basis for comparison on how well these brothers have "made over" the "dining room." The lighting is dim (likely for atmosphere), but assorted wooden paddles still hang on the walls in no particular pattern, no care taken to beautify a cracked empty trophy case in the far corner; and although the cheap fold-out tables are covered with plain white tablecloths to give the illusion of a "first-class restaurant," the tables themselves are set with clashing silverware, sloppily folded paper napkins, and thick candles that rest on the tablecloth, wax collecting in puddles on the cloth. Not exactly the level of sophistication I'd expect from Carolina Baptist or Cornell or EU, and LaFaber might even question how this décor impresses in its new members the mission to build socially responsible leaders ("Is this the best you can do?"), but it's a fraternity house Etiquette Dinner in a town without much money. And tonight, it feels fine to me.

Maria sits across from me—I pull out her chair and help her into her seat, and upon seeing me perform this small act of courtesy, several other pledges around the room bumble from their own seats and attempt to do the same. Beside me is the pledge who asked for a light just fifteen minutes ago. His name is Michael, he tells his date, and I now notice that his violent red shirt (and black tie, black pants, black shoes) is complemented by a pair of white socks. It's as if he has an image in mind of who he wants to look like, some rapper or hip-hop artist who stands on boats or pops from the sunroofs of limos with outstretched female limbs clutching any piece of him, titties smashed against him constantly, champagne bottle in hand, always wearing sharp blacks to show the world that he is a man of the night life. But Michael has missed the most subtle elements of the costume: matching socks, for instance.

Maria takes a sip of water, regards me from across the table. "You look... older."

"Ouch," I say for the second time tonight.

"That's what I said outside!" Michael shouts, nearly spilling his water as he thrusts it forward to point at me. "Looks fucking older!"

"Yes," I say. "And thank you for putting it so kindly."

"Sorry," Maria says, "I didn't mean—"

"No, I get that a lot. I took a couple years off after high school. Boring story, but anyway..." And now it's a race to frame the conversation, to make sure *I'm* the one asking questions, not the one caught in a domino set of lies. "So where are *you* from?" I turn my back to Michael so that he's forced to converse with his own partner.

"Santa Fe. You?"

And Michael is sopping up the spilled water now, his partner asking if he's all right.

"I'm from Florida," I say.

"You're kidding."

"Not kidding. This entire state is brand-new to me. Have you lived here your whole life?"

"Yes." She runs her fingers through the ends of her highlighted hair, letting it fall lightly on bare shoulders. "My parents moved here from California."

"Long way away."

"Not as far as Florida," she says. "I don't think I've ever met anyone from *Flor*-ida."

"You've never been to Orlando? Disney World?"

"Once, but this is different. I've never met anyone from Florida out in *New Mexico*. Why on Earth did you come all the way out here?"

"My story's not too interesting," I say and look down at the table, shrugging. Thinking of a story. Beside me, Michael is now struggling to find any response longer than three words to satisfy the polite questions asked by his partner, a girl with intricately braided hair and a complexion so smooth that she looks too young for college; were I not seated at a fraternity-sorority mixer, I might have guessed her a high school student. She's asked four or five questions, but she looks bored and exhausted already, folding and re-folding her napkin and searching the ceiling for something more noteworthy than her partner, who has again pulled out an unlit cigarette and is twirling it around in his fingers.

"Tell me your story," Maria says. "I'm sure it's interesting."

Back in Florida, Jenn is piling into a car with her sorority sisters, and they're on their way to Central, to Tango's or Hem-Haw's, and for the second time today she will drink free beer and vodka tonics purchased by frat guys at the bar who maybe have a shot with her.

"Well," I say, "Florida's a fun state, but I needed something different. It's so humid sometimes that you sweat a gallon just walking from class to class."

"Wow," she says. "So, where do you live out here—"

"How is Santa Fe?" I ask. "I've only been to Las Cruces and El Paso, so far."

"You haven't even been to *Juarez* yet?" She holds her hand to her mouth.

"Juarez?" I ask. "Like, Mexico? No. Should I have been?"

"Oh my God," Maria says and she taps the high school girl beside her and says in a quick burst, "oh my god shelley, charles hasn't even been to juarez."

Shelley brightens immediately, turns her attention from spiky-haired Michael and smiles at me and says "Oh my God" dramatically, like she was just saved from a burning building, pulled from the window by a firefighter on a ladder.

"He's from *Flor*-ida," Maria says.

"Oh my God! What are you doing out here?"

"Just...still getting used to a different state, is all," I say.

"Yo, I'm still over here, for fuck's sake," Michael says. "S'posed to talk to *me*."

"Florida," Maria says. "We *have* to take you to Juarez. I can't believe you've never been. I mean, it isn't the greatest place, but you can drink. It's nuts. You have to go."

"I can drink anywhere," I say.

"What do you mean?" Maria asks. "You're not 21, are you?"

I'm silent for a second, hear my heartbeat growing louder. Just another pledge, I'm thinking. "No. I've just been to a lot of different places. How do I know Juarez is better than going to, say, LA or Fresno?"

"Fresno?" Shelley asks. "Eew."

"Fresno's awesome," Michael says, and now he's leaning over onto our side of the table, arms and elbows on the tablecloth, hair almost poking me in the face, the plastic-alcohol odor of hair gel and the stale smell of cigarettes settling over me. Shelley rolls her eyes.

"Juarez," Maria says. "We're going. You'll love it."

"What happens if I get really, really drunk in Juarez?" I ask. "I've seen those shirts that say, 'I was drunk and left for dead in a Mexican prison.'"

"There are Mexico horror stories, Charles," Maria says, scoots her chair a bit to the left to show her disinterest in Michael. "That's why you go with a group."

"Yeah!" Shelley says. "It's more fun that way, too."

"But you have to find the *right* group," Maria says.

"Who are you?" Michael asks me, but he looks at Maria. "I don't know who you are, bro. Never seen you before. Who *is* this guy?"

I adjust my napkin, wonder if I should just end the performance and make a formal introduction to Michael, if there's any going back now.

"I like your tie," Maria says. "And that suit? What color is that?"

"Silver-black," I say. "It's supposed to be the next big thing."

"It's very classy."

"Thank you. I'm glad you like it."

Michael turns away, still eying me suspiciously, then exhales loudly before scrolling through his cell phone. "Whatever," he says.

Soon thereafter, a short Hispanic guy in blue jeans walks from a doorway at the back of the room, carrying four styrofoam bowls of salad balanced uneasily on his wrists and palms. He arranges them in front of each girl at the far table, then heads back through the doorway to the kitchen, a moment later returning with more salad bowls, and he continues, over and over to the kitchen, until all thirty of us have been served. I joke with Maria and Shelley about how a single tray would be more efficient to carry all these plates, about how it's great that we've broken out our finest china for tonight, and while I worry my jokes are contrived, they laugh with such honesty that I wonder if I might somehow sparkle with the same energy that attracted Jenn so long ago. Meanwhile, Michael continues to mutter under his breath. "A thousand comedians out of a job," he mumbles.

*

Dinner: Michael plunges into his salad before Maria and Shelley are even finished folding their napkins in their laps. I wait to pick up my fork until they've taken their first bites, and Michael says, "Fucking show-off." Still, I ask them how the food is, and I don't chew with my mouth open, and I swallow and wipe my mouth before speaking.

Michael again asks if he knows me, now has his hand on my shoulder.

I brush his hand away—Maria and Shelley staring at this scene the way you'd regard parents reprimanding their children in public—and I whisper so loud that it probably isn't a whisper: "*Come on*, Michael. Quit messing around."

"Is he all right?" Maria asks, fingers at her temples to keep her curly hair from slipping over her eyes. Minutes before, she didn't seem to mind the spontaneity of out-of-place hair, but now the tension has become a tangible thing seated at our table.

"He's a joker," I say. "Funny guy. Heh."

"He seems…" and she lowers her voice to a whisper: "angry."

"No no," I say. "See, they're talking now. Everyone's having a great time." But Shelley is still staring at the two of us, and Michael is now on his cell phone, telling someone about *Transformers*.

After we finish our salads, the server in the blue jeans brings out styrofoam plates of steaming spaghetti and lumpy meat sauce, and plates stacked high with garlic rolls.

"What are you studying here?" Maria asks.

"Business," I say. "But I'm already thinking about changing."

"To what?"

"College. I can major in *college*, right?"

She laughs. "Do you have a girlfriend?"

A plate of spaghetti is slid before me, sauce spattering on the tablecloth.

"Girlfriend," I say.

"Yeah. You have one?"

"I don't even know anyone around here."

"Good. Guys without girlfriends are more fun."

"Yes they are, aren't they?"

After the spaghetti is delivered, Michael thankfully turns his full attention to Shelley, quizzing her on NBA stars and statistics, Dwight Howard vs. Shaq. Kobe vs. LeBron. Her eyes going wider and wider and her hands flapping around in frustration as she says, "Look, I don't *care*, okay?" But somehow, I've got something going with Maria: I'm commenting on differences in weather between Florida and New Mexico, in landscape, in student attitudes, and amazingly, she remains engaged throughout dinner. I slip once or twice, first telling her that I'm from Fort Myers and then telling her I'm from Cypress Falls. But the cities are right next to each other, I reassure her. Parents bought a new house. We moved.

"So does everyone, like, have orange trees in Florida?"

"Orange trees?" I ask. "Where'd you get that idea?"

"Don't laugh," she says, laughing herself, and both of our hands are above the table and she stretches out her fingers and taps my hand playfully. A curl of hair falling across her forehead and settling like a dark lightning bolt over her right eye. She doesn't lift her hand to brush it away, just lets it sit there framing her face in shadow, just keeps her fingers intertwined with mine. "It's a real question," she says.

"Real question? I don't ask you if all New Mexicans have cacti in their yards."

"You *do* have an orange tree back home, don't you?"

"Yes," I say. "Everyone's got orange trees. And everyone lives on the beach. And Mickey Mouse is our governor."

"Don't laugh." She play-hits me again.

"This is good stuff. I'll have to remember this." And I can't stop smiling, because everywhere I've been, I've only noticed those things that are different from my home state; I've viewed the world through the lens of Florida, and now suddenly I'm being viewed through New Mexico.

But the dinner, and all conversation, ends abruptly when Sam and Nicole reappear at the front doors of the chapter house, Sam with his arms folded before his body, Nicole with her hands at her waist and her foot tapping an impatient rhythm. "All right, gentlemen," Sam says, "I need you outside *now*. Out the back door. Courtyard."

And there is no explanation following this statement.

The pledges rise from their seats, fifteen confused young men with spaghetti-full mouths, marinara-stained napkins falling to the floor as they stand. One of the pledges on the far end of the room tries to continue his conversation with his sorority partner even as he rises, but Sam just says "*Now!*" and he jumps forward as if poked by a cattle prod.

"Thank you gentlemen," Nicole says with a fake sing-tone in her voice.

So I tell Maria and Shelley "Thank you for a wonderful time," and shake both of their hands (but only the very ends of their hands, their fingers, not a full-hand grip like Michael gives) and I join an awkward line of pledges out the door and into the back courtyard.

I realize, also, that I didn't stain my shirt with marinara. Score.

*

For a moment—here outside in the fraternity house courtyard (there's no *yard*, just pavement and sand and cacti), where it has grown dark and where the distance affords only jagged black outlines of miles-away mountains, no city lights—all is quiet. Fifteen young men stand with hands in pockets, disappointed looks on their faces because they can't believe the Etiquette

Dinner has come to such an abrupt and anticlimactic end. The same kind of look you might see in a theater when a movie cuts off unexpectedly, some electrical failure ripping the audience from the experience. They wanted phone numbers. They imagined themselves wooing their women, winding up back in dorm rooms beneath bedsheets: for 18-year-old men, the mind inevitably unveils this scenario whenever conversation is struck with an attractive female, no matter the occasion.

But the disappointment lasts only a moment.

Soon, the scattered pledges converge in the center of the lot to re-form their fifteen-man Pledge Clump, and quickly it becomes a jubilant mass of howling laughter, of "Yo, that was *money*, baby!" and high-fives, pats on the shoulder, fist-pounds and "I almost got her *number*, man," and even spiky-haired Michael is high-fiving his pledge brothers, bragging as though he was the model of "true playa," as though he wasn't reciting Shaq's rebound totals for Shelley or slurping his spaghetti and splattering the meat sauce across the tablecloth.

I stand on the periphery to avoid drawing attention to myself, but I can't help loosening my tie and unbuttoning my wrists, my own minor victory celebration. For one night, I was a pledge at a college party, not an angry storm trooper blasting his way inside the house.

After a few minutes, though, Michael breaks free of the Clump. "Yo," he says, "I would've fucking had my girl's *number*, too, bro. She was all up *on* me. But this other guy, yo, he fucking cock-blocked me *all* night."

This other guy. Cock-blocking.

"I kept trying to talk to her," Michael says. Has a cigarette in one hand, and this time it's lit, a trail of smoke swirling about as Michael makes wide slashing gestures with both hands. "Kept trying to work my way into the convo, but this fucker kept brushing me off, knahmean?"

"Brushing you off?" someone asks. "Who was it?"

And outside, here in the unlit parking lot, I suddenly feel the need to tighten my tie again, to button my cuffs. Just another pledge? I hide behind a section of the Pledge Clump and scroll through my cell phone for nothing in particular.

Michael glances in several directions, looking for me. Takes a drag of his cigarette.

The New Mexico night growing colder, but still I can feel dried sweat and desert dust caked over my skin. Waves of it, like this state wants to bury me one sand grain at a time.

"Yo," Michael says, and he's located me in the crowd. He walks to me, motioning for a companion—a heavy-set kid with spotty facial hair over smooth cheeks—to follow him. Michael's body sways from side to side, boxer style, the sort of pose he probably saw on a 50 Cent video. Wipes fist across dry lips. "Yo, who the fuck are you, man?"

Silence in the Pledge Clump. Heads turning to watch the three of us. Smiles creeping across faces. Elbows nudging ribs. Whispers: "*this is gonna be good!*"

"Um. My name is Charles," I say. "We met."

"No, no," Michael says. He waves his index finger at me. "Who *are* you?"

"We sat at the same table. I'm Charles."

"Course we did. You think I don't know that?"

All eyes on us, the Pledge Clump breaking apart like a patch of scattered seagulls on the beach taking flight, all sorts of flapping noises and "Come on, come on," and "Let's go!" and they charge forward and re-converge quickly around *us*, surrounding the three of us in the same way that a mob might form around a middle school fight, almost as if they've been waiting for a confrontation all evening. Like they've known all along that I'm too polished to be authentic.

"Who the fuck *are* you, bro?" Michael asks. "I never seen you before. Never seen you at any parties, at any pledge meetings, nothing."

His finger in my face, ember-tipped cigarette centimeters from my eyes.

"I'm Charles," I say. "*Charles.* What do you want me to say?"

"I don't know what you're trying to pull, yo, but I know my pledge brothers. I know that this is Tony, right here. I know that that's Ro, over there. That's Miguel. That's Richard. But *nobody* knows who the fuck you are."

And I don't want to lose this night, don't want to reintroduce myself as "someone from Nationals," but all eyes are on me, violence in the glares, and so there's only one thing I *can* say: "I'm an Educational Consultant from the Nu Kappa Epsilon Headquarters." Vague looks from the Clump. "You might have read about my position in your pledge books. A consultant? From Headquarters?"

"The fuck...?" Michael says.

"Yo, this guy's a fucking spy," Tony—the stocky sidekick—says.

"The fuck?" Michael says again, head shaking.

"Brothers were testing us," Tony says.

"Oh, *shit*," Michael says and his chili-colored face immediately drains and his anger is gone and I could swear his pupils dilate and his spiky hair deflates and he looks like he's going to throw up. "Oh shit, oh shit, oh shit."

"Hold on," I say. "It's, um..."

"I'm so fucking sorry, man," he says and takes my hand and tries to shake it, but he looks like he was dipped in wax, barely moving or breathing, and—startled—I pull my hand away. "Oh shit, *sorry*, man. Don't tell the brothers. Don't tell the brothers I didn't know who you were. Oh shit. Don't tell them I stepped to you, bro."

"Stepped to me?"

His cigarette has fallen to the ground. He ambles backward, crushing it.

And, for some reason, the rest of the Pledge Clump is shrinking away, too, faces white with terror. One of them has turned around, is digging his fingers into his hair with the sort of stressed-out "I've lost everything!" panic that I'd expect of a stock broker after a market crash. Another has closed his eyes, is breathing super-slow, gripping his chest.

"Oh God," I say. "What just happened? It's all right. Don't worry."

I feel like I knocked into a fire alarm accidentally, like I just set something in motion that cannot be taken back, sounded an evacuation and killed the entire workday.

"My life's over," Michael says. His knees have gone weak. He's shrinking.

"Yo, yo," someone says. "Michael's a little slow. He's not usually like this."

"He doesn't usually make these kinds of mistakes," Tony says. "He's a good kid. He just has…you know…issues. We'll work it out, man, *really*."

"The brothers are good to us," someone else says. "They don't do nothing wrong."

"No, I'm just here to have a good time tonight," I say. "I'm not spying on you guys. I'm not here to get you in trouble or tell the brothers anything. All right?"

Silence from the Clump. They don't believe a word I'm saying.

Michael still isn't moving, breathing, so I repeat, "All *right?*" and finally he nods and some color appears to re-enter his face. All around me, I see the same debilitating and senseless fear on every face. Maybe I did pull an alarm, and this is the resulting loud-speaker blare that this fraternity chapter *hazes* with reckless abandon: Etiquette Dinners are the *fun* activity, but on any other Saturday night? Maybe the pledges are woken up in the middle of the night, herded here to the house backyard for hundreds upon hundreds of push-ups and jumping jacks and dehumanizing drill instruction, then briefed on how to keep secrets from authority figures, how to protect their own suffering. I should ask questions, right? I should take Michael aside, ask him if he's been hazed, if he's suffered physical abuse? I should stop this charade immediately, call LaFaber, find the necessary forms—

But inside the house are Maria and Shelley, and maybe the Etiquette Dinner isn't over…and these kids have only been in the fraternity for weeks… they wouldn't be hazed yet. That was the Fun Nazi talking, and he's not here.

"Oh fuck me," Tony says. "Look. It's Sam."

And we all look back to the fraternity house, all of us at once, as though we're a group of high school kids caught smoking in the bathroom by the campus rent-a-cop, and Sam Anderson stands in the open doorway of the house, a featureless silhouette framed by the muted orange light of the dining room. The pledges back away from me quickly—I'm the cigarette butt they've tossed into the urinal. *Nothing to see here*, smoke hidden behind puffed-out cheeks.

"*Gentle*-men," Sam says. "You may now re-enter the house. And let's make this quick, 'kay? No pussy-footing around."

The pledges form a single-file line, myself at the back, and smiles are finally—*finally*—returning to their faces. Like the threat of push-ups and air chairs and whippings has ended because there is still an Etiquette Dinner to be finished. There are *girls* present. Brothers can't haze when girls are present. I breathe easy. Sam wouldn't haze, I'm thinking. Jose wouldn't haze. Much too disciplined. Not reckless. I was wrong, I'm wrong.

*

We march through the front doors, myself at the end of the single-file line, and when I pass Sam at the doorway he gives me a handshake and says, "I hope they haven't been *too* much trouble for you, man," and I shake my head and manage a good-natured shrug, and then I'm inside the living room again and it has changed considerably in the last ten minutes. Sorority girls gone. Tables folded up, shoved against the wall.

The eerie emptiness of this chamber is broken only by a single chair in the center of the room, sloping brown plastic and uneven rust-eaten metal, a piece of furniture that looks as if it was swiped from a condemned elementary school. A single broken chair at the center of a dark room: looks like the scratchy minimalist poster for a *Saw* movie.

But as my eyes adjust to the darkness, I see that there are at least ten older fraternity brothers standing behind the chair, grouped together along the room's far wall near the entrance to the kitchen, some with their arms crossed over their chests, others with their hands on their hips. Jose, chapter president, foregrounds this thick side-by-side mass of intimidation, this Brother Wall, collective glares fixed intently on the line of pledges entering the empty room.

As soon as he sees the chair and the brothers, Tony skids to a stop and says, "Aw, shit."

Jose steps forward and waves his hands in a calming manner, smiles in a friendly way to reassure the line of pledges, but somehow he still looks military, unimpressed with the sudden burst of terror the young men are feeling; somehow it still feels like a "quit acting like pussies" smile, a "be a man" smile. As if the fear is unwarranted, and the brothers have done nothing to deserve such a reaction. And maybe they haven't: no matter how innocent the fraternity chapter, a pledge semester can be scary, rumors and stories of other chapters' horrendous physical and emotional tortures constantly circulating, parents and friends and fellow students sharing clipped newspaper articles detailing the Big Brother Night mishaps from Arizona State or Southeast Missouri, movies featuring ultimate pledge humiliation seeming to play endlessly on HBO —*Van Wilder, Revenge of the Nerds,* old episodes of *Tales From the Crypt* where pledges are locked inside haunted houses and then disemboweled by malevolent spirits. No matter a student's safety, the pledge drifts through his semester in a culture of fear and paranoia. That happens everywhere. And here in this room, even if nothing bad happens, these young men are processing thousands of embedded mental images from Court TV, *USA Today, Rolling Stone,* each concocting different scenarios for his own imminent abuse.

But it's just an empty room. Just a chair. It's nothing.

"Everyone, if I could have your attention please," Jose says from the Brother Wall, his accent more pronounced now that he's projecting so loudly. "I would like to introduce you to our Educational Consultant, Mr. Charles Washington. Everyone is familiar with the duties of our national consultants, yes? He will be staying with me for the next few days. Attending our meetings, observing our fraternity. Please make him feel comfortable."

257

And it feels as if he says "comfortable" like a warning to all of the brothers: *The Nationals Spy is here! Watch what you say! Watch what you reveal!* My hands fumble in an effort to loosen my tie, but I realize I've already loosened it. Now that everyone knows that I'm a consultant, the suit works against me, widens the age gap between us all. When I try to smile, only half my mouth will cooperate.

"Thanks, Jose," Sam says. "All right. For all our pledges who don't know what an EC is, make sure to read up in your pledge books. There'll be a quiz later."

Laughs from the Brother Wall. Big heaving laughs from the shadowy figures.

"'Kay," Sam says. "You might be wondering what happened to the girls. That's a legitimate question. Here's your answer: they're gone. While you were out back, their sorority sisters picked them up in the front parking lot. Poof. Gone. So the social part of tonight's activity is over. Before they left, though, we asked each of them to fill out a short questionnaire so we could *assess*"—he lets the word linger, like he's proud of using it—"your progress as pledges."

Tony, the stocky pledge in front of me, says "shiii-iiiittt," grinds his teeth together and forms his hands into such tight fists that he eventually has to shove them into his pockets to retain some composure. "I knew it," he whispers to no one. "I knew it. This was a test. Whole time, this was a test." He looks like a student after a final exam, bolting out of the classroom to confirm his answers in the textbook and then learning that he was dead-wrong on more occasions than he'd expected.

"Without further adieu, we will begin with my favorite douchebag pledge," Sam says, holding the stack of etiquette questionnaires. He reads from the top sheet: "Michael Garcia, step to the front."

Michael, he of the spiky hair and the red shirt and black pants and white socks, gives a *who me?* look, eyebrows raised in utter disbelief, and Sam responds with his own twisted facial expression, the intractable kind that says, *yes, Retard, YOU.* Sam points to the chair and Michael shuffles over with heavy feet. "Stand on the chair," Sam says.

Michael obeys; he steps reluctantly up, stands atop the seat of the chair—creaking noises as he climbs, the sound of strained metal—and glances over his shoulder at the dark figures behind him—they snicker, and one says "What the fuck are you looking at?"—and then back at his pledges, searching for support. Spiky-haired Michael is on display in the center of the room, a limp shadow of a man standing at Sam Anderson's mercy. More accurately, of course, he stands at *Shelley's* mercy, since Sam holds a paper filled with her questionnaire answers.

"Heard you were giving our consultant a tough time tonight, Garcia," Sam says.

"Wha...?" Michael asks, trembling hands rubbing his red shirt. "Wha...?"

"Being a little troublemaker."

"Wha...?" Michael asks again, wobbling. "How'd you...?"

"No," I say from the back. "No, he—"

"Don't need to defend him, brother," Sam says, and the Brother Wall laughs, shadows bouncing. "Just giving him a hard time. Only way these fuckers learn, you know?"

"Well," I say.

"We will keep it clean," Jose says. "No need to worry."

I close my eyes for a moment, rub them. Many of the hazing stories that earn headlines— whether it's a college lacrosse team, a high school soccer team, or a fraternity—are the sort that involve physical abuse, that result in injury and lawsuits. The true definition of hazing, though, includes not only "bodily harm or danger or disturbing pain," but also any activity that "causes embarrassment or shame in public" or makes someone into "the object of malicious amusement or ridicule." Name-calling, silly late-night tasks ("Go get me a burrito, pledge!"), scavenger hunts. This type of hazing generally goes unreported, but it's just as illegal as paddling or push-ups or thumb-up-the-ass "elephant walks." As a consultant, I should raise my voice. Stop this.

But then again, this could be nothing, right? Back at EU, the fraternities were heavily monitored by the university. We could host parties, sure, but the RAs would have noticed any hazing. We joked with our pledges about the terrible hazing that they'd endure ("Better watch out, pledge, we make you eat your own shit during Hell Week!"), but it was just jokes, just boys being boys, never anything serious.

This is nothing, I tell myself finally. Just loosen up and go with it or else—once again—I'll find myself in a dark backyard surrounded by orange construction netting, bass thumping from the chapter room inside and signaling that the party is just moments from becoming reality. I'll find myself once again yelling desperately at Adam Duke—six-pack in hand—to just end it, *please*, just end it, *I need this!* "All right," I say. "Okay. You're fine. Keep going."

"Excellent. So, Michael Garcia," Sam says, reading from the paper. "Your date for the evening was a girl named Shelley DeJesus." Sam looks back at the Brother Wall. "Pretty fucking hot, too, tight little ass. Got a good look at her when she came in. Garcia here is a lucky cat. Even got to sit right by the consultant, so he should've been able to get some pointers. So let's see how well you did tonight, Mr. Garcia. 'Kay?"

Michael holds his breath. Maybe choking. Chair straining.

"The first question on this sheet. Did your date introduce himself and shake your hand? Let's read what Shelly wrote." Sam pauses for dramatic effect. "'No. He just matched up with me and told me to come inside with him. Didn't know his name until after we sat.'"

Atop the chair, Michael stares at his shoes, says "Heh," swallows.

"That's not very good etiquette, is it, Garcia?"

The Brother Wall laughs, but the Pledge Clump manages only thin smiles, tension relief against their own approaching fear of the chair. Michael, still wobbling, lets his shoulders drop, his own smile fading. Up on the chair, he stands high above everyone else in the room, but somehow I still feel as though I'm staring down at him.

"The next question on our *assess*-ment. Did your date help you into your seat?" Dramatic pause. "Hey. I'm no psychic, but I bet I can guess this answer, too."

The Brother Wall cackles again, laughter that is perhaps not so much earned by Sam's lackluster wisecracks as it is by Michael's gushing embarrassment each time a new questionnaire prompt or response is read.

"Next question: 'Did he wait for you to eat first before beginning his salad?' Oh, big surprise here. Another 'no.' I feel like a broken fucking record." Despite the cliché, Sam again receives an unlikely amount of laughter from the dark Brother Wall behind Michael. The questions continue, too, from obvious—"Did your date ask you how the food was?"—to odd—"Did your date chew with his mouth open?"—(and Michael attempts to protest Shelley's answers several times, but Sam silences him with a thunderous "*Shooosh!*") before the climactic clincher of a final question: "Would you go on a second date with this man?"

Michael's face is now bloodless, lips quivering, spiky hair rattling. Once again, he rubs his shirt, the metal legs of the chair rattling and threatening to slide as he fidgets.

*Stop this,* some part of me screams, the consultant part of me, the Fun Nazi part, but I stifle the scream, shift my weight from left leg to right, position myself near a closed closet door far from the action, a shadowy stretch of space where no one else is standing, where no one can see my facial reactions, where perhaps no one will even remember I was here.

"Let's take a quick survey of the room, shall we? What do you guys think? Would you give him a second date?" Sam asks, and several brothers make exaggerated "hmm" faces; one shadow-brother strikes the Thinker pose, fist under chin; several others are less subtle, dark silhouettes shaking their featureless heads with unapologetic vigor. The laughter builds, then from the Wall a "*fuck* no," then a collaborative "psshhhh" noise and some dismissive waves, a "get the fuck *outta* here," a "*boooo,*" and then Jose quiets the crowd and says: "Be nice to the pledge. Remember we have company." And amazingly, at just a quick word from their chapter president, all the brothers go submarine silent, hands dropping to their sides, their outrageous pantomimes ceasing. Jose looks at me, face black in the shadows of the room's far reaches, and shrugs his giant shoulders. "Sorry, Charles."

"Um," I say. "No problem."

"Tell us, Sam. What did Shelley say?"

"Shelley wrote just one word," Sam says. "'Sorry.'"

"Oooohh," I hear.

"That fucking hurts," I hear.

"Blue balls, baby, blue balls!"

"Douchebag pledge!"

"La chica," someone says, and speaks several Spanish sentences, and I don't know what he's saying but he gets a grand applause, and all of this effects deep failure in Michael's eyes.

"The Etiquette Dinner was lesson number one for you, pledge," Sam says and points up at Michael. "But lesson number two? You don't fuck with the consultant. Hear me? You don't start shit with your own fraternity brothers. I hear about this kind of shit again, we'll put you in the Dark Room till the fucking sun comes up."

"Um," I say. "What's the Dark Room?"

But now Sam is helping Michael down from the chair, has his hands on his shoulders as if giving him a rough massage and is whispering something in his ear; then he gives Michael a good-natured shove that sends him careening across the room and into the waiting Pledge Clump where he's received with back-pats and ass-slaps and hair-ruffles that immediately lift his flopped-over spikes. "Fuck that girl, man," Michael says.

"Yes sir," Sam says. "This is brotherhood in here."

"Bros before hoes," Michael says, standing tall again.

"Bros before hoes," Sam repeats. "Yes sir. Brotherhood."

The other pledges laugh and agree, and when the brothers laugh, the pledges laugh harder. And this isn't quite the ending that I expected: even though the fraternity put him through the humiliation to begin with, the aftermath is familial. Warm. So yes, if anyone asks about my involvement, this is what I'll point to: this image, brothers hugging and laughing.

But it's just a moment. A single sand grain swept away and displaced. Here, gone.

"Remember: you're still a dirtbag pledge, pussy," Sam says. "Remember that."

The moment fades into five minutes ago. And now Sam is saying, "Joseph Santiago, step to the front," pointing at the chair, and a lanky basketball-player-type with a shaved scalp is emerging from the Clump, stepping forward, standing on the chair, his head almost touching the ceiling and he is raising his arms and grabbing the ceiling fan just to maintain his balance. "Another fucking pledge," Sam is saying. "Let's see if you're as big a fuck-up as Garcia."

And it's starting again, this roast of unsuspecting pledges. And I have to watch this thirteen more times? Have that many experiences to record in my mind, that many opportunities for something to go wrong, someone to feel "emotionally" hazed, or remember that I'm here and question why I'm not stopping it?

"*Duncan!*" one of the brothers catcalls and pumps his fist.

Santiago smiles and responds with a fist-pump, also.

Jose now stands beside me, his face glowing with enthusiasm, and he tells me that this pledge plays for the chapter's intramural basketball team and that his nickname—Duncan—is a reference to the San Antonio Spurs' All-Star center, Tim Duncan. "Is all of this a bit much?" I whisper, and he tells me no, this activity is a great "break 'em down and build 'em back up" exercise. He tells me that the pledges love it. Trust me, he says. This is the sort of thing that makes these kids into men. These are military kids running the show, after all, tough and disciplined and well-aware of the rules, and their actions can't be bad if they're influenced by time-honored military tradition, right?

Jose laughs, leans back, takes a deep breath and stands tall. "We all remember the Etiquette Dinner. It is a good memory for all of us."

"We all know you got a mean hook shot, Duncan, 'kay?" Sam says. "But let's see how well you play the ladies. First question: did your date introduce himself and shake your hand? His date, her name was Cyndi, she wrote, 'He told me his name but he tried to kiss my hand. Very polite, but come on. Who kisses hands? Is this 1950?'" Sam stops, makes a face like he just took a whiff of a bad fart, and holds the paper a few feet away like it was the fart's source. "*Duncan*! Wow. This girl sounds like she was way *into* you, bro. And you ruined it off the bat."

Duncan smiles, head still lowered so he doesn't knock into the ceiling fan. "Heh."

"'Did he pull out your chair and help you into your seat?'" Sam reads, and now he speaks in a high-pitched girl voice, too, puffing out his chest with mock boobs and rubberizing his legs and wrists to give himself an effeminate stance. The Brother Wall laughs. "'No. Joseph just sat down. Didn't help me into my seat at all!'"

And one after another, the pledges take their place on the chair. The questions continue, all of the answers feeling like an unending horror story that could be submitted to *Men's Health* for some "social disaster" column. "He swore at the dinner table!" one questionnaire says, and another says, "Someone should tell him to match his shoes with his belt. A woven belt does *not* go with dress shoes, and a plaid shirt does *not* go with a striped tie." Every few questions, a pledge wins a small battle—"He was very friendly"—or even the entire war—"If he asked, I might go on a second date." But mostly this is a forum for ridicule, improv comedy night for Sam, his material growing more inventive as the night progresses. At one point, Sam tells a pledge that he is dressed like a disposable background gangster from *Scarface*. He pulls jokes from sources as varied as *Spaceballs* and *The Dukes of Hazzard*. He manages to both alienate the pledges and earn their favor. Questions continue. Answers continue. One pledge after the next. On the chair. Off the chair. Humiliated when it's their turn, relieved when it's someone else. Until finally Sam motions for the last pledge, a skinny white kid with red hair and thick glasses and an atrocious red-and-green-striped dress shirt (the sort of thing you see only at thrift stores and Christmas parties), to step off the chair and rejoin the Pledge Clump.

"Better luck next time, Ronald," Sam says, and this red-haired kid *does* bear a striking resemblance to Ronald McDonald. Just give him red overalls and big floppy shoes and he could have a career as a ribbon-cutter at McDonald's grand openings. Just good-natured boys-will-be-boys jokes. Nothing more. "All right," Sam says, "we've got just one more. Could I have our honorable Educational Consultant, Charles Washington, step to the front of the room, please?"

"I'm sorry?" I say, and I'd forgotten I was even a part of this. I stand in a corner, watching the activities from neither the Pledge Clump nor the Brother Wall. I've become so silent, in fact, that even Jose—still beside me—seems to have forgotten that I'm here.

"Come on, Charles," Sam says. "Right up here."

"I don't know if this is a good idea," I say, fingers picking at my suit jacket's buttons.

"Come on," Sam says. "It'll be fun." He stands beside the empty chair, a stack of crumpled questionnaires at his feet, only one sheet of paper remaining in his hand: mine. He smiles with the power of the untouchable because he knows he's in charge here. He is the sarcastic drill instructor from *Full Metal Jacket*. Fun, yes. But about a hundred reasons *Why I Shouldn't* bottleneck at the entrance to my brain. I'm thinking that I'm a consultant, I'm thinking LaFaber, standing at the window in his office and staring out across the country and spotting me on the chair. But *all* eyes are on me. Daring me.

Michael Garcia at the forefront of the Pledge Clump…a tiny figure against so many well-muscled ROTC students…his once-crushed face has regained all of the antagonistic biting fight that it had when he "stepped to me" outside. His dream come true.

So I take a step. Another. One foot in front of the other until I'm beside Sam, until I'm climbing the chair, until I'm looking down at eager sets of eyes that are measuring me against everyone else in the room. I'm the consultant, the Marathon Man, the ideal Nu Kappa Epsilon brother, and all eyes are on me, and the pledges—Michael especially—probably want me to be broken down in the same way that they have been.

"Charles Washington," Sam says, and his tone is different now. Softer, sedated, like he has a full shelf of personas to choose from and he's re-shelved Pledge-Humiliator and pulled down By-the-Book New Member Educator. "Your date—and in case any of you guys don't know who she is, let me just say that you're missing out, 'kay—your date was Maria Angelos."

"Oh, *shit*," someone says.

"That's some retarded-ass shit," someone else says with real awe.

"You are a lucky, lucky man," Sam says.

I smile, but I think that everyone was hoping for a more dramatic reaction.

"Hopefully," he says, "you could teach these kids a few lessons, huh?"

"I hope so," I say.

"First question," Sam says. "Did your date introduce himself and shake your hand? What did Maria write...?"

I struggle to remain still atop the chair, but the metal scrapes along the floor.

"'Yes,'" Sam says, and he doesn't use the sarcastic high-pitched girl-voice again, instead opting for a sultry and sexy Jessica Rabbit voice. "'Charles was, from the start, a true gentleman. He never stopped smiling, and was very polite in his introduction.'"

Behind me, the Brother Wall—that mob that had formerly been composed of whispers and snickers and rude remarks and shadows—laughs lightly, several brothers singing praises: "Not bad, man. Representin' Nike in here, man. Rep-re-*SEN*-tin'!"

The Pledge Clump remains a mixture of straight faces and forced-respectful smiles, slumped shoulders. As though this could all end in a split-second, and any one of them could be called back to the chair for another un-manning.

"Next question," Sam says. "Did your date pull out your chair and help you into your seat? Maria answered: 'Yes. Charles made sure I was comfortable throughout our date.'"

Select smiles from the Pledge Clump.

"Straight P.I.M.P.," a brother says behind me.

"No doubt," Sam says. "Made her feel *comfortable*. Looks like we could all learn something from our man, here. Ready for the next question?"

I brush a bit of fuzz from my suit jacket, straighten my off-center belt. I say, "Sure."

"'Kay. Here goes. Did he wait for you to begin your salad before he started eating?" And Sam keeps making little quote fingers each time he reads

Maria's words. "'Yes,' Maria says. 'Charles even asked if it was good, and if I needed salt or pepper.' Damn, Charles. I think *I'm* falling in love with you."

Michael still stares back from the Pledge Clump, on edge, still hoping for Sam to deride me, for Maria to dispense with me. But each of the questions is answered in a similar manner, with a "yes" and an adoring explanation of my gentlemanly prowess, and suddenly I feel like it could have been *any girl* on that side of the table and they would've melted under the heat of my conversation. Anyone. Bring on Angelina Jolie! Bring on Jessica Alba! Jenn is doing her thing in Florida? Fine. I'm doing my thing out here.

"Final question," Sam says, "and this is the best, trust me." He nods spastically, licks his lips with the sort of comic hyperbole of an old Loony Toons short, the one with the starving prospector who sees his own friend as a turkey. "Would you go out on a second date? And I think everyone already knows the answer to this one, don't we? But listen to what Maria wrote. 'I would *definitely*'—and she drew a smiley face, too—'go on a second date with Charles. Who wouldn't? He needs to call me, and Shelley and me will show him Juarez for the first time.'"

Sam stops, a reverent silence falling upon the room.

Pledge Clump stuck on pause, no movement whatsoever. Michael's hostility appears broken, shoulders crumpled and face overtaken with futility. A loud noise might shatter him.

"And she left her number," Sam says, staring directly into the pledges. He holds his arm out, stiff, and dangles the paper before me. "Bravo, my friend. You have shown these scumbag pledges the way."

I shouldn't need the awed smiles—*real* smiles—and the applause that follows. But I haven't seen a friend, a real friend and not a "business associate," in months. I haven't seen Jenn since the summer. Six months ago, I sat in a country club banquet room for Alumni Ball, my own fraternity brothers and alumni clapping and congratulating me and thanking me for my dedication to the college and to Nu Kappa Epsilon for four undergraduate years. Graduation was fast approaching; my name was being etched into plaques; I was being given a respectful farewell by the undergraduates, "Thanks for the memories!" and all that. What a moment! What a stage! All eyes on me, and in the best way possible.

But that was a *goodbye* moment. Right now, this is a *hello* moment. *Welcome back.*

So instead of correcting Sam for saying "scumbag pledges," I pluck the paper from his hands, take in the sweetness of Maria's responses, the smiley face, the phone number, and wave from my place atop the chair as the applause grows.

# Open Space
## CHAPTER SEVENTEEN

First time that Jenn and I got together. Like, *together* together, a date and not just drinks on the fraternity house lawn. Her sorority's Grab-A-Date function, a bar called Icy Jack's.

We sat on barstools beside the gigantic Iron Tee arcade game, the DJ's heavy bass beats forcing us to lean close to talk. And every word we both said, every comment we made, we leaned just a little closer, until finally she had her fingers firmly on my arm and her lips nearly touched my ear as she spoke. Icy Jack's is one of those bars that's cast in the glow of blacklights so that everything around you feels like a photo negative. Jenn and I had been drinking, and the world around us—awash in these cold blues and purples—seemed not only different, but mystical. The normal rules of science no longer applied that night; time either slowed or sped up, depending on the moment, and gravity lost its hold. We floated through the crowd, onto the dance floor, Jenn leading me, holding my hand as she cleared a path. I don't remember any songs from that night, and I don't remember how she looked as she danced, what I looked like. I remember only that the entire room, so many bodies under blacklight, no longer looked like a room. I might have been wedged between Jenn and forty or fifty people I didn't know, between walls and beertubs, but I wasn't suffocating; I was moving in a space of dark blue, earrings and wristwatches and rings sparkling here and there like tiny Earth-captured stars. The world opened up.

From the front lawn of the fraternity house just days before, just chatting with Jenn, to barstools at Icy Jack's, to the dance floor, to…well, there seemed to be so much possibility, and even though I'd set no goals and had outlined no real plans or life structure, I felt like I was in complete control. Not some rigid "Marathon Man" back then, no. But a Frat Star?

Anything I wanted to do, I could.

Now, I can see for miles in every direction out here in the desert, all this open space. No one is creating my schedule here.

# **Night Off**
CHAPTER EIGHTEEN

On Saturday night, after the Etiquette Dinner ends and after I drink a six-pack with Jose at his apartment and watch the last bits of the Hawaii football game, I sleep on his pull-out couch. But it is in the waning moments before sleep that—as I charge my phone—I scroll through the last few texts I received from Jenn during the day, most of them while I was on the plane:

> Where r u?
> Answer ur phone Charles!
> Where r u?
> We lost the football game. And u didn't call once the entire game.
> This is not funny. U need to call me.

And yes, just as she said when we talked on the phone earlier, there are at least ten text messages stored in my cell. But here, now, there isn't a single message to which I will respond.

*

When I wake up the next morning, I find a hand-scribbled note from Jose telling me he's gone to help his father with chores.

Without a car, I've got no way to leave, and my body is aching for the sort of go-go-go activity in which I've been whipped about for the past three weeks. I feel anxious when I sit on Jose's balcony and drink coffee and stare into the distance without purpose; I cook eggs in his kitchen, and it's been so long since I've cooked—so many restaurants, meal plans, fast food drive-throughs—that it feels strange to see and to know what's actually going into my food, to wash my own dishes.

Jose returns for lunch, and we spend the afternoon at a restaurant called El Sombrero. His sister is good friends with the owners, so we sit in a screened-in patio with wobbling ceiling fans where we are joined by several other chapter brothers and alumni, and we talk and eat chips and salsa. "Have a beer," Jose says. "The first round is on me." Okay, I tell him, and with a beer in my hand the fraternity brothers sit more casually, swear more easily, share their budget difficulties and "operating procedure" problems without any hesitation. Ben Jameson's prophecy come true. Eventually I don't bother to hide my Tecate cans when a new brother arrives; I just take a sip, introduce myself.

"I should call the Executive Board together for a meeting tonight," Jose says.

"Yeah, probably," I say.

"That is what you said in your emails. An official Executive Board meeting."

"Right," I say. "Official. We do need to have a meeting, right."

"The last two consultants, they came here and they acted like they were better than us. Like we were below them because we are always behind on our national dues payments. It is not our fault, you know?" Jose has a notebook with a printed-out Excel budget on the table before him, and it shows that nearly all the New Mexico State brothers are delinquent in their dues payments. "Money doesn't come so easily for us as UCLA."

"Those consultants were assholes," I say. "They graduate and they think they know everything. Half the time, they don't know what they're talking about."

"It is good," Jose says, "that you act more professional than they did."

We sit and drink for hours, the tables at El Sombrero filled all afternoon long with Nu Kappa Epsilon brothers. My body is still aching for activity, and she's on my mind: Maria. The light curls of shiny hair that fell just past her shoulders, that fell into her eyes (and she didn't *care*, that was what made it so sexy)...Maria, whose number I programmed into my cell phone, whose body radiated sex—*built for fucking*—and bad college decisions and I have no doubt in my mind how it would feel to rub against her, hard. Her breath against my face, hot, needing me. I haven't hooked up with a girl, haven't made out or kissed or touched or groped, not since...early July, the last time I saw Jenn. When I drove back to Florida for the Independence Day weekend.

*Maria*, I'm thinking even as we leave El Sombrero half-drunk on Tecate to meet up with the other NMSU officers for a Sunday evening Executive Board meeting. Sixteen straight weeks of travel—one full *year* of travel—and I spend my time amidst sweaty males, gym shorts and cut-off fratty t-shirts and the smell of Certain Dry deodorant, stale French fries; I spend my time on grimy beds, slimy couches; with football and rugby players, with gruff alcoholics and spoiled pretty-boys. No women, and it's Sunday night, and Jenn didn't call today, not even a text.

When I arrive at the fraternity house for the Executive Board meeting, seated once again in a room full of brothers and pledges, I'm showered with praises for my performance at the Etiquette Dinner. Pats on the back, cat-calls, howls. These kids have had a full day to discuss my questionnaire with one another, to discuss my "playa status" (as one pledge says), to elevate me to Legend. The out-of-town brother that came into Las Cruces and entranced the beautiful Maria Angelos! Diamond Candidate. Beacon. Tony, the stocky kid, is playing ping-pong in the chapter library when I arrive, but he drops his paddle and rushes to me. "You're a god," Tony says. But Michael remains at the ping-pong table, arms crossed over his chest, glaring across the room.

Jose notices the commotion I cause in the fraternity house and tells the Executive Board that it'd probably be best to meet somewhere else. "He has not been to Buenos Noches," Jose says. "We can meet there."

"They've got great salsa," Sam says.

"Another Mexican restaurant?"

"What else?" Sam asks.

So just as quickly as I arrive, I'm whisked out of the house.

We take two cars, and because I'm still haunted by the styrofoam-and-spoiled-onion smell of Jose's car, I ride with Sam, hoping his vehicle will be more pleasant. I'm wrong. There are six of us in Sam's Honda Civic—*six*, because Jose had room for only three in his equipment-cluttered car—and only Sam and I can claim front-seat spots. The other four Executive Board officers scream in discomfort from the backseat, piled atop one another, yelling for Sam to turn the air up, accidentally stepping on one another's feet. One says, "Did you just touch my fucking *cock*?" Another responds in a meek voice: "Bro. Our Educational Consultant is in the car." "He's heard *swear* words before, dude."

"And he's going to hear more if he doesn't give Maria a fucking call," Sam says.

"I'll think about it," I say. "I don't know if it's a good idea." Because there remains the possibility that she wrote those responses out of politeness or cuteness, or that—worse—she knows the truth by now. I'm a Fun Nazi, a liar. And she was deceived.

The drive is short but bumpy, someone's knee or foot pounding the back of my seat, and I've moved up my seat as far as it will go, but out of courtesy I've asked, "Do you have enough room?" maybe four times, and the response has always been, "If this was an *orgy*," and everyone's laughed each time. So I keep asking, and everyone keeps laughing. Finally we enter the cramped parking lot of Buenos Noches, greeted at the entrance by a hand-painted wooden board shaped like a green pepper. Another Mexican restaurant, and I can still taste the refried beans on my breath from this afternoon. As the six of us crawl and squirm from our seats and into the parking lot, Sam's car rises several inches off the ground.

Inside Buenos Noches, our table is large and round, looks like it would make a perfect flotation device after a shipwreck, like it could save fifteen people from tumultuous post-wreck waters. And it's topped with so many baskets—*buckets*—of tortilla chips and deep bowls of salsa that the entire restaurant sounds as if it's in a constant state of crunching. Around me are the eight Executive Board officers, and in heavy contrast to the chapters I've visited thus far, Sam is one of only two white men: four are Hispanic, one is black, and one is Asian. From their initial conception in the mid-1800s as secret literary societies, fraternities have always been clubs for "Good Ole Boys," exclusive societies where status is a primary factor in member selection. I've heard stories about fraternity life in the 1950s and 1960s (even the '70s and '80s), when chapters split divisively (or voluntarily closed themselves and disbanded) over the issue of admitting black men. These are regrettable memories today, of course, though the tradition certainly survives in racist bedrock states where members whose fathers and grandfathers wore Nike Red still shudder to think that they could call any black man a "brother." But Nu Kappa Epsilon's mission includes an initiative called "Diversity of

Brothers," page 51 of the *Marathon* handbook, stating: "Every chapter should take extra efforts to seek out potential members from diverse backgrounds. Chapters will be stronger through their difference, and each brother may learn from his fellow brothers about new cultures and backgrounds." Most national fraternities have made similar proclamations, and some have even revised this statement to include an open-armed addendum on homosexual men.

Seated here in Buenos Noches and thinking about all of this, I realize that I haven't said a word about the Nu Kappa Epsilon mission statement in hours, and it suddenly worries me: today, these guys have seen me drink at least eight beers over the course of the afternoon, but I haven't offered a single piece of leadership development wisdom. Jose, in fact, looked annoyed when he led us away from the fraternity house like maybe I wasn't doing the job he'd hoped I would do. So after we order our food, I say: "It's great that you guys are really fulfilling the Nike Diversity Initiative."

They give me sandblasted stares, all eight of them.

"What do you mean?" Sam asks. "Diversity initiative?"

I search the table—white, black, Hispanic, Asian—and look for a glimmer of recognition. "I mean, it's great that you guys are so *diverse*, you know?"

Sandblasted stares. Silence.

"Some chapters aren't quite so…full of people from different backgrounds."

"Almost everyone in our chapter is from New Mexico," Jose says. "So…?"

"I mean, like, backgrounds. You know?"

They look to one another, eyes squinted, many of them shaking their heads or shrugging.

"It's not…*this way*…at other schools," I say.

"You mean we are not white?" Jose says, and now the others are smiling.

Sam laughs. "Chapters out in Iowa just a bunch of white farmboys, huh?"

"They have never seen a Mexican," Jose says. "I would scare them."

"No," I say. "That's not I what I meant."

"Sure it was," Sam says.

"No. It's just…some chapters are traditional."

"White is traditional?" Jose asks.

"Tradition, ha," says Brandon, the short and (by his own admission) enchilada-fattened black Treasurer for the chapter. Earlier today, while we drank on the porch at El Sombrero, Brandon and I talked for over 45 minutes about the Tampa Bay Buccaneers and the Arizona Cardinals; he's had Cardinals season tickets since he was a boy, he said, and they were the sorriest sports franchise you can imagine ("The Bucs had a rough stretch, too," I argued, but he wouldn't budge). But he's fiercely loyal, kept telling me that dedication is the most important quality of a good citizen. It pays off, he said. Hell, if Arizona can win a Super Bowl, it'll mean more to the dedicated fans because *they stuck with it*. "We've only been chartered for ten, twelve years," Brandon says now. "There *is* no tradition here. That's what I like. We're *building* it."

"That's what I'm saying," I say. "You have a choice of what you want to be."

"We met the brothers from LSU at the last National Convention," Brandon says. "Five feet from us, and one of these pricks says, 'They're letting beaners into Nike now?' Beaners, this guy said. I almost socked his ass. Who even uses that word?"

"Like he memorized an episode of Carlos Mencia," Sam says. "*Psssh.*"

"Hmm," Sam says, rubs his chin. "Diversity Initiative."

"Diversity Initiative," I say. "Whether you know it or not, whether you planned it or not, you guys are making good choices. Setting good traditions."

"Obviously you don't know us very well," Sam says, and the table laughs.

Jose turns to me. "Tell us about the 'traditional' chapters."

"One of my first chapter visits," I say, "was at Green Valley, a little college in the mountains of Virginia. Town of about 5,000, including students. Southern kids who grew up in town, graduated, never left. Nike's been around Green Valley since the '40s, so half the town is Nikes. The furniture store owner, the gas station owner, the mayor, the police chief. It's like a country club. Lots of pressure in that school to be a Nike."

"Fucking inbreeding," Sam says. "And I thought our school was bad."

"The more tradition, the more uptight everyone gets. Serious money on the line, and everyone's fighting over it. The students, the university, the alumni, nationals."

"No money to fight over out here," Sam says.

"Just wait a decade or two. Until you're an alumnus, and some 18-year-old kid is spraying beer all over the ceiling fan that you just installed in the chapter house."

"So this is a real job, then, Charlie?" Sam asks. "No joke?"

"Yes," I say.

"You get paid?"

"Yes."

"You're not in school, still?"

"I graduated."

"Real job. And you just go house to house, hanging out? Is this fun?"

"It has its moments. But it's still a job."

"You're visiting fraternities," Sam says. "*Frater*-nities."

"I bet you get to see a lot of shit like our Etiquette Dinner, huh?" Brandon asks. "I bet you get to see some pretty cool parties."

"Chapters are scared of me," I say. "They think I'm there to spy on them."

"You're not?"

"Doesn't matter why I'm there. Most chapters hate me as soon as they meet me."

"That sucks. I'd go crazy if I were you."

"What do you mean?" I ask.

"If I had to always be a bad guy."

The Fun Nazi business card, I'm thinking. Keep it flipped.

"I'm not a bad guy," I say. "I don't *want* to be a bad guy, anyway."

"We gotta take you to Juarez," Brandon says. "That settles it. You're going. We'll treat you like a brother, not a fucking spy."

"Okay?"

"Seriously," Sam says. "Take the night off, 'kay? Have fun."

"I can't take a night off," I say. "I'm always on."

"I've seen you drink a dozen beers today, bro," Sam says. "Can't take a night off? Shit, if this is the working life, where do I sign up?"

"No, honestly, I've got a Code of Conduct and everything. I can't go overboard—"

"Have another beer," Brandon says.

"We'll call up Maria," Sam says. "We'll have a grand fucking time."

"Give this Maria stuff a rest, will you?"

"Come on. This is a fraternity. Brothers take care of one another."

"It sounds nice," I say. "But I could get in a whole lot of trouble for hooking up with some undergraduate girl. This is bigger than just, you know, a few beers. Dicey stuff."

"Don't be a pussy," Sam says. "How's anyone going to take you seriously if you don't hit that shit, yo? From, like, a professional standpoint, I don't even think you've got a choice."

We talk "new member education" for a few minutes, and I slip in the possibility that, you know, maybe the Etiquette Dinner could've been intimidating, and maybe tone it down so you, like, don't get in trouble. You know? This isn't me, I say. If it was up to me, hell, do whatever. I trust your judgment. But if a school administrator saw that: that's what you've got to do, I say, think about how it looks to an outsider.

"Sure," Sam says. "I gotcha. Makes sense."

"Just wanna keep you all safe," I say. "You're already my favorite chapter, and I don't want you getting in trouble for something so ticky-tacky."

Dinner ends. Beer at the house, they keep saying. A couple beers on a Sunday night, and so we pile back into Sam's car and I'm given the front seat again but now there's no end to the swearing. No caution flags, no loudspeaker warning that "THE EC IS IN THE CAR!" Now, it's green lights and gas pedals to the floor and Sam saying, "I always have to fucking drive you clowns around," and Carlos in the back saying, "I'm going to get so fucking ripped tonight, bro," and someone else adding, "That Phi Mu is working bar on Tuesday night, man, and she is so fucking banging," and "I want to bang the shit out of her," and it's a race track jam-packed with speeding swears and zipping 200-mile-per-hour disregard for professionalism, but it doesn't matter because now I'm living on the blank side of the card.

\*

I wait to call Maria, wait until I've been asked—"you're going to do it, right?"—and urged—"bro, she was all up on your D"—by every brother and pledge in our NMSU chapter, wait until I'm absolutely convinced that, if I do call her, the result will not shatter the illusion of "Charles Washington" that I've built. I wait all Sunday night. I wait through a two-hour-long chapter meeting on Monday (during which I earn a round of applause when Sam introduces me as the "Nationals Pimp," and Jose says "Quiet, quiet. Okay, quiet. There is business to be done."). I wait through three or four officer one-on-ones (during which the conversations quickly derail from Nu Kappa Epsilon policies and procedures to *Iron Man* and Lil Wayne and USC's killer season). And I almost wait through Monday night, too, but I'm sitting in a Mexican restaurant called Green Chile with Sam and four other brothers— all native Mexicans, and they tell me why this is the best *New* Mexican (not *Tex*-Mex) restaurant in Las Cruces, and then they won't let me continue waiting. Monday night, they're assertive.

"Do you have her number *right now*?" asks a pudgy-cheeked kid with curly black hair and a blue Adidas shirt. His name, I think, is Andy, but I've been afraid to call him by name, just in case I'm wrong. The name might be Alejandro, and I don't want to say the wrong thing and look culturally insensitive, as if I always hear "white names" no matter what you tell me.

"I saved it in my cell phone."

"Listen, bro," Andy (?) says. "You're only here for two more days."

"I'll call her tomorrow."

Andy (?) curses in Spanish, speaks an entire Spanish sentence. An entire paragraph. All night, when they haven't been extolling the benefits of green chile salsa over tomato-based salsa ("New Mexico is green chile country, amigo," they've said a thousand times) or bragging about their fathers' gamecock training pens, they've been drifting into Spanish or Spanglish as though I'm fluent in either. "Como?" I keep asking, jokingly, and they laugh. "You're from Florida," Jose said to me last night. "How is it that you do not speak Spanish?"

"Give me the phone," Andy (?) says.

"Why?" I grab a tortilla chip from the large black bowl in the center of our table. I've come to expect free appetizers at every restaurant, and I'm sure I'll miss them when I'm back in New Jersey or Delaware.

"If you don't call her, I will," he says.

"I'll do it. Just not now."

But before I know what's happening, Sam has me in a headlock, and the tortilla chip flings out of my hand and lands on the floor, and I make a desperate *unngh* noise, flail for a second, but Andy has my phone and he scrolls through the numbers and says, "This is what brothers are for, homeboy." And then he says, "A-ha!" and his face lights up because he's found Maria's number in my phone and he's hitting "dial" and until now, it's been pure fantasy, just another in a long line of "things I want to do but never will," but when Andy says, "Is this Maria? Oh. Oh, good, good," the fantasy itself is just a fantasy, because Sam lets me loose and Andy says, "Charles lost your number, so we called you for him. Here he is."

He hands me the phone.

Released from the headlock, I flop forward in my seat and take the phone hesitantly, hear Maria say "hello" and I clear my throat and speak. Five minutes later, I have plans to go out to Juarez on Tuesday night.

My schedule on Tuesday looks like this, but I only keep track of it because Jose prints a copy from his computer:

    9 AM - Wake up
    10 AM - One-on-One with Alumni Relations
    12:30 PM - Lunch with Vice President (Rancho's all-you-can-eat)
    4:00 PM - One-on-One with Greek Advisor
    6:00 PM - Dinner (Taco Bar)
    8:00 PM - Juarez

I spend the day at a second-hand boardroom table in the fraternity house chapter room, scrolling through ESPN.com. Sometime in the afternoon, though, I receive a phone call from Walter LaFaber. Very rarely does LaFaber call me outside of our scheduled "one-on-one" phone conferences. Just for emergencies. But I answer the phone and muster a super-excited Disney World voice. "Hey Walter!" I say.

"Great news about Illinois!" LaFaber exclaims.

"Oh yeah?"

"They've been completely evicted from the house. Completely removed!"

"What?"

"The house is empty! They've been removed!"

And just like that, my voice is deflated. "Holy shit. It's been how long? Three days?"

"They were issued eviction notices on Friday morning," LaFaber says.

"The chapter has only been closed for a weekend," I say. "That seems too quick to pack up and find a new place to live."

"They knew it was coming," LaFaber says. "It was in their lease. They were warned."

"But still."

"And the house is absolutely destroyed, too!"

"You sound happy. Why is this good news?"

"We can go after these punks, Charles," he says. "Do you realize how much history is in that Illinois house? Since 1921, that chapter has stood for the ideals of our organization. On the final walk-through this morning, the Housing Corporation found severe structural damage to the support beams in the basement. Water damage in the top floor. Beer stains the size of watermelons. Dog fur. *Dog* fur! Urine stains. Missing doors. Cracked windows. The charter is missing, too: that's an irreplaceable artifact. The list goes on and on. We can go after them. We have the last laugh with these clowns."

"That's ridiculous," I say. "They couldn't possibly have done all of that. That house has been in continuous occupancy for decades."

"They signed leases. If they didn't create the damages, they should have reported them when they first moved in."

"Structural damage, Walter? That takes *years*. That's not a one-night party."

"Calm down, we won't sue them for *everything*," he says, and I can picture him in his office, a thick manila folder before him, complete with grainy black-and-white photos of damages, complete with spreadsheets and checklists and signed and verified documents. All the things I could have sent him as I investigated Shippensburg. I can picture his face, thick Alabama football player cheeks pulling back in uncontainable smiles, rich hair shaking as he laughs and twirls in his chair and attempts to stay professional despite his victory over the Illinois undergraduates. Scar on his forehead glowing as it does when he gets excited. "We have the sort of list that can make a statement," he says. "A reminder that we are a leadership organization, not a drinking club, and we hold our members accountable. We dodged a bullet with Illinois."

"Those kids. Where are they living, now?"

"Not our problem," he says.

I've collapsed in my chair. "This doesn't seem right."

"Remember the *mission*, Charles," he says in a gravelly voice, and he's back: LaFaber, the man who can stifle his emotion in a split-second and revert back to a walking and talking leadership book. "Our fraternity lives by a lofty set of standards. These men at Illinois, they did not live up to those standards. They violated every bullet-point of their lease. This is justice."

And, yes, my mind is still an Educational Consultant manual when it needs to be. Job responsibilities, Page 4; Visit Expectations, Page 8; National Hierarchy and District Structure and Suggested Bylaws, and Page 1, black spirals touching the edge of the text:

## THE MISSION
## NU KAPPA EPSILON FRATERNITY

**We will actively strive to better ourselves and
our communities, to uphold the values set forth
in custom and law by the honorable Founders.**

**We will improve ourselves through diversity of
membership, through steadfast dedication to
scholarship and an unwavering integrity. Nu
Kappa Epsilon will develop our members into the
socially responsible leaders of tomorrow.**

"Listen," LaFaber says. "I want to talk. We need to get caught up. I have a few concerns with those guys out at New Mexico State. But I've got an important conference call with some Illinois alumni, have to give them a timeline for our return to campus. Give me a call sometime tomorrow, could you?"

"Whatever you want," I say. "Whatever you want."

*

On our trip to Mexico, Sam drives. He jokes that he's the "DD" for the big-shot fraternity consultant, and I give a dry chuckle and say, "No, no, I won't drink more than a beer or two, I'm still working," but as soon as Maria enters the car and I'm sitting with her in the cramped backseat while Shelley sits in the front with Sam, I tell her that—hey, check this out!—Sam has agreed to be our DD for the night, no worries, what a great fraternity brother and chapter officer, etc. Jose follows behind us, driving Brandon and two other Alpha Alpha sorority sisters, a convoy headed to Mexico. I've already had a beer, so when the Black Eyed Peas blast from the stereo, singing "Tonight's gonna be a good night," I sing along.

This is the same route that we took the other day when Jose first drove me into town from the airport in El Paso, a long drive across a wasteland of charred desert. Now, though, the sky is dark save for stars speckled across the blackness so brightly that I think, for the first time, I can actually see constellations, dots connecting in purposeful patterns. The world is so dark and unending, and out here in the desert, with only an occasional blinking light, a radio antennae, a car on some distant road ...aside from these things, aside from the highway itself, there are no distractions. No office buildings. No billboards. No development. No Blazers. Just...space. And Maria beside me in the backseat, smelling like raspberries and wine and sex.

Sam pops in a hip-hop mix CD, and now Nelly is singing, "It's getting hot in here, so take off all your clothes," and the girls are singing along, and it's just a song but the way they move I know they want us to imagine: clothes off, sweat rolling down bodies, skin, heat.

Just thirty or forty minutes ago, Sam and I stopped into Hanson Hall, a co-ed dorm, and walked through the hallways with the sort of self-assurance born of several years of Frat Stardom. Look at us, our stride said. Destructed jeans. Crisp button-downs, sleeves folded up halfway to our elbows, top two buttons unbuttoned. Faded brown belts. Flip-flops. (For me, an ensemble made possible by an afternoon trip to the mall, my packed clothes still office-building awful). Sam made stupid jokes about the male freshmen we passed in the hallways, cocky laughs at their expense because they still wore high school graduation t-shirts. The same sort of jokes he made at the Etiquette Dinner, but now I have no trouble joining. And we met Maria and Shelley on the third floor, where they stepped out of a room so pink and purple it hurt the eyes.

"Do you drink tequila?" Maria asks, here in the backseat.

"Shots?" I ask. "Or, like, do I sip it like a drink?"

She laughs, glitter on her face sparkling. "Shots."

"I try not to. Tequila is bad news."

"Oh, no. Tequila makes good memories."

"Are you sure?"

"Positive."

"What the hell," I say. "This is Juarez, right? First time in Mexico for me. It'd be an offense to *not* drink tequila."

I meet Sam's eyes in the rearview mirror. "Tequila?" he says. "Careful."

I shrug. It's hard to argue when a night takes on a life of its own.

We pull through the border check-point, then drive through a city that's all lights and dust and dark alleys and surly congregations of homeless Mexicans on street corners beside flashy tourist-stop restaurants. I've never been to Mexico, but I *have* been on a cruise, and Juarez reminds me of the grimy-glitzy port cities of the Caribbean, those places like Nassau and Barbados whose subsistence depends on the constant loads of cruise-ship passengers, those places that are used and abused by American travelers who disembark and stay for a day and get trashed and then ship off. Yes, that is Juarez. A border city where, Sam tells me, impoverished Mexicans will create jobs where none are available. Some stand on corners and count the seconds until the next bus will arrive, or until the streetlight changes, and, for a nickel or a quarter, tell the time remaining to any interested passersby. When we park at a bar called "Dios Mia," Sam hands a limping, unshaved Mexican a twenty and the man nods and stands on the sidewalk beside Sam's car: Sam has just hired this man as a security guard for his vehicle.

The other car—Jose's—has not yet arrived, but Sam assures me that this man has also agreed to protect Jose's dusty Toyota Corolla.

"You're not scared, are you?" Maria asks me. We walk behind Sam and Shelley, sexual energy pulling their bodies together, Maria walking close enough beside me that she continually brushes up against me, sometimes places her hand on my forearm as she did at the Etiquette Dinner, and her skin is so cool and smooth—almost slick—in comparison to the rock-hard, hairy hands I've shaken in the past month.

I think briefly of Jenn, of her hand leading me to the dance floor and the world going dark blue and so much possibility appearing in front of me, so I keep touching Maria, however subtly I can, and hope that she doesn't object or recoil. A hand grazing her waist as we enter the bar, a palm on her upper arm after I laugh at one of her jokes. An arm around her shoulder as I say, "I'm really scared, but I think I'll be all right as long as I have you for protection."

"Right," she says. "I'm so intimidating."

"You *can* be, yes."

"I look like one of these guys on the street corners?"

"No," I say. "Intimidating in a different way. Like, when we were in the parking lot outside the Nike house, just before the Etiquette Dinner, I think all of the other pledges were scared to pair up with you."

"Scared of me? Why?"

"Because you're out of their league."

"And you weren't scared?"

"I was. But you were the only girl left. I had no choice."

*Dios Mia* is a Mexican dive bar, but somehow it's also a college bar. All the way out in Juarez. Servicing the students of NMSU and UTEP and the El Paso community colleges and probably many other Texas universities within an hour's drive. A college bar. A typical college bar. Sweltering, packed with girls wearing short skirts and low-cut tops with thin straps, belly-buttons and lower-back tattoos showing; packed with guys wearing slogan t-shirts ("FBI: Female Body Inspector" and "College" and "Your Retarded" and "Let's do the NO PANTS dance") and torn jeans and baseball caps. Mike Jones playing so loud that you can only hear the pounding bass and an occasional hint of the chorus (*Back then they din't want me, now I'm hot they all on me*)…not that it matters what's playing…if you know the words, you gyrate and sing, and if you don't know the words, you just gyrate. Typical college bar. Hundreds, *hundreds* of kids too young to drink legally in the states, chugging and yelling and dancing, plastic cups all filled with the same watered-down beer, this pattern broken only by an infrequent pink mixed-drink. Floors so sticky with spilled beer and liquor that you wonder if they've ever cleaned this place. The bar—a long wooden counter-top behind which two super-quick bartenders pour beers and splash alcohol into sugary cupfuls of punch or orange juice—is so busy that it looks like a mosh pit. Cramped, but that just means that Maria is pressed against me.

"Drinks are on me tonight," I say to Maria and she looks at me again like she did at the Etiquette Dinner, like I'm some rare breed of New Mexico Man, one that actually buys a drink for a lady, and she touches me on the wrist and says, "Thank you," and it doesn't occur to me until after I order two Coronas (I flash a twenty, am immediately served by a bartender) and hand one of them to Maria and watch her drink half of it, that she is 18 and I am five years older than her, that I've seriously broken American laws by giving her this drink, that I've broken so many NKE policies ("No dating, no drinking!"), but it's Tuesday night and we are alone, no fraternity brothers around to impress. Jose is gone, Brandon is gone.

I do spot Sam and Shelley out on the dance floor, grinding in the crowd, and there's a strobe light flashing over the dance floor and then it stops and it's a slower song now, a nasty song, "Freek-A-Leek," the place now submerged in blacklight, Maria's fingers on my belt, pulling me close, Maria saying something about dancing.

Dancing. Fuck. I'm an embarrassment. A white-boy embarrassment.

I say, "Let's get some tequila first, right?"

"If you insist," she says.

Philadelphia to Illinois.

Illinois to Philadelphia. To New Mexico State. To El Sombrero. To Green Chile. To Juarez. To Dios Mia. To Corona. To Jose Cuervo. To Jose Cuervo. To Corona. To the dance floor, where Maria bends over in front of me, quickly, ass against my crotch, and then she stands and we're front to front and her face is in my face and then she moves like Shakira, all hip shaking like she-wolves and hot sex, and then her face in my face, lips on my lips, tongue in my mouth and she bites my lower lip.

To the bar. To Corona.

To the dark corner of the bar, where we kiss more and my hands are at the small of her back, at the bare skin below the lowest length of her shirt and above the highest length of her tight black pants, and her hands on my traps and boom boom boom, this is it, right here, and she bites my lip again, tongue, skin, and this is it.

New Mexico State to Texas Tech. To…fuck it, wherever.

■ ■ ■
## CHAPTER NINETEEN

With.................................................................................................................
............................................................................................................................
............................................................................................................................
............................................................................................................................
.........................the.................................................................................................
............................................................................................................................
...................................................................................................................
........................................two of those...........................................................................
............................................................................................................................
............................................................................................................................
............................................................................................................................
and he...................................................................................................................
............................................................
.............................................................................................................
............................................................................................................................
............................................................................................................................
............................................course...............................................................
Jose and the other one.................................................................................................
............................................................................................................................
............................................................................................................................
............................................................................................................................
............................................................................................................................
............................................................................................................................
............................................................................................................................
............................................................................................................................
............................................................................................................................
.....................................
"Hello, ........................................................................................................
............................................................................................................................
............................................................................................................................
............................................................................................................................
............................................................................................................................
............................................................................................................................
.................................under the impression that I wasn't.........................

..................................................................................................
..............................................................................................
..........................................................................................
......................................................................................
..............................................................................................
..............................................................................................
......................and.........................................................................
..............................................................................................
................................................................................
..............., three more of those."
..............................................................................................
.............................................................and he..............................
..............................................................................................
..............................................................................................
..................................................
............................................................................................
..............................................................................................
..............................................................................................
..............................................................................................
.......................because.........................................
..............................................................................
..............................................................................................
..............................................................................................
..............................................................................................
..............................................................................................
..............................................................................................
..............................................................................................
..............................................................................................
...................
"Hey, ..................................................................................
..............................................................................................
..............................................................................................
..............................................................................................
..............................................................................................
..............................................................................................
..............................................................
........................................................................
..............................................................................
..............................................................................................
..............................................................................................
..............................................................................................

...................................................................................

...................................................................................

...................................................................................

...................................................................................

...................................................a crashing noise against the bar

.............................................

.......................................................BULLSHIT!!!!"

"!!!!!!!!!!!!!!!!!!!!!!!!!!!!!!!!!!"

.........................................................

...................................................................................

..............................

...................................................................................

...................................................................................

...................................................................................

...................................................................................

...................................................................................

...................................................................................

...................................................................................

...................................................................................

...................................................................................

...................................................................................

...................................................................................

...................................................................................

...................................................................................

...................................................................................

...................................................................................

...................................................................................

...................................................................................

...................................................................................

...................................................................................

...................................................................................

........................

...................................................................................

*

...................................................................................

.....................................

.................................pink and purple..................................

...................................................................................

...................................................................................

...................................................................................

...................................................................

285

..............................................................................................................
..............................................................................................................
..............................................................................................................
..............................................................................................................
..........................................................................................
..............................................................................................................
..............................................................................................................
..............................................................................................................
..............................................................................................
..............................................................off my shirt.....................................
..............................................................................................................
..............................................................................................................
...........................
...................flesh........................................................................................
..............................................................................................................
..............................................................................XXX...............................
..............................................................................................................
...............................hand on..........................................................................
..............................................................................................................
..............................................................................................................
..............................................................................................................
...................XXX..........................................................................................
..............................................................................................................
..............................................................................................................
.................................................................
...........
..................the sink and I grab.......................................................
..................................................................
..................
..............................................................

# Charles Wakes Up

CHAPTER TWENTY

I slide out of the bed and stumble toward the door to Jose's bathroom so I can piss-puke-shit/whatever-the-fuck-my-aching-body-is-screaming-that-it-needs.

But then the black shapes throughout the room start focusing: posters on the wall, colors, purples and pinks, an Alpha Alpha picture frame atop an end-table next to the bed.

Blackout night. Just a series of strobe-light snapshots. And just before I open the door, I remember the most vital snapshot from last night: this isn't Jose's living room, this isn't Jose's pull-out couch where I've been sleeping. I came back to *Maria's* dorm room. And there, across the room, buried beneath the fluffy purple comforter, pressed against the far edge of the bed, is a young woman, swaths of glittery dark hair spilling from underneath the blankets. Maria. And on the other side of the room, close to the door, is another bed and another shape under the blankets: two bodies: Shelley and Sam Anderson. Everyone sleeping.

It's sometime early in the morning in Maria's dark dorm room, so early that it might still be last night, so dark that almost everything seems indistinguishable from everything else.

These are the only snapshots I remember:

The bar in Juarez. Dios Mia? The dance floor. Packed, hundreds of bodies brushing against mine throughout the night; barely enough room to breathe, but I didn't feel crushed under any collective weight. All those bodies, and still my legs were free to move however I wanted to move them, still my arms were free to slide around Maria's waist and bring her close, still my pelvis was free to grind, my head was free to nod to the music. We moved with ease through the crowd and to the bar, we floated.

Then: crawling into bed with Maria, sloppy-drunk sex, and—after she fell asleep—vomiting in the community bathroom at the end of this dorm floor's hallway. And not just "vomited," like into a toilet, but, like, a spectacle...across sinks and mirrors.

I shouldn't be here, and yet I am here. The cold certainty of my morning.

\*

I creep through Maria's dorm room, hunched over, patting the dark carpet and searching for the shirt and jeans I tossed on the floor. Random shapes across the floor, boxes and giant plastic bins and folders and textbooks, maybe even a bean bag against one wall. Tequila hangover right now, but I *do* remember what this dorm room looked like in daylight: a pink and purple mess, notebooks and envelopes of developed photographs scattered everywhere.

Lumber forward, head spinning, and finally bump into what I thought was the bean bag, but when I lean to touch it I discover that it's actually a waist-high clothes pile. Dirty, clean, I don't know. These girls either don't have a hamper, or they don't have a dresser. Stick my hands into the clothing mountain, hope my jeans and my shirt lay somewhere on its slopes.

I grab a white skirt. Toss it. A black halter top, a studded belt. Toss them. Girl's clothing: all of it. I toss each item into a separate pile so that I don't keep searching through the same clothes over and over again, but soon I realize that I *am* grabbing and inspecting the same clothes, and I'm spinning and can't tell one pile from the other.

Across the room, the blinds are shut tight, not a single slip of sunlight sneaking through. And there are sounds on the other side of that window, cars driving past, distant lawnmowers, the noise of the world grinding back to life for the Wednesday work day.

Something in my stomach gurgles. Almost a full week of Mexican food and beer and mixed drinks coursing through me, and I need to get back to the bathrooms. In a hurry. But—oh for fuck's sake—I can't run through the girl's dorms in just my boxers.

Stomach groans again.

I give up on my clothes. They're lost, at least until the lights come back on. But I've got to get to the bathroom, quick, so I look for a temporary solution.

Across the room, Maria turns in the bed, makes a mousy noise, and finally comes to a rest facing me. She can't wake up now. Let me get my head straight, get to the bathroom, purge whatever is rebelling against my insides, clean up the mess I made so the entire floor doesn't notice, and then let me figure out how to sneak out of here.

Maria moves again, this time brushing away the blanket.

Eyes still closed, but she faces my direction as though watching my every move. Meanwhile, I'm standing in a stooped position in the center of her dorm room, one hand in a clothing pile and the other holding a pair of her panties—a lace thong?—and so I fling it away and make an innocent face in case she wakes. She doesn't.

I toss aside a pair of Capri pants and finally find a T-shirt, a small powder-blue baby T. Why not? I struggle into the shirt and it's so tiny that every flabby curve of my chest pops out. The shirt barely covers my stomach, stretches only to my belly button.

But no matter how much I rummage through the clothing, I can't find any pants large enough to manage around my waistline, so this baby T and this pair of boxers will have to suffice. I head across the room to the door, remember that—because this is a university dorm—it's the sort of door that automatically locks as soon as it closes. I grab a sandal from the floor, turn the door handle softly, and as I squeeze out—hallway light flooding into the room—Maria wiggles her nose and coughs—I hurry out into the hallway and stuff the sandal into the crack between the door and the doorframe so it stays open.

*

Another snapshot from last night develops in my mind. Brief, indistinct, the sort of photo taken with blinding sunlight in the background. Perhaps useless?

After the dancing, there was a corner booth. Maria's tongue in my mouth, my hand on her ass. Looking out across the bar, Jose staring directly back at me as he sipped a drink and nodded to the beat of an Usher song. Shelley dancing in front of him, but he barely acknowledged her: he was looking at me, face as humorless and unforgiving as a sand-trap.

Sipping the drink, staring at me like an *outsider*.

So I moved my hand up Maria's back, let it rest on her shoulders instead of her ass, and finally he turned his attention elsewhere.

*

The dorm's hallway is lit orange by overhead lights, the same exhausted pharmaceutical color of over-the-counter cold medications. Doors run both walls—heavy metal bedroom doors, so strong they could survive a battering ram attack (this is the type of "security" that fathers demand for their college daughters, but it's rendered pointless when a daughter *invites* a young man to her room). To break the industrial intimidation of the hallway, the RAs have lined the cinder-block walls with colorful bulletin boards; they've taped cut-out construction-paper New Mexicos just below each door's peephole, occupant names written in bubble letters within the cut-out: Maria and Shelley on the door I just closed, Christy and Angel on the door across from me. Many of the girls on this floor have also decorated their doors with glossy photos taken in these first few weeks of school, sprawling collages of party-time craziness, nights at El Sombrero and afternoons at Aggies football games, snapshots of long lunch tables at the campus cafeteria, ten girls to a photo, hugging, cheek-kissing, "sorority squatting," making their fingers into *Charlie's Angels* guns, holding red plastic cups and smiling like their days never have dull moments or tiring routines, and it's college college college, some of the photos cut in cute shapes, in hearts or circles or zig-zag outlines, and some of them have thought-cloud and word-balloon stickers stuck to them, too, with smarmy captions like "Who needs boys when you've got the girls?!?" and "Girl's Night Out!"

But my stomach tightens: posted on the door across the hall, a weekly class schedule: Christy (the room's occupant) apparently has class at 8:00 AM on Mondays, Wednesdays, and Fridays. My cell phone is stuffed in the pocket of my lost jeans and I have no idea if it's 7:00 or 8:00 or 9:00, but I know—just from the sunlight and outdoor sounds—that it's Wednesday morning, and even though I journeyed to Mexico last night, the rest of the world went about its usual business and the work/school day is definitely beginning. Christy and the rest of the freshman girls on this floor are ready to enter this hallway to head to class, and they are *not* ready to see a 22-year-old

289

man standing here in skimpy boxers, gut hanging out of a powder-blue baby T with a screen-print Anne Geddes photograph of a little boy wearing an over-sized suit and holding out a flower to a girl in a sundress.

I place my hand on the wall, steady myself, and—running my fingers over bulletin boards and doors and posters—I make my way to the end of the hallway, several times stepping barefoot on discarded staples and tacks, several times biting my tongue to keep from swearing. And when I'm mere feet from the bathroom door, an electronic beep rings out from the opposite end of the hallway: the patient and unnerving noise of an elevator changing floors. Followed by the clinical swoosh of the elevator doors opening, someone coming home.

I dart toward the bathroom, baby T ripping under the arms as I run.

"Totally bombed that test," says a girl from inside the open elevator, keys jingling in her hand. "Like, none of that shit was in the notes. How am I supposed to know what a *macro* is?"

She steps out of the elevator, into the hallway.

And I run, and the bathroom is right here and I skid to a stop, a couple heavy rattling steps as I change direction, and I look over my shoulder and she's standing still and looking into her purse, and I fling open the bathroom door, hope she didn't see me, hope I'm safe, but before the door closes, the girl says, "Can I call you back? Gotta hit the bathroom."

The door shuts tight behind me. And not only is *that* girl on her way down here, but I suddenly realize that this is a women's floor, that there is only one bathroom, that this is the women's bathroom, that this room could be full of girls already. Really fucking smooth, Charles Washington. You just trapped yourself in here.

*

The bathroom is no friendlier than the hallway, suffering under honeycomb lights so muted that they seem to darken rather than illuminate the space, the floor a moist expanse of tiles punctuated down its center by grimy gold drains that long ago lost their sparkle. The wall to my left is cold gray cinder-blocks, and the wall to my right is lined by five or six stalls; lucky for me, they're all unoccupied.

At the far end of the bathroom, thirty feet away, is an unlit cave of showers and faded pink curtains, all of which (lucky for me, again) also appear unoccupied: I have not walked in on some 18-year-old in a bathrobe, ready to scream like a horror movie victim. I step forward, bare feet on cold wet tiles, and to my right are the bathroom sinks, five total, yellowing formica countertops and rusty faucets and...and...

Vomit across the counter, vomit splashed on the mirror and caked on the floor, up, down, across, in the sinks and hanging from the faucets...

And this is all *mine*. Every drop.

Maybe no one knows it yet? But word will get around on the women's floor, questions asked, fingers pointed, names volunteered, word eventually traveling from Las Cruces to Indianapolis. And, insult to injury, I can't even clean it, not yet, can't use the toilet either, because even if I slip into one of the stalls to wait out the girl from the elevator, she'll still scream when she sees the sinks, or (at the very least) when she sees my hairy legs under the stall door, and her screams will bring the RA, the Hall Director, and then the dorm will have its culprit *immediately*. Caught at the scene of the crime! Could I lock the door, then? Lock the bathroom and keep everyone out until I've cleaned this mess? But I inspect the door, and there *is* no deadbolt.

I search around, looking everywhere for escape, footsteps outside the door now, and there, just feet away, right behind me, across from the mirrors and the sinks, so close that I can't believe I didn't see it sooner, is an open door: a janitor's closet.

The footsteps in the hallway clack louder, and I sneak into the closet, a tiny dark space smelling of bleach and passion fruit, crowded with rolls of paper towels. I pull the door closed behind me and try to settle into the clutter, leaving just one open inch between door and doorframe so I can watch, a broom poking into my back.

*

We left the bar, I remember, myself and Maria riding with Sam, and I remember looking around for Jose, thinking that I was escaping him somehow...I was just happy that he hadn't stomped across the dance floor to forcibly remove me from Maria. And Sam's driving didn't feel drunk/ dangerous, maybe because I wasn't paying any attention, and we wound up at another bar called "Pub," a hole-in-the-wall where we drank Tecate out of cans, crunched the empty cans in our fists and tossed them into a giant mesh-metal bin. Maria curled into my lap in our booth, just as effortlessly as if we'd been dating for years. Sam ordered a bowl of hot pecans from the bar.

But this is foggy. I don't remember how we got back to the dorms. Hazy memories of me and Sam bouncing into the hallway walls here in the dorms late at night. But I do remember Maria staring up at me while we were in the booth, interested eyes peeking out from beneath the shiny black hair falling across her forehead and into her face, hand on my thigh just inches from my crotch and fingers creeping upward; I do remember that she said, among other things, "You seem older, but in a good way," and "Everyone tries to get out of New Mexico, but you came *here*," and every time we kissed, it wasn't just the quick lip-to-lip starter smooches, nor was it the middle-school variety tongue-all-over-the-place make-out, but she instead pressed her face into mine and bit my lips softly and I could feel heat, real heat as if someone not only wanted me, but *craved* me, and it was something I haven't felt in so long.

*

From the tiny crack in the door, I stare directly into my mess...the bathroom mirror, the sinks, the chunks, the culmination of last night's exploits, the raw reminder of how far I traveled.

The bathroom door opens, and the girl from the elevator—librarian glasses, brown hair still in early-morning tangles—turns the corner for the stalls without even a cursory glance in the direction of the mirrors and the vomit, and she shuts her stall door and I can hear her tearing off sheets of toilet paper and placing them on the toilet seat, and I think *NOW!* Now is the time for a getaway, the time to escape back to Maria's bedroom. I place my fingertips against the closet door, am ready to push it open and run, but stinging bladder pains shoot through my body again; I clench my stomach and picture myself actually clearing space inside my body, rearranging my spleen and my kidney to allow my bladder to expand. And all of these sinks, all of these toilets, seem to be engaged in constant draining and dripping, water flowing freely through pipes. Get out now, and what? Piss in the corner of Maria's room?

Before I can move, her stall door opens, the toilet flushes, and this girl—who, I conclude, looks just like *Lisa Loeb* of '90s alt-rock fame—is still buttoning her jeans as she leaves the stall, still buckling her belt, has her shirt pulled up over her stomach to adjust the jeans around her waistline, slips her fingers into her pants and grabs her panties and pulls them this way and that, adjusting. And fuck. This is no longer simply an "embarrassing moment," a 22-year-old man trying to clean up puke at a sink. Suddenly I'm a pervert, a peeping predator surveilling the women as they dress. If caught now, I'll look downright depraved.

"What the hell?" Lisa Loeb says.

She now stands just inches from my janitor's closet door, back to me, and as she stares into the sinks and mirrors and takes in the gross grandeur of the vomit, a helpless strand of dangling matter hanging from a faucet, matter collected in the drain of one sink...as Lisa sees it all, absorbing the magnitude, I am inches from the back of her maroon t-shirt. She might even hear my breathing, my rustling among the mops and towels. She stands still, hand over chest as if bracing for a heart attack, taking quick-burst breaths.

I'm pressing against the closet door in such gut-clenching anticipation that it creaks open about four inches under my weight. I step back, startled.

Lisa Loeb lifts her head, gaze shifting from the vomit to the reflection of the closet door in the mirror. Did the door just move half a foot, she's wondering? By itself? Did she really just see that?

I retreat deeper into my cave, but now my left foot lands on something that makes an awful rattlesnake noise—bristles at the end of the broom—and the handle of the broom shifts, knocks into a shelf, and the noise is quick and explosive, like someone dropped a handful of those white 4th of July snap-crackers.

Lisa Loeb steps closer to the door, real fear in her eyes: maybe imagining something furry, something slithering through brooms and toilet paper, but maybe she knows that I—

The bathroom door opens, another girl enters, and Lisa backs away from the janitor's closet. "Hey."

"What's up?" the new girl says, rubbing tired eyes and walking in a crooked line as if barely awake. She's tall and athletic, black hair, wears a Santa

Fe Invitational T-shirt and has the look of a high school basketball player who wasn't quite tall enough for college ball.

"I think there's something in the closet," Lisa whispers.

"Something?" the basketball girl asks, still rubbing her eyes. "What do you mean?"

"The broom just fell down in there."

"Maybe it wasn't placed right."

"I really think there's something in there, Tara. I think it's a rat or something."

I'm crouching in a corner now, far from the door so that I can't even see them anymore.

"Fine. Let's open the door, then," Tara says. "We can shoo it out."

"Shoo it *out?*"

"Yeah."

"That makes no sense," Lisa says. "It's in *there.* Why do we want it out *here?*"

"I don't have time for this shit."

Lisa sighs. For a moment, neither says a word. Just that same steady drip.

"Shit," Tara says finally. "I have to take a fucking shower. I have to work in an hour."

"Take a shower, then," Lisa says, sounding both relieved and victorious, perhaps sensing a chance to escape the bathroom without having to face the closet creature. "There's nothing in the showers. Only in the closet."

Silence. That dripping noise again. My bladder.

"I'll tell Linda about it," Lisa says. "And about *that*, too."

"Holy shit. Who puked on the mirror?"

"Some of the girls on this floor are disgusting," Lisa says. "I can't wait to move out of here."

"I can't deal with this," Tara whispers. "I need to get a shower."

"Okay, listen. Temporary solution. You shut the door and hold it closed, and I'll grab the trash can and barricade it. You can take a shower without worrying about...whatever it is...and I'll tell Linda to have maintenance check it out."

A barricade? I back up against the shelving unit (almost knocking over a bottle of Liquid Plumber) and try to stay as far out of view as possible. I hear some minor metal-dragging noises, a 1-2-3 count, and I can picture a complicated operation out there in the bathroom, the sort of ultra-timed system that might be employed for a SWAT raid of a crackhouse, one girl creeping toward the door while another scoots the trashcan into *just* the *right spot*, both of them poised and ready like this is a life-or-death mission. And then the door bangs closed and the trashcan crashes and Tara says, "Shit, the can fell over!"

"Not our problem," Lisa says. "Let the maintenance crew clean it up."

"I don't want those nasty janitors in here while I'm in the shower," Tara says.

"They'll wait for you to get out."

293

*Siiii*-ghhh, from Tara. Then: "I'll stop by your room after I get dressed."

And then—mercifully—the conversation stops, and seconds later the sound of a shower echoes through the bathroom. Tara might still be waiting for the water to warm, and Lisa might still be roaming the room, but I have to take a chance. I have to get out of here. If I stay in this closet, the RA or the maintenance men will find me.

*

Did we see Jose again last night? I remember text messages. Who did I text? How many? Will they appear on the billing statement that our Financial Director receives? And at some point in the night, I used the word "rebound," also, I remember that much, but in what context? "I'm rebounding from a relationship," is what I said. That's right. I said that?

"Who?" Maria asked.

"Some girl in Florida."

"Poor baby," Maria said.

And I thought that would be the end of it, but when I checked my text messages throughout the night, both Maria and Shelley looked at me in a strange and pitying way. Waiting for a message from the ex-girlfriend? Had I become *pathetic*?

And I talked to Shelley for awhile, too, didn't I? A heart-to-heart. At a Burger King?

"You're not on Facebook?" she asked. "We have to set up an account for you."

"No, I can't do it," I said.

"Seriously. We'll do all the work. We'll show that bitch how much fun you're having."

*

I push open the closet door, reintroduce myself to the fluorescent lights, and along the floor is a scattered pile of brown paper towels, q-tips, tampon wrappers, strings of floss, a used condom, and a toppled trash can, and I hop over it and take a long look down the far end of the bathroom: Tara is in the shower, so I've got ten minutes, tops. I rush into a stall, spend two minutes, four minutes, five minutes—fuck, *it never ends*—emptying every ounce of everything from my body, then rush back to the closet for paper towels, Windex, buckets, gloves.

Feeling lighter and quicker, I lean over the sinks and hold my breath and spray the mirrors with Windex, spray the sinks, spray the floor, Windex everywhere, slip my hands into the pair of yellow rubber gloves, pick up the orange chunks in the sink first, then make wads of brown paper towels and scoop up the rest. And I spray again, scoop, spray, wipe, minutes passing, stretching to the mirrors, leaning over drains, my ass crack hanging out of my boxers.

Spray, wipe, shower still going strong...shower stopping...then the sound of Tara opening the curtains—I freeze, still crouching—and her hand creeps between the half-opened curtain, grabs a towel, slips back into the shower.

294

I toss the crumpled paper towel wads into the trash mound at the foot of the janitor's closet, leave it all as it lays, leave the Windex and the yellow gloves under the sink, leave the entire area a sparkling fresh masterpiece, better than new, stand, sprint to the door (shower curtain opening again), dash into the hallway and back to Maria's door, open it, creep inside, pull the sandal from the doorframe, close the door—

And I'm safe! Safe again! Clean bathroom! Empty bladder!

I can only imagine what Tara, this freshman girl who only wanted to get ready for work without any hassle, must think when she sees the sink and mirrors spot-free but the closet door hanging open and the trash mound remaining. The janitors cleaned while girls were still showering? And it's exhilarating to picture her face, to know that I got away with it all!

\*

Last night, once we got back to the dorm, there were no awkward moments between me and Maria. I know that. I hadn't become pathetic with my text messages, only more deeply sought-after. A mission. A prize. No questions about what I wanted to do, whether she wanted to do this; when we slipped into the room, Sam and Shelley behind us, we said very little, just breathed heavy and turned out the lights, each couple pulled to their respective bed, Maria turning on the radio, loud, and in no time we were under the blankets and I was sliding her black pants from her legs, hands traveling over smooth thighs and then sliding her thong from her waist and pulling it over her feet and around her toes and tossing it onto the floor and her hands were working at my belt, at my zipper, and my head was spinning and I unrolled a condom that I got from somewhere—I know I had a condom, please say I didn't imagine this—and I barely saw her naked body and she barely saw mine in the darkness, but she dug her fingers into my ass and pulled me forward and we fucked under her sheets, still drunk, laughing and whispering "shhh" even though the radio covered our noise, and we moved, tried to change positions, and there was no grace to the sex and I can't even say if it was satisfying. I can't say how long it lasted, if I came, if she came, if I went limp or if I had an explosive orgasm, savoring sex secondary to simply *having sex*. The act, and the knowledge that it had happened: the exclamation point on the evening: that was most important.

Later in the night, of course, I woke up and tossed the condom into the trash and puked in the sinks and, well, we all know the story there.

Right now, I am a man in a girl's dorm room; my clothes are missing, my wallet, my cell phone, all of it, lost under a pile of sorority t-shirts and sports bras and Five-Star notebooks. But I am *there* again. The blank side of a business card.

\*

When I step forward into the dorm room, my foot lands on something sharp—another thumbtack or a staple—and it slips into my skin with such ease, such painful ease, that I'd swear I stomped on the little—

"Fucker!" I shout, knowing my foot must be bleeding. Bleeding all over the carpet, bleeding all over Maria's jeans and camisoles and gym shirts.

I stand on my free leg, raise my injured foot into my frantic hands, hop to steady myself, bang into a bed, fall against a wall, raise my foot to chest level, squint, still can't see anything—dark, dark—fumble for the spot where the pain is sharpest.

Lights now flooding the bedroom.

"Charles?" A high, perplexed voice from the corner of the room, but I don't look that way, can't, because my foot is finally visible and I spy the offending object, position my fingertips—my fingernails—around it like tweezers, can't get a good grip—

"Charles?"

—looks like green glass, and I think I've got hold of it now, yank—

"Charles, what are you doing?"

—and in my hand, I hold a bright green sword, the kind which skewers maraschino cherries and orange slices and pineapple chunks on the rims of fruity cocktails...a green sword with one side striped red in blood. I drop my foot to the floor, holding the sword before me, and it's a broken sword, actually, only half a sword, not very large at all. Plastic.

"Charles, bro," A male voice from the bed beside me. "You all right?"

I wipe my forehead, don't drop the sword.

"Yeah," I say, huffing. "Yeah. I got it. I got it out." And a laugh escapes my mouth, the same sort of relieved laugh that spiky-haired Michael made on Saturday night when his humiliation had concluded and he stepped down from his chair.

But no one joins my laughter; only silence around me.

Across the room, Maria stares at me from her bed; she's slipped the sheets and comforter from her upper body, sits upright and unblinking. On the other bed, Sam's head pokes out of the sheets, and his eyes are filled with ripped-from-REM-sleep puzzlement...he seems to be coming to a gradual understanding of the scene before him: A dorm room? And Shelley is not in the bed with him? Shelley is on the floor! On the floor beside the pile of clothes, just inches from the spot where I grabbed the baby T I currently wear, so close that I probably came inches from touching her as I searched the floor earlier. On the floor, curled up, backpack as a pillow.

"I went to the bathroom," I say finally. "And then I stepped on this sword."

"Fuck, Charles," Sam says.

"Are you all right?" Maria asks, and her voice is not heavy with shock: she remembers enough of last night that she isn't frightened by two men in her room. "I have band-aids."

I examine my foot. Strangely, it isn't bleeding.

"I think..." I say. "I think I'm okay."

"Poor baby," Maria says.

"Gaahh," Sam says. He looks left-for-dead, has a prickly growth of facial hair. "So bright in this room. What time is it?"

"Nine," Maria says, checking her cell phone.

"Fuck," Sam gurgles.

"Guess I missed my Psych class," Maria says.

"It's too early to be conscious." Sam closes his eyes.

"The early bird catches the worm," I say, forcing a goofy smile.

Sam snorts and falls back against the pillow, but Maria scoots up on her bed, revealing a bright orange "Powder Puff" T-shirt, and she squints hard and runs her hands through her hair. Wait, did I just say, "The early bird catches the worm?" And I didn't even have an ironic edge to my voice? And I've been giggling, stepping on plastic swords, acting like a maniac. Tangles of hair fall across her face, and I can't tell what she's thinking.

"You're sure you're all right?" she asks.

"Never felt better."

She pushes the hair from her forehead. I hold my breath.

"So, um. You have a good time last night?" I ask.

"Of course," Maria says. "You like Juarez?"

"I'm never going to Juarez again," Shelley moans from the floor.

"Yeah, don't know if I have the energy to go back," I say.

"You'll always remember your first time, at least," Maria says, and now—*yes!*—she *is* smiling, has that look in her eye, the one that regards me as the Most Interesting Man in the World, the one without suspicion. She scoots farther up in the bed, against the wall and out of the sheets completely, and she's wearing pink and white booty shorts, maybe just regular old sleep-wear but they're the ass-hugger type so skin-tight and ultra-short that they might as well be lingerie. Maria stands and stretches, sheets collecting in a lump at the foot of her bed, her bare arms stretching skyward as she faux-yawns, her legs viewable in their entirety, and she stretches some more, eyes closed, and Sam and I are taking it in, breathing it in, ignoring the growing buzz of traffic outside, ignoring the noise in the hallway, the smell of dirty laundry and dorm floors, channeling all of our energy and our focus into this…absorbing that gorgeously proportioned shape before us.

She opens her eyes, glances at Sam. His arms are crossed behind his head as though he's settled in to watch a movie. She knows we've been watching. She lives for this. Maria sighs. "I shouldn't have taken a roadie last night," she says through still-glossy lips.

"A roadie?" I ask.

"That's where the sword came from," she says.

"She took a margarita for the drive home," Sam says, gaze fixed prominently upon the smooth fabric rounding Maria's ass. "A *roadie.*"

"I got pretty drunk." Maria gives a flirt-frown. She walks to me, takes my hands, takes the sword from my hands, examines the stripe of blood. "Sorry."

"It's fine," I say.

"I haven't been that drunk in a while. You brought out the worst in me."

"Oh, ha. Don't say that."

She kisses me on the lips—we press together—and it isn't a goodbye kiss; she thinks this is the start of something. That *last night* was the first of many times that I'll wake up in her room and use the community bathroom and sneak back under the covers to hold her. She doesn't know that I'm leaving for Lubbock.

"Plenty of time for that later," Sam says. "We got class, Charles."

"You're leaving?" Maria asks.

"We got *class*, Charles," Sam says, and *shit*, my flight leaves El Paso at noon. He remembered, but I didn't. "We need to get home. Just looking out for you."

"Right," I say. "I need my clothes."

They're somewhere under the sheets, and Maria digs for them and holds them out for me. But when I try to grab them, she says, "Not so fast." I pull back, unsure what I've just done.

"You're too cute in that outfit." She reaches across her dresser and picks up her cell phone. Opens it, pushes a button, and it clicks and flashes. Camera phone. All the world has gadget phones except me. "Had to get a picture. Facebook?"

I scratch the back of my neck, then struggle into my jeans.

"You're not keeping that picture, are you?" I ask before we leave.

"Charles in a baby T," she says and laughs. "Call me later."

# Away
## CHAPTER TWENTY-ONE

We plod through the dorm's hallways, Sam and I, bumping into walls. Sam slams into a door, hard, grabs his elbow but doesn't make a pained grimace, just keeps holding it as we walk. Finally we exit through the main lobby, burn under mid-morning sunshine in the parking lot as we trudge to Sam's car. The world around us is in perfect working order, an achingly perfect machine, sun still shining in the same spot as this time yesterday as if it was programmed by some technician somewhere for the sole purpose of keeping the business day on schedule. Professors and administrators, dressed in starched shirts and dry-cleaned blazers, walk to offices and classrooms, retracing the same steps as the day before.

Meanwhile, students move in packs, girls holding notebooks and textbooks against their bodies, each in the same flimsy way, boys tucking their notebooks under their arms as if to say, "I don't care about class and I damn sure don't care about this notebook." They walk in packs, four or five of them together, purses and shoulder bags and occasional backpacks, paths unsure, floating in life's sweeping unpredictability. Eyes, like mine, glossed with the effects of last night.

"Did you drive last night?" I ask.

"You don't remember?" Sam fumbles with the keys, almost dropping them, but seconds later he unlocks the doors and we climb inside and he starts the engine.

"Just the ride home. It's foggy."

"Ha," he says and even though he doesn't smile, I can tell he'd like to show some amusement; like me, his brain isn't working properly yet, his facial muscles have apparently short-circuited. "We had a pledge drive us."

"A pledge? Everyone was drunk?"

"Wasted," he says. "Shit, I spent sixty bucks at Dios Mia. Kept buying Shelley drinks cause she played that I-forgot-my-purse card. Must be great being a hot girl."

"We didn't have any pledges with us," I say. "It was just the four of us in your car, and then Jose and Brandon in the other car."

"You really don't remember?" he asks, pulling out of the parking lot. "We made some calls."

"Who? *I* didn't make any calls, did I?"

"I saw you on your phone a couple times," he says, "but no, you didn't call the pledges. That was all me. Didn't think I'd drink so much, thought I'd be good to drive. But I was breathing Jack by the time we left for Pub, and Shelley was a mess. Shit, that backfired on me."

"When did you call the pledges?"

"End of the night. You said you were cool with it."

"We had them come all the way to *Mexico* to get us?"

"That's what pledges are for," Sam says in the same authoritative New Member Educator voice he used when he read the critiques after the Etiquette Dinner. A voice sharp with humor, but thick with military seriousness. "Designated driving. Teaches them respect."

I force myself to breathe easy.

According to Sam, *several* pledges actually made the drive to Juarez at 2 AM so that Sam's and Jose's cars would not be left in Mexico. And when we arrived back on campus, Sam—craftily, cleverly—asked the pledge driver to drop us off at Hanson Hall. "Maria and Shelley *had* to invite us back up to their room after that," Sam says. "Our ride was gone."

"They didn't want us to come up?" I ask.

"They probably did. I just needed an insurance plan."

Our conversation is interrupted briefly when Sam stops at Jose's apartment so I can pack. Thanks to yesterday's mall shopping spree, I'm leaving Las Cruces with more clothes than I brought, and my suitcase feels heavier, lumpy in certain spots. When I toss my luggage into Sam's backseat, my bag crunches and rattles (notebooks breaking? shampoo bottle cracking open?), and I have to force myself to not check the damages.

Jose is at work, so I don't get to say goodbye. Apparently, though, I gave him a bear-hug last night and told him he was an amazing president, he was my "dog" ("Yes, you actually said that," Sam informs me). Last thing I do before I leave, I change shirts and give myself the "Axe shower": a quick spray of deodorant.

"Those were tiny beds," I say when I get back into Sam's car. "Back in the dorm?"

"Shit, yeah," Sam says. "Dorm beds are the worst."

"Move an inch, and you're on top of someone."

"Shelley slept on the floor."

"You hook up?" I ask, but I realize that in the heat of last night, I never stopped to think about what I was doing and if Sam might have been watching. And as I ask, "You hook up," I'm also aware that I've lapsed back into college-speak, into the sort of slang that came so naturally as a student— "that's tight," "just made hella cash," "what up, yo?"—but that I tried to banish from my vocabulary as soon as I spent my graduation money on that Ralph Lauren suit.

"I barely hooked up," Sam says. "She was damn-near passed out."

"Oh."

"Obviously *you* weren't paying attention," Sam says. "You were busy. I don't even remember how it happened, but Shelley crawled onto the floor just a little while after we got back to the rooms. I passed out, too. Didn't even realize I'd passed out until *you* got up an hour or so later for the bathrooms, woke me up."

"When I puked?" I ask.

"You puked?"

"I mean…I'm not sure."

"You puked," he says and nods. "You covered all the bases last night, didn't you? Went to Mexico, got wasted, hooked up, puked. Grand Slam, bro."

"Well, I try."

"Got a question for you, brother, a serious one," Sam says as he pulls to the curb beside the Departing Flights doors of the El Paso International Airport. "Why are you doing this?"

"Why am I doing what?"

"Consulting. You say you don't make any money. So what made you decide to do it?" His voice is disarmed, low and confidential, so honest that I don't even know how to respond.

So I say that: "I don't know."

"You don't know?" he asks. "Seems like a hell of a hassle, all this flying and the meetings and what-not, if you don't even know."

Others have asked, and for the last several months I've had a script from which to read my answer: "I believe in the mission of this fraternity. I believe that a fraternity is something powerful and influential in the lives of young men. I believe that we needed to protect the institution, save it from those who have the wrong priorities." That is the recorded response that so many have heard. And it was true. But now things feel more complicated, missions and motives not so clean.

"There's a lot of reasons, I guess."

"Why did you take the job to begin with, then?"

"Fraternity," I say, looking at the dashboard, where the vinyl has begun to peel away at the edges, cracking and wilting under the constant sun. I don't ever admit the real reasons, do I? "It was my life. For four years, it was all I cared about."

Behind us, someone revs his engine, honks.

"I could recite *The Marathon* backward and forward. I could tell you the GPA of every member in our house. I went to every intramural game, showed up at every Dead Week study session to help our pledges. My degree should have been fraternity. That's the only thing I was really pursuing in college."

Sam doesn't move, doesn't speak, the fever of realization slowly burning through him.

He rubs his chin and stares out the windshield, where a baggage handler is mouthing "What's the hold-up?" and is holding his palms out impatiently. But Sam raises a finger in a just-a-second gesture and continues to rub his chin. "It's funny, you know?" he says. "Cause I keep thinking about it, ever since you first got here."

"Thinking about what?"

"We're similar, you and me."

"Are we?"

"Yeah, bro. We're practically the same fucking guy. I mean, we woke up in the same place together this morning, know what I'm saying?" And he smiles and hits my arm.

"We did."

"This is *my* life, too," Sam says. "This is like the only thing I care about."

"But I don't know that this is a good thing," I say. "There's a lot more…"

"No, fraternity is the only thing keeping me in school, bro. This is it. If I didn't have the fraternity, I don't know where I'd be. If I'd be anything. Fraternity is the best thing that ever happened to me."

"Sam," I say. "I'm sure that isn't true."

"This is all I care about," he says again. "And it's over come next semester."

My God: he sounds just like *me*, back in the hot tub.

"It's never over, Sam. The friends you have, the house, it's always there."

"But I'm not living in it."

"No. But you'll get a place off-campus. You'll keep your friends. Then you'll get married or whatever, and you'll get a good job, real money."

"You think I'd make a good consultant?" he asks. Quiet and patient voice, not the loud wise-cracking smartass who forced each pledge to stand on a chair and absorb his insults at the Etiquette Dinner. And I see him perhaps for the first time. A world opens up. A whole life flashes before me. This is a boy whose father served in Iraq or Afghanistan, died probably, whose high school years drifted by in a haze of duplexes and double-wides and six-week stints at the houses of sympathetic aunts and uncles who quickly wearied, a boy who squeaked into college but never really wanted to be there, only went because he needed to get away from wherever he was, and then suddenly he was in a world of 100-person lecture halls and professors demanding papers and RAs patrolling dorms as if the 10 PM quiet hours were a life-or-death matter, and fee deadlines and a mother back home who said only, *Don't ask me for no help, you made your choice what to do with the money your father left you*, and recruiters calling and a world collapsing and then…fraternity was there. Jose and Brandon and all the rest of them, best friends delivered by God himself, and the implosion halted, his life saved.

I see him. For the first time this semester, I'm seeing someone.

"Be honest," Sam says. "This is all I got, brother."

"It doesn't pay well," I say. "And it's tough on the road. Away from everyone."

"I don't care," he says. "Look. You come out here, you have a blast. It's like a second family for you, and they listened to every word out of your mouth. They took notes. We made a *budget* for the first time ever. That'll save us… how much money?"

"Over ten thousand a year, the way we have it structured," I say.

"All I'm saying is, you made a difference, you know?"

"Are you being serious?"

"Totally. What could be a better job? Working with fraternity brothers. It's all win-win. This is my life, and I just…I need it."

And I shouldn't say it, but he looks as fragile as a sand castle on a shifting dune, and I owe him. "If you apply to be a consultant," I say, "I'll write a letter of recommendation."

"Thank you," Sam says. "Oh God, thank you."

And as I make my way to the airline counter, as I'm processed from one checkpoint to the next, a long line of Blazers, I wonder how any of this happened. None of it feels real anymore. How did I get here? Alone? El Paso, in the middle of September, holding this luggage? All of it—the Etiquette Dinner, Mexico, alcohol, sexual intrigue, bathroom hijinx, Sam Anderson in the car, near tears—feels like the sort of thing I'd watch in a bad *American Pie* rip-off, not my own life. I hand over my baggage to the woman at the United counter, and for a flash of a second, as I lift my suitcase, I worry that all the extra clothes I bought at the mall, the bottle of souvenir green chile salsa from Café Ranchero and the six-pack of Dust Storm Amber Ale (brewed in Las Cruces) will push the weight of my bag past the allotted 50-pound limit that the airlines set...that I will have to pay a $50 or $75 extra fee for this flight... and then again for the flight to California...and again for the flight back to Pennsylvania.

But there's no problem at the counter.

As I head to the security checkpoint to walk through the x-ray machine, I briefly worry about my necklace, too, about my shoes, about getting selected as the random passenger for a full search...and then I worry—as they screen my laptop—about what criticism I could possibly write in my report for NMSU (How can I write anything negative? When I was there, when I was participating the whole time?)—

—but I'm through the checkpoint without a beep.

*

Just before boarding, my cell phone rings: Walter LaFaber.

"How was New Mexico, Charles?" he asks.

He is picturing me in shirt and tie right now, isn't he? He's standing at his window and staring out and picturing the Diamond Candidate, just finished with a chapter visit, just finished with workshops, set to write reports on his flight from Las Cruces to Lubbock.

"Fine," I say.

"You sound tired."

"No," I say. "That's the sound of life, Walter. Hard work."

"You must have gotten a lot accomplished, then?"

"Some big strides in Las Cruces."

"It's always great to be exhausted," LaFaber says, "but in a *good* way."

"Right."

"Just wanted to drop you a phone call. Make sure all is well with you. When you're so familiar with the driving lifestyle, taking a detour through airline country can be jolting."

"I'm good," I say. "Healthy. Listen, though. I'm about to board. Can I call you back? Later today, maybe? Or tomorrow?" And he agrees, and I hang up, and it's that easy. There is no lecture, no "change the culture" call-and-response, no catalogue of fraternities-in-the-headlines, or alcohol infractions or famous alumni or lists of accomplishments from former consultants, no praise, no warnings, and I hold the phone in my hand and wait for it to ring again but it doesn't.

# PART III

## Onward
CHAPTER TWENTY-TWO

New Mexico State to Texas Tech.

A thousand miles from Indianapolis, from the Nu Kappa Epsilon Headquarters, and now—back in Las Cruces—Sam Anderson likely daydreams a consultant's life. Parties every night, he's thinking. Girls' dorm rooms in Pennsylvania and South Carolina and Colorado. Oh, living the dream! What could possibly be better? So he needs me, Sam Anderson does, and any talk of Charles Washington—*Charles Washington?*—cavorting about with sorority girls, shooting tequila in Juarez—*Charles Washington? The guy with all the goals?*—any talk that would tarnish my reputation will only tarnish the recommendation letter that I write.

Texas Tech.

After hours of surprisingly productive one-on-one meetings and database updates and an emotional "Confront Your Brother" workshop that sees old friendships in the chapter rekindled, old conflicts extinguished, the students whisper among themselves, planning and conspiring to take me out to the bars and get me wasted, and I respond with a lackluster protest ("No, no, I represent the National Headquarters, I'm responsible for enforcing alcohol rules") but it's mostly for their sake, so that the fraternity brothers—when they actually succeed in getting me loaded—can feel as if they've achieved some small victory against the rule-imposing Evil Empire of "Nationals."

And for some reason, Texas Tech is a Miller Genuine Draft chapter, and so we split an icy bucket of MGD bottles at my Wednesday night Executive Board dinner in Lubbock, and down 2-for-1 MGDs during a Thursday night Happy Hour at Wanda's (voted one of the top tequila bars in West Texas). "I can't believe he's going out with us," I overhear one of the brothers say. "This has been the best consultant visit ever."

Wednesday night at Texas Tech to

\*

To Thursday night, when I get so drunk that I have to cancel the Alcohol Responsibility workshop that we'd planned for Friday afternoon. "It wouldn't be right, talking about alcohol abuse when I look like this," I tell their president, rubbing my eyes and sipping water. "You guys got lucky. It's a long fucking presentation." We understand, we understand, he says. That's cool, bro. You're the best. "Just don't say a word of this to anyone," I tell him. "I don't ever get drunk on chapter visits." No, no, he says. Not a word. "And I can transform back into a Fun Nazi in a heartbeat," I say. "Then it's workshop workshop worksop. Investigations. Infractions. You know what I'm talking about." I know, he says, and we're both referring to the kegs that they hide in the chapter lodge, an offense which could end them...if I pushed the issue.

Thursday night in the Texas Tech lodge, to

*

To sometime after 1 AM, and I'm standing outside the lodge in the chilly darkness of a mid-September night, MGD in one hand and cell phone in the other. Inside, the brothers are blasting Kid Rock and howling together in a sloppy chorus of voices that they're "Drinking whiskey out the bottle, not thinkin' 'bout tomorrow, singin' 'Sweet Home Alabama' *all summer long*!" Jenn has been leaving messages all week, but I've avoided the call-back because I'm afraid of how I'll sound when we speak. Is it possible that she'll sniff out the *other girl* still lingering on me? Each of Jenn's messages has grown more frantic than the last, and out in Florida the bars have closed, she's home, so finally I call her back, though I try to give the impression that I'm tired, that my days have been filled with meetings, that I'm living in constant jet-lag, and that my hectic schedule has made it difficult to find time for a phone conversation. A real conversation. You know, Jenn? One of those talks that *matter*, where we talk all night about *Seinfeld* and *Futurama* and fathers and future families and all that? Jenn's voice, by contrast, sounds scratchy, and she explains that it's because she cheered so much at the Homecoming Spirit Rally the night before. "Do you even realize what time it is?" she asks.

"I didn't," I say. "I forgot about the time difference."

"I forgive you," she says raspily. "What time does your flight get in tomorrow night?"

"My flight? I don't leave here until the weekend."

"Well, I'll be at the game on Saturday. Who's picking you up from the airport?"

"I haven't thought that far ahead," I say.

"You haven't been calling me back. You don't tell me things."

"I've been busy," I say. "I don't have my Explorer, so I can't get a second to myself."

"Is that Kid Rock in the background?"

"Huh? Oh, right. These guys love that stuff."

"So what time"—she coughs, clears her throat. "So what time are you flying in?"

"Not sure. Noon, maybe?"

"Who's picking you up?"

"I need to call the guys at Fresno," I say. "I don't know."

"Fresno? What does that have to do with anything?"

"My next visit is Fresno State."

306

"That's..." she starts, scratchy voice suddenly inflamed with emotion. "That's not what we're talking about, Charles."

"That's what *I'm* talking about. I'm in Lubbock, and I'm flying to Fresno."

"Homecoming, Charles. *Homecoming* here at Edison."

I rub the stubble on my cheeks, run my fingers along my smooth forehead, perhaps waiting for the world to offer some interruption, a car horn, a plane overhead, but although an occasional breeze rolls past there is only quiet here in Lubbock. Homecoming. In *two days*. The single mid-semester weekend on which I'd promised Jenn that I'd return home. I've forgotten to clear my schedule, to book plane tickets. And while I know that what she *should* really care about is seeing me, and while I *could* promise to fly back three weeks from now instead (a compromise!), I also know that this weekend has become symbolic for her.

It was supposed to have been symbolic for me, too, I realize suddenly. Just months ago—was it only *months?*—I was imagining a crowd of fraternity brothers surrounding me to sing the Sweetheart Song, Jenn crying as she ran her fingers over the lavalier. I'd imagined sour milk over my head. Hog-tied. A glorious ass-beating. I'd imagined myself tied to the light pole on Greek Row, with Jenn working furiously to free me so that we could go back to the hotel room I'd booked across town...I'd imagined something nice, the Ritz-Carlton, even though I don't have money for plane tickets let alone for a nice hotel... and I'd imagined the kind of sex I would remember. Not the hot tub kind, not the tequila-drunk kind. Not romantic-comedy sex, either, or '80s action movie sex, blue-light special with drapes blowing in the breeze and silhouettes making window-shadows while "Take My Breath Away" breathed behind us. I'd imagined the kind of sex where maybe I'd shower the crap off myself, the yolks and the OJ pulp slipping into the drain and Charles Washington feeling cleaner than he'd ever felt, renewed, and Jenn would be waiting in the room in a hotel robe with only the lavalier around her neck, and then she'd walk slowly to me and I'd slip my hands beneath the folds of the robe and brush it back from her shoulders and it would just be her and the necklace and before I pulled her face to mine and pressed my body against hers I would say, "This is the start. When I get back to Florida, I'll have a different piece of jewelry for you." And then—oh, you can imagine the sex *then*.

"I can look up some prices," I say. "Hotwire.com. Bad flights, crazy expensive at this point, but I'm sure there are spots."

"Oh please," she says. "I just want to hear you say it, Charles."

"I can make this happen. I'll get back there."

"I want to hear you say that you didn't book your tickets," she says.

"I'm looking for solutions, Jenn," I say, and there's a sudden urgency to my voice that I didn't anticipate. "*Solutions.* Come on, help me out here."

"I want to hear you say that you forgot."

"No, I remember. I was just waiting."

"Waiting for what? You don't care. Just say it."

"I do care, Jenn. I'm trying to take care of this right now."

"Are you high or something?" she asks. "What's so important about your fucking job that you can't even call me, that you can't visit on the one day I care about?"

"I'm not on drugs, Jenn."

"Just say it, Charles. Say what it is."

"Jenn, *really*."

"You never booked the tickets. That should tell me something, right? This isn't like, 'Hey, remember to call my sister for her birthday,' and then forgetting. You could have bought tickets back in July, when you *were* at your office. And you lied about it."

"I didn't know the itinerary for my other flights yet."

"Keep telling yourself that."

"I'm telling you the truth, Jenn. This is...you don't understand life on the road."

"Here we go. Really, Charles, I'm through with this crap."

"Through with what crap? This is my life."

"You're really not coming?" she asks.

"Just...it'll be fine. Homecoming will be *fine* without me, okay?" And now *I'm* angry, like she's the one who ripped the dream from *me*. Look at what I was willing to put myself through: a flight from Texas, the baggage, the lines, the security checkpoints, the Blazers and their leadership books, the take-off, the landing, the decompression headache, the hotel room and rental car, the lavalier, the eggs, the swollen wrists and rope-burn and near-suffocation from the hog-tie. Look at what I was willing to do, to go through, and she didn't appreciate it? "You'll be just fine. Dancing, drinking to your heart's content. You've got the *Jenn Outlook*, after all."

"Are you making fun of me?"

"I want *you* to hear yourself," I say. "This isn't the Jenn I know. I'm offering to come back, to make this work. If you don't want me to, that's on *you*."

"Enjoy the fucking desert," she says and the line goes silent, and I'm standing outside in the eerie stillness of West Texas with the phone pressed against my ear, Kid Rock having faded to Uncle Kracker or the Zac Brown Band or something. Seconds pass, then minutes, and I know I'm not talking with anyone anymore and I know that there's no reason to continue standing here like this, but a month ago this would have shattered me, my future consumed in a destructive blaze: all those mature images I'd dreamed of the way life was supposed to be post-college, Jenn as my sorority-girl wife, the two of us living in a downtown condo and driving back to EU for Homecoming every year, wearing NKE and KΔ "Alumni" shirts, young professionals, world figured out. But now, here where the sky is crisp blackness stretching from one horizon to the next over the undeveloped curvature of the Earth, I breathe deeply and try to convince myself once again that blank space is better. If we work it out, we work it out.

Thursday at Texas Tech to

*

To Saturday night, which passes without a single phone call or text from Jenn.

Convince the brothers to drive me somewhere with cheap drink specials.

Wedge myself into a crowded college bar called "Moonshine," blonde hair and skirts and glitter everywhere, girls in cowboy hats and boots, asses bursting from the bottoms of their shredded jean shorts, near-riot breaking out on the dance floor when the country music makes way for Rihanna. Keep myself surrounded, MGD in hand, head nodding, so that I don't think about her, so that I don't think about the way my life was supposed to be when I returned home. Saturday night at Moonshine, then Sunday morning at Lubbock's airport to

*

To Fresno State, and now I've arrived at a Bud Lite chapter.

Loosen up, loosen up, you don't want to be the only guy in the house without a drink.

By day, I help the Fresno State brothers create and fine-tune their budget, help them fill out Delinquent Forms for members past due, help them research collections agencies for members who owe more than $500, help them research online dues-paying sites, OmegaFi. We update their decades-old chapter bylaws to comply with new university regulations on membership and housing, and I collect checks for National Headquarters dues and national insurance. "We just got more accomplished in, like, two days, than we had all year," their president tells me, and I nod and tell him that I'm happy for him.

"Friend-request me," he says. "Join our fraternity's group page."

"You have a Facebook page for the chapter?" I ask.

"It's a forum. We post questions, updates, that sort of thing. I'm sure our officers will have, like, a thousand questions about the budget."

"I'm not on Facebook anymore," I say.

"Dude," he says. "Get with the *times*. You don't have internet or text messaging on your phone? You don't have a profile? Even my mother is on Facebook."

LaFaber's speeches about digital footprints seem less dire now, articles in the *Washington Post* and *New York Times* chronicling Obama's social media strategies, the first political candidate to fully embrace and absorb himself in Web 2.0. I've gone from a world where Facebook and MySpace are liabilities, dirty autobiographies to drag you down and ruin whatever future you might want to write for yourself...to a world where the technologies are Potential! Potential! Potential! "Yes we can!" speeches reprinted in their entirety atop photos from the civil rights era, photos of white and black hands clasped together, shared and re-shared and re-shared, 20-year-olds changing their profile pictures to the Obama "Hope" graphic. Friendships suddenly blossoming between kids and their corporations, all at the click of a "like" for MSNBC and FoxNews. Amazon.com and Microsoft and MTV and Kellogg's, "liked" and friended and shared. It's clear now: there is no way other than this.

309

"You don't even have any mp3s on this shitty laptop," the president says. "How do you survive?"

"Our Tech Director warned us," I say. "He told us not to download anything, that they could track it when we got back to Headquarters."

"You're shitting me," he says. He clicks a few buttons, weasels his way through my internet settings and my control panel. "Well, this laptop probably doesn't have the memory for iTunes anyway. But I can change a few settings, download Kazaa for you. Then you can listen to songs on the Windows Media Player, at least."

"I don't know," I say.

"Just delete the program before you give the computer back," he says. "Transfer your songs by flashdrive or Ethernet cord or something. Simple, brother. A man without mp3s can hardly be called a man. Do you even have an iPod?"

"Come on," I say. "You're making me feel shittier by the second."

That's my day. But it's a Bud Lite chapter, and so—by night—I travel with the brothers to a shack-in-the-woods bar called Jimbo's on the fringes of Fresno, a musty-brown building at the end of a dark choppy road; it's adorned with flickering Budweiser neon signs, spattered with caked mud kicked off the tires of pick-up trucks. To get here, I've stuffed myself into a car with six or seven other fraternity brothers, and we all tumble out and walk a quarter-mile gravel road from parking spot to bar. "This place is a dive," one of the guys tells me, "but we're all going to get ripped, *ripped.*" Jimbo's looks built of driftwood, feels like we're crawling inside a beaver dam: boards creak as we walk across a shaking front porch to show our IDs to a mullet-haired security guard. But inside, it's packed with beer tubs and girls and bars and the guys all wear jeans, torn jeans, faded jeans, vintage Twinkies and Spam T's and striped button-downs and "Trojans" caps and trucker hats, and it's irony overload, the bar itself and the apparel, everyone looking like they just stepped off the set of *The Real World*, and I'm dressed just like them.

"That girl's checking you out, bro," one of the Fresno State chapter brothers tells me, yelling over the unlikely (but seemingly sincere) boyband/gangsta rapper combo of Justin Timberlake and 50 Cent, as they sing about technology ("Hey-oh, I'm tired 'a usin' technology. Why don't sit down on top of me?"). Words to live by.

"Checking me out?" I ask. "Introduce me."

Here at Fresno State, the one-on-one meetings pop past so quickly that the days seem to turn to night in half the time. I ask the students to complete any/all reports for me because it's just details, formalities. "I won't make you do any workshops if you don't want to," I say, so we see a movie, go to the mall, go out to eat, tour the city. Sunday through Wednesday at Fresno State, and not a day passes that I don't help a group of brothers rip open a box of Bud Lites and fill their recycling bin with empty aluminum cans, and then I fly to

*

To Cal State-Highland, and they are an Anchor Steam chapter, and it feels good to drink something distinctive. Like getting drunk is a cultural endeavor.

I mark reports with the same gusto that I reserve for filing taxes and completing credit card applications. I do no background checks or investigations, even when I know that alcohol infractions are rampant. I do not repeat that "The mission of Nu Kappa Epsilon is to build our members into the socially responsible citizens of tomorrow" because even when they listen to me, the message thuds in the members' minds with the same empty phrase-to-remember cadence as the Pledge of Allegiance or the Lord's Prayer...just words. I do not wear my silver-black Ralph Lauren suit and my Tommy tie into any more fraternity houses, and I do not recite the "Four D's" or show the "Circles of Danger." They drink Anchor Steam, and this is why I feel good as I drink with them: you can drink Bud Lite like water, ten Bud Lites out of a cooler at a football game, drink till you puke; but the better and more expensive the beer, the more you appreciate it, savor it. Quality alcohol—not afternoon-long workshops—has made these fraternity men into responsible drinkers. I recognize this. I tell them congratulations.

"We started our Awards Packet for Nationals," the President says.

"Fuck it," I say. "Do you want to be a *paperwork* chapter? Let's get out of the house. Let's do something. Fresh air, you know?"

Daily, I scroll past Jenn's number in my cell phone and send text messages even though I'm past my limit and each will cost me more than I want to imagine.

> Charles: Listen, really sorry about homecoming. U understand right?
> Jenn: [No response]
> Charles: Just saw a girl at the airport in a KD shirt.
> Jenn: [No response]
> Charles: Got a call from Edwin. Said he saw u at Hemhaws?
> Jenn: [No response]
> Charles: Can u call me? This is silly.
> Jenn: [No response]

I want to call her, but I can't, and I don't know why. Am I afraid that I'll have to listen to her voice, so happy, on the voicemail message? Am I afraid that I'll have to leave a message, that my own voice will be recorded and saved for her, some sad desperate kilobytes crossing the continent and captured forever in her phone in a way that feels more real—more human—than the easy letters of a text message? Am I afraid that I might actually have to *talk* to Jenn, that I'll be forced to speak more than a single sentence, a single question, a single observation?

I discover Maria's number in my phone, am surprised that it was still saved. Am surprised that she didn't save *my* number when I first called her, that she hasn't called me since I left New Mexico, but I think this was her dorm number maybe, not her cell, so maybe she never had my phone number? I delete Maria from my cell phone.

From Thursday afternoon in CSUH to

*

To Friday morning, waiting for a meeting in the Cal State-Highland chapter room, and I'm using their high-speed internet to download T.I., "Live Your Life," a song that surges through me like an anthem. I download Kanye, "American Boy." I visit Billboard.com and download the entire Top 50, most of them pop songs I've only sort-of heard at bars and in the staticky in-out crackle of radio stations as they fade from Illinois to Indiana to Ohio to Pennsylvania. The more I download, the more I realize how incomplete my life has become, a once-full profile now drained to empty questionnaire ("What's your favorite song, Charles?" "What was the last movie you saw?" "What is the most pressing issue in the current election?"). A man who suddenly knows nothing about the world.

It's only inevitable, then, that—with all those songs downloading in the background of my slow-moving laptop—I find myself on the Facebook home page, typing in the old familiar email address and password, entering the familiar domain once again. I change my privacy features so that the world cannot search my photos, double-check that I am "EU – Graduate" and that my employer is kept vague, just "Higher Education," and soon my entire life appears once again on my computer screen. I am restored. I need updates, yes, but I also wonder: could I have ever truly made it disappear? It was always saved somewhere, just waiting patiently on some server. It wouldn't ever *let* me stay away.

"Charles is…back," I type.

My first Facebook status update in four months, five months? I download a photo of Ryan Reynolds in *Van Wilder*, make it my new profile picture.

And there in the Highland fraternity house chapter room, I spend the entirety of my morning calling auto shops in the greater Philadelphia area, pricing tires and wheels, doing some mental math, deciding that I can put the tire on my credit card but I'll pass on replacing the dinged-up wheel because the price is approximately equal to a full month's salary and my credit card bill has already grown substantially larger than my bank account can ever be as long as I'm in this job. I set an appointment to change the tire but don't tell the mechanic that my wheel is damaged.

When the afternoon turns to evening, I suggest to a couple of the Highland undergrads that we drive to the Save-Mart and grab a couple Anchor Steam 12-packs. "On me," I say, because I can pay with my NKE credit card and lose the receipt and try to report the expense as my lunch or dinner.

The clerk scans the card. I sign my name to the receipt,

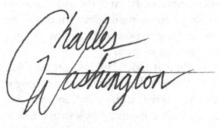

then crumple it and toss it into the trashcan. The cold worries of back East are thawing, cracking apart, melting away.

\*

"Dude, a girl can't *bone* a guy," the President says. We're drinking Anchor Steam in the backyard of the house, a guy chasing a screaming sorority girl through the grass with a lit sparkler. Someone else is shooting bottle rockets. I don't know if these are left-overs from July, or if the Highland brothers just keep fireworks around for lazy backyard nights.

"It's just an expression," I say. "*Boning*. No different than screwing, or fucking."

"No, no. Boning implies that you're doing work with a bone," he says. "The best a girl can hope for is *getting* boned."

"But a guy and a girl can *bone*. Like, together."

"No, if a girl is talking about sex, she's got to say 'We were having sex.' She can't say, 'We were boning.' The *man* bones. The woman *gets* boned. You see what I'm saying? The only way a girl can bone is if the dude's unconscious and she has to do all the work. You see?"

"An astute observation, sir," I say and reach my hand into the ice to find another bottle.

\*

This is the difference between driving and flying. Driving: I have an entire snap-shut case filled with maps and directions and every mile is necessary and planned, and I hit the gas and then the brakes and then the turn signal and then check the map and then hit the brakes again because someone cut me off and then the gas and then swerve and then move into the center lane and my fingers grip the steering wheel under the stress of a seven-hour drive and then I collapse into a jagged pot hole. And flying? I just settle into a seat and look at the window, and maybe there's turbulence but it isn't my problem.

\*

Jenn's page: new photo, and she's smiling wider than the old one.

That's what she wants the world to see, anyway.

Jenn's new photo: dressed in her costume for the Homecoming Skit Dance, an event taken so seriously by EU sororities that tens of thousands of dollars are spent, choreographers employed. In sorority Rush, cheerleaders and dancers are treated like top draft picks; the Kappa Deltas are notorious for scouting them all, for recruiting the one former Miami Heat dancer now attending EU, the two Bucs cheerleaders, all for the purposes of a Skit Dance worthy of YouTube immortality. And the girls…the girls dress like they're auditioning for a Vegas show, tight silver pants, or short skirts that fly up when they spin around and expose asses almost in total, breasts gleaming, a single shade removed from *strip club*.

So yeah, there's Jenn at Skit Dance. Costume. Hair streaked with pink and black like she's a Pussycat Doll, the picture burning with hot sex. The type of picture that, after you take it, a girl says "Holy shit, I look fucking *hot*!" like she didn't ever think it was possible to look so good, and you can tell that her first thought is that the world needs to fucking see this, men drooling and fantasizing and—

Whatever. Back to my own page.

*

Friend requests on Facebook from the chapter presidents at Texas Tech and Highland.

"Your profile is back up?" Edwin—from back at EU—writes on my wall. "Nice."

Jenn writes nothing, but I notice her relationship status has become "Single."

At first, I'm afraid to write anything…it seems as if no one noticed that I was ever gone.

But one typed letter leads to another, one status update to another.

"Charles is…living the dream, fighting the good fight."

*

While I'm sitting at a Karl Strauss bar at the airport, my father calls. First time in over a month. I answer. I don't know why I answer. Possibly because I've had three Red Trolley Ales.

"Your mother said you haven't called her back."

"I'm in California right now," I say.

"What does that have to do with anything? You have a phone."

"Things are crazy. Traveling."

"Call your mother back. She worries."

"She doesn't worry."

"She thinks you're upset with her."

"So the two of you are talking now?"

"We never stopped talking."

"Always a surprise with my parents," I say. "I never know the real story, do I? I never know the *real you*, do I?"

"What are you talking about, Charles?"

"Nothing."

"She thinks you're shutting her out. Shutting *us* out. Have you booked tickets for Thanksgiving yet?"

"Can't afford it. I'm on my own now, remember?"

My father sighs. "Charles, I told you. I'll buy your ticket. We want to see you."

"Yeah," I say. "Well, anyway. They're boarding."

314

*

Cal State-Highland to Long Beach State.

To San Francisco State, where I spend a full day at an outdoor café, thinking about typing up chapter visit reports for Walter LaFaber but really just page-hopping on Facebook, following links to *Daily Show* clips and watching and re-watching Katy Perry videos and pretending that I'm doing it in an ironic way.

"Charles is…loving the Tina-Fey-as-Palin skits. Whoever said that SNL was dead?"

"Charles is…now friends with Sam Anderson."

"Charles is…now friends with Tamara Jones."

"Charles is…waking up at noon today."

Answering questions about national dues payments and alumni relations programs via Facebook chat with the officers at Pittsburgh, Grand Valley College, Texas Tech, St. Joseph's. *This is so easy*, they say. *Why haven't we always done this?*

*

Then, back on a plane to Philly for my visit to Delaware.

Cross the country. Two connections, two airport bars. I even find Ethernet connections.

When I roll my luggage through the parking lot at the Philadelphia airport and finally spot my Explorer, I stop for a moment, afraid to approach the door.

Finally I walk closer, touch the surface of the vehicle, warm but not hot, the handle of the back hatch, dusty but not dirty; it makes a crackling noise when I lift the door, sleep crust snapped upon opening. I slide into my seat and behind the steering wheel, the leather so familiar, the snap-shut cases, the scattered hangers and fallen backseat rod and it's a mess but it all feels right, only takes a moment for the seat to conform to my body once again, and I start the car and the air-conditioning blasts out and Britney Spears screams from the speakers, and I shiver and cough and…I realize I'm crying, also. I don't know why, but for a full minute, I stare at the center console…the maps, the goal sheets, the blank flipped-over business card, the rearview mirror, and I cry. There in the parking lot of the Philadelphia airport, in my Explorer, crying, to

*

To an afternoon at an auto shop in Philadelphia as the new tires are installed, the mechanic telling me that he's worried about the condition of my wheels. The metal, he says, is so twisted that it could destroy the rubber; he's surprised, in fact, that the spare isn't already toast.

"This is like a ticking time bomb, kid," he says.

"I wish I could afford new wheels," I say. "My credit card is maxed out."

"Cost you now or cost you later," he says. "I'm telling you now, cause this don't look good. You're going to want to get them."

"Just the tires for now. That's all I can do."

After my Explorer is repaired, I drive slowly and carefully to a hotel, eat and relax at an Applebee's a block away because it's already 7:00 PM, and I won't drive nights. Not anymore. The stress of the potholes is bad enough during the day. So I will be a day late to the Delaware chapter house, but I don't think anyone will stay up waiting for me.

Several times throughout the night, I part the drapes and stare out at my car.

It looks pained, still, and I want to ask if it's all right. If the tires were enough. But just like a dog after a visit to the vet, you can ask questions but you'll never get a response.

I spend three days in Delaware (a Dogfish Head chapter), then drive to Marshall (a Yuengling chapter) in Huntington, West Virginia.

My Explorer rattles worse than it ever has before, hangers shaking, the framed Illinois charter from 1921 banging against my suitcase, and I try to ignore it all.

\*

"Charles is...out for a night at the Hall of Fame bar and grill!"
"Charles is...THUNDERRRRING HERRRRDDD!"
"Charles is...now friends with Randy Jung."
"Charles is...now friends with James Neagle."
"Charles is...ha ha ha! WHOOOOO!"

\*

"Dude," the Treasurer says. "Don't tell me you've never jerked off while driving."

"No," I say, laughing. "Jerked off? Come on."

"Oh, you gotta. All the driving you do?"

"How do you even...the logistics of it?"

"You buy a pack of tube socks, is the thing."

"When did you do this?"

"When I drive back to Cleveland for the holidays. On the road for how many hours? You need something to occupy your time. Anyway, listen: you buy a pack of tube socks. Don't just grab some old sock from the bottom of your drawer. Don't be cheap. Buy the full pack. You need at least two."

"At least two socks. Got it."

"Roll the sock over the cock, see," he says, "and do your thing. Jerk off and don't worry about it, you know? Don't worry about getting anything on you, don't start looking down or anything. You don't want to crash while you're jerking off. Talk about tragic, man. So let the tube sock do its thing. Roll it back off, stop at a rest area, a McDonalds, whatever, dump it in a trash can. Boom. No worries."

"Okay," I say. "So why do you need two socks?"

"The other sock," he says, "that's for the trip back."

\*

Marshall to Miami University in Oxford, Ohio, and most of the fraternity brothers are out of town for some football-related road trip, so I have the house to myself. Fridge full of Samuel Adams. Then north, through the down-and-out Great Lakes cities of northern Ohio and eastern Michigan. Miami University to Toledo (Wild Turkey, unfortunately). To Central Michigan in distant Mount Pleasant (Mickey's malt liquor), where the brothers get me a hotel room near the local casino. To the University of Michigan, where I visit five different college bars in one night, probably a personal record, and I'm never even sure what type of beer I'm drinking.

*

Here in the Midwest, away from the t-shirts and flip-flops and sunshine of the West Coast, away from the stacked-on-top-of-one-another cities of the mid-Atlantic, the universities feel different. The campuses themselves are secluded kingdoms of limestone castles and thick brick buildings, rocky facades emblazoned with donor names, wide open grassy spaces graced with statues of past presidents and administrators, each campus encircled by neighborhoods of fraternity and sorority mansions as old as the school itself, then surrounded by hundreds of square miles of cornfields. Though the schools burst with Chicago and Indianapolis and Cincinnati and Cleveland kids, these Midwestern universities feel far removed from the crowded urban centers of each state. Worlds unto themselves.

But the weather is turning now.

The sprawling green campus quads have gone autumn yellow, ready to be frozen and covered in snow. Trees are changing, shaking off red-orange leaves, afternoon air growing cold, smoky. Living in Florida all my life, never having experienced any season but endless summer, this has happened quicker than I imagined. And everywhere I go, I'm the only one who regards this change of season, this cold, as…as anything to be regarded. It was always supposed to be one way, and I'm the only one who wonders why it doesn't stay that way.

The students are changing with the season, also. The once-naïve freshmen have donned an extra layer of clothing, thick university logo sweatshirts, thicker skin after having suffered humbling first-year embarrassments, the excitement of *FREEDOM!* and *INDEPENDENCE!* settling. The world no longer sparkles with newness. Now, college is life, that's all. Midterms approaching. Homecoming Weeks ending at campuses everywhere, the semester's final stretch before Thanksgiving.

Excitement over. Unpack that peacoat I bought, those gloves and that sweater, prepare for my first-ever winter. The past month—plane-hopping the West Coast, then region-hopping from Atlantic to mid-Atlantic to Midwest—seemed to pass more quickly than I could've imagined, but now the cold is coming and I'm slowing down.

*

Todd Hampton, the new President at EU, has posted a McCain photo as his profile picture. Every few hours, he posts a new status about war heroes and patriots, "Ted Nugent is so fucking right" and "Obama isn't even a citizen!!!" and "A vote for that man is a vote for terrorists."

317

Everywhere there are arguments, long comment threads of vitriolic virtual finger-pointing, socialism and Godlessness and stupidity and hockey moms and Vietnam and Muslim faith and "I can see Russia from my house," an election approaching and the Facebook world suddenly a room full of hungry zombies fighting over the squirming-dying man on the floor, yanking out his intestines and ripping scraps of flesh from his face. It's nearing the end of October, and I don't want to hear this shit. I don't want any of it. This is not what it was supposed to be. This is like going home to Cypress Falls on holiday break, seeing some new area where I played as a kid now gobbled up by a condo development or a Wal-Mart, bull-dozed, chain-link-fenced, world of Florida hotter, pavement multiplying, power lines multiplying, Facebook no longer a magical portal back to the wonderful world of college but instead a window to the world beyond.

The future President of the United States of America with his own Facebook page? Has he ever visited, do you think? Would he update the page himself, the occupation title, when elected? Does he even know his own motherfucking password?

I try to ignore it all, try to focus on the comments about food, about vacation, about movies, about last night, about

*

And I am driving south once again, Explorer making noises so loud that I have to crank up my stereo to an unhealthy level and I don't even hear when someone honks behind me; I drive south, away from the lakeside industry and smokestacks and back into the quiet cornfields of northwest Ohio. To Bowling Green State University.

And I've still made no attempt to organize my car.

Just keep moving, just keep moving, just keep

# Bowling Green
## CHAPTER TWENTY-THREE

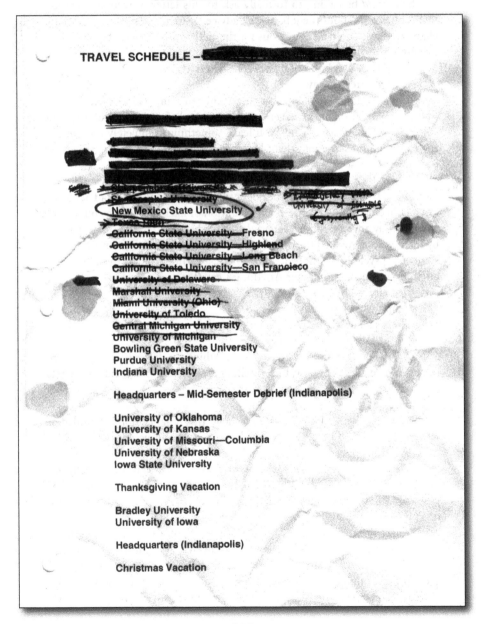

TRAVEL SCHEDULE – ~~[redacted]~~

~~[redacted]~~
~~[redacted]~~
~~[redacted]~~
~~[redacted]~~

~~[redacted] University~~
(New Mexico State University) ✓
~~Texas Tech~~
~~California State University—Fresno~~
~~California State University—Highland~~
~~California State University—Long Beach~~
~~California State University—San Francisco~~
~~University of Delaware~~
~~Marshall University~~
~~Miami University (Ohio)~~
~~University of Toledo~~
~~Central Michigan University~~
~~University of Michigan~~
Bowling Green State University
Purdue University
Indiana University

Headquarters – Mid-Semester Debrief (Indianapolis)

University of Oklahoma
University of Kansas
University of Missouri—Columbia
University of Nebraska
Iowa State University

Thanksgiving Vacation

Bradley University
University of Iowa

Headquarters (Indianapolis)

Christmas Vacation

As I finish my drive to Bowling Green, I receive a phone call from Sam Anderson at New Mexico State, the first in three weeks (except for a few Facebook messages). The roads here in southern Michigan are mostly flat, sometimes rising/ falling in prairie rolls, but the hangers suddenly rattle on my backseat rod.

"Got a question for you," Sam says, no pleasantries.

"Would love to hear it," I say.

Sam *could* be calling to formally ask for his letter of recommendation, to ask questions about the job, to seek advice, or to give me an update on his chapter…these could all be reasons for the call, positive news…but somehow I doubt it.

"I just read that blindfolding is considered hazing."

"That's correct," I say.

"*Blind*-folding?" he asks, a high-pitched Jim-Mora-*Playoffs!?*-style squeak in his voice that I've never heard from him before, the sort of desperate voice crack only possible when you learn something completely unexpected, the truth behind some long-kept lie. "Just a piece of fabric? Just a shred of a bed sheet? Or a sock?"

"Sam," I say and I pull off the highway, onto the shoulder, hoping the hangers stop shaking. I try to speak gently, delivering the law as a friend and not a policeman. "The by-the-book definition of hazing mentions blindfolds. It doesn't say anything about *material*. Just the blindfold itself is considered— by those who developed the definition, not me—they say it's a way to demean someone psychologically. To scare them." Gentle, supportive: "Is there anything you need to tell me? Anything I can do?"

"Just fabric?" he says. "Not physical abuse or any of that shit."

"Sam. I can help, really."

"There's a rat," Sam says. "Fucking snitch."

"Who? What do you mean?"

"Every day, I tell these pledges that this is a *fraternity*, 'kay, a *secret* society. We're all adults now, I keep telling them. We don't reveal our secrets. Am I right?"

"Sure."

"'Kay," he says. "That's all I need to hear. This organization is founded on *secrecy*. Our letters. Our ritual. We don't run and tell our parents what we do."

"What happened, Sam? Tell me. I can help."

"We've always blindfolded," he says. "It's always been like that. It was never against the rules *before*. When I came into Big Brother Night three years ago, they blindfolded *me*. I didn't complain. *Nobody* complained. You don't fuck with tradition."

"You're right, Sam," I say. The rules haven't changed, but I don't argue.

"Last Friday, we do the same thing as always. We blindfold the pledges and have them march into this dark room. We're in the fraternal robes, all the brothers singing 'Song for a Brother' just like it says in the New Member Education manual. I mean, it's in the manuals that *you guys* gave us. We quiz them about one another," he says and pauses. "I can't believe I'm telling fucking Nationals about this."

"Don't worry. You're right about the manuals, Sam." This entire ceremony, blindfolds included, is outlined in the national officer binder that we give each chapter delegation at our annual Transitional Leadership Conference; the undergraduates are *supposed* to do all of this, even though another manual—the Risk Management Handbook—forbids the blindfolds. The Initiation Ritual itself, a twenty-minute experience for each pledge, is a highly scripted and choreographed performance involving candles and fires, tricks in perspective, trust, quick scares, and is dependent upon blindfolds. Historically, the pledge is also supposed to "walk Initiation free of spirit and unencumbered by earthly burden." Butt-naked, in other words. To enhance the experience, or...I don't know what. Generations of Nikes were forced to undress and walk Initiation in the nude, and although some old-school chapters still do it, the National Headquarters now sells "fraternal robes," a more popular option. But hell, you can do whatever you want in the Initiation Ritual. Why the fuck not? It's a ceremony hidden behind of veil of secrecy for more than a century, the idea of secrecy sworn by oath in the ritual itself, *blood oath* at some chapters (*naked* blood oath at others)...*I will never betray the secrets of Nu Kappa Epsilon...* if the ritual ever became public, the meaning of the letters public, it would be almost worse than some alcohol lawsuit because it would mean that the national brotherhood had failed. In the eyes of the National Headquarters, it's *leadership development* that makes us a fraternity and not a drinking club. But in the eyes of many of our brothers and alumni (especially the oldest among them), it's the shared rituals; they bind the generations togethers, and no one will change a *single* motherfucking detail of any of them. "Go on," I say. "Tell me what happened."

"They're blindfolded in this dark room," he says, "and we give them these far-fetched questions that they can't answer. A test of brotherhood. Like, 'Name the hometowns of your pledge brothers,' shit like that. Every time they get one wrong, all the brothers get, you know, *loud*, and yell at the pledges about how they should know these things about their brothers. They're blindfolded, so it's scary for them, but it's"— silence— "it's *nothing*."

"Is that it, then?" I ask. "You get loud, and that's the whole ceremony?"

"After that, we pretend to have a fake blackball session. Pretend to kick them all out. We tell them to *get the fuck out of*...I mean, we tell them to *leave* the room so we can vote on whether or not to keep 'em in the fraternity. Just then, though, a brother walks behind each pledge—this is the Big Brother— and he whispers the information into their ears, the answers to the questions, and he argues for a second chance. They answer correctly this time, see? With a little help from their new Big Brother? That's when we remove the blindfolds and reveal the pledge's Big Brother for the first time. And we sing the song again, go through the explanation about how real brotherhood isn't just memorizing stuff, but *being there* for your brothers."

"That sounds acceptable," I say, but I suspect that the New Mexico State version of these events includes additional layers that Sam keeps hidden behind his chapter's veil. "And one of the pledges was upset by this? Even after he heard the positive message of the Big Brother ritual?"

"Wasn't just him. Some pledge told his *parents* the ritual."

"Okay, well—"

"The *entire* ritual!"

"Relax, Sam. Headquarters will defend you on this."

"Shit."

"And anyway, that's a pledge ritual, not the Initiation Ritual. It's not one of the Higher Secrets."

"Well, fuck," he says. "That's not all of it, you know?"

"There's more?"

"Yeah," he says. "I guess."

"Tell me, Sam. I can help."

After talking evasively for another minute or so, finally Sam is ready to reveal the rest of the narrative. "This has got to stay between us. I'm not kidding." Yes, I say. I can keep your secret. Trust me. Sam exhales. Tells me, Okay, listen: before the ceremony, he sat the pledges—fifteen of them, blindfolded—in the backs of pick-up trucks and hauled them to a pecan farm on the periphery of developed Las Cruces; like prisoners-of-war, he had them all march single-file through the rows of pecan trees, arms outstretched and clutching the shoulders of the man walking in front of them. Occasionally one of the pledges would trip over a root or over upturned soil or get smacked in the face with a renegade branch, but finally they all came to a creek or an irrigation canal or something (all Sam knows is that the farmer is a Nike alumnus who looks the other way when the brothers use his property, or so they've always been told), and Sam marched the pledges onto a modest wooden bridge with low railings, twenty feet over the rock-cut water. And there, with boards creaking below their feet, a steady stream rushing below the boards, Sam made each blindfolded pledge—one at a time, "so it was *safe*," he says—climb a stepladder that he'd positioned in the center of the bridge, stand tall, fold his hands over his chest, turn around, and fall backward.

"A trust fall," Sam says. "They thought we were making them walk the plank, you know? Into the water? But we had a bunch of brothers who caught them when they stepped off the ladder. Teaches the pledges to trust that we wouldn't put them in harm's way?"

"That's not in the manual."

"Nothing's ever happened," Sam says. "We would never hurt them, all right? I would never…I've got a younger sister, a younger brother, and fine, I'll pick on them and give them a hard time or whatever, but if anyone touched a Goddamn hair on their heads, I'd"—voice trembling and growing louder—"I'd beat his face into the fucking ground, do you hear me? That's how I feel about our pledges, 'kay? We love them, do you hear me?"

"I hear you."

"It's just…one of our pledges told his parents, see, and they were pissed. *Pissed.* How could someone blindfold their son on a bridge, he could have died, blah blah blah. They called the university and got our Greek Affairs Director on the line. He called me—*me*, personally—and asked if the whole deal was true."

"You didn't confirm it, did you?" I ask.

"I said *maybe*, and he started talking about hazing, about suspensions. Student Conduct Board."

"Does the kid want to pursue this? Or is it just his parents?"

"His parents," Sam says. "Our pledges fucking loved the ceremony. Aren't you listening to me? The thing is, there's a picture."

"Of, for fuck's sake. A picture? Of what?"

"When we had the pledges in the back of the pick-up truck? Blindfolded? Someone took a picture of us while we were driving back to the fraternity house. The Greek Advisor emailed me a copy of the picture. All these kids in white shirts, hunched over, heads down, black blindfolds on. Looks so much worse than it is."

"The Greek Advisor has this picture?"

"He gets pictures all the time, that's what he told me," Sam says. "Every time there's anything weird going on around the university, people take pictures and assume it's a fraternity. Could be the fucking football team, but the Greek Advisor files the pictures away in case he hears anything else. In our case, he gets a phone call from some parents, and all of a sudden he's got a story that matches the pictures. Knows who it is."

"Sam. How could you let a *picture* get taken?"

"They're using the blindfolding charge to put us on 'exploratory suspension' for the rest of the semester," Sam says. "And they want to conduct some big investigation."

"Investigation, fuck," I say. The further this situation progresses—another lawsuit for Nu Kappa Epsilon in addition to the Sandor Lawsuit, LaFaber said during the summer, and the entire National Fraternity could be wiped out—the greater the chance someone will uncover all the details of *my* visit, too, the Etiquette Dinner and the pledge humiliation that *I* watched, the trip to Mexico, the pledge DDs, the sex in Maria's dorm room, the vomit in the sink. Hell, if the university administration takes Sam Anderson down, he'd hand me over without a moment's hesitation. *Our Educational Consultant condoned all of thi*s, he'd say. *Take him! Take him*! And Jose—based on what I remember from Juarez, Jose looking pissed because, why? because I was dancing with Maria, his dream girl maybe?—Jose might not even need to hear someone ask before he sold me out. "Let me handle this," I say. "Make sure your Greek Advisor has *my* cell phone number. Don't say another word to him, no matter what he says. Without confession, without clear evidence, all is hearsay. *Refer all questions to me.*"

But still I'm thinking: have the parents called the National Headquarters? Has LaFaber heard about this? If so, he'll want to know if I saw anything suspicious in New Mexico. "And tell your Greek Advisor *not* to call Headquarters," I say. "I'm the national representative. Let me handle it, and this thing won't last another week."

"You're sure?" Sam asks.

"Blindfolding is against the hazing guidelines, but it's not serious," I say, knowing that this single situation, like the fabric, is only superficial. It's what lies beneath—the details an investigation might reveal—that is damning. "Don't worry. I'm not worried."

Sam exhales. "All right. I trust you."

"That's right, Sam. We're good?"

"I hope so." He exhales again. "So where you at these days?"

"Heading to Bowling Green State in Ohio," I say. "It's getting cold. But ya'll don't have that problem in Las Cruces, do you?"

"Little bit," he says. "Nights are chilly. Gets cold really quick, soon as the sun sets. Happens so quick, you freak. What about the women out there in O-*hi*-o? Any honeys?"

"We'll see."

"Oh," he says. "That reminds me. Maria keeps asking me about you."

"Maria?"

"You didn't forget about her already, did you?"

"No, no," I say. "Of course I didn't forget about her. What—" and I scratch the back of my neck, smooth my pants, scratch the back of my neck, "what's she saying?"

"I don't know. I only ran into her once. She was like, 'why isn't he calling me' and shit. I don't know. I played it off. Said you had family issues in Florida. Your mom died."

"Oh God, Sam," I say, but Sam is reassured that I'll do everything in my power to deflect the Greek Advisor and the parents and bury the blindfold situation, so I let it go. "Keep me updated," I say. "Everything, no matter how minor." And then we hang up.

But all of this came from nowhere, came like a cold night in the desert.

I pull my Explorer back onto the highway, every bump in the road pounding into my new tires, my dented wheels, reverberating through the cabin.

*

The day is dark and wet by the time I arrive on the Bowling Green campus, only dim sunlight behind a wall of granite-gray clouds cemented across the sky. Everywhere, students walk uncertainly, some holding up umbrellas and others carrying them at their sides. But the rapid-fire rain starts and stops without pattern, twenty-second spurts, two-minute spurts, usually pouring at the very moment when everyone has folded and re-sheathed their umbrellas.

This is a campus dripping in browns and oranges, the "BGSU" banners flapping from lampposts and the football posters taped up on windows all printed in colors that match the slushy piles of dead leaves collected along the sidewalks. The concrete buildings are stained dark with rainwater, seeming to glower down at students instead of welcoming them inside; the library—a towering building, eight or nine floors—is decorated along one exterior concrete side with some sort of funky, graffiti-like artwork that feels like a foolish experiment in modern art rather than a striking and inventive "statement." On another day, perhaps, this campus might convey the same historic authority as Michigan or Illinois, but today it seems only a pale and depressed distant relative.

It is a cold Sunday in Bowling Green, and before I leave the warmth of my Explorer to walk a puddle-spotted sidewalk to the Nu Kappa Epsilon fraternity house, I rummage through my backseat for my Edison University windbreaker. Since I left the Headquarters in late August, I can't remember a single day of rain, and I can't even recall if I stuffed my windbreaker under the seat or into my duffel bag or if, maybe, I left it in Indianapolis. But finally I find it, then make my way through a rain that seems to grow heavier and louder as I walk to the front steps of the NKE chapter house, a non-descript brick structure identical to several other non-descript brick structures across campus, each of them bearing Greek letter combinations.

The president of this chapter, Bradley Camden, meets me at the door and invites me inside. Bradley is short, slouches as he points me down a long hallway to a special guest room that actually says "GUEST" on the door. "In there is where you're staying," he says, but doesn't lead me to the room, doesn't help me with my bags.

Not a frat star: Bradley has the sort of pudgy face and stomach that come not from excessive drinking but from a lack of exercise, from all-night video-gaming, posture shaped by office swivel chair, spine curved perfectly to fit the seat. And I don't know why, but I'm disappointed.

*

After I've dropped off my bags, I meet Bradley in the chapter room where he paces with Harvey Pekar jitters, hands stuffed in pockets, occasionally touching a couch's armrest before turning around and walking ten steps in the opposite direction.

"I've got a strange question," I say and sit, but still he stands and shuffles about, still can't make eye contact for more than a split second. "You all right?"

"Huh? Yeah."

"I've been wondering since I got here. Why do all the houses look the same?"

"Huh?" he asks.

"Sit down," I say. "You're making me nervous."

He does, and I ask again.

"The school owns the fraternity houses," Bradley says. "They're just converted dorms with Greek letters on top." Each house, he tells me, eyes darting about, has a live-in Graduate Assistant and a Resident Advisor—two paid staff members—on the first floor. Bowling Green likes to refer to itself as a "learning laboratory," he says with a shrug, and so the fraternities and sororities and clubs and organizations are supplied with seemingly limitless resources and graduate student advisors who are completing Master's degrees in College Student Personnel.

"Do you have guests very often?" I ask him. "Enough to justify a guest room?"

"A lot of grad students." Bradley scratches his neck. "Every time they have a conference or something, they use all these guest rooms to house the attendees."

"Just random people, staying with you on random nights?"

"Huh? Yeah, sometimes."

"Do you have *any* control of this house?" I ask, setting my laptop computer onto a plain table so smooth and scratch-free that I wonder if anyone has ever used it. The cinderblock walls throughout the fraternity house are painted off-white, the color of used-up toothbrush bristles, the texture bumpy and sloppy.

"The university owns it," Bradley says, words melting into mumble. "They think the house is, like, one of their resources. So they tell us when they need to use the chapter room or the guest room. Then they come and use it."

"They can use your chapter room, too?"

"Sometimes," he says again.

"They just tell you, and then they take over your house for a night?"

"Huh? Oh. Yeah."

*

Later, I sit with the Executive Board in a pizza restaurant near campus. Bradley kept suggesting Subway for dinner, but I wanted a place that might serve beer on a Sunday night. Loosen this kid up. Loosen them all up, because they've all got the jitters, the shrugs, the nervous eyes. But we wait twenty minutes for a table to be cleared; they stare at the floor, scowls on faces, looking a bit like 7-year-old boys dragged to the dentist.

"Do you want to just order a pizza take-out, then?" I ask. "Grab a 12-pack, chill out at the house? We can have our meeting there. More casual."

"Huh? University doesn't allow alcohol in the fraternity houses," Bradley mumbles.

"We can be discrete," I say. "We're not getting a keg."

Bradley shrugs, says he doesn't care one way or the other.

So we stay at the restaurant to eat pizza, but after I pour out a glass from the Miller Lite pitcher, the undergraduate fraternity brothers shy away from the beer as if a mere touch might burn them. I asked for seven cups, and all the others remain empty.

"So, um," I say, "what does everyone do for fun in Bowling Green?"

Huh? Oh, there's a lot going on at BGSU, they tell me. All the time. But over the next twenty minutes of conversation, they never get specific. Parties? Football tailgates? Bars? They just shrug, tell me that the university is always doing "stuff." They're always busy, they say.

*

On my laptop in the guest room. Everyone else in the house asleep. And I've never been in a guest room (or a fraternity house) so quiet. Doesn't feel right. Where am I?

"Charles is"—and I'm typing my status—"bored in Bowling Green."

326

Earlier, Bradley and several of the other officers asked if I wanted to watch some *Clone Wars* cartoons they'd downloaded on one of the computers upstairs. "We've got, like, a thousand movies on this computer," someone told me. "*Battlestar Galactica* episodes, *Lost* episodes, every episode of *Adult Swim...*" "No, thank you," I said. "I've, um, got work to do."

Three more Facebook friend requests awaiting my approval.

Billy Goodwin, a brother from the University of Delaware.

Ray Hudson, a brother from the University of Michigan.

I accept the requests.

But the third request: Maria Angelos, from New Mexico State University. A thumbnail-sized profile picture accompanying the name, a brunette girl in pajama pants hugging her blonde roommate and beaming at the camera, pink clothing mounds surrounding them, purple and black posters on the walls behind them, all of it looking like the bedroom of a high school cheerleader. "Confirm," it says, or "Ignore."

Maria Angelos.

I click on the picture and follow the link to her Facebook profile, but her page simply tells me that I'm not allowed to view Maria's pictures or information due to advanced privacy settings. She has more sense than I do, it seems, because when I check my own privacy settings, I see that all of my information—my employer, my interests, my educational history—and all of my friends, all of my wall posts, all of my photographs, all of the collected Facebook information for the last five years...all of it is viewable to the general public. But I thought I'd...? And so Maria has seen everything. Maria knows my age, Maria knows that I'm a fraternity consultant.

I ignore the friend request.

\*

"You're a consultant," Bradley says when I see him in the kitchen the next morning, "so you should check out the CSP program at Bowling Green." He's dressed in the same ash-gray hoodie he wore yesterday, and he's eating one of those fast-food productions that includes several different breakfast foods—eggs, cheese, sausage, and pancakes, I think—all smashed together. I've scoured the kitchen for cereal, for orange juice, for granola bars, anything, but I find only discarded McDonalds and Burger King bags.

"Grad school?" I say. "No, I'm not sure I want to do that."

Bradley shrugs, tosses his McDonalds bag into the trashcan where it lands on a heap of other fast-food bags. "Didn't you say you had a Communications degree?" he asks. "What else can you do? Don't you *have* to go to grad school?"

I force a laugh and say, "Not at all, bro."

He winces when I say "bro," so I say in a slightly more stilted tone, "Not at all, Bradley."

\*

The living room of this Bowling-Green-owned-and-operated NKE house carries all the warmth of a DMV lobby. The three couches—green-cushioned blocks situated in a sort of amphitheater square around a 32-inch

TV—are so exceedingly ugly that they almost seem like a sketch-comedy joke, something from the set of *SNL*. It's an indestructible room, meant to withstand fifty years of annual move-ins and move-outs: doors and walls that can never be broken, couches and carpet so bright and hideous that their very ugliness makes them stain-proof.

Just the same as in the hallways at the New Mexico State girl's dorm, though, the brothers of this fraternity house have added touches of humanity, wherever possible. A metal tube runs the length of the wall around the living room—interrupted only by two red doors, one which leads to the main hallway and the other which leads to the live-in Graduate Advisor's room—and encased within the metal tube is a thick strip of cork. The cork, apparently, is the only part of the wall on which the brothers may hang any wall decorations, and in a straight line around the room are hundreds of social event photographs and multi-colored flyers for various campus and Greek Life events ("Welcome Back Expo," "Swing Club Dance-Off," "Greek Anti-Hazing Speaker").

It's now Monday night, and it is in this living room that I again sit with the fraternity Executive Board, all of us eating our Burger King drive-through quietly, dabbing our mouths with our napkins, clearing our throats, munching softly. They look at me with "you're not one of us" distrust, something that has lately been easy to shake. But not here.

"So," I say eventually. "Do you guys cook very often? You have a kitchen, right?"

"No," says Bradley.

"No?"

"No, we don't really cook."

The living room TV is on, playing old *Seinfeld* reruns.

"Why not?" I ask.

"I don't know," he says, shrugs. "Time?"

"What do you mean?"

"We don't have a time to get together. Everyone's got different schedules."

"You could still hire a cook, though. Late plates for anyone who works."

"University won't let us. They told us that we'd have to use the campus meal plan, have it delivered. Meal plan sucks."

"Why don't you take turns cooking? You can buy food in bulk."

"You serious?"

"A lot of alumni tell me that this is how some houses were run just ten, fifteen years ago," I say. "You guys have all this kitchen equipment in here. Industrial stoves and what-not. You could put it to good use."

"None of us can cook," he says.

"You can learn, right?"

"Did you ever do that at your house?"

"Not exactly," I say, and I suddenly have this image of my father searching the hallways of the EU house, trying the doors and looking for Windex and a mop, asking me if I could really call this *responsibility* if I couldn't even get into my own kitchen. "We had a cook."

"Listen," he says. "I can't even make scrambled eggs. We're not the kind of guys that are going to cook meals for each other, okay?"

And after we finish our Burger King, these kids spend their night immersed in video games. All of them, it seems. Seven or eight of the fraternity brothers drag their wireless laptops into the living room, plug in power cords, and they play *World of Warcraft* together. "Who's going to GAMMA tomorrow?" Bradley asks as a scream erupts from his laptop speakers. Then the sound of swords clashing. Then a gurgle. GAMMA stands for "Greeks Advocating the Mature Management of Alcohol," and it's one of the many weekly programs that BGSU mandates for each fraternity.

"I killed the fuck out of this guy!" another of the brothers yells.

"I'll go to GAMMA," someone else says. "Got nothing at that time."

"You guys don't drink. Why are you going to GAMMA?" I ask. But when I speak, the entire living room suddenly feels like the quiet floor of a library, the silence punctuated only by the completely-in-synch video game music of *Warcraft*.

No one answers my question. It's as if, in this setting, I'm not allowed to speak.

"Intramural flag football tomorrow, too," Bradley says, explosions blasting out of the computer. "Daniel, could you make a flyer for the bulletin wall? Remind everyone of the game?"

"Gotcha," Daniel says.

"You guys don't go out?" I ask. "Out to bars? Clubs? No parties or socials?"

Bradley sighs as if distracted. "Sometimes. Not really."

Then silence again in the room, as they all hunch over their computers.

"Oh," Bradley says. "Chris"—the live-in Graduate Assistant—"wants to have a meeting with the Executive Board on Thursday. Everyone can make it, right?"

They all nod, never tearing their eyes away from their laptops.

They don't leave the house, don't leave the room. This is a cave for them.

After awhile, I drive to a local gas station, buy a six-pack of Yuengling, sneak it back into the guest room and drink by myself, and it feels forced, routine. I don't even know if I'm buzzed by the time I finish the six-pack; I have no point of reference, no one to talk with. I sit on the bed, typing out a joyless report, *Warcraft* sound effects echoing from down the hallway.

\*

Monday morning, sometime after I shower, I notice the voicemail indicator on my cell phone blinking, so I check my messages. There is only one:

"Yes, yes, um, Mister Charles Washington," says a clumsy male on the other end, "this is Donnie Ackman, from the Office of Greek Life at New Mexico State University. Yes. Well, I was referred to you by Sam Anderson, the...what was it? The New Member Education Chairman? Of the Nu Kappa Epsilon chapter here at State? Well, it looks...and I don't know if you've heard about this, but it looks like we've got some real issues with the chapter here. Some hazing issues that I fear you—and your entire Headquarters—may be interested in. Or, rather, concerned about. If you could give me a call back as soon as you get this message, hopefully we can get this worked out. Thanks a lot, Mr. Washington."

*

Before I can return Donnie Ackman's call, my phone rings again: Walter LaFaber.

"You missed our scheduled one-on-one call yesterday," he says.

"I'm sorry, Walter. I had car trouble."

"Yesterday wasn't a travel day."

"No," I say. "I…I'm having trouble remembering what day it is. Where I am."

"Yesterday. Start with yesterday."

"I was…I needed new wiper blades? And an oil change. So I forgot to call."

"You weren't overdue, were you?"

"No. Well, a little. A couple hundred miles."

"Take care of your car," he says. "That is your office, Charles. Take care of your body, take care of your car. You'll find it difficult to accomplish much without either of those. Dr. Wigginton always says: you can tell everything you need to know about a man from his shoes and his car."

"Yeah, I—"

"And do not miss another one-on-one call."

"I won't. It's just—"

"I get the feeling that you're slipping."

"Slipping? No. I'm fine, I'm fine."

"We're deep into the semester. Are you slipping?"

"Walter, everything is—"

"I don't have your last several reports."

"Right. I've just been jam-packing my days with meetings, so it's been tough to find extra time to sit down and type. But I think I'm winning a lot of battles out here, Walter."

"Are you?"

"Definitely."

"We haven't talked lately."

"I know." I walk toward my suitcase, toward my laptop bag and my paperwork, but LaFaber continues responding so quickly that I barely have time to process/answer/move/think before he's snapping back once again.

"I haven't received any reports. So tell me. What battles you are 'winning?'"

"Um. Organizational stuff, mostly? Budgets? Goals? You know."

"Do I?"

"Winning hearts and minds, Walter." Scrambling through a series of print-outs, but don't even know what I'm looking for. Something I can read back to him? Something tangible that will prove that I am who I should be? "Accomplishing the mission on a personal level," I say. "It's not always the workshops that are, you know, going to reach everyone. Sometimes, it's just the one-on-one conversations—"

330

"I still don't have a report from your visit to New Mexico State University."

"You didn't get that?"

"No."

"I thought I emailed that to you."

"No."

"I have it on my computer. I can email you."

"Tell me about New Mexico State," he says.

"Why?" I ask. "That was, like, a month ago. I barely remember."

"Barely remember? A month? I hear you shuffling through papers. Stop that. Just talk."

"No, I remember. It's just...why do you want to hear about it? Why now?"

"Is that a problem?"

"Listen, I'll get the report finished."

"I thought it was finished already."

"They were fine, Walter. They were good kids. I'll get more specific in my report, but they seemed like they really had it together. There's nothing to worry about, so I didn't feel like I needed to be in a hurry to finish the paperwork."

"That was your impression, Charles? Good kids?"

"Maybe some little things to work on. We made a budget."

"No evidence of hazing?" he asks.

"What?"

"Hazing. Physical violence? Harassment?"

"Of course not," I say. "Walter, I would have told you right away if I'd seen—"

"I didn't ask whether you'd *seen* it. I asked for your impression. Often, as consultants, we're forced to piece together a picture of a fraternity chapter based not simply upon observations, but also nitty-gritty research and investigation. Interviews, reactions."

"I didn't have a bad impression, then," I say. "No."

"What about their New Member Educator? Sam Anderson?"

"Sam Anderson?"

Hangers shaking. I smooth my pants. Eyelid twitching.

"I don't, um, think I remember him...specifically."

"That's too bad."

"Too bad?" I ask. "Too bad that I didn't find evidence of hazing? Or too bad that I don't remember Sam—um, what's his name?—Sam Anderson?"

"Both," he says and exhales, a noise that—through the phone—sounds like nails falling against particle board. Hundreds of nails. "I received a phone call this weekend, Charles."

"A phone call. From who?" I miss Donnie Ackman's call this morning, and Ackman immediately phones the National Headquarters? "Was it the Greek Advisor who called?"

"The Greek Advisor," LaFaber says. "I haven't talked to him yet."

"You haven't?"

"Not if I can avoid it. Not yet. You know by now, Charles, that these Greek Advisors are a bunch of hacks. No need to stir the pot until we know what we're cooking."

"I thought…"

"You thought?"

"Never mind," I say. "Who called?"

"I received a phone call from an irate mother of one of the pledges."

"A mother. Something serious?"

"Nothing terrible, not from what I could understand. No deaths, no injuries."

"So there's no problem? Just something minor?"

"No problems, as long as we take the proper actions."

"But even then, we're not talking about anything major?"

"We cannot afford another lawsuit, Charles. Not with the Sandor suit hanging over us. We've got to act quickly, but we've got to take retroactive action, as well."

"You never even told me what happened," I say.

"No, I did not."

"What did she tell you, the mother?"

"You don't need to know."

"Did she give names? Was it…I mean, how specific did she get?"

"I can't tell you. Rest assured, I can handle the situation, but we need your assistance with that visit report that you haven't submitted."

"All right, all right," I say. "I'll email you the report. But I told you, I never saw any indication of hazing while I was in Las Cruces."

"It's not what you see, Charles."

"Okay. I get it. It's all about the 'impression.'"

"You're not hearing me. Give the report extra-special care. Print it. Overnight it to me by tomorrow. Do not email it."

"I hear you, Walter. But email is easier—"

"You're not hearing me. *Do not* email the report."

"Why not?"

"I want the report to be dated as it should have been. The day after your visit. If you email it, the current date becomes record."

"So what? It's the same report."

"It might be the same report, but the date of the writing is what is most important. With a mailed package, I can lose the envelope."

"Still not understanding. Maybe I had too many beers last night."

"Excuse me?"

"Joke. Just joking."

"Listen to me, Charles. You saw something in New Mexico."

"I didn't see anything. I told you."

"You saw something. You saw several things that were unsettling. The way that the brothers spoke to the pledges, perhaps. Maybe they made embarrassing jokes at the expense of the pledges. Maybe they seemed capable of physical cruelty. *Capable.* Maybe you saw paddles at the fraternity house. Maybe you saw a box of blindfolds."

"Walter, I didn't see any—"

"I don't give a damn what you *did* or *did not* see, Charles," he says, and now his breathing is hard, grating, the fuming nostril exhalations of a dragon, and there is a crackling noise. He wants me to hear these things, to picture him in his office in a way that I've never before seen or heard him. Suddenly, he wants me standing on the chair in the center of the room as he paces and screams behind me. "When I see that report in my office, I want to be scared of what that New Mexico State chapter might be doing to its pledges. I want your impression of that fraternity to convince me that—even though you saw nothing directly incriminating—I should suspend them."

"You want me to lie?"

"For the good of the National Fraternity, for the good of thousands of young men across the country, you will emphasize certain features of this chapter that we know to be true. And if the report is dated properly, I'll be able to claim that all suspension paperwork was filed at least a month ago. I can convince that Greek Advisor that I sent him a copy of the report weeks ago, that he must have lost it…with the dysfunction at some of these schools, that isn't too hard. If we can claim that we suspended this chapter a month ago, we can tell our attorneys that we acted out of obligation to our mission *prior* to any hazing allegations. We can tell the mother that punishment was swift, that she has nothing to worry about."

"Wait. This isn't right."

"It isn't right or wrong. It's just paperwork."

"Walter, I can't. For God's sake, I can't do something like this."

"They did indeed haze," he says, words breathed with fire. "The dates are just numbers on a page, and you *will* make those numbers work for us."

"But if they didn't? If they didn't actually do anything?"

"Get to work, Charles. I look forward to reading your report."

*

Tuesday afternoon, and I have a meeting with the campus Greek Advisor in a building that looks like a brown flying saucer. When I enter the lobby of the Greek Life Office, I'm greeted not by one lone Graduate Assistant at a receptionist-style desk—as is usually the case—but by a crowd of graduate students, a full Last Supper of seated disciples at a long wall-mounted computer desk, and all of them rise and rush to me and shake my hand and tell me how much they admire what I'm doing, that I'm making such a big difference in the lives of students everywhere. Saving the culture, saving the world.

"I wish I could travel to different universities," one blonde guy says sadly. "My fraternity didn't select me as a consultant."

"That's too bad," I say.

"It's always exciting to meet new consultants, though," a curly brunette reassures me. "It's so *ex*-citing."

"You look excited," I say.

All around me. They're all around me.

"We are excited!" she says.

Someone is gripping my shoulder, slapping my back.

"So this is, um, a full office," I say. "What do you all do?"

"I'm Todd, and I'm the GA in charge of IFC," the blonde guys says. "And that's Lisa, the Special Events GA. And Tamara, the Panhellenic assistant. Rodney is the GA for NPHC. Shannon is the Department assistant, and Sheryl is the Recruitment assistant."

All of them surrounding me, a funhouse of smiling faces everywhere.

"That's a lot of assistants," I say and they laugh and continue smiling. Wider now, and after I say it, I realize that this is probably a comment that every visitor makes, that the GAs probably laugh every time it's said, have learned how to laugh with appropriate volume and vigor at this specific joke. *Everywhere*, these Bowling Green GAs, all around me since the moment I arrived: in the fraternity houses, in the dorms, on every floor of this building, in every office, these graduate students who still look awkward in their suits and ties, who scurry about with clipboards and portfolio binders and to-do lists for their departmental supervisors. It's consultant orientation *all day everyday* in here. Every major "student life" department at Bowling Green is the same, they tell me, from Homecoming to Orientation: GAs, GAs, GAs. The best program in the country for student personnel! You're guaranteed to get experience and good job placement. Whether you want to become the Director of Orientation at the University of Maine or the Coordinator of the Office of Student Involvement at Memphis, BGSU is *the place* for CSP. And, like me, these graduate assistants were all students who'd been tremendously involved in campus life during their undergraduate college careers. They were all Diamond Candidates who chose to fashion their undergraduate social activities into their careers, and now—whooooo, hold on!—they're *climbing!*

I should go back to grad school, they tell me. Consulting gives me an edge on the application process! And this was the plan all along for me, wasn't it? they ask. To use my experience as an Educational Consultant to propel me into a career in student personnel?

"I don't know," I say.

"You don't know? You don't have a plan?"

"No, it's not that," I say. "I just wanted to work for my fraternity. That was why I took the job as a consultant. No grand ambitions. I loved my fraternity. So."

"No grand ambitions?"

They all laugh softly, and I try to join in.

"What about afterward?" one of them asks.

"Afterward?" I say.

"After your consultant contract has expired?"

"I, um, want to keep working? No retirement plans yet."

"Well, you'll need solid references and a squeaky clean resume to get into *this* graduate program," Lisa says, "but I'm sure you've got all of that."

"In other words," Todd says and play-elbows me, "kiss all the right asses, and don't piss off the wrong people. It's a small world, this field, and nobody gossips like CSP."

"Right, ha," I say.

"This *is* what you're planning to do, right?" Lisa asks. "Grad school?"

All around me, all around me.

"Sure, that's a goal."

"Let's get you in to see Dr. Vernon," Todd says, voice reverential. "He's ready to receive you."

*

And I'm led into a large office that feels more like a cave carved into the thick of a million-year-old tree, everything around me wooden. Mahogany desk, I think, with matching mahogany pencil holder and "outbox." Mahogany bookshelf, mahogany end-table. Furniture so strong that a tornado couldn't move it. Reminds me of Dr. Wigginton's mountain cottage, but here the lines are contemporary, surfaces smooth, handles of steel.

Dr. Vernon, the Greek Advisor, sits behind his desk, but when I walk into his office he continues staring out his floor-to-ceiling window at the crowds of students scattered on the wet pavement below, back to me. Slowly he turns his chair around, motioning with one thick hand for me to sit at the dark-cushioned wood chairs before his desk, his gold cuff links reflecting his lamplight like sparks on copper wires. He is better-dressed than every other Greek Advisor I've met so far, French-cuff shirt so starched that it doesn't even bend or fold as he pulls a folder from the top drawer of his desk, slides it onto the desk's surface to rest beside a couple hardcovers (the book on top is called *Generation X in the Job Market* by (surprise) Dr. Harold Vernon), and then he folds his hands before his face. "Charles Washington?" he asks.

"That's me." I sit.

"So good to finally meet you." He examines my face, his eyes seeming to drift between colors as he squints, brown to hazel to bronze. His face seems heavy, skin dark and tough like one of those middle-aged Florida natives I'd sometimes see at the beach early in the morning, their entire days spent under the sunshine, 7 AM to 7 PM, bodies browned and weathered not from exhausting outdoor labor but instead from the simple desire to be beach bums…but this is northern Ohio, and Dr. Vernon is not spending his mornings on a beach towel on Lake Erie.

"Are you hung-over?" he asks.

"Me?" I pat my chest, my arms, ruffle my hair, checking to see how I put myself together this morning. "What do you mean? No."

"I know how things get on the road," he says, still squinting, perhaps trying to see beyond my eyes and into my mind, trying to confirm or deny his suspicions. "Surrounded by college kids? Every chapter, a fridge full of beer? Parties. I'm sure it's tough to stay sober and serious…girls everywhere, beer everywhere."

"What? No." I start to stand again. "I must not've slept well."

"You have a guest room when you stay on this campus," he says. "I hope you'd let us know if the accommodations are poor."

"It's a nice room. Just. A lot of time on the computer last night?"

"So you haven't been drinking while you've been here?" he asks.

"No. I mean. What have you heard?"

For some reason, the world around me no longer feels real. For some reason, it doesn't feel as if I'm really here. In Bowling Green, in the mouth of a prehistoric tree, the world outside crackling to cold. Dr. Vernon squints harder and then finally leans back, fingers interlaced before him, and smiles like a tycoon. "I got you," he says and laughs. Then holds out his hands in an I-couldn't-resist pose. "I got you, Charles Washington."

"Got me?" I smooth my pants.

"Only joking, young man. I've heard good things about you from my colleagues. Don't worry. You don't look a mess."

"From your colleagues?" I sink back into my seat and let out a wispy laugh that sounds like a deflating air mattress. Hanging from the wall to my right is a plaque that reads, "For 20 Years of Distinguished Service at Bowling Green": with twenty years of continuous employment, Dr. Vernon must be well-connected in the world of higher education and Greek Affairs. A small world, those GAs said. And Dr. Vernon's colleagues? He probably knows—probably taught—many of the Greek Advisors I've met throughout the country. "Someone at this school?" I ask. "Or somewhere else?"

"My colleagues are everywhere," he says. "All corners of the country. They say you've got a good head on your shoulders. That you truly care about the students you service."

"This isn't a joke, is it?"

"No, no. This is real. Forgive my sense of humor earlier, but this is real." He opens the manila folder on his desk (they *always* have a folder or an envelope during meetings, always wet their finger and flip through pages of data and spreadsheets and photos and printed news stories, like criminal investigators attempting to scare a suspect in the interrogation room), and pauses on a printed email, laughing softly. "My colleagues also say you're a bit—how do I say this?—unorthodox in your approach to consulting?"

And what might he have heard to lead him to this conclusion? I think the worst: Buenos Noches and El Sombrero, cans of Tecate at student meetings, destructed jeans purchased at a New Mexico shopping mall, worn at night in Juarez, worn the next day on a flight to Fresno, worn during every chapter visit while my khaki slacks and silver-black suit remain packed. There is an image in my mind of Charles Washington sleeping until 11 AM at the University of Delaware, legs spilling over the armrest of the living room couch, shoes still on my feet from the night before. Unorthodox? A stolen charter in the backseat of my Explorer, an artifact I was proud of saving from that Illinois chapter house but now can't admit to anyone that I've taken because I never should have gone back the next morning.

"Unorthodox, what does that even mean?" I ask.

"You have a Facebook page, I'm told," he says. "I've never heard of a consultant friend-requesting the chapter presidents."

"You know about that?"

"I hear everything."

For weeks, I used the Van Wilder image as my profile picture...probably the reason it took Maria so long to find me, to confirm the page as mine... and although late last night—shaking from a 64-ounce gas station fountain drink I'd finished in fifteen minutes—I changed my privacy settings, there are dozens of images that Dr. Vernon could have found, that all of these Greek Advisors could have found, that even Walter LaFaber could have found in the stupid interval between re-activation and privacy protection, if only they'd searched my name and clicked my page. What have they seen? Hell if I know.

"Who doesn't have a Facebook page these days?" I ask finally.

"This takes some getting used to, these new mediums," he says, leans back again. "Five years ago, I thought it was strange when a consultant would text the chapter president to schedule a visit. Five years before that, I thought it odd when consultants set up AOL instant messaging accounts to interact. What's unorthodox now will be mainstream in months. A good topic for graduate research. But in the meantime, be careful with it. The more knowledge you have, the greater your responsibility."

"You're right," I say, and now I'm thinking of the wall post I received from Sam Anderson early this morning: "Hey, dude, gotta talk about that hazing thing." I'd been—what had I been doing?—trying to type the report for New Mexico State, that's right, stuck after only one awkward paragraph, and I hadn't noticed Sam's comment for several hours. Later, I deleted it, but still: the comment was there for anyone to see. *That hazing thing.*

"Have you ever thought of continuing in this profession?" Dr. Vernon asks.

"Consulting?"

"Higher education," he says. "Student personnel. A career in anything from Greek Life to Residence Life. Bowling Green has an excellent program, you know? What's your degree?"

"Organizational Communication."

"Wonderfully vague," Dr. Vernon says. "Perfect for grad school. With your experience, you could make a tremendous Greek Advisor."

Usually, the campus Greek Advisor is some kid fresh out of grad school who takes the job with high hopes and endless energy, until fraternity and sorority undergraduates begin ignoring or disregarding him even while he works weekends, late nights, organizing programs for the Greek community, compiling reports for various deans and student-life administrators. Then, twelve months later, the kid will be job-hunting with such panic that you'd think the Greek Advisor office was set to explode. Very rarely is the position as prestigious as Dr. Vernon's appears to be. Very rarely do they write books. A career as a Greek Advisor? That can't be what my life has led to: Fun Nazi at a desk? "Something to shoot for," I say.

"You don't look excited."

I shake my head, still my twitching eyelid. "Sorry. I promised myself I wouldn't be a climber."

"No apology necessary." He leans forward, face intense with curiosity or offense, eyes going amber, hands still folded before him, dark skin etched with age but not worry. "Are you familiar with our programs here at Bowling Green?" he asks.

"The students told me about them."

"They're all very exciting to *us*, you know? Even if *you* don't care."

"No, I didn't mean—"

"Simply put, we offer our students more programming than any other Greek Life office in the nation," he says, voice hypnotic as Walter LaFaber's... and then he lists off the names and goals of alcohol awareness workshops coordinated by this office; he lists academic success workshops, scholarships specifically for Greek students, recruitment conclaves, leadership conclaves, and I hear the words "conclave" and "symposium" and "convocation" and "conference" and "workshop" and "retreat" used so often that I try to keep a mental tally but eventually lose track. The office and its graduate assistants plan Diversity Pot Luck Dinners and Faculty Luncheons, resume-building sessions and study skills presentations, Greek-wide service events, Greek-wide "Unity" barbecues. And as Dr. Vernon speaks, I get the feeling that he has this entire boilerplate speech memorized for the benefit of traveling consultants and school administrators; it slides out of his mouth as easily as the Alphabet Song.

"Yeah, that's a lot of programs," I say.

"You still don't seem impressed. This is the pinnacle, Mr. Washington. This is what *you* do, but to the *next level*."

"No, I'm properly impressed. It really sounds like a lot of programs."

He grins again. "We're catering to the Millennials." He taps his fingertips together.

"The Millennial Generation." I rub my temples.

"Absolutely," he says, his hand sliding a few inches to the left to tap one of the books on his desk, a thick hardcover published by Yale University Press. "We are the undisputed experts on Millennial Generation research."

"Sounds like a big deal."

"You can say that again," he says, and—just to be a smart-ass—I almost do, but once again he's off and running: "Parents are programming their kids from an early age, you see: team sports, foreign language lessons. Once they get into high school, kids are taking AP classes in their *sophomore* year. I read recently of a student entering UVA with 72 credit hours! College enrollments are at their highest levels ever. These are high achievers. All of these students we see around us, these Millennials, their generation has the greatest potential *ever*, is what we hope. A Hero Generation, capable of changing the world."

I think of Sam Anderson at New Mexico State, of students standing on a chair in the center of a dark room. I think of Adam Duke at Illinois, his

big-screen TV and six-pack of Anchor Steam. I think of Bradley Camden
in the empty kitchen, tossing a McDonalds wrapper into a trashcan full of
McDonalds wrappers. I think of Pittsburgh, the stain on the ceiling fan. I
think of my own Senior Send-Off, the lonely boy standing on the curb while
the Night Patrol rolled up.

"Our programs at Bowling Green will directly influence the rest of the
universities in this country." Now he sweeps his hand outward to indicate the
vastness of the North American continent. "Our research, our practices, shape
the way that students go about their daily lives. Their residence halls. Their
clubs, their fraternities. We are with them 24/7, and we shape their behavior,
their attitudes. Do you see the magnitude of it all? We will chart the course of
this *entire* generation."

"Sounds like a big deal," I say again—

—but he's saying "We are going to soon be living in a *compassion boom*,"
and then he's talking about privileged young people who could take high-
paying jobs, but who choose—*willingly* choose—to work for non-profits, for
social services, for schools. He's reciting statistics on the number of unpaid
positions that young people are assuming for a full year after graduation in
order to *change the world*, and he's clapping like he's the reason for it. "We
have a generation who has easy access to information, who knows what's
wrong with the world, who wants to *save* the world," he says. "The graduate
students you see around you? They are part of it."

"Compassion boom." I think of my father, casually dismissing the term.

"Compassion boom," and he taps the book again. I notice the title:
*Fraternity Man as Community Champion.*

I say nothing. I open my mouth. I shrug. I came to this meeting out of
obligation, to finish some basic paperwork for my visit report. I'm not in the
mood for anything more.

"So," he says, fingertips pressed together again. "You don't look like you're
buying my bullshit."

The world stops.

"What? Bullshit?" I start. "I wasn't trying to be disrespectful."

But I was. And he saw it.

"Let's talk about *you* for a moment, Charles Washington," Dr. Vernon
says. He moves the book aside, shuffles through those papers on his desk
again, finds something that intrigues him. "With whom have you met so far
on your visit?"

"Wait. This, like, isn't about me."

"Sure it is. We're talking. I'm getting to know you."

"Okay, fine," I say. "I've met with the Executive Board."

"One meeting in two days? That's pretty light. Is the road wearing
you down?"

"I've done a lot of informal stuff."

"Tell me about your average chapter visit, Charles Washington," he says.
"Your schedule. Your activities. What do you do out there?"

"Why does that matter? Aren't we supposed to talk about the chapter here at Bowling Green? I'm confused."

"I know about the chapter here," Dr. Vernon says. "We have a graduate assistant *living* in the house. But I want to know more about *you*. After all, these students are paying for your visit, are they not? What are you offering that the university isn't?"

"You've had this job for twenty years? I thought you'd know about all of that."

"Humor me. Pretend I know nothing."

"Fine," I say. I throw up my hands. We can both play the "boilerplate" game. "I'm an Educational Consultant. I have a specific set of responsibilities." I tell him the mission, even though I'm sure he's heard it before. I tell him that Nu Kappa Epsilon is building socially responsible citizens, that we offer more leadership development programming than any other young men's organization, Boy Scouts included. I tell him that I pledge allegiance to the flag, I tell him that Our Father, who art in Heaven, I tell him that A-B-C-D-E-F-G, H-I-J-K-LMNOP, I tell him that one-on-ones, alumni, meetings with advisors, I tell him that Marathon Man and Diamond Candidate and polo shirt, I tell him that I'm not even listening to myself anymore, or maybe I just think that last comment, but who knows, because when I talk about fraternity life now, it just feels like a voice recording projecting from my mouth. In mid-sentence, I'll start to wonder why anyone even takes this shit seriously. I mean, people write books about fraternity life? Can you imagine dedicating *years* of your life to writing a book about this shit?

And here, now, I say something that surprises myself: "Sometimes I don't know if I'm doing the right thing even when I am," I say. "Sometimes I'm doing the wrong thing, but it feels like the right thing. Sometimes I get so mixed up that I don't even care."

"Interesting," he says.

"Interesting?" I ask. "Shit, I shouldn't have said any of that. It's...that's not something I want repeated. What did I just say?"

"What wrong things have you done?"

"I misspoke," I say.

"Then what did you mean to say?"

Finger to my eyelid. How do I hit *backspace* on this one? "It's not...it's not that things were wrong."

"No?"

"It's just, everyone has these different definitions of what makes a thing right or wrong. That's what I meant, I guess."

"Please don't feed me bullshit," he says.

"No, no," I say. "What I mean is...we try to make things simple by saying 'this is right' and 'this is wrong,' but it's never that easy, you know? It's always changing. One moment at one school, something is endearing or harmless, and then suddenly it's dangerous and unacceptable. It hurts my head."

He places his fist at his mouth as if to cough, but he chuckles instead. "I like your skepticism," he says. "I like that you're thinking critically."

"You *like* that I'm critical?" I ask. "I would've thought that this is blasphemy."

He nods. "So much better than the consultants who just give me the company line. I meet with far too many robots."

"I'm not a robot."

"Prove it. Tell me more, Mr. Washington."

"Tell you more?"

"Tell me what you've seen out there, on the road."

"I don't know."

"Unless you want to leave the impression that you're just like the rest of them?"

"I'm not," I say, and before I know it I'm telling him everything that I've been thinking for the past month. I'm telling him that I thought everything would be textbook-pretty—

—but it took me too long to realize that no matter the "mission," everyone's got an agenda. And too often they clash. The students have a reason for joining a fraternity: some of them probably *did* want the leadership development angle. But others? They could care less about leadership, just joined because they just wanted friends to play video games with, or—hell—maybe they did want a drinking club. Sure. We make it sound so nefarious, I tell him, but these things aren't *all* terrible. It's just kids, and they join for a specific reason. But then here comes the National Fraternity, and we say: *No, there's only one thing you can be, and that's what we want fraternity to be.* If you aren't with us, then you're a *problem chapter.* And so there's this animosity, *us* vs. *you,* and then you throw in the alumni, and now there's another 80 years' worth of ideas of what *they* want the fraternity chapters to be. Sometimes it aligns with the students, sometimes it aligns with the National Fraternity. Sometimes neither. "And then, shit," I say, "then there's *you.*" I hold up my palms: we had to get here sooner or later. Every Greek Advisor on every campus wants something different, too, I'm telling him. Maybe you're in it for yourself, your research. Maybe you only want to advance to some other campus position. I close my eyes, shake my head, try to visualize all of these groups competing over the same institution, an army of men in polos and Greek letters all reaching and grabbing and reaching and grabbing. "I always thought my parents' marriage was like a tug-of-war," I say. "Always going back and forth whenever one of them won some little domestic battle. But this? The fraternity world is like a four-way marriage tug-of-war, for God's sake, and there's no chance for divorce."

He leans forward, tie piling like folded deli meat atop the manila folder, and makes a faux shock face. "You think Greek Advisors are part of the problem?"

"Greek Advisors." I shake my head. "At one campus, I met a fraternity—they'd gotten in trouble because *two members* were underage drinking at a social event—and this entire fraternity chapter, sixty guys, had to take an online alcohol education program. That was the punishment that the Greek Advisor recommended. What the hell is that all about? What does that do?"

"Well," he says and looks about to deliver some data on—

"Another campus," I say, and I'm not going to let him say a damned word. Suddenly he has become Dr. Jacobs at Illinois, George Samuels at Pittsburgh, Donnie Ackman at New Mexico State; he has become every Greek Advisor I've ever met, a hundred books on his wall, a dozen binders filled with reports and surveys and typed-out programs, a gallon of ink spilled on signatures and tear-away presentation-board sheets, a thousand hours of workshops and motivational speakers...but not a single hour on a fraternity house couch. "I saw a group put on probation for conducting an *unregistered* community service event. Listen: they were holding this book drive for a local high school, but they hadn't filled out paperwork with the Greek Life office, and so they all—again, we're talking about sixty or seventy guys—they were *all* punished by the Student Conduct Board and had to write these stupid apology letters and..." I shake my head. "There are other examples. Dozens. Campus administrators who think everything is solved"—I make like I'm clapping the dust off my hands—"because we filed paperwork, or because we had everyone go to see an anti-hazing speaker one afternoon. They're just trying to create the illusion that they've done something."

Dr. Vernon's cuff links sparkle again as he motions toward me. "Useful commentary," he says, and I thought he'd be pissed, seething that I'd just attempted to crash the scaffolds of his life's calling..."So how are *you* different?"

"How am *I* different?"

"How are you different?"

"I'm right there in the house," I say. "I sit with them. I talk to them."

"About what?"

"About *everything!*" I say, and suddenly I realize my voice has become loud and uncontrolled. *I don't know* what *we talk about*, I tell him. House occupancy? Dues payments? Jay-Z? LeBron James? Tina Fey? Thirteen or fourteen waking hours, breakfast-lunch-dinner, trips to Subway or Quiznos, movies till midnight, a 12-pack. Who knows what we talk about in all that time? But *that's* real work, I tell him, growing angrier with each new word. That isn't just a formal one-on-one meeting in an office, Greek Advisor with Student Leader. That isn't just typing on a computer. You've got to care about these kids as something more than spreadsheet cells, I say.

Dr. Vernon hasn't blinked in the last minute, doesn't break his stare as he listens to me. But eventually he leans forward in his seat, calm as ever, body casting shadow over his desk, and says: "So. Are you trying to convince *me* that you've done good work, or are you trying to convince *yourself?*"

"I don't know what you mean."

Vernon exhales. "You still can't admit it. You're no different than the ones you're criticizing."

And I wipe my forehead. "*I'm* no different?" I ask. "I see what you're doing here. You just want to talk about *me* because *you're* the one who doesn't know what the hell he's doing. You're fucking clueless! All of your pointless programs? Millennial Generation research? You're just another climber, using these fucking students for your own gains. *I'm* no different?"

Ordinarily, this is only what I would be *thinking*. Today, this is what I just *said*.

Charles is...stepping over the line.

"Ahh, ahh!" he says as though I've hit upon some important point. He claps, cufflinks briefly clinking against one another like toasting champagne glasses. "Now you're talking!"

"I called you clueless, and *now* I'm talking?"

"You called me 'fucking clueless,' actually," he says. "But you bring up a good point. How do I know that these programs are effective?"

"Exactly. What's the point of any of it?"

"Millennials crave programming, Mr. Washington. I told you. All their lives—youth soccer, Key Club—each hour designated to a different planned activity, a different club or organization or sport. Never a wasted moment. That's what we're trying to replicate."

"For God's sake." I smooth my pants. "Listen, I've *seen* them during the programs."

"Ahhh. So tell me: what have you seen?"

"An average alcohol education workshop?" I say and laugh. "Half the room looks at me like I'm a prison guard, and the other half won't make eye contact, they're so angry that they have to sit through it. There's a pocket of students who are hung-over, but the majority of them can't wait to go out and get their night started. They have these, 'What did I do to deserve this?' looks on their faces. It's the same with the Chapter Scholarship Workshop I've presented, the same thing with the mandatory Executive Board meetings. Programs. Please."

"Oh?"

"And this isn't a judgment, not against the students," I say. "I'm asking for their free time, and then I'm telling them how to live their lives. If they resent me, that's their right. But that's what your fucking programs are good for," I say. "That's how your Hero Generation responds to programming."

"My programs?" he asks. "Well. Do you think you've uncovered a flaw in programs in general, or the specific programs that *you* are facilitating?"

"Does it matter?"

"You've been honest so far, Charles. Critical. Don't shut down now."

"I'm not. I don't think it matters."

"Interesting," he says and nods. "Because I'm afraid you misunderstood me earlier when I said that *you* were no different. I didn't mean *you*, specifically, though you seemed to take offense. I meant the *national fraternities*. Answer honestly: aren't paperwork and programs and workshops *your* bread and butter, too?"

And I know now that he just set me up, that he was waiting for this moment to spike the ball in my face. "Listen," I say. "I'm paid by Nu Kappa Epsilon, and I don't think I need to say anything about our institutional failings."

"Just tell me this. One thing, since you had so much to say about *our* programs. What is the goal of *your* national fraternity's programs?"

"Leadership development," I say. "You know that."

"You conduct Alcohol Responsibility Workshops because you want to build leaders?"

"That's part of it. There are two types of fraternities—"

"Let me guess. Those who get it, and those who don't?"

"Yes."

"And it's the drinking clubs, the frat stars, that fuck everything up for the good guys?"

"Yes."

"It sounds to me," he says, "as if you're being reductive about your membership. Talking like a robot, Mr. Washington."

"It's just an expression." I wave my hand around as if expressions float in the air and land in your mouth unexpectedly, as if none of us have any control over our clichés.

He nods. "Let me just make sure that I'm understanding your argument. You think that *our* programs at Bowling Green are unnecessary. But you honestly think that a generic workshop commissioned by a national fraternity, then delivered to students on a Friday afternoon by a 22-year-old traveling consultant, will change a drinking club into a group of socially responsible citizens?"

"No. I told you: it won't happen. What do you want me to say?"

"Good. So what is the purpose of the workshops, then, Charles? Answer that question. If they do not impact the students, what is their purpose?"

"You tell me."

"The national fraternities have a reason for what they're doing. It wasn't always like this, I can assure you. What is the purpose behind the workshops? Think, Charles."

"You're not my fucking professor, all right? You're not Socrates. Stop."

"Again, let's be clear, Charles. All of this traveling? A full year, and God only knows what sort of pressure you've placed on yourself to achieve measurable results? All of the family pressure, too? Parents who think you're wasting your livelihood? Fiancé, or girlfriend, or even just best friends back in—where was it? Florida?—friends in Florida with whom you've fallen out of contact? And now you're a year behind your peers in the job market? And you're certainly not making any money in this labor of love you've undertaken."

"And my car is fucked up."

"And your car is fucked up. Anything else I'm missing?"

"Probably. Debt."

"Debt. You're not the first, Charles Washington. How many other young leaders have been drawn to the beautiful lie that is fraternity consulting?"

I rub my eyes.

"All of this, and what do you have to show for it? Three days on one campus and then you're gone, and you know that the impact you've made…is there an impact?"

"Thank you for brightening my day. Now I'll go spend the afternoon in the rain."

"The leadership development, the workshops: it's not a service to the students. It's *branding*, Charles, and that's all it is. You know it, whether you want to admit it or not. No different than a billion-dollar corporation donating a few million to breast cancer research to create a loving, community-friendly image for themselves."

I shake my head. "And how is it any different than your degree program here at Bowling Green? Your Millennial Generation research, your brand?"

And Dr. Vernon is silent and I think I've landed my own in-your-face spike, and I'm about to jump out of my seat and punch the air and scream that I beat him, that I'm right, and *fuck you!*, but then Dr. Vernon claps. Slaps the desktop hard and his cufflink creates a metallic ringing in the room that sounds as loud as a university bell-tower's between-class clanging. "Excellent, excellent!" he says.

My mouth is open.

"This stuff about Millennials," he says, smile now gone, tanned face smooth, the ringing in the room replaced with dead silence. "You're right. That's the sexy stuff. It brings in the money and the graduate students. We believe in it, certainly, but it is undeniably our *brand*. But truthfully, do you know the research I'm most interested in?"

I tell him that I have no idea.

"In this program, we want students to ask difficult questions about fraternity life," he says. "We want students who will ask, what sort of positive gains are *actually* made by fraternity consultants in just three days? And further, what is it that makes men so loyal to the institution of fraternity, to the point that they refuse to acknowledge any flaw? You—even *you*, two minutes ago—seemed intent on defending your own work even as you dismissed ours.

Fraternity men will go to extraordinary lengths to defend behavior that, in any other context, they would find reprehensible...all in the name of their Greek letters. Why is that? In this program"—and he leans forward again and stares at me with Walter LaFaber intensity—"we allow nothing as sacred. We ask, why do we even have a system of 'pledging' when we know that it creates division, when it is bound to give rise to hazing? Why keep it? In our program, we find ways to *re-think* fraternity life. Everything about it. Why such an emphasis on large chapter size, on massive recruitment classes and quotas? Why do we consider it a good thing to have 150-woman sorority chapters? Why such an emphasis on housing, on physical structures? We look at motivations, however hidden. We look at—to use your word—*agendas*."

"You can't change these things. You know that, right?"

"If we truly want to be leaders, we'll make unpopular choices. And the most unpopular question of all: why do we even need the institution of the *National* Fraternity Headquarters? Why do we need this sprawling empire of chapters across the country? You said it yourself, Mr. Washington: it's a four-way tug-of-war. Couldn't we simply alleviate the conflict by removing one of the four antagonists, allowing the campus—rather than some unknowing headquarters—to dictate its own culture? Wouldn't we be better served with stronger Greek Life offices on each individual campus, the national dues that students pay—the money that currently goes to fund fraternity and sorority consultants—staying right there to fund campus initiatives that are shaped to that specific student population?"

"That's ridiculous."

But in this moment, it doesn't sound ridiculous. My fight has left me.

"There are no easy answers, Mr. Washington. But on this campus, we study every single program that we offer, which ones work and which do not. We study student responses. We care about programs that will *actually* service the students in the best way possible, programs that will change the culture of fraternity life, not just the *perception* of fraternities." He taps the folder. "We don't care about pumping more money into some faraway headquarters."

"That's all very noble," I say. "Thank you for all of this."

"You ask tough questions about the Greek Advisors you've seen across the country, Charles, but you might be better served asking those same questions about your own employer." He lets his hand drop to his desktop, shakes his head, then looks me in the eyes. "Do we want to change the culture? Not just *say* we're doing it."

"Of course," I say. Softly.

"We haven't had a consultant in the program in a few semesters," he says. "Most national fraternities are now telling their consultants to avoid us; they know we're onto something. But we could benefit from someone with real-world experience, someone who knows the institutional failings. Someone who wants to create change on a big scale."

"I don't know."

"There's a grant available," he says. "But we need someone from the inside. You do still want to change the culture, don't you?" His cuff links flicker once again as he folds his hands before his face, assuming the sort of distinguished pose that one might see on a book jacket. "That's why you took this job to begin with, correct?"

"Change the culture," I say, whispering now.

"I'm glad we're on the same page, Charles. We can make this happen. Trust me."

*

When I leave, we shake hands, and then I'm immediately met by an army of graduate assistants outside Dr. Vernon's door. World no longer spinning, just uneven, off-balance.

"What did you think, what did you think?" Todd asks me.

Dr. Vernon's door shuts behind me.

"He's amazing, isn't he?" Todd asks.

I open my mouth, can't think of a way to respond, so I just raise my palms.

"Still processing all of it, I understand," Todd says. He hands me a copy of *The Chronicle*, on the cover of which is the title, "How we can help Millennials discover their future," by Dr. Vernon. "Read it," he says. "It's so frickin' inspiring! It'll make you a believer."

*

My remaining time at Bowling Green passes uneasily, a mild case of indigestion after a so-so dinner that you're still not quite sure how to judge. The chicken was cooked well, but was it cooked well enough? Did you bite down on one pink squishy piece, or was that just your imagination trying to account for your stomach ache?

"Charles is…staring at a blank report on his computer screen."

"Charles is…eating McDonalds again."

"Charles is…out of toilet paper in the bathroom. Sitting here on the toilet, I called the chapter president, but he can't get to the bathroom supplies. They're locked in a janitor's closet somewhere, he says. Really?!"

"Charles is…facilitating an Alcohol Responsibility Workshop, my first in several weeks. Blank stares. A few of the kids brought laptops. They're gaming. I shouldn't have bothered."

*

At some point, I leave the chapter house and head to a gas station to get a soda. While I'm filling the cup at the soda fountain, my cell phone rings, surprises me, and I spill most of my Super Big Gulp across the metal countertop.

I sneak away from the spill site, dig in my pocket for my vibrating cell phone, and when I finally pull it out—expecting an 800 number or an Indianapolis area code (LaFaber)—it is instead a 505 area code. I recognize the code, but can't remember from where. California? Indiana? Pennsylvania? Michigan? So many places. I flip open the phone, and am greeted by a female voice burning with acrimony: "I know who you are," she says. "I know who you *are*, Charles."

"Excuse me?" I ask, peering into the fridge. "How did you get this number?"

"This is Ma-*ri*-a," she says. "Don't act like you don't know who this is."

"Maria?" I ask. "*Maria*, Maria?"

"Maria, Maria."

"Maria," I say. "I didn't recognize the number."

One of the employees has noticed the spilled soda on the counter, shakes his head and says "Fucking savages." He goes off in search of a mop, and I distance myself further from the mess I created.

"Of *course* you didn't," Maria says. "You probably deleted my number, didn't you?"

"I…" Shit. *I know who you are*, and yes, she's seen my Facebook page. She knows that I'm a consultant, that I lied to her, and she isn't calling to plan Date #2. "Yeah." I exhale. "I deleted your number. Sorry. I honestly didn't think we'd talk again."

"You're a fucking *ass*-hole," she says.

"I am. You're right. I had to—I had to leave town, Maria. I'm sorry. I should have called, you know? That was really…an asshole thing to do."

"You left town? That's an interesting way of putting it."

"That's what happened. I don't know what you were told." I swallow again. Remind myself that this is just some college freshman halfway across the country, that there should be no worries, not now. I can handle this. "It was"—what did Sam say?—"my Mom died."

"Bullshit. You were here for a *week*. Left town? You were never here to begin with."

"All right, all right," I say. "Let's slow down."

"Bullshit, slow down."

"What have you heard, Maria?" Calmer, now. I head for the front door of the gas station, empty-handed, ready to squeak out of here with no purchase. "Tell me what you've heard."

"It's what I didn't hear, *Charles*," and she says my name mockingly, almost as if she believes it to be a lie. "We go to Juarez, I invite you to my room." A pause. "But I never—I swear to God I didn't think this would happen—not so much as a *phone call*? Not a word. And why was that, I wondered? I can handle a run-of-the-mill asshole, Charles, 'cause at least I can tell my girls to stay away, but you fucking *vanished*. It was like you'd never existed."

"It wasn't, you know, my intention to—"

"How do I get back at an asshole that isn't around to face consequences?"

"You don't have to get *back* at me."

"Didn't accept my friend request," she says. "That was too bad. I could have let bygones be bygones."

I'm out the door of the 7-Eleven, heading back to my car while behind me a mop squeaks my spilled soda. The wind is cutting so sharp that tears streak across my face.

"You want to know how I found the Facebook page, Charles?" she asks. "See, you told me you never had a page. And at first, I just kept seeing this page with Ryan Reynolds as a profile picture, and you *damn sure* aren't Ryan Reynolds. But I *googled* you, Charles. And funny, the things you find online. Full profiles of Educational Consultants at the Nu Kappa Epsilon National Fraternity web site."

"Wait, hold on," I say, back inside the Explorer.

"Your entire bio. Your degree, your honors and accomplishments, your travel territory. Do you want me to read it to you? You're at *Bowling Green* right now, aren't you?"

"You know..." I start. Hotter in here. Blood in my head beating quicker, quicker, almost pounding as I hold the phone to my ear, and it's the same sound that my tires make these days as they rattle on my busted wheels. And when I speak, trying to sound calm and rational, trying to remember that I'm the adult and she is just an emotional college girl, trying to convince her that this is all a miscommunication, I can only manage this: "Um, how did you get my cell phone number?"

"I called the phone number on the web site."

"What web site?"

"The Nike national web site."

"My phone number isn't listed."

"I called the Headquarters. The 800 number. Some guy answered—"

—*who* could have answered? A guy? Not one of the secretaries, obviously. Maybe she hit an extension number, got one of the interns? LaFaber himself?

"What did you say?" I ask, mouth dry.

"I told them I had to get in touch with you. Easiest phone number I ever got."

"What *else* did you say?"

"Oh, you're worried, aren't you?" she asks. "You're not supposed to sleep with little sorority girls, are you? Big no-no. I asked the Alpha Alpha traveling consultant about it when she came to our sorority house. She said there are strict policies against that: no dating, mating, or relating, she said. You're scared, aren't you, Charles?"

"Listen," I say. "Listen. I was wrong, all right?"

"Easy to say afterwards, isn't it?"

"What do you want, Maria?" I ask. "I told you I'm sorry. But I'm in Indiana right now. There's not much I can do out here. What is it that...I mean, what do you *want*?" I realize, after I say this, that it comes out sizzling like acid—*what do you want?*—like I'm some action hero who finally finds the dastardly villain who's been threatening to blow up the city for no real reason.

She's silent for a moment, considering the ridiculousness of the question. "I want more than some half-assed apology," she says eventually. "We'll talk again, player. Till then, be easy on those little Ohio bitches." And she hangs up; the car suddenly grows cold, a light rain hitting the windshield and then rising in violence, the long road back to campus falling dark.

*

Long after the fraternity house has gone silent on my final night at BGSU, I type the final letters on my visit report for New Mexico State University. It's late, so late that many of the local gas stations have closed until sunrise, and outside the guest room window the campus appears so windy, wet, and desolate that I feel as if I'm in the middle of a Florida hurricane. Middle of night darkness made darker because the rain and the shaking tree branches obscure the street lamps. Everyone on lockdown, not a car on the streets, not a smoker on the park benches.

Nobody, it seems, wants to watch me finish this report.

"I did not witness hazing in Las Cruces," I typed on the first draft, "but I recommend further investigation/ temporary suspension. I saw clear signs of bullying (brothers making jokes at the expense of the pledges), though one could dismiss such activity as 'boys just being boys.'"

But this wouldn't have been good enough for LaFaber.

So I added, "I saw boxes full of blindfolds. Unclear whether these were to be used in a ceremony, but I feel it must be recorded." Then, "I was unable to attend any chapter events, but..." But I strike it out because LaFaber wouldn't believe it, replace it with, "I attended a chapter Etiquette Dinner for a few minutes, and many of the pledges seemed terrified when they learned that I was a national representative, perhaps indicating that the member education process is flawed? Warrants further investigation."

LaFaber needs specifics, individual incidents and observations. So I type, "I overheard a brother call the pledge class a bunch of 'dirty scumbags.' I overheard one pledge complaining about having to do push-ups all night long." And, "I think they have some alumni connection to a pecan farm they use for pledge activities. Didn't see anything, but this seems suspicious." But I also write that it is "important to note that individual brothers—Sam Anderson, the New Member Educator—seemed committed to doing the right thing," but "the overall chapter culture seems influenced by ROTC/ military training tactics. This is a problem chapter."

"Charles...is typing the wrong date. The date: one month ago."

"Charles...is printing the report."

And then the visit report is in my hands, paper-clipped, all six pages. I shake it and expect it to be heavy.

I remember a time, back when I was in high school, 14 or 15 years old, and my father was involved in a long and bitter battle over a sizable chunk of land along a few of the twisting brackish creeks and rivers that fed into the intracoastal waterway. I don't know who he was working with, which investors or holding companies, but the plan was to transform the mud and palmetto scrubs and spiderwebs and snake pits into long rows of condos, town centers, boat clubs, docks, seafood restaurants..."Coastline" was the name of the development...undesirable land turned into waterfront property...but an organized political push from the Sierra Club was holding them back. Something about tortoises, pelicans. And I heard the daily updates from my

Marine Biology teacher, Mr. Foster: how we would never get these wetlands back, how this was Corporate America at its worst and today they just got another permit approved, how there was a march at the Super Wal-Mart the next weekend and a letter-writing campaign and we need to stand up and do what's right, how the people in charge—"Suits" and "Blazers," he called them, but you knew he wanted to say "Greedy Bastards" or "Shady Sons of Bitches," that he had faculty-lounge conversations with the other teachers where his face grew red and he pounded his fist on desks—were fudging documents, commissioning environmental studies showing that there were no endangered tortoises anywhere close and *they were lying*, Mr. Foster said, he'd seen them! One morning in class he read aloud an article from the *Cypress Falls Herald*, and my father was quoted as saying that "it had been a long struggle" but "it was a big win for the local business interests." Coastline was a reality. *Thomas Washington*, my teacher said, throwing the paper down. *Thomas Washington! Who is this guy? How can he sleep at night?*

I didn't say a word. To Mr. Foster or to my father.

But I remember thinking: no one would ever say the same thing about me. I just wanted to do *good* in the world, to have everyone acknowledge that and say, "Yes, Charles Washington is doing good. This world's a better place because of him." It didn't seem like that tough a mission.

I flip through the report, looking not for typos but for some sign of the damage I will do, as if the text will suddenly have turned red, bolded, surrounded by blinking lights and arrows that denote each individual lie, as if I will see the wetlands drained and all the pelicans and tortoises and deer and foxes slaughtered, but…it's just paper. Black and white. Just text on paper, and paperwork isn't action, right? I stuff the report into a FedEx envelope.

Just paper, I tell myself. Just paper. Just paper.

And I don't know if I know where I am now. If I know who I am, what I'm doing.

# Purdue
## CHAPTER TWENTY-FOUR

I leave Bowling Green on an afternoon when the sky has again taken the color and texture of cracked cement, and I drive to Purdue University in West Lafayette, Indiana, where the world seems even darker, more jagged, the campus painted with grayer grays than BGSU, the cold sidewalk puddles longer and deeper. Students burrow into gray Boilermaker hoodies as late October winds slice through campus, tearing apart piles of leaves in the grass and sending the leaves rocketing through the air until they eventually smack against kids in their hoodies and leave muddy leaf-prints. Winter is hungry, and Purdue is experiencing its first bite.

Just the same as Illinois and Michigan, the fraternity houses are spread throughout the campus, and it takes me half an hour to find the correct one-way street, pull into the proper alley, and park in the correct lot for the sharp-edged limestone Nu Kappa Epsilon Fraternity house, a structure built from stone blocks as large as the parking spaces.

I dart through a steady driving rain, wearing my EU windbreaker over a long-sleeved Fresno State t-shirt I bought in California, but as soon as I make it to the front door the chapter president tells me that I've got a meeting with the Greek Advisor in twenty minutes. Face is cold and wet, my hair dripping in matted-down tangles. Dress shirts still packed.

"I've got a meeting?" I ask. "In twenty minutes? You're kidding me."

"Yeah," he says. His name's Bryan O'Reilly, a thick Irish kid—half fat and half muscle—with a shaved head and fiery goatee, and he takes huffing breaths after every sentence he speaks. "Only time he could meet. I can take your stuff upstairs, though."

"I look awful. I need to clean up," I say. "Didn't you think to call me?"

"No," Bryan says. "You didn't tell me I was supposed to."

*

I change into an NKE polo, stick with the destructed jeans I've been wearing nonstop, sprint across campus to the Greek Life office, and dry my hair with a brown paper towel from the building's first-floor bathroom. The Greek Advisor here at Purdue—Grant Farmor—is just another 23-year-old kid with a Master's in CSP: soft face, pale white and marked with acne scars on the cheeks, hair such a thin fair blonde that it looks like it might fall out at any moment. Grant rolls his chair to his scuffed desk, boxes and boxes of folders and papers and disks and network cables at his feet, and with an energy level sustained by grande Starbucks coffees, he introduces himself and lists his accomplishments: he is the *Greek Advisor* of Purdue, the man in charge

353

of the third-largest Greek Community in the country! He is only 23! He has presented at conferences as diverse as SEIFC and SROW and the Beta Theta Pi National Convention! The first ten minutes of our conversation feel like a spoken-word performance of Grant's resume, and then suddenly he looks me in the eyes and shifts focus: "And you," he says. "I've heard about *you*."

Heard about me. *Again?* All of these advisors: do they just spend their days instant messaging one another? I'm about to throw my hands in the air, about to toss my laptop bag across the room. *You know* everything, *don't you? So why don't you fill out my reports, and let's just call it a motherfucking day!*

But Grant leans forward, lowers his voice: "I mean, you closed the Illinois chapter."

"Illinois?"

"For that keg party? You walked inside and closed that chapter, right? I heard about it." When I nod, he leans back a little in his cheap creaking chair, and he says, "Oh man, that takes some serious..." hushed tone "...serious *balls*, brother." Hands miming the act of holding some serious balls, face pure delight, as if he doesn't get the opportunity to use the word "balls" nearly enough. He seems like the sort who would also jump at the opportunity to pantomime masturbation if we were talking about someone he considered a jerk-off.

"That wasn't exactly the way it happened," I say.

"That's a wild campus, my man," he says. "Usually, when I hear about chapter closures, it's always sort of..." Leans forward again, whispers: "Always sort of *pussy*-ish, you know? An email that says 'Oh, by the way, your chapter is closed.'" Leans back, mimes the ball-holding again. "Nobody goes *into* a chapter house, pistol drawn, and lays down the law. You've got a reputation as, like, some kind of cowboy. Let the legend build, brother. Let it grow."

"I tried to *save* that group," I say. "That's what happened."

"Some chapters are beyond saving. You either get it or you don't, you know?"

"That's what they say."

"In any case, it's better this way."

"I suppose."

He looks at me with squinted eyes, like some unspoken dialogue is now taking place. He pats his thinning hair, makes it cover a bright spot on his scalp. "You don't think it's better?"

"The house is empty, trashed," I say. "The kids were evicted in the first month of the semester. Doesn't seem like it worked out for anyone."

"Incidental casualties. If what we're hearing is true."

"What you're hearing? Is there something I'm missing?"

"There's been rumblings from Illinois...?" he says, squinting hard, perhaps gauging me, what I know, what I don't. Hands spread out across his desk.

"Rumblings?"

"Rumblings. You really haven't heard? Come on, brother-man."

"Good or bad news?"

"Both," he says. "I'm friends with a grad assistant over in Cham-bana. Did our undergraduate together at Iowa. He told me about…" And he looks around, like someone is spying on him through the wall vents or from under his crumbling green desk…"Nu Kappa Epsilon's interest group."

"An interest group?"

"An *interest* group," he says, closes his freckled hands into fists. "You know? An interest group?" When I give no response, he finally divulges: "Haven't done any colonizations yet? Still new to the game? There are two different ways that a national fraternity can start a chapter on a campus. The first way, you're probably familiar with." He gives me a prompting look, stretches one hand out, palm facing me.

"National colonization," I say.

"At Purdue, we allow one national fraternity to colonize each Spring. Generally, a chapter that closed down a few years ago, and we re-colonize to keep the old alumni happy."

"I thought we already had a colonization deal with Illinois. Five years from now, after all the evicted brothers graduate."

"That's what most universities prefer," he says. "But every now and then, you get a group of non-affiliated students on campus who want to start their own fraternity. Like, let's just say you're some sophomore, and you start thinking how cool it might be to get your friends together and start a fraternity from scratch."

"How does that relate to Nike?"

He grins and leans forward, and for a moment he looks like a little boy trapped in his father's suit, a little boy cursed with thinning hair and the early effects of old age on his skin. As he shakes his head, I picture him in a sandbox, on a baseball diamond, on a bicycle. He doesn't look old enough for this position, for a desk, for these clothes or that hair or those wrinkles, but here he is. Educating *me*.

"When a new fraternity forms, they usually declare themselves a 'local' fraternity, some combination of letters that doesn't exist on a national level. We've had this happen at Purdue…they'll call themselves something ridiculous, like Tappa Kegga Miller. Those fraternities don't last long. They collapse after football season. If a group is serious, it'll ask a national fraternity to be their sponsor. The plot of the original *Revenge of the Nerds*, the white-boys asking the all-black Tri-Lambs to be their sponsor? Anyway, this is what we call an 'interest group,' and rumor has it that you've got an interest group at Illinois petitioning the Nu Kappa Epsilon Headquarters to become a colony. And it's causing an uproar in the fraternity community there."

"Only a *month* after we closed the old chapter?" I ask.

And again, his face cracks into childish delight as he recalls his conversations with graduate assistant friends from the University of Illinois; "rumor has it," he says twice, thrice, then twice more, and "word around the grapevine," and "word on the street," and the cherry: "from what they're saying on the inside…" *Uproar*, he says with red cheeks. *Uproar!* The Lambda

Chi Alpha Executive Director had assurances from the university that they'd be the next fraternity to colonize at Illinois, and now this NKE interest group has thrown off the entire expansion schedule. And the Lambda Chi Alpha fraternity house on campus, vacant for the past four years (thousands of dollars sucked out of the alumni Housing Corporation bank account on a monthly basis), will remain vacant *even longer* because *Nu Kappa Epsilon* has an interest group forming. *An interest group*! Ready to move back into the house immediately and replenish the bank account. Illegal maneuvering, clandestine deals! Oh, the conflict between national fraternities, where millions of dollars are now at stake, he says. This is the big-boy leagues, he says. Getting things done!

And Grant Farmor relishes every gossipy syllable he spills; he's no longer a child in a sandbox; now he has the excited eye twinkle of a 19-year-old headed off to the bar with his new fake ID. Gossip gossip gossip, as though this is still college he's talking about—who hooked up with whom last night, and when's the next big party, and who got a boob job, and who talked shit about Danny. This is the same conversation, conducted in the same way as if he was still the Vice President for his undergraduate fraternity at Iowa.

But I also realize: this kid's got a job. A real job. An office. And a solid career ahead of him after he finishes what will likely be a two-year stint as a Greek Advisor. He's going places, using this position to go somewhere. And what have I got?

"I'm sure you'll have everything lined up if you apply for grad schools, but if you need a letter of rec., let me know." Twirls again. "It's a small world, higher education, but you got to know the right people."

"Kiss the right asses, don't piss off the wrong people, that's what everyone tells me."

"You're a fraternity consultant, after all. Natural transition into Collegiate Student Personnel."

"That's what Dr. Vernon told me," I say.

"Dr. Vernon," he says and chuckles. "Good old Doc Vernon."

"He told me to apply for Bowling Green's program."

"You'd do well," he says. "Good head on your shoulders."

"Just wait till you get to know me."

"Ha." He twirls in his chair. "Really, though. Consider it. It's fun to work with students, help them to realize their potential and all that."

"I do that right now," I say.

"Yep. And you met Dr. Vernon already, so…looks like you got your bases covered." And he laughs, has an in-joke grin on his face. Knocks on the table. Nods. Takes a beer-chug-sized gulp of his coffee.

"What's so funny?" I ask.

"Dr. Vernon? Dude's a quack," Grant says. And now he's pointing at the surface of his desk, finger making a dull thump with each impact, and it seems that the coffee is forcing him to constantly move, constantly keep his hands busy. "Don't get me wrong. I got mad respect for him, but let's get realistic, you know? All the learning laboratory stuff. Come on."

"He seemed to have a good thing going," I say.

"People worship the guy," he says. Hands swirling. "But it's all because he publishes a few articles, a couple books, gets a bunch of grant money."

"That's a big deal, though. Right? He had a lot of research."

"Research, right. The stuff he's doing on campus? Psssh. Dude has been there forever. Who works as a Greek Advisor that long and doesn't get a better job offer, you know? Shit, talk to *anyone* who works there, and they'll give you the inside scoop: head-in-the-clouds theory, you know, all these programs and symposiums and what-not. None of it really accomplishes anything. Just gives him material to write more journal articles."

"I didn't get that impression," I say. "He seemed—I don't know—honest. Like he saw through all the head-in-the-clouds stuff. I don't see honesty very often."

"Talk to the grad students. When they first start the program, they love Dr. Vernon, think he's a celebrity or something. By the time they're done? Hate his guts. Makes everyone work 60, 70 hours a week on all this B.S. programming." Shaking his head, shuffling papers. "The way I see it, it's people like you and me doing the real work, am I right?"

*

The next day, during the lazy hours of an early Thursday afternoon at Purdue, rain crashing against the roof of the fraternity house and turning the tall windows of the chapter library into dark smears, I'm again scrolling through Jenn's Facebook page to examine each change she's made in the last few weeks.

Her profile picture is new, it seems, a photo taken late at night, Jenn standing in a parking lot with her friend Tina, both of them wearing sparkling black shirts with low neck-lines, matching white skirts, ready to head inside some bar. Jenn smiles at the camera, her body turned at such an angle that much of her face is in shadow, one arm hidden behind Tina; over her other shoulder she carries a golden Louis Vuitton purse, has it pushed out toward the camera as if displaying it. It's an accessory I've never seen her carry before, this purse, a designer label she never seemed to care about. In fact, when I suggested buying her an LV purse for her birthday, she scoffed. "Don't spend that kind of money, Charles. That's such a waste. People who buy that crap are insecure." But here it is. Here she is. Not wearing the same thrift-store vintage t-shirts she used to wear, not the same tight gray jeans and black cloth headband, the contrast to the super-serious Princess look of her sorority sisters. There's no longer any corniness in her clothes, no longer a feeling that she will not be absorbed or consumed by the cynical world around her. And the smile. Shadowed, dark, mischievous, happy but not "Jenn Outlook" happy.

There are three new photo albums uploaded, also: "Homecoming," "Out with the Girls," and "Single and Mingling!" We haven't spoken in weeks, so Jenn is long past the days of an "It's complicated" relationship status. She is "Single," and she wants the world to know.

Outside, the rain slashes at the windows with greater violence.

I click on the "Single and Mingling!" album.

I expect the worst, don't know why I'm even doing this, and so I'm rightfully rewarded with punishment. Pictures of Jenn with college guys of all shapes and sizes: sitting on barstools with a spiky-haired blonde boy, taking shots with a kid in a Boston Red Sox hat, smooching the cheek of a Kappa Sigma fraternity brother, on the dance floor in a purple dress at some fraternity formal. Some of the guys are easily recognizable for me, faces glimpsed in hallways and classrooms and intramural baseball diamonds in a past life that no longer feels like it really happened. Others are strangers. These are the ones that hurt; these are the ones that show me how little I know about her.

In one photo, she holds a box of SQWorms, the sickeningly sweet gummy candy that would always surface from the depths of her purse late at night when we were drunk. She is holding the box, but she is not eating them. She is alone, also. This is the sort of photo in which I used to appear, nuclear-green SQWorm in my own hand, and the sugary strands would be hanging from both our mouths and our faces would be crackling with laughter.

I smooth my pants, search for an older photo album—"House Party with Charles"—and hope that it will make me feel different. But even this isn't what I expected. It's an album full of photos taken at my Senior Send-Off.

The first photos seem innocent enough, Jenn with her arm around my waist, a picture of my parents standing together in the fraternity house living room, a few pictures of the barbecue, the cake. Innocent, ordinary. But on the weekend before I left for Indianapolis, when Jenn was uploading the photos to Facebook, we had a long conversation about which to upload, which to exclude. "I don't want anyone seeing that," I said, pointing to one of the more harmless photographs.

"Which one?"

"The one where I'm trying to cut the cake."

"That's cute, Charles," she said.

It wasn't. The picture was taken around 10 PM, shortly after we'd sorted out the barbecue fiasco, and I'd unveiled the giant Publix cake, a rich castle-like construction with frosting spires and the iced message of "Welcome, Best Parents in the World!" By this time, the fraternity house smelled of pulled pork and spilled rum, and in the first picture that Jenn had loaded on her computer, I was holding a mixed drink at an angle, the alcohol spilling out from the top. "I look like a sloppy drunk in that picture," I said. "I don't want anyone seeing that."

"You *were* a sloppy drunk at the party."

"Jenn, please."

"We'll mark it as a 'maybe.'"

The next picture was of the cake itself, whole, as yet unspoiled by knife or human hand. Jenn had been our official photographer at the Senior Send-Off, gathering parents with their sons, making mothers hug fathers or stand next to their sons' thumb-sized photos on the large composites hanging in the hallway. She'd slipped in three photos with my parents, as well, all of which she'd made me take.

Later, the two of us clicking through the photos on the computer, it was strange to see these images, the authority with which I'd taken the photographs, the authority with which Jenn had stood between my mother and father, as if perhaps she was already their daughter. I said, "Those look nice" even though she knew nothing about what was happening between them, and Jenn uploaded them to Facebook, tagged them, waited for the obligatory "You're so cute!" comments from friends. And I remember thinking that—as horrified as I'd been to see myself so drunk in all the other photos—I'd also been eager to upload and immortalize any picture that could continue to tie me to Jenn. What girl would cheat on her boyfriend, leave him while the relationship was long-distance, if the Facebook photo albums were full of pictures of her with his parents? It was like moving in together, buying a car together; it was all I had, all I could think to keep her, as I planned my inevitable trip to Indianapolis for a year of consulting.

But yet, even now, after she has changed to "single," here they remain.

Even after my parents have divorced, they stand together with my ex-girlfriend.

"A lot of pictures of the cake," Jenn told me as we scrolled through all of the possible pictures to upload: a photo where I was holding the cake at this angle, at that angle, flash, no flash, close-up, the sort of pictures that no one would have taken in such quantity before the advent of 4 GB photo drives and digital cameras. And then, suddenly, the cake pictures ended, and there *I* was, attempting to cut the thing with a plastic knife.

"Not this one," I told her. "Don't upload this picture."

"Why not?"

"My finger is in the frosting. That's disgusting."

"Charles, only *you* would notice that."

"Don't you remember?" I asked. "It was a big deal."

"I don't remember, no. Your finger in the frosting was a big deal?"

"We didn't have large utensils. The caterer didn't give us any, remember? So I had to cut the cake with one of those little plastic knives. But the cake was, like, too tall, too thick."

"Okay?"

"So when I made the first cut, my entire hand smashed against the frosting."

"We'd all been drinking, Charles. Nobody will even notice. Or care."

But I cared. Because it wasn't simply that I'd destroyed those spires of frosting on the cake's southernmost wall…it was how it had happened, and what came afterward, the things Jenn hadn't seen but which were still raw and painful for me.

And it is only after I view the final photo in this "House Party with Charles" album that I notice a button at the top of Jenn's Facebook page. "+1," it says. "Add as friend."

We're no longer friends. At some point, she deleted me as her friend.

"Really?" I say aloud, and maybe this shouldn't bother me. It's just Facebook, after all. Jenn has moved on, and it's just Facebook, and what am I?, some it's-the-end-of-the-world-because-I-can't-go-to-the-party-on-Friday-night high schooler?, but it feels like something very wrong has happened, is happening, and I can't control myself and it's irrational but I'm nevertheless fumbling for my phone and I'm dialing and there is a click and suddenly—for the first time in who knows how long—I'm on the phone with Jenn.

"I see that we're no longer friends," I say.

"Well, hello," she says, voice light as if she thinks I'm just joking. "Good to hear from you, stranger."

"Good to hear from me?"

"It's been a little while." Are these the same happy high-lows that I remember? Or is this a new woman, one who will chirp with happiness on the phone just to placate me, all the while rolling her eyes and making "gag me" motions for anyone watching? This was a girl who ate GORP and yogurt for her lunches, who shopped the organic Greenwise section of Publix, whose iPod was filled with Wilson Phillips and the Bangles and Soul for Real; this was a girl who never apologized for her tastes, for her opinions, who valued honesty above all else, breezing through the pretension of private-school EU on scholarships rather than on her parent's cash; this was a girl who cringed when we drove past Wal-Mart, as if the big-box corporate stores might grow gigantic concrete legs and chase her down the highway like some prehistoric creature from *The Mist*; this was a girl who never needed an excuse to go shopping for a new dress, but who preferred second-hand to department store uniformity, who loved her conformist sorority sisters mostly because they were so different from her, a girl whose own eccentricity and distinctiveness should somehow have prevented her from ever joining a sorority to begin with. And yet the profile picture: Louis Vuitton. Do I know her?

"Good to hear from me?" I ask. "Are you just fucking with me?"

"What?"

Outside the chapter library window, a strong wind gust. A pelleting of hard rain producing a sound like crushed ice falling into a plastic cup. A branch smacking into the glass.

"No, I'm not *fucking* with you, Charles."

I'm pacing the chapter library, now have one hand on the outdated window drapes. Fabric tight in my fist. "You're sure?" I ask. "You're sure you're not...I get the distinct impression that everyone has been...I don't know how much more of this I can take, Jenn."

"Sensitive today? Wow," she says. "Listen, I wasn't sure if I'd hear from you again."

"Wasn't sure if you'd...? You didn't think we'd *ever* speak again?"

"I don't know, Charles. God, calm down. It was just a comment."

"Ever?"

"It was just a comment! I'm graduating in a month. There's a lot of people I might never see again if I take the job in Atlanta. It's just been on my mind. I didn't mean—"

"A job in Atlanta? You never told me about this."

"Well. We haven't talked. You shut me out."

"Trying to start over, then? Some new life? Jettison your old friends?"

"Jettison?" she asks. "Who says that? Why are you—"

"You're single, I get it. But we're not even *friends* anymore?"

Jenn is silent for a moment. When she speaks again her voice has lost the light and happy tone with which she answered, has lost the momentary sadness with which she mentioned her own future, has lost the confusion that weighed down her questions. When she speaks, it is in a tone that no longer drifts between notes, but instead slices uncompromisingly. "Oka-*aaa-aayy*," she says, drawn out in a way that I've never heard from her before, the pampered sorority girl tone that can take the simplest word ("okay") and make it sound cutting, that can pump four simple letters full of *are you serious?* and *that was the stupidest thing I've ever heard* and *you don't deserve to be talking to me*. "This is about Facebook, is it?" she asks.

"I'm all the way out in Indiana, and you want to forget that we ever happened," I say. "Don't you remember that you encouraged me to take this fucking job?"

"You're upset that I deleted you as my friend. Is that it? You want to know why."

"Yes," I say. "Yes. You're quick today, Jenn."

"You don't need to be nasty."

"I get deleted as your friend, and *I'm* the one who's nasty? Facebook is the story of our lives. You can't delete someone."

"Really, Charles? I thought it was a web site. And I think I *did* delete someone."

One of the Purdue chapter brothers enters the room, perhaps because we have a meeting scheduled, but I wave him away angrily and mouth "not now." He backs up as if I've swung at him, then shrugs and says "Whatever, dude," and he's out the door and it's just me and the cell phone again, a new wave of hard rain against the window. I finally loosen my grip on the drape, let it hang limp against the dusty windowsill, and I exhale to fill the silence.

"Who are you?" I ask. "Really. Who are you?"

"Who am *I*?"

"A fucking Louis Vuitton purse?"

"What does that have to do with anything? It was a gift."

"The Jenn that I know. She wouldn't act this way."

"What way?" She pauses. "Wait, why do I even have to explain anything to you? What does it matter to you what I wear? Who the fuck are you to say anything to me?"

"Hey, just remember. People can change in bad ways, too. That's what you told me, Miss Single-and-Mingling."

"You're absolutely right, Charles. People can change in bad ways. And that's why we aren't together anymore. That's why I deleted you. Satisfied?"

"Oh," I say, *"you're* the same girl, but *I've* changed?" And it's a stupid response, I know that as soon as it's out of mouth, and so now it's her turn to exhale into the phone, and I grab the drape again to steady myself, to stop from pacing the library, and I know now that nearly everything I've said so far has been stupid, that this entire conversation, if transcribed and read aloud by a semi-reasonable individual, is stupefyingly juvenile. But that doesn't change the way things happen in real time.

"You wanted to be the man, Charles," she says. "That's what you said. Way back when we were packing your car."

"So what?"

"You wanted to be the man. Same thing my father said, but you said you that if you were going to do a relationship, you were going to do it right. All sorts of proclamations, Charles."

I see the faintest possibility of reconciliation beneath this all. The faintest glimmer of the future I wanted, then forsook. To be with Jenn again is to be the Diamond Candidate again, to have no fear and to have done nothing wrong. To step out into the world and to save it, not to be halfway through with the job and to have failed. "Maybe a long-distance relationship wasn't realistic?" I say. "Maybe we got ahead of ourselves. Maybe we're both to blame?"

"Both to blame, Charles?" Jenn asks. "I told you I was ready. But I don't give myself to someone who talks a big game and then doesn't deliver."

"Fine," I say. "Fine. A thousand times. Fine. I'm sorry that I—"

"Don't start with the apologies," she says. "I get it. You're feeling guilty."

"I'm not. I'm just trying to do what's right."

"What's right? I've heard you talk about doing what's right for the past six months," she says. "The noble hero out to change the world? Making socially responsible citizens? Save it for someone else. I've read your Facebook updates. I know what you're doing."

"Please, Jenn. That's nothing. I've gone out a few times, but—"

"Ha! First you delete *your* profile, then you use it to brag about waking up at noon."

"Hey, listen"—anger now—"I've seen *your* profile, too. The shit *you're* doing—"

"Don't play that card. I never made a big production of trying to be some crazy-intense role model. I am who I am, and I never made any claims otherwise."

"Come on. Single and mingling? Come on."

"I didn't think it could be true, honestly," Jenn says. "I saw your name on my Caller ID, and I thought...I *know* Charles Washington. This is him. He'll prove me wrong. All this other stuff I've seen and heard: it's got to be a mistake, it's got to be wrong."

"All this other stuff?"

"And now, after this conversation, I know," Jenn says. "She wasn't lying."

"Wasn't lying? Who?"

"You really did, didn't you?"

"I really did *what*? What are you talking about?"

But I know, don't I? I know where she's going next.

"I don't want to fight," I try. "This is not what I wanted."

"You called because you were angry at me about the Facebook thing, but really you're mad at yourself, aren't you?" she says. "Guilty conscience. So tell me. Maria? Is it true?"

No defense. No response. "What," I say. "Maria."

"I didn't believe her email," she says. "A freshman girl in New Mexico? But if it's really true, then you know why we aren't friends, why I want nothing to do with you. You're not the man I thought I knew. You're my worst nightmare come true."

Outside, a thin tree shakes and bends in the wind, one of its long bare branches reaching almost to the muddy ground in a blast of wind, then stretching back skyward as the trunk straightens and strengthens, then reaching down again in another gust...reaching, almost touching the ground. And I wonder if there's a point at which the branch—or the tree trunk—will snap. Which will snap first.

*

Later in the night, while the rain continues, I sit with a scattered group of Purdue fraternity brothers in the type of warm wooden living room that one would expect from a typical Hollywood "frat house" movie: deep brown leather couches; a pool table at one end of the room; wooden floors that, as you cross them, creak and smack like the sound of fingers flipping through stacks of cash, ghosts in the walls and in the spaces between; composite photos dating back to 1955 lining the hallways and leading to a long fireplace, above which hangs a painting of (what else) the house itself, the limestone castle illuminated by summer sunshine; a spiral staircase at the far end of the room, leading to the next two floors; a coat rack, too...a fucking carved, wooden *coat rack*! Everything you'd expect of a fraternity house that's stood since 1948.

All is quiet tonight. The rain outside. The big-screen television at the front of the living room. All sounds like soft static, and many of the brothers stretch out on couches as though drugged. Some have opened textbooks, but they don't appear to be reading or studying.

Into the silence, I say, "Anybody want to grab a beer with me?"

Around the room, all heads turn to regard me.

"It's sort of quiet around here," I say. "Anybody want to, like, just hit up a bar or something for an hour? Let off some steam?" Blank-faced stares. "You've got some good bars around here, right? Or, we don't have to go to a bar. We could just go to Applebee's or something. I need a drink. It's so..." Stares. "Quiet."

But now the stares seem to take me in from head to toe, from my mall-purchased shoes to my faded American Eagle jeans to my untucked long-sleeved t-shirt. "You're a con-*sul*-tant, right?" one of them says, upper lip curled in this disgusted look like he just accidentally stumbled upon his parents naked.

"Just one beer," I suggest. "Just half an hour? Anyone?"

But they all, one by one, shake their heads and then open their textbooks or type text messages on their phones or engage in some other low-energy activity simply to avoid eye contact. "We've got a mid-term tomorrow," one of them says. "In Statics."

All of you? What the hell is going on here? Why is everyone so concerned with textbooks and school and mid-terms, I want to ask. Just go out and relax. *Loosen up!*

*

And so I leave the house, leave them all to "studying," and I head to a bar called "Brother's" and sit at the bar and it's busy, clusters of frat guys in backwards-turned baseball caps gathering under the wall-mounted televisions to watch college football, and I order a pitcher of Bud Lite and ask for three cups and turn to a couple of girls beside me. "Hey," I say.

Both have been talking to one another conspiratorially, pressing lips to ears in order to be heard over the loud beat of…Ludacris? Or is it Lil Wayne? Or some other rapper I haven't heard? *If you* are *what you say you* are…*a superstar*…*then have no feeee-arrrr*…Both are brunettes, also, wearing jeans and black shirts, and they turn to me in unison with faces bereft of amusement. "We're talking," one says.

"Sure," I say and hold out the two cups. "Thought you might want a beer?"

She holds up her own cup, a lime-garnished cocktail that is by now mostly ice. "Already got a drink, so…"

"Looks empty," I say. "You sure?"

The other girl leans forward, says, "We've got boyfriends." And then they turn their barstools so that they're no longer facing me, and they are speaking into one another's ears again, their bodies barely registering any interruption.

Heavy ceiling fan. Mold breaking through.

The beer goes warm before I can finish it, the crowds of college students seeming to all stand at a distance from me, as if I've fallen into a crater and one false step might send any of them tumbling down here with me.

# Toxic
## CHAPTER TWENTY-FIVE

After I pay my tab at the bar, I consider driving back to the Purdue chapter house, consider whether they'll still be awake—it's past 2 AM, but this is a fraternity house—and consider what they'll see when I ring the doorbell and ask to be let back inside:

Or:

When I pull into the parking lot, the lights on the limestone castle's first floor are all dark; the second floor seems alive, soft music seeping from one room, lamplights in three windows and blacklights in a couple others. I park, leave the Britney CD on low volume, "Toxic" again the soundtrack as I stare through my windshield at a fraternity house.

I know what they'll see.

I'll walk to the front door, and when they answer the ringing bell (and who will hear, who will answer?), there I will stand, shifting from foot to foot. Dark blue jeans with holes in the knees. EU windbreaker over a black graphic tee: an Express t-shirt I bought last week, the screen-printed image of some sort of winged creature snarling in the center, an angel maybe?, feathery wings consuming the entirety of the shirt's front and sharpening as they wrap around the back. A pissed-off angel. Beer spilled onto the white graphic. The smell of cigarette smoke so heavy on my clothes that I feel encased in a gray cloud. Rain water matting my hair, two-day stubble on my cheeks, and have I brushed my teeth since yesterday morning? I don't know anymore.

Oh, I know what they'll see.

This is what has been printed on the blank side of the business card, and I can't let anyone see me, not like this.

So I stay in my Explorer, waiting for another car to pull in. "I'm on a ride," Britney is singing, and if someone parks and walks to the front door and opens up ("You're toxic") then I will jump out, catch up ("I'm slipping under") mumble something about how lucky I am that we both arrived at the same time ("Don't you know that you're toxic?") and slip inside and slip to my guest room and no one else will notice. Things will work out: the Etiquette Dinner, the bathroom at New Mexico State. Things will work out.

But I'm alone in the parking lot for a long time, the rain and wind breathing strong bursts, and at some point, that long tree branch in the fraternity house front yard—bending for the last several days, bending in the gusting wind—splinters and collapses to the ground.

*

I'm awoken early in the morning by someone tapping on my passenger-side door. The car is still grumbling, heat still blowing, and I've been sleeping in the driver's seat for the last several hours.

"You okay in there?" I hear.

"Huh? Fuck," I say, and try to stretch forward, slip back against the seat.

"You the consultant?" At the window is a youthful Jeff Goldblum lookalike, dark hair and glasses and inquisitive eyes, palms pressed to the glass, face just centimeters from leaving a nose print. "Shit, it's the *consultant* in there. He's sleeping in his car."

"No," I say. "No. I'm…ugh…I'm fine."

I force myself to lean as far forward as possible—stretch—and there are pains in my neck and back that are brand-new to me, spots on my body that have never before registered a moment's thought now aching with the sharpness of just-purchased dress shoes worn for a long and heel-scraping walk.

And then there's another face at the window. Bryan O'Reilly: chapter president. Boston Celtics sweatshirt, beanie pulled over his shaved head. "You want to, like, go inside?"

"Yes," I say. "I do need to."

The clock reads 7:04 AM.

"Well hurry up. We're already late for class," Bryan says.

I shut off the car. Not sure how much strain I put on the battery. Open the door, shiver in the early-morning cold, slump out onto the pavement. "Glad you guys have early classes," I say and rub my eyes. "I…I didn't want to wake anyone up last night."

"Shouldn't have gone out to the bar by yourself," Bryan says.

"You sleep out here all night?" Goldblum asks. "Fuck."

I nod and we walk through the front yard, the fallen leaves and dead grass and broken branches and mud. There is no wind right now, but still the cold feels as if it is finding new ways to penetrate me. Shouldn't have worn jeans with knee-holes.

"Everyone's got early classes," Golblum says. "Only time they offer some of the engineering pre-reqs."

"That sucks," I say and wipe my nose with the sleeve of my windbreaker.

"You look like shit," Bryan says. "But at least you're up for breakfast."

"Breakfast?"

"You missed breakfast the last couple days," he says, opens the front door, and straight ahead, there in the dining room where I've eaten lunch and dinner with the chapter throughout my visit here at Purdue University, are twenty or thirty fraternity brothers at the long cafeteria-style tables, trays before them, bowls of cereal, cups of orange juice, plates of toaster-friendly waffles or Pop-Tarts. They turn, they see me, a collection of heads swiveling in unison.

"Everyone, it's the consultant," Bryan says. And then he's back outside and heading to class and the door is shutting behind me and I'm standing in the hallway alone and they—the dining room full of hoodie-clad fraternity brothers, their hair pillow-messy or hidden beneath Boilermaker baseball caps—are shaking their heads and making "whoooo" noises, and one of them says, "Really fucking professional, dude. Really classy."

*

There is a community shower in the second-floor bathroom at the Purdue chapter house, what the brothers call a "gang-bang shower," and I've counted my blessings these last few days when entering an empty bathroom at 11 AM. At Edison, we had individual showers, each separated from the next by cinderblock walls, closed off from public view by plastic curtains. At most of the universities I've visited, the bedrooms have shared attached bathrooms with other bedrooms, or—best case scenario—the guest room has enjoyed its own shower. And no matter how disgusting the tile floors or how impotent the water pressure, I've always been able to at least savor my privacy; no matter what the fraternity brothers thought of me, how they saw me, I could at least preserve an image in their minds of a man fully clothed. This morning, though, when I slink into the bathroom, it seems as if every brother who wasn't eating breakfast is now standing naked at the long row of showerheads. One after the next, they turn their heads to see me walk in, towel draped over my arm, toiletry bag in hand, frozen at the sinks.

I can't leave, not now that they've seen me. The only thing worse than a naked wannabe-professional is a Fun Nazi too *scared* to get naked in front of the boys.

One of them—a blonde-haired wrestler-type—shuts off his shower, waits for a moment as the water slows to a dribble and swirls into the drain below, and then he turns around fully, proudly, not a flinch of shame or embarrassment. He shakes his hair from his eyes, blows the dripping water from the tip of his nose; there are towels stacked here at the sinks, and so he walks—one leg dragging as if hobbled by a sprained ankle—straight toward me, settles beside me, the air around us suddenly thick with humidity and hot flesh. "You can have that shower," he says, slaps my back. "I'm all finished." He grabs a towel, ruffles his hair, trudges out into the hallway still wet and still naked, rubber flip-flops squeaking as he goes.

"Hey, it's the consultant," says one of the guys in the showers, staring back at me with giant puffs of shampoo in his hair.

"No way," another says. "We get the honor of showering with the fucking consultant."

"Heh," I say. "Quite the privilege."

"Lather up! Plenty of room for you right here!"

They're laughing now, an echoing room full of steam and jet-spray and bare asses, naked men who have seen a hundred times before the swirls of hair on one another's chests, the pimples on one another's backs, the white nether-regions of one another's thighs, the sadness or exuberance of one another's penises. Every single day, every single morning. Just skin, by now. But me? I'm different. My every pore is new to this room.

"Don't tell me that you consultants shower in your pants! Ha!"

"Heh," I say. "No." I pull the shirt over my head, try to take my time in folding it and sliding it to one empty section of the sink. It's a stupid thought, but I find myself hoping that—maybe—this might all end if I stall long enough. Staring straight ahead into the mirror, I unfasten my belt, roll it as tightly as I can, place it atop my shirt.

"Hope you brought soap on a rope, bro. Crazy things happen in the Purdue showers."

Slip one leg out of my jeans, then the other.

"Better have a big Nationals-sized cock, homey. Only big cocks allowed here."

Hold my boxer shorts in front of my crotch for a moment.

But no one is looking at me; they're washing the soap from their eyes, scrubbing their legs, working the conditioner into their scalps, rinsing their bodies one last time. I toss my boxer shorts into my pile of clothes on the counter, walk slowly and cautiously forward into the community shower with my toiletry bag blocking the view of my Headquarters cock. My feet have never been colder in my life, and my chest has broken into goose flesh, but I eventually take the shower vacated by the wrestler. And when I turn the faucet, the water that hits my forehead is such a perfect temperature—feet thawed, chest thawed instantly—that I already know it will be difficult to shut off and creep back into the cold to grab a towel.

"Best part of the day," the kid beside me says, his eyes closed as the hot water hits his face. "After this, I gotta walk halfway across campus for my first class. So fucking cold, the wind between these buildings."

"Hot water doesn't run out?"

"No, sir," he says and spits. "I feel like Kevin Spacey in *American Beauty*. After my morning shower is over, it's all downhill from here."

But then he shuts off his shower, squeaks away in his flip-flops.

Then, a moment later, another shower shuts off.

And another.

Brothers flopping away, chatting at the sinks, towel-drying, leaving.

And soon, it's just me in the community shower, standing under the water and trying to wash the dirt away, and there is no more laughter, no jokes, no comments, no greetings or goodbyes, no adjusting of handles and water temperatures, no more squeaking of sandals, no more rustling of towels or clothes, no blow-dryers, no scratching of razors. Just one naked man in the second-floor bathroom of a limestone fraternity house on a cold autumn morning, not another sound in the world but the rush of hot water over my head and in my ears, one naked man now shutting off his own shower, tip-toeing across a chilly floor, searching for clothes on the counter. Gone. Searching for a towel, clean or dirty, anywhere. Gone.

Alone, and it's all gone.

I stand at the sink, dripping water now chilly on my skin, cold wet hair in my face.

"What the fuck?" I say, hoping some merry prankster will laugh and toss my clothes back into the bathroom and this moment will end. But there's no response.

I hold my toiletry bag over my crotch again, poke into the hallway, and it is there—naked and still wet, eyes wide and terrified—that the laughter begins and the camera snaps and then my socks are flung back into my face, and I say "Fuck!" again as they clap and hoot, scampering away and retreating into separate bedrooms, knowing that I won't run—dick flopping—after them, knowing that all I've got is a pair of dirty socks, so what else can I do? I ball up the sock over my crotch and I lumber through the hallway, knocking on doors.

"My clothes!" I yell with each knock. "Give me my fucking clothes!"

"Whoop whoop whoop!" someone yells from somewhere, hyena-voiced.

"Who the fuck?" I cry. "Just…Who fucking stole it? This is juvenile."

Inside one of the bedrooms, a stereo clicks on, heavy bass suddenly shaking the door. So I slam my fist against the door, try the handle, slam and knock again and again. "Open up your door! Open up the fucking door!" I scream.

"Go away," someone says from inside. "Studying."

"Open up your door!"

"Gonna call Nationals, dude. Tell 'em you're hazing me, not letting me study."

"Just give me my clothes. That's all I fucking want!"

And then another picture snaps from the opposite end of the hall, and sock over cock I dart that way, the flash still registering in my eyes, but the photographer has ducked away like a sniper after a successful kill, and then a picture from the opposite end, and I charge that way, and there is music coming from another bedroom, another, and I stand in the center of the hallway, wet argyle-patterned cloth in hand, balls aching from having been clutched so damn hard, and I say, "Fuck it. Fuck it. Take your fucking pictures, you pieces of shit." And it's at that moment that I hear a noise behind me, a sound like dirty sheets tossed into the dryer, and when I turn I see a pile of clothes. Not mine. But someone has taken mercy, tossed a gray Purdue sweatshirt and some jeans and a hand towel into the far corner. "Fuckers," I whisper. "These fuckers."

After I grab the stack, I retreat back to the bathroom sink to dry off and to warm myself in the sweatshirt. "Facebook, yo!" I hear someone shout from far away, laughing, and I want to storm out there and scream again, defend myself, defend my image as the National Fraternity Educational Consultant—*"Keep that off the internet!"*—but I know that whatever they captured on film: it is accidental brilliance: because you can find no better image, six months after my own fraternity brothers saw me carrying my mother out of the house, six months after my father saw me in the rearview mirror with the Night Patrol, to show the world what has become of Charles Washington on his mission to save the world.

\*

It's still Friday morning and my visit is supposed to stretch into Saturday, but I pack up and drive as quickly as I can.

Pack up and drive. Without ever finding my t-shirt, my jeans, my belt.

Battery making a pained noise, engine rolling over, Explorer unhappy at having spent a full night idling in the parking lot.

But I pack up and drive. Away from Purdue University.

According to my schedule, I'm now supposed to travel to Indiana University. From here in West Lafayette, straight down south to Bloomington.

Directly through Indianapolis, home of the Headquarters. But I find a hotel south of Indy, know that I can't step foot into another fraternity house right now. Not now.

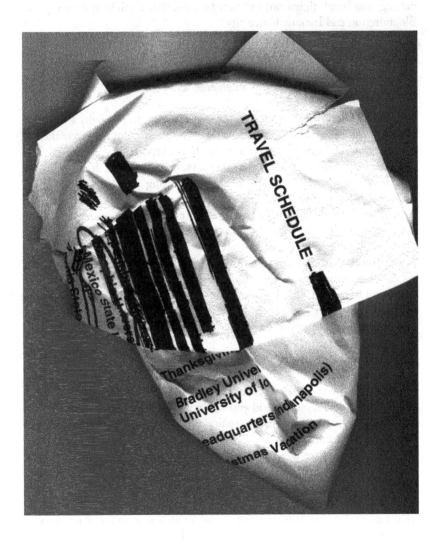

Just as I'm unlatching my suitcase and staring once again into the tossed-about wreckage that I've still not sorted, my phone rings. And it's Walter LaFaber. Even exhausted and aching from last night, my breath is still caught in my throat for a moment. Was he standing at his window, same as always, tall and military-proper, hands clasped behind his back? Did he watch me drive through Indianapolis? Does he know that I left Purdue early, that I'm putting two hotel nights onto the credit card, that I might not even go to Bloomington and Indiana University?

"I've got your New Mexico report here with today's mail," LaFaber says.

"You do?"

"Why else would I be calling you on a Friday?"

"I thought maybe there was an emergency," I say.

"An emergency?"

"Never mind." I lean back into the stiff mattress, the scratchy sheets, but still this feels more comfortable than any of the guest room beds over the last two months. "Did I do what you wanted? In the report?"

"I've just finished reading," LaFaber says, then clears his throat.

"It was tough to write. I'm, like, really putting myself out on a limb," I say, and I don't know why I feel it's necessary to remind him. He knows. A man who's made his career marketing himself as the Leadership Guru, the man who can show you how to *Put Values First* in your organization, a campus legend at Alabama, a fraternity legend at Nu Kappa Epsilon, a legend amongst all national fraternity legends, but also a man who has made his career painting over dirty ceiling fans. Yes, he knows what it means to fabricate a report; after all, he's likely done it a thousand times in order to get where he is now. "I don't usually do these sorts of things."

"These sorts of things?" he asks.

"I mean, like, lying about—"

"I didn't ask you to lie," he says.

"Didn't you—"

"Charles, I just finished reading this report." He clears his throat again. "If something is inaccurate, and you know it's inaccurate, that would reflect very poorly upon *you* if anyone was to find out, and especially upon *me* if I was aware of the inaccuracies."

"No," I say. There is a slight fold in one corner of the wallpaper above this hotel room's television, almost like a dog-eared page in a book, where the glue must have loosened. I can't stop staring at it. When I look away, my eyes return just seconds later to the wallpaper to see if it changed. "It's accurate, is what I mean. I was just making sure it was detailed enough for your purposes. For the, um, good of the National Fraternity, I mean."

He exhales, and now I wonder if even this—acting annoyed when speaking to me, sighing when I "just don't get it"—has been part of his performance all along. As if he needs me to feel deflated, reliant upon his expertise. "For right now, this report will work," he says. "We'll be able to suspend the chapter. You did fine, Charles."

"Have you talked with them lately?" I ask. "About the hazing?"

"Nothing new has developed, if that's what you're asking."

"There are good men at that chapter, you know," I say. "One of them would actually make a good consultant. If anything happens at New Mexico State, I'd recommend that a few of their members be kept—"

"Probably won't happen."

"Probably won't...? Well, if you need me to go back out there?"

"It's expensive to send consultants out there," he says. "And to send a consultant out there for a National Review, or a Re-Org? Better off just closing them. They're dead weight."

"Is that why you really—"

"You're back at the Headquarters next week for our mid-semester debrief," LaFaber says. "We'll talk about it then. Might need you to sign the official paperwork authorizing the chapter closure and the expulsion of their membership. But that's next week."

"Next week," I say.

"They rent their house, so we won't need to worry about evictions. We've got no real financial obligations at New Mexico. Anything else you'd like to discuss, Charles, while you have me on the phone?"

I'm thinking of the last two weeks. I'm thinking of Bowling Green, of Dr. Vernon and the CSP Master's Program and an extra spot reserved for someone from a national fraternity, of the too-young-to-have-this-job Greek Advisor at Purdue, of the bar from last night, of the parking lot and the broken branch, of Jenn, of Maria, of the black-and-white photo of the house fire at Florida and my father telling me to avoid things I couldn't handle, of the man I wanted to be and the man I've become because I couldn't avoid it, of the gang-bang showers and the missing clothes and the photos and the Purdue sweatshirt that I'm currently wearing and I don't even know who it belongs to.

"What are the chances that we could suspend the Purdue chapter?" I ask. "If I had some rock-solid evidence that...I don't know...hazing, maybe. Worse than anything we've heard from New Mexico State."

"That house?" LaFaber asks. "Their membership numbers look pretty good. In fact, they won the Chapter of the Year award at Purdue last year. Last year's consultant helped them with their Awards Binder, and they cleaned up."

"This chapter? An award?"

"It's all about presentation. You know that."

"What if there was a party at this house, a really bad one? Worse than Illinois."

"This is all hypothetical?"

"Maybe."

"We're living the mission, Charles," he says. "If a chapter isn't living the mission, then we might consider our options. We are values-based."

"But what would it take?" I ask. "That chapter. Purdue. Profitable, historical, great awards packets, a hell of a house. What would it *take*, Walter?"

He's silent for a moment. Perhaps he wasn't expecting an outburst, not today, not a Friday afternoon. "If you know something, tell me," he says. "But otherwise, that chapter is operating very efficiently. Alumni contributions from Purdue..." He pauses, and I can almost hear him lick his lips. "Their values, so far as I hear, are just where we like them. Their charter is safe."

"That's all I wanted to hear."

"Okay, then. I suppose we'll see you back in the office next week?"

"Sure."

"Keep fighting the good fight out there," he says. "Remember: one chapter at a time. You are a leader, Charles Washington. You are a leader, and you will—"

"So," I say, "is that all you needed from me? I've got work to do."

"Oh," he says, and I hang up.

*

Late in the evening, after a few drinks at the hotel bar downstairs (all of them purchased with the Nu Kappa Epsilon credit card: "Charge it to the room," I said), I google myself. What has changed, I wonder, from the days before summer training when I first tried to clear the muddy shit-clumped footprints I'd left across the world wide web?

The old familiar 18th-century Charles Washington, the younger brother of the nation's first president, no longer leads the google search results, I learn.

Now, suddenly, it is my Facebook page that appears first.

"Charles Washington," the search result's summary reads. "Network: Indianapolis, Indiana. College: Edison University. Facebook is a social utility that—"

And I click onto my own page, try to view it as the outside world might view it.

"Charles is...boilermakin'," my status says.

That's what I wrote two days ago. It was supposed to be clever, a reference to Purdue's athletic mascot, but it just seems stupid now, stupid like my black screen-print pissed-off angel t-shirt. And my profile picture? Charles Washington in a tuxedo at the Alumni Ball, rose pinned to jacket, looking off in the distance as if this was a staged head shot. This has always been my "classy" picture, chosen for my profile because... what? I expect the world to believe that I dress in black tie every day, that when I drink, I do so at galas and banquets, that I eat dinner rolls with every meal and that I only use butter shaped to resemble butterflies? I look at the photograph now, the forced certainty, the three-drink glaze in my eyes...

I hit the "back" button, which deposits me again on the google search results.

Farther down the page, I appear once again: the Nu Kappa Epsilon National Fraternity web site, the "Meet the Staff" page that Maria was able to find so quickly and easily. "Full bios for each Educational Consultant," it says. "Click here to—"

And yes, I click the link, and now I'm looking at the NKE staff page, the photos taken on our third day of summer training. "Brock London," buzzed blonde hair and intense eyes, "Nick Bennett," spiky black hair, looking surprised that someone just flashed a photo, and "Charles Washington," combed brown hair looking too stiff for comfort, eyes focused so hard on professionalism that you'd think I was starring in a law firm commercial. "Each of our consultants is a proven leader from a rich and diverse campus community," the text reads. "They know what it takes to make a student organization successful, and they will visit nearly fifty schools over two semesters in an effort to keep all chapter operations running smoothly. Educational Consultants are our front-line warriors—"

And I click on my picture.

Those eyes.

Focused on professionalism.

"Charles Washington is a graduate of Edison University in Fort Myers, Florida, and holds a BA in Organizational Communication. During four years as an undergraduate member of Nu Kappa Epsilon, Charles served as the president of his—"

He is the missionary who visits the brothel as soon as the sky goes dark.

Back, back, back. And I'm on the google search results page again.

18th-century Charles Washington is still there as a search result. A thumbnail-sized image, a portrait of Charles Washington standing in the warm study of some mansion in Virginia or Maryland or Pennsylvania. I used to think that he was just an irrelevant relic of American history, his painted portrait so forced, so obvious. The wig. The silly clothing. The sword at his beltline. Expression straining at regality. He's playing dress-up. But there is his Wikipedia page directly below my own Facebook page, more than 200 years separating our portraits…we're in this together, now, the two of us. This is how the world knows us, these snapshots.

And then I'm back on my Facebook profile, scrolling through comments left on my wall.

"Charles is now friends with Amanda Garrison and Boyd Fulton."

"Charles was tagged in Edwin Cambria's album: SENIOR YEAR."

From an old fraternity brother, Brandon Seders: "Bro, you still traveling? Give me a call. I'm headed to Chicago for business. We should meet up."

Message from Sam Anderson: "We need to talk, man. No joke. I got a call today, dude. This is not what you promised! Why haven't you called me back?"

And then I'm on Sam Anderson's page, where his status update reads, "Sam Anderson is…sick of all the bullshit."

His page is filled with comments from other New Mexico State fraternity brothers:

"What's going on with Nationals, Sam?"

"Are we getting closed?"

"Are they pulling our charter? This is fucked up, man!"

"BULLSHIT IS RIGHT, SAM!"

"Hey, did you ever talk with our consultant? He said he'd help us out, right?"

And farther down Sam Anderson's page:

"Sam was tagged in Maria Angelos' album: JUAREZ."

And yes, I should have known that they would be Facebook friends.

And there are thumbnail-sized pictures of Sam and Maria hugging in a dark bar, crowds behind them, blackness and multi-colored club lights co-existing in the background, and I remember taking this picture.

I click on Maria's online "JUAREZ" photo album: 85 total photos.

And as the images load, I see my own face developing, pixel by pixel. Corona in one hand. Another image: Coronas in each hand. Another: arm at Maria's waist. Another: my face on her face, my tongue in her mouth. One photo where the two of us hold tequila shots in a toast, and another photo where the two of us are tilting the shot glasses back and the tequila is rushing into our mouths. And her captions tell the world all that the photographs have left to mystery: "And this was my first college lesson about never trusting men," and "Charles Washington, the esteemed Nu Kappa Epsilon fraternity consultant, buying drinks for an 18 year old!!!" and "Never let a man sleep in your dorm room, or he'll steal your clothes!" and there I am in the baby T and boxer shorts, the morning after Juarez, stunned face, surrounded by the purple and pink nightmare of Maria's bedroom. Nothing I can do to erase this. Only a matter of time, wasn't it?

\*

The next morning, I know for sure what I've got to do.

After I've re-organized my suitcase—any Fun Nazi business cards now thrown into the trash, everything neat, just the way it was two months ago—I make another phone call. Dr. Vernon at Bowling Green State University.

"Yes," he answers. "And who is this?"

"Charles Washington," I say. "The consultant. We met last week."

"Ahh. Charles Washington. On a Saturday?"

"Your contact sheet had your cell phone number. Did I catch you at a bad time?"

"I'm very busy today, actually. I'm supposed to meet up with a friend in a few minutes."

Then: silence.

I've been pacing the room for the last few minutes, trying to script what I might say to the man who could offer me a second chance, a new future. I walk quicker, flipping through the pages in my mind, searching. "I was wondering about the CSP program," I say. "If there are openings for the Spring semester?"

"One," he says.

"One."

"One in Spring, and one in Summer," he says. "We've already got applications for next Fall, and it's going to be *extremely* competitive."

"I want to do this. Can I...what do I have to do to get that spot?"

"Well. I need to know that you're serious."

"I'm serious," I say. "I need to get out of here. Out of consulting. Out of my car."

"Grad school isn't easy. Our program isn't easy."

"Listen. I just had my clothes stolen out of the shower at Purdue, okay? Chased through the hallways, kids taking pictures of me. Somehow, I don't think grad school is going to present the same challenges." And now I've stopped at the hotel room window, am peering into the parking lot at the hanging clothes and snap-shut cases in my Explorer, all that I've crammed into my traveling office. "I need to get out of this, and I am serious—*serious*, okay?—about doing something positive, something that's going to, like, make a *real* difference. Serious."

"All right," he says. "I believe you."

"So what happens if I…I mean, could I just drive out to Bowling Green this weekend?"

"Classes in the Spring are a bit premature, don't you think?"

"Right, but—"

"And you're not the only consultant we've targeted. The only one applying."

"There are others?"

"You have potential," he says. "But there are five or six that could be useful subjects for the program. Not enough spots for everyone."

"Useful subjects," I say. "What if I…what if I quit? What if I quit my job with the Headquarters and just started working with you *right now*? Like, even before classes? You said you had a grant to explore the national fraternities, right? I could quit. I could come right now."

"No. You can't quit."

"I can call LaFaber right now. Tell him—"

"You can't quit," he repeats. "You won't be a useful subject if you have less than a single semester of experience. No no no, Charles Washington. You need to finish out the Fall."

"I don't know if I can do that," I say, and let the drapes fall shut.

I don't know if I can smooth out the paper:

TRAVEL SCHEDULE – ~~████████████████████~~

~~████████████████████████████~~
~~████████████████████████████~~
~~██~~ ~~████████████████████████~~
~~████████████████████████████████~~
~~St_____ie University~~
New Mexico State University ✓
~~Texas Tech~~
~~California State University—Fresno~~
~~California State University—Highland~~
~~California State University—Long Beach~~
~~California State University—San Francisco~~
~~University of Delaware~~
~~Marshall University~~
~~Miami University (Ohio)~~
~~University of Toledo~~
~~Central Michigan University~~
~~University of Michigan~~
~~Bowling Green State University~~
~~Purdue University~~
~~Indiana University~~

Headquarters – Mid-Semester Debrief (Indianapolis)

University of Oklahoma
University of Kansas
University of Missouri—Columbia
University of Nebraska
Iowa State University

Thanksgiving Vacation

Bradley University
University of Iowa

Headquarters (Indianapolis)

Christmas Vacation

"You need to finish the Spring, also."

"The Spring? But I want to apply *now*. I need to get out of here."

"Are you really *serious* about this opportunity?" he asks, and for a moment I can almost hear the smile in his voice, the demanding lilt of those final words speckled with the same cruel delight as when Walter LaFaber asks a question that is really no question at all: just another chance to let everyone know who's really in charge.

"Very serious," I say.

"Then you'll finish the semester. And you'll lobby for that Illinois expansion in the Spring," Dr. Vernon says. "Lobby hard."

"You know about the Illinois colonization?"

"A small world we have here in higher education," he says, again too gleeful, and I think of Grant Farmor, the Greek Advisor at Purdue, the kid who seemed to burst with excitement over the nitty gritty gossip of the national fraternity world. After he learned about the interest group, did he immediately call Dr. Vernon, fill him in as if he was Vernon's little frontier outpost spy? Or has Dr. Vernon known all along, even before Farmor told him, even before Farmor told me, even before I met with Dr. Vernon last week, even before...even before I was sent on an emergency visit to close the University of Illinois chapter to begin with? How long has Dr. Vernon known? How *much* does he know?

"I don't know that there's going to be an expansion, not officially," I try. "No one at Headquarters has told me anything about it. For God's sake, I still have the old charter in the back seat of my car."

"Oh, it's coming, the colonization," he says. "No doubt about it. Just convince your superiors that you would make a phenomenal Lead Expansion Consultant at Illinois. You closed the chapter, after all, so you'd make the perfect consultant to organize the colonization."

"I...I'll try."

"Get that position, and you've got a guaranteed spot here for summer," he says.

"If not?"

"We won't talk about that," Dr. Vernon says, lower by several octaves. "We want to document the inner workings of these colonizations, from a national fraternity perspective. Everything. In order to change the culture, we've got to change the institutions."

"Change the institutions," I say.

"You've got it, Charles Washington. You've got it."

*

Charles is...packing up his bags on a Sunday morning.

Charles is...leaving his hotel room, missing it already.

Charles...has two months left. Pack up and drive, pack up and drive.

Charles is...heading south to Bloomington. Indiana University. Hoosier Country.

Charles is...breathing. Two months. Smoothing his pants.

Charles...has one last chance.

Okay, here goes. Pound chest.

Charles...will walk straight into that house at IU, yessir, no question, his pants dry-cleaned and pressed and looking just as crisp as the day he bought them, and he's got a new belt now, too (and maybe his dress shirt is still tainted by pizza stain but who will notice?), and he will walk straight into that house, and they will say "MARATHON MAN!" and Charles will nod in the affirmative and he will step from foyer to chapter room, running his finger through the dust on the mantel, unacceptable, unacceptable, and Charles will gather the brothers in the chapter room and he will ask them why they have let their house go, and why they are drinking so much beer that the trash cans out back are over-filled, and…and…shit…they will not quake with fear at the sight of the Big Bad Consultant, will they?, probably won't say "MARATHON MAN!", might not even quiet enough to let Charles speak a full sentence at the Alcohol Responsibility Workshop, might even say "Aw shit, the fucking consultant is here" and might drop stacks of "Fun Nazi" business cards in his suitcase, but does it matter?, because no, Charles is not out to change the culture, not today, not tomorrow, not at Indiana University. That much was clear before Charles ever began typing this status update.

But Charles can pretend. He's good at that.

So.

Charles…will go to bed at a reasonable hour from now on, and he will wake up at 6 AM each morning, Sunday, Monday, Tuesday, Wednesday, and he will salute the National Fraternity Headquarters and Walter LaFaber will look out his window and he will see Charles and he will be proud and he will think that Charles is doing a bang-up job out there, writing reports, facilitating workshops, etc., bang-up job, and then, later this week, Charles will drive north once again to Indianapolis, back to the Nu Kappa Epsilon National Fraternity Headquarters, to the office, khakis and dress shirts, and it will be such a magnificent reunion with his fellow consultants Nick and Brock, with Walter LaFaber himself, the mission of NKE, a three-day "debrief," three days, where everyone will talk of student potential and achievements and "I stormed into that chapter house and I told them that we would not tolerate this destructive behavior anymore" and "We have standards, we have values!" and "We are not stereotypes, that's what I told them" and Charles will smile and smooth his pants and nod and hope that they trust their eyes and the image they see before them, the flesh-and-blood image, the thunderous voice and the passionate fist-pump, and not the images they might see on their computer screens should they perform a 0.13-second google search, all those digital images—jpgs and bmps and gifs—all those kilobytes and all those thousands of colors and all those faces and arms and hands and beer bottles and balled-up socks and naked Charles Washingtons in second-floor hallways that tell the true story about the students he has failed, the Pittsburghs and Shippensburgs and New Mexico States, images that tell the true story about how he has failed himself most of all, but he will never forget that it wasn't *really* his own fault, this mess, no no no, because—somehow, for some reason—he still believes he is capable of great things if only everyone would stop stealing his clothes from him, if only the computers everywhere would crash and cripple google and the search results would vanish, and hell, maybe he can call Jenn and summon the energy to sob and tell her that he's so sorry and that he's been a wreck, a real wreck ever since his parents revealed their divorce and you're the only one I can talk to and I've been keeping this to myself and I'm sorry I never told you about the divorce but I'm telling you right now and I need you, Jenn, and maybe this will work, and maybe he will be honest for once, and then Charles will argue to become "Lead Consultant" at the Illinois expansion and he will keep quiet about the Master's program at Bowling Green where he'll tell Dr. Vernon everything he wants to know about the "inner workings of national fraternity colonizations," and by next year maybe he can change his entire Facebook profile again—photos, career, everything—and who will even care about the footprint he left from some other life? This is possible, right?

Back to the Headquarters.

Where they build the socially responsible citizens of tomorrow.

"Change the culture," they will say and Charles will echo the words, but he will have something different in mind.

# The National Fraternity

## CHAPTER TWENTY-SIX

Nu Kappa Epsilon was founded in 1910 at Carolina Baptist, but Dr. Wigginton was right: it didn't truly become a "National Fraternity" until franchises swept North. In the first decades of the fraternity's existence, there *was* no Headquarters, and only semester-by-semester postal correspondence between the brothers at their respective schools kept the fraternity from dissolving or from splitting into wildly different operations. But the National Fraternity kept growing, Carolina to Georgia to Virginia to Pennsylvania and Illinois and Nebraska, and so, to keep track of all of these new NKE chapters, Jackson Cohen (now 29 years old, the fraternity still his foremost concern) proposed in 1922 the creation of an "Executive Secretary" post, and a "National Headquarters." Archives would be maintained, tradition written into record, correspondence between chapters formalized, conventions held, Sacred Laws voted upon. Like some towering and respected oak in the center of a sprawling woods, the National Headquarters would watch over and protect the entire forest.

National dues, of course, would now be necessary.

And houses? The Headquarters would solicit alumni to help purchase fraternity houses at each campus. Housing to entrench the groups into the campus culture, to make them permanent.

And more new chapters? Like an empire establishing colonies, the Headquarters would establish new chapters at schools across the country. An NKE flag flying in every state, that was the original goal. Build the brand. Grow the HQ revenue stream.

And insurance for those houses, for intramural sports, for legal issues?

And more staff members to assist the Executive Secretary?

And a National Headquarters building, of course, of course. 1952.

From a tiny dining hall idea to strengthen friendships at a small college came a National Headquarters for a National Fraternity called Nu Kappa Epsilon. It seems improbable, this development, the math of chapters and members and alumni—multiplying from one tiny group of eight at Carolina Baptist—as explosive and surprising as the growth of the billion-dollar fantasy football industry from one tiny "rotisserie baseball league" in the early '80s. But it happened.

When I was a kid, my parents used to take me to the Thomas Edison House and museum in Fort Myers every summer; vacations, my father told me and gripped my shoulder, should be enriching. We traveled to Kennedy Space Center at Cape Canaveral, also, and the fort in St. Augustine, and the

Everglades. (It took awhile before I got Sea World or Busch Gardens, let alone Universal Studios in Orlando.) But mostly, it was the Edison House. And I hated the museum, the smell of sawdust in the old cabins, the yellowing note cards describing various artifacts, the moss and algae growing over Edison's "historic" swimming pool behind the house. But out in the sprawling yards, there was a giant Banyan Tree that I'd spend the entire afternoon exploring. From one original trunk, the Banyan Tree had grown and spread to cover more than a full acre of land. Each time a new branch of a Banyan Tree grows and extends, vines drop from the branch and plant themselves in the ground and strengthen and thicken and form into new, sturdy, independent trunks capable of growing their own branches. Over the course of more than a century at the Edison House, the Banyan Tree had consumed the yard, had invaded and ruined some of the sidewalks when the vines and branches ran amok. And I'm sure *someone* knew the spot where the acres-large tree had started, but I wasn't sure which had been the tree's original trunk. It was impossible to sort out.

It's the same with the National Fraternity, I've decided. Those vines, those branches, those roots of power. As the Headquarters has grown its finances, its staff, and its influence, creating new programs and buying new properties, it's no longer some independent oak keeping vigil, its motives single-minded, values-based. No, the Headquarters is that Banyan Tree, its origins forgotten behind a system of trunks and branches and vines that obscure 1910 and 1922 and 1952. The National Fraternity Headquarters, an institution made stronger by the thousands of lifelines dropped from branch to ground, thousands of alumni with competing interests, hundreds of chapters whose motives cannot be grouped so simply into "get it" and "doesn't get it," an interconnected manifest destiny that no one can slow, let alone topple.

The National Fraternity Headquarters: that's where I'm headed right now.

\*

On the night I drive into Indianapolis for our mid-semester debrief, the skies are the color of old German war helmets, and the highways at rush hour are a long crackling strip of red lights one way and bright-white headlights the other, a thousand plumes of exhaust meeting the cold air and vanishing high in the charcoal sky. The "Mid-Semester Headquarters Debrief"—two days of meetings conceived, LaFaber says, to update Headquarters on what's happening "in the trenches." Not quite "mid-semester," since November is just days away, but it gives me a shot to tell LaFaber in no uncertain terms that *I am his man* for the Illinois expansion. One last chance to step into a future bright with promise. Because if the worst happens and, while I'm here at the Headquarters, I'm fired for Code of Conduct violations, then I'm unemployable in higher-ed, only a broken hyperlink to a future at Bowling Green with Dr. Vernon.

Unemployable: a future where I'm pulling up to my father's driveway in my Explorer, stepping out as he waits for me on the front porch, his head lowered, one hand in his pockets and the other holding a mug of coffee, entire body radiating with I-told-you-so. A failure with no money and no home, forced to return to the father I defied with a job I couldn't handle. Just another kid in his quarter-life who crashed and burned when he thought he was soaring through a Compassion Boom. "You're on your own now," he said, and there would be no recovering from such a pathetic homecoming.

When I pull onto Founder's Road, the scene on National Fraternity Row is much different than when I arrived for orientation in bright cheerful May... The road is dim, the parking lots mostly empty at this hour, only a workaholic financial director lighting a front window of ZTA or ΛXA. Each Fall, once consultant training is over at each headquarters and the semester begins for colleges, the consultants disperse across the country and the Row becomes silent, populated only by full-time secretaries and chapter services directors and CEOs and interns. And damned if they'll work consultant hours during the semester.

At the far end of the road is NKE, that stealth fighter of a building, concrete triangle pointed directly at you. In summer, the front lawn was colorful, blooming, but now the fountain is ice on metal, the plants and grass just fossil versions of former selves. The "Headquarters Lodge" (the residence hall for NKE consultants, interns, and visitors) sits a hundred feet behind the Headquarters, behind a smattering of now-bare trees and beyond a gravel parking lot empty at 6 PM save for a single car. My Explorer bounces more than usual as I grumble across the gravel.

When I first step into the Lodge, I'm blasted by nostalgia. *The Lodge!* The fraternity house for professionals. Where every NKE consultant stays during summer training, where *I* spent two months of this past summer, where I slept and ate and read once training had finished for the day. Two months. My belongings (the few things I brought from Florida to Indianapolis that I couldn't fit into the Explorer) still stacked in cheap plastic storage cases in the basement: some CDs and DVDs, my bed sheets, an extra pillow, some leadership books, and extra clothes.

The nostalgia is brief, though. We left Indianapolis in August, and now—the end of October—the Lodge walls are already covered in different posters than I remember—Linkin Park, the Cal Golden Bears, a Barack Obama "Hope" poster with a Hitler mustache drawn on—probably because the summer interns have gone back home to their own campuses, and new fall interns have attempted to impose a new personality upon the place, the Lodge a constant patchwork project of always-new residents. Nobody stays here longer than a year, so the Lodge is never completely cleaned, and never completely lived-in. The living room's three sofas do not match in size or color, and the television is an old 27-inch CRT monitor likely gifted to the Lodge when some full-time staffer no longer wanted it, a black bar encroaching upon the picture and advancing a millimeter toward center each day; the kitchen is a Goodwill mess of mix-and-match silverware sets, of steak knives and spatulas. Dust and carpet-fuzz is ancient, and old porno mags sit sticky beneath the second-floor sink like the sad reminders of long-gone adolescence you hope to never stumble upon again.

I drag my suitcase through the empty living area, bump it up the stairs.

No, I never called this place "home," never could. The Lodge might as well be a hotel or another chapter house; I still have to unpack when I arrive, find my sheets in the basement storage, find an empty bunk bed and prepare it for my stay. "Home" should be comfort. The Lodge is just empty space.

As I push my suitcase onto the second-floor hallway, I hear a quick thumping noise, increasing in frequency and in volume, and when I look up I'm broad-sided, lifted, slammed into the wall and into a bear-hug embrace, and I can't breathe and I'm choking—

"Charlie Washington!" A bellowing Texas voice.

"Ugh," I say. "*Brock.*"

He releases me and I flop backward, catch my breath.

Brock London, everyone's favorite cowboy consultant, bred on red meat and whole milk, a childhood of smashmouth sports and hunting, face like a hammerhead shark. Brock London is here, has unpacked already, and apparently there's something in his Texas blood that converts all of the steak and ground beef and bacon into pure muscle, because now, three months into his life as a road warrior, he looks as dense and powerful as ever. "How the hell are you?" Brock asks.

"Ugh," I say again. "Hanging in there."

"Nick's somewhere in Indiana right now," Brock says. "Crossed over the border from Kentucky, last time I talked to him."

"Oh," I say, huff. "Super."

Brock likes to wrestle, to bear-hug, to fart, to eat six hot dogs in a single setting. But I know that he's also the kind of guy who hasn't taken a drink all semester, the kind of guy who'd pin me against the wall if he knew what I've let so many undergraduate chapters get away with, if he knew what I've done on my own time.

"We haven't talked in weeks, buddy," Brock says, slapping my back and leading me downstairs to the lifeless living room, his arm around my shoulder and determining my direction. "You sound so busy whenever I call you. Like you never have time to talk."

"I'm not a big *phone* guy," I say.

"You look tired," Brock says, and he slaps my back again. It's something he does unthinkingly and without after-thought, an impulse that—if I told him to stop—he might question whether he'd ever done it. "We need to get you some caffeine? Some eats? Grill House has all-you-can-eat on Wednesdays, remember?"

"I'm not hungry," I say.

"All right, all right, that's fine," Brock says, and now we both sit on the clashing sofas of the Lodge living room. Despite Brock's enthusiasm and attempts at friendship, the two of us will always remain as different as these couches. He has the Ashton Simon Tragedy, a best friend lost to binge drinking, a world colored by heartbreak and then by the undeniably productive reaction to the heartbreak. He lives in a fraternity world as black/white, good/evil as a

*Lord of the Rings* movie: *evil* is always easy to spot and must be punished, and the punishments imposed by the *good* are always appropriate, just, effective. To even say that I watched a (potential) hazing activity at New Mexico State, or drank a Tecate with Sam, would be to peg me as evil as Sauron himself. "Tired or not," he says, "just good to see you. Heard you had it rough, busting up the bad guys."

"The bad guys?"

"*Charles Washington* takes no prisoners. We all heard how you stomped into Illinois at the zero hour, gave them what-for. Dirty Harry hisself. Never would have expected that from you."

"Thanks. A real compliment."

"Wasn't an insult," Brock says. He raises his hand as if to slap my back, but I'm too far away and so he slips it back onto his lap. Again, I wonder if he even knows that he's done this. "It's just that you didn't seem like a hard-ass during the summer. Always reading those leadership books? I didn't know you had it in you, closing chapters and what-not."

I stare at him emotionlessly, scratch my chin scruff. I don't know what he's heard, who's been giving him his information, but I've certainly never known Brock London to be sarcastic. He honestly believes I've been a model employee. "Tough job," I say, "but someone's gotta do it."

"Hell yeah, buddy," he says and smacks his own knee. And then he asks about my semester, my stories. "Come on," he says, "you gotta have some good ones. I want to hear what else you got into." And sure, I've got stories. But they're nothing like his: he is *truly* Dirty Harry: like, probably he walked into the University of Houston chapter house and found a keg in the living room and picked it up with his bare hands and tossed it into the dumpster and grabbed a mop and made the chapter president clean the muddy tiled floors. "Unacceptable!" I can hear him shouting. Or maybe he stomped into McNeese State University and ripped down the Budweiser poster from the wall, replaced it with an inspirational Lance Armstrong poster. Or maybe he roared through Colorado State University's basement and commanded the brothers to sweep the floor, take out the garbage, repaint, stand up straight no slouching, have some fucking respect, act like men.

But we don't get as far as his stories, not even as far as my own, because Nick bumbles through the Lodge's front door just a few minutes later. He isn't unbridled energy like Brock, doesn't lift anyone off the ground, doesn't bear-hug the life from us. Nick is a five-ten California boy, laid-back but not timid, gay but low-key about "gay pride"; he doesn't have an Equal Rights bumper sticker or talk-squeal like a sorority girl; often, Nick tells people that he doesn't want homosexuality to define him, and in the fraternity world maybe it doesn't. So what if he reads *The Advocate*? So what if he owns the entire DVD collection of *Queer as Folk*? So what if he has a poster of a shirtless Abercrombie model tacked to his cubicle wall? He's a dime a dozen, one gay man among a sea of higher-ed gay men. No, homosexuality doesn't define him in the fraternity world, but—as much as I don't like to admit it—it *does* define Nick for *me*, because his motives as an Educational Consultant are as pure as Brock's. Homosexuality, in fact, is the very reason that he's a consultant. Like many fraternity men across the country, Nick came out during college, sophomore year, after he'd already started living in the UCLA chapter house; there were 55 brothers in the chapter, and together they negotiated and worked through a situation that elsewhere might have descended into the blackest of hate. What did it mean to have a gay brother? What did it mean—as an 18-year-old who'd always told gay jokes and squirmed whenever he saw two men holding hands—to live with a gay man? The results weren't always happy and sunny, of course: and in other chapters, sometimes the gay brother is forced to move out of the house, surrender his pin, give up the fraternity. But because Nick's experiences in college were so positive, so encouraging, he's made it his mission to help other college men through this transition, to work with chapters to understand rather than judge; after his consultant contract expires, he'll move on to another job in higher-education: a lifetime of helping young students to realize themselves without the harassment or negativity they might have encountered in high school or in their myopic hometowns.

Nick tosses his duffel bag onto the hallway floor, wipes sweat from his forehead, oscillates a hard stare between Brock and me, on the living room couches. "So-ooo..." Nick says. "Here we are again."

It takes Brock a moment to summon his unrestrained enthusiasm, but when he does, Nick doesn't stand a chance. "Get your ass over here!" Brock says, shoves himself from the couch and wraps his arms around Nick, squeezes. "Aw," Brock says, tousling Nick's hair, "you look like you've lost that California tan."

"Okay," Nick grunts, prying at Brock's hairy arms, "okay, okay. Playtime's over. I get it. You're glad to see me."

Brock finally lets Nick loose, and Nick tumbles toward me, bumping his hip into the armrest; he stands upright, then, and brushes his long-sleeve t-shirt, brushes his jeans.

"And you," Nick says to me, waving his hands to indicate my ensemble. "Looks like we're really gonna be mistaken for brothers now." That was the running gag over the summer: the California boy and the Florida boy, both of us with dark Caucasian skin and short, black hair. For the old ladies who'd worked as administrative assistants for thirty years and had seen a hundred consultants (and who would forget about us the moment our contracts expired), it was just easier to lump us together into one man: "Nickorcharles." The more perceptive Headquarters staffers would describe Nick as the "Laid-Back Consultant," the one who rarely tucked in his shirts, who styled his hair with a bit more wild college zest. By contrast, I suppose I was the "Uptight One," though no one ever said that to my face.

Now, though, except for his two-day-old facial hair overgrowth, we look nearly identical.

"Never seen you wearing jeans before," Nick says. "Looks like you turned over a new leaf."

"That's one way of putting it," I say.

Minutes later, we're at the dining room table so Nick can open the sliding glass door and smoke. This has always been an unspoken agreement: our conversations follow Nick wherever he goes, wherever he can smoke. "Tell me about your semester, Charles," he says, words mumbled through the cigarette. "How's Jenn?"

Oh, she's fine, I say.

"Fine?" Nick asks, cold air swooshing inside as he opens the door wider. "You get back to Florida to see her at all? You never call us. I have no idea what you've been up to." Nick taps the ash of his cigarette out the window where it likely falls into a patch of dead vegetation. "Hope you've been calling *her*, at least. Gotta make sure you hit your two-call daily goal, or whatever."

"You knew about that?" I try to smile, but I don't want to tell them anything else. Both of these guys are good friends, the sort with whom I'd share a dinner, stories from college, even a couple beers, but neither values my friendship over his job as an Educational Consultant.

Brock turns to me, shrugs, looks as though he's about to say something— and I can tell, just by the way he's raising his wide shoulders and stretching his face in that curious way, that he's going to ask another question about Jenn, or about my travels, my chapters, *my stories*, how I handled Illinois, everyone's heard about Illinois, about how I take no prisoners, and so I head him off. "Tell us about *your* semester, Brock. You look like you lost weight."

"Me?" he asks and pats his belly. "Ha ha. Nossir. Put on fifteen pounds, been eating so many hamburgers. Everywhere I go, someone says they got the best hamburger in the state. Or the best barbecue. Or whatever. Can't call 'em liars unless I try it, right?"

But he's been waiting for this moment, a prompt, someone to give him the green light: and Brock is off to the races, listing his top visits and his worst, unfurling a lengthy narrative of the worst sleeping conditions he had to endure. Most interesting visit was West Alabama, he says, where he slept in the freshman dorms for a night (*"Men's* dorms?" I almost ask, but swallow the comment at the last second, because why would anyone but *me* wind up in the women's dorms?) and was then kicked out by an RA who claimed that residents couldn't have visitors, and then spent the next three nights at the president's *mother's* house ten miles away from campus. "Hell of a cook, that woman," he says. Brock is still wearing a dress shirt right now, and his underarms have gone wet with sweat despite the cold air cutting inside from Nick's open window.

"That's nothing," Nick says, lighting his second cigarette. He tells us that when he visited the College of Charleston, nobody was at the house. *Deserted.* He called every number on their roster and no one answered. It was late at night; he had nowhere to go. "And this is Charleston, too," he reminds us, "where the cheapest hotels are, like, 150 a night." And Nick tells us that he drove thirty miles before he could find a reasonable hotel, and he learned the next morning that the chapter had taken a road trip to Florida for a mid-semester break, and he wound up spending three days in an empty fraternity house. The conclusion of his story is interrupted by Brock's laughter, and he's slapping the table with *been there, done that* gusto. Did I tell you about Labor Day, how I forgot it was a holiday and no one was on campus?

And then Nick's telling us about a water balloon fight at Clemson, and when he's finished and tosses his cigarette butt out the window, Brock's got another story. And when Brock's finished, Nick's got another story: he stole one president's sandals so he could walk across the scummy floor of the UNC-Wilmington shower. *Ha ha!* Brock says. Well, Brock had to take a shower in the community "gang-bang" shower at Texas A&M, and while he was shampooing, the cleaning crew came in and mopped and sprayed and cleaned and stared at him, and they were all women and they didn't even say *hello*! I laugh but not too loudly, don't say a word about Purdue or my stolen clothes or the pictures. I keep waiting for each story's secret sub-plot, an Easter egg or a deleted scene that will reveal Brock or Nick as a Frat Star, also. Like, did Nick ever get friendly and fraternize with the *undergrad* brothers at any school? Did Brock allow himself once—just once—to polish off a 12-pack with some good old-fashioned All-American Texas-sized Nu Kappa Epsilons? *Just once*? A couple beers? *Come on!*

I stay quiet through their stories.

They say that their lives are enriched, that they've seen places—schools, national monuments, historical markers, natural beauties—they never would have seen otherwise. They've eaten things…oh, the places they've eaten! "I had no idea pimiento cheese was so awesome until I went to UNC – Charlotte," Nick says. "Most gigantic ribs I've ever chomped into," Brock says. They've met people who have *already* changed their lives. "And we get *paid* for all this!" Brock howls. Say, Charles, did you stop by Gettysburg while you were in Pennsylvania? "Um," I say. "Sure." You go to Chicago while you were in Illinois? Go up the Sears? "Sure, sure, sure." They list museums that were on my route, obscure off-highway attractions that are world-famous and that I *had* to have seen, right? ("Largest model train set in America! Saw a YouTube video of it. So amazing.") "All of that, yes. That's what I did," I say. And I just nod, agree, and then stay quiet, because the less I talk the more they fill the silence with their own experiences. Maybe this isn't so tough, I realize. They're a couple of old ladies sharing vacation photos, and they could go on for days and barely notice I'm here.

*

Late on Wednesday night after everyone has gone to sleep, the late-October cold seeps into the Lodge, seeps under the windows, seeps up from the basement. I unpacked my sheets but couldn't find my comforter in the basement storage bins, so I wake up shivering at 3 AM. And I'm not the only one. Across the dorm room, Brock is curled up into himself, his sheets pulled over his head, a series of pillows piled over his body like a makeshift blanket; Nick appears to have ripped loose his fitted sheets from the mattress and has cocooned himself in these, as well as his flat sheets, combining both sets so that the sheer thickness might warm him. Everyone is wearing sweatshirts, several pairs of socks.

Half-asleep, still shivering, I shed my sheets and grab a left-behind Colorado sweatshirt from the closet. I've got to crank up the heat, but I can't find the temperature control. Downstairs, perhaps? I tiptoe out of the room, through the hallway, down the staircase, through the living room... the kitchen. Nothing. The basement? No. At this hour, in this cold, I am *not* walking down into the basement. But here in the living room, even though all is early-morning dark, I can still see the outlines of the couches...the rich, soft cushions...and the thick Nu Kappa Epsilon quilt draped over the back of the sofa. Teeth still chattering, arms still prickly, I bump through the living room and climb onto the couch, pull the quilt over my body, and something about the couch feels ordinary, natural, warm. I consider taking the quilt back up to my bunk bed, but that isn't *my* bed up there. This couch...this makeshift living room sleeping spot...this is mine.

# Debrief

CHAPTER TWENTY-SEVEN

Thursday morning is bright through the windows of the Lodge as I iron my khakis, but the sunshine is deceiving; when I step outside and walk across the pavement of the courtyard to the Headquarters building, my still-wet hair feels like it's crackling into a quick freeze, my breath spreading from my mouth in a frosty puff that almost feels solid. The Indiana sky a blue canvas streaked with white, exhausted brush strokes from a paintbrush starved for paint.

The three of us—a Californian, a Texan, and a Floridian—huddle into ourselves as we dash to the Headquarters. Brock and Nick have been traveling along the Gulf Coast throughout the Fall; this is probably the first morning that either of them has tasted temperatures below 30 degrees. Me, I've *been* living in the cold.

Inside the Headquarters building—at the vanguard of the "V"—is an impressive lobby, Merlot carpet, walls a waxy blush color, your eyes drawn first to a leather-bound guestbook, pages tied together with gold string; then to the "Chapter Book," a three-ring notebook filled with page-sized composite photos from each chapter slid into plastic sleeves; past the notebook to the ten bronze busts of our National Hall of Fame Alumni; and finally to a banner the length of two SUVs, draped from the ceiling, cataloguing every "Chapter of the Year" winner since 1975 (Edison University making the list in 2001, just before I began my freshman year). At the very back wall of the main lobby, a yellowing NKE flag, proportions of 10 feet by 19 (the same, says *The Marathon*, as the proportions of the American Flag), signed in one corner by the eight original founders of Nu Kappa Epsilon Fraternity. The letters and symbols were hand-stitched onto the dyed cloth by Marjorie Mayweather, the wife of Carolina Baptist's esteemed President Edgar Mayweather, who helped the young group in its early years. There are also tall portraits of past Executive Directors of NKE, and framed pencil drawings of fraternity houses from across the country, and Donor Roll plaques, and—

The Headquarters lobby is a showcase of fraternity history, of the size and scope of NKE, and even the bookstore-smell ensures that you are inhaling Grand Tradition. From eight young students at Carolina Baptist...to this, a *National Fraternity*, a Headquarters! A true Nike Man should get a boner.

Of course, I've only just now noticed: this lobby is so focused upon asserting the importance of Nu Kappa Epsilon that nowhere does it mention the friendship of those eight men in 1910. Who were they, other than black-and-white photographs, names to memorize for the Pre-Initiation Exam? Did they care about one another, or did they only care about crafting this institution?

In any case, this is only the lobby. The rest of the building is more modest.

Beyond the decadent display of fraternity splendor, two doors open—each at opposite ends of the lobby's back wall—into the two separate "office wings" of our stealth fighter. The left wing is never opened to the general public; it's just a three-floor office building of inestimable unimpressiveness: rows and rows of cubicles that rival the *Office Space* set in their monotony, filing cabinets and cardboard boxes and stacks and stacks of three-ring binders, plastic crates filled with carbon-paper order forms, a full first floor simply called the "Warehouse," where conference materials (t-shirts, cups, keychains, easels, notepads) are dumped onto metal shelving, and on every floor there are the closets...the *closets*! The left wing of the Headquarters, it seems, was built more for closets than for offices (occasionally, a closet is even cleared out and converted into a makeshift office). Past the cubicles sit four closets in a row, *four*, nicknamed the Ducks (someone, years ago, having mentioned something about keeping all necessary files in order, like "ducks in a row"), all overflowing with chapter files. Here in the Ducks, you can locate the entire financial history of our chapter at the University of North Carolina, including tattered budgets from 1974 and consultant financial reports from 1982. You can find correspondence from the National Headquarters to the University of Tennessee regarding a hazing incident in 1989 (and, for some incidents, there is a great deal of correspondence regarding these matters). Of course, nothing is easy to locate. Every semester, Walter LaFaber assigns an intern the unenviable task of organizing the Ducks. Every semester, the intern barely makes a dent.

The lobby's other door, the right, leads to a wing of a different sort. One that *is* available to public viewing. Here are the seven "real" offices of Headquarters, each of which exudes a power and opulence to match that of the lobby; here are two boardrooms and one library, filled with alumni directories dating back to 1920, old pledge manuals, books written by alumni.

And in these "real" offices, you'll find Dr. Simpson (Executive Director), Walter LaFaber (Director of Chapter Services). You'll find our Financial Director, our Ritual and Special Ceremonies Officer, our Director of Alumni Relations, even our administrative assistants, everyone in this wing with a real salary, with health insurance.

When I came through the National Headquarters on a tour during my interview, I was shown only the lobby and the "real" offices, not the disheveled "other half" which exists in a state of constant turnover—interns every six months, consultants every year, just the same as the Lodge—and where the only consistency is disorganization.

"I forgot how this place smells," Nick says.

"You're right," Brock says. "Smelled so much beer and piss this semester."

"Smells like paper and reconstituted air," Nick says, fanning the air toward himself with one hand.

"And you can smell Betsy's perfume," I say. "She's not even here yet, but it stays in the air. Even if this place was abandoned for twenty years, you'd probably still smell it."

Out of the far end of the lobby, a crisp and commanding voice: "*Gentlemen*, so good to see you this morning."

We freeze, all three of us, hands in mid-air, mouths open, and we stare at the doorway of the right wing from which Walter LaFaber has emerged. He stands tall, the massive muscles in his shoulders stretching his white dress shirt to the limit. His black hair is combed meticulously into the sort of young professional mold that one might expect from a *serious* contestant on *The Apprentice*. Black pants, thin gray pinstripes, not a single wrinkle. Silver belt buckle, smooth and blank, the size and weight of a Zippo lighter. Walter LaFaber. Cheeks as hard as granite. He stands like a statue, waiting while we take him in, the American Fraternity Man.

Brock is the quickest of the three of us to return to life, and he lets out a haunting Texas cackle—"Haw! Haw! Haw!"—and stomp-runs across the lobby. "Walter, buddy," Brock says and collides with LaFaber (neither moves), the two of them flexing as they embrace, the shirt over LaFaber's shoulders so taut that it looks ready to rip. "Been too long! Too long!"

"It *has* been, yes," LaFaber says, smacking Brock's back. Both smile violently, a war of happiness. "I'm glad you all made it back safe." His voice is warm with understanding, like he knows all the "Road Horror Stories" that we—*Brock* and *Nick*, actually—were telling last night, like he knows it because he lived it. Because he's one of us. Fifteen years ago, LaFaber was a consultant. *Before* consultants carried cell phones and laptops, he's quick to remind us.

Nick is the next to come out of his trance. He saunters to LaFaber, and they engage in a firm handshake. No hug. "Good to see you. Is it casual day? Did I miss something?"

Nick wears a powder-blue polo, untucked, with his flat-front khakis. "UCLA game this weekend. Just wanted to show some Bruin blue. You know me, Walter."

And then LaFaber's gaze slips from Nick and finds *me*, and his smile shrinks as though I've sucked the energy from the room. "Charles Washington," he says, and it's a deep vibrating voice, the kind best suited as a voice-over in a horror movie trailer.

He walks toward me, Brock and Nick still standing together behind him but now engaged in their own private conversation, barely attentive to either of us. LaFaber's clothes crackle in just the right way as he walks, perfect folds appearing and then disappearing with each new step, lobby's lights lending no shadows over his face.

Charles Washington, on the other hand: I look like…well, like I *always* look in relation to Walter LaFaber. An amateur. I wasn't able to iron the hanger crease out of my khakis this morning (haven't worn them in weeks); my belt is scratched and old, a relic damaged during my travels; my hair has grown long and shaggy, and I shaved this morning in a hurry, nicking my neck four times.

"The consultant All-Star," LaFaber says to me, inches away, sticking his hand out…and I grip it, shake. "You should see the evaluations we've been getting for you. Students and Greek Advisors alike."

"I can't imagine," I say.

"We've got a lot of things to talk about, Charles."

"Only good things, I hope?"

"Sure," he says and slaps my shoulder. Then he adjusts his sleeves, adjusts his tie even though it's perfect. Pulls it tighter, so his neck bulges out of his collar even more. His cheeks seem to have gone harder, too, shoulders grown larger. He's breathing through his nostrils, bull-like. "Lots to talk about, you and me," he says again. "For now, get settled at your desks, but get ready for the all-staff roundup. We've got a big day ahead of us."

*

Soon thereafter, Dr. Simpson's voice—that old, Southern, Dr. Phil voice, the one rich with experience—crackles over the office intercom, calls all staff to gather at the Cohen Conference Room. Without thinking, I rise from my chair at my empty cubicle, and I meet Nick at his cubicle, and the two of us meet Brock at his cubicle, and we weave our way through the mess of boxes and crates and stacks upon stacks of binders, and we walk to the conference room, interns also rising from their chairs and joining our march, and we look like an assembled *Gangs of New York* mob by the time we trudge through the main lobby and into the East Wing, filing eventually into the Cohen Memorial Conference Room. It was in this room that we consultants spent our summer training, learning the "in's and out's of Nu Kappa Epsilon," learning how to facilitate workshops, learning every decimal point in the National Budget and the individual chapter fees and assessments. This was our training room, and I remember sitting at the boardroom table everyday, staring at my reflection in the thick glass tabletop, thinking *I've made it*, thinking *Diamond Candidate*, thinking I could be the next Walter LaFaber. Thinking, as I looked at several etched platinum plates underneath the glass—the names of our founders, the names of the first Headquarters staff—thinking that this was my first step to something great.

"Good morning, everyone," Dr. Simpson says to the full staff of the National Headquarters gathered here in the boardroom, "and welcome back to our Road Warriors!" He stands at the head of the table, wearing his nicest navy suit and French-collar shirt, gold cuff links. I wonder how often he interacts with the undergraduate men who currently populate the NKE student chapters, if he even likes them, or if fraternity for him has become something so spreadsheet- and numbers-driven that he can't even remember how he got swept up into it back in college. Dr. Simpson is smiling, blinding-white hairs matted on his scalp, and he begins a thunderous applause for the consultants, an applause immediately joined into by Walter LaFaber (who rises half out of his seat to put extra strength into each clap), by Dr. Simon Eckstein, by Janice Nevin, by the interns, by everyone.

"We look forward to hearing everything you have to report back to the National Fraternity," Dr. Simpson says. "Fraternity is a special institution, and it is you three—not any of us in this office—who maintain the fine tradition and the fine vision set forth in 1910."

Applause again.

And then Dr. Simpson is talking about the grand tradition of Nu Kappa Epsilon National Fraternity, about the many men who have come before us, about the legends whose names we view under the glass tabletop. And it goes on like this for the duration of the catch-all meeting, eloquent welcomes from each of the staff members, aggrandizing the mission of the fraternity and the "necessary work" of the consultants. "Brothers," Dr. Simpson says as the meeting comes to a close, "You have done more to preserve our national family than you even know."

But then the day gets more serious.

*

"I want the slackers and the trouble-makers *gone*," LaFaber says in our 10:15 AM Group EC Meeting, and he refuses to sit, palms pressed against the boardroom table, the entire surface shaking as it absorbs the weight of his anger. Here in the conference room, it's just the three of us and LaFaber, and I try to make myself comfortable in one of the padded leather chairs, but every time LaFaber speaks I flinch.

"Procedure be damned," he says. "I. Want. Them. Gone. I want the under-performing chapters *closed*," he says. "I want the drugs and the alcohol *purged*. I want a world without *hazing*. This is our mission, gentlemen, changing the culture one chapter at a time."

There—that single word slipped into the middle of his speech—did you catch it? One second he's saying "trouble-makers," and the next it's "under-performing." How easily he conflates "dangerous" with "unprofitable."

And now LaFaber smiles, more sinister than joyful. "So. Would the three of you like the good news first, or the bad news?"

"Good news," Nick says.

"Good news," LaFaber confirms. And he pushes up from the table, stands tall and holds out his hand as if prompting me to rise and take a bow. "First and foremost, we owe a special thanks to Charles Washington, who did his part at the University of Illinois this semester, expelling some trouble-makers from the brotherhood. Just one closure this semester, and Charles handled it brilliantly."

Brock claps like a madman, slips his fingers into his mouth and lets loose a glass-shattering whistle that the interns can likely hear in the west wing. For a moment, I actually do smile, actually do feel like I accomplished something. "Thanks," I say.

"We'll talk about the other trouble-makers in a minute," LaFaber says. "But here's the positive news." And it's a moment that I've known was coming ever since my visit to Grant Farmor's office at Purdue. "We are returning to the University of Illinois," LaFaber says, "re-colonizing, changing the culture by starting over from scratch. And listen, it won't happen in four or five years, as is typically the case, but *next semester*." Unprecedented, he says, and the next five minutes is a speech that I could have written one week ago. According to LaFaber, the alumni Housing Corporation couldn't handle an empty house—a financial drain—for five long years, and they'd opened negotiations to sell it…thus making an eventual NKE return to the Illinois campus impossible. Something had to be done. And fortunately, LaFaber says, a godsend opportunity appeared out of nowhere. An interest group. And this is where the speech veers from the predictable.

LaFaber tells us that a young man at the University of Illinois, the son of a Chicago stock broker and Nu Kappa Epsilon alumnus, heard of the chapter closure, and after speaking with his father about the way the chapter *used to be* ("before the party," LaFaber says…but does a group of men become hopeless overnight?), he rounded up twenty other young men on campus in an effort to resurrect the chapter. An interest group, ready to pick up the pieces and form a new NKE chapter and move into the house as early as next Fall.

Brock and Nick are both on the edge of their seats. For them, this is exciting. A brand-new fraternity chapter! Godsend! Saving the Illinois house!

"So what's the process?" Nick asks.

"We meet with the interest group and coordinate a full-scale *colonization*," LaFaber says, and he describes each step in detail. First, the National Headquarters sends two Educational Consultants to visit the interest group; the consultants interview the students, making sure they are "men of character"; then the consultants coordinate a leadership retreat for the interest group, and the "interest group" becomes a "colony." Finally, the Headquarters stations a single consultant with the colony for a full semester; this consultant assists the men with recruitment and groundwork, helps them to meet the requirements necessary to earn a charter by the end of Spring so that the "colony" can be recognized as a "chapter."

"One consultant stays with the group for a full semester?" Nick asks. "No traveling?" Right now he is imagining himself as the lone consultant assigned to the Illinois colony. Brock took this job to be a sheriff: to clean up the fraternity world and punish the bad guys. Nick, on the other hand, relishes the chance to work with students on a one-on-one basis, to coach, to provide guidance, to help them realize themselves in the same way that he did. "God, that's a dream opportunity," he says.

"If we invest enough time and resources at the start," LaFaber says," then this will be a mission-oriented chapter. A chapter that gets it…*forever*."

"When does this start?" Nick asks.

"Spring," LaFaber says.

"Who goes?"

"We'll talk specifics this afternoon, in our one-on-ones," LaFaber says, and his hard cheeks barely move to accommodate the folds of skin as he smiles. "But don't forget. I've got some bad news, also."

"Excellent!" Brock says and licks his lips, perhaps anticipating a dirtier, grimier discussion. He slaps the table. "Let's get down to business!"

Nick already had a pack of cigarettes out, was probably looking forward to a quick break, but now he replaces the pack in his pocket.

"We only closed one chapter so far this semester," LaFaber says, "but that doesn't mean there aren't a few more teetering on the edge." LaFaber opens a manila envelope and slips out four sheets of paper; he distributes them around the table, keeping one for himself, a solemn act with the feel of ritual. "This is the procedure for a National Review," LaFaber says, and he sits erect, holding the paper perfectly straight before him, willing us through his silence to appreciate this paper, to regard it as we might a war memo detailing a coming invasion. Even the thin scar on his forehead seems to have faded, its color smoothing from seashell white to a flesh tone indistinguishable from his skin. He straightens his sheet so that the text must be perfectly level before him, not even the slightest angle, no.

"The National Fraternity Headquarters has a number of disciplinary tools at our disposal," he continues. "We can suspend a chapter or revoke its charter, if we feel that we have enough evidence of Sacred Law infractions. Sometimes this is the best way to go, especially when the chapter poses a threat"—and LaFaber looks in my direction and nods, perhaps indicating Illinois...or maybe New Mexico State? "But we also have the power to conduct a National Review if the circumstances are more complicated. To conduct a formal investigation, formal interviews, and to make a recommendation better suited to the nuances of the situation. We can still choose to suspend or close the chapter, of course, but we can also choose to expel individual trouble-makers, or to—"

"Re-org," I say.

"Correct," LaFaber says. "We can conduct a 're-organization,' hand-picking the members we keep, and purging the rest. Working intensively with the remaining members to create a changed chapter."

"Illinois went through a re-org just a few years ago," I say. "Never recovered."

"It's a risky proposition. Expensive. And in the end, the re-orgs can create zombie chapters. We might keep ten brothers, and expel fifty. At that point, those 'keepers' might not have much motivation to continue the fraternity, and so it becomes a lurching, living death."

I scan the document, the lists of different punishments, the "questions to consider," the copy/pasted Sacred Laws giving the Director of Chapter Operations the authority to make any decisions he deems necessary, and finally I come to a section on the page that reads, "Chapters Scheduled For National Review." And, of course, I see the words "New Mexico State University: Hazing Violations," and I sink a bit in my seat, suck in my breath, cross my legs, uncross them. There are five or six other chapters listed ("Eastern Washington: Low Membership Numbers," and "Baylor University: Continued Failure to Meet GPA Minimum") before I finally see "Edison University: Hazing," and then it is no longer mere discomfort: suddenly I cannot breathe. Brock, on the opposite side of the table, stares down at his sheet with squinted eyes, fingers stroking his chin. And Nick looks at LaFaber, not at the paper, with a look that says either "I don't understand" or "I understand and am amused."

"Edison University?" Nick asks, eyes suddenly sad.

Blood filling my head, and is this a joke? Is this retribution? Karma? *Edison University?*

And it's twenty or thirty seconds before I can look back up, and LaFaber is staring at me as if he just asked a question and is now waiting for my response. He still pinches his paper, still hasn't changed his stolid expression. But no one says another word to me; no one mentions my home chapter or the circumstances that forced them onto the page.

"Each of you will be assigned a National Review," LaFaber says. "Some of the reviews can be conducted via conference call, and we simply have alumni volunteers take care of them. Eastern Washington, for instance. No need to fly all the way out there just to lecture them about low numbers. For others, we'll book plane tickets this afternoon after our one-on-one meetings, and you'll be leaving in the morning."

I stare at the glass tabletop. "C. Anthony Croke," reads the nameplate under my reflection. Who the fuck *was* this guy? Would he want this boardroom, this nameplate, this table, these National Review sheets, this casual discussion amongst graduates of eliminating the fraternity chapters to which young men belong?

"I want the trouble-makers gone," LaFaber says, "and gentlemen: it's bad news that we've got to conduct these hearings, but I couldn't be more delighted to know that you're on top of it, and that we're gonna change the culture."

Change the culture. Right.

"Come on, say it," LaFaber says. "I want to hear that you still believe. Say it."

\*\*\*

Next up: my one-on-one meeting with Walter LaFaber.

And his office is the sort of open and impersonal room befitting an ultra-successful guru at the top of his game. Dr. Vernon's office at Bowling Green glimmered like an expensive symbol of professional achievement, but it was also warm despite its opulence. LaFaber's office, on the other hand, is a cold beacon of modernity: a glass coffee table supported by a silver frame (*Fortune* and *Architectural Digest* magazines spread across the top, along with copies of *How to Win Friends and Influence People*, and *Band of Brothers*), two stiff black visitor chairs teetering on thin silver legs, a triangular throw-rug the color of arctic water, and a black wire-frame bookshelf lined with alumni magazines from dozens of schools, with long rows of psychology and leadership journals (all with the same blank white spine, a message to outsiders that there is dense text inside, that there will be no attempt to entertain the idiot masses with colors and photos). On the walls: only two metal-framed pictures, one of which is the *College Chronicle* depicting LaFaber on its front cover, and the other a photograph of LaFaber shaking hands with Dick Cheney at some gala or banquet. Otherwise, the walls are an untouched industrial gray, blinds pulled down over the single window on the far wall.

400

When I step inside and take a seat at one of the visitor's chairs, I squirm and try to get comfortable but find it impossible to do so.

"Good to see you this morning, Charles," he says, delighted by my discomfort. "Sleep well?"

"Not really. But I'm used to bad sleep."

"I always sleep well," he says, "when I know I've worked hard."

I smooth my pants, cough.

LaFaber's desk is a sweeping L-shaped, glass-topped unit, a mesh steel wall attached to the front to shield visitors from viewing his legs. For some reason, it makes me feel like I've been detained.

"Is that what we're here to talk about?" I ask. "Last night's sleep?"

"You used to be so much friendlier. Has road life hardened you?" The scar on his forehead is shining brighter now, like the red "ready" light that blinks on when the oven has pre-heated. The scar tells me that he's just getting started, that the past ten weeks on the road were nothing: today he's got plans that will put all of that to shame. He knows what I want, too, doesn't he? He knows that he's got me in his pocket. "Down to brass tacks, then" LaFaber says, staring at me with a numb but patient expression. "You want to know why Edison University made the list."

"It crossed my mind," I say.

"Nobody knows about this," LaFaber says. "Not your alumni, not your administrators. Not even Brock, and he's set to visit Edison University in the Spring. The only people that know about this are the officers of your chapter, who have been told that they'll receive a visit from a couple national representatives tomorrow."

"So what happened?"

"I got a tip about some hazing activities," he says, "and it doesn't look good."

"Hazing? There's no hazing at EU."

"Hazing," LaFaber says. "Your boys got carried away."

"What was it? Blindfolds? Was it something...silly?"

"There's a full packet I'll give you," he says and then folds his hands in his lap. "Print-outs of Facebook photos. That's the irony here, Charles. We never would've known about this had they not posted pictures on Facebook. And not just vague pictures where maybe it could be hazing, or maybe something else. It was an entire photo album dedicated to an event in a hotel room. The brothers yelling at pledges, kids doing push-ups, covered in vomit. Some really disturbing stuff. Captions, too, like 'This is how you treat a scumbag pledge.'"

"They posted it *themselves*?"

"Your boys couldn't just..." He closes his eyes and runs his hands across the glass surface of the desk. "Couldn't just *shut* their *fucking* mouths. And now this is something that we can't ignore."

I shake my head. He isn't making this up; this is not something concocted simply to punish me; already I can tell that this is real, that this is something that LaFaber didn't anticipate and didn't want, not just some manipulation of national bylaws or Excel spreadsheets in order to make a point or to get what he wants. What the hell had *Todd* done since I'd graduated?

"Charles," he says, "I need you to go to EU."

"A National Review for my own chapter?" The room is still cold, the metal shelves still icy and the world outside still dead, but suddenly I feel heat in my body. "That's against procedure, Walter. Consultants aren't supposed to go on formal visits to their own chapters, and they're especially not supposed to conduct investigations or reviews—"

"Procedure be damned," he says. "This is critical. This isn't some podunk Shippensburg or Las Cruces group. EU has been one of our best-performing chapters for more than a decade. That campus, that house...you know it by now, the places you've seen...that chapter is a dream come true. Never a problem, never a violation." He stops, takes a moment to sit up straighter and to try to steady his breathing. "I need *you* to save that chapter. Strike the fear of God into them. Whip them back into shape. We cannot"—breathes heavy, scar bright as blood—"cannot let this become an issue, not there of all places."

Here's the deal, LaFaber says: Brock and I will go to Florida, while LaFaber and Nick conduct the other reviews via telephone. LaFaber will take Nick to meet with the interest group at Illinois next week...Nick is perfect for the colonization, don't you think? So dedicated to the personal growth of the men, so empathetic. *Perfect.* Anyway, if everything looks like a "go" at Illinois, then we move forward with a full-scale colonization for Spring.

"I chose to speak with *you* first," LaFaber says, "because, well, Brock is a great consultant, very dedicated, but he's a bit headstrong. A hot-head. I admire his determination, but I need someone who understands what it means to be flexible."

"What does that mean?"

"I need you to save EU, Charles," he says. "You understand what real problems look like. The mess at Shippensburg? The party at Illinois? And hell, those guys at Delaware and Central Michigan are just asking to be shut down. I don't know how you got out of there alive. Edison University is a steady revenue stream with no expenses. You know what I'm talking about. You see it. We send a consultant to Florida once a year, as mandated by Sacred Law, and that's it: not a peep from them. Always 80 or 100 men in that chapter, sparkling facilities, and they send—you sent, when you were president—sixteen men to Regional, another fifteen to National Convention. EU is... with the bullshit we deal with? New Mexico? EU is like an A+ student in a room full of delinquents."

So *this* is who I am. *Flexible.*

It occurs to me that LaFaber has known me all along, that we three consultants were split up the way we were for a reason: Brock to the efficient chapters that just needed a kick in the ass, Nick to the well-performing schools where no one was needed, and me to the schools where...where a push-over consultant was needed, someone malleable, someone to look the other way if need be, or someone to take an action that values and good sense would prevent another man from taking. I was needed in places where the consultant could be controlled.

And that's why I'm going to Edison University. To look the other way. To give tips on how to hide the hazing, perhaps? With Brock to "strike the fear of God into their hearts," but Charles Washington to make the final recommendation to the National Headquarters—something light and harmless to ensure the future prosperity of a profitable chapter.

"Okay," I say. "I'll do whatever you need."

And LaFaber leans back and cracks his knuckles. Once again, he's gotten exactly what he wanted. Once again, he's seen into the very souls of the people around him, has figured them out so completely that—

"But I need something from you, Walter. Two things, if I'm going to do this."

"You need something from me?" Walter asks. His hands were behind his head in triumph, but now they're sinking back to the desk surface. The scar was bright, but now it's gone a chilly white, a smear of hardened glue across his forehead. "All right," he says. "What can I do for you, Charles?"

"First," I say, "I want you to call off the New Mexico State review."

"That's crazy," he says. Shakes his head, laughs. "The hazing is rampant, and it's palpable. You wrote it in the reports, wrote it yourself. I could have shut that chapter down based solely on your reports. But the diversity angle…a review is going to happen."

"No, it won't," I say.

Part of me wants to stop talking, to once again nod and give up and take direction: just delete the photos from my investigation, or write the fabricated report, or—hell—just cave under the chop-chop-chop noise of Helicopter Parents circling above. But not now. Not anymore. It terrifies me to speak this way, but I tell LaFaber: "This is what you're going to do with New Mexico State. You're going to give them a semester of probation. Let me work with them. Or Brock, or Nick. They're good kids, and they can change. But that chapter's going nowhere, and that's non-negotiable."

LaFaber smiles, snorts. "Or?"

"Or I call the Greek Advisor, call the campus newspaper, tell them that you made me falsify the report."

"A campus newspaper? Please."

"This isn't 1998," I say. "Medium doesn't—"

"You're lucky I don't terminate you right here."

"Medium doesn't matter," I finish. "Campus newspaper, blog, whatever. Story goes viral overnight."

"Weak threat," he says. "You need to think long and hard about what you say next."

"Viral. We'll see how quickly there's a 'Save New Mexico State' Facebook group," I say, "how long it takes to have a hundred thousand members. How long before the word 'racist' gets thrown out, regardless of whether you take that extra step and conduct a token review before closing them. How long it takes the collective membership of the national fraternity to align against you. That's the thing about viral stories, Walter. At some point, outrage overtakes truth."

LaFaber breathing heavy. Perhaps for the first time considering my position.

"You talk to me about Google search results?" I ask. "Whenever someone searches 'Walter LaFaber,' this is the first thing they'll find from now on."

"Fine," he says. Shrugs. "Fine. Fine, fine, fine. You can have your New Mexico."

"New Mexico *State*."

"Whatever. But they'll be *your* problem."

"The other thing," I say. "I want the Illinois expansion."

"Charles," he says and laughs. It's hoarse and dry, sharp as a machete. "A colonization requires a lot of resources, financial and staff. It takes almost a full semester, plenty of blood, sweat, and tears. The University of Illinois is *big* for this fraternity, and Nick is going to be willing to work for sixteen weeks without sleeping."

"You can make it work, I'm sure."

"But why *would* I, Charles? To avoid another of your threats?" The machete laugh again, and now he's standing, glaring at me dismissively with fingertips pressed into the desktop. Shit. He's getting his groove back. It was only a matter of time: Walter LaFaber, larger than the stage on which he walks. "It wouldn't be too tough for me to fire you right now," he says, "to paint you as some rogue Frat Star consultant. Very easy, in fact. And if I do that, every story you tell will be tainted: sour grapes from the fired employee."

I smooth my pants. "This isn't a big request."

"Charles," he says. "Charles."

"I want to do the right thing, Walter. This expansion would let me make up for—"

And somehow, in the span of a heartbeat, he's won.

"Even if I wanted to put you on that expansion," LaFaber says, "there's so much that would need to be rearranged." Sighs, considers me from the corner of his squinted eye, looks ready to start taking back every inch he'd conceded...

"I've got their charter," I say suddenly.

"Their what?"

"From 1921," I say.

"The Illinois charter?" Eyes wide open.

"The Illinois charter."

"Well," LaFaber says and now his fingers are wrapped through the blinds, squeezing. "Well shit, Charles. Go get it. What...why didn't you *tell* anyone? Where is it?"

"I snuck into the house the next morning." I smooth my pants again, wonder if I even need to say anything else. "Maybe I wanted to save something," I say, "because everything else I'd done was so pointless."

"Where *is* it?"

But now I'm standing up, too, and I'm walking to LaFaber, walking behind his desk and he's twice my size but I don't care. "I have it," I say. "You put me on Illinois, and you get this artifact back. One of the original charters from the North? That's priceless."

"Well. It's not worth *that* much."

"It's signed by our founders. You told us during training: there's only three or four *original* charters left from the fraternity's first two decades."

LaFaber shakes his head, tries to conjure a smile and a laugh.

"I get New Mexico State, and I get the expansion," I say, and I point in his face, "and you get EU, safe and sound, your little ATM machine. And when the expansion is over, you get the charter back."

He hasn't moved. My finger is in his face, and he hasn't moved. "I had other plans for you in the Spring, Charles. Big plans. I could've made you into the next Walter LaFaber."

"Not anymore. *Illinois*," I say.

He waves away my finger as if it hasn't bothered him. "You give me what I want at EU, Charles, you won't have to worry about a thing. You'll be lead consultant on the Illinois colonization. You and Nick will work together, but you're the lead." He holds out his hand for me to shake, and I do, and then he leans over his keyboard and types a short message and says, "Go visit Janice's office. She's booking your flight, and it leaves in the morning."

"All right," I say.

"Finish up here, and get packing."

And I smile, but for some reason the smile hurts my face.

*

Much of the remaining Thursday afternoon is spent completing reports that various staff members have dropped off at our desks, responding to hundreds of emails from alumni, volunteers, and university administrators who have all been notified (in a mass email from LaFaber) that we are off the road, in the office, and available for their every need. Outside, the sky grows dark with clouds, then turns to a soft white during the sun's last hours above the horizon. Online weather reports confirm what everyone in the office, through our windows, can see developing: Halloween snow flurries. Unexpected, some of the reports and forecasts say, but not unusual. A cold front drifting in from Canada. My first snow ever: and I picture white snow blanketing the ground like puffy pillows. A winter wonderland. Candy canes.

Before he leaves the office, LaFaber stops by the cluttered west wing of the Headquarters to say goodbye to us all. He stands a fair distance from our cubicles, from the mess that overflows from the hallway and spills into our work spaces, as though we created all of this disorder and he refuses to become entangled within it; he holds his coat over one shoulder, his pose more akin to a model than an office executive. "Save them," LaFaber says to me. "Save your chapter, Charles. This is win-win."

405

When Nick, Brock, and I walk back across the courtyard to the Lodge after business hours, the wind is piercing—my ears, my entire head, hurts after only a couple seconds outside—but the snow is light, melts as soon as it touches the ground. All is cold and wet on our final night in Indianapolis. What I thought would be a pristine white wonderland is instead a sleeting gray dusk.

# National Review
CHAPTER TWENTY-EIGHT.

But then, just like that, snap my fingers and shut my suitcase and—*whoosh*—I'm back in Florida in my Nu Kappa Epsilon polo, shivering when I leave Indy but sweating when I land. Rental car with Brock, and we check into an off-exit hotel, grab some lunch at a local Panera, then head out to campus, world green and bright around us as we pull onto Greek Row, but the NKE chapter house looming dark and glowering like some still-shot from *Amityville Horror* or *Poltergeist*.

Through the front doors and the bodies part around us like bystanders at a crime scene. Here in the house, there are faces that feel familiar, like Facebook friends you can't remember adding and whose status updates you've learned to ignore. Their names could be James or Joe or Jason, and as Brock and I walk swiftly from the foyer to the living room to the chapter library, I can hear them whispering as we pass. "Old president," someone tells a new member. "Gonna help us out," someone else says. "*Sweet*," and a high-five, but a high-five like they're watching me on TV, like I'm some field-goal kicker trotted onto the field and they could care less about the man beneath the helmet.

The older brothers—the ones who would say hello and ask how the road's been—aren't here. Not hanging out on the lawn furniture in the living room, not watching TV, not reading or studying. Maybe they were told not to come. Maybe they're avoiding me. Maybe the chapter has changed so completely in six months that they no longer want to be part of it.

I think of all those declarations I made, in public and in my own head, how *Fraternity is Family!*, but this house—a place I lived for four years—is as cold to me as the Headquarters Lodge. They're glad to see that it's Charles Washington walking through the door instead of some other consultant they've never met, but really I'm regarded no differently here than I was at Pitt, or Ship, or Illinois, the Nationals scab to wait out, something not of the body.

*

The eight officers of the Executive Board are waiting for us in the chapter library, but they think that an arrangement has been struck, that Charles is here to save the day. Maybe LaFaber has consulted with the alumni already, and the alumni have called the officers to ease the anxiety of the National Review. These guys are all smiles, ready for a wrist-slap and a "bad dog" and then a "Well, talk to you later! Keep on keepin' on!" They understand, in a way that I never did, how perfect Edison University is, how perfect and lucrative and important their individual fraternity chapter to the National Headquarters. University of Florida in the early '70s, defended by the National Fraternity despite a hazing activity that nearly resulted in a dozen dead 18-year-olds. After the fire was over, those guys had to know they were invincible, right? *What would it take to shut them down?* Well. These guys know it, too.

But here's something they don't know: right behind me, a wrecking ball is about to swing through the doors.

Todd Hampton is seated at the far end of the boardroom table, playing with his cell phone, saying "Oh hey, Charles," but not looking up at me, and the next thing he knows he's dropping the phone and yelping like a high school girl at a horror movie because Brock plows through the room and into his face and says, "You the chapter president?"

"Um, yes," Todd says and half-stands, but falls back into his seat.

Brock is hovering over him. Brock is 250 pounds of *don't-fuck-with-me.* Todd raises his hand meekly.

"Don't wanna shake your hand," Brock says. "Put it away. I wanna know what I'm dealing with here."

Todd tugs at his collar. His phone is on the floor now, an unfinished text message on a screen whose brightness is slowly fading to black.

The seven other officers are speechless, faces gone ashen. They're sophomores, mostly, Todd one of only two or three juniors elected to the Executive Board. These were men who joined while I was already an officer, whose short NKE existence was lived in my shadow. During elections last Spring, there was nothing out-of-the-ordinary about them, no red flags that this group of eager young Nikes was plotting some dramatic introduction of hard-core hazing practices. For all I knew, they were just like me during my own freshman year, decent kids with all the promise in the world. Looking from face to face, though, they seem even younger than I expected, younger than anyone should expect when using words like "elimination" and "suspension" and "expulsion." Across the country, I've seen what seasoned frat stars look like, and at worst, these are kids still trying to play the part. Perhaps they're shocked at Brock's entrance, rolling through here with the weight and physical presence of a Marvel superhero, or perhaps they're just surprised to see that they aren't in a favored and coddled position, that my presence won't save them. Were they expecting fist-bumps? Twenty minutes of bull-shitting about the EU football season before we got down to business?

"Here's what's gonna happen," Brock says. "We're gonna meet with you one at a time. We're gonna get the full story, damn it, and then we're gonna see what's to be done about it." He's standing with his weight against the table now, trying to look each man in the eyes as he talks...but by the time he gets halfway around the table, he notices that someone has brought a Super Big Gulp into the room, and it's sitting in a wet ring on the glossy surface of the boardroom table. A Super Fucking *Big Gulp?* In a *National Review?* Brock grabs it—no one reaching to stop him—and sighs heavily like he's fucking told these kids a thousand times not to bring drinks in here...told them! And then he stomps across the room and slams it into the trashcan, the sound of its impact like a glass-shattering car crash. "Way we see it at HQ, you guys could be *closed* by tonight if we don't hear what we want."

Brock is a pitbull let off the leash, and I'm doing nothing to rein him in.

"Charles," Todd says softly, "Charles, is this true?"

"You don't believe Brock?" I ask. I look across the room, where Brock still stands over the trash can, winded-looking, hands on his hips like it's taking every ounce of energy he has to prevent real violence from erupting.

"No, it's just...*closure?*"

"Are you calling Brock a liar?" I ask.

"Charles..."

"Who the fuck do you think you are?" I ask, and he's half-standing again and this time it's my turn to rush over to him but unlike Brock, I shove him back into his seat and his rolling chair skids backward and collides with the bookshelf, a stack of alumni directories spilling over and crumbling onto the floor. "Calling a *consultant* a *liar?*" I say.

"Geez, Charles—" He's holding his elbow, but he isn't hurt. He's fine.

"We meet with *you* last, Todd," I say. "You better hope your brothers don't turn on you."

And we send them all out, everyone except the Chapter Secretary, lowest on the totem pole. They shuffle to the door with backwards glances at me, like kids hoping they can get away before their father decides he wants to spank them. Brock puts his arm around my neck, whispers into my ear, "I don't think we're, uh...I don't think we're supposed to *touch* them, right, Charles?"

I nod. "Probably not. But whatever."

Brock backs away, and suddenly he doesn't look so terrifying anymore. He stares at his own hand, in fact, the condensation from the Super Big Gulp cup still on his fingertips...he's wondering if this was too much, the spiking of the drink. He doesn't know *too much.*

"Secretary," I say and I walk to where he's seated and grip the armrest of his chair.

He's a scrawny class-clown-type nicknamed "Taint." And hell if I know how the nickname came about...it's something silly and endearing to his other 19-year-old friends, no doubt, but it doesn't help him in his National Review. Tell us about the night in question, *Taint*, I say. Leave something out, or lie to us, *Taint*, and you're the first to go. We take your pin, *Taint*, and we strike your name from the records of our brotherhood. *Taint.* Anyone with a nickname of *Taint* can't be trustworthy. Why should we trust you, *Taint?* Your brothers aren't going to save you. Stop looking at the door, *Taint.* Hey. Look at me. You're accountable for your own actions, you know that, *Taint?* We could expel you from Nu Kappa Epsilon. Hell, we could turn you in to the Campus Conduct Board, have you expelled from the university. What do you think about that, *Taint?*

He's damn-near crying by the time I'm done yelling in his face. He's the youngest of the officers, was a pledge just nine months ago; whatever he thinks and whatever he knows, he's still years away from truly understanding the machinery of the National Fraternity.

"I wasn't *there!*" he says at one point, breaking down. "I had no idea they were going to do that!"

"Do what, Taint?" I ask, and slam an alumni directory onto the table so hard that the glass gives an anguished cry, a whisper from cracking. Brock has gone rigid beside me, seems afraid to move, afraid to say a word. Who is this Charles Washington, he's wondering. What really happened at Illinois? For that matter, what really happened at Grand Valley College, at New Mexico State, at Delaware, at Pittsburgh? Has he snapped? Is this what it looks like when someone *snaps?* For God's sake, *I* was supposed to be bad cop. Brock is a pile of fat and muscle, but in this moment he's afraid of me: in the Lodge and at Headquarters, Charles is the boy concerned with ironing his khakis and drafting goal sheets, but there's something dark inside of this man, isn't there? An anger. A rage that's suddenly exploding like a geyser here in the library. This guy's like one of those *Alien* movie creatures, acid for blood, a whole other face waiting to scream out from the face he shows the world.

And Brock, if this is all you're thinking, you don't know the half of it.

"Get the fuck out of here, *Taint*," I say. "Send in the Treasurer."

And one after the next, we call them into the room. There is no chair in the center of the room for them to stand on, no Brother Wall and no Pledge Clump, but still the officers of my old chapter tremble like pledges at an Etiquette Dinner. I am Sam Anderson suddenly, slapping the table and yelling, "I didn't *ask* that. Don't you fucking get *clever* on me!"

"I'm not trying to be clever, Charles!"

"Look at this, Brock," I say. "A thousand comedians out of work, and this joker's got the nerve to try to be funny."

"Ha ha!" I say during the next interview. "We've got another crier!"

One after the next, the full story assembled bit by bit, new details pulled from each new officer: the event was called "237," and really, it's been going on at EU for at least five years. I've heard of it. As President, I knew that there was something called "237," that each year a small crew of Big Brothers took their brand-new Little Brothers to a hotel room at a ghastly place called Seaside Inn. The "No-Tell Motel," we called it. A place meant to inspire fear, water stains on every ceiling and cracks in every window, bodies hunched over curbs out in the parking lot twenty-four hours a day. 237: it was the room number from *The Shining*.

But the event was supposed to be a bonding experience. Big Brothers and Little Brothers spending the full night together, downing a case of the nastiest, scariest beer on the market: Natty Light or Milwaukee's Best, one of those terrible value beers so disgusting it had earned a frightening nickname, "The Beast," or "The Liver Killer" or whatever. Just eight total men, that first year. Eight the next, as the former Little Brothers now became Big Brothers to a new group of pledges. I wasn't part of it when I was a pledge, and so—as a sophomore, when I had a Little Brother—he wasn't part of it, either. No one talked much about 237; there wasn't really much to share, as far as I knew. Just a bunch of bros hanging out, drinking more than they should, and watching bad horror flicks all night long: that was the other thing: they would watch bizarre '70s horror movies, Dario Argento, maybe some '80s slasher flicks, *Sorority House Massacre* and *Peeping Tom*, and they'd spend the night performing a drunk version of *Mystery Science Theater*. Stupid, but harmless.

But in the fraternity world, there's something called the Law of Threes. Whatever you start doing in your chapter, it will be three times worse, three years later. Start an annual party with a single keg, and three years later the kegs will be stacked and there will be two DJs and three bands and a *Girls Gone Wild* camera crew. And I learn here in my old house that the Law of Threes has proved true once again.

I wasn't paying attention, I guess, when the number of participants in 237 went from eight to ten to twelve to—this Fall, while I traveled—the entire pledge class, stuck in a single hotel room. Twenty-five men. And how was I supposed to know? I never called Todd Hampton to see how he was doing; no one called *me*, either; this entire Executive Board felt like a group of cousins I hadn't seen grow up, personalities etched without my influence…

The context sharpens with each new officer Brock and I interview.

A couple semesters ago, the event had transformed from "brother-pledge bonding" to full-fledged hazing. Big Brothers forcing Little Brothers to chug. Big Brothers quizzing Little Brothers on fraternity history, threatening push-ups for incorrect answers. "C. Anthony Croke!" they'd scream at the pledges. "Get the names right! Your founders would be ashamed!"

Still small, still hush-hush while I was president, but meanwhile there'd been rumblings rippling through the chapter. "Charles has made us a bunch of bitches," Todd Hampton had complained. "Come on. Not allowed to fuck with the pledges, not even a little bit? He's more concerned with some stupid *Family Weekend* bullshit than he is with running this chapter the way it needs to be run. More concerned with awards packets. Things need to change."

He'd been joined by a chorus of malcontents, a song I was too busy to hear. "The pledges don't respect us, that's the problem." "They fucking walk all over us!" "Pledge looked at me funny." "Pledges need to be taught some fucking *respect*." "Goddamn inmates running the asylum, thanks to Charles, the Pledge Lover." Pledge Lover? I'd been the only thing protecting the 18-year-old new members from boot camp and near-torture? As far as I knew, we'd all agreed that hazing was pointless; as far as I knew, we all wanted a brotherhood, we all cared about one another. But I was some relic, the last of an old guard dying off to graduation?

This Fall, 237 was no longer some "aw shucks, we're just drinkin' a few beers and gettin' to know one another" type of evening. Hell, there *were* no brothers in the hotel room. Just the 25 pledges stuffed inside, A/C turned off, curtains shut…and oh, such a perfect setting, too…you could do whatever you wanted to these little fuck-tards…the Seaside Inn was an establishment so shady that it wouldn't mind all-night scream-fests in the rooms, or stains on the sheets, vomit on the carpet…hell, they barely cleaned, so could they even prove which occupant had done it, and when? Take a blacklight to the room and you'd find come-spatter from the Carter administration.

The Law of Threes.

237 was now a night in which 25 men were imprisoned in a stuffy hotel room, white t-shirts and jeans the dress code, and in the center of the room a single Gator-Ade cooler filled with the most unimaginable filth you could imagine. Everclear mixed with OJ topped with diced tomatoes, heaps of garlic, oysters, Natty Light, a slop-bucket that could probably kill cockroaches. Our New Member Educator, Danny Boller, organized the event with the promise to his chapter brothers that *we will teach them respect for their elders*. Locked the door, told the pledges, "You got three hours to finish that jug. Get started, bitches."

And of course there was no way it would be finished. No way. The jug was hell itself.

So, at 2:37 AM, a gang of older brothers poured into the room, Todd and Danny and fifteen others, and they said, "You didn't finish your jug? Oh shit. This is the dedication you show? You want us to initiate you into our fraternity? *Ooooooh*, shit."

And then there were push-ups, and air-chairs, and human pyramids, and jumping jacks till there was vomit across the walls, and the room was a sauna of sweat and slop and screaming, a scene worse than any American detention camp overseas, terror stateside, terror because these little shit-bags couldn't just learn some simple motherfucking respect for the fraternity.

And you know what? The pledges hadn't even snitched. Nope, not the now-terrified EU freshmen who could probably still taste the hell that they'd tried to drink. It wasn't even the hotel. They were fine with fifty men in a room, even when the *prostitutes* were calling the front desk to report noise complaints. The only reason they'd been caught was because Danny Boller had posted a "237 – Best Night Ever" photo album to Facebook, bragging to the world about how they'd abused their pledges. As if Facebook was still some secret message board shared between a couple dozen students on a single dormitory floor, as if you couldn't read a status update from Barack Obama and Amazon.com and the city of Tampa, back to back to back, just before you stumbled upon the album of hazing photos.

"This is bad," Brock says before our final interview, Todd Hampton. "Charles, brother, I'm sorry."

"Sorry for what?"

"For what happened to your chapter, brother."

"No apologies necessary," I say, filling in small boxes solid-black on the official form that I was supposed to be using to take notes during their interview responses. There are other doodles, too. One looks like a spike, another like a burning house.

"You're not upset?"

"I am," I say. That my own fraternity could become something like this in less time than it took to complete a single three-credit-hour course at Edison University. That this had been everything in my life, my home and my family and my future, that I'd felt I knew it so entirely and yet behind the doors there was this darkness, the hate and malevolence of the Overlook Hotel's Room 237 itself surging through my house and my brothers. Upset? I am. But: "But it isn't the most surprising thing I've learned this semester," I tell Brock.

"What do we do?" he asks.

"You're asking *me*?"

"Shit, Charles. You got the experience. You *closed* a chapter. I follow your lead."

"You want me to close this chapter? You want me to make that call?"

"No, I just…" He hangs his head. "Is this *fixable*? Charles, I only know how to bust heads, buddy. I'm a big dumb animal." He slaps the bookshelf and another stack of old hard-back volumes tumbles. "I don't know…"

I consider the moves that I'm supposed to make, the stern talking-to that I'm supposed to give Todd Hampton just before I tell him that, well, *this time* we're not going to take action. You're off the hook. But, oh boy, if there's a next time?

I consider what LaFaber wants me to do. Put the fear of God into them, or whatever, and then just let them go about their business? Walk away, fly back to Indianapolis, knowing that they're no longer amateur frat stars but instead hardened Headquarters Haters ("Nationals doesn't *get* what we're *doing* here!"), having learned only that they were idiots to post the pictures, now determined to find more clever ways to hide what they're doing…and if they're spending so much time hiding it, well shit, they'd better make it worth it. Why stop with one event? Law of Threes. Make 237 into a weekend-long affair.

I consider all of this, and again I feel like screaming, like punching the wall. Like I want to bring Todd Hampton into this room and make him my piñata for every fucking thing I've learned this semester, for my every failure, for my every frustration. But—

Charles…knows this will never end. Never the right thing, always a fuck-up waiting to happen.

Charles…just remember, buddy, it's all for the greater good! Illinois! Grad school! You can do it, buddy! Change the culture! Change the institution!

Charles…wants to punch the fucking wall.

Charles…wants to break every bone in his hand.

Charles…wants to punch the wall so fucking hard that his wrist breaks, too, that every bone in his arm is pulverized, ground to chalk, that his insides are liquefied and he's a puddle on the floor and better yet: he's blank space, and he can—please, can he?—start over, just motherfucking *start over from scratch*? Clean slate. A *new* Charles Washington, the man he's wanted to be all this time, without this fucking footprint following him, *please*, can we just…

Charles Washington…will do what he's always done, won't he?

Charles Washington…remembers an old t-shirt from National

Convention, back in 2006. On the front, "If you do what you've always done, you'll get what you've always gotten." On the back, "Nu Kappa Epsilon: Re-Defining Fraternity, Re-Defining Excellence."

Charles is…

Charles is…?

"I know exactly what to do," I tell Brock.

"Okay, good." He slaps my back. "What are we doing?"

"Grab Todd. Bring him in, and follow my lead."

Brock nods, lumbers to the door and tugs Todd into the room.

"Sit," Brock says, and Todd tumbles into the chair like a man about to be executed.

"This is what's happening," I say. "You're going to turn in your pin."

Todd holds up his palms, makes a half-smile/ half-shocked face. He thinks I'm joking. "Oooo-kay," he says and laughs. "Well, um. What's really—"

"You're finished," I say. "I'm serious. No discussion. You, every one of your officers, all finished. We'll collect the pins and your membership placards before we leave, along with the pins of every brother involved in 237. And we know who was there. The photos are on Facebook. You tagged 'em. You made my job easy."

"You can't do that!" he screams. "That's half the chapter!" He looks to Brock, like the pitbull is going to save him, but Brock is following my lead. Brock might never have done anything like this, but you know what? He likes it, and he's not going to give a fucking inch.

"Eyes on Charles," Brock says. "He's talking to you."

"Your other option," I say, "is to surrender the charter. Your choice. But if you surrender the charter, remember that this university co-owns these houses, and there's a waiting list a mile long for new fraternities here at EU. Lose the charter, we lose the house. And do you want to go down as the man who *killed* Nu Kappa Epsilon at Edison University? Call me Pledge Lover all you want, Hampton, but do you want *that* to be your legacy?"

"Charles," he says. "There's got to be some other—"

"Choice is yours, Todd. Turn in your pins and placards, and shit, we'll even offer you this deal: instead of marking you as 'expelled,' we can make you 'alumni' in our national database. Ten years from now, no one will know the difference."

"Alumni?"

"That's right," I say. "Your time as an undergraduate member of the fraternity is done. You aren't worthy of it. You'll clear out of the house. You'll never attend another social event, another chapter meeting. Never talk to another pledge, never participate in another initiation. Nothing. And if you push it and choose to appeal before National Council, I'll make sure that they revoke your charter, your brotherhood pins, erase any trace that you were *ever* a member…You'll be disowned, Todd. A bigger disgrace than you could ever imagine."

And just minutes later, Brock is walking Todd from bedroom to bedroom to collect the brotherhood pins for all 33 members whose names we've gathered, Todd explaining—through tears—that this is their only option. "I'm gonna fucking *appeal*!" I hear from upstairs more than once, but there is no chance of that. Really, we don't even need the pins or the membership placards in order to take action; I just *wanted* them, wanted to hand them over to Headquarters so there would be no chance of turning back.

And I know this isn't what LaFaber wanted, but you know what? EU is still alive, still kicking, and once the reports are written, LaFaber won't be able to complain. Maybe this kills my shot at the Illinois expansion, at grad school, and maybe one good action doesn't make up for all the wrong that I've done—shit, maybe it was even wrong to demand that New Mexico State be left alone, maybe it was selfish and dangerous, maybe this one good decision is canceled out because I defended another group of hazers—but I also know that right now, I only have control over this moment, and *one good action* is a hell of a lot better than making *one more mistake*.

Whatever happens, I'll figure it out.

Whatever happens, I know that I'm not willing to crumble ever again.

While Brock and Todd are upstairs gathering pins, I'm on the phone with the pledges, one after the next, to tell them that this is their fraternity now. It's theirs, and they can make of it what they will. There's no more dead weight, I tell them, no more trouble-makers. This is it, I tell them. Your chance to change the culture.

*

Our flight leaves the next morning, but there's one more place I've got to go before I can leave town. I leave Brock at the hotel to finish the final paperwork and catalogue the pins and placards he's collected, leave him to draft the formal memo to the alumni which will instruct them to evict the punished brothers. "I'll be back," I tell him, "but I have to…"

"I know," he says. "You want to see your girl, don't you?"

"Jenn," I say.

I know it's over, know that the things I've done have made it impossible for the two of us to ever have the life I'd imagined. But I can't leave things the way they were. I need to see her, convince her that the good things she saw in the old Charles Washington do still exist. That I'm capable not just of mean disappointment and injury, but also of…something better.

Jenn doesn't know I'm coming for her, but Facebook has made it impossible to hide. "Bored at the KD house," she wrote ten minutes ago as her status update, and so that's where I go.

Park, ring the doorbell, and a girl named Elizabeth Safron answers the door, recognizes me, puts hand to mouth. "Oh my God, *Charles*." She's wearing a bright orange t-shirt with a black screen-printed jack-o-lantern face smiling wide and gap-toothed, the shirt three sizes too large and sweeping down over her black leggings like it's a skirt. "What are you *doing* here?"

"Hoping Jenn was home," I say.

"Well," Elizabeth says. She closes her eyes, likely searching her mind for an alibi, somewhere Jenn can be instead of right here, but she wasn't prepared for this.

"Can I come in?" I peek my head through the doorway. There are plastic pumpkins lining the hallway, each stuffed with Lemonheads and snack-sized Snickers, each pumpkin painted with the letters of a different fraternity. Beyond the hallway is the living room, and from this angle it's all hair spilled across couch cushions, legs on arm rests, flashes of denim and cardigan.

"Um. Sure," Elizabeth says, but I'm already inside, not even waiting for her to walk me to the living room and the couches and the TV and the girls.

I know this house almost as well as my own, remember when the wallpaper was stripped away and the walls were re-painted lavender, remember when the plantation shutters were installed in the new cafeteria. I remember each couch, the way they feel when you're the only man on them surrounded by a dozen sorority girls. I remember evenings after date nights, watching *Eight-Legged Freaks* or *Scream 3*, and I remember the drunk girls who would walk into the house late-night, coming home from the bar with boys they didn't know, douche-bags who'd plop onto the couches and make comments like, "This is what a sorority house looks like?" and "What's it gonna take to get some three-some action, eh?", the other girls on the couches going nervous until I said, "He tries to get past the stairwell, I'll tackle him," and then the relief. Charles to keep us safe. Charles the good boyfriend. Charles the Protector. I remember the boxes of Cap'n Crunch that seemed to appear magically whenever the girls sat down and turned on the TV, conjured from hiding spots behind the couches, Goldfish too, and Oreos, the accompanying "I'm such a fat-ass" remarks while girls stuffed face with Crunch bars. Other comments, too: "Ahh, these panties give me such a freakin' wedgie!" and "Oh my God, Dana is passed out naked on her bed upstairs! Can someone go wake her up or something?" Days when they forgot a boy was present, days when I was transplanted into the sorority world, followed by nights when Jenn faced the same at the NKE house: dozens of dudes watching Monday Night Football and throwing Doritos at one another and farting and wrestling one another in the grass of the backyard, comments like "I'm *soooo* gonna fuck that Ashley girl. Oh, shit. Forgot you were sitting there, Jenn."

The living room—the long sweeping couches, the HDTV mounted to the wall but still surrounded by a massive and unnecessary espresso-colored entertainment center, shelves and cabinets lined with stuffed animals and framed photos. This feels more like home than anywhere I've been in the last six months.

When I turn the corner and enter the frame, there are only three girls seated before me, and all three gasp.

"Charles," Jenn says. She might be the last to see me, to register that it *is* me, as she was looking down at her cell phone and typing out a text. She has an iPhone now, and I remember some September conversation when she told me she was going to the Apple Store, but this is the first that the unseen moments of time away have connected with the visible, the here, the unexpected now. Her hair is shorter, so light that it's damn-near platinum, bangs falling over her black headband and slashing down her forehead like icicles. "What...what are you *doing* here?"

"In town for the day," I say.

"Yeah, but..." And she looks at the clock on the wall, as if it contains the answers she's struggling for. In her mind, she is flipping the pages of a calendar, finding the holidays. "Thanksgiving is not even until...why *now*?"

"Not glad to see me?" I force a sheepish shrug, my posture and face suddenly like the Monopoly Man when forced to pay his poor tax.

"Charles, I..." She's wearing an old Eddie Money t-shirt and a pair of black yoga pants; the hair has changed, the purse has changed, but maybe there's more *same* here than I thought.

The other girls are still staring with the same faces they'd have if someone came into the house and told them that Florida had split from the continent and was now drifting on a collision course with Cuba. Ten minutes before, they were thinking of Halloween parties. Spread out on the empty cushions are the bits and pieces of half-costumes, a tall pair of clear heels, a Hooters shirt, a pair of bunny ears. Ten minutes before, they were timing the exact moment they'd need to leave the living room and head upstairs to start getting ready for the night's parties, cramming their tight bodies into fishnets and long white gloves and three inches of glittery top or bottom. And then: Charles Washington appeared.

"Maybe we should get out of here," Jenn says. "Talk somewhere else."

"I've got a car in the parking lot," I say. "I'll probably get a ticket if I don't move, so..."

The Lindsay Lohan girl—Edwin's girl from the Senior Send-Off—is sitting on the other couch, wearing a set of vampire teeth in her mouth. She spits them out into her hand. "Don't go with him, Jenn," she says. "Nikes are all assholes. Your boy"—and she's pointing at me, now, spit-strands from fingers to still-clutched vampire teeth—"your boy *Edwin* never calls me back."

"Edwin," I repeat.

"Edwin," she says caustically. "Your best friend."

"Well, he never calls *me* back, either," I say. "So you won't get any arguments from me. Not about Edwin, not about any of those assholes."

She sits back, makes a "harrumph" noise, and stuffs the teeth back into her mouth.

"Jenn?" I ask. "Wanna go?"

Jenn looks at her sorority sisters, unseen thought clouds bubbling throughout the room. It's a moment that no one saw coming, and there's something to be said of such surprises in life. No one can form any other defense to stop Jenn from leaving—they never thought they would need to, that I would ever be back, perhaps thinking that I'd actually taken some *real* job in Indianapolis and I lived there and had a real apartment and did real adult things—and so Jenn's moving from couch to hallway to door to front porch to parking lot to passenger seat of my car, and I am cranking the A/C and we are leaving her sorority house.

And then we're in the car together, and I'm driving us out of the Kappa Delta parking lot and down Greek Row.

"What are you doing here?" This might be the first time I've seen her so emotionless, holding her purse in her lap no different than if she were a woman riding the subway by herself and trying to avoid human contact.

"It's a National Review," I say.

"Is that like—did the Nikes do something wrong?"

"Hazing," I say. "You'll hear about it. We're kicking a bunch of guys out."

"Wait. They sent you back here to kick out your *own* brothers?"

"Wouldn't be my first major purge as a Fun Nazi."

"A what?"

"Never mind."

Outside, Halloween has begun. Kappa Sigmas are walking Greek Row in the president masks from *Point Break*, waving like political candidates at intersections and shouting nonsense at passing cars: "Death or taxes!" and "Abort my bill!" and "Amend your own asshole!" Down the street, someone is dressed as a ghost in front of the NKE house, just a bed sheet with eyeholes and arm-holes, and he is standing all alone, an eerie image through my rearview mirror as we roll to the stop sign. I expect him to move, wait a few extra seconds at the stop sign before the driver behind me grows impatient and mouths "*Come on!*", and then we're going again.

"Where are we going?" Jenn asks. She holds up her hands as if our stillborn conversation has already exhausted her. "Where are you driving me?"

On the rental car's radio, the afternoon DJ's relaying some news update about McCain, the election just days away now. Then the DJ laughs and the music takes over, "Misery Business" by Paramore. Maybe there was an election joke tying into the song, who knows?

"I don't know where I'm driving, Jenn," I tell her.

"Okaaaay," she says in the sorority-girl voice that I can't stand. "Well, can we go…I don't know…*somewhere?*"

"I can't stop at my own chapter house," I say. "They hate my guts now."

"Well, we can't just keep driving to, like, nowhere."

We roll to the final stop sign at the west end of campus. Behind us are the parking garages, the faculty office buildings, the classrooms, the campus quad, the dorms, the fraternity and sorority houses. Ahead is a long avenue lined with pine trees, medianed by marigolds, the beautiful boulevard by which you enter or exit campus, the buffer zone between "real world" and "college world." In a quarter-mile, the trees disappear and the commercial glut of Mid-Sized American City takes over: long plazas of textbook stores and liquor stores and coffee shops, edge-of-university Applebee's and Chili's, a half-mile away you can go from Best Buy to PetSmart to Kohls all in an afternoon but you need to drive from parking lot to parking lot in order to do so.

"I want to talk, Jenn. And if I stop somewhere, you'll get away."

"That's creepy, Charles."

"No, I didn't mean it like that. I just…there's so much I want to talk about, and I really"—how does one say it, that he is only comfortable in a moving vehicle? That he has forgotten what it means to sit somewhere, to open up in conversation, to be honest about who he is? How does one say that his home is now *couches* and *car seats*, his friends only memories? "I don't want it to end, Jenn," I say.

"What do you mean?" she asks. "It's already over."

"If I keep driving, I don't have to think about that. We can just talk. It can be…I don't know. Like it was."

"Oh, for God's sake, you're about to cry."

"I'm not," I say. "I'm not."

We pull onto University, and all is silent in the car. It's November in Florida, but there are only occasional dead leaves on the ground, nothing that would constitute "foliage" in the Northern sense of the word. The trees along University are still full-canopied, the road heavily shadowed here in the last gasps of daylight.

"What do you want to talk about, Charles?" she asks. "I'm starting to feel like I'm Kim and you're Eminem."

I turn from University to Central, the short "campus town" district jam-packed with the bars and restaurants that carried me through my four years at EU. Hem-Haws, Sangria's, Bang-Shots. And the old Campus Theatre, too, where we'd go to occasional concerts. Maybe this is some sort of hopeful test: will Jenn ask me to stop so we can go to dinner? Will she be the same Jenn I remember, and point at Supernova where we went to '90s Night, tell me that she wants to check out the Presidents of the United States of America Cover Band Cover Band? Will she keep quiet, and just hope that I take her home?

"There's a Zombie Walk that ends at Indie Saloon," she says. "Let's go there."

"A Zombie Walk?" I'm not sure whether this is a good thing or a bad thing.

Indie Saloon is at the far end of Central, around the corner on a moldy side-street. But if that's where she wants to go, that's where I drive us. Far from the glitter and stripper outfits of the frat-tastic bars at Central and University, a place far less sexy.

"You've never seen a Zombie Walk?" she asks.

"Nope."

"Obviously, I failed as a girlfriend."

"This is a real thing? Something that's been around?"

"A Zombie Walk is when, like, there are dozens of people…hundreds, sometimes, in the bigger cities…and they all dress like zombies, do elaborate makeup jobs, and they just walk together down a city street like the apocalypse has started."

"That's…bizarre," I say. "Nobody shoots them?"

She laughs, the first time today. "Maybe if they did it in Mississippi."

"So there's a Zombie Walk at Indie Saloon?"

"It *ends* there," she says. "I don't know the full route, but it ends there, and they've got all sorts of undead drink specials."

"What time do the zombies get here?" I shut the car off.

Jenn checks her cell phone, swipes through a web page or a Facebook event or something, then says: "Fifteen minutes. We better get going so we can get drinks before they stumble in."

"Any of your sisters doing it?" I ask, and now I'm hurrying to catch up with her as she speed-walks down the sidewalk. "Dressed as sexy zombies or something?"

"No," she says. "You can't make a zombie sexy."

"Your boyfriend?" I ask, and she's at the door to Indie Saloon. And it occurs to me that—in the next minute—I could lose her for the night, lose her for good. It's here where she can slip away and maybe find some new pack of friends in whom to take refuge. Wedge herself in, turn her back to me. We've left the car, and I'll never get a chance to say another word to her.

"I don't have a boyfriend," she says. Shows her ID, and the bouncer lets her through to the thick darkness of the bar. "You've stalked my Facebook page. You should know."

The bouncer stops me, hand to my chest. "In a hurry?" he asks, and it's just the two of us out here and Jenn has vanished. He stares at my card for what seems a very long time, and I picture myself searching frantically through the crowd, trying to spot that flash of frosty hair but seeing ironic slogan t-shirts everywhere, no Jenn.

When I finally manage inside, the crowd isn't thick at all, just twenty or thirty hipsters scattered at scratchy booths and on sticky barstools at high-top tables. Long hair, tattoos, beards, flannel, the antithesis of *frat star*.

"Nice costume," a guy says to me.

I'm wearing the Nu Kappa Epsilon polo.

"Tuck it in," he says. "It'll be more fratty that way."

"Right," I say, and push the front of the shirt under my beltline.

"Front tuck!" he says and claps. "Perfect, man. *Perfect.* Might as well do the popped collar, too, right?"

"Absolutely," I say and flip my collar.

"Ha ha! This is the best," he says.

Jenn is waiting at a table, already has a cranberry-vodka but there's no second drink for me.

"They know you here," I say. "Wave you inside, have a drink ready for you."

"They've always known me here," she says.

"I didn't know you were still coming to these bars."

"Why wouldn't I?"

"I don't know. Maybe…the Louis Vuitton doesn't go over very well in a place like this."

"I didn't bring my Louis Vuitton purse."

I sigh and hold up my palms. "All right. I guess I'm an idiot, then."

Jenn reaches over to the next table and grabs a Miller Lite bottle, slides it over to me. "Here you go," she said.

"Did you just steal that from someone?"

She laughs again. "No. I bought it. I just didn't want you to *expect* that I'd get you a drink."

Fifteen feet away, a guy dressed as Sarah Palin is arguing with a girl dressed as George W. Bush. Someone else is dressed as Jared from the Subway commercials, and someone else as Hillary Clinton, but none of the white hipster crowd seems daring enough to go black-face and dress as Barack Obama. There's someone dressed as the Verizon guy, too, going from table to table to ask the girls "Can you hear me now?" The monsters are coming, a hoard of zombies in what Jenn assures me will be professional and stunningly grotesque make-up, and yet—here in the bar—every costume is just a different celebrity or public figure.

I rest my elbows on the high-top. "I need to tell you something," I say.

"Well, I already know you cheated on me," she says and holds up her glass as if to cheer me, "so it can't be much worse, can it?"

"My parents are divorced," I say.

"*What?*"

"They lied to me," I say. "For months. I don't know why. Maybe they told me the reason, but I don't care what it was."

"Divorced." Jenn puts her drink back on the table and exhales slowly. "God, Charles, I'm sorry. I had no idea."

"Because I lied to you, too," I say.

"What do you mean?"

"They told me at graduation. When we went out to lunch. But I kept it from you."

"Back in May?"

"I've barely spoken to them since," I say. "When they call, I don't answer."

"My God, why didn't you tell me?"

At the front door, the Palins and the Jareds and the Bushes are clumping together and yanking cameras from pockets and purses, fighting for position to photograph the approaching zombie mob.

"I wanted you to think I was someone else," I say. "That's as honest as I can be." I swirl the Miller Lite in the pools of condensation that have formed on the table-top. "I spend all my time trying to be these personas. But I don't even know which one is the real one anymore. It's like being in a house of mirrors, but as an out-of-body experience…and you can't find the real *you* anymore. Every time I turn around, there's some other *me* that I want to be, or some other *me* that I hate and want to erase, and…it isn't supposed to be like this, is it? I mean. Is it this way for you? When do we grow up and be the people we're supposed to be for the rest of our lives?"

We hear the first groan, a guttural growl that sounds exactly the way it should: like a response to my rant. Following it are a series of less-impressive (but still adequate, I suppose) expressions of pain and flesh-hunger. Someone out there is screaming "Brains! Brains! Brains!", a zombie more picky than the rest.

"I don't know what to say, Charles."

"I'm crazy," I say. "You're scared of me. You think I've snapped or something."

"You're not crazy," she says. And she stands, taps my chest with her fingertips, and motions for me to follow her. We settle at one of the front windows, where—through the scuffs and spilled beer and hardened bubblegum deposits—we can see the first wave of zombies braving the crosswalk and coming toward the Indie Saloon, confused drivers at every corner watching the grim procession.

"Thank you for telling me that," she says.

"That I'm crazy?"

"Thank you for being *honest*," she corrects.

Beside us is a man dressed as Kurt Cobain. Or, at least, I *think* he's supposed to be dressed as Kurt Cobain. He has his painted-black fingernails pressed to the window, forehead nearly touching the glass as he watches. "That first one," he says. "Oh man. That first zombie." And there's a touch of wonder in his voice, as if there's more beauty in what he's seeing than he was even able to imagine.

"Can I tell you something?" she asks.

"Tell me anything."

"You're upset that your parents got divorced," she says. "But all semester, I...I didn't tell you that my parents got back together."

"Did they?" I ask and gulp my beer. "Well, shit. Good news for one of us, at least."

"No," she says and looks down at the terrible floor, a timeline of a hundred thousand hipster footsteps smeared and caked into the surface. "He hit her, you know that?"

"He *hit* her? When?"

"Always?" she says. "I guess. We didn't know, my sister and me. We didn't find out until after he was out of the house. My mother...maybe she thought it was normal? Or maybe she wanted us to think that everything was normal, that he was as good as any other father? After he was gone, she finally talked to us about it."

"You never told me."

"I've never told *anyone*," she says. "How do you even *start* to tell someone that? I've never even talked about it with my father. It's like this secret that we all know, and that we were all supposed to keep, and maybe it was okay when they were divorced and we never had to worry about the two of them in the same room. But now we're out of the house, and he takes some anger management class, and she puts herself right back there."

The bar is swimming in the irony of John Mayer's "Your Body is a Wonderland," the zombies overtaking the security guard at the front door; he just steps aside, laughing, doesn't even attempt to check their IDs or mark them with wristbands. The zombie in the lead—the one that mesmerized Kurt Cobain beside us—is indeed a masterpiece of both makeup and performance: both arms outstretched, one leg twisted around unnaturally as if it was crushed by a truck, stumble-walking and biting the air, a long piece of fake flesh—a piece of pulled turkey? a painted pasta noodle?—hanging from his mouth. One of his eyes is yellow, and the other appears to have been ripped from its socket, leaving only a chewed-up red-black cavity.

"You need to call them back," Jenn says. "Your parents."

I pretend not to hear. I watch the apocalyptic procession. The next zombie is a nurse, her white outfit splashed with blood, one sleeve missing. Another is dressed as a Hare Krishna, blue skin and orange outfit pulled straight from *Dawn of the Dead*. There are construction workers, policemen, truckers, an Indian, as if a group of guys bought Village People outfits and bloodied them up into zombie costumes. There are tattered shirts, long cuts down faces and arms. One zombie is even carrying a frighteningly realistic severed arm, and he digs his face into the appendage every few seconds.

"Everyone's a house of mirrors, Charles," she says. "You, me. Our parents. But I know the way that you think about family, how much you care about them, and you'll regret it forever if you cut yourself loose from your parents."

I look deep into the faces of the zombies until they no longer seem strange or menacing, until it feels like this is just life, just an ordinary night on the town with zombies hanging out in a bar. "My father," I say, "he told me: if you're in a situation that you know is destructive, you should remove yourself from it. That's what I'm doing. Just following his advice."

"That's what you want to *think* you're doing," she says. "You might not like all their drama, but are they really destructive? What's worse? Making a phone call and being honest with them, too, or holding a grudge for the rest of your life?"

Long sip of my beer. That damned Jenn Outlook again.

Then: "Whoops!" Jenn says, as a zombie in a Superman costume trips over his own cape, face-plants into the sidewalk. But he rises and bumbles forward without breaking character, and everyone inside the bar's clapping, Jenn's applause the loudest.

And I understand now that I don't really know Jenn, that perhaps I never did. Not the way I should have, anyway. The Jenn that I thought I knew—the Britney Spears, the NKOTB, the Poison t-shirts, the '90s Nights, the old-school slap bracelets she jokingly wore to semi-formal dances, the '80s-era ColecoVision she had in her bedroom—it's part of her, but it's all surface-level stuff. What did I avoid? The confusion and the pain she feels from some other life, a life that I never thought to ask too deeply about? I wanted perfect, and so I made her perfect, but she never asked for that. *Everyone's a house of mirrors*, she said. *You, me. Our parents.* But I never bothered walking through.

Charles is…telling Jenn that he's sorry.

Charles…doesn't want to make this moment cheesy, okay?

Charles is…not going to ask you to say anything. And he knows that this is over, the two of us, and that you only left the house and came here with me because…well, because you're a decent person. But I'm sorry, Jenn. For what I did, yes, but most of all for what I didn't do. For the things I never tried to talk about, or cared enough to realize.

Jenn nods, closes her eyes.

And when she opens them they are brighter, and she's pointing to the bar and saying, "Let's just watch the zombies, Charles."

Tomorrow I'll be back in Indianapolis, and by next week I'll be back on the road, but tonight it's zombies, and it's Jenn smiling again as the zombies mock-fight to pass through the open doorway. "Ohhh, look at that one!" she says and points with her drink to a zombie with a sword through his head. Another zombie has cleverly dressed as a dead alcoholic so that he can sneak his own beer into the bar: in one hand, he clutches a six-pack of Pabst, and no one stops him as he shuffles through the door. Jenn's smile turns to a laugh, and she's clapping again, and it's a tiny moment, this smile, the zombie, the beer, the applause, but suddenly I can't think of anything in the world that could be better than this, and then I'm tipping back the last of my Miller Lite and groaning like a dead man and I allow my whole body to go rigor mortis, and I pluck the raspberry lip gloss from Jenn's purse and paint sparkly blood trails from my mouth to my chin like I've been eating super-excited sorority girls who bleed sparkles, and then I'm lurching toward the bar, a Zombie Frat Star in pursuit of another beer, and Jenn is laughing and following me and I'm growling "Brains! Leadership! Fraternity! Brrraaaains!" and Sarah Palin claps me on the back and says "Nice!" and Subway Jared screams "Hide the pledges!" and when I go so stiff that I accidentally bang into a barstool, Jenn steers me back in the right direction.

And it feels good to be dead for a little while, and then—just like initiation night—to know that I'll soon wake up reborn, this time maybe in skin that's all my own.

# **Acknowledgements:**

Some readers—particularly those who have visited any of the university campuses featured in the novel, or who work for a fraternity or sorority headquarters in Indianapolis—will notice that minor liberties were taken with either geography, institutional hierarchy, semester scheduling, or academic offerings. No disrespect intended, homeys.

Additionally, I think it's important to reinforce that no character in this novel is intended to represent any real-life student, alumnus, or higher-education professional. This isn't *Primary Colors*. The Nu Kappa Epsilon National Fraternity does not exist, nor is it patterned on any one specific national fraternity, and any reader attempting to match real-world fraternity/ sorority figures with characters in the book will be disappointed. There are some nasty people in this book, and if you're currently reading this, chances are that you're not one of them.

On the contrary, I have many people to praise for their hard work in molding the lives of young men and women on college campuses. The culture of Greek Life is highly complex, always evolving, and heavy with baggage, but there are a lot of people who have made it their life's mission to be forces for positive change. A thousand thank-yous to T.J. Sullivan of CampuSpeak, who does more to "keep it real" for fraternity undergrads than anyone I've ever met. Thank you to Mark E. Timmes of Pi Kappa Phi, for leading a fraternity that does challenge the worst elements of the culture, and to my own fellow traveling consultants with whom I've collaborated and commiserated: Dave Corey, Sean Mahoney, Kevin Yania, Matt Hunt, Todd Cox, Brandon Tudor, Josh Carroll, Kyle Longest, Lyle Dohl, Cal Majure, Tom Mosher, Dustin Alexander, and Ira Katzman. Special thanks also to the countless other fraternity men I've met who do honestly strive be role models for the next generation: Steve Whitby, Jeremy Galvin, Andrew McCarthy, Adam Nekola, and Abel Garcia, among many others. If this book at times shows the worst, I want this page to acknowledge the men who represent the very best.

Thank you to my own fraternity brothers, also, the ones who have known about this book for years and have never discouraged my writing on the subject. These are men who know that human relationships are more important than protecting intractable institutions: Brandon Lee, Chad Feaster, Alex Scharf, Justin Pachota, Stu Chalmers, Adam Sich, Mike Gross, James Long, Mike Pigford, Mike Hayman, and Mark Mestrovich.

Thank you to the super-supportive writing community of Orlando, Florida: Ryan Rivas, Mark Pursell, Hunter Choate, Jared Silvia, David James Poissant, Ashley Inguanta, Jonathan Kosik, Teege Braune, J Bradley, Laurie Uttich, Susan Hubbard, Craig Saper, Jocelyn Bartkevicius, Pat Rushin, Phil Deaver, Susan Lilley, and John King (and a hundred other great writers whose names would swell the word count of an already-gigantic book). Thank you, especially, to Jay Haffner, my Detroit writing homey, Lavinia Ludlow, my West Coast writing homey, and Lindsay Hunter, my Chicago writing homey. And, of course, the late Jeanne Leiby, who helped me to craft and shape the original draft of this book; and Matt Peters, who believed in the book's potential and helped me to shape the final version you now hold. I can't tell you all how grateful I am for having you.

Finally, this book would not have been possible without the love and support of a family way cooler than the one Charles Washington was stuck with: my parents, John and Pam Holic, who gave me far more encouragement than I deserved; Aaron, Patti, Jason, and Crystal; my baby boy Jackson, who—someday, while on full scholarship somewhere (fingers crossed)—will face the decision of whether to join a fraternity, and who has a father that promises to tell it straight, but will still stand by him no matter his decision; and most important, the world's biggest "thank you" to my wife Heather, who kept me positive and who believed in me for the full seven-year duration of this project. It ain't easy being married to a writer. We have odd habits, and disappear for long stretches of time to the dark office at the far end of the house, emerging only to grab a new Fresca from the fridge and make odd comments about semi-colons; then we disappear again, and you likely start to wonder if your husband is ever going to finish this thing, if it's even a worthwhile project, if it's ever going to see the light of day, if it will all just result in seven wasted years...but you don't say any of that, do you? Just: "Stay positive. It'll happen. You'll do it." Not even a second thought. And that's why you're so fucking awesome.

# About the Author

Nathan Holic teaches writing courses at the University of Central Florida and serves as the Graphic Narrative Editor at *The Florida Review*. He is the editor of the annual anthology *15 Views of Orlando* (Burrow Press), a literary portrait of the city featuring short fiction from fifteen Orlando authors. His fiction has appeared in print at *The Portland Review* and *The Apalachee Review*, and online at *Hobart* and *Necessary Fiction*.

*American Fraternity Man* is his first novel.

Find him on-line at: http://NathanHolic.com/